the ▊▊▊▊▊▊▊▊▊

D0628476

Twelve bearded, filthy G.I.s wait behind barbed-wire, prisoners of their own army. Murderers, thieves, rapists—they wait to be sentenced to death, or a life at hard labor. They are the damned of the American Army.

Suddenly—almost miraculously—they are given a gamble for a kind of salvation. . . .

Their savior:
A cruel, cynical OSS Captain qualified to forge them into disciples of precision killing.

Their mission:
Parachute into the heart of a German rest camp for officers, just before D-Day.

Their chances:
One in a million—but the damned don't count.

METRO-GOLDWYN-MAYER

Presents

A KENNETH HYMAN PRODUCTION

THE DIRTY DOZEN

Starring

LEE MARVIN   ERNEST BORGNINE   CHARLES BRONSON

JIM BROWN   JOHN CASSAVETES

RICHARD JAECKEL   GEORGE KENNEDY   TRINI LOPEZ

RALPH MEEKER   ROBERT RYAN

TELLY SAVALAS   CLINT WALKER   ROBERT WEBBER

Screenplay by
NUNNALLY JOHNSON and **LUKAS HELLER**

Produced by **KENNETH HYMAN**

Directed by **ROBERT ALDRICH**

IN METROCOLOR

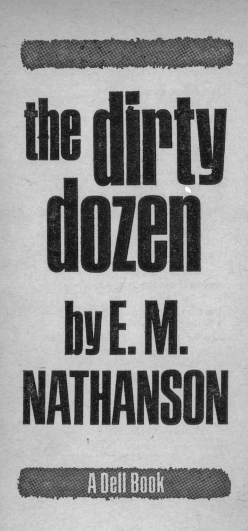

the dirty dozen

by E. M. NATHANSON

A Dell Book

To Marianne, my wife

Published by
DELL PUBLISHING CO., INC.
750 Third Avenue
New York, N.Y. 10017
Copyright © 1965 by E. M. Nathanson
Dell ® TM 681510, Dell Publishing Co., Inc.

All rights reserved under
International and Pan-American
Copyright Conventions.

Reprinted by arrangement with
Random House, New York, N.Y.

This story is fiction. I have heard
a legend that there might have been
men like them, but nowhere in the archives
of the United States Government,
or in its military history
did I find it recorded.

—E.M.N.

Previous Dell Edition #1945
New Dell Edition
First Printing—May, 1967
Second Printing—September, 1967
Third Printing—September, 1967
Fourth Printing—November, 1967

Printed in U.S.A.

Partake my confidence! No creature's made so mean
But that, some way, it boasts, could we investigate,
Its supreme worth: fulfils, by ordinance of fate,
Its momentary task, gets glory all its own,
Tastes triumph in the world, pre-eminent, alone.
Where is the single grain of sand, 'mid millions heaped
Confusedly on the beach, but, did we know, has leaped
Or will leap, would we wait, i' the century, some once,
To the very throne of things?

—Robert Browning
Fifine at the Fair
XXIX

part
one
THE
GALLOWS

1

Selections from the service record of Private Enos Gardiner, 32149763, classified Confidential and entombed in the Army records repository in St. Louis, Missouri. . . .

HEADQUARTERS
SOUTHERN BASE SECTION, UNITED KINGDOM BASE
EUROPEAN THEATER OF OPERATIONS
UNITED STATES ARMY
A.P.O. 490

20 Feb 1944

General Court-martial Orders No. UK73

Before a general court-martial which convened at Camp Chiselden, Swindon, England, 30 November 1943; pursuant to Paragraph 1 Special Orders No. 74, Headquarters Southern Base Section ETOUSA, 25 November 1943; was arraigned and tried Pvt. Enos Gardiner, 32149763, Company A, 501st Inf. Bn., 4th Inf. Div.

a) Charge: Violation of the 92d, 96th, and 69th Articles of War. Specifications:

(1) In that Pvt. Enos Gardiner, 32149763, Company A, 501st Inf. Bn., 4th Inf. Div., did at the Wiltshire Arms, Wootton Bassett, England, on or about 20 November 1943, with malice aforethought, willfully, deliberately, feloniously, unlawfully, and with premeditation, kill S/Sgt. George Trainor, 15368492, Company A, 501st Inf. Bn., 4th Inf. Div., by shooting him with a carbine.

(2) In that Pvt. Enos Gardiner, 32149763, Company A, 501st Inf. Bn., 4th Inf. Div., did at the Wiltshire Arms,

Wootton Bassett, England, on or about 20 November 1943, with malice aforethought, willfully, deliberately, feloniously, unlawfully, and with premeditation, kill one Beatrice Elizabeth Rosamond Hawley, an English female human being, single, by shooting her with a carbine.

(3) In that Pvt. Enos Gardiner, 32149763, Company A, 501st Inf. Bn., 4th Inf. Div., when apprehended in uniform in a condition of drunk and disorderly behavior, did show grave disregard for human life and contempt for authority by resisting arrest and pointing a carbine at members of the Wootton Bassett Constabulary, and members of the 322d Military Police Bn.

(4) In that Pvt. Enos Gardiner, 32149763, Company A, 501st Inf. Bn., 4th Inf. Div., did willfully maim himself in the head by shooting with a carbine, thereby unfitting himself for the full performance of military service.

b) Pleads the accused to all the specifications and the charge: Not Guilty

c) Findings of all the specifications and the charge: Guilty.

d) Sentence: Accused to be hanged by the neck until dead.

e) The sentence having been approved by the convening authority, confirmed by the Commanding General ETOUSA, and Article of War 50½ having been complied with, will be carried into execution on 25 Feb 1944, at United Kingdom Guardhouse No. 1, Marston-Tyne, Somerset, England. The act of execution will be under the direction of the Commanding Officer of the 51st Disciplinary Training Center, Marston-Tyne.

> By Order of Commanding General ETOUSA
> F. S. Bryan, Major General USA
> Deputy Chief of Staff

L. D. Partch, Brigadier General USA
Adjutant General

HEADQUARTERS, 51ST DISCIPLINARY TRAINING CENTER
SOUTHERN BASE SECTION, ETOUSA
A. P. O. 490

26 Feb 1944

SUBJECT: *Digest* of a Report of Proceedings at the execution of General Prisoner Enos Gardiner, formerly Private, 32149763, Company A, 501st Inf. Bn., 4th Inf. Div.

TO: Commanding General, ETOUSA, APO. 400.
(Thru: Commanding General, Southern Base
Section, UK Base, ETOUSA, A.P.O. 490.)

In compliance with letter, Headquarters, Southern Base
Section, ETOUSA, File No. 171—Gardiner, Enos—dated
20 Feb 1944, Subject: "Execution of Death Sentence,"
and Paragraph 9, Standing Operating Procedure No. 54,
Headquarters, ETOUSA, dated 5 March 1942, the execution having taken place, the following report is submitted:

1) The site of the execution was the gallows room in the
town prison at Marston-Tyne, Somerset, which is now
United Kindom Guardhouse No. 1 under the jurisdiction
of the 51st Disciplinary Training Center Overhead Detach-
ment. It is a high-ceilinged, oblong room approximately for-
ty-five (45) feet long by thirty-five (35) feet wide. The
walls and floor are of stone. Extending across the breadth
of the ceiling is a stout oak beam approximately twelve
(12) inches by twelve (12) inches, from which the noose
is suspended. Directly beneath the noose is a wood trapdoor approximately six (6) feet by five (5) feet, opening to
a room below.

2) The hour of execution was 0300, chosen by the Commanding Officer as least likely to give offense to the townspeople, arouse any of the other prisoners in the building,
or disturb condemned men in nearby cells.

3) Due to an extended period of wet weather, the interior of the gallows room was very damp and quite chilly. At
the hour of execution, there was a gusty wind from the
west and a steady downpour, audible and viewable from
other parts of the building, but not from the execution
chamber.

4) At 0240 hours, 25 Feb 1944, the Commanding
Officer 51st D.T.C., Lt. Col. Simon R. Tarbell, O-2473629,
assembled in the execution chamber twenty officials, witnesses, and authorized military and civilian spectators and
observers. He read to them General Court-martial Order
No. UK73, Headquarters, Southern Base Section,
ETOUSA, dated 20 Feb 1944, and gave proper instructions and precautions as behooves their duty at this
formation.

5) The witnesses and spectators were then placed in
their proper positions, viz., the official witnesses were in a
single rank at a position five (5) paces from the southern

11

border of the trapdoor, while the military observers and English civilians were in two (2) ranks at a position seven (7) paces from the western border of the trapdoor. The medical officers were four (4) paces from the northern border of the trapdoor.

6) At 0250 hours, an escort consisting of the Commanding Officer, the Official Recorder, and two M.P. guards entered the cell of the condemned. One M.P. guard, carrying the braceboard, was posted outside the door.

7) The escort party found the prisoner in prayer with the chaplain, 1st Lt. Thomas C. Pines, O-5375923, ChC, Hq and Hq Co., 4th Inf. Div. The Commanding Officer informed them it was time to proceed. The two guards bound the prisoner's hands behind his back. The procession left the cell at 0252.5, Colonel Tarbell leading, 1st Lt. Pines on his left, praying softly, followed by the prisoner with a guard on either side, and the third guard behind carrying the braceboard.

8) At 0252.75, a disturbance from another prisoner in a neighboring cell halted the procession. The procession was able to proceed again in a military manner at 0254.5.

9) At 0254.75, the procession entered the execution chamber. The command: "Attention!" was given by the Recorder. The prisoner was led to the center of the trapdoor. The guards assisted the executioner in binding the prisoner's feet and tying the braceboard to his back.

10) The Commanding Officer took his position in front and to the right of the prisoner. The Chaplain took his position in front and to the left of the prisoner. The Commanding Officer read to the prisoner the specifications of his court-martial and the order directing his execution, and then addressed the prisoner as follows:

"Private Gardiner, do you have a statement to make to me before the order directing your execution is carried into effect?"

The prisoner made no reply.

The Chaplain then addressed the prisoner as follows:

"Private Gardiner, do you have anything to say to me as Chaplain?"

The prisoner made no reply.

The Chaplain intoned a prayer. The executioner fitted the black hood onto the prisoner's head, lowered the noose around his neck and tightened the hangman's knot over his left ear as prescribed in AR 633-15.

11) The executioner stepped to the wooden handle controlling the trapdoor release. The Commanding Officer nodded to him and the executioner threw the handle at 0258.5. The trap mechanism operated perfectly and the prisoner was precipitated through the opened trapdoor clearly and hung suspended in the room below. The command: "Parade rest!" was given by the Recorder.

12) The body hung suspended with no sounds but with slight muscular contractive movements of the lower extremities. The witnesses and observers stood silent, some with heads bowed. There were no visible or audible signs of emotional reaction from any official or observer.

13) At 0303, the Commanding Officer commanded: "Medical Officers, make your examination!" At 0309, the Senior Medical Officer, Capt. Paul L. Gordon, O-1954372, MC, 51st D.T.C., reported to the Commanding Officer: "Sir, I pronounce this man officially dead." The formation was dismissed at 0309.5 hours.

14) The elapsed time from the entry of the prisoner into the execution chamber to the springing of the trap was three-and-three-quarter (3.75) minutes. The elapsed time from the fall of the prisoner to the pronouncement of death was ten-and-one-half (10.5) minutes.

15) Each official performed his task in a highly efficient manner. The proceedings were conducted with dignity, solemnity and military precision.

LeRoy W. Strom
1st Lt., DC, O-1638815

Approved by:
Simon R. Tarbell, O-2473629
Lieutenant Colonel, CMP
Commandant

WESTERN UNION

WAR DEPARTMENT
WASHINGTON, D.C.
26 FEB 1944

MRS. AILEEN GARDINER
BOX 17, ROUTE 3
LOVELAND, TENNESSEE
WE REGRET TO INFORM YOU THAT ON

25 FEB 1944, ENOS GARDINER DIED IN SERV-
ICE.

ADJUTANT GENERAL
UNITED STATES ARMY

—

2

—

THERE HAD always been a gallows at Marston-Tyne.

It lay deep within the bowels of the old prison that had immured the flushings of Saxon generations and now confined the useless dregs of the great American Army that had come to the United Kingdom from across the sea. An aura of quaint country charm concealed the building within the limits of the old market town.

The gibbet room was the dark womb of the place, primly covered by its damp stone walls. Things said about it were hushed, mysterious, secretive. It was entered only on special occasions. Among participants in the rigid ceremony that custom and military directive decreed for its use, anticipation of its function generated a complex pattern of emotions building to an unbearable denouncement. It was said by the priests who knew these things that it was a place of gestation, and they spoke of it in this way to soothe the trembling of men brought there for execution.

There was another scaffold, a portable one of serviceable Vermont pine stamped USQMC, which the transient Army had brought with it across the Atlantic. Some logistically clairvoyant brain had worried to include it among the engines and stores of war, certain that it would be needed. But it was hidden away, packaged and unused, as though in fear of offending the host nation with the tactless suggestion that better gibbets were made in America.

It was of the old gallows that Hump Edwards and Albie Salmon spoke to the Yank Captain in the taproom of The Butcher's Arms in the dark, moist town beyond the prison walls.

"You cood tell when there wuz to be a hanging in the oold dayz," said Albie. He leaned close to John Reisman,

14

the sweet smell of the good "Zumerzet Zider" on Albie's breath, his dimming blue eyes holding Reisman with an old man's tenacity. "They did it at dawn then," said Albie, "a proper hour. None of thiz zneaking aroond in the middle of the night like I oonderstond you Yanks are doing."

The American Captain gripped his whisky glass strongly and nudged Albie's cup. "Drink oop, oold mon," he mimicked. "I'll buy your poison." He ordered another whisky for himself, his drinking deliberate and planned to dull the fears about his night's commitment.

You will proceed to the 51st D.T.C. at Marston-Tyne on 24 Feb 1944 to witness an execution . . . Just like that. Go ahead. It is easy. You've done worse things yourself. That is why we value you so highly. Go watch the Army string some screaming bastard up by the numbers.

The order had reached him at 10th Replacement Depot in Lichfield, where he had been burrowing for qualified volunteers for a new Special Operation coded Rosedale. But the relationship between the hanging of a criminal and the carrying out of espionage behind enemy lines escaped him.

Reisman hadn't even known the Army was doing that sort of thing, and it had come as something of a shock, which in itself baited him, for he had come to believe in his own brute toughness of mind and emotion, as well as in his wiry, scar-conditioned body. He had wanted to protest, to ask why—for in his business the why sometimes took the stink from the what—but he knew better. Often the reasoning of the great brains at OSS headquarters in London was as obscure as Army, and their orders as unfathomable.

With the fifth drink in his belly and the alcohol doing its soothing job in his bloodstream, he felt less of the anger and fear he had brought into the pub with him and more of his usual detached air of curiosity toward life and death. Death was not new to John Reisman—nor violence. Not crude and misdirected violence, but slick and shrewd and clever and well-placed violence. This had been Reisman's business for years. He was a professional maker of violence, and so it bothered him that on this night he should be disturbed to be an invited guest at a hanging. He had a terribly acute awareness of himself that taunted him and allowed him no rest, particularly when he perceived himself wanting in some quality such as courage.

The door of The Butcher's Arms opened and Reisman felt a coolness touch his neck, as of the malevolence he had conjured with his thoughts, and momentarily fill the room until it, too, was warmed by the fire. An American soldier had entered, wearing a bulky issue overcoat and a field cap. Moving with exaggeratedly precise, almost theatrical gestures, he removed the coat and cap and hung them near the fire. He was a stocky man in his middle thirties with a thick face going soft and jowly around the edges and small limpid eyes that reached out quickly to every corner and person of the room as he moved softly to a table and seated himself. He wore the stripes of a Master Sergeant on both sleeves of his jacket, not the brief new-style jacket but the old-style blouse that fell in a straight line and covered waist, hips and buttocks. On his lapels were mounted the crossed pistols of the Corps of Military Police.

There were few other military in the room, for it was the sort of night that kept most men at home in dull but dry quarters in the camps and airfields of the Wessex downs. Of those that were there, Reisman noticed others who wore the crossed pistols and took them to be from the prison unit. None of them greeted the Sergeant, yet their very denials—eyes darting away, chairs shifted, sudden immersion in soft conversations—was recognition of his presence, acknowledgment that they knew him.

"Aye, it's him . . . Morgan," said Albie Salmon. "And look at the ztripes he'z wearing. They give it to him like he zaid they would."

A girl Reisman had not noticed before came from the kitchen doorway to the soldier's table, and Reisman followed her with his eyes as she moved, tempting his mind away from its preoccupation with violence and death. She had a very full woman's body that was immediately sexual, more startling for her very young face.

An unexpected wistfulness caught at Reisman as he watched the girl coquettishly lift her thick gray skirt a trifle above her knee and twirl half a step to the left, the right and then around, while the Sergeant stared at her legs. Reisman could not hear what they said to each other, but the girl was smiling broadly, almost laughing. Reisman noticed then that she wore flesh-colored silk stockings, which in those times denoted great acumen and sacrifice on the part of the giver, and often the receiver.

The Sergeant seemed embarrassed, yet he reached out, lightly touched the back of the girl's knee as she twirled, and as quickly pulled his hand away. Her pirouette over, she fluffed neck-length, sand-brown hair over each ear, the better to show cheap bright PX earrings that dangled there, each a large imitation pearl caged in thin, gilt filigree.

"Coom for hiz bacon poodding and hiz milk and a look at the wench like any oother night, I guez," said Hump Edwards. "It'z a woonder he can do it." Hump sucked on a large black pipe gripped in toothless gums and poured the strong tobacco smell and smoke into the air in short thick clouds.

"Doozn't seem no different to me," said Albie. "Doozn't look the part of the job neither. The King's man, Poindexter—I zaw him in the flesh, you know—now he looked like a dooctor or an oondertaker. He wuz a zkinny one in a black county zuit and a Loondon hat. Jolly az a funeral to zee. Mon, he looked the part."

"Who is he?" asked Reisman.

Albie Salmon snapped his head down onto his left shoulder, distended his tongue and bulged his eyes. With his right hand, he held an imaginary rope above him.

"The hangman," he said.

Enos Gardiner, nineteen, white, redhaired, freckled, was nervous but still not scared. The officer who had defended him at his court-martial had told him not to worry about the verdict. "A lot of guys get the death sentence, Gardiner," he had said, "but few of them are carried out."

It was the last time he had seen the officer, who had been sent off on another assignment. Lawyer one day, gunman the next, Indian chief the next—that was the Army, everybody an expert. Gardiner wondered how he would have made out in a trial back home with a real lawyer. At home they only hanged niggers anyhow for killing a white man, or for looking slantwise at a bit of white poontang.

It was the Colonel who had come to him and told him the sentence had been confirmed, but that still didn't mean anything to Gardiner. He knew what they were gonna do. They were gonna scare the shit out of him right down to the last minute, then put him in jail for the next twenty years.

"Do you want a Chaplain?" the Colonel had asked. "Anyone in particular?"

Sure he wanted a Chaplain. He wanted anybody who would come into that lousy cell and sit with him and talk to him. There was some crazy wop in a cell down the hall who kept saying he was Al Capone's kid cousin and Capone would fix everything and get them all out of there. His name was Victor Franko, and they talked to one another through the bars, but the guards didn't like their yelling and told them to shut up whenever they came around. He didn't know what the hell Franko was talking about half the time anyway. If he wasn't a foreigner, he'd figure him for a Yankee. Enos told the Colonel he only knew one Chaplain, and he'd just as soon have him come as anybody. That was the Lieutenant Pines from the 4th Division, who used to come to see him when he was up to the hospital. He was some kind of crazy Catholic or something, and they'd always spoke against the Catholics at home, but this one talked like an American from down around home, and he sure as hell was a convincing preacher. If he was gonna get religion, this guy would be the one to give it to him.

Now Pines was there and Gardiner listened to him talk about God and Christ and Kingdom Come, but he knew he wasn't going to die that night. They weren't going to take him out of that cell that night, put a rope around his neck and string him up. Because if they were, they would have let him die four months ago when he'd been shot. They said he'd tried to kill himself, but he didn't believe that. One of the MPs must have done it. He remembered getting crazy drunk, going AWOL when Trainor told him he was restricted to camp and said don't you worry little buddy boy because I'll be taking care of that girl friend of yours myself tonight! He remembered going to look for Bea-Bea and her landlady saying the Sergeant had already come for her and taken her out. But Bea-Bea was his. "You're my little red fireball," she had moaned from the wet white cushion of her flesh beneath him. "Fireball, fireball, fireball, fireball . . . !" And she had screamed in the agony of pleasure he had given her. He had never had a woman like her. He had never had a woman—until he had her—and she was his. Seen her first that time in Wootton, with Trainor following after like a bull in heat, coming around when he wasn't wanted, playing up to her, trying to pull his lousy stripes. One night in Wootton, he'd gone to the latrine to piss out all that lousy hot limey beer, and he'd come back to the lonely dark booth in the back of the pub and found Trainor sitting there with his fly open and that big thing of his stuck out into her lap, with her drunk and all, and her hand on it, going, "Oooo, oooo, oooo!" trying to push Trainor away, and that's when he'd pulled him out of there, hit him and taken her away from the lousy pig. But then the next night, Trainor had put him on the duty roster, and the crazy fear of what was happening outside the camp had made him drink, and then driven him out, and then he must have come back and gotten the carbine and the ammo and gone looking for them, because the next thing he remembered was going into that bedroom in Wootton and the ugly white nakedness of the two of them entwined, and the explosions and the awful screaming of Bea-Bea with the dead Sergeant in her, only he didn't know he was dead because he just kept pulling that trigger blasting the guts of him all over her and that's when she'd finally kept quiet. And he'd taken her in his arms and talked to her softly, telling her not to be afraid of Trainor no more because he couldn't hurt her, and crying over her because she was so still and awful-looking, and then the red fury coming over him again when the MPs came and tried to take him away, and then the blackness and the awful pain when he woke up. That was what he remembered and he started to cry now, for thinking of Bea-Bea, and the beautiful soft motherly flesh of her.

"Cry, my son," said the Chaplain. "It is good to cry. Our Lord cried too, for his sins and the sins of others. Cry, and empty your heart of all bitterness and hatred, and fill it only with love of Our Lord, Jesus Christ, and you will be saved."

"They're not really gonna hang me, are they, Lieutenant?" Gardiner said. "I told them I didn't mean to kill the girl. They're not gonna hang me. They saved my life. I must have pulled the trigger and I didn't know it, just like with Bea-Bea, and the doctors said I almost died, but the Army saved me. Why would they kill me now? I told them I was sorry, didn't I, Lieutenant?"

"Call me Father," said Lieutenant Pines kindly. "Or

Padre, if you like. That's the way men say it in the Army. Would you like to pray with me?"

"Yes, Father, I'd like to pray," said Gardiner, "I'd like to pray for Bea-Bea. I loved her."

Captain Gordon and Lieutenant Strom waited in the medical Quonset within the prison compound. The fire in the pot-bellied iron stove made it warm and cozy, but they sat back tensely in their chairs, feet on Gordon's desk, trying to look relaxed and casual, sipping brandy from the medical stores.

"I wonder what they'd do if no one came?" asked Gordon. He was the older of the two—a tall, gaunt man with thick gray and black hair, and steel-rimmed Army spectacles that made his eyes disappear if he caught the desk light just so.

"Who's *they*?" asked Strom.

Neither question was really a question. For Gordon it was just the sort of wild thinking he indulged in on nights like this for his own amusement, or possibly to keep his sanity. There had been other executions, both black and white, but somehow the hanging of this dull ignorant kid seemed to him more criminal than the others, more criminal than the act of violence that had precipitated it. They had done such a damned good job on him up at Taunton, bringing him back to life.

Gordon stared at the blond, fresh-faced young dentist. "Who's *they*?" he repeated. "That's a good question. The ineffable . . . the elusive *they*. Tarbell, you, me, Sergeant Morgan, take it all the way up to the Commanding General if you like. What if the weather was so goddamned bad the roads washed out? Or the Germans bombed us? I wish the hell they would. Just one little bomb in Gardiner's cell and his mother would get a different kind of telegram and everybody'd feel better."

Gordon heard the staff car pull up outside and knew what he earnestly wished for wouldn't happen. Events set in motion weeks before, maybe years and centuries, ground inexorably to their finish.

Strom dropped his feet from the desk and rose to peer out the window into the rain. "It's them," he said. "I must remember to add a little literary flourish to my report of these mundane proceedings this time. Something about the weather perhaps."

"Then try submitting it to your *Dental Journal*, my friend," said Gordon, "as a curious by-product of the war. It might do for them to give a brief course in hanging in the medical and dental schools in the future—or, in your case, in the proper recording of hangings. Maybe it ought to be done in Latin, like a prescription."

Strom opened the door and five men dashed into the Quonset. Captain Keller from the General Hospital at Taunton was in the lead.

"Evening, Doctors," he said, striding to the stove.

"Evening, Doctor," said Gordon. "Nice night for a hanging."

Keller gave him a dirty look and there was no humor in it. "That's not funny, Paul," he said, shaking out of his wet coat and hat. "I never thought they'd let it go this far with this one. If I had, I think I would have let him die on the operating table."

"And violate your oath?"

"My oath be damned," said Keller, moving closer to the stove and holding up his hands. They were hands that had been described in medical circles as having a brain in each joint of every finger. Keller was an unbelievably skillful surgeon who had volunteered the day after Pearl Harbor, and detested the Army as much as he loved his country. "I've taken many oaths in my day and I'm violating most of them tonight," he said.

Lieutenant Strom introduced himself and Gordon to the other men who had come in with Captain Keller. There were two MP Captains and a Deputy Provost Marshal from Camp Chiselden, and an infantry First Lieutenant from the outfit Gardiner and Trainor had been with. Others would be along later to meet in the Commandant's office.

"Don't let it get you down, gentlemen," said one of the MPs. "It will soon be over, and Gardiner is only getting what he deserves. I wouldn't waste any sympathy on him. You didn't see what he did up there in Wootton. What a bloody-assed mess! Then the son-of-a-bitch stuck the carbine in my face when I came to get him. He could have killed me or one of my boys just like he did Trainor and the girl. If you're giving away sympathy, save a little for them."

21

"Don't be too hard on the doctor, Captain," Gordon said. "Gardiner as he now stands or sits or does anything, for that matter, is solely the creation of the learned doctor and his skillful assistants. That boy should have been dead four months ago. I know. No artist likes to see his most triumphant work destroyed."

Keller walked to Gordon's desk and sat on the edge of it. He was a short man, with a round, gentle face and clear brown eyes that mirrored concern for the world. "It's not the verdict I dispute, Captain," he said to the MP officer, "and I fully understand your own position in the matter. But surely after all the boy has been through, there has been enough punishment and retribution. Surely there are some grounds for commutation. I didn't expect a pardon, or to let him go scot free . . . but I didn't expect this either." He turned to the infantry Lieutenant from Gardiner's company. "You know the man, Lieutenant," he said. "What was he like before this?"

"Not a bad kid," said the Lieutenant. "Kind of slow and stupid, but he'd never been in real trouble before he took up with that girl. AWOL a few hours, I suppose, but that was all."

"Think he deserves hanging?" asked Keller.

The Lieutenant was a cautious man who knew his own business and that was all, and he damned well wasn't going to commit himself. "Well, now, I don't know," he said. "I couldn't say. I hate like hell to lose any of my men, but I don't know about that sort of thing. He was brought up on charges, and if the charges stick, I suppose that's the way it's got to be."

"How about Trainor?" Captain Keller persisted. "What was he like?"

"A good man," said the Lieutenant, "real tough with the men and kept them in line." He paused a moment and almost smiled. "Funny how he used to bait Gardiner. Rode the hell out of him just for practice, I guess. Never thought the kid would come back at him."

"You know your Bible, don't you, Doctor?" said the MP Captain. "An eye for an eye—a tooth for a tooth. Gardiner's lucky. He knocked off two people, but he's only getting hanged once."

"I would suggest, speaking of the Bible," said Captain Gordon with a strong bite of sarcasm in his voice, "that none of us know what the hell we're talking about. Maybe the poor kid is going to be hung and hung and hung, on into eternity—unless the Reverend gentleman who's been with him for two days can fix him up a special pass."

Lieutenant Strom knew it was time to change the subject. He was lowest in rank, but their extra bars didn't awe him in the least. He'd fill or yank anybody's tooth with the same happy-go-lucky air of nonsense. "Beds, gentlemen, beds!" he called, indicating the cots in the tiny ward, which was empty of patients. "You might want to catch a little snooze till it's time for prayer meeting. For those who feel a bad cough coming on, I'm sure the Captain will allow me to prescribe some of this cure-all we've been sipping."

While the others moved into the ward to pick their cots, Captain Keller stayed with Gordon. "How is he, Paul?" he asked.

"Can't really say," said Gordon. "He doesn't really believe he's going to be hanged tonight. Who knows? Maybe he's still in some kind of deep shock. Maybe it's better that way. I've got to go up and give him a final check now. Want to come along?"

"No," said Keller. "I couldn't bear it."

Gordon got up from his chair and picked up a portable scale from the floor nearby. "Make yourself comfortable, Fred," he said. "I'll see you in a while."

"What's that for?" asked Keller, indicating the scale.

Gordon had tried to make the move seem as casual as possible, almost unrelated to his errand, but Keller had spoiled it, and Gordon spoke now with the bitterness he would ordinarily intend for others, not for the doctor, whom he admired. "Got to check his weight again," he said. "For Sergeant Morgan, so he gets the drop just right. They don't want to strangle him to death or yank his head off. Just a nice quick break and sudden oblivion."

He that is without sin among you, let him first cast a stone . . .

The words teased at Reisman as palpably as though they were substance and not reverie. He had been staring at the Sergeant for many minutes, uncertain of the reaction he should exhibit, or even what he truly felt. There was reality to the chill the man had brought into the room, yet Reis-

23

man denied the repugnance and anger that started to rise within him, and forced his mood to one of academic interest.

The girl came by Reisman with a tray of food and he stopped her. "Tell your boy friend I'd like to buy him a drink," he said.

Up close she was disturbingly pretty. Her skin was marvelously clear, reminding him of the texture of exquisite china. Her hands might have been the same, except that the work they had done had taken the softness from them and colored them darker. Her eyes were a gentle blue, and very lovely. "I have no boy friend, sir," she said, smiling. "Who do you mean?"

It seemed to Reisman that what she said was meant pointedly, almost coquettishly for him, and some small part of him was relieved, although he couldn't explain why. He liked her voice, too. It was sweet and lyrical and it wasn't Somerset.

"The Sergeant over there," said Reisman. "Tell him I'd like to buy him a drink to celebrate his promotion, and to give him strength for his night's work."

She was back in a moment. "The Sergeant says he drinks only milk, but he thanks the Captain for his kindness."

"Let him have milk then."

"I'm afraid you are both out of luck, sir," said the girl. "Some crazy Jerry got the dairy night before last, and we've had no milk since."

Reisman rose from his bar stool and walked to the table, beckoning the girl to follow. "There's no milk, Sergeant," he said in a voice louder than he'd planned. "What will you drink? Whisky, cider or a pint, if you like?"

Carl Morgan was bent over his food, cutting easily with the edge of his fork, chewing slowly and deliberately. When he had swallowed his mouthful he looked up at the officer and spoke.

"May I ask the Captain what outfit he's with?"

"No outfit. I'm just a tourist passing through, Sergeant. Will you drink with me or won't you?" Reisman looked for a cutting edge in the man's words, but could not honestly say that he had found it.

"The reason I ask the Captain that," said Morgan, "is that I know that fraternization between officers and enlisted men has been expressly forbidden. And though I thank the Captain, I cannot comply with his request."

"It's not a request, Sergeant . . . oh, shit, never mind," muttered Reisman. He grabbed a few shillings from his pocket and handed them to the bewildered girl, who still stood by the table. "Get him another pudding and keep the change," he said, turning back to the bar where the two old farmers watched him with interest. "He'll need his strength tonight." Reisman knew what he had done was childish, but he had a momentary feeling of triumph, small as it was.

Morgan watched the officer retreat. "You can keep the money," he said to the girl. "I don't want any more pudding." He knew the mood of the others in the room, but he didn't really care. There were those that begrudged him his stripes. There were those that feared him and because they feared him hated him. But he was no longer just a buckassed Private available for any jerk with a stripe or a bar to tell what to do. He was *somebody* now in this whole goddamned shapeless mass of an Army. He was special and there was nobody else like him. He didn't need drink or poontang, anything or anybody. He liked the fat steaming bacon pudding and the fresh creamy milk that he missed tonight. He liked the little girl who waited on tables —Bess or Tess, he could never remember her name for sure. Rank didn't make any difference to her either. She had been nice to him since he joined the 51st to help Poindexter. The snotty limey bastard hadn't taught him a thing. He could have taken right over in the beginning and done the whole job instead of just watching. But tonight was his night. He'd show them something good. In the beginning the men had been friendlier. They figured him for another guard with a tough-shit assignment, but then they found out different, the lousy hypocritical bastards. The girl always had a smile and a friendly word for him. That was why he bought her the stockings and the earrings. It pleased him that it made her happy, and he wanted nothing in return.

At the bar Reisman ordered another whisky and sipped it slowly, withdrawing within himself in a secret way he had, away from the Somerset men, away from Sergeant Morgan, away from the girl. He thought of dead Germans lying in the snow of the Mottarone above Lake Orta. The death of Germans was particularly good and sweet and exhilarating, a major driving force in his life. His mission among the mountain guineas had almost come to grief because of his zest for blood contact with the Nazis. It was one of the reasons he suspected he had been moved from the immediacy of Secret Intelligence to the organizing of Special Operations.

The death of Italians was not quite so good, for it reminded him of his Italian mother and all her inbred family who had made the journey to Chicago and, except for her, had never quite realized they'd actually arrived and could come out of their protective cocoons.

The death of Englishmen was regrettable, as was the death of good Frenchmen, Belgians, Hollanders and Scandinavians, and those other nationals of the European heartland who fought the Nazis.

The death of Russians, Poles, Hungarians and Romanians left him unmoved. They had their own brands of viciousness, unaided by Germans, which he had learned from the lips of Aaron Reisman, his father, confirmed by the full ethnic and geographic range of his father's circle of friends and relatives, and reaffirmed by personal experience among the offenders.

The death of compatriots in war was a sad fact over which few tears were shed. He hoped they would shed those few tears over him when his time came. The years of his wars had been many, and he felt overdue for his comeuppance. There had been crazy Latin wars while he was a runaway in his teens. They had been his first, south of the Rio Grande and around the Caribbean, in which either side could have been right or wrong, but to him it was all hot fun and games. There had been Spain, in which he thought he had found a cause, but had not been really sure —because the Communists had clouded the issue—until it was all over. China had been weird, strange, exotic and brutal, and completely hopeless—better to be out of it, because he didn't really understand it. And in Palestine he had found again some meaning.

He was only part *Landsmann*, but he had never felt this part so intimately before, or so happily, on a tribal if not a religious basis. He had taught men who had never before raised their voices in anger to shoot and knife and garrote. Some of them, discovering a latent talent, he had taught to relish the fight itself as he did, and some day they would be formidable. And he had gone out on missions for their struggling leaders and weak but tenacious organizations, into the slime of *Mittel Europa* to find and save their brethren and bargain with the gatekeepers. They had been good years, and someday he knew he would go back.

Reisman summoned the years of his wars to mind in moments like this to reassure himself who he was and what he'd done, much as a salesman of another line of merchandise taking stock of himself to bolster status, if not integrity.

The girl came up behind Reisman, and he smelled the fresh sweetness of her as she touched him.

"You don't have to give me this money, sir," she said, one hand extended with the shillings. "The Sergeant didn't want anything else, and he thanks you." Her other hand rested softly on his arm. Either in her naïveté she didn't know what she was doing to him, or in her ingenuousness she did and wanted it that way.

"Then you keep it."

"I couldn't, sir."

"Then let me buy you a drink."

"I couldn't sir, though I wouldn't mind a pint, and to talk to you. Not while I'm working. My uncle wouldn't like it. This is his inn."

"Then give it to your uncle and tell him I need a place to stay the night," he said.

She started away, and he called her back. "What's your name?" he asked softly.

"Tessie Simmons, sir," she said. She couldn't withhold the smile or the pleasure of him in her voice. She knew she was bold, maybe too bold, but at least she was honest and did no one harm, and maybe some good. It was the sweet goodness of life that she wanted for herself and for others as well, and if she was the means of bringing it, then both of them shared it, and it was doubly good, like mercy which was twice blessed and was little enough left in the world. "I'll go now and tell him. We have five letting bedrooms. He'll be glad to have you."

"And you, Tessie?"

"Of course, sir. I too will be glad to have you," she answered demurely.

She had noticed the Captain at the bar earlier, talking to Mr. Salmon and Mr. Edwards. There were so many different kinds of Americans, she could never get them quite straight. She thought the Captain handsome, but so were all the men in uniform who came to The Butcher's Arms, except that funny one who had just become a Ser-

27

geant and bought her the gifts but never seemed to want anything more of her, not that she would necessarily give it. People in the pub were saying he was a hangman up at the prison, but she didn't believe that. She knew they were just teasing her, like the ghost and goblin stories they told to children to keep them frightened and behaved. But she was not a child anymore.

She liked the Captain's looks. He was dark as a Spaniard or Italian without being swarthy. His face was young, yet already set and mature in its lines and hollows, and with tiny wrinkles at the eyes, mouth and forehead that belied his years. He had been angry with the Sergeant, although she couldn't say why, and his eyes were a cold gray. Then at the bar, to her, they had been soft brown. Maybe he could change them like a chameleon or maybe they changed by themselves to cover his mood.

She found her uncle in his room, spinning the wireless and getting mostly static. He was a London man who many years ago had come to Somerset, as a holiday booklet urged, and had liked it enough to stay and buy The Butcher's Arms for a living. He was a widower now, a simple, satisfied, pleasant man, apart from the world. He supervised the running of the place with a friendly, impersonal scrutiny, but kept mostly to himself in his room, or when the weather was good liked to stroll on the country roads. He kept his hand on the accounts, but the separate parts of the establishment were in the care of a cook, a barkeep and a maid. He had given Tessie refuge during that horror-laden London winter four years before, but now that she was grown it was she who looked after him.

Tessie told him they were to have a guest for the night, and he nodded agreeably and pointed to where he kept the room keys. She picked the one she knew was the nicest and coziest, with a good fireplace and a plump down comforter on the bed, and felt an exciting warmth run through her, a bit guiltily.

The Captain waited for her at the foot of the stairs, leaning on the banister.

"You owe me four and six for the room," Tessie told him.

"Don't you trust me?" he asked, turning and smiling at her.

"Of course I do, but it's custom to pay in advance. You gave me four shillings, and the room is eight and six."

Tessie took the money from him, watched him sign the register, and walked beside him as they mounted the stairs. He was half a head taller than she, though not really tall for a man, and he had dark hair with waves in it that she wanted to reach out and touch.

"Don't you have a bag?" she asked.

"Yes. But I left it somewhere else. I didn't know I was going to stay here. I'll bring it when I come back."

"You're going out?" She tried to hide the disappointment in her voice.

"Not now," said Reisman. "I have to be somewhere later."

"Devil's work no doubt on a night like this," said Tessie.

"Yes, devil's work," he said curtly.

She had meant to joke, but something about his voice and the look of his face made her sorry. He seemed suddenly tense again—fused of the molten, unstable things that made strength, that needed softness against it to surround and protect it; fused as a bomb to ignite and explode, and she knew the horror of those. She felt weak as she opened the door to his room. If he came too close, if he touched her, she would tremble for him.

Reisman watched her plump the pillows on the bed and stoop at the grate to light the fire. Without trying to stir anything within himself, he admired again the fullness of her woman's body, and the sensual gracefulness of her movements. There was an eagerness in her face, a soft, trembling fear in her eyes.

"I want to sleep a few hours," said Reisman. "Will someone be up about one-thirty? I want to get up then. I have to get up. It's very important."

"I have a clock in my room," she said quickly. "I'll wake you."

"No. Lend me the clock," said Reisman. "I don't want to put you to that trouble."

"No," said Tessie. "I don't mind. You might not hear the clock. I'm used to it. You might go back to sleep and miss your appointment. You'll need someone to see that you get up."

"All right," said Reisman.

He got up from the bed where he had been sitting and went to the door. She passed close to him, the slightest look of disappointment written on her face, and he

29

touched her shoulder lightly, stopping her. When she turned her face to him to see what he wanted, he bent quickly and kissed her cheek.

"Stay as sweet as you are," he whispered, and it was remarkable how easy the words came. Then he closed the door after her softly.

The small fire had begun to warm the room, and Reisman kicked off his shoes, and fully dressed threw himself on the bed. He was exhausted by the long journey of the day, his senses dulled by whisky, yet sleep stood off awhile yet.

Who was it they had hung in the morning?

Danny Deever? Yes, that was it, wasn't it—Danny Deever, the good soldier.

> They are hangin' Danny Deever, you must
>   mark 'im to 'is place,
> For 'e shot a comrade sleepin'—you must look
>   'im in the face . . .

Should he weep for Danny Deever? Would he weep for him? Or would he be afraid?

But what was fear to him now and why did he think of it? Surely not concern for personal safety. He had long ago discounted that. Emotional involvement in action left no room for personal fears. It was what they stupidly called bravery. But where was the action here, the heady excitement, the singing of the blood? To stand and watch a man die horribly and show no concern; to do nothing, neither for it nor against it; to be expected to be uninvolved emotionally; this was his dread. There were, too, the old, old memories. The violent sickness spewing from his belly, the involuntary emptying of bowels. No, it had not really been all hot fun and games. If he had conquered the innate, generations-bred fear of savagery and grisly terror, he could still lose the victory in one unexpected, unguarded moment.

Victor Franko lay on his cot and he heard the screws coming for Gardiner. He had fought sleep to be fully awake for this moment, and he heard them now marching down the hall. Quickly he darted to the door of his cell. Their uniforms were different, their methods were different, their punishment was different, even their right and wrong was different. But to Victor Franko they were screws, no different from the guards and wardens he had known at Sing Sing, Dannemora and Leavenworth.

Before them, there had been the soft, monotonous litany of the priest, and an occasional word from Gardiner. But Franko could not see them, or hear them well, and though it seemed in the beginning that Gardiner would not go easy, it seemed now he might go strong.

That he would not go at all, was what Victor Franko willed. For if Gardiner didn't hang, then he could be certain Franko wouldn't hang, and could turn his wild thinking to things more useful than the myriad plans for saving himself he had built in the eye of his mind.

It was evil that had brought him here, and he knew that somehow, some way, it would be evil that would save him. For long ago Victor Franko had made his pact with evil in that corner of New York called Hell's Kitchen. He was a child, but had known . . . *Good will destroy me, as it has destroyed others or allowed them to rot, as it allows my mother to rot, my father to rot, my brothers and sisters and friends and enemies to rot. And so I will be evil, recognize evil, court evil, develop evil and make it work for me.*

This was his vow, and though he had sufficient mentality to draw strength from his evil, he hadn't the intellect to make it work for him successfully. Ten years of prison life attested to that, though he would never admit it.

Evil had worked for him that day in Leavenworth when they had come to him and offered temporary parole if he went into the Army. Sure he'd be a good boy. Just let him out of there to a place where he could have a woman and breathe clean air and eat and drink what he damned well pleased—and be free! Freedom—that was a joke. What the hell kind of freedom did they offer in the Army? Five thousand cons had come to England on the boat with him —good boys who had promised to behave from then on and do their duty for God and Country, for the privilege of being cannon fodder. Christ, to have been General of those five thousand men—a regiment of evil, schooled in evil, commanded by evil. Sail the high seas, plunder, rape, unallied, uncommitted, invincible.

But where were they now? Dispersed to outfits all over the place, and Franko had worked only his private little evil and been caught again. Caught big. Caught so big they said they were going to hang him this time. But not yet. His case was still on review. And if that didn't work, there were other ways. He knew the book. He knew their book. He knew their *Manual for Courts-Martial,* and their *Articles of War,* and there were ways of getting out of this that they hadn't thought of. And if that didn't work, there were other ways. He would get sick. He would maim himself. You had to be healthy to be hanged. It said so in one of their other books. He would break every finger, one by one. He would smash his arm, mutilate his leg, crack his skull, if necessary. He would use his very flesh and bone and muscle, but they would never do to him what they were doing to Gardiner.

Christ, how quickly they moved. They were coming out of the cell now, that asshole Colonel in the lead, looking properly grim. He wondered where that hangman was, that slimy-looking son-of-a-bitch he'd seen skulking around the corridors for days, a Private one day, loaded with stripes the next, asking questions of the guards, peering through the window slots like a vulture.

The procession was moving away from the cells now.

"Colonel!" he yelled. "Colonel, let me say goodbye to him. Please let me say goodbye!" He hadn't known what he was going to do, but now that he had shouted, he felt carried away by his act.

Startled by the sound, Colonel Tarbell halted the procession. "Silence that man!" he ordered.

"Just let me shake his hand, Colonel, that's all," begged Franko. "Father, make him let me say goodbye to Gardiner. There's no law against it. God knows, the kid needs a friend."

The Colonel looked quickly at Gardiner. His unbelieving daze seemed broken for a moment, but he was not really conscious of what was happening. There had been no last supper, no special requests—Christ, let's get this damned thing over before I puke! thought Tarbell. He looked to Lieutenant Pines for help, and the priest nodded.

"Take him over there for a second," said Tarbell.

Franko reached one hand through the bars of the little window, groping for Gardiner's, but saw that his hands were bound behind his back. He grabbed Gardiner's shoulder roughly, but now that he had him there, what in hell did he say? What in hell did he say? Be brave, kid!

32

Stay strong, kid! Don't let them get you down, kid! Screw you, kid! Why don't you fight them? Kick, claw, bite, scream, but don't let them do this to you, you stupid son-of-a-bitch! He said nothing. He tightened his grip on Gardiner's shoulder while the man looked at him with that crazy, uncomprehending stare. He tightened his grip harder, starting to twist. If he twisted hard enough, maybe he could break it. Then they couldn't hang Gardiner. They'd have to put him back in his cell, take him to the hospital until he was better!

"All right, Franko, get it said!" the Colonel said. "This isn't your party. You'll have your chance soon enough."

"Hypocrites!" screamed Franko in a sudden burst of fury. "Lousy, goddamned hypocrites!"

"Silence that man!" snapped Tarbell. "Goddamn it, shut him up!"

Franko fixed his fanatical gaze upon the startled priest. "You, you holy-rolling son-of-a-bitch, you're the worst of all! Talk of God, talk of Christ, talk of Salvation, talk of Right and Wrong, and you're helping them crucify a kid!"

The MPs tried to pull Gardiner away and get at Franko while the man flung a stream of curses at them. They beat at his hand to make him let go, and in the melee Gardiner hung there relaxed, not even seeming to hear or to feel the pain of Franko's fierce grip.

Suddenly it struck Tarbell—the glaze of the man's eyes, the numbness, the docile following of orders, the almost catatonic movements. It wasn't just some sort of beneficent shock—the doctor had given him something. Against orders, against rules and regulations, Gordon had given him a sense-dulling pill to lull him on his way.

Well, the hell with him, the hell with them all, the hell with the Army for the stinking job they had given him! He smashed at Franko's wrist with the hammer-edge of his hand.

Franko felt his grip loosen. One of the MPs opened his cell door and shoved it back with a bone-jarring crash, breaking his hold on Gardiner. The MP hit him hard, catching him low on the cheek, and he fell to his cot and lay there, breathing hard but no longer speaking. He heard his cell door slammed and the key turning in the lock, and the procession marching quickly down the corridor, but he said no more. He had no more to say.

He felt exhilarated, Godlike—he had done what none of

them could do. He had done what God couldn't do, if there was a God—and Franko had led his life as though there were none, only his antithesis. He had given a man life. He had given Gardiner two more minutes of life than he had coming to him.

But they had him now. They had him in that room. He could hear the distant talking, and the praying, and then that final, unrecallable crash of the wooden trap . . .

. . . and he cringed. He cringed on his cot with the wet stink of the fear he rejected.

Reisman rushed from the execution chamber the moment the order for dismissal was given, stopping only to retrieve his bag from the Commandant's office. Outside the prison walls he removed his hat and held his face up to the rain, drinking it in, absorbing it hungrily through his pores, urging it down deep into his welcoming flesh so that it would fill him with nothing but cleanness. How good it was to be alive.

He found the road to The Butcher's Arms and raced along it, his suitcase slapping irritatingly against his shins, past the streets and lanes, the hedges, the black gardens of night, the tight clusters of dark stone walls that sheltered the slumbering populace of the old, old village, good people here and there and everywhere for whom justice had been done this night.

A hungriness propelled him, a hungriness that had forewarned him that evening, a pitiful need for softness to squeeze gross death from his mind and body. Why had it taken the boy so long to die? Toward the end he had wanted to rush down into the pit where the body hung and finish him off himself.

The inn was dark, and he tried the door. It was locked, and he turned away again and then back, like a man uncomprehendingly rejected, wondering if there was perhaps another way in, or if he had the right to wake them up since he had paid for his room.

Tess opened the door. "I forgot to give you a key," she said softly. "I worried about it all this time."

In the moment of seeing her, Reisman realized how pathetically relieved he was, how grateful for the sight of her, how necessary to him it had been for someone like her to be there—waiting for him, to give shelter and succor.

He brushed quickly into the dark entrance hall, past her, feeling that she wanted him to say something more to her than "I'm sorry I woke you," yet wondering if he sensed her mood or merely his own wishful thinking. Maybe it was her job to wait up for all stray dogs in the storm.

A big cozy blaze burned in the dark, empty taproom, throwing dancing fireshadows into the lobby that lit and darkened their faces.

"Look at you!" she cried suddenly as they moved closer to the light.

The water ran from his clothing in rivulets and formed little pools on the floor around him. His hat was soggy with the rain, and when he took it off, his hair was soaked and matted in disarrayed clumps. He stood by the stairs, wondering if he should go right up to his room, but he didn't want that. The night couldn't end for him with what he'd already done, already seen. Another few minutes and he was certain there were men in the prison room who would have passed out from the strain. He had watched their faces, seen the sickly whiteness and the cold sweat, and known that despite his fears, he was strong.

Tess took command of him. "You'd better take your things off, Captain," she ordered. "You're a sight! Come to the fire and warm yourself. I'll bring you something hot."

"Thanks," said Reisman. "I'd like that. The fire looks good." He couldn't just stand there like a fool, invoking the need of her. He had to say something, besides thinking it is you who looks good, so good, in your ludicrous, heavy wool coat buttoned to your neck to hide you from me chastely or warm you, it makes no difference . . . in your silly flannel nightgown flapping around your shoes . . . with your disarrayed hair the color of sand on a lonely beach . . . your pretty young face . . . your fine woman's body . . . you are good to see.

He dropped to the floor beside the fire and found a few books there beside a pillow. She hadn't been asleep then. She had been reading. Romantic stuff by firelight—two novels, one American, the other set in some far-off magic island; a collection of travel articles on the United States; and a thin book of poetry—*A Shropshire Lad* by A. E. Housman.

Tess came from the kitchen carrying two steaming mugs, and bent to him holding one out. "This will do you good," she said.

He put the cup to his mouth and pulled it away quickly, the heat still stinging his lips. "What is it?" he asked, his head enveloped in the steaming, spiritous essence.

"Pure fire," she said. "Fire of rum, blaze of cider, ignited by sticks of cinnamon. An American once told me, 'It'll kill ya or cure ya.' He spoke strangely, even for an American."

"Do you know many?"

"Oh . . ." she said, laughing, "hundreds. I feel sometimes that the entire American Army has come through here."

"How many are privileged to enjoy this middle of the night service?" he asked, and then was sorry he had said it when he saw the look of hurt on her face. He had not meant it as it sounded.

"Very few," she said, looking at him directly, her eyes catching little glints of firelight.

"I'm sorry."

"That's all right. I know you weren't being spiteful."

They were quiet for a while, staring into the blaze, taking little sips of the steaming brew. Was this then to be their little byplay, wondered Reisman? Where was the time for hellos and goodbyes, and then hello and goodbye again, and each meeting a closer coming together that reaffirmed what went before and set something new between them?

Reisman picked up the book of poetry. "I thought only moonfaced American boys read Housman."

"Were you moon-faced when you read him?"

"Yes . . . many times, regrettably. But I survived each one of them, and now I feel no pain."

"I don't believe you."

"About what?"

"That you feel no pain. It would be awful to feel no pain, for then you could feel nothing else." She paused and sipped from her cup, and then put it down on the raised hearthstone. "No goodness, no love."

How terribly wise she was for one so young, thought Reisman. "Did you mind my kissing you before?" he asked. He had asked a girl that once when he was fourteen, and received the strangest look from her. He had never asked again, and it had always been right. But now he was thirty, and Tess no more than eighteen, and so he felt fourteen again for a moment.

Tess turned and looked at him fully. "I thought you'd

forgotten," she said. "Because you were drunk and it meant nothing."

Reisman reached out and drew her to him, hearing the breath escape from her as she came softly to him, feeling himself grow strong. He was caught up in the compelling rhythm again—happily, yes—but was he enjoying life or celebrating death?

Tess pulled away from him. He had started to unbutton her coat. Even through the thickness of her clothing, how good it had been to hold her, to feel the soft warmth of her flesh. What an unbelievably marvelous construction was woman.

"Not here," she said softly. "Are you warm now?"

"Yes."

"Take your drink then and go upstairs . . . "

Reisman felt a sudden, hopeless loss and wanted to cry out *No!* ". . . I'll come to you soon," she finished.

His room was warm. She had kept the fire going there too. Reisman skinned out of his damp uniform and hung it over a chair near the fire, shaking with the heavy, expectant beating of his heart. But lying there alone under the soft thick comforter was no good. His mind fled away again and the specter invaded his senses. It had been a clean drop, but no one would ever know if the boy had suffered. Why hadn't they shot him quickly, instead of allowing him to dangle there for an eternity?

Tess came into the room, moving softly, standing over him before he even knew she was there. Reisman sat up and held out his hand to her and she fell beside him and kissed him. She tasted of the fire they had drunk, but still she did not let herself go completely. He started to unbutton her heavy coat again. "You don't wear this to bed, do you?" he said.

"No," she said, smiling. "Let me take it off."

When she came back to him, her nightgown still hid her. "Is it bright enough to see?" she asked. There was only the firelight in the room.

"Are you embarrassed?"

"No, not that," she said. "Will you read to me?" She picked up the *Shropshire* poems which she had carried upstairs and dropped beside the bed.

"Not from that," said Reisman, seeing what it was.

"Why not?"

"There are other things in there besides moon-faced lovers and willing girls," he said. "There's too much of death and hanging." The barbarity of it was not so much the fact of a youth alive a few minutes ago now being dead— Christ, there was a war on and they were dying all over the place!—but the absurd ritual accompanying his dying.

She lay against him again, this time trembling. "Then it's true," she said. "They hanged a man tonight. The Sergeant did it. You were there."

"Yes, I was there," he whispered. "That's right. Weep. Weep for him. Weep for the boy. Weep for the Sergeant. Weep for us all."

She kissed him again, and he looked at her a moment in awe, grateful, absorbed in the wonder of her, and when he pressed her against him, when he made love to her, made her whimper, laugh, writhe and call out, it was as though he were committing some private, instinctive act of memorium to the departed.

part
two

LES
ENFANTS
PERDUS

3

IN THE QUIET dignity of a London town house that was the headquarters of Special Operations, Office of Strategic Services, Major Max Armbruster sat at his desk, hunched over an ordered confusion of papers, maps and books. He was a scholarly-looking man in his early forties, with a high mop of brown hair combed straight back, and an impressive mustache he had nurtured to lush fullness since landing in England, in the virile style affected by stalwarts of the local forces, and which was the pride of his personal life.

It was Saturday morning, the twenty-sixth of February, 1944. On the college campuses where, before the war, Major Armbruster had taught political science, government and history, there had always been a hushed pause in the grind on Saturday mornings. However, the rules of warfare as determined by civilized peoples some years before at Geneva had not allowed for a five-day academic week. Professor Armbruster was still an important middle man, an organizer of information, purveyor of facts, and mentor to others, but now the lives of many men and the course of the war could be affected by his scholarship, and his physical presence on the job and alertness of mind were sometimes required seven days a week, twenty-four hours a day.

The project he brooded over now, tentatively entitled Amnesty, was one he realized had to have been cleared in the very top echelons of command, but Major Armbruster would never have suspected SHAEF of coming up with it,

41

it was so completely unorthodox: Select twelve General Prisoners convicted by courts-martial and doomed to be executed or serve lengthy prison terms for murder, rape, robbery and other crimes of violence; train and qualify them in as much of the clever and dirty business of behind-the-lines operations as they could absorb in a brief but unspecified time; and then deliver them secretly onto the European mainland just prior to the Invasion, to wreak havoc upon segments and personnel of the Nazi war machine. This was Project Amnesty.

It was not a directive, in the sense that it did not follow standard operating procedures for such missives, but was more a tentative outline of a tentative plan, and it was not signed. It was not by anybody's order; it just was brought to him by the young Lieutenant of Psychological Warfare who, also without precedent, had been attached by Supreme Headquarters Allied Expeditionary Forces as liaison and special project officer, with the full authorization and approval of OSS Base Headquarters in Grosvenor Square.

That the plan had been brought to Major Armbruster's branch for implementation was not unusual, for that which was unorthodox, unbelievable and untried elsewhere had always been the rule in his office. Yet he wondered if he would ever know the origin of the project. He would have to get next to Lieutenant Kinder, the liaison man, and try to find out more. It would be a good indication of the man's ability to preserve secrecy and a test of his own cleverness at finding things out.

Captain John Reisman bought a Third Class ticket for London at the Marston-Tyne station. Ordinarily he preferred the likelihood of comfort in a less crowded First Class compartment, but now he actually sought the possibility of human companionship.

The isolation he had felt from people, the revulsion at their sight, their touch and smell was gone. The pores of his senses were open again; the tendrils of sentient nerve endings once again sought active experience. The girl had cleansed him, made him whole again. He would buy her something in London and send it to her at the inn. It would mean something more to her than to him, and, therefore, it would be good. For him it would be a gentle kindness which it gave him pleasure to contemplate, and a way to say I know you, I do not think of you as being less, but being more. What we did together was more to me than you knew, though because I am me I cannot make of it anything more. For her the gift would be a sign that she was recognized and acknowledged as self, a symbol by which this acknowledgement could be conjured at will, brought up in joy, not sadness. For though there had been nothing of tears or remonstrations when he told her he was leaving that morning and didn't know if he would be back, there had been something of wistful regret written on her face.

"C'est la guerre!" he had said, cringing at its triteness. Was it the hundredth or thousandth time he had said that to a girl?

Waiting there on the little station of the Great Western Railway, Reisman watched another train come in on the Down side and passengers debarking. There was no town name on the station, as there were none in all of Britain. They had been taken away to confuse the enemy. Reisman wondered how many passengers these last years, not hearing the conductor's announcement and never having been where they were going, had missed their stops and been hopelessly lost in a nameless world. Someday they would put the names back on and for the survivors there would again be identifiable homes and roots.

It had never really troubled him before, this interminable and unending pursuit—almost a worship—of constant travel, excitement and adventure purely for its own sake, to which he had fallen victim. In fact, just now was the first instant in which he had ever thought of the adult years of his life in terms of the word victim. But in these last weeks, since escaping from Italy, he had felt the tiny and unaccountable crack in his supposedly impregnable make-up. Waiting in Bern for the courier plane, after slipping across the border into Switzerland on foot, he had marked his thirtieth birthday. Maybe that was it—old age; there was an energy-sapping dullness of routine, even to excitement, that brought tiredness and satiety. He wasn't a happy-go-lucky kid anymore. Now, of course, he couldn't get out of it if he wanted to. He was in for the duration, and his way of life was now an official way of life and highly prized. But what about afterward, if there was an after?

Thinking of the nameless towns, he remembered vividly one of the terrors of his boyhood, but whether it had been

43

daydream or nightdream, or even fact, he couldn't remember. Nevertheless, it had been a thing like this—the boy on a train, going to a place that was not a stop on the line but was accessible from somewhere along it, and being filled with a terrible panic of wondering How will I know when to get off?—as station after station went by, landscapes and lights blurred in swift passage, and people milled around him, embarking and debarking, knowing exactly from where they were coming and to where they were going. There was no terror in contemplating a thing like that for him today—but enough of a residue of memory for him to see a current simile of application.

It was early afternoon when the train arrived in London. Since Reisman had been away, a bomb had scored a direct hit upon the great translucent glass cupola over Paddington Station, leaving the stark, giant girders with no other function than to frame the open sky. There were still little piles of rubble around, and tiny shards of glass sparkled back the bright stream of light that poured through the shattered cupola onto the platforms. He caught a taxi in the tunnel and gave the driver the address of the house in Baker Street.

The weather was amazingly clear and warm for February in London. The sky was almost blue, the sun struggling to be yellow, and the dismal grays that had prevailed for weeks were suddenly revealed to have hidden colors that brightened the textures of faces and clothing of the great moving crowds, and the streets and buildings. Staring skyward in a puckish fantasy as the taxi carried him through the crowded streets, Reisman played with the notion that it was really the city that was held in place by the hundreds of barrage balloons that strained upward on taut cables—a floating fairyland in space, the *pièce de résistance* at some cosmic children's party, that would otherwise float away if it was not held down just so. Everything and everyone about him seemed to have absorbed the bright new mood of weather, seemed quicker, surer and infinitely gayer.

In Baker Street, Reisman tipped the driver more than was necessary, a habit he was always promising himself to stop. Americans were ruining the cab drivers and the British economy with their friendly open-handedness, and he was no different from the rest of them. He showed his special pass to the MP at the door, and entered the finely furnished reception hall of the building.

It was the town house of a Lord-something-or-other, now on duty with His Majesty's forces in In-ja, and it was on loan to the government for the duration. Lord-something-or-other was a man of some wealth and considerable taste, all reflected in the fine furnishings and decorations in the many rooms of the five-story, stucco-front building. One of the absolutely delicious and sensual pleasures of Reisman's life was to loll in a steaming tub in the large black marble bathroom adjoining Major Armbruster's office. He had been introduced to the habit when he had returned from his first mission, and hadn't been able to beat it. He would have loved to have had Max's pretty English secretary scrub his back and pat him dry, but had hesitated broaching the subject for fear of ruining a good thing.

"Hello, Mox'll," said Reisman, as he entered the Major's dark-paneled, carpeted office. "Tub ready?"

Major Armbruster took off his heavy-framed reading glasses and stood up to grip Reisman's hand. "Save the bath for another time, John," he said. "You look pristine pure." He sniffed the air a few times, wrinkling his nose. "No apparent body odors . . . You even look surprisingly cheerful."

Reisman tried to continue the flip mood. "Why shouldn't I be?" he said. "Nothing like a good public hanging to cheer one up. Wasn't it a sort of recreation once in Merrie Olde Englande?" But he had a sudden horror of memory, and he knew that it would always be with him and that he cared—cared more than he did when he thought of those times when he had been the purveyor of death. "I didn't realize we were also in the entertainment business. What's it all about?" he asked.

His flipness didn't cover up for him completely. Armbruster knew. There was uncertainty, if not anger, in his tone, and if so, then what he had witnessed had had the desired effect. If some deep and unprotected part of Reisman had been touched, maybe seared, then Armbruster's assessment of him had been close to being correct. Lieutenant Kinder had said the key man for the assignment must be composed of equal parts of brutality and compassion. Major Armbruster was well aware of Reisman's deadly

45

efficiency in matters of combat and espionage, and had great respect for his high intelligence. He had long suspected, too, that softness and compassion lurked somewhere far below the surface of his friend's tempered exterior.

"It's something new," said the Major, "quite new." He sat down and pointed Reisman to a leather chair.

"What about the Rosedale missions?"

"I am taking you off that. Forget everything you have learned about Rosedale. I don't believe you were in so deep as to compromise it." Armbruster paused, opened a desk drawer and rummaged around. "Before I forget . . . a letter came for you while you were away."

"Probably my draft board wanting to know why I haven't reported," Reisman said. But he was more than curious. He wasn't used to getting letters. When he saw whom it was from—Aaron Reisman of Chicago, Illinois, U.S.A.—it was more shock than surprise. He could hardly remember when he had ever before received a letter from his father. He slipped it into his coat pocket casually, eager to read it yet wanting to be alone when he did.

"The business in Marston-Tyne is part of something new," said Major Armbruster again. "It's quite unusual— even for us."

Reisman was suddenly all professional interest, leaning forward in his chair, senses alive. Armbruster told him about Project Amnesty.

"I want you to run the show, John," he said in conclusion. "You pick the prisoners you want, and give them their choice—execution of sentence or train for the missions."

"Seems to me there's not much of a choice," said Reisman, lighting a cigaret. "Particularly for those condemned to death. It's a gift. What's the catch?" He blew a stream of smoke at the ceiling and waited, a vacant expression covering the turmoil he felt building.

"I don't really know if there is one or not," said Armbruster.

"What's their reward if they pull off the jobs and get back? Do they get turned loose?"

"No rewards have been promised. Later on, the Review Board or the Commanding General or even the President might consider their records in the light of their new service. For now, it's an even trade, a temporary amnesty for the good of the service, as Lieutenant Kinder would say

. . . oh, you'll be working with Kinder, incidentally. You'll meet him shortly. You rank him and all that, but you'll be receiving some of your instructions from him. He's our direct channel topside. I don't mind telling you he strikes me as the sort who goes overboard quite easily on something like this. You may have to use some of your uncustomary diplomatic tact to keep both of you under control if you are going to work well together."

Armbruster reached for a pipe and tobacco pouch on his desk and leaned back comfortably in his high-backed chair. While his fingers expertly pushed and tamped the tobacco into the bowl, he continued to look directly at Reisman. "Well, what do you think of it all?" he asked.

"It stinks!" said Reisman in disgust. "Why don't we go to the troops and ask for real volunteers like we did for the Jedburgh teams, like I was doing for Rosedale, instead of resorting to jerks like these?"

"You know the difficulty we had filling the Jedburgh quota, John," said the Major, "and you were scouring the bottom of the barrel for Rosedale. The orders have come down about the type of personnel to be used, and we can't change that."

"I don't like training jobs, Max," Reisman said. "You know that. I want to go in somewhere again. Anywhere."

"That's out of the question. You won't be going in anywhere for a while."

"Why not?"

"I didn't think it would be necessary to go into that."

"I've got my own thoughts on it, but it's never been put into words by anyone."

"Very well," said Armbruster. "They were very disturbed at Base by what happened during the last big arms drop in the Mottarone before you came out. Your orders were to avoid contact with the enemy at all cost, merely to pick up the equipment and see that it got into the right hands. Luring the German Army into a pitched battle, causing casualties among our partisans, was not part of the plan. Base felt it was time to give you a rest."

"How come they're willing to trust me with this?"

"That was my idea."

Reisman inclined his head toward the Major in mock graciousness. "Then I'm not in bad with you, too?"

"No."

"My compliments, Major," he said, smiling. "What

47

makes you think I'm the man for this? Why not the MPs or the Disciplinary Training people?"

"This is an espionage mission," said Major Armbruster. His pipe had gone out, and he struck another match, got the pipe going and blew out the flame with a stream of smoke. "You wrote the text on what these men will have to learn, and you have been out there doing it yourself."

He didn't mind Reisman's protesting questions. They were more a searching out of himself, an airing of his doubts, than they were excuses.

"I can't picture myself playing warden, Max. I wouldn't know how to deal with men like these. The people I've always worked with have been topnotch boys—brainy, sharp, tough, patriotic as all hell, all the Boy Scout rules and regulations, and pure volunteers. How can we depend on a bunch of slobs when the chips are down?"

"In the end," said Armbruster quietly, "that would be entirely up to you to decide, John. If they were not ready, we would not send them in. *You* can make it work, otherwise I would not have interrupted your work on Rosedale. Whatever the Powers That Be have in mind, it may be of terrible consequence for the Invasion."

"What happens to the condemned men I don't pick? Pronto kaput?"

"I understand they'll hold off any further executions until after we land, except in certain instances. It will depend entirely upon the circumstances of the case."

"All right," said Reisman without conviction. He could turn it down and it would be all right, he knew, but he had never yet turned down an assignment, and there was always the chance that if he did well on this one, they would let him go in again.

The officer who bustled into Major Armbruster's office wore an exquisitely tailored Savile Row uniform and carried a briefcase chained to his left wrist. He was a short, thin young man with good cheer on his boyish face, as though it had been pasted there. Reisman was certain that he would also be able to paste a grim expression there, if it became necessary. He strode up to Armbruster's desk and saluted.

"First Lieutenant Stuart Kinder reporting as ordered, sir," he snapped out in a strong voice.

Reisman thought Max looked suddenly uncomfortable.

"No need for the formalities here, Lieutenant," said Major Armbruster. "I'd like you to meet John Reisman. I have told him as much about Amnesty as I could."

"Pleased to know you, sir," said Kinder, turning his smile to Reisman.

"You can dispense with the sir business with me, too," said Reisman. "We're all blood brothers in this racket. Besides, the way things go in this man's Army, it may not be long before you outrank me and I don't want you to hold it against me."

"Very well, Captain," said Kinder, still smiling. "Major . . ." He turned back to Armbruster. "The General and the others are ready and would like us to join them for the briefing."

They walked downstairs to a drawing room that was used for conferences. Reisman had been there often. His eyes wandered over the ordered luxury of the room—walls hung with a soft, textured fabric, probably silk; the thick rug, the fine lamps and paintings, and the marble mantelpiece. He loved the mood of this room, so alien from his beginnings. A number of large tables, extra chairs, and wallboards and cases for maps had been added to serve its present function. Three officers were there at a table. Reisman had rarely come this close to a man with a star on his shoulder, and for some strange reason his mood was immediately antagonistic—All right, show me why you're a General!

"You know Major Armbruster, sir," said Lieutenant Kinder to the General, falling comfortably into his role of liaison. "May I present Captain Reisman."

Reisman didn't know whether to salute or put out his hand. He never knew when the hell to salute or not.

"General Worden of the Judge Advocate General's office," Kinder explained, and the gray-haired gentleman stuck a fine-looking cigar into his mouth and extended the hand which had been holding it, ending Reisman's confusion. "Colonel Gould of Military Police," Kinder continued, "and I believe you know Colonel Denton."

"Of course. How are you, sir," said Reisman, shaking hands with each of the men. Denton was from Base Headquarters in Grosvenor Square, privy to the top policy councils of OSS.

General Worden took over immediately.

"Because of the unusual nature of this assignment," he said, directing his speech to Reisman, "we felt that you were entitled to as complete an explanation of it as we are at liberty to give you just now. Please feel free, Captain, and the rest of you, too, gentlemen"—he waved his cigar over them as though it were a papal scepter giving dispensation—"to disregard military formality and speak your mind here. Interrupt or rebut as you are moved to.

"Understand, first of all, gentlemen, we would not be going ahead with something like this unless we had the approval of the highest authority. My own feeling concerning Project Amnesty is that it is a simple matter of human logistics. These men may have gotten into trouble in civilian life, but in another way you might consider them casualties of the war. There is a certain amount of philosophical practicality to the whole idea. Better to use them than to waste them. As an example"—he paused so that the more startling part of his sentence would strike them with proper effect—"few people are aware, and I am sure that includes you gentlemen, that some months ago five thousand convicts paroled from Federal prisons to go into the Army were landed in the United Kingdom from the *Empress of Scotland*. Very few of that number have given us cause to regret their paroles. They are now an effective part of the Army."

The looked at each other to see who among them might wear the smug look of foreknowledge, but none of them did. Reisman was surprised, and so were the others, including Stuart Kinder, who looked petulant.

"Though it may be considered extending an interpretation somewhat," continued the General, "there exists within Army regulations and directives the grounds for undertaking a project such as Amnesty." The General waved his left hand toward Lieutenant Kinder and snapped his fingers twice. "Kinder, do you have that?"

Kinder opened a manual to a marked page. "Yes, sir. Right here. Paragraph seventeen, Army Regulation 600-375: 'Commanding officers having appropriate court-martial jurisdiction will give due consideration to the timely granting of temporary paroles or suspension or remission of unexecuted portions of sentences whenever it is in the best interest of the service to do so.' " He picked up a mimeographed paper and placed it on top of the manual. "Here is an excerpt from a directive concerning the Salvaging of Manpower and Clemency for the Good of the Service. It reads: 'Others of a criminal type, but who are intelligent, robust fighting men should be organized into special combat teams or construction units for duty at or near the front. These would be on the pattern of the French Foreign Legion.' "

"Thank you, Lieutenant," said General Worden. "Whether we will be able to find these 'intelligent, robust fighting men' among prisoners convicted of crimes of serious moral turpitude remains to be seen. My function in Amnesty ends with the judicial aspects of policy. The Army is leaning over backward to be fair to these men. For those who are contrite, here is a chance to make amends. For those facing long years in prison, here is a chance to beat the rap, as they say, at least temporarily. For those condemned to die, here is a better way to do it, if that is their fate."

The General had been talking to all of the group at the table, but now he spoke directly to Reisman. "You have a grave responsibility, Captain," he said, "and I must impress upon you the need for tact and secrecy, which I am sure you and your organization are accustomed to working under. Colonel Gould of the Military Police, who is also an experienced attorney, will assist you in gathering your personnel. Lieutenant Kinder will be your direct liaison with those other branches of the Army that will have an interest in Amnesty, including SHAEF, his own Psychological Warfare, and Colonel Denton's operational planning at your Base Headquarters. Lieutenant Kinder, please take over."

Stuart Kinder unchained the briefcase from his wrist, unlocked it, and removed a fat stack of folders. He was immediately all business.

"What I have here," he said, glancing up at Reisman, "are the service records, including courts-martial transcripts, of a sampling of the type of men you are authorized to use on this assignment. If you are not satisfied with these, the Judge Advocate General's branch will open its files to you, and you are authorized to choose any group of prisoners you want. I also have here JAG indices and charts of courts-martial proceedings broken down into various categories of crimes in relation to background, education, race, religion, age and other measurable aspects of personnel brought up on charges ranging from AWOL to murder. We, of course, are more interested in the harder types, as I will elaborate in a moment."

Kinder had the rapt attention of every man in the room, including the General, and was in firm control of himself, his material and his audience.

"I also have here," the Lieutenant continued, "an outline of the type of training these men will need in order to qualify them for the missions to be assigned."

"I take it, then," interrupted Major Armbruster, "that this is not to be a group operation, but a series of individual tasks?"

Colonel Denton intervened. "As of now, that is the plan, Max," he said. "But you are well aware of the many factors that can change between initial planning and final implementation in an operation of this sort. The actual missions are now undergoing study. All that can be said is that there will be certain dirty work to be done, important to the Invasion, and these are the men who will do it. The nature of the missions will not be revealed to anyone until the status of Captain Reisman's group is ready to be changed from Training to Operational, and that will probably be shortly before they go in—if they do, of course."

To Reisman this kind of fuzzy briefing meant that there were no missions as yet. There was only an idea.

Lieutenant Kinder picked up the ball as though it had never been borrowed from him. "I would like next to speak of the role in Amnesty of my own particular branch, Psychological Warfare," he said. He slipped one folder off the top of his pile, revealing some handwritten notes. "The fact that Psychological Warfare was brought into it is a bit out of the ordinary, yet it offers us a unique opportunity to test our thinking and methods at two ends of the same project. While Psychological Warfare, as you gentlemen know, is concerned with weakening the enemy through the use of propaganda—attacking, confusing and subverting him mentally—it is also, in a less known and more subtle area, concerned with motivating our own forces to fight even better. To have under working control a uniquely low caliber sociological group such as the one we propose to set up, will give us the opportunity to work out certain theories in actual practice, discard those that are unworkable, and inculcate others into the Information and Education programs of the Army. Programs that will work with this group will certainly work even better with individuals who have never suffered from their disciplinary problems. At the other end of this project, the target end, so to speak, these men will have tasks to fulfill against the enemy, of both a physical and psychological nature, the effectiveness of which we also hope to be able to evaluate."

Lieutenant Kinder reached for his briefcase and began returning his papers to it, indicating his part of the briefing was over.

"May I ask a question here, sir?" asked Reisman, addressing the General.

"Of course."

"I gather from Major Armbruster's talk with me earlier and from your remarks and Lieutenant Kinder's briefing that these are not just delinquents I am authorized to use, but murderers and rapists condemned to death."

"Colonel Denton," said the General.

"That's right, Captain," said the Colonel. "There are a number of factors involved which seem to dovetail nicely. From our point of view, the operational side, because of the nature of the missions being considered, it is precisely this type of individual that is wanted."

Reisman had committed himself more or less to Max, but not yet to these others. If he was to succeed in the assignment, then he would explore every facet of the plan and squeeze every drop of information from them that he could, whether it was science, clap-trap, opinion or fact. He wanted to be convinced and so far he wasn't.

"It has always been my understanding that criminal types generally are basically cowards," said Reisman. "How can we ever be certain of their loyalty?"

"That, Captain," said Colonel Denton, "will depend entirely on the man who trains them. If you do not feel that this assignment is for you, I will suggest to Major Armbruster that another man be assigned."

"That's all right, Colonel," interrupted General Worden. "I believe the Captain is within his rights in asking that question." He turned to Reisman. "Colonel Denton's response, however, states the situation succinctly and accurately. Everything will depend on the man who trains this group. You will probably find that your best candidates are those whose cases are still on review. Some may want to take their chances on the Review Board finding legal insufficiency in their trials—but you don't mention that. Those not under death sentence might even prefer the rela-

53

tive security of a Federal penitentiary to the insecurity of Project Amnesty. You must use your own ingenuity—possibly with the help of Lieutenant Kinder, who is trained in these things—to meet such a reaction from a man you feel will be an asset to your group."

"May I add one more important point, sir?" asked Lieutenant Kinder.

"Go ahead."

Kinder turned to Reisman and the grim expression was there, as Reisman had predicted it would be. "You must enlist men," he said, "to whom the possibility of death in these missions is actually a salvation. Men completely without hope, and this provides the hope. That is why we thought it best that you go personally to Marston-Tyne to witness a hanging—so that you would know from firsthand experience what it is like, and through you, your men will know."

"How much time do I have?" asked Reisman. What he wanted to say was, That was a cheap, stinking trick like the rest of this business! But he contained himself, beginning to use what Max had aptly termed his uncustomary diplomatic tact. Besides, despite his grousing, there was an unorthodoxy to the project that seemed more challenging than anything he had done before.

When the meeting was over, Reisman knew that at best he would have three months, at worst two. For if there was to be an invasion soon, it would be in May or June. Nobody knew, of course—probably not even the Commanding General—but this was the mood of the times, and this was the goal of the buildup.

In those meager weeks he must make soldiers of men who had lost their right to be men. He must instill in them a will to fight and then teach them how. And he must teach them how to parachute from an airplane into a black void of fear. The conduct of the training, the location, the methods, would be left more or less up to him. Lieutenant Kinder would stay in London and only come out into the field when needed, or to implement or report on one of the motivational schemes he might create.

Kinder left Reisman in possession of the briefcase of material. "I have copies in the safe in my office, of course," he said, handing him the keys.

Alone with Armbruster again as they walked back upstairs to his office, Reisman voiced a thought that had been teasing him: "You don't think it possible, do you, that that brilliant young man could have cooked up this whole thing himself?"

"I kept waiting for him to use that classic line," said Reisman, " 'There is no such thing as a bad boy.' "

Armbruster smiled at him. "And of course," he suggested, "you could have immediately refuted him with yourself as an example."

Reisman wondered if Max had any idea how close to the truth he was. But then he couldn't really know, for Chicago and that first youthful, confused run-in with violent death and the cops was a long time away.

4

IN A ROOM of the town house of Lord-something-or-other in the beleaguered city of London, so many miles and years from what he might think of without longing or pleasure as *home*, Reisman read the lines of his father's letter and smiled with a pang of old love.

February 4, 1944

Dear Jacob my son,

Here is a surprise which I hope is not a shock. Yes it is a letter from your father.

How come you do not write to me more often like the other boys in the neighborhood who are in the Army? Mothers and fathers show me the letters and pictures (the son of Mrs. Ellenstein, my landlady, I am renting his bedroom till he comes home from the war, he is a flyer out in China which I think is farrer away from Chicago than you yet he writes to her two times a month). They all ask me how come my son don't write and I tell them he's busy with the Army and he's alright because if he wasn't I would hear from them.

I still have your letter from more than a year ago from England and I take it out and read it sometimes. When are they going to let you come home on a furlow like the other boys? Five years I haven't seen you. I hope you are still in the same place and this letter gets there. I know I don't write you often, maybe even this is the first, and maybe you should ball me out. But to write a letter for me is hard (excuse the spelling and bad writing). But I didn't write you to ball you out. Only that you should remember your old father once in a while, like you do sometimes. I got the birthday card and the Jewish New Years. Thanks. But write something next time. Take a picture so I can show Mrs. Ellenstein your goodlooking not like your old man.

You know what today is? Today I went to the synagogue to say *yahrtzeit* for your Mother, may she rest in peace. You know what is *yahrtzeit*, you *shagetz* you. (I'm only joking). A prayer we say for the dead on the day they died so God will remember them and be kind to them. You probably forgot, but if you can go to a synagogue and ask the Rabbi to help you say a prayer.

You should remember your Mother, Jacob, and honor her. I have not loved a woman like her before or since. She was to me a Jewish woman. It wasn't her that *hocked* me about priests and churches and bringing you up—it was those gangsters. She knew the story of Ruth in the Bible. Ruth was also a *shiksah*, although excuse me for using that word. I don't like to use that word. People say it too much like a curse, only I don't mean it that way with your mother. Ruth said to Naomi, her Jewish mother-in-law: "Whither thou goest, I will go; and where thou lodgest, I will lodge: thy people shall be my people, and thy God my God." Who knows? Maybe I wasn't strong enough in my God then. Only lately now since I'm older and everybody is dying and I'm so much alone do I go so often to the synagogue.

Two days ago I went to a funeral. Diamond. Remember Diamond the delicatessen man where I use to take you to eat sometimes. He died. I went to the funeral because we belong to the same synagogue. I'm all the time going to funerals now. I should only be late for my own (ha ha).

I am no longer a spring chicken, Jacob, and I want you should remember. I'm alright. Healthy with a flat belly like you use to say proudly when you use to make like you were going to hit me there in fun when we went to the Oak Park Beach, and besides the akes and pains and *kvetchis* of an *alta cocker* I'm okay. But I'm 61 now and I want you should remember in case something happens. There is so much I never told you like I should. Your my son and I want you should know I have feeling for you. I don't know why you never settled down and got a job and got married and raised a family. But who should talk? I was past 30 when I married your mother, and she was a few years older, so maybe theres hope yet for you, huh kid?

I don't know why you go running away all the time. Maybe its my fault I never got married again and gave you a mother who would make a real home. I don't even know what it is you do for a living or if its honest accept now I know you are in the Army, or how come you go running off and going to places where its none of your business and fighting in wars. All I can think is like Errol Flynn in the movies and if you want to be like Errol Flynn thats your business. Now its okay because I understand what your doing. Its a war against Hitler and the Nazis and all they have done against the Jews and if the army would take me I would go myself.

I think a lot about all the good times we had together going to visit the relatives, going to the park, the beach, the movies, even to the synagogue was fun to go with my son when we went sometimes. Maybe we should have gone more often. You were a good boy, John, a good son, and I love you. What happened to make the *accident* happen, I don't know, maybe it was my fault it happened, and after that you ran away. That a father shouldn't be able to know a son 16 and help him is a terrible thing, I'm sorry.

Which reminds me I have news to tell you. Remember Osterman the detective who helped you. What do you think that *alta cocker* is in the army. I

57

use to see him sometimes in the neighborhood and he always asked for you. He came to see me special and said he is going overseas and wants your address to look you up. I gave it to him a couple weeks ago so maybe you should expect him if he went to England. If he went or not I don't know because President Roosevelt, God bless him, don't tell me all the inside stuff where he is sending our boys. I wish he would only tell me about you, I would be happy.

So that's the end of my story for now. I never wrote such a letter in all my life, its so big. I hope not too much for you to read. The old neighborhood is going to hell, not like it use to be, with the *shvartzes* moving in, but you should know that anytime you want you have a home here with me, kid.

Write to me and send me a picture.

Lots of love from your father,
Aaron

Reisman leaned back in a deep leather chair, eyes closed in nostalgia, the pages of blue-lined schoolpaper covered with painfully neat broad script spread on his lap, his hunger in devouring their contents still not appeased, but more so than he had ever expected.

How familiar the word patterns and rhythms. His father had been born in Chicago and spent a few years in its school system, but the older he got the more he sounded as though he might have been born in the Polish-German village from which his own father had emigrated back in the Eighties. It was not so much a matter of accent, but the words and ethnic perspectives and prejudices of the huddled-together old neighborhood around Roosevelt Road where he had always lived.

Half of Reisman's life had been there—unimportant now, for he had wrenched himself forcefully from it and thrown himself open to the neighborhoods of the world, and it was the thousands of other times and places and people of his more instant memories that formulated him as he was and maintained their stronger influence over him; yet his father wrote to him as though his world had not turned, as though it centered there on Roosevelt Road, as though he was in and of that neighborhood and had left from there to go to war.

Maybe it was so. Maybe his father knew better, and he was still in and of that narrower world. Though he hadn't thought so. Certainly there were things there that had influenced the course of his life by propelling him out and away. He may have severed the roots but they were still there, if somewhat dim and vague . . .

. . . February 4 . . . the disturbingly familiar date of the letter . . . but he had not remembered what it was until he read farther, and marveled that his father should sanctify a wife dead all these many years and mourn her in a place sacred to him but alien to her knowledge and beliefs . . .

. . . Winter in Chicago, icy winds born in the vast Canadian northland whipping in from Lake Michigan, ricocheting through the crowded streets . . . Influenza across the country . . . His mother—dark, gliding doer of household tasks and sometimes comforter—lying incomprehensibly sick . . . What was it but a lousy bad cold she had nursed him through with medicines and broths? . . . A terrible silence and grimness in the tenement apartment that knew none of the niceties of life and lacked some of its necessities . . . his father in a dark corner praying with tears in his eyes . . . The doctor coming out of the bedroom looking helpless . . . The Donatos suddenly filling the apartment . . . And the priest with his holy oil and Latin pronouncement of irreversible doom, while the boy of seven watched in curious terror the ancient rite of extreme unction and heard his grandmother cry *"Povera disgraziata tornata ad Dio!"* and sob that she had brought into the world not only life but death . . .

. . . The memories filled him suddenly with a vast emptiness, a terrible sense of once-upon-a-time loss, seeking some remembered softness, some leftover image of Mary Donato.

Her death never softened the relationship between his father and the Donatos. Stranger to their ways and language and religion, they had never forgiven him for marrying her, for being the instrument and partner of what they considered her sin, and they held him accountable somehow for her death. The boy, though, was their flesh and blood, baptized "in the name of the Father and of the Son and of the Holy Ghost." Though he was tainted by exterior contaminations they could neither understand nor accept, John also went to their church and had begun instruction for his first Holy Communion. And from them and his mother he had learned with a child's quick mastery a child's share of Italian. But they aggravated Aaron's grief by demands beyond compromises he had already made with his wife in love. They feared backsliding now that the boy's mother could no longer oversee the Catholic share of his upbringing and education.

Reisman read the first words of the letter again. *Dear Jacob my son* . . . And he remembered . . .

. . . "This is my son Jacob."

"Please, Pop . . . it's John."

"John, Jacob, what's the difference? What kind of name is John for a good Jewish boy?"

"I'm also a Ca—" No, skip it, he knows, don't hurt him. Softly, "It's on my birth certificate . . . John."

"A wonder *they* didn't try to name you Jesus!"

. . . Stubbornness, righteousness, and go-to-hell-with-you-ness, all in the face of unbending reality. These were among the strains he had inherited from his father. The Donatos had always been *they* or *them,* and sometimes *those gangsters,* because Uncle Pete carried a gun and was supposed to be a driver for Al Capone. But Pete had been a great guy—he called him Johnny-the-kid, and told him wild cops-and-robbers and adventure stories, and was his favorite relative, even though the Donatos had considered Pete as much a black sheep as the daughter who had married beyond the pale.

As a boy Reisman hadn't minded being segmented—part of the Jewish world of his father, the Italian Catholic world of his mother's domineering family, and the externally imposed norms of surface Americana to which they all paid homage while fighting to foster their identities within him. Baptized John, circumcised Jacob, he had once had a child's exhilaration at being special, at being part of so much. What he had to avoid was the conflicts between his worlds. He would not be made a battleground!

Reisman remembered a time when he was eleven or twelve. He and his father were at the Donatos on a Sunday, where the large clan always gathered, drifting in and out, depending on which Mass they went to. A woman cousin, either oblivious to the presence of Aaron and his son, or not caring, was talking about how it was the Jews who had all the money, they were crooks, so never give one an even break in business, rob him blind if you get a chance. The boy stood up and shouted: "You're full of shit! My father's a Jew and I'm a Jew. Do we look like we got all the money in the world!" Tears of anger filled his eyes and he trembled with rage. A shocked silence filled the room, and he was amazed that he, a child, had command in that moment of every person there. He rushed out of the house, catching Uncle Pete's smile and wink as he went past him, that made him feel good all over. His father rushed out after him, took him by the hand and walked silently beside him for a few seconds. "You shouldn't use such words, John," he had said.

Aaron didn't help much, either, in the interfamily rivalry. He would never eat in a Donato household—"No, thank you, I just ate!" Not that he was so very strict when it came to the ancient dietary laws, but dammit, if they were forever going to think of him suspiciously as a foreigner, he would show them how stubborn and unbending and different he could be and make them rue it. The day they started serving gefilte fish, matzo ball soup and meats from a kosher butcher, on ritually cleansed and separated plates, was the day he would join them in eating. And Reisman could remember, in humor, his matriarchal grandmother angrily saying to his father, "Wassama, you think I poison you? No good enough for you?"

When his father finally decided to limit his own visits to the Donatos to maybe once a year, and to let John go himself whenever he wanted to, he mimicked some of the milder elements of their Sunday talk that alienated him: "You been to Mass? You made a Confession? You going to take a Communion? It's Greek to me. You'd think maybe they was related to Cardinal Mundelein or the Pope or they was the biggest angels in the world the way they talk! They want me to go to church. Why don't they come to the synagogue with me? Even your mother, may she rest in peace, wouldn't come with us. It was against her religion, she said."

Then how had they met, those two? So different in their backgrounds, and so much alike in their loneliness. How many times had he heard that romantic story from his father, and he could even remember back far enough to when his mother would laughingly correct and add details or tell her own version of it. He had heard the story again that last summer before the war when he had sailed back to the States from Europe, thinking the World's Fair in

New York might be something worth seeing, and had gone on to Chicago for a few days, feeling like a stranger.

He had found his father in another rented bedroom then. Shorter and thinner than his son, with the old shock of wild brown hair going gray and sparse, and glasses then, with speckled brown thin frames—"only for reading," although there was never any evidence of it around except newspapers. He had long since given up the old apartment —"What do I need such a big place myself for?" But it hadn't been big at all. It had been lonely. And rather than have a place of his own, he preferred to board and become involved at least partly in other people's lives.

"Why don't you get married again, Pop?" Reisman had asked casually.

"Married! Huh? From you too?" he muttered. "All the family keep saying, 'Why don't you get married again, Aaron?' Even the dead ones in my dreams like your Uncle Bernie and Aunt Rose and more uncles and aunts and even cousins are dying younger than me, I see them ten years ago saying, 'So when you going to get married again? You got a girl friend, Aaron?' Nobody but cockeyed Jennie I tell them. They should mind their own business. I don't want to get married again. When my son gets married then I'll get married."

And he had told the story again, how he had been on a Fourth of July boat ride to Benton Harbor and had seen a woman leaning against the rail, looking as though she was about to cry. "She looked Jewish with the dark skin and the thick black hair tied up in back, and you put together in the same group sometimes Jews and Italians and who can tell the difference, maybe not even God."

She told him her name was Mary and she was about to cry because she was angry that she should be seasick because all the time she never did anything exciting and she had been looking forward to the boat ride for so long. Everybody had come with a group—"churches, politics, like me the Workman's Circle, everybody friendly together celebrating their American holiday"—husbands and wives and kids, and boys and girls on dates, and singles like Aaron Reisman and Mary Donato, hoping they would find somebody. She told him she had come with a church group. In a sudden, unaccountable and inspired moment of braggadocio, he told her his name was Tony.

They stayed together and he bought her a lemonade and

they talked and she wasn't seasick anymore. At Benton Harbor they walked around together and had fun and pretty soon they were holding hands. "Then I knew I should tell her I wasn't Tony because she was asking me questions like where I lived and what church I went to and where I worked and what my last name was and I had to make up some pretty fast stuff. But she looked so happy, if I told her I wasn't Tony maybe she would be mad or cry and spoil her day, so for the day I would be a big deal *shagetz* named Tony and who would know the difference?"

But that night coming back on the boat . . . "You're old enough already to know how it is by moonlight at night on the water with a girl you like. I knew already it was too much. Your mother was talking to me like all her life she knew me, telling me what was in her heart and soul, and I felt so much I had to take this poor girl in my arms and hold her and comfort her."

He asked her how come a beautiful girl like her didn't have a husband or a boy friend and she told him she had one once, in Italy. "And you know something, she never saw him since she was a baby, only she wrote to him in Italian. She was born in the old country and was brought over here a little girl and you know how it is in the old country how parents say to a neighbor or friend their children will get married and it's a promise. Anyhow, that's what happened to her and for years she was waiting for this guy to come over and marry her, only he never showed up, and her mother and father made her wait. She was scared of them like a little girl. Finally she heard that this guy got married over in the old country and was never coming and it was like hearing her husband died only he died before she ever knew what it was like to have a husband. She said she was going to be a nun only her mother screamed like she was dying and her father said he wouldn't let her do it. She had to stay home and take care of them, that's what God meant for her to do. She wanted to get married so bad, only by that time all the men she knew were already married with families. I kidded her. I said I'd marry her myself if I thought I had a chance."

Reisman remembered how very serious his father had become as he said the next lines. They were in his room, Aaron sitting on his bed, smoking, slumped forward, reminiscing; Reisman in the one comfortable chair, the *Tribune* in his lap telling of the latest Nazi demands and weighing the possibility of war in Europe. "About such things I should advise you, Jacob," he had said, "if I never tell you nothing else, don't joke. It's a serious business with them. She asked me if I meant it and I said yes. You never saw such love and hope in a woman's eyes, Jacob, and tears. And I thought I must be crazy I didn't even know this girl an Italian *shiksah*, God bless her, and I was asking her to marry me and she was saying yes. Girls I knew I asked to marry me they said no because they were all the time interested in prospects, what's a man make, what he does, what kind of future. Me right away they knew had no prospects, no ambitions and I wasn't even such a big good-looking guy to make them happy. Mary Donato, may she rest in peace, in one day was happy and in love with a *shlump* like me and she wanted to marry me. Only she was calling me Tony so now I had to tell her the truth I was Aaron Reisman and I came from a different kind of family and religion. She was confused and even a little afraid, but she said, 'You know, I didn't think you was an Italian.' Then I said I guess you want to forget what you said, and she looked me right in the eye and said, 'No, I wasn't kidding. I never had so much fun with anybody like I had with you today, Aaron. I never told anybody the things I told you. It's like you knew me already like we were already married.' All of a sudden I really meant what I almost meant before when I was kidding her, I had such a feeling for her. I really felt good, big, like a man for the first time.

"You know, Johnny"—he had hardly ever called him Johnny or John and it sounded strange coming from him —"how you talk about adventure and going off and doing different things because the world isn't only where you were born and live and the same kind of people you know. Maybe to marry your mother was my adventure."

Mary Donato never went home that night because she was afraid she would change her mind or she wouldn't be able to get out, or that Aaron would change his mind. The next morning they were the first customers at City Hall to get married. "The families, they could scream their heads off all they wanted, both sides, we were married and happy and that was that. My family, too, was no bargain. I was working then for my brother Bernie in the store on Maxwell and he was all the time talking about how I stabbed him in the back and insulted Momma and Poppa.

He was supposed to give me a raise but he wouldn't do it out of spite so I left the store and you don't remember you were too young then but after that I had all the time different kinds of jobs and never made enough money to get along the way I should except always we ate and had a roof over our heads. And those gangsters, they made your mother feel bad all the time saying she wasn't married unless she went to a priest. Me they hated, like I stole her from them, a woman past thirty who was all the time staying home taking care of the house and her old mother and father and the brothers and sisters and the rest of them. You know I'm broad-minded and not so kosher religious but not even for your mother I wouldn't go to a priest in a church and that was that."

It had been funny then, in the summer of 1939, to hear him rant about *those gangsters,* for the old Donatos had already gone to their heaven, and even Uncle Pete was gone, shot to death in an intergang squabble, and it was for Pete, more than any of them, that Reisman felt sorrow, for he would have liked to see him and tell him exciting stories then of his own, and maybe have him be proud.

But his father had rambled on, and Reisman had wondered why it was that some men got mellower as they got older and others became more bitter. "I know you used to go to church with her when you were a little boy and it's not so terrible. That much I said they could do. They could take you to church if they wanted, but you also went to synagogue, remember? You should know what a tumult they made when they found out I had a *bris* made on you in my own apartment with my own relatives there, and your mother who was resting in the bedroom from having you said it was okay because even the doctor said it was a healthy thing to do. Did I make such a fuss when they took you to be baptized? Only they shouldn't drown you in all that holy water. To be twiced blessed maybe isn't such a bad thing, anyway, I figured . . ."

That was it. In the beginning John Reisman had thought too that he was twice blessed, with his child's exhilaration and wonder at the beauties and mysteries of his segmented worlds. But in time he had come to dislike the ritual devotions in church and synagogue—not only with the frustration of a boy who has discovered more compelling interests and is made fidgety by having to sit still and clean and silent, but also with sudden awakenings to conflicts and confusions and big fat holes in reasoning, and hypocrisy, that were the stuff of dogma.

When it had come time for his Confirmation in the church and *bar mitzvah* in the synagogue, he had rebelled and refused to cooperate, for he could not commit himself to either with a pure and honest heart. And he had felt better, and stronger in his private resolves, too, when he got through that period, for with something of the childhood fear of the omnipotent anger of God still within him, he had allowed for the possibility that he might be untimely cut down for his sins of omission.

And later, when it was demanded of him that he make a stand—not by his father, nor even by the Donatos, but by the peculiar prejudices of forces he didn't understand—when he realized he wouldn't be allowed to be a complete person in his segmented worlds, that he had to be identified as one thing or the other, or even as something completely different; when he was attacked for being one thing or the other—only then had he begun to lose his belief in God, his respect for *status quo,* and forever after created identifications of his own.

Filled with memories conjured up by the letter, Reisman tried to picture Aaron as he had written it. He would be sitting at a small painted desk in his rented bedroom, with a wobbly little lamp of china or Colonial maple that didn't give enough light. He'd have on his longies—it got pretty cold pushing a hack around those streets, even with a heater in the car—and pants, socks and slippers, and a robe hugged tight up on his thin chest; and there'd be the smell of steam heat in the room, a little table radio playing softly, and the knocking of the radiator pipes as they gasped and struggled to function.

Pop! You wonderful old character, he thought. I am glad that Mary Donato didn't marry some old country guinea, for though I have met many, loved some and hated others, I would not have had you then as a father, and this would have been a loss. You who marshal within yourself all the inbred, innate, inertial tenacity of all the sundered tribes of Judah and Israel and say, I believe! Therefore, it is so! There never was any *accident.* You know there was no *accident.* You know because you underline it as you do your wonderful Yiddish words, telling me in secret that it

66

is special with special value and meaning, as they are special. You know there was no accident. I killed a man. In blind, righteous fury, I killed a man with the strength of remembered cowardice, because the first time I had been called out, as every man or boy in his lifetime must be called out, I turned and ran, and swore that I would never run again. And never did.

5

LIEUTENANT COLONEL Simon R. Tarbell looked up from the personnel shipment order he was reading and muttered softly to himself, "Thank God." The involuntary trembling of his hands stopped, and he was able to soothe the nauseous sickness of his soul. It wasn't the order itself that elicited gratitude to his particular deity, but the thoughtful note appended by a friend at Southern Base Headquarters in Salisbury who suspected, but had never been told, the true depth of Tarbell's suffering in his job as chief warden and lord high executioner.

Among the prisoners coming into Marston-Tyne that day—Wednesday, 1 March 1944—were maximum security convicts awaiting review of death sentences. Ordinarily that would mean work for Sergeant Morgan within a few weeks, and new nightmares for Tarbell into eternity. He knew already that he would never be the same man again, as a result of his duties of the past year. But the personal note said, "I have it on good authority that executions are being put off until after the Invasion, despite any conclusions you may draw from prisoners on enclosed roster."

In the windswept airport at Belfast, Ireland, Samson Posey broke from his armed guards and ran. Now they would shoot and it would be done!

He ran fast, but awkwardly—head depressed into shoulders, back muscles tensed for the smash of bullets he hoped would end his life. He was not afraid to die, but he must not hang. How could his soul fly free and away on his last breath if it was imprisoned, if he was strangled like a dog, at the end of a rope?

But the brute pain he expected didn't come.

Had they missed?

He was a big man, an easy target. He slowed. He heard no sounds of firing. And in those few more seconds of running, prepared and eager to die this way, he thought of Billy Three-legs, whose power was strong; and of Old Charlie, his grandfather; Yucca, his father; Anna, his mother; Eva, his wife; and Little Charlie, his son; and of The People —and he was ashamed. This, too, was wrong. He was fleeing, turning his back, as The People had turned their backs and fled, until the ground in which to run was smaller and smaller, and desolate as the emptiness of their lives.

He stopped in a patch of lush green grass, gasping in the sweet wetness of it which alone might be the secret of the white men's strength as Billy Three-legs said. The wonder of its wetness and color! If they had grass like that at home to feed their emaciated cattle and sheep, to feed themselves, then maybe he would never have had to leave.

He turned, a giant again and not a turtle; head erect, shoulders squared, as the soldiers always demanded; massive chest out to take the bullets, so that he faced his enemies and would die in this way, and they would know, and those at home would know he had not died a coward. Billy Three-legs' power was strong to come this far and turn him around. He'd always thought so, but now he knew for sure. It would be good to die there in the thick green grass, breathing in the wetness of it, mingling his blood with its strength and willing both back to The People.

But they didn't shoot. They smashed into him—the three guards who had brought him from the Base stockade and the others who answered their coyote barks of angry alarm. He fought with the strength of the bear, but they smothered him and chained him, and carried him trussed like a sheep for the slaughter into the growling belly of the airplane.

It rose up like the eagle, screaming with fire and thunder, bearing him with it, and he marveled that he was flying . . . really flying. Never had he done anything like this . . . and suddenly the tension within him eased, he stopped straining at his chains, and he was calm . . . remembering when he was called Suh-gatz . . .

The scream of the eagle startled Suh-gatz. He was alone with Yucca's sheep in a scrubby canyon on Ute Mountain. He had expected no strange sights or sounds, certainly not eagle, for in the ten summers of his life he had never seen one there, though he knew about eagle.

Sheep bleated with fear and little ones ran to their mothers. Big for his age and strong, Suh-gatz was still a boy and frightened by the unexpected. He grasped his stick tighter and whirled his eyes around the rim of the canyon, searching the clear sky, the crevices, the green stands of piñon and juniper.

There! There was eagle! The sight of him filled Suh-gatz with the exultation of discovery, and fear again for the safety of the sheep. Yucca could not afford to lose any, not even one little one. Suh-gatz raced to his tent and snatched up the ancient rifle Old Charlie had taught him to use. He did not want to shoot eagle. He would not shoot him unless eagle wanted to take Yucca's sheep. But what a tale he would have to tell when he returned to camp. How big was eagle, what great noise he made, what wind he stirred with the beat of his great wings as he swooped down and up, down and up near the top of the canyon, as though calling to somebody, as though shouting, "Come fly, boy! Follow eagle into the sky!"

It was then that he saw something else and laughed, as much with the pleasure of being witness to so great an event as with the realization of his great error. Eagle was not *he*, but *she*. Sighting along the barrel of the rifle, Suh-gatz saw something else move up there on the mountain. There were little heads, and wings flurrying in imitation, and little cries, and he knew eagle really was calling, "Come fly! Follow me into the sky!"

Then suddenly eagle swooped down into the place where she lived, where her babies were. And as if one visitation were not enough for him that day, another sound came to them—*them,* for Suh-gatz and eagle were truly together in that awesome moment when airplane glided over the ridge preceded by its noise. Eagle didn't know what it was. She hovered in her aerie, wings spread protectively over her young. But Suh-gatz knew, after that first shock of recognition, for he had heard about white men's birds of wood and cloth and iron, though never before had he seen one.

For weeks, Suh-gatz told everybody he met about eagle and airplane, but nobody got as excited about it, or had anything as interesting to say about it as Billy Three-legs when he saw him down at the Towaoc trading post. It was before Billy got the power real strong and started to walk again with a cane, so he was still called Billy No-legs. But he was smarter than anybody else around, and he had some power even then, although he was only six or seven years older than Suh-gatz, not really old enough to be respected like the strong medicine men.

It wasn't the airplane so much that interested Billy—he'd seen a lot of them all those times he'd gone away to the white hospital to get his legs fixed up—but he wanted to know more about that eagle and her babies. They spoke in Ute. Billy knew English pretty good, but hardly anybody else did in that part of the reservation. Suh-gatz didn't. He knew the language of The People, and only a few words in English and Spanish picked up from sheepherders, cattlemen and traders.

"You show me where that eagle is, I'll teach you how to play poker," said Billy.

Billy was pretty good at gambling. Like most of the Utes around Towaoc, he spent a lot of time playing poker and Spanish monte. Even Yucca, who knew about sheep and cattle, and Old Charlie, who knew more about the old days than anybody, couldn't have taught Suh-gatz about gambling better than Billy Three-legs.

So they made a deal, and on the way up Ute Mountain together on Billy's horse a few days later, Billy told Suh-gatz what he really wanted was to get one of those baby eagles for himself and train him. He told how in the old days The People kept eagles for pets. They'd file their beaks and talons with a stone, and pluck their wings. The eagles stayed near camp to be fed scraps and grasshoppers.

"There's a lot of power in eagle," said Billy. "You don't know about these things yet, but I do. You know I've got power. But if I have eagle, it will make me stronger. Maybe I can walk."

They rode quietly awhile, beginning to climb out of the sage-brush barrens into higher country, a little greener. They moved along at an easy walk so as not to tire the horse. Suh-gatz held the reins, and he was big enough already so he could easily see around Billy, who sat in front of him.

"We getting close?" asked Billy anxiously.

"No, not yet. Still a long way."

Then Billy started to talk about what Suh-gatz had seen on the mountain. "If you had power, you'd understand," he said.

"What do you mean?"

"First eagle calls to babies, 'Follow me!' Then airplane flies over and says the same thing, only to you. That airplane probably belonged to the Army. It's easy to tell what it means if you have power like I do."

"What does it mean?"

"Will you help me catch eagle? You'll probably have to climb up rocks or go up on a cliff to get to the nest. Will you do that?"

"Sure!" he answered readily.

Billy read the signs for him then. Great eagle was the government that had taken away the ancient tribal lands and left them in poverty; airplane belonged to the Army their fathers and grandfathers had fought; together they meant there would be a time Suh-gatz must join the soldiers of the eagle, fight beside them and bring honor to his people.

Such a thing was so far beyond his comprehension that Suh-gatz didn't know what to say. Finally he asked, wide-eyed, "How'd you get power, Billy? Sun Dance? You eat peyote?"

"No, not yet. I will some day, but not yet. You can't go too fast with these things or it'll kill you," said Billy. He smacked his blue jeans where they covered his shattered legs, and then the two crutches lashed to the saddle. "I got it from here. From the white men's bullets. That time I got shot when I was a baby, that's when I got it, only I didn't know it then. The white men shot it into me with their lead. If you've got that in you and you live, then you're real strong."

Suh-gatz knew the story. All The People knew about that time when Billy was a papoose and his camp was attacked over in Utah by a white posse that wanted to arrest a Ute they said had killed a Mexican. It was just five winters before Suh-gatz was born, and that was the last time The People had fought a real battle with the white men.

They reached the scrubby canyon where Suh-gatz had been with Yucca's band of sheep. "There!" he said. He pointed. "That's where I saw eagle!"

71

Billy stretched himself erect and forward and fastened his eyes hungrily on the spot. They saw nothing but the rocky canyon walls, the clear sky, the crevices, the green stands of piñon and juniper. There was a tall, deep silence within the high valley. Billy turned in the saddle so that his eyes were level with Suh-gatz's.

"I spoke the truth," said Suh-gatz.

He urged the double-burdened horse upward. Soon he got off and led her carefully through the treacherous rock-falls until dirt and stones started to skitter away under her feet and she balked.

"Help me down," said Billy. "I'll stay here."

Billy leaned on his crutches and looked anxiously up the mountain. There was disappointment written in his face, and Suh-gatz felt sorry for him.

"Maybe they have flown away," he said softly, and then he wished he hadn't said that, even though it seemed to be so.

He tethered the horse to a large rock, took his rifle and began to climb. He didn't really want to hurt eagle with his rifle, or steal one of her babies so Billy could do to it what he said The People used to do, but if it would help Billy, okay.

It was dangerous climbing, and any second he expected to hear eagle's scream and maybe be attacked—but there was nothing. He got as close to where he thought the aerie was as he could, and then he was stopped by an outcropping of cliff. He couldn't go any farther. He threw rocks and called "Eagle! Eagle! Eagle!" hoping to stir them up if they were there, but nothing moved on the canyon wall except Suh-gatz.

When he climbed down empty-handed to where Billy waited and saw with what great disappointment he was greeted, he was sorry he had ever agreed to the deal.

"You don't have to teach me poker," he said.

Billy smiled—and to Suh-gatz this was a wonderful thing, for he had hardly ever seen him do that before.

"I will teach you poker," Billy said, reaching out his hand and grasping Suh-gatz's shoulder. "Will you look for eagle with me again?"

"Sure," he answered.

But they never found eagle, and Suh-gatz was secretly glad.

So this airplane did not frighten Samson. It brought back the boyhood times. It was eagle speaking to him through the power of Billy Three-legs who had read the signs—telling him not to despair, this was his true way, he had not been forsaken. For things had happened that had worried him to think the boyhood signs had been wrong or misread.

He knew with great pain that he was ignorant and un-schooled. They had taken him into the Army but had not taught him very much of the skills of a soldier. He had been put aside as though crazy, put to work like a Navajo, lifting, carrying, digging, piling. And then, so long, so far from home, from Eva, out of his great loneliness and need, he had gone in search of a woman, risked catching the love sickness he'd escaped at home by marrying only Eva, and had been goaded into an anger that killed.

If only the woman-seller hadn't pulled the knife! To be cheated, to be insulted, this he was used to. But to be a coward before a knife was something else. He had beaten the man with his bare hands—and he had been dead before Samson realized it.

In the soldier's court, when the officer who spoke for him had pleaded for mercy, the officer who spoke against him had told the judges about that other time . . . when he almost killed two soldiers cheating him at poker. So, it had gone hard against him. Maybe harder than if he had never hurt those other men. And in a small way he saw that there might also be some justice in the way it had gone hard, for few men knew the tricks Billy Three-legs had taught him with cards. The little tricks that were also cheating, which he used with great pleasure only against white men, and which had never been caught.

So the soldier's court had said he must hang. Why they did not do the deed there he did not understand. But it was only one thing of many that Samson Posey did not under-stand about the alien world into which he had foolishly al-lowed himself to be caught up and swept away. Now there was nothing left but the old bitterness that was his heritage, the inbred hatred against them—the Belegana, the pale-faced iron-makers from the east with hairy mouths and ears sticking out. And knowing the way the soldier-judges said he must die, he hoped airplane would carry him into the sea above which they flew now, and he would die in that way—better than hanging.

But that too was in vain. They landed, and he could not help feeling a great exhilaration at the way airplane glided down from the sky.

In the truck he dozed fitfully, thinking of home, wondering where the soldier-policemen were taking him. He felt the truck slowing, and as it turned, his huge body tightened against the chains that held him to the frame. The truck stopped and Samson heard boots against stone, the coyote bark of questions and answers, wood banging against wood, wood banging against metal. One guard awoke startled and angled his rifle at him. The other guard lifted the canvas flap and peered out into the gray day wetness where other soldier-policemen gathered. They were in an enclosed place, for the wind had been cut off. All Samon's senses were alert. Once he had wished he knew more of the language of these men, and he had tried hard. Now he didn't care. His ears heard everything and knew meaning if not words. The hush of rain spoke to him; the wind moved elsewhere, but not against the truck, for walls or buildings broke it; his nose was filled with the wet smell of canvas, sickening to his empty stomach, alien to the hot smell of canvas under burning sun, which was the way he remembered it, although there had been many winters of wet and snow and cold.

If this was the place, if this was the time, he would know it, and he would do something to make them shoot him. He was not afraid to die, but he must not hang. How could his soul fly free and away on his last breath if it was imprisoned, if he was strangled like a dog at the end of a rope?

The guards rose and came toward him along the bed of the truck in a crouching position, one on each side of him. The flaps were up now and the tailgate down, revealing a crowd of curious soldiers gathered around the truck.

"What in hell you got here, boys?" asked Sergeant D'Alessio.

"Special dee-livery all the way from Belfast, Ireland," said the Staff who had been riding shotgun in the cab, "and it ain't Irish whisky."

"How many you got?" asked D'Alessio, taking the personnel manifest. "Bowren, get that goddamned guard detail lined up in a hurry!" he yelled to the Corporal.

74

Corporal Clyde Bowren gave them the quick "Ten-hut! Dress ri-i-ight, dress! Pa-ra-a-ade rest!" left them that way and turned to see what else was bugging the Sergeant at the tailgate.

"Only one!" D'Alessio bellowed. "For shit's sake, why all the artillery!"

Bowren strained his attention into the mildewed interior of the vehicle. He heard one of the truck guards order, "All right, Chief, let's get your ass out of here! Behave yourself and nobody's gonna hurt you!" Then he heard chains clanking, and—he couldn't help himself, and it was all right because D'Alessio did the same damned thing—he gasped and involuntarily stepped back from the truck.

"Holy Mother of God!" The Sergeant whistled. "What is it?"

"Watsamatta, you never seen an Indian before?" said the Staff, laughing. "This one no speaka da English, so you gotta point. He must be something real special. They gave us a whole goddamned airplane to take him across the Irish Sea. I'll sure be glad to get rid of the son-of-a-bitch. Tried to make a break for it at the airport."

"Get him outta those goddamned things," said D'Alessio, pointing to the chains.

The Staff handed him the keys and stood back. He didn't voice it, but his expression said Go ahead, wise guy, it's your funeral! An expectant hush fell on the prison yard as D'Alessio bent to the shackles. He glanced up just once into the broad, walnut-brown face of the man who towered hugely above him, and whatever assurance passed between them was silent.

"Fall in the guard in two files, Corporal," said D'Alessio. "Take him to the dispensary with the others."

Waiting for the processing to begin in the medical Quonset, what Kendall B. Sawyer wanted most was a shave and shower. He felt ratty and unclean, and standing among the others, who probably didn't give a damn one way or the other, seemed to compound it. If the Army had taught him one thing, it had taught him the daily ritual of cleanliness, so that he had actually come to enjoy it and miss it if everything were not just so. Face scraped pink and shiny, hair never longer than a quarter of an inch, ODs pressed to perfection, fatigues that belied their name, summer tans starched to brittle stiffness, shoes gleaming so bright the inspecting officers used to kid him they could check their own appearance in them, decorations proper and in their place, and two beautiful stripes on his sleeves, just high enough to keep him out of the crap details and low enough so he didn't have to worry.

It had been that way for three years, except for the months in combat in Africa, Sicily and Italy, and even then a tank gunner had a little more of the conveniences of home with him, a little more of a chance to take care of himself. The stripes were gone now, and so was Kendall B. Sawyer, good soldier, and it was nobody's fault but his own, and for this he was truly sorry. In his rain-damp and rumpled coat and uniform, his layer of travel dirt and stubble, he missed the good soldier.

"Call the roll, Sergeant," said Captain Gordon. There were eight new prisoners in the room now, men who had been brought to Marston-Tyne in ones and twos from all parts of Britain, and had been arriving all morning, awaiting his pleasure to certify them alive and healthy. He wondered how many of them he would be certifying dead at the end of a rope in the weeks to come. Later, when he had more time, he would read over their service records and courts-martial transcripts. He always found that fascinating, and sometimes enlightening. It was a strange and motley group this time. He looked at the giant and thought of Queequeg the savage harpooner of *Moby Dick*.

"When I call your name, step forward and answer Present," ordered Sergeant D'Alessio. "Jimenez, Luis."

"Present!" A boy, nineteen, twenty, maybe twenty-one, short, thin and dark.

"Lever, Roscoe K."

"Present!" A little older, but not much. A little taller and broader. Brown hair going high at the temples. Thin lips that he was forever wetting with his tongue. Eyes that shifted shyly, and then suddenly said Screw you!

"Maggot, Archer."

"Present." It was a softer response, one that said maybe he was there, maybe he wasn't, but if he was, he didn't belong there. A blond man with a red neck and watery eyes, in his mid-twenties. Gordon would bet anything that he was a Reb.

76

"Odell, Myron."

"Here, sir!" Also blond, combed to the side with a part that looked as though it had been put there with an axe. A thin, nervous, frightened man, peering eagerly around through steel-rimmed GI glasses. Probably in his mid-twenties, but the kind who looked younger and acted even younger.

"I told you to answer Present!" said D'Alessio. "And can the sir, buddy. You don't see any brass on my shoulders, do you?"

"I'm sorry," said Odell, flustered.

"Posey, Samson."

He came forward slowly, but said nothing, staring straight ahead of him, seeing other things, other people. D'Alessio looked up, waiting. Everybody in the room had his eyes on the Indian—awe, respect, fear, curiosity.

"Sawyer, Kendall B."

"Present!" He stepped forward smartly, yet shame was written on his firm-jawed, stubbled face, shame for being there and having to answer, and his eyes were cast down, seeking no one else's.

"Smith, Calvin Ezra."

"Present!" There had to be a Smith, of course. Salt of the earth. Everybody and nobody. This one was tall and round-shouldered, with a long face and pointed chin, and blue eyes that had sun crinkles around the edges, and skin that had hardened in the weather. He may have been a little older than the others.

"White, Napoleon."

There was only one left—the colored man. The mere act of stepping forward and identifying himself was an indignity for him.

"Present," he said softly.

There was a snicker in the rank, and even Doctor Gordon felt an unwilling smile coming on. It was an unusual name.

"Sheet, boy," muttered Maggot, catching the wind of the room, "Yo pappy color-blind?"

Napoleon heard it. Everybody in the room heard it. Napoleon turned and spotted the insulter, and before anyone could stop him, he was on Maggot and they were wrestling on the floor.

D'Alessio and a couple of the guards pried at the flailing bodies. Maggot was getting the worst of it, and trying

77

to pry the Negro loose was like trying to pull a steel vise apart with your bare hands. D'Alessio let him have it in the back of the neck with a couple of vicious rabbit punches, and they held them apart then, both panting, the Negro's eyes hot with fury. A trickle of blood ran down from Maggot's lips, and there was a reddening bruise high on his cheek, yet he, too, was willing to go at it again and jerked at the men to turn him loose.

"You! Big mouth!" barked D'Alessio, landing on Maggot. "Keep your big mouth shut unless somebody talks to you!" For the Negro, he didn't soften his voice, though he wanted to. "White, you'd better control yourself. That temper of yours probably got you here in the first place."

Napoleon shoved his glistening face up close to D'Alessio's, and all the rest of the angry bile came spilling out between deep gasps of fury. "You're right, white man!" he panted triumphantly. "I killed a man the color of scum! I put a knife in the belly of a nigger-hater and so help me you keep that son-of-a-bitch away from me or I'll kill him! You can only hang me once!"

D'Alessio felt the spittle spray of the man's passion, and though entitled now to his own anger, he said nothing, guiding the prisoner firmly back into the rank with his hand on his arm. He had known nothing of past and future of these men, they were merely his charges, to be treated with his usual mixture of profane, courteous and military contempt. But now that the confession of crime and punishment was out, and grounds for the man's new whiplash so apparent, he felt that compassion he had felt for the Indian in chains. Their destinies were already sealed.

Maggot tried to jerk toward the Negro then, in answer to his outburst, but the guards held him. "You got a deal, black boy!" he challenged. "Come any time!"

D'Alessio looked at him with disgust, then turned to the medical officer, glad that he had stayed out of it. "Sorry, Captain. Do you want to recommend discipline?"

"No, that won't be necessary, Sergeant," said Captain Gordon. "Just keep them apart and watch them closely."

Myron Odell had flinched and darted away from the melee when the fight began. His heart pounded rapidly. He felt ill with the passion and crudity that had been unleashed in the room. A guard ordered him back into the

78

rank, and he smiled hopefully at the prisoners on either side of him, the thin little Mexican, Jimenez, and the husky guy, Sawyer—he had made a point of remembering all the names.

Jimenez shrugged his shoulders and stood to attention at an order. Sawyer caught the smile, uncertain, and turned away. Odell wondered if he would have bunkmates or if each one got a separate cell. He would need a friend. Desperately he wanted a friend, someone to tell his story to. The sight of the giant Indian in the room had terrified him, and then the fight had given him the shakes.

The Sergeant was talking. "Strip down to your bare asses for a shortarm and general. Any of you have anything of value with you, now's the time to turn it in for safekeeping. You never know who your friends are here."

D'Alessio had hoped for a snicker, but didn't get it with this bunch.

Taking his clothing off, slower than the others, Odell got the same feeling of delight and fear he always experienced. All his life, it seemed, there had never been anything but long lines of naked flanks and backs and male organs. First little, innocent, playful, unaware there was anything else—hospitals, shower rooms, dormitories, and always the lines of naked boys. Then adolescent bodies with new size and muscle and tone and growth and hair sprouting and puzzlement and embarrassment, and the terrible curiosity and wonder about where everything went, and the wonder and mystery of what they said about the female. And then the full-grown bodies of size and dimension and challenge and demand, dormitories and shower rooms, and then lines for physicals and barracks and latrines. And somebody like him they had put in a pro station in Glasgow to ram in the syringe and listen to their stories of conquest. How could they have imagined somebody like him capable of killing, of killing with lust, of killing that which he had feared to know, to see, to touch . . .

He moved through the ordeal of the physical, the fingerprinting, the prison issue clothes, the photographing. He searched for the face of the man who was kind, the man who would help, and he saw that face in the doctor, speaking to them again, gently, in a group, sermonizing them like a priest. Of course! The doctor was a man of compassion, he would understand, he would know how to help. He was an older man—maybe he was a father, maybe he had children somewhere whom he loved, who looked to him for guidance and love and strength, and therefore he would know what it was to have never had a father or a mother . . .

Gordon was finishing his standard indoctrination speech: "I'm here to serve you men, to look after your welfare, help you when you need me . . ." He put the proper firmness back in his voice. "But there's one thing I won't tolerate, and that's gold-bricking! If any of you answer sick call, you'd damned well better be sick!"

When he had finished he turned them back to the Sergeant, and they filed out of the Quonset. Any individuality they had before was lost in the amorphous mass of green prison fatigues they now wore, with the big white P's on legs and backs. One of them hung back and moved toward the doctor. It was the thin, pasty-faced kid with the glasses. Gordon was about to say "What's wrong, soldier?" when he remembered they were no longer soldiers and were not to be addressed that way. The man seemed nervous and agitated, and bent over conspiratorially to whisper.

"Doctor, I've got to talk to you," begged Odell. "You've got to help me, please. I'm Innocent. Nobody will believe me. I'm Innocent!"

"Hey you!" boomed D'Alessio from the door. "Gold-bricking already. Let's get the hell out of here!"

Gordon, dismayed, watched him scurry like a frightened bug through the door after the others. He reminded him of a locust that had always fascinated him—the bronze locust —that could bleed at will when threatened, that could shed great drops of blood as a bid for compassion. He shook his head, annoyed yet not unsympathetic, as he settled down to read the service records of the new prisoners.

———

6

———

REISMAN SHOWED his credentials to the MPs at the gates, returned their salutes, and drove his jeep within the walls of Marston-Tyne prison. Platoons of cadence-counting prisoners moved across the compound, some shuffling, few singing out with anything resembling martial fervor and spirit, many eyeing him with envy and suspicion as he drove slowly past them to a parking place near the administration section.

There was a cold drizzle in the air, but they wore no coats. The white P's on their backs and legs danced along disembodied, the brightest element in the dismal aura they exuded. It smacked him with the here-and-now quality of the job he had to do. He still doubted the efficacy of the scheme, but after days of poring over records in London and Salisbury, issuing orders and pulling strings, he had come up with twelve possibilities for what he was coming to think of as his personal legion of the damned.

The French had a word for it. They always had some clever word for it. *Ah! le petit enfant!* they clucked at the sight of the gurgling baby. And took this same *enfant* when he was grown, had balls and muscles, gave him a uniform and gun, sent him off to do a lost and impossible job, and called him *l'enfant perdu*—lost child. How well that had fitted in the days of the phony war, and when he had helped them fight the losing fight as the Nazi juggernaut swept on to Paris. Lost children, lost soldiers, lost cause— *les enfants perdus!*

It might fit again. Four of his prisoners had been there at Marston-Tyne already, one waiting for confirmation of his death sentence, three beginning long terms they would have finished in Leavenworth or some other Federal penitentiary back in the States; and the rest were either fresh from the legal lists or had been languishing in temporary jails awaiting their fates in various parts of the Kingdom. He had briefly considered extending his search to other theaters of operation, even to the Zone of the Interior tucked safely back across the Atlantic, but Lieutenant Kinder had conveyed orders from some mysterious *above* that this was not part of the plan.

Surfeited on the damning records of their backgrounds and crimes, Reisman felt no more than contempt toward most of the prisoners he had chosen. Yet there were those two or three in whose backgrounds he saw persons other than what they had become, men who, in more ordinary circumstances, he might also have considered for such an assignment.

He had taken without question those doomed to die, feeling the first hint of godhead in him. He would give them all their chance and they would either make something of it or be restored to the hangman. It was the proven capability of these men for viciousness, Lieutenant Kinder had lectured him, that he must cultivate under rigid controls—to bottle, as it were, ready for instant use when the Army commanded. Yet they both agreed there was a certain absurdity to this—that he was motivated once to the ultimate violence of murder and rape did not mean a man could push a pre-educated button to do it again under other circumstances. Kinder wanted to run a series of Rorschachs and Thematic Apperception Tests on the group as soon as it was organized, for he did believe there was a predisposition to what he termed "this kind of emotional outlet" in such men, and he wanted to check out his theory.

As he was about to enter the building, Reisman stopped and returned to the jeep. He removed the rotor from the distributor, slipped it into his trench coat pocket, and headed for the Commandant's office.

"Too bad this didn't come in time for your last visit here," said Colonel Tarbell, tapping the orders Reisman had handed him.

"You mean the redheaded kid . . . Gardiner?"

"Yes." Tarbell let the silence fill the room, and then went on. "I don't suppose you're at liberty to tell me what it's all about . . . No . . . that's all right. Don't try to explain. It says here the men are yours and I'm to help you in any way you require. That will do for me."

"Thank you, Colonel," said Reisman. He caught a little of the man's relief, and thought he understood why. "They're not really mine yet. I can only give them the pitch I've been ordered to give them, and see if they go along with it. It's a matter of either or . . ."

"You mean either they go along with you . . . or the court-martial sentence?"

"Yes."

"That's rich," mused Tarbell. He slid out from behind his desk and stood at the window, peering out. The cadence count of drilling prisoners bounded up to them. "For most of them, it's probably better than they deserve. I don't envy you. You've got a bitch of a job on your hands, whatever it is. There has already been a fight in the bunch that came in this morinng. Colored boy let some sap have it in the kisser for baiting him."

That would be Napleon White, Reisman realized. From what he knew about the man, he was not surprised. As a matter of fact, he was pleased. Better to get the internal tensions out of the way in the beginning, so that they could get to work.

"How about the Indian coming in from Belfast? Is he here?"

"All the men on your requisition are here now, Captain," said Tarbell, turning away from the window and strolling back to his desk. "They're all a little afraid of him, I think. My men too."

"What's he like?"

"The no-o-oble savage?" Tarbell dragged out the phrase to emphasize its ludicrousness. "Either he refuses to talk or he doesn't know English, but so far he's been following orders. He must know something to have gotten through the Army this far." The Colonel dropped his broad, tired body back into the swivel chair. "What help will you need, Captain?"

"Lots of it," said Reisman. "To start with, a dozen experienced MPs and a Sergeant to keep them in line. One or two of them could be Corporals if you're top-heavy on Corporals, Colonel. It makes no difference to me. I just want a guard for each prisoner. They'll be on detached service with me to go wherever I need them. Once they join me, they're stuck until it's over."

Tarbell whistled. "You know what you want, Captain, but that's a lot of men to give up," he said.

"Go ahead, haggle," offered Reisman, smiling. "But it's a lot easier for you to get them and train them than it is for me. I need men right away who have been working with prisoners and know their jobs."

They haggled, and Reisman settled for six Pfc's, a Corporal, and a Sergeant. "Who's your best top kick?" he asked.

"Sergeant D'Alessio . . . but that's where I draw the line," said Tarbell pleasantly. "You can't have him, Captain. I depend on him too much."

Reisman was pushing, but he knew when to stop. "Whom can I have?"

"There is one man of that rank who is free now, and will be for a while . . . I guess."

"I'll take him."

"Carl Morgan?"

"The hangman?"

"Yes."

"I'll take him."

The idea hadn't occurred to Reisman before, but there was a certain peculiar logic to it. If by his own strength and leadership he couldn't win the cooperation and respect of the prisoners and make them behave, then he would fill them with the terror of Morgan, and the man's ghoulish presence would be a constant goad.

"I'd like them kept in separate cells now, if that's possible," Reisman continued, "so they can't communicate with each other. I'll talk to them one by one after I have a general look at the group."

Tarbell explained the schedule of the prison. The men rotated through drill, calisthenics and workshops. "All except the condemned men. We take them out for a little exercise once a day, but that's it. They're not required to do anything else."

"Can you make an exception now?" asked Reisman. "Get all twelve of my prisoners out, including the condemned men, and put them with a platoon on drill. I want to see how they respond to a few simple commands."

"You're going to have trouble if you do that," said Tarbell. "Why don't you make your pitch first?"

"I'm going to have nothing but trouble from now on, Colonel," Reisman replied. "But I've got to start somewhere. This is the best way I can think of. No promises. No hopes. Nothing new to make them smart. We start even, and see what happens."

Victor Franko was suspicious, but elated. There was a change in his routine, the kind of change he didn't understand but interpreted in his favor, for it had removed him momentarily from the isolation of the near-dead. They had taken him out before this, but only to retrace the same steps each day like a dog on a leash looking for the place he had pissed last, always in some isolated little part of the prison yard where he was permitted to communicate with no one. Even the two lousy meals a day were brought to the loneliness of his cell, so it was exhilarating to be with other men again, to see new faces. He did not even know if he would like or approve of what happened next, but he waited, biding the time for his next move, his next emotion.

The rain had stopped and the air smelled cool and clean. Corporal Bowren dressed the platoon, and they stood at ease in four ranks of twelve, ringed by what seemed to Franko to be an unusually large detail of guards. Franko's eyes darted over the prisoners and guards, evaluating by facial expression and stance their strengths and capacities. Some of the prisoners he had seen before from a distance, but none in his rank. He saw strength there, blind indomitable strength, like the giant who stood stiffly, staring straight ahead of him; he saw the dregs of what once had been strength; he saw the power of cunning, but none so cunning as he; he saw mediocrity, that same mediocrity of body and spirit that had always been the most futile and depressing emanation thrown off by cowed and passive cons in every prison in which he had done time; he saw weakness, and the rancid look and smell of cowardice. He saw all these things, for they were all in him.

The guards stood alert, their carbines at the ready. Some of them Franko recognized. Corporal Bowren, who often exercised him, wore a heavy .45 on his slim hips, and Franko's mouth went wet with the envy of it . . . till his eyes fell in a sudden fear of recognition upon the stocky Master Sergeant who hovered silently on the fringes of the platoon, looking morose and ill at ease. But the terror passed in a split second to be replaced by rancor. You won't get me, you son-of-a-bitch, he screamed within himself.

Quickly he fastened his attention on the prisoner beside him, without actually looking at him. There was a skittish, haunted look about the man, an anxious questioning in his eyes as they sought to make contact with Franko, as they sized him up.

"What's this crap all about?" muttered Franko, not even turning his head. They were not supposed to talk.

"I don't know," whispered Odell joyfully. How good it was to have someone seek him out. "I was hoping you did. I just got here this morning. I guess they're going to drill us."

"The hell they are. They're not turning me into any goddamned tin soldier."

"What do you mean?"

Franko didn't know what he meant, but he knew he had to mean something now. He was an old hand and he would show it, and he knew the rules and regulations.

There were niggers all over the place. Maggot spotted the one he'd had trouble with that morning. He was at the other end of the line. The guards had made a point of keeping them apart, but putting him next to the indian was almost as bad, worse in a way because he knew he'd never do or say anything to provoke the giant. His nose twitched with the smell. He knew the answer now to the question the boys asked around home, "What stinks wors'n a nigger?"

Being lumped together with them, and with indians, mesicans and foreigners, was what bothered Maggot most about what had happened to him. There weren't any jews because jews didn't have the guts to get into his kind of trouble. The sentence of doom worried him, sure, but that smart jew lawyer had said he stood a good chance of having it commuted, and there was still time to worry about that if it came to being hanged. But he'd known—get into a jail and there'd be a nigger in it sure as hell, and he'd known there were places away from home where they put white men and niggers together, and he'd always thought of that with fear and revulsion.

When they were assigning cells, Maggot had listened to the talk of the guards and caught in one the honey-sweet accents he had hoped for. He had gotten the guard aside.

"You a Georgia boy?" he had asked.

"Shaw . . . Savannah . . . so what?"

"You see ah doan get put in with no nigger, y' hear?"

"What in tha hell you think this heah is, the Savannah-Peachtree?" the guard had mocked. "You all go wheah we tell you to go!"

But they had given him a cell by himself up on the third tier of the building, and that was something.

Reisman stood up there in front of them feeling like a goddamned football coach at a scrub session. He had taken the salute from Corporal Bowren, while Master Sergeant Carl Morgan stood to one side watching, not certain of what to do or where he belonged. "All right, you men, we're going to do a little marching!" They looked at him coldly or curiously. "Rearrange the ranks you're in by size, left to right, and snap it up!"

Reisman could tell Morgan recognized him from the night at The Butcher's Arms, and that it bothered him because he couldn't figure out what Reisman was doing there or why he had been ordered out to join him. It was apparent too that whatever else Colonel Tarbell had told him about his transfer, he had probably told him of the moratorium on his technical services, for Master Sergeant Morgan wore the petulant look of a vicious child from whom a frog has been snatched as he was about to eviscerate it.

Seeing Morgan, Reisman thought for the first time of Tess Simmons. How could he have emptied his mind of her so completely? It had been as though she never existed for him. Later, he told himself, he would go to see her.

There was some confusion in the ranks as they rearranged, but they finally got it. His men were in front, as he had ordered, dominated by the figure of Samson Posey. It was his first look at them and it gave him a queer feeling to know what he knew, and know that they didn't. Their appearance was no different than the ranks behind them, or the other prisoners he had seen around, yet he found himself staring at the twelve almost defiantly.

Reisman's voice was deep and articulate, and he was satisfied by the sound of it as it boomed across the field: "When I tell you to, count off left to right, front to rear!" He liked the heady feeling of command: "If I have reason to talk to you, I'll call you by number. If you have reason to talk to me, the name is Captain, or sir! All right now, count off!"

Few of them sounded as if they meant it, and there was the usual hesitation when numbers jumped ranks, but Reisman had never yet seen a raw platoon count off well if they hadn't done it before. When they had finished, Reisman turned to Morgan.

"Take over the platoon, Sergeant, and drill them!"

Morgan came up to him and saluted. "May I speak to the Captain in private?"

"Sure."

They walked away from the platoon. Reisman pulled his head back in disgust as Morgan leaned close to him in secrecy, so close he could hear the man breathing.

"What's on your mind, Sergeant?"

Morgan whispered it to him in embarrassment, and Reisman wanted to laugh out loud, except that he realized he now had an additional problem on his hands.

"Well, you'd better watch closely then, and learn fast," he said stiffly, "because that's going to be part of your job from now on."

Reisman walked back to the men, the Sergeant trailing disconsolately behind. Morgan had never before drilled a platoon.

"Corporal Bowren!" Reisman called.

Bowren came up to him and saluted smartly. "Yes, sir?"

"How are you on close-order drill?"

"Pretty good, sir."

"Then take over and run them through their paces."

There was trouble from the first "Right face, forward march!" The rear ranks moved off okay, but one man in the front row stood his ground, upsetting the flow of the line.

"Platoon halt!" Bowren commanded, and he looked quizzically at Reisman.

"Fall them in and try it again, Corporal."

The same thing happened, and this time there was a scuffle. Bowren rushed in and separated the men.

"Son-of-a-bitch won't move," said Sawyer.

Reisman singled out the wiry, olive-skinned prisoner who stood his ground, glaring at them.

"Something the matter with you, Number Seven?" asked Reisman.

"Sure there is," said Franko arrogantly.

"Sure there is, *what?*"

"Sure there is."

"Sure there is, *sir!*" Reisman snapped.

"I don't have to sir you or anybody else, Captain. And I don't have to march if I don't want to. Those are the rules, and you know it."

"Why don't you have to march, Number Seven?"

The rest of the platoon stood around staring and nervous, dumfounded by the exchange. The beginning of a smug smile played on Sergeant Morgan's lips. Corporal Bowren wanted to slam his fist into Franko's yellow teeth. He had known the man was a troublemaker from way back, but it looked like the Captain was inviting trouble.

"Condemned men don't have to drill," Franko said.

Others in the front rank heard him and wondered. Reisman could see the struggle begin within each man and flow outward unspoken to test the group. A back door of trifling protest had been opened, and if they could believe it was true they still had rights, they would rally to them zealously.

"What did you do? Run over the Colonel's dog?" Reisman mocked.

Now Franko wanted to say it, to scream of murder, and the rage of his thoughts made his fingers tremble to bury themselves in the Captain's throat. But to cry out that he had murdered was to make confession and invite the retribution they had decreed, and that he would never do.

"That's right, Captain," he said.

"Do you refuse to march?" asked Reisman.

"That's right."

"What's your name?"

"Number Seven."

"His name is Franko, Captain," interjected Corporal Bowren.

"Come on over here a minute, Franko. I want to talk to you," Reisman said, his voice conciliatory.

Franko shrugged his shoulders and ambled out of line in the direction Reisman indicated. Reisman smiled, walked with him and put his arm around Franko's shoulder. Height and weight, they were the same size. Reisman leaned close to Franko's ear.

"Look, you wop bastard. You don't march, I'm gonna beat the shit out of you," he whispered matter-of-factly. Then he dropped his arm, turned on his heel and walked back toward the platoon.

He knew Franko was coming. He felt it as a rush of air behind him, and he dropped on one knee, tucked his head and reached up. Franko bounced on the hard-packed sod, his head next to Reisman's knee, gasping for air. Bringing his hand across, as though to help the man up, Reisman chopped him viciously at the side of the jaw. Franko lay there unconscious, Corporal Bowren now leaning over him. The other guards had moved in on the platoon.

"What did the Corporal see?" asked Reisman.

"I saw the Captain attacked by this prisoner and forced to defend himself," answered Bowren.

"Thank you, Corporal," said Reisman. He called to

Morgan. "Cart this man back to his cell, Sergeant. Take one of the guards."

But if he had hoped for acquiescence on the part of the others, he was mistaken. There were mutterings in the ranks.

"Any of you others have anything to say, out with it," said Reisman. "I'll listen to you."

"If what he says is true, ahm not gonna march either," Maggot ventured tentatively. "Wha the hell should ah? They say they gonna hang me anyhow."

"All right, Johnny Reb," ordered Reisman. "Step out of line."

Maggot moved forward cautiously. "You doan try nothin lak that on me, Cap'm," he said, indicating Franko's limp form being carried away. "Thas grounds for caught-moshall. You wind up heah with us, you gonna be in real trub'l."

Reisman could see the alliance of the damned beginning. In a way it was good, in a way it made him look like a fool. "Any of you other jailhouse lawyers who don't think they're supposed to drill, step out of rank," he challenged.

Odell didn't really know what he should do, but if it was true about the condemned men not having to march, then why should he? Franko had talked to him, he was a nice guy, maybe he ought to protest too. Sawyer wanted to march. He wanted to put on a crisp new uniform and march and march and march, so he waited. Napoleon White stepped forward. It was no protest, but the less he had to take from any of them, the better he'd like it. Jimenez stepped forward. He'd march to the gallows; that would be enough. Odell stepped forward, feeling a new excitement. Sawyer stepped forward, finally. Samson Posey saw the man next to him move and he moved too.

Six of them stood out now, and the others in the first rank held their ground. He knew their records, but not the men who went with them, yet Reisman was certain they had split in ranks of life and death.

"Corporal Bowren," he called. "Assign a guard to take these men back to their cells, then drill the platoon for thirty minutes and dismiss them."

The prisoners were finished with their second and final meal of the day by three o'clock, each bitching to himself about the monotony of Brussels sprouts. Reisman went up to the catwalk of the third tier and began his rounds. Master Sergeant Morgan had been sent out again to learn close-order drill under First Sergeant D'Alessio. Corporal Bowren and an MP escorted Reisman to each cell, with orders to shove off ten paces and close their ears until he came out or called for them.

Victor Franko eased off his cot when he saw who had come into his cell, and sat ready to spring.

"Hello, Franko," said Reisman. He looked around for a place to sit, but there wasn't any except the bunk, so he stood in the middle of the cell letting his eyes roam comfortably over everything there. "I want to talk to you about something very important."

"I'm gonna do my talking to the Colonel," declared Franko, glaring. He missed nothing. He knew what he would do. Wait and see what happens. If the review goes against him, scream about brutality and try to force a court-martial—an officer couldn't strike an enlisted man and get away with it. Even Patton couldn't do it. Ike had chewed his ass out and made him apologize. When they brought charges against the Captain, they'd need him for a witness. A dead man can't talk. It would take time—time in which he would live to think of something else.

"We'll forget about this morning for now," said Reisman. "How would you like to get out of here?"

"Stop pullin' my pud, will ya?"

"Al told me you were a tough one."

"Al who?" His mouth hung open, questioning.

"Capone . . . your cousin Al. Didn't you tell all the guards you're Al Capone's cousin?"

"Hah! That crap! What the hell do these farmers know!"

"What would you say if I told you Al fixed it up for you to get out of here?"

"I'd say your were full of shit and knew it."

Reisman could understand arrogance of pride, and know how to deal with it, but Franko's was the insolence of a weasel. He knew well the Frankos of the world. There had been a time long ago in Chicago when they had reached him with their talent for producing fear. But he had been a lot younger then, and had only to learn that they, too, bled, screamed, were fearful, and died, to become equal to them or stronger. With this one, he would enjoy the game and the challenge to come, as he had enjoyed his superiority of mind and body that morning. He longed to grab him and beat him from wall to wall and leave him broken and whimpering on the floor, but that would be childish and would accomplish nothing.

"As a soldier, you stink, Franko!" he said softly. "I saw it in your record, and you demonstrated it this morning. They should have left you in Leavenworth. Why'd you make the trade? You didn't mean it when you said you'd take the Army."

Franko said warily, "Say, what the hell is this anyway? You a lawyer or somethin'?" Then his voice softened suddenly. "You don't have the report from the Review Board, do you, Captain? They're gonna let me go!"

"No, I'm not a lawyer, and I don't have any report, Franko," said Reisman flatly. How the hell do you say it, he wondered? How do you tell a man, even a slob like this, that you bring him a new lease on life? Do you let him have it, boom, right between the eyes, or do you savor it awhile yourself, building for dramatic effect? "What would you say," he continued, "if the Army offered you another chance to make good."

"For Christ's sakes, get it out, will you, Captain!" Franko said. If only the thinnest ray of hope, get it out, you Captain son-of-a-bitch. But watch him, oh Christ, watch him, he is tricky! Say then what you are expected to say, and say it in the way that you are expected to say it. "Oh, yes, sir, Christ, yes, sir!" It came out as a faint cry, slightly disbelieving.

"Only this time you don't go into any regular outfit. You leave here just as though you're dead to the world already, and you work your ass off like you never worked it before. Marching, hand-to-hand, guns, demolition, parachute jumps, and then you go in somewhere the Army tells you, and maybe you'll get killed quicker than the rope, and maybe not even as pretty. If it goes all right, you get nothing . . . nothing but a maybe. There's still the rope!"

"I'd say, Yes, sir!"

"Yes, *sir!*" echoed Reisman. "Yes, I guess you would . . ." for now, until you saw which way the wind was blowing. But you would mean it like you meant it at Leavenworth. "This has nothing to do with your court-martial review, Franko. Make this deal and the review is temporarily suspended."

Yes, yes, yes. Mr. Captain, sir! What the hell you expect me to say . . . No? "I'll do it, sir. Just give me the chance!"

"All right, Franko," said Reisman softly. "The necktie party is off." He drew a package of smokes from his coat and offered it. "Have a cigaret."

"It's against the rules."

"It's all right, go ahead, you probably need it. We're going to break a lot of rules from now on, but you break only the ones I tell you to. Keep your nose clean and stay out of trouble and we'll get along." Reisman realized how soon he was beginning to sound like some unimaginative jerk whom he could easily detest, but what other way was there? It was one of the penalties of the job, and things would get worse.

Franko flicked the cigaret up with his lips and drew on the lighter held in Reisman's hand. "Thanks, Captain," he said. Oh, Christ, I'm going to do it! I'm going to beat them again! But I know you, you bastard! You want something from me! The Army wants something from me! You don't come to Victor Franko unless you need Victor Franko, and no matter what I say or how I say it, you need *me*, Mr. Captain, sir, and that makes us even again from here on in.

Reisman left the cell, and each, on some unconscious level of communication beyond their spoken words, understood the other, and each had taken new measure of the antagonist with whom he would have to contend.

7

"YOU GOT A BUG up your ass so big it's reached your brain and won't let you think straight, Lieutenant," muttered Reisman. He knew his approach was all wrong with Napoleon White, but he couldn't help himself. The man was making himself unreachable.

Napoleon lay on his bunk, hands crossed under his head, staring gloomily at the ceiling. "I'll tell you something, Captain," he said, speaking to the ceiling. "I say to you what Flavius Honorius, the last Roman Emperor of the West, said to the natives when he pulled out of these parts: 'Look to your own defenses!' " He rose up on an elbow and looked angrily at Reisman. "And don't mock me with that word Lieutenant. I am not a Lieutenant. I am a General Prisoner." He dropped down again, staring at the ceiling.

"I don't understand you, White," argued Reisman. Of all the men he had picked, this was one of the few he genuinely wanted to help, one of the few he thought he could work with man to man, soldier to soldier. "Why the hell did you join the Army? Why did you volunteer for OCS? Why did you bother with any of it, if it didn't mean anything to you once?"

"Once," mused Napoleon softly. He sat up and swung his feet over onto the cold stone floor. "I joined the Army for the same reason you did, and let me tell you, that very act takes a lot out of a colored man. There was a war on and they told me I was on their side."

"You're not on the other side now, are you?"

"I'm on nobody's side. It's not my war. If an army of black men were marching on Washington, I would be on their side. And I volunteered for OCS because I had four years of college behind me and I thought I knew something, and they told me I would be an officer and a gentleman. Look at me, Captain," he said, holding up his arm. "I am a nigger. I shall be a nigger even after they put that rope around my neck, or if they don't put that rope around my neck. And you know something—I am proud of it at last. My life doesn't mean that much to me to sell out what little I've got left. Give me the opportunity again to kill a man like I killed and I will." Napoleon sized him up disdainfully. "I could kill you, Captain."

Reisman smiled. "You couldn't," he said. "Because I am the better man, White. I know things about fighting and killing that you don't know. I'm not offering you life, because I can't promise you that. But I would teach you these things, and give you the opportunity to satisfy your blood lust. Now you are just a man feeling sorry for himself."

Napoleon lay back again, staring at the ceiling, saying nothing in retort. He was depleted of anger, tired of the fight.

"I'll come back later, Lieutenant," Reisman concluded. "You'll have your last chance then. Take it or leave it.

Leave it and you're a damned fool." He went out onto the catwalk again, picked up Bowren and the MP, and went on to the next cell. If White said no, he'd have to waste more time scrounging for a replacement and he couldn't afford that. Though there was the probability of racial conflict, the group would be better for it once it was licked. And White had brains, was a leader, and had lived by the fiery passion of honest convictions that might be kindled again. Reisman needed a man like that to counter the pollution that Franko and some of the others would bring. If they could ever learn to respect and follow a Negro as their internal leader—not because he was black but because he was the best of them, if it so proved—then that would be a sign that they had truly risen above their petty perversities, and would outdo themselves.

It took awhile for Napoleon to get back there in his mind. It always took long now, for he had been so high up, so far and away in his enlightened, protected world; he had fought so tenaciously to hold onto his ivory tower, and had crashed so cruelly to the bottom. But the Captain had helped. He had brought the stimulation of literate talk, the goading urge to probe. Once, Napoleon had never even had to think about who or where he was in the world, it had been so good, and he had accepted it as his just due.

Was it that Thanksgiving Day, that incomparably magic day that had been his high point? Or was it magic only because he thought of it that way now out of the depths of his misery. No, it had really been magic . . .

Warmer than it had any right to be in late November, yellow morning sun filling the stadium with promise, blue sky unclouded, a light breeze blowing into the football field fresh off the rivers of New York and carrying with it authentic nostalgia of autumn country smells. He stood with champions in tunics of violet and white, maroon and gold, facing each other joyfully and proudly, with a clutch of exhilarating fear. The turf grass was heady with a new-mown smell despite patches bare and brown, and the air carried the taste of burning leaves that held older memories of Washington and high school days when those who played and those who watched were one vast sea of unbroken brown faces. It had been good then, too, delicious to be cheered, to be Number One.

But on this field he was the only Negro, and that was both a joyous and frightening thing. In the vast stadium—like the vaster, more complex life he had chosen and mastered—the brown faces of family and friends were lost in the roaring white sea. Yet the greater wonder was that amid that white sea, multitudes cheered for Napoleon, and the jeerers were not all enemies but merely cheerers for the maroon and gold.

"Na-po-lee-on! Na-po-lee-on! Na-po-lee-on!" How they chanted that day! And how he played that day!

Time! Spoletti lay on the sidelines kicking his legs in agony. They all rushed up to him from the field and bench, and Napoleon went sick inside with the sight of the blood spurting from his alternate's eye. Napoleon was fast and clever and uncatchable in the open. Spoletti was heavier and could drive harder through walls of bone and muscle, and that was what they had needed when the coach had sent him in to replace Napoleon at left half. The clock was running out, the violet and white were one touchdown behind. Third down, four yards to go for a first, twelve for a touchdown.

Someone said "Oh God, look at him!" and bent to try and stem the flow of blood.

"Leave him alone!" yelled the coach, hovering over Spoletti. He saw them gripped in the weakening sight of the blood, the anguished, flailing arms and legs, the moans of pain. "Goddamn it, you guys, get the hell out of here and get back on the field. Napoleon!"

Napoleon rushed up to him and the coach leaned over and whispered in his ear. "Get the hell in there and do something, Nappy!" he begged. And they took Spoletti off the field, holding the sliced eyelid in place, and the game went on.

In the huddle he told them, "Coach says Number Seventeen!"

The captain looked at him quizzically. "It's a hell of a time for tricks. We've got to bust that line wide open!"

"No. He says Seventeen."

"You gonna be a football hero?"

"Maybe."

"Okay, Nappy, Seventeen it is!" The captain slapped him on the ass as they came out of the huddle. "Go to it!"

Seventeen was a razzle-dazzle with variations. They'd worked on it all year, but had only used it once or twice in key spots, and the variations were still to be seen. It was that kind of a play. Use it too often and it was finished because everybody would know about it.

The captain took the snap at quarter, spun and handed the ball to Napoleon as he crossed with the right half. But Napoleon didn't hold it. He drove hard, with long strides, as though going for a right end run, and handed the ball under his armpit as the right end came around behind him going the other way. Napoleon kept going, right over the goal line, without the ball, thinking he'd sucked the maroon and gold into following him, giving the ball carrier a free run on the other side. But the maroon and gold were fired on "Hold that line!" and they came in fast—too fast —and smeared the right end with the ball seven yards behind the line of scrimmage.

Fourth down, eleven yards for a first, nineteen for a touchdown!

In the huddle they were morose, bitter, fired up with frustration. "What else did the coach say, Nappy?" asked the captain.

"He said stick to Seventeen."

"You're kidding?"

"No. That's what he said. Let's try the pass variation this time. They're all tightened up for a line plunge. If I miss it, at least the clock stops."

"Seventeen again," said the captain. "Make it the pass, and it's got to work this time. It's got to!"

Napoleon stole a glance at the clock as they got into position for the hike. Thirty-three seconds, and the stadium was on its feet. The line-up was tight, like they were going to try to break through or go around end with all their power. The maroon and gold were tight too.

The ball came back. Napleon took it from the captain on the run and handed it off to the right end coming around. Only this time, instead of faking a wide end run, he cut sharply between center and guard, and headed for the goal line with every ounce of speed he could muster.

Suddenly there was a mighty roar from the stands, half hope, half anguish. He was clear, the ball was in the air, going beyond him in an easy curve that drew him to it, away from defenders who had suddenly caught on. He darted, leaped, enfolded the beautiful leather in his chest, and dropped to the ground, bracing his back for the crash of bodies.

Oh, what a roar! What a mighty roar of exultation filled the stadium. They pounded him, hugged him, kissed him, and the referees had to call the cops to clear the field of spectators to let them kick the extra point. And they made that too! Fired with victory, they made that too! And then they turned to him again and hoisted him on their shoulders, and danced him round the field, their joyful white faces bobbing beneath the handsome, glistening brown face of sweat and tears. The goal posts rocked and cracked and fell, bedlam surrounded him, and through it all, they chanted:

"Na-po-lee-on! Na-po-lee-on! Na-po-lee-on! . . ."

Oh, God, it was good, so good . . . Tossing on his hard cot of memories in his cell at Marston-Tyne, remembering the glory of it, Napoleon wept . . .

And afterward, they wouldn't let him go. Everybody wanted to take him home to Thanksgiving dinner. "No, my folks are up from Washington," he said. "Some other time, maybe."

His family was taking a train right back and he went to the station with them. They had hoped he would come with them for the long week end, but they had understood earlier when he explained he wanted to stay in New York to study. He was getting B's and A's and he wanted to keep it that way. Though they were struggling and scrimping to help him, it was the scholarship he had won that was carrying him through the university, and grades were as important to him as football.

Then he was free.

Zelda was waiting for him in the darkness of the Tropicana, sitting in a booth, smoking a cigaret and drinking coffee. It was funny how the Tropicana had become their rendezvous—for chili or chicken-in-the-basket lunches with cold beer; for coffee after classes before he went up to the Bronx for football practice; for beer and dancing to the juke box in the evening when she stayed downtown to wait for him to come back. They had never talked about it but they had understood that this was their place, that they melded into it, that everything was the same color in there. They came with groups of other white and Negro students, and when they were alone, the friendly bartenders and waiters had already accepted them, and the feeling was that they were waiting for the others to join them. Sometimes others did, often they were quietly alone.

The few far-spaced dim lights that did as much to hide as illuminate the phony tropical décor, made little glints on her glasses as she looked up. Why hadn't they picked a bright place where they could be seen by everybody? They just hadn't, that's all. This was a college hangout. What the heck made the difference? He walked with her outside, didn't he? She took his arm when they crossed streets, sometimes they held hands quickly.

"No. Sit here beside me," said Zelda, as Napoleon started to slide onto the bench opposite. She gripped his wrist and ran her hand firmly, possessively up the length of his arm under his jacket sleeve, feeling its strength, its power. "Oh Nappy, Nappy, you were mighty! How proud I was to know you . . ."

A surprised, sensual tingle raced along his spine and settled in his loins. They had held hands before, even kissed each other's cheeks, but there was never such sensuality in so innocent a gesture as her hand on his arm.

"Not because of the game;" she continued. "You know I think it's silly, a waste of time, but because you conquered them all. You were the best, the tops. What a blow for your people."

Napoleon hated it when Zelda spoke of *his people* like that, as though he were a prophet or something right out of *Green Pastures*. But he knew she meant well by it. She was young and filled with the injustices of life, while he was too busy with personal accomplishments and winning victories to give the larger issues much thought.

"How long can you stay?" he asked. "Do your folks expect you for dinner?" If she asked him home for dinner, he would go. He would like to meet her folks, for despite his popularity at school, his social life was limited to students and student functions. It would be a worthwhile experience to meet parents and friends, to socialize with an older, non-university group.

"They don't," said Zelda. "They've gone to Lakewood for the week end. Isn't that wonderful? I've got the apartment to myself."

He felt a sudden clutch of fear.

"Would you like to come up?" she asked. And then, to make it sound more innocent, "If you don't have plans, that is. We can't stay here all day," she said, almost giggling. "There's nothing to do. After all, it's Thanksgiving."

Napoleon had known that there must come a time that would take them beyond the threshold of casual intimacy. But how innocent and natural she made it sound. "No. I don't think I ought to go up there," he said slowly. "You all alone with me. It wouldn't look good for you. People would talk. I know how they are, seeing somebody like me in a nice white neighborhood."

It was the first time he had ever broached the subject that he was black and she was white, but it was necessary now. Necessary out of his own fear of an incident, and necessary for her own protection. Her father was in business. He made good money and they probably lived in a swanky building. It was on Central Park West and probably had a doorman and an elevator man who would ask questions and carry tales.

"Napoleon, how can you say something like that?" Zelda insisted. "It's my home. I can take anybody I want there."

But he knew he wouldn't, couldn't go. The added fear would spoil anything there might be. Yet he certainly couldn't take her to his place. He had a cheap room with a family in Harlem. If she came up there with him, there would be nasty talk too. And if some of those punk gangs caught her around after dark with him, they'd work him over, and there'd be a gang bang. It had happened to others. Harlem was as perversely rockbound in its morals and mores as the rest of the world.

But though not an eager, panting pursuer, Napoleon was not totally innocent that day. "How about going over to Rex's place?" he suggested. "He's away. I've got the key. He said I could use it any time I wanted to." Things like this were accepted in the Village.

"Okay," she said. "Let's go now."

University Place was almost empty. They entered Washington Square and crossed the brown, leafless park diagonally toward the warren maze of cold-water and semiluxury apartment buildings that spread out south and west. Rexford Mace had fixed up a cold-water flat there as good as anything on Park Avenue once you got past the dirty street and the dank smell of garbage in the hallways. It was a building inhabited mostly by friendly, open-minded bohemians, bisexuals, students and intellectuals, so there was never a problem over the fact that Rex, who was the son of a wealthy West Indies family and spoke with an astonishing Oxford accent, was probably the blackest Negro in New York.

If Napoleon envied and respected anybody, it was Rexford Mace. He had even taken to imitating his friend's precise, Oxfordian way of speaking, as a continuation of his own self-improvement plan that had long ago rid him of his Southern drawl.

"Where did you ever get that name, Napoleon White?" Rex had kidded him after they had gotten to know one another. "It certainly is pretentious—or precocious—or even precious, depending how you look at it. Your father must certainly have had some plans for you when you were born."

Napoleon had found it easy to laugh, too—easier than usual in discussing himself and his background. "I think there was a Cajun lover loose on the plantation back about a hundred years ago," he had said, trying to be serious but finding it difficult with Rexford's infectious laughter. "My people are from Louisiana, not far from New Orleans. Anyhow, that Frenchman was apparently my great-grandpappy."

"Well, we know where the White came from now, but did they have to be so damned patriotic, or un-American about it?" Rexford had joked. "Me, I'm all black, as you can see, but choice!"

"It's sort of a family tradition," Napoleon had explained sheepishly. "I guess all Frenchmen were Napoleons in those days. There's been a Napoleon in every generation since."

In the way Rexford thought, acted and lived, he never seemed to be conscious of the fact that he was a Negro. His color seemed to have imposed no limitations on his life, other than a few minor annoyances occasionally which he destroyed with humor, ridicule and hauteur. Rexford knew what he wanted in life and had the means and manner to get it and enjoy it. He was a brilliant pre-medical student, who had not even bothered to apply for admission to an American medical college, which he considered beneath him, but had already been accepted at Edinburgh. He might have preferred Heidelberg or some other Ger-

101

man school, but had shrugged them off, knowing Hitler's racist policies, when the subject had come up. "They couldn't possibly be good schools anymore, anyway," he had said.

Rexford was a charmer and girls a very necessary and important part of his life. They were as likely to be white as colored, coloring to him being merely a sensual adornment, as the shape of a breast, the size of a buttocks or the clean, slender lines of a leg. "I really prefer the Oriental women," he had said once, as he lay on a divan, indolently smoking a Sobranie in a black onyx holder. "They are so marvelously submissive, so eager to please, such wonderful lays." As for the white girls, he had admitted he was in the position of a vampire. Whether they pleased him sexually or not, he needed them to fortify and sustain something within him.

Napoleon didn't have that need, but he wanted to try it.

"Rexford has such good taste," said Zelda.

"And the money to go with it," Napoleon said.

Zelda had come into the small kitchen where he was mixing martinis. She had a frilly black negligee draped over one arm and was holding it up for Napoleon to see.

"I've never been able to snoop around here before like I wanted to," she said mischievously. "Found it in a bedroom closet."

"Zelda, you shouldn't. That's not nice."

The tinkle of the ice cubes against the side of the cocktail mixer, as he stirred, gave them a gay, festive, holiday mood; and he didn't really care if she snooped. Rexford wouldn't care either.

"You don't suppose he wears this, do you?" She giggled. "In some mad, secret moment known only to himself."

"No, Miss Innocence," he said, smiling at her, but feeling weak, "that's for overnight guests. Rexford is very considerate and attentive."

"I'd love to try it on. If I bought anything like this, my mother would kill me."

He looked up casually from pouring the martinis. "Go ahead," he said. There was a catch in his voice. "You'll probably look like Hedy Lamarr."

"I like Josephine Baker," she said. "Paris . . . I wish we were in Paris now. It's different there."

"Vive la différence!" cheered Napoleon, clinking the glasses together and handing her one.

"Do you really want me to?" asked Zelda, staring at him.

They sought and found each other's eyes and held them as though wanting to travel down deep within and make certain of what the other thought. He was very fond of her, but whatever selfless love of a woman was, he doubted that he felt it. She was a challenge to him, a flattery to his ego. But it was strange, he didn't even know if she was pretty. She looked like other white girls to him. Were they pretty, or were they just women of another race?

"Yes, I do," said Napoleon softly.

"Okay," answered Zelda gaily. "I will. Be back in a minute."

She turned and started from the kitchen, taking her martini with her. He wondered if it was to give her courage.

"Zel?" he called.

She stopped a few feet into the living room, her stockinged feet soft on the deep-pile rug. The apartment was filled with exciting, new, modern things—soft and firm, yet clean-lined and colorful, and she liked it, so welcome a difference from the stiff, old-fashioned, and rather formal dark elegance of her family's large apartment.

"I have a confession to make," said Napoleon. "Come here." He opened the refrigerator door. "Turkey, cranberries, stuffing, all the trimmings. I had sort of hoped we would do this. We can have our own Thanksgiving dinner. Can you cook?"

"Can I!" She kissed his cheek happily and rushed off to the bedroom.

Napoleon was sitting on a couch, sipping his martini nervously, when he heard Zelda say, "Well, what do you think?"

He wolf-whistled as he looked up at her standing in the doorway to the bedroom. When in doubt, stoop to the common denominator, follow the masses, do what you might be expected to do, do what they do in the movies. Only movies didn't cover things like this.

She struck a pose—high heels and negligee. "Sexy, isn't it? Do I look like a vamp?" Zelda was being coy now, he knew, to cover her own nervousness. He wondered if she had ever done anything like this with another man, if she had made love, if she knew what she was doing, if she was a virgin.

She had taken off her glasses. Her thick black hair was unpinned and combed out so that it swept over her shoulders. The negligee covered her but was sufficiently transparent so that—because of the way the lamps were lit in the living room and the way the soft light came through the bedroom entry in which she stood—he could see her fleshy, full breasts. Napoleon had been aware of her womanliness, but he had never been aroused just because of it before, the way some of the guys at college were always talking about the sizes of tits and look at that ass and boy how I'd like to have those legs wrapped around me. She had kept on her panties or girdle. He could see the outline of it through the negligee.

"I can't see a thing," said Zelda, squinting. "Say something, will you? Don't just sit there with your mouth open."

"You look wonderful," said Napoleon. "Very exciting . . . very sexy . . . very . . ."

"Stop there," she said, coming toward him. "Wait, I want to get my drink." She went back into the bedroom where she had left it, returned, and plumped herself down in an easy chair across from him. She crossed her legs, and kicked one up and down a few times, examining her ankles and her pumps. She sipped her martini. "Mmmmm, this is good. My, this is cozy. Just like we've been doing it all the time."

Napoleon had a wild, fleeting, nauseating thought. Why hadn't she sat down on the couch beside him? He had patted the place next to him with his hand as she came out of the bedroom, indicating it was for her. Was it all a tease? Did she mean to go no further? If that was it, then all right —he didn't need her that badly. But he had heard of girls like that—white girls who did that to boys and then yelled Rape! when the guy tried something. Oh, Christ, no, not Zelda. She wasn't like that. He wished she would get dressed again. They could have a nice dinner, listen to Rexford's calypso records, then each go home. That would be a good day.

"Shall we start dinner now?" asked Napoleon, getting up. "I'll help you. You tell me what to do."

"You men, always thinking of food," said Zelda, winking at him. She held out her empty glass. "How about another drink?"

They went around again twice, while they talked of friends and school and the football game, and their families. It was really a sparring session, each feeling alternately distant and close to the other, seeking that intimacy they felt when they were with others, when they didn't have this larger thing to contend with. Zelda was trying to gain the strength of her convictions. Napoleon didn't know what he was to do.

He had had his share of women. He was good-looking and sought-after. The Frenchman's genes had lightened his skin and altered his Negroid features somewhat. Ever since he had been old enough to have one, he had groomed a thin mustache that made him feel suave and sophisticated. And with a few good clothes bought from part-time and summer earnings, he had always managed to be neat and well-dressed. At home the sex had started early in spite of family discipline and church membership. Around the university there were a few hot high yellows who went for him, but except for an occasional lay for kicks, he had committed himself to none of them; and there were plenty of girls around where he lived in Harlem who were quick and ready for a good time—so his purely sexual drives had never gone wanting. But there had never been a white girl.

"Nappy, honey, I feel woozy," Zelda said, finally, rising slowly and gliding toward him. "Oh, my, I drank too much." She dropped into his lap and it was a shock to him, feeling the soft fleshiness of her against him so suddenly through the thin negligee. Her head lay on his shoulder and her heavy perfume overwhelmed him. "Oh Nappy," she said, "kiss me. Don't you like me?"

He kissed her neck, her cheek, then found her full, damp lips. Her tongue came out and raced into his mouth, and she moaned and dug her nails into his shoulders. It was crazy, but maybe it was the game that had done it to her.

"Oh, that was good, that was good," she said. "Like you meant it."

"I do, Zel," he said soothingly, smoothing her hair. He wanted to touch her white flesh underneath the fabric, but he didn't dare. "Mmmm, you're heavy," he said, easing her up.

"Too fat," said Zelda, kissing his lips lightly and smiling at him. "But not for you, Nappy. You're strong. You're a star. I saw that today." She ran her hands along his arms again, kneading his flesh, testing the strength of his muscles. "I bet you can carry me. Go ahead, carry me, Nappy."

He picked her up, and she lay against him submissively.

"Carry me in there," she said, pointing to the bedroom. "I feel so faint. I'm going to pass out if I don't lie down."

Napoleon carried her to the bedroom. She was heavy in his arms. He didn't like it when a girl got drunk, though whether Zelda was or not, he couldn't tell. Maybe she wanted it to appear that way. Everything seemed to be moving according to some prearranged plan that he couldn't stop if he wanted to.

"We'd better start dinner," said Napoleon. "That will fix you up. A turkey takes a long time, doesn't it?"

"In a minute, Nappy," Zelda whispered against his ear. "Please let me rest a minute . . . pleeez." He put her gently down on the bed, somehow managing to keep the negligee closed around her. "You go take the bird out of the refrigerator . . . oh, that's funny . . . bird out of the box . . . it has to warm up, you know . . . Go ahead . . . I'll be there in a minute."

Napoleon went into the kitchen and fussed around for a while. What the hell did he want to mess around with a white girl for anyway? Because it was a dangerous challenge, because it was exciting? Maybe it was only that in anticipation and would really be nothing. Maybe it was too easy with Zelda. He had never made an overture more than friendly. Napoleon brewed a pot of coffee and stayed in the kitchen until it was ready, then carried two steaming mugs into the living room.

"Zel," he called. "Here's some coffee to fix you up. Come on out."

He heard her sob, put down his coffee and went in to her slowly. "What's the matter, baby?" he asked. But when he saw her in that instant, everything vanished from him but heart-quickening desire.

Zelda was lying on her belly on the large double bed. The borrowed negligee was tossed aside. She wore only a pinkish girdle of some sort, the little garter things sticking down from it against the back and side of her thighs. Napoleon's gaze swept over the tender smoothness of her naked back, the high rise of her covered rump, her open white thighs and curving legs, and where her breasts were squeezed against the spread. The dark shades were down, hiding the outside world, and whether it was day or night didn't matter.

"Nappy, Nappy, what are you doing to me?" Zelda said, sobbing, her face turned the other way. "Don't you see what you're doing?" She pushed herself up on her elbows and turned her wet face toward him, imploring. "I want you . . . so much . . . to feel your body . . . your strength . . . against me . . . Don't you want me?"

"It's all right, Zelda," whispered Napoleon, leaning over her. "It's all right now. I'm here." He felt the quickening within him so strong it seemed it would hammer him apart. He reached out and touched the small of her back and caressed it with circular motions. Zelda sighed in a long moan as though all the air had gone out of her, and she collapsed on the bed and pressed her back up against his hand. Napoleon's fingers touched the top of the girdle, pried under and his hand spread over the soft fullness of her body there, and then both hands went under, he kissed the small of her back, and peeled the girdle down her thighs, past her knees, her ankles, and threw it to the floor. He saw no color now, no reservations, only that she was a girl who had made him ache for her and wanted him, for whatever reason it might be.

Zelda stared at him hungrily, straining to see, as he started to undress. Napoleon turned away, embarrassed to show himself. Nude, he started next to her, one knee up on the bed, the rubber hidden in his hand. Zelda's wide-open eyes searched for him with a voracious, straining, awesome eagerness, and when she saw what she had done to him, she reached out and held him there. "Oh, my God, that's what it's like . . ." she murmured. "Come to me, my Nappy . . . oh, come to me . . ."

Still for him there was an instant's hesitation, a glimmer, then a sure awareness that, unbelievably, he was the first for this girl.

"Put something on, Nappy . . . pleeez," cried Zelda. "I don't know anything . . . you do it . . . oh, my God! . . ."

Napoleon's loins ached now to think of it, and he

pressed his fists into his eyes, feeling anew with this memory the pain of once was but nevermore. She too had been part of that magic day, those wondrous years. Yet, if he had thought, as Rexford must have thought in those days, that making love to Zelda would give him some new and invincible status within his own awareness of his being, then he had been mistaken. There had been no great hunger satisfied that day, for he had had no great hunger. He had been high up in a cocksure pipe dream that had nothing whatever to do with the rest of the world. The hunger had come later, and had nothing to do with women.

And poor Zelda. What a bubble they had burst for each other that day, and on the other days when she had begged him to try again, and he had wanted so very much to make her happy, to see if he could help her reach those sensuous heights she strained for futilely. But gradually they had stopped seeing each other, even at the Tropicana, and though he still liked her and thought well of her, it was all right with him because their relationship had become an exhausting physical and mental strain. For him the danger was always there; for her the satisfaction wasn't.

It wasn't until much later that Napoleon had finally come to understand completely about Zelda. He had graduated, spent months futilely trying to find a halfway decent job, then enlisted immediately after Pearl Harbor, the war at last giving him a sense of direction. On furlough he had gone up to New York and dropped by unexpectedly to see Rexford . . .

Zelda was there with Rexford in his apartment and they both acted embarrassed, as though they had been caught *in flagrante delicto*, as they probably had.

"Nappy, how wonderful to see you," she said, ill at ease. "Tell me about it. You look . . . hmmm . . . marvelous!" She raised up on her bare toes and kissed his cheek.

Her presence there disturbed Napoleon, but he was too puffed up on pride again to let it show. "Well," he said casually, "I've just finished basic, and I've been accepted for OCS."

She put a damper on it. "What's it like . . . I mean . . . you know, training in the South and all that?"

"Oh, all right," he said. He knew what she meant. The

segregated training unit, the crap you had to take from some of the white noncoms and officers under the guise of military expedience and respect, and the squeezing-out jobs they did on you in the towns despite—or maybe because of —the uniform.

Zelda left in a few minutes, saying an innocuous, "Thanks for the book," to Rexford, and, "Call me, Nappy, if you have time," to Napoleon. It was silly because even when they had been going together, he had never telephoned her at home.

"You're not angry, are you?" asked Rexford sheepishly, coming back from the door. "About her?"

"Heck, no," said Napoleon, "that was over long ago."

They had drinks and talked. The war had canceled Rexford's voyage to Edinburgh, and he was staying on at the university medical college.

"Maybe by the time I'm qualified to dig out bullets and patch up blasted bodies, the civilized races will have stopped shooting and blowing each other up," he said. "If I'm lucky, that is, and either His Majesty's Government or the Great White Father in Washington don't decide that I would make better cannon fodder than a doctor."

The talk came back to Zelda, as they both knew it had to.

"If you'd rather I didn't talk about her, I won't," said Rexford.

"No, go ahead, tell me about her," said Napoleon. "I'd like to know. Maybe I feel a sense of responsibility. I don't know."

Zelda had worked up quite a reputation as an easy lay around the Village. There was always a new man in her life. "Whatever that girl is looking for, she'll drive you crazy trying to find it. Even I have failed," admitted Rexford, "and with my reputation! She drops in every now and then for me to console her, and to see if maybe I've thought of something else. It's too bad, really. I'm sorry to see her go this way."

All at once, his entire affair with Zelda became clear to Napoleon. He understood her. She had looked upon him only as some potentially marvelous *chef de cuisine* of sex, as some goddamned stud who was going to service her because she was ready, wanting and needing, and who could be counted upon to start her off right the first time. He felt no malice or bitterness—there never really had been any.

There was only a wistful poignancy and, yes, even a little humor, too, though of a rather pathetic sort, for he really felt sorry for her . . .

Those were the good memories . . . that Thanksgiving Day, those years, those people, that girl . . . but they had coursed through him now, leaving what there was of sweet residue, and brought him closer to the hunger and vengeance and hate . . .

—
8
—

REISMAN LOATHED what he had to do those hours moving through the gloom of the dank old prison from cell to cell, refining his dialogue, offering his slender thread of hope. He wished somebody else could have gone through the scenes he had to play, and then merely presented him with twelve soldiers ready to go to work.

On the drill field earlier in the day, when he did not know individual identities, he had played a game with himself—match the crime to the man. He had studied their records. He knew their crimes, and something of their sociological, psychological, military and medical histories, but he didn't know the men. Posey stood out, of course, and he knew that Napoleon White was the Negro, and then he quickly knew who Franko was, but as for the others, there was no way of matching them up, except by intuition.

Now, Corporal Bowren told Reisman the name of each prisoner as they came to his cell. Before, there had been a disembodied crime and a disembodied man, now he could associate the men with their crimes. But in their cells, their faces and bodies in repose, they registered no passion that gave them away as killers, murderers, rapists, thieves. Reisman found this almost shockingly strange, as though he had expected them to denounce themselves in some evil cast of the eye, vicious set of countenance or position of body, like the ancient lepers who went about with bells ringing on their necks, warning the blessed of the world, "I am unclean! Unclean!" But they did not, as he did not openly wear the guilt of men he had killed. And with Reisman, as with these men, it was not a conjecture of maybe I have killed with my rifle at two hundred yards, or maybe I have killed with the bomb I dropped impersonally from the sky, but he had seen life turn to death under his hand, and though he remembered, he was not haunted. Why should they be? Why should it show on their faces? Why should they be haunted, if he was not!

Luis Jimenez took it best of all, from Reisman's point of view—clean and uncomplicated.

"Sure, Captain. Why not?" said Jimenez. "I got nothing t'lose."

Jimenez was a good-looking kid, with bright, even teeth that gleamed white against his smooth olive skin. He always looked as though he was about to smile, but never quite did. He was unemotional, untalkative in his simple commitment to Reisman, showing no interest in the control of his life, but still not passive.

Jimenez had killed a Lieutenant who chewed him out for protesting extra hours of guard duty. He was a likeable kid, a California fruit-picker who had always minded his own business and had never been in trouble until the night he pointed his M-1 at a man's heart and murdered calmly. Why? ¿Quién sabe? Maybe because he had a loaded rifle in his hands like he was supposed to; maybe because the stupid Lieutenant wouldn't let up on him, like Jimenez said afterward.

Yet it was this very unknown quantity in Jimenez that made him dangerous—he belonged to the sleeping, brooding, seemingly passive mass of the uncommitted— and Reisman knew that he could never let himself forget that for a minute.

Kendall B. Sawyer was the only one of the group who had combat experience, and this was mainly what interested Reisman about him. His IQ wasn't much, but he had apparently been a good soldier once. He had been with the Fifth Tank Destroyer Group when it was pulled out of the line in Italy and sent to England to provide muscle for the new invasion. Sawyer and T/5 Claude Bonner, a tank jockey, went out on the town in Plymouth. But the shift had been too quick for dull minds still conditioned by the nervous tension of combat, that still heard the roaring engines, thundering guns, screaming 88s coming in; that felt the coffin-fear of the teeth-rattling ovens of death they rode; that smelled the acrid stink of cordite, terror and dead bodies. There had been no de-doctrination, no psychological and sociological reorientation from the rapine life where you grabbed what you could when you wanted it and it was usually all right as long as it was German or Italian and there weren't any bird dogs around. They attacked Plymouth in the same frame of mind they had come up the Italian boot, and somebody had forgotten to tell them the British were on their side.

Sawyer told about it later and there was no way to know differently. They ran out of money and were staggering around the bomb-leveled streets near the big clock in the middle of town. "Let's take some off one of these stupid limeys!" said Bonner, and Sawyer shrugged his shoulders in acquiescence, sheeplike, in an alcoholic haze. They hailed a cabby and got in, planning to rob him.

According to Sawyer's testimony at his court-martial: "I stopped the taxi and walked off about twenty yards to urinate. When I got back, the driver was dead and Bonner said, 'Let's get the hell out of here!' He wasn't supposed to kill the guy. I never meant that to happen. Bonner must have grabbed him from behind and squeezed too hard."

But Bonner was dead too, by the time of Sawyer's court-martial. They'd stayed AWOL and then split up, feeling the hot breath of the CID agents on their tails. Bonner had gotten a gun somewhere, tried to shoot it out, and been shot to death. Sawyer, already in custody, had cursed him for dying and leaving him to take the blame.

"I'll do a job for you, Captain," Sawyer swore to Reisman. "So help me, I'll do a job for you. You don't know what this means to me. I had a good record. I don't mind dying . . . but not like this. Give me a chance and I'll do anything for you."

Sawyer was bawling and Reisman looked away in embarrassment. Not once in the minutes he spent with him had Sawyer been able to meet his eyes, but of them all, Reisman thought he might be able to turn his back on Sawyer safely.

112

Archer Maggot wouldn't settle for a simple yes or no. He wanted all the whys and wherefores, what they were going to do and who else was going to be in the outfit.

"Ah doan spect this charge gonna stick, Cap'm. That girl say ah rape her was lyin. Hell, ah nevah haftah rape no one in mah life," he said. His chuckle was bravado and sickening gall to Reisman. "You jus ass them bout Archer Maggot back in Russell County, thas all. Wha should ah stick mah neck out and go long wi you?"

Reisman turned wordlessly to open the cell door and leave.

Maggot came off his cot anxiously. "Hol on dere, Cap'm," he said. "No sense gettin riled up. I din say no."

"You didn't say yes either, Maggot. Say it now or shut up. I've got no time to waste on you."

Maggot was a gambling man. He was twenty-seven and had been bully-boy in an empire of rackets and vice that ran from Fort Benning, Georgia, through Phenix City, Alabama, all the way to the state capital. His take had been from thousands of little penny ante guys looking for fun and an easy buck, moonshine whisky and corncrib sex, but Maggot fancied himself a big gambling man and liked to play an occasional high roller coming through Phenix City, though he was mean if he lost. This time, however, the stakes were too high. Somehow, some way, he wanted to get back to the banks of the Chattahoochee River and get even with the friends and neighbors responsible for his being in the Army, just another dogfaced sucker like all the others he'd squeezed those first lucrative years of the war.

Maggot looked into Reisman's face and smiled. He said, "Well then, ah guess you bettah count me in, suh!"

With Samson Posey, Reisman never knew for sure that the man understood all of what he was saying. He sat squat-legged on a dung-colored blanket spread on the stone floor of his cell, his eyes lidded as though he was asleep, while Reisman stood above him, then crouched, and finally sat, trying with the intensity of his stare, the careful choice of his words, to elicit a sign of understanding and acknowledgment.

When Posey finally spoke, he asked incredulously, "I will not hang?"

113

"No, you will not hang," said Reisman softly, staring into the heavy, walnut-brown face, and in this instance, he was glad that he brought hope. "But you must understand that I cannot promise you anything after your mission is completed. That is out of my hands. In a way, it depends on you." Reisman wondered again if the Indian really understood. He spoke English haltingly, and at least they would be able to communicate, but did he really understand?

A look of terrible relief flooded Posey's face, softening his features. "I will fight . . . die maybe like you say . . . but I will not hang," said Posey. He stood up, and Reisman could not help feeling a fractional second of fear as the man towered over him. Posey held out his hand. "Thank you," he said. "I will follow you."

Reisman took the Indian's proffered hand, and though he didn't want to, though he fiercely rejected the arrogant thought, he could not help feeling the power of what he had done.

Roscoe K. Lever ran his tongue over his lips and shifted his eyes away from Reisman's direct look. Though Lever tried to keep his manner calm, even forcing a phony, blustering, upper-hand edge to his voice, Reisman saw the struggle going on within him.

Lever had a tougher decision to make than some of the others. The crime for which he was convicted did not doom him to the noose. Yet Reisman found both the man and his crime more despicable than the others.

"Nobody ever did me any favors and the Army ain't starting now, that's for sure. Not after the rap they handed me," Lever said.

"You were guilty, weren't you? What's the bitch?"

Lever didn't answer. He was guilty . . . of stupidly getting caught, of making a mistake, and he didn't want to make another. His mouth was so dry his tongue felt like a swollen lump of clay. He wished he had a bottle of cold beer. He was always wanting something cold and wet to drink now. The Captain was waiting for his answer and Lever felt trapped like that day in Birmingham . . .

He was a Pfc with the 37th Ordnance Battalion, working in a motor pool, and had spotted the little jewelry store as an easy mark. It wasn't his first holdup—they didn't know about the others—and he hadn't planned on it being his last. But he never stole from anybody in Service—only civilians; anybody not in uniform was making money because *he* was in, and he was entitled to some of it. His system had been foolproof: armed robbery; pick a small place, a filling station or store—the small ones added up and were easier; walk, or drive a stolen car; wear civvies, a mask or disguise; cache a uniform along the escape route; park an Army vehicle on official business within walking distance of the uniform. Opportunities were limited, timing was critical, but the limitations were its safeguards. It had worked all over the States . . .

"Well, were you guilty or weren't you?" prodded Reisman.

"Not thirty years' worth."

"You were lucky," said Reisman acidly. "The British would have hung you. You can't use a gun on a job over here and get away with it. You should have studied the customs of the natives before trying anything" . . .

He had gone by the store a number of times, casing it, and had always seen either an old man or a girl behind the counter. They had never been there together, and there had rarely been a customer. He picked a time when the man was on duty, figuring the old guy would be easier to deal with, and came into the shop with his face and hands blackened, wearing rough workman's clothes, a cap, and a kerchief pulled over his nose. The fat Luger threw terror into the old man—it always did, and it was strange how that exhilarated Lever as much as getting the money. The storekeeper stood there trembling, his eyes bugged out, his hands glued to the counter where Lever ordered him to keep them, in what he hoped was a cockney accent. "It is a small shop. I have little money . . ." the old man gasped. Lever turned up the terror. He brought the gun down on the man's hands, then up across his face, knocking his glasses off. The man collapsed where he stood, trying to yell but only managing a whimper . . .

"What do you say, Lever? You with me on this or not?" asked Reisman.

The Captain interrupted his chain of thought. Lever was remembering, coming to the part that went wrong. He answered quickly, not a decision, just something to keep the

Captain guessing, while he thought it through: "If I go with you, I stand a good chance of getting killed, don't I?"

"Maybe," said Reisman impatiently. "But if you'd rather rot in prison for thirty years that's your business!"

"That's all right," Lever mocked, "nobody's locked up for thirty years. The Review Board will cut it, then after the war, when the pressure's off, it will be cut again. I'll be sitting pretty, and the heroes will all be dead . . ."

He'd be sitting pretty because before Birmingham everything had gone so well. He had been clever enough not to live beyond the means of a Private First Class when he was on pass, but he had never wanted for money for a drink, a good meal, lathering up some dame or paying a prostitute. Not like the other soldiers, the suckers, always hard-up—they weren't buddies, for he had no buddies, and that's why everything had gone so well. The greatest part of his loot was still waiting for him in savings accounts and safe-deposit vaults under various civilian identities. And he had seen no reason to suspend his successful forays into crime when he had been shipped to England. As far as he was concerned, that which was happening in the world—and was most glorified, provided it was done by *their* rules—was all crime. It suited him to believe the Army, the country, the whole world was involved in the biggest goddamned crime in history, and he was making sure he got his share . . .

"Then your answer is no, Lever?" Reisman insisted.

"I didn't say that, Captain," he snapped back. He needed time to think, time to stall . . . but stalling hadn't done him any good in Birmingham. That was what had gone wrong . . . he had stalled . . .

He had moved quickly to the big old iron safe. It was locked. He rushed back to the semiconscious storekeeper, futilely trying to get him to open the safe. But he was spending too much time. He had to go. He grabbed the little money from the cash box and was sweeping armfuls of jewelry into a sack when the girl came in. She started to scream, but in her terror it came out a gasp. Before she could try again, he was on her, his hand over her mouth, dragging her behind the counter with the bloody old man. When she saw the storekeeper, her mouth began to work again, soundless, like a hooked fish. He had to go, but he couldn't take his eyes from her . . . something about the

116

pleading terror of her face, seeing the unconscious old man she must have thought was dead . . . something about the absolute helplessness of her . . . her very smell . . . he had no intention . . . he had never before . . . he ripped at her clothing, overwhelmed by a lust such as none he had ever felt, driven by a compulsion he had to have her then, in that moment, in the unbelievably supreme mastery he had created! And it was then she had screamed . . . and screamed . . . and screamed! And he had turned to run . . . into the arms of people from the street and neighboring storekeepers, the police, the MPs, the court-martial . . . Charges: Armed robbery, attempted murder, attempted rape . . . Findings: Guilty on all counts . . .

"I should have known you didn't have the guts for something like this," said Reisman with contempt. "Guts enough to pistol-whip an old man, to terrify a girl, but not enough guts to do an honest job of soldiering, which is what you swore an oath to do. They say a man turns yellow in prison, Lever . . . his skin turns yellow if he stays there long enough. They won't notice the difference on you . . . you're a cheap coward!"

Reisman hadn't wanted to get angry. To become emotionally involved in what had to be a coldly skillful job, was bad. It had to be either/or, with no vituperations, but he was fumbling it this time.

Lever heard *Coward!* hurled at him with absolute scorn. And of the Captain's entire unexpected and uncalled-for abuse, it was this word *Coward!* that reached him. It was kid stuff—*you're a bigger one than me*—but he was not a coward. A burglar was a coward, a sneak-thief was a coward—but not Roscoe Lever. He planned his work. It was face-to-face confrontation that he relished, a headier element of danger that made the fruits sweeter. Tempting fate, call it what you will. Sure, he used a gun, and he picked his victims and time in his own favor, but the odds were always against his taking by force that which belonged to another, and he was merely improving the balance.

"What the hell you flying off the handle for?" Lever blurted out. "I was thinking, that's all." He paused, hesitant before the final commitment, but he could no longer stall. "I'll do it, dammit," he muttered. "Just to show you, I'll do it!"

117

Reisman felt the tension ease from him. A challenge was something he understood. "Then begin now," he commanded. "How do you address an officer?"

Lever stiffened to a phony attention. "Sir!" he said. "I volunteer for your outfit, sir!"

But both the *sir* and the *volunteer* were a mockery, and that was the way Reisman heard them.

When he left the cell of Myron Odell, Reisman felt crawly all over, as though lice had invaded his clothing. Odell had fallen to the floor and wrapped his arms around Reisman's knees, blubbering in a combination of gratitude and supplication when he finally understood what Reisman was offering him. Yet his first words still struck at Reisman —"I am Innocent!"—for none of the others had made such a claim, though all their court-martial transcripts recorded pleas of Not Guilty.

Odell was a strange one, his records indicated. The only girl he was ever known to have been friendly with—a simple-minded, half-witted girl—had been found dead, raped and mutilated, in the prophylactic station T/5 Odell ran in Glasgow.

His guilt or innocence was not Reisman's concern, and he refused to dwell upon it. But how was he to turn a wretch like that into a man, much less a soldier? He had selected him on the basis of impersonal, written records, as he had the others, but wondered now if he even would have considered Odell if he had met him previously? Probably . . . if only to save the poor son-of-a-bitch from his fate. For, having been given this power over life and death, to have chosen one doomed man and not another would have left him with an irritating guilt. Odell was no less deserving than some of the others and maybe more, and was truly of *les enfants perdus.*

For the rest, the choice was as difficult as it had been for Roscoe K. Lever. They were convicted under Article of War 96 for crimes of violence, but did not have to face the hangman as did the seven doomed for rape and murder.

Calvin Ezra Smith, Vernon Pinkley, Joseph Wladislaw, Glenn Gilpin—Reisman knew them too as he came to see now that he had known all of them. Some special only because of the violence they had done; none because of who they were or might have been, or who had preceded them and given them life.

He had seen them in country roadhouses, village cafés and city taverns across the face of the nation. In the Bible Belt towns where they rejected National Repeal and the bootleg was secretive and dishonest, and they brought their own and ordered mixin's, and the room was always tense. On narrow, wooded, mountain New England roads where they grew up angry at the cities and there wasn't a goddamned thing to do Saturday nights except roar their old jalopies through the hamlets, picking up girls, scaring the tourists. In neighborhooded Chicago, where they stepped across the street and were in a foreign country, and the juke box music and small talk were different, and God help them if they were in the wrong place when the natives were feeling mean. On the vast Southwest plains and prairies that fed and fueled an empire that was running ahead of it, where they brought their own loneliness and frustration to share, and finding no takers, went away meaner than ever.

Smith, Pinkley, Wladislaw, Gilpin—that was where they had come from and would have stayed forever but for the war. To Reisman, they all said yes, for they did not like the trouble they were in, and this was a way out, maybe an easy one, maybe the vaunted path to glory.

Smith, clutching a Bible: "I've been sitting here, Captain, praying to the Lord to show me the way, and now He showed me."

Pinkley: "We get any time off? You know . . . go to town or somethin'."

Wladislaw, on being told Reisman's birthplace: "Wattayaknow, Chicago! Say, you know . . ." as though there weren't over a million other people there.

Gilpin: "One part of the Army ain't much different than another. What the hell!" It still hadn't struck him that he was not in the Army, but in prison.

There were others like them Reisman could have picked, and he would have been at a loss to explain why these. An intuitive feeling, a word or phrase in their records, an old skill, an indication they might be the best of the worst. They were the men across the face of the great question mark of America who seemed always to be seeking something they never found, always ready to argue or fight, or join some scheme to make a quick buck. Men who sat vacantly at bars drinking in the mornings and in the late hours of the night, or argued, or talked boastfully, or got into fights. Not drunkards, but men who always seemed to be in those places, though they must have had jobs or some means of support to pay for the drinking and the hours they spent doing nothing.

Hewers of wood, drawers of water, little men in little places, with the unattainable goads of wealth and fame and sensation rammed into the orifices of their beings by the modern god-devil, the monster-tyrant Communications! And so they detested their work, and unexplained bursts of savagery were protests at their lots in life.

They might have girl friends or wives—good women who whimpered for them or slatterns who bled them. They might have children whom they patted or punished as their inclinations dictated. But this was really their lives, this sitting around, waiting, for excitement, for stimulation, enthusiasm, for someone stronger to point the way to the next lot of trouble.

When he was finished, Reisman knew why Lieutenant Kinder had insisted that he personally offer each prisoner the choice. A strange, emotional link had been forged with each in the moment of his revelation to them. Odell, Sawyer, Posey—though each at vastly different marks of a measure of competence and manhood—had made him most aware of the psychological advantage accruing to him by performing this function himself. And with the others it was probably also true, though they gave no sign and would deny it. Their allegiance would be to him, as would be their hatred. White, to whom he must now return for his answer, was still an enigma.

Reisman remembered what Lieutenant Kinder had said: "In a way they will be like newborn babes and you will be father and mother to them, bringing them life and nurturing them in their first moments of recognition."

It was a frightening thought. Aside from the dangers of his own emotional involvement, what kind of strength could he possibly weave from strands so brittle?

9

MASTER SERGEANT Carl Morgan sat alone at a table in The Butcher's Arms, stuffing himself with food and drinking glasses of cold, creamy milk. The others knew now what had happened to him. The rumor had spread that there were to be no more executions for a while, and there was no man who was not relieved—secretly, or publicly with glad words. Sergeant Morgan was superfluous and no longer had a function in the Table of Organization of the 51st Disciplinary Training Center.

They had seen him on the drill field in the late afternoon, helplessly directing a guinea-pig platoon into patterns of confusion. The prisoners, at first irritated by the extra drill, had, when they realized his inadequacy, thrown themselves into their marching with snickering disdain, fighting him subtly, compounding his errors with feigned ignorance. The soldiers and prisoners of Marston-Tyne had feared him, now they were laughing at him. And he brooded that it was Captain Reisman who was responsible, and the Captain therefore bore the brunt of his hatred.

Tess brought him another glass of milk, and he caught at her wrist and held her as she started away. She too was no longer as friendly as she had been. Well, they were all alike, after all.

Tess tried to pull away. He was hurting her. "What is it?" she asked.

"What's the matter? Don't you like me anymore?" he said. She was bare-legged and wasn't wearing his earrings. She hadn't worn his gifts since the night of his first meeting in The Butcher's Arms with Reisman, the night of the execution.

Anger was alien to her being, yet Tess flushed now and, with a final effort, jerked her arm from the Sergeant's grasp. He had never really touched her before, and she had seen no harm in being nice to him, even flirting with him to cheer him a bit, but now she felt dirty where he had

121

touched her. "My likes and dislikes are my own affair," she said haughtily.

"Your wise-guy friend is back," mocked Morgan, "but I suppose you know that already." She looked surprised, suddenly curious. "Or do you?" he added tauntingly. "I know your kind, and I know his. There's other inns in the village, you know, and other girls."

Tess flushed deeper. He couldn't know. He was only guessing. Unless the Captain boasted—but she didn't believe that. "What friend?" she asked, trying to hide her eagerness.

"The Captain that was in here last week. The one with the big mouth and the big nose. I put him in his place then and I'll do it again if he tries to make trouble for me, and you can tell him that when you see him."

Morgan stopped, aware suddenly that he was ranting nonsensically. What did the girl know of the Captain? What did the girl know of anything? If he fought Reisman, if he told him off, he had the power to court-martial him, to break him. Working under him, how long could he put up with it, how long would they let him keep his stripes? He wondered if the Captain was a Jew or something, but he had never seen a Jew in a job like that.

Tess moved from the Sergeant's table without answering him, happiness and fear surging through her at once. The Captain was back, and the memory of their night of love surged through her deliciously.

In the tormented gloom of his cell, Napoleon hardly noticed day had turned to night. Since the Captain had left, one memory had given way to another, and it was now where the golden dream had been smashed with such finality, where the unspeakable thing had been done to him, that he feared to think. Yet he forced himself, for the good memories had made him weak to think of life and hope again as the Captain had offered it, and he must conjure the rest of it for strength . . .

How proudly he wore his golden bars. He was Plans and Training officer of the best Negro outfit at Fort Huachuca, Arizona, and that made them the best in the world, eager to go, to show what they could do.

They went east to Louisiana to the giant maneuver area where the incubating armies began to flex their muscles in mock combat. Tanks and trucks and massed formations wheeled and turned and gnashed their teeth at one another across the plains and swamps and roads. They popped their guns and boomed their booms and thought up all the clever schoolboy tricks they dreamed they'd use if they were ever called to war. Now was the time to get rid of the nonsense, for later it would hurt too much.

It went well. It was good to work with the white boys, to show pride in self, allegiance to the same flag, competence of training. Napoleon took a salute well, and gave one back that was smart and sharp, and many a white boy had give him the salute, and he had answered, *I read you loud and clear. I'm with you and you're with me, and though it is only the bars you salute now because you are required to do so, maybe some day, if I am lucky, you will also salute the man.*

Then in Davisville one night, they saluted the man.

The maneuvers were over. The armies were at rest and play and they swarmed into town. Napoleon skirted the edges of the Negro community, unable to bring himself actually to enter into it. There were no streets, no lights, and from the stench that rose up from it, probably no sewers. Dark, ragged shapes materialized out of the squalor and stared curiously, enviously. Sounds of anger, sorrow and pain erupted from hovels and alleys and open lots and assaulted the summer-still night air. A false note of laughter sounded close by. Whatever he was looking for to ease the tiredness of the field, to satisfy the desire for change, relaxation, maybe stimulation or excitement, it wasn't there. He wandered over to the streets of the white honky-tonk, knowing that he didn't belong there either, wasn't wanted, but wanting to test this thing—feeling a tremor of danger even as he dared—wanting his mere presence to serve as a protest.

He told himself he was being coldly curious and clinical, and as he moved along the noisy, uniform-crowded, neon streets, he contented himself with the knowledge that here too there was nothing for him. As a somewhat condescending outsider, he saw beneath the women, booze and excitement to the filth and vice and avarice, and knew that for white man or black man there was really nothing there.

Soldiers jostled against him, those few who saluted doing

so half-heartedly and in confusion for they saw him now out of context and weren't too sure of the proprieties. He passed a café door just as a group came charging out. A woman staggered against him and he put out his hand to steady her.

She turned, her overripe face fixed in a smile, starting to say, "Scuze me, soldier . . . I . . ." and ending with an injured, "Oh . . . for crying out loud . . . look at him, will ya!"

"Get yo goddamn han off dat woman!" a soldier shouted.

There were five in the group—two women, two enlisted men, and a fat civilian. The one who spoke was a tall Corporal with a harelip and a pushed-in nose. He wore a tanker patch on his shoulder.

"What you doin here, nigger?" demanded the civilian.

Napoleon saw that they were drunk and fired up, and he knew that a man on his way to get laid or earn money didn't like to be interrupted. He ignored the civilian and addressed himself to the uniforms. "Sorry, soldier," he said naturally, not knowing what he was excusing himself for, and feeling shame because of it.

He started to move on.

The Corporal blocked his way. "You scuse yusef ta that gal, ya hear!" he ordered.

The other soldier stared at him and shook his head. "Jeezus Christ!" he said. "It's one of them nigger lieutenants!"

"That's right, boy. You pologize and git the hell outahere," said the civilian gleefully. "You tryin ta git a cheap feel a sumthin."

"You didn't see it right, mister," said Napoleon, feeling the anger rising within him. "Your girl friend was falling and I helped her." He turned back to the two soldiers. Now he wouldn't let it go. "You two had better review your military courtesy," he said hoarsely. "You address an officer as sir, and you salute in passing. Let's try it again now!" There was no exhilaration in this, no triumph—only a stomach-turning sickness, and a fear that he forced himself to reject. He was combat-ready now, but not for this, please, not for this!

"Of all the uppity nig'ras ah evuh . . ." blurted the woman in amazement.

Movement around them on the hot, dirty sidewalk began

124

to slow and then stop, as other soldiers and townspeople saw what was happening. Napoleon saw the ugliness of the crowd and his anger fought with the fear—more the fear of so unwanted and stupid an incident than the fear of personal safety. A Military Police patrol car pulled up to the curb, and a Sergeant, billy club dangling from his wrist, hopped out of the rear, two other MPs following him.

"What's the matter here?" he demanded, facing the tall Corporal.

"Thisyere nigger insulted mah girl," said the Corporal, reaching out and pulling the woman toward him protectively. Her mouth was open and she was shaking her head up and down, smiling eagerly.

The MP Sergeant turned to Napoleon, and only now spotted his gold bars. He saluted and Napoleon returned it.

"Jeezus Christ!" said the civilian, watching.

"May I see your pass, Lieutenant?" asked the Sergeant. He took Napoleon's pass and ID card and stepped toward the car. "Sir, I think you'd better handle this," he said.

An MP First Lieutenant opened the car door, annoyed at having to trouble himself. Then he saw the Negro was an officer and knew he had to end the trouble quickly and quietly.

"Let's talk in here, Lieutenant," he said, indicating the front seat of the car.

Napoleon stepped in without protest, knowing the man was trying to be tactful.

"Yaay-aay, they restin the son-of-a-bitch!" yelled a voice in the crowd.

"All right, break it up, get moving!" ordered the Sergeant. "You two stay right here," he told the two soldiers.

The fat civilian protested, "You no police aroun here, boy!"

"Tell your friends to get moving, Corporal, or you're gonna be in real trouble," said the Sergeant.

"You go ahead back in dat ca-fay," said the Corporal anxiously. "Yo hol dem girls dere now, yo hear. We be along."

The crowd was moving again, and the tension eased. To those who passed the patrol car now, it was just another bunch of snooping MPs. The town was full of them.

Napoleon related what had happened, but he felt chastised and small at having to detail his moves and motives like a little boy caught in the cooky jar. Then he listened in silent fury while the two soldiers tried to make him sound like a liar. If they had been completely sober, it might have gone better for them.

"Will you accept an apology from them, Lieutenant," asked the MP officer, "and let it ride? I think it was all a misunderstanding."

The two soldiers stood at the car door, separated from the passing crowd by the MPs. Their civilian companion and the two women stood in the café doorway, waiting to see what would happen. Other soldiers going by were giving the women the big eye, and they were returning it with coy smiles.

"Yes, I'll accept an apology," said Napoleon in resignation.

"All right, you two, make it!" ordered the officer.

The Corporal and his companion looked at each other and at Napoleon and the MPs to see who would say it first, and their eyes flitted nervously back to the café doorway.

The Corporal wiped his mouth with the back of his hand. "Yeh, weuh sorry," he mumbled.

"You're sorry, *what?*" coached the officer.

"Weuh sorry, Lieutenant," said the Corporal, but he looked past Napoleon to the First Lieutenant as he said it.

"All right, move along," said the officer.

They both saluted. "Yessuh," they said, and walked quickly toward the café.

"We won't make any report of this, Lieutenant," said the MP officer. "I hope you'll do the same and overlook it."

"Yes. Thanks for your help," said Napoleon. "It was getting pretty ugly."

Napoleon started to get out of the patrol car, but the officer put a hand on his arm and stopped him. "Can we drop you somewhere?" he asked meaningfully.

"No, thanks," said Napoleon, "I think I'll take it right from here." He got out, saluted the MP officer, and started walking back in the direction from which he'd come.

He walked quickly at first. Then, seeing that nobody took particular notice of him, he slowed his pace again, and tried to relax and see the things and people he was passing. He was extra careful not to jostle anyone or be jostled. The acuity of his sense of touch was heightened so that it overwhelmed sight and sound, and it seemed that the touch of another person, a white person, would burn him.

The glare of the honky-tonk receded, the noise was behind him, the crowd gone. Napoleon was alone on a quiet residential street. An old car moved slowly behind him and he became aware of it as a voice called, "Give you a lift, Lieutenant?"

He moved toward it to see the face of the Samaritan and say No, thank you, and as he did he saw behind the wheel the fat civilian who had been with the soldiers. The back door burst open, and they rose up from their hiding place rushing at him, faces contorted in exultant rage. The tall Corporal with the harelip and pushed-in nose swung his arm in a giant arc and Napoleon had but the fraction of an instant to dodge his head and take the full impact of the tire iron on his shoulder. He felt the bone crack and wanted to scream out with the pain, but sound and breath strangled in his throat as an arm encircled and jerked his neck from behind.

The iron clanged to the roadway from the force of the blow. The Corporal smashed a fist into Napoleon's mouth. "Black nigger bastard!" he spat out. The words were vomit that had rumbled and ripened and sickened in the man's gut, and only by their spewing out could there be relief. "Yo los dem girls fo us!" Curse flooded after curse as they beat him, tripped him to the ground, and stomped on his body.

Weak, and senses reeling from the surprise and fury of the attack, Napoleon lashed out with arms and legs, but they held him tightly, dragging him into the car.

Idiotically, over and over again, as his fists smashed at Napoleon, the other soldier yelled, "Lieutenant, Lieutenant, Lieutenant, Lieutenant, Lieutenant, Lieutenant . . ."

"Yo got im?" blurted the driver. He threw the car in gear and it leaped forward. "Git da knife, git da knife, dem niggers allus gotta knife!" he warned.

Napoleon fought with all his strength to get up from the floor of the moving car, to throw them from him and cry out. A heavy boot crashed into his skull, another in his groin, and then again, and he lost consciousness with the mockery of " . . . Lieutenant, Lieutenant, Lieutenant . . ." sounding dully in his ears.

Negroes of the town found him at daybreak moaning and semiconscious in a sewage ditch in the colored section of Davisville, covered with human excrement and slime. He was naked, more dead than alive, his body a mass of blood-clotted bruises. Strewn around were the shreds of his uniform, the Lieutenant's bars ripped from his collar There was a terrible pain in his groin.

In the hospital a doctor told him what the pain was. A razor or sharp knife had been drawn deliberately through his scrotum. He would recover, said the doctor, for they had failed if they intended worse—but for Napoleon that final, unspeakable act of derision screamed in his brain, and in the convoluted layers that governed vengeance a picture was seared.

All that he would tell the Military Police was that a car had suddenly loomed out of the night and struck him as he walked on the road. That was all he remembered, he said. In the weeks of pain-racked, bitter recuperation, bone and tissue healed, but not the mind he had committed to his own and singular purpose. He didn't want the fat civilian, or the soldier whose face he couldn't even remember; vengeance centered on the tall Corporal with a harelip and a pushed-in nose, and an armored division number he would never forget . . .

Seeing him now, Napoleon wanted to scream, but who would truly hear him? He turned violently on his cot . . . swift, despairing, as though he could escape a memory that harassed him on one side but not the other. His chest collapsed in a deep sob, and the damp cold of English winter laid him bare beneath the blanket. Had he not exorcised that face? Erased it forever with steel and blood? But he still saw it . . . haunting him . . . mocking him, as it had mocked him then. That was the trouble with an obsession so vile . . . there was no cure . . . there was never a cure . . .

He told no one—neither police, nor friends, nor superiors—what happened to him that night in Davisville. He returned to duty. It was his own affair and justice would be his own, for the little left to him of pride and honor could not survive the glare of publicity and personal revelation that would surround an official investigation and the public processes of the law. In his work he was adequate, but without that warmth and joy he had felt before and communicated to others. He moved with a shadow over his shoulder, looking back suddenly to catch it. He awoke startled in the night, sweating and trembling from his dreams. Stabs of pain assaulted him unexpectedly where he had been beaten and cut.

He became a great storehouse of the anguish of his people. Yes, they were now his people, he was in and of his people. He scoured newspapers and magazines and clipped from them stories of Negro suffering and persecution. His mind, his eyes, his ears opened up to stories of abuse. He listened to—and only now did he hear—the uneducated patois of his men as they griped and repeated their Jim Crow tales, and he remembered with grim nodding of his head.

He remembered Harlem, and the absurdly ludicrous rantings of black *Führers* on the street corners of Lenox Avenue . . .

"Heil Hitler! . . . I like Hitler . . . yeah, I like Hitler for what he is doin'. He is doin' all right. Let the white man kill his brother white man. It'll leave fewer whites to bother with later—when the black man can step in and get justice for himself."

Black Nationalists! Unbelievable then . . . funny . . . embarrassing . . . because he was a college student, educated, well-spoken, well-dressed, moving up in a friendly, open world. That he was a Negro was incidental. Sure there were limitations because of it—he knew that and had experienced them, but everybody suffered from limitations: Jews and Catholics and Irishmen and Italians and Poles and Germans, American-born and foreign-born, black and white. It was a country of limitless limitations. He listened to a street-corner harangue . . .

"Jews are all Communist, and Communism wants to exploit the Negro just like the white man. I wouldn't lift my finger to save a Jew . . ."

No! It's not so! he wanted to cry out. *Some of my best friends are Jews.* But he didn't. The embarrassment of involvement . . . the fear of reprisal from the toughs who watched. And the speaker, having dropped one unrelated piece of hate, had already gone on to another.

Once he went to a meeting in a basement hall, wondering at the extent of the sedition that went on when they were off the streets, in the privacy of their own hovels. The speaker seemed to be looking directly at him when he lashed out: "The blacker the Negro, the finer the Negro.

The blacker the Negro, the greater credit he is to his race. Mulattoes are bastards. They will side with the white man. They are enemies of the black Negro. We want an empire of Blacks in Africa. We want nationhood based exclusively on black men. The salvation of my race is a religion with me. What Hitler said about the nobility of the Aryans also applies about the nobility of the Negro" . . .

The Frenchman in him curled up and wanted to hide. Napoleon slunk out of there feeling unclean, apart . . .

But maybe they were right, those ridiculous, uneducated black *Führers*. Look at what had happened to *him*! And he had played *their* game by *their* rules! . . .

One obsession governed his life in the months after Davisville. He studied the clues and official reports of troop movements, knowing at any given moment the location of his quarry's division, feeling the quickening excitement when he thought their paths might cross, festering the bitter wound when it did not happen. There were times he thought of taking leave, of going AWOL, of going after the Corporal and ending it, for fear the man might be transferred, die, be killed in the war, be lost forever in some other way and thereby leave Napoleon as half a man, unmended. But he waited. Even dreading that it was the torment itself he relished, and not its end, he waited. For he knew there had to be a better way, a right time that would come if only he could will it into being with the overwhelming power of his hunger.

In the late fall he was offered a new assignment, to go to England where small Negro units were being partially integrated into larger commands for the Invasion buildup. But even here, the choice was not entirely his. Where was the Corporal? What would he be doing? Where was his division going? He made inquiries, and only when he knew for sure, did he make his own decision. His life was irrevocably entwined with the other, as would be his death, if need be.

The train carried him northeast to New Jersey and New York, their port of embarkation. Through the window he stared at the face of the land and hated it in its winter of white. It made him feel more alien than he was by birthright. Why didn't it snow black? Why did it have to be white like everything else of the world into which he had been born? If it would one day snow black, then all would be right with the world, and he would abort his vendetta. He hated the ugliness of white—snow white of winter cold, soon dirty. Black never became dirty, it was just black, and he felt that logically there ought to be some innate prestige in this. Or maybe his hatred of the land of winter white was a simple physiological reaction to temperatures strange and uncomfortable, bred back in generations of naked black men in jungles of a far place from which the line had sprung.

He could have gone home to Washington, but he didn't want to. He could have called Rexford in New York, his friends from the university, his teachers, but he didn't. He was unclean . . . he was apart . . . he wanted to see no one . . .

The *Île de France* sailed out into the North Atlantic. Napoleon moved through the decks and corridors of the vessel, incredibly jammed with the men and machines of war. In the places where he wasn't supposed to go, he schemed and challenged and bluffed so that he could. He saw the shoulder patches of the armored division and moved among them searching their faces. It was broad daylight when he saw the tall Corporal with the harelip and the pushed-in nose. There were many witnesses.

"Bird dog!" somebody whispered. The Corporal looked up from his poker hand, looked back when he saw it was no one important.

Napoleon reached down, grabbed him by the hair and twisted his head to make sure—to see the mouth, the nose, the angry face he remembered. The others sat there dumfounded, cards loose in their hands, money on the deck, uncertain what was happening.

"Do you remember me?" asked Napoleon. He moved fast, before any of the others could recover. With his right hand he smashed back and forth across the Corporal's livid face.

The Corporal struggled to rise, he clawed at the hand that held his hair in a painful grip. "What the hell yo think yo doin, nigga!" he yelled.

"Davisville . . . last summer . . ." said Napoleon. His hands were steady, his voice unbelievably calm. He reached into his pocket and the Corporal's eyes bugged in terror as he heard a click and saw the flashing blade—and remembered! "Here's the knife you were looking for!" Napoleon's voice rose exultantly. "I bought it for you, knowing you'd want it!" He brought it across the man's throat and then back, and as the others came out of their stupefaction and reached for him, he thrust it with all his might into the Corporal's chest . . .

. . . hearing his own scream and that of the Corporal, even now in his haunted cell at Marston-Tyne, feeling the sticky warmth of the man's blood as it flooded out, despoiling his hands, his uniform, his life.

Reisman came into his cell and found Napoleon beaten by the struggle with his memories, lying damp and weak under his blanket. His face seemed softer to Reisman, no longer grim in its angry certainty, but the electric light came from one low-wattage bulb in the ceiling and was conducive to that sort of hopeful projection.

"My conscience returned," said Napoleon in recognition. "I was just beginning to mix you up with my bad dreams."

"No, I'm real," said Reisman. He too was weary. "May I sit down?"

Napoleon moved his legs to the far side of the cot, and Reisman sat down. He had dismissed Corporal Bowren and the other guard, and then reread the service records of Napoleon White before returning to his cell, seeking a clue to that something which would touch Napoleon and make him respond as Reisman desired. If there was one thing that had characterized the man's life before, it had been vitality.

"Why didn't you put up a better fight at the court-martial?" asked Reisman.

Napoleon sat up, startled. "Were you there?"

"No. But I've had to read about it."

"I told them my story and that was that. I had three strikes against me, anyhow, when they took me off the boat in chains. I was guilty until proven guiltier. A dozen men saw me kill him—in cold blood, they said."

"Was it in cold blood?"

"The temperature of my blood was far from normal at

the time, I assure you. But it wasn't cold. I had wanted re-
venge against that man for so long, I would have died myself if I did not have it. I was worthless as a soldier by
then, anyway . . . certainly worthless as an officer."

"But your responses in the transcript were so listless, as
though you didn't care. Why didn't you fight?"

"I told them my story. That was all. If that didn't do it,
there was nothing that could."

"Yes, I read your statement to the CID in Greenock
when they took you into custody. Your lawyer should have
had the civilian from Davisville and the other soldier
brought over for the trial."

"He tried that. The civilian gave a deposition saying he
didn't remember anything."

"How about the other soldier you said attacked you?"

"They couldn't find him. It could have been anybody,
anywhere. I didn't know his name or his outfit or anything.
Even if they had found him, he would have denied the
attack."

The officer who defended Napoleon had been sharp
enough to introduce hospital records and a statement from
the doctor who had treated him, concerning the extent of
his injuries. As far as the court-martial was concerned,
however, that was another story, and not grounds for self-
defense. The concurrent plea of Innocent by Reason of
Temporary Insanity was futile, for it was shown by the
prosecution that Napoleon had conducted his military duties in a competent manner in the months after recovering
from the attack upon him, and that his killing the Corporal
aboard the *Île de France* had been deliberate.

"So you gave up!" said Reisman reproachfully. "And
now there's nothing else you want to do with your life."

"Only to be permitted to hate," said Napoleon. "To hate
you because you are Caucasian. A crazy goddamned word
if I ever heard one for describing what you are. What the
hell has a province in Russia got to do with the color of a
man's skin? Hating will make my dying more bearable. If I
was free to act again, it would be only for myself and men
the color of my skin . . . against the white master race."

"Horseshit! How about yellow men and red men?" Reisman asked. "There's an Indian sitting as lonely and miserable as you are down the hall. You gonna hate him too? For
surely it wouldn't end there. What's to prevent black and

133

yellow and red from fighting each other dividing the spoils of a white world, if it ever comes to that?"

Reisman was on his feet now, pacing nervously back and forth in the narrow confines of the cell. He could never sit still when he was filled to bursting with ideas and arguments. Napoleon watched him, alert, the blanket cast aside, following Reisman hungrily with his eyes and ears.

"And what do you mean, act for yourself?" Reisman argued. "What the hell do you think you've ever done? Everyone does. I do. You are no different from anyone else in that department. I don't believe in your grand and magnanimous hate and I don't think you do either. All I can think of is you had one hell of a shock and haven't gotten over it yet. I don't know. Maybe you got hit in the head too hard. This crap you're handing me has become a familiar and useful piece of cant to you, that's all. You want to hate? You want to fight? You want to kill? All right! I offer you such an opportunity. I offer you a chance to fight Germans! To kill Nazis! The rottenest slime of the white master race."

Napoleon found himself swept along in the Captain's angry monologue. It was crazy. The Captain was now the Defense, telling him why he should live, but also how he *would* live; and Napoleon was some stiff-necked, grim judge and prosecutor combined against himself. He had already given up, that was true—only a matter of weeks, but it seemed so long ago.

"You've got family, haven't you?" Reisman continued urgently.

Napoleon nodded. Good family, hard-working, respectful, respected. He had tried not to think of them these weeks. Selfish? Maybe. He had not even written, except a brief note before sailing, implying that he was going overseas and they would not hear from him for a while. They had done well by him, and this affair had nothing to do with them. Yet how could it not help but touch them? Wound them deeply? There would be a message saying he had died, and they would want to know more. Would they be told the truth? What was the form? In knowing—yet not really knowing—how could they not help but feel dishonor and disgrace that in a time when sons were honored for killing, theirs should be damned; when sons were dying gloriously, theirs was executed in infamy.

"You think I don't want to get out of here?" Napoleon

blurted out passionately. "But not your way . . . not the Army's way. I want to get out of here, man, and go . . . go clear out of this life of hypocrisy. Hell, I'd even go to Hitler . . . or maybe Africa and take off my clothes and just disappear back wherever the hell my ancestors came from."

Just then Reisman became aware of the discordant sounds of the prison orchestra tuning up down in the compound, and remembered that Corporal Bowren had told him it was the night of the weekly entertainment. It was so goddamned stupid and irritating. What in hell did that have to do with the making of war? What did music and entertainment and all the half concessions to humanity and sanity and niceness and peace have to do with a prison full of slobs? What did it have to do with the seven men destined for the rope, and their five companions in his legion of the damned? Yes, Mr. Colonel, sir, there's nothing I'd like better my last night on earth than to have Mr. Rudy Staritus and his Starlights play for me; and then couldn't you put off this nasty business a week or so, because there's gonna be Highlights and Hilarity with Hank Ladd of the Phil Baker Radio Show, and he just may bring one of those full-hipped, deep-bosomed blonde All-American tootsies with him and there's nothing I'd like better than to hear her singing *To Each His Own* as I go through that big wide hole.

Napoleon heard the music too. Their overture was a medley of dance tunes . . . Glenn Miller . . . Tommy Dorsey . . . Jimmy Dorsey . . . Harry James . . . It made him ache for times past—for school dances and college balls, for Village joints and Cab Calloway in a smoky night club on 125th Street—nice times, good people, good things. He was weakening, and he wanted to weaken, for who was it that would not want to live, or even die a different death than that at the end of a rope? But he said, "Show me the way out of here with no strings attached and I'll go, but to live a life even more debased than before, that's not for me. Death at least would be clean and final, and no pain beyond the first, and even there, I understand they've got a clever little monster handling the ropes and he fixes it so that the trip is over before you even know it's begun."

Reisman didn't want to argue anymore. He was in deeper now than he had any desire to be or right to be. This

135

was what he didn't want—this angry, emotional involvement. Yet, one more thought occurred to him, one final word, a snatch of wisdom he had once read and latched onto hungrily. "You're a clever man, White," said Reisman wearily. "Educated. That quotation you threw at me this afternoon, 'Look to your own defenses!' Very good. But here's a better one: 'It is required of a man that he should share the passion and action of his time, at peril of being judged not to have lived.' Spoken by Oliver Wendell Holmes, Justice of the United States Supreme Court, and if that doesn't have meaning for you, then I leave you to stew in your own mess of self-pity. What's it to be, yes or no?"

Yes or no? Could it really be that simple? Napoleon struggled in those seconds to know. How much of that which was exclusively and privately himself, and which he jealously guarded, now hung on those words? Which was the coward's way and which the hero's? No, not the hero's, but the right way, even if it was cowardly.

He opened his mouth, even then not knowing what it was that would come out. His body sagged with exhaustion, and only his eyes moved, white and gleaming.

"Yes," he said.

Reisman's face hid whatever feeling of gladness he had. He stood up and extended his hand. Napoleon's was slippery wet, his grip limp.

"We'll begin in the morning," said Reisman. He turned and left the cell, feeling as though he had just come through some great physical battle.

—

10

—

IN THE LATE EVENING in the Commandant's office, after the USO people had left, Reisman told Lieutenant Colonel Tarbell what he had accomplished. He was outlining his plans for the following day when the telephone rang.

Tarbell picked it up, listened for a moment, then said to Reisman, "It's the OD at the main gate. There's a girl there asking for you."

"I'll go," said Reisman, standing up. "You understand about the uniforms and field equipment we'll need tomorrow."

Tarbell looked at Reisman as though he was going to snap at him, but took a rank-soothing breath and changed his mind. "Our supply is pretty good," he said. "We've been restoring men to active duty right along." He paused to weigh his words tactfully, then went on pleasantly, "You know, Captain, they really ought to give you more rank for this job. If I'd pushed Colonels around like you when I was a Captain, I'd either have a couple of stars by now or I'd be a buck-assed Private."

"I don't mean to offend, Colonel," said Reisman quickly. "I'll be out of your hair soon enough."

The Commandant got up from behind his desk and walked with Reisman to the door. "Oh, I'm not offended, son," he said, "but there are Second Looies who would be . . . not to speak of Majors, Colonels and Generals. When do you expect to move your group out?"

"Sunday the latest . . . even if we have to sleep out on the moors under canvas."

"Good night then," said Tarbell. He put out his hand and Reisman took it. "Good luck, Captain."

Tessie Simmons was in the small guardroom by the main gate, her face pressed eagerly against a glass pane. Reisman almost knocked her down when he opened the door, for she had seen him through the window and rushed to the door to open it. She poised on a flood of demonstrative affection, her face radiant, touched with a flush of pink— whether from the cold of the night, the warmth of the room, or shyness of this second meeting that rekindled private memories of the first, he did not know.

The soldiers in the room looked from Reisman to the girl and back again, alert to what would be said and in that way establish the relationship between them.

"Hello," said Reisman, and seeing the radar-alertness of the room, he took her arm and guided her outside. He closed the door behind them and Tess stood up on her toes and kissed him softly, her lips and cheek warm against his face, shattering his natural reserve and fear of embarrassment.

Reisman drew her against him tightly and they kissed with the eager expectancy of young lovers.

"I've missed that," said Tess when they drew apart.

Reisman wanted to say something to equal it—something more to nurture the gentle fire she brought him, but it came sputtering out as, "What are you doing here?"

"I heard you were back and I was afraid you weren't coming to see me," said Tess.

They began to walk, holding each other about the waist.

"I would have. I was on duty until now. Who told you I was here?" he asked.

Tess thought of Morgan, but decided not to mention him. "Oh, some of the men were talking at the inn," she said.

There was too damned much talking around Marston-Tyne, thought Reisman in irritation. Most of it might be inconsequential, but sometime it might not be and there was no way of knowing the ears to which news would be carried, or the cleverness with which someone might put isolated facts together. He would have to mention it to Tarbell and get him to put a gag on his troops, for everybody's protection.

"Are you angry?" asked Tess.

"No. Of course not," he replied. "I'm glad you're here. We can stop somewhere for a spot of something, and then I'll take you home."

They walked along the road into the village, away from the prison, close against each other. The wind was stiff in the branches of the yew trees that lined the way; out in the open places, the moon made the night bright and illuminated the winter clouds hurrying here and there across the sky.

"Will you be staying the night?" Tess asked softly. "Your room is ready."

Reisman turned to her. "So it's become my room now, has it?" Yet what she had said, the way she had greeted him, made him feel strangely as though he had come home.

"Yes," said Tess. "Mine too. I've slept there since you went away." She reached up and brought his face around and kissed his lips quickly. "John? Is it John or Johnny? What do people call you besides Captain? It's silly that I shouldn't even know that."

"Which do you prefer?"

"John. I think you're a little too forbidding to be called Johnny."

"I don't think I like that," he said.

Again she kissed him quickly. "John," she said, "thank you for the robe. It came yesterday and I've worn it almost every moment since. I'd have it on now, but it wouldn't be *prooper*, as Mrs. Culver would say. She's our cook at the inn."

"It fits all right?" he asked. "I'm not used to buying things for women."

"Nor I to getting presents from London. And from Selfridge's! I love it!" she said. "You must see it on!"

"But that wouldn't be *prooper*," he mimicked.

"But it would," she said simply. "I love you."

Reisman pulled her to him again, the excitement of their by-play permeating his body. He kissed her neck. "And if I want to see you again without?" he whispered.

"That would be good," she said. "Do you think I am wanton?"

"Yes," he answered quickly, but his mock frown was so serious they both laughed. They were on the lane to The Butcher's Arms now and Reisman wondered if he ought to go back to the prison first and get the jeep and his things, and then he thought the hell with it.

"Mrs. Culver says so too," Tess said, "but I hardly know what the word means." She stopped suddenly in her skipping, arm-swinging walk and pulled him behind a tree to whisper against his ear, sending shivers up his spine: "You introduced me to something new and wonderful, you know."

"I introduced you?"

"Yes . . ." If he knew how she had longed for him . . . five days . . . four nights . . . wondering if he was coming back . . . "I know I am wanton, but there was no one before you . . ." She kissed him sensually and sprang away, but he held her hand and she spun back into his arms and they fell against the private shelter of the tree trunk.

"Then . . . since I introduced you, I have a responsibility to you . . ." said Reisman. And they went on together toward home, having their by-play after all, thought Reisman, like proper adolescents and foolish young lovers, and Tess with her fullness of heart chased much of the grimness from his own.

They lay together in the wide bed, the comforter thrown away to the floor, and in the cozy warmth of the dancing firelight Tess explored Reisman's body with her fingertips. She came to a place on his right thigh where a channel of scar tissue showed through the soft black hair that grew there, the cut running from just above his knee around into the swell of his buttocks.

"You've been wounded," she said tenderly, and brushed her lips along the scar.

"Yes," he said, "sometimes I forget. It was a long time ago. I'm not very fond of that one. It makes me look as though I was running away. I wish their aim had been better and they'd brought the shot around a bit to the front."

"No, please God, no." She shuddered. "Don't say such things." Then she laughed and pointed her finger and said, "But then it would have been there and that would have been terrible."

Reisman picked up his head and looked where she was pointing and said, "Yes, I guess that would have been worse. Though you might say I was wounded there once too, intentionally. The wound of faith. The sign of the covenant between old Abraham and his God."

"Does that mean you're Jewish?" asked Tess.

"That doesn't," said Reisman. "It's done in the best of families now. But I am half Jewish. My father tried to raise me in the faith, but it didn't take. My mother was a good Christian of noble soul, but that didn't take either." He reached down and tousled her hair. "But how do you, in all your previous innocence of men, know about such things? Or have you been telling me tales that I believed?"

"Oh, no," she gasped. "What I said was so, but I am not a child, and I've heard things." She ran her fingers lightly back along his thigh to where his legs joined. "How did it happen?" she asked, touching the long scar again.

"Shrapnel . . . in Spain," said Reisman, remembering drowsily.

"Is it all right to talk about . . . ?" asked Tess hesitantly. "You don't mind? I mean, sometimes when a person has had a horrible thing happen to him, he doesn't like to talk about it. I haven't done much in my life, but there are things I won't let myself think about . . . much less talk . . ."

"I'll tell you if you tell me," he said, speaking to her as though she was a little girl.

"All right," she said.

He came fully awake now. "I was with the International Brigade there in Thirty-six," he said, and remembered . . . Franco pressing down on Madrid and there were some of them who were tired of falling back all the time. They wanted to see what it was like going the other way for a change. It was a stupid thing to do. They had no support, no artillery worth speaking of, their few tanks no match for the Germans and Italians who had moved in. But it was a stupid war anyway. All mixed up. You never knew who was really in charge or what you were supposed to do or how you were supposed to do it. Sometimes everybody was a commander, sometimes there were no commanders, and there was always the politics going on around them that did more damage than the enemy . . . "I was running across an open field with the others, toward some Fascist tanks . . ." He would never forget the sight of the guns lowering on them point-blank as though they too were tanks, for a brave man with a bottle of gasoline and a match could do as much damage to tanks as a cannon . . . "I remember running and shells exploding around us, and the next thing I knew I was in an aid station back in the city. A friend of mine had picked me up, put me in a truck and carried me back."

"Weren't you afraid?" she asked.

"No, not when I was moving. Only later, when I saw the mess they'd made of my leg and I was afraid somebody would come along in the hospital and cut it off. Everything was so damned primitive then. But it really looked and felt worse than it was. No bones broken. Just a lot of flesh chewed out of my hide and a lot of blood gone. It knit up good enough in a few weeks and I got the hell out of there . . . out of Spain."

Tess shivered against him. "How awful," she whispered.

"Not really," he said. "Worse things have happened to me. I've got other little souvenirs too, if you're interested." He felt himself running away now with playing the role of the old soldier—old blowhard, he accused himself—but no matter. He seldom talked about these things or had a chance to display his wounds under circumstances so rewarding for the knight-errant.

He showed her the thumb that wouldn't work properly since it had been broken and the tendon cut; the salt-and-pepper lacing of grenade fragments in his right forearm;

the tunnel where a pistol bullet had gone cleanly in and out of the top of his shoulder; and the other places where his physical being had been assaulted and he had delighted in the wounds, other than the pain—the honorable wounds of his wars, and the memorable hurts of dirty brawls in bars and docks and back streets of the cities of the world where he had sauntered, sometimes looking for trouble, sometimes not, but always ready for it and reacting with a violence, a viciousness that was unexpected by his opponents or himself, and a competence that got him through.

"And this?" Tess said, touching his navel.

"The worst . . . the wound of birth," he said.

"Are you not glad to be alive?"

He thought about it a moment. "I guess so. I don't know anything else."

"But why are you at all uncertain?" she asked.

"No purpose . . . no objectives . . . no ideals," he confessed.

"But that's not true!" she said indignantly. "Of course you have a purpose. To win the war, is it not? And go back home to America, and have a home and a family and . . ." She faltered at that, not fully realizing what she was saying until she had said it. "Why look at you . . . you were in the war from the beginning . . . from before the beginning. You have strong ideals! You were fighting the Germans in France before your country was ever at war! And Spain! A man without purpose and ideals doesn't do that."

"But he does," said Reisman. He reached out for her, kissed her cheek tenderly, and she snuggled to him so that he really felt her now in this moment when private needs and passion did not intervene . . . touch against touch; the smooth softness of skin; the warmth that came from her and surrounded him; the pliant nakedness of her flesh seeming to fit part by part against his taut, muscled body. And then, in that instant, the old driven guilt came suddenly upon him—the guilt of full and sated senses—as he had felt it often in such fully savored, unguarded moments of pleasure, these last years. What right had one man to eat or drink or play or breathe clean, unworried air, or copulate to a moment of exquisite exhaustion as he had done, while another hungered, thirsted, froze, suffered with pain, took a bullet in his gut, or lay on a pariah's cot in a dank English prison, trembling to think of the noose?

But what an absurd fanaticism of compassion that was!

Sometimes when it darted in on him like this, he wondered if he should have become a priest to save men's souls and order their behavior, but then he never could have been a routine Catholic priest anyway—he would have had to be one of the fire-breathing hell-and-damnation kind of preachers so that he could properly scream at the world and give vent to his passions, as well as his compassions. He was not gentle enough by nature to have become a rabbi—for all rabbis, he knew, were supposed to be gentle men, learned and dedicated.

"I wasn't an idealist in Spain," he said. "I was an adventurer. I'd been going to sea on and off for years and I'd been in a couple of little wars you never heard of, and then that one came along and it was something to do."

"But you were on the right side, weren't you?"

"I suppose so," he answered. Then he chuckled, remembering something. "You know, once in Mexico . . . that was my first time out . . . I was actually on the wrong side."

"What in the world were you doing there?" Tess asked. "Did the Americans fight a war there?"

"No, not then . . . we did back around 1846 . . . and there was all that messing around when Pancho Villa was raiding . . . but this was different. I was a kid and I'd been going to sea about a year. We had a shipment of agricultural implements in the hold, out of New Orleans bound for Veracruz. Only it turned out they weren't agricultural implements and we unloaded machine guns and rifles and some mortars and plenty of ammunition in a crazy place called Tabasco . . . you know, like the hot sauce you put on chili . . ."

Tess looked at him quizzically. "Chile . . . that's in South America, isn't it?"

"This chili you eat," said Reisman. "I guess you've never had it here in England. It's beans with ground meat and tomato sauce and hot spices . . ."

"Sounds awful!"

"There was this little Mussolini guy down there named Cannibal or Cannabal or something like that. You know how it used to be in Mexico where one General would get hold of a state or a town and he'd run it like it was his, like he owned everything and everybody in it. Boy, was he named right for the job. He had two kids and he called one of them Lucifer and the other Lenin. You have to give a guy like that credit. He was so bad and he wanted everybody to know it. There was none of this phony posturing that you get from Mussolini and Hitler about the good of the people. Whatever happened down there had to be for the good of Cannabal. He had a private army they called the Red Shirts, and that's why he'd bought up all these weapons at a pretty stiff price, what with the smuggling and all. There were some Americans and Englishmen and a German or two working for him. All the foreigners were officers with fancy uniforms and good pay. While we were unloading the stuff, I found out he was looking for more men, so I decided I'd join up and see what happened. They fixed it up with the captain and I signed off the ship."

He was making it sound like nothing, not like what it really had been for him then—a kid driven to test out this thing of fear and bravery in himself. Because, though he really had no interest in the affairs of Tabasco, and no mental, physical or emotional part of him had to get involved in what was going on down there, once he was there and the opportunity had been presented to him, he would have curled up and cowered within himself, suffered mental, physical and emotional anguish if he had sailed away. For him, it had been a bigger step in a pattern that had already been started and tested, yet one that fed on itself and promised no surcease.

"You mean you just signed on . . . to fight for a man like that?" asked Tess.

Her voice echoed against his chest, where her head lay, and it held a note of accusation. He had wanted to make it sound like a lark, which it really had been at first, with good food and drink and plenty of *mestizo* and Indian girls to service them, but now he was sorry he had gone off on this tack.

"I wasn't fighting for anyone, or any thing or cause, for that matter," he answered lamely. "It was just a job."

"What happened?" she asked. "What did you do?"

"Oh, I just stayed around a couple of months, drilling troops and teaching them how to use their new weapons." And learning himself, bluffing his way through and picking things up as he went along, finding to his delight that he had a talent for that sort of thing. And he hadn't really known what was going on there politically at first. It had taken him awhile to find out that the trouble Cannabal was expecting was from an oppressed and disenchanted citizenry. The reality of the situation had given pause to his romantic daydreams about freebooters and soldiers-of-fortune who had taken over some little foreign country or primitive island tribe and earned glory and gold for themselves.

"Was there a war?"

"Not really a war. Just some fighting . . ." But he didn't want to tell her what had really happened . . . that the army which finally had come against them had not really been an organized force, but a ragtag mob of political outs, peons and students armed with more zeal than weapons . . . how watching them move against his entrenched position he had felt fear upon fear rising within him that he would be killed in that unbelievably ridiculous place where no one even knew him or cared, that he would be hurt and maimed, that he would turn and bolt or cower in hiding and thereby be maimed worse, for he would have to live with it . . . how he had wanted to go out and reason with them, tell them to go back, and had known a greater thrill of fear, almost seeing and smelling the palpable hatred that rolled up from them.

"Were there people killed?" she whispered sadly.

He started to say, I don't know . . . I suppose so. But what was this sudden compulsion of his to shield her from reality that was yes or no, black or white, good or evil and the infinite admixtures of them all? "Yes," he said. "Some on both sides."

Tess shuddered against him. "Why must there be war?" she murmured.

"I'm afraid it's as old as the world and will last as long. That's neither new or profound." But he couldn't confess his culpability in the pattern, or tell her how he had reaffirmed—in that moment when firing and explosions began and he had known death was aimed at him, had seen bullets strike near, heard their whine and smack, smelled burnt powder, tasted cordite, heard men scream with hate, fear and pain, crumble with silent disbelief, fall with blood spurting from their bodies—that *enemy* was anybody who went for *him* . . . and that to test out this thing in himself he had always to inflict terrible sacrifices upon others.

"You sound so callous . . . so uncaring about life and people," said Tess. "But I don't really believe you are like

145

that, for if you were, then I couldn't love you. I hate violence."

"I do too," said Reisman. "Against animals as well as men."

"What do you mean?"

"Bullfights, cockfights, horseback riding, hunting and, naturally, slaughterhouses."

"You're making fun of me," said Tess.

"No, not really," said Reisman. "Why, do you know that in India there are Jains who sweep the path as they walk so they won't hurt the wee bonnie craytchoors they can't see? *There* is supreme reverence for the sanctity of life. Yet people laugh at them. I laugh at them, though I respect and envy them."

She stirred in his arms and sat up. "Look! How lovely!" she cried. The moon had moved around in front of the large bay window, and its bright, cold flood spilled through, fighting the yellow firelight for attention. She put on her new robe and went to stand in the moonlit window.

Reisman watched spellbound as she extended her arms in what might have been a gesture of homage and devotion and recited:

"All hail, new moon, all hail to thee!
I prithee, good moon, reveal to me
This night who shall my true love be;
Who he is, and what he wears,
And what he does all months and years."

"That's lovely," he said.

She came running back to him then and leaped lightly on the bed, opening her robe so that her breasts pressed warmly against him and then closing it protectively around both of them. "Are you my true love?" she whispered.

"Yes," he said.

"Then tell me, sir, who you are and what you do all months and years."

"No. Now it's your turn to tell me," he said.

"What?"

"The terrible things that have happened to you," he said, laughing, for then he really didn't think there had been any. "Remember, we agreed . . . 'I'll tell you if you tell me.' I've told you about Spain, as I promised, and more."

146

"Must I?" she begged. It was a little girl's voice . . . a whimper, as though she had been caught out at something and was sorry.

He said, "Yes . . ." without even thinking, and then was sorry, for she took a deep breath and began, "It was the bombings in London . . . my mum and dad were killed there . . ."

"You don't really have to tell me if you don't want to," he interrupted, too late.

"I think I want to," Tess murmured. She had rarely talked about it—once with her uncle after it had happened and she had come to live with him, and once years later with Mrs. Culver when the cook had discovered her sitting alone in tears during a sudden, unexplainable, agonized mood of loneliness, and had comforted her.

So she told him about the big blitz by the Nazi bombers in August 1940. They had lived in the bustling, densely populated East End. As soon as she mentioned it, Reisman knew what would be coming, for he had seen the unbelievable and senseless destruction and desolation there. It was as though the Nazis had executed personal vendetta against the poor, working-class people who had lived there. At the time of the first blitz, shelters had been inadequate and many thousands had still not developed the habit of fleeing to them nightly, preferring to take their chances at home or feeling confident that since they were not a military target they and their homes would be spared. In pitiable detail, Tess told him of her night of terror . . .

The air-raid sirens starting up in the distance, in the South End from where the bombers were coming . . . pitch low, pitch high, pitch low, pitch high, whooping musically up a scale of panic, racing across London ahead of the planes . . . the sirens of Stepney and Wapping taking up the alarm and passing it to the city beyond, and going silent, superseded by the *boom* and *crump* of far bombs falling, and distant thunder of antiaircraft guns . . . then the tempo of bombing and firing quickening, the awesome crescendo of noise and fear rushing closer, punctuated by the wind-slicing cut and thud of shrapnel that had burst high in the fiery night sky and rained back down upon the city and the gunners who had propelled it upward . . . then the bombers . . . wave after wave of them grinding, filling her eardrums until she thought they would burst,

147

conjuring unbelievable visions of monster airmen ordered from Berlin that night to get her, only her, Tessie Simmons . . . She had started from bed, trembling and shaking as the building itself rocked and trembled with shocks . . . She had called to her mother and started toward her, for it was most terrible to be alone, and had heard her father answer from their room . . . and then there had been the most horrendous noise she had heard in her life and she had been smashed to the floor, her room tumbling around her . . . Hours later, rescue workers had found her trapped in the precarious rubble of her room three stories above the ground, where she had huddled in horror, alternately screaming for her parents, for anybody to help her, weeping convulsively, and numbed by this unimaginable thing that had happened to her . . .

In the unpredictable, unexplainable fashion of bombs, one had made a direct hit in the inner courtyard of their block of tenement flats. Tess had come through with slight bruises to her body and a permanent scar in her memory; her parents had been killed, smashed to the courtyard below with tons of rubble on top of them.

"They were gentle people," said Tess. "My father was a good man . . . hard-working and honest . . . my mother a dear woman, contented with her man, and with me, though she had little enough of the comforts of life . . ." A sob of terrible loss racked her body and Reisman comforted her.

"I'm sorry," he said. "I shouldn't have pried."

"I wanted to tell you," she said, and then, "Do you believe in God?"

"No," he answered too quickly.

"I don't either," said Tess seriously, "for if there was a God then he wouldn't have let happen what happened. My parents believed very much in God. He wouldn't allow there to be any war . . . any suffering . . . any evil. But I believe in believing in God," she added. "I believe in goodness and in beauty . . . and in evil."

"Then I believe in you . . . very much," said Reisman, kissing her.

"Now tell me," she said, pulling back, and sitting up on the bed Indian-fashion, as though preparing for a long and serious discussion, "what you do."

He was silent a moment, wanting to tell her, wanting to share himself with her, but he knew he couldn't. "I can't really," he said, "except that I suppose it has to do with good . . . and with evil . . . and with the relative merits and uses of both." And he realized that he had hit upon something, with her help, at least as far as the war was concerned.

—

11

—

VICTOR FRANKO heard the screws coming down the corridor at 0500. It seemed like a whole army of them, like when they had come to get Gardiner; only he wasn't afraid anymore. Sure, now he could admit he'd been afraid, but he wasn't anymore.

Corporal Bowren was surprised to find him awake and alert, standing at the door when he opened it. "Get your toilet kit and join the parade," he ordered.

Franko fell in behind the file of prisoners in the dimly lit corridor. He recognized them, the same men who had been in the rank with him on the drill field the day before—the nigger, the Indian, that weasel who looked like somebody's pratboy, the rebs and the farmers—and he knew then that he hadn't been the only one who'd had a talk with the fink Captain; these others were in on it, whatever it was. Morgan was there too, warily bringing up the rear, and though in that fraction of a second in which he saw him he was afraid again, it was only for that instant, for whatever the hangman was doing there, the necktie party was off.

In the washhouse Bowren counted out a shaving blade to each man. Steaming hot water came boiling up from the sinks as the taps were turned on.

Kendall B. Sawyer, tasting the stink of himself—though not as bad as it had been before his new hope of redemption—eyed the shower stalls. "Time for a quick one, Corporal?" he asked.

"Sure, fella, sure," said Bowren. He bellowed out to the others, "Captain's orders! Everybody take a hot shower and shave and change into Class A uniforms. He wants you looking and smelling like a rose."

Franko spat out a mouthful of water into a sink. "Where we suppose ta get Class A's from, General?" he muttered.

"Your duffels'll be up in a minute, wise guy," Bowren said. He didn't know the others well enough yet, or why they had been tossed together, but he knew they were his babies from then on, and he knew Franko. Of them all, this one would bear the most watching.

In the mirror Franko saw Morgan slinking around like a goddamn cockroach, taking in everything, saying nothing, just looking. He made him nervous—those fucking eyes. He didn't look at you. He didn't see you. He looked right through you like he could see the bones in your body. Like you were a skeleton. A nothing. Franko pulled at his lathered cheek and started to run the razor down from his right sideburn. The lather came off, but not the dark beard. He tried again and it didn't work.

"Son-of-a-bitchin blade don't work," he complained to Bowren.

"What do you mean it don't work?" said the Corporal suspiciously. "It's a new blade, fresh out of the pack."

"Try it yourself you don't believe me. You want me to shave, gimme another blade." It wasn't Bowren he was ranting at. It wasn't the blade. It was Morgan. But all he succeeded in doing was drawing attention to himself. Morgan stopped his slow, incessant dissection of the room and focused on him while Bowren reluctantly held out a new blade. Franko took it and turned back to the sink.

"Hold it!" Bowren ordered. "Give me the other one!"

Franko gave it to him. He would have liked to have kept it. It was a nothing, but it would have made him feel stronger.

Samson Posey bent low to the mirror and inspected his walnut-brown face for hairs that might be visible. There were none, and he laid the blade, still in its wrapper, on the long tray that ran above the sinks. It was one advantage of being an Indian—the white men with their hairy mouths and faces and ears sticking out had to shave every day.

Roscoe K. Lever saw Samson put the blade down. Out of the corner of his eye, he watched the Indian bend into the sink to fill his cupped hands with icy water that he brought up again and again, with bearlike sounds of satisfaction, to his face. Lever looked quickly from side to side and behind him, picked up the blade and dropped it into his toilet kit.

Franko finished shaving and waited in front of an occupied shower stall. Somebody grabbed his arm from the side and yanked him toward another stall.

"Hee yah, boy," said Archer Maggot. "Take this'n. Ah'll wait till it's cleen!"

Franko pulled his arm loose. "Get your goddamn hand off me, Reb!" he spat out. Then he saw the dark figure step out of the other shower and he understood—and was ready when Bowren came at them from across the room.

"What in hell is it this time, Franko?" demanded Bowren.

"Didn't like what he said about the colored, that's all." Franko glanced up quickly. Napoleon waited there tensely, towel hanging loosely in his hand, looking like he was getting ready to pounce. "We don't go for that kind of crap where I come from."

Maggot wore a confused and hateful look on his ruddy blond face. Napoleon leaned closer, listening, watching, uncertain.

Bowren turned to Maggot. "Knock off that Mason-Dixon stuff, fella!" He shook his head in disgust. "You can't even go to the goddamn can without getting into trouble! Move along!"

Franko moved. He gave a friendly little nod and wave to Napoleon and stepped into the shower. Now the nigger would be lined up on his side. In every prison in which he'd done time, there had been the leaders and the led, and this time he was getting the jump. This time he would be Number One. And he'd let them know about Morgan— how he'd given it to Gardiner—how he'd give it to them. The others didn't know. He was sure of that now. They hadn't been around long enough.

Napoleon moved. The tenseness drained out of him. Another time he might have laughed at Franko's curious buddy-buddy act, but now he was wary. That jerk hadn't struck him as the noble, generous type when he'd tangled with Captain Reisman on the drill field.

Maggot hesitated in front of the shower. Another guy came up behind him, and he grabbed his arm, urging him forward. It was a very white arm that fell away from his fingers like jelly. "Here, kid, take this," he said. "I'll wait."

"Thanks," said Myron Odell in amazement. He kept his towel on around him until he'd stepped into the stall, and

151

then he had no place to hang it and had to lean out again and toss it on the floor.

When the duffel bags were brought in, the prisoners lingered over their belongings, fondling and repacking things few of them had expected to see again. Bowren read off a list of authorized clothing and equipment. Items they didn't have were brought up from Supply. Personal stuff that had managed to survive inspections, pilferage and regulations was to be left behind.

Calvin Ezra Smith hesitated as he was wrapping the heavy black book in a sweater to stuff in his duffel. He moved up to the Corporal sadly. "I've just got to take this with me, Mr. Bowren," he said. "You don't know what it's done for me these weeks."

"Let me have it," said Bowren. For all he knew, there could have been a shiv encased within the Bible. The pages made a whirring, whistling sound as he riffled them quickly. A piece of paper fell out and they both stooped for it. Bowren recovered it.

"You've just lost my place, Mr. Bowren," Smith accused.

"Place, hell!" said Bowren. "I bet you can't even read. And stop calling me Mister. It's Corporal."

"Well, sir I can too read," said Smith indignantly. "And I remember pretty good, too."

They were all quiet in the room now, watching and listening.

"I'll tell you what, Smith," said Bowren. "You tell me just one thing you remember from this book and you can take it with you."

Smith stood at attention, hands loosely at his side, chin tilted heavenward, eyes focused right through the ceiling of the washhouse upon some magnificence on high. "The Lord is nigh unto all of them that call upon Him, to all . . ."

Bowren wanted to laugh but found he couldn't, that he was involuntarily assuming a stance of repose in that unbelievably ludicrous place of worship.

" . . . that call upon Him in truth. He will fulfill the desire of them that fear Him; He also will hear their cry, and will save them."

Silently Corporal Bowren handed the Bible back. Smith

wrapped it in his sweater and stuffed it in the duffel bag.

When they were all finished, the prisoners lined up in the washhouse, wearing Class A's, overcoats draped over their arms, duffels at their feet. Bowren moved down the line picking up their shaving blades. When he got to Samson, the Indian looked at him bewildered.

"Your blade, Chief," said Bowren. "You gotta turn in the blade. Nobody's allowed to keep em."

Samson shook his head.

"You shaved, didn't you?" asked Bowren in exasperation.

"No," said Samson.

Joseph Wladislaw, remembering hot, boisterous Chicago afternoons in the Independence movie theater, momentarily forgot who and where he was. "Hey, Corp, ain't you never seen an Indian pitcha?" he blurted out. "Indians don't have no beards."

Some of the others started to snicker.

Master Sergeant Morgan, silently watching and listening to the proceedings with growing excitement, suddenly strode purposefully to the point of command. His finger waved at Samson. "What did you do with the blade?" he asked.

Samson pointed to the shelf, walked over there and looked around, confused. Bowren stayed with him, trying to help, then he turned to the others and demanded, "Who lifted the blade?"

Nobody said a word.

Morgan felt the tremble of excitement rising within him. "Empty your bag and get undressed, Chief," he ordered. Then to the others, "I want the blade or nobody leaves the shithouse." He spoke softly.

Samson stood in the middle of the washhouse naked, while the guards went over his clothing, his toilet kit and the contents of his duffel, examining them minutely.

"All right, bend over and spread your cheeks," said Morgan. His voice was hoarse, barely audible.

Samson did what he was told without anger or remorse. The Captain had promised him he would not hang, and nothing else mattered, though they insulted him, though they made a fool of him. When the guards were finished, he dressed again silently.

Morgan moved down the rank of prisoners, studying their faces for a clue. "I want whoever took that blade to turn it in now . . . no questions asked."

They were quiet. Nobody moved. Nobody said anything.

Lever knew he'd never be able to keep the blade now. He knew he'd made another mistake the minute they started on the Indian and wouldn't let up. They'd find it on him if they kept looking. He had to get rid of it.

Franko, his eyes straight ahead, felt Morgan stop in front of him, fill his field of vision to monstrous proportions, yet he didn't see him, he refused to focus on him.

"You!" said Morgan.

You! Like I was some nameless crud, thought Franko. Christ, didn't he even know my name? And in that same inward bleat of horror—No! That's good he don't know my name!

"Your turn," said Morgan softly. "Dump your stuff and strip."

To Bowren, Franko might have protested Why the hell does it have to be me? I didn't take your goddamn blade! I gave you mine! But for the hangman he got undressed and stood naked and shivering while they searched him and searched his duffel.

Corporal Bowren wondered how much longer Morgan would revel in his authority without obtaining results. There were better ways to handle this, but officially it was Morgan's detail, and though the slob had let him run it till now, Bowren knew better than to protest in front of the prisoners.

When they finished with Franko, Morgan suddenly looked tired and defeated. "Take over the detail, Corporal," he muttered. "Find that damn blade or no chow for them . . ." And he left it hanging that way, going out the washhouse door and closing it softly behind him, as though he, at least, was satisfied with what he had accomplished there.

Bowren stood in front of them silently, trying to figure out what to do. If they were really going to live and train together like the Captain said, then this kind of crap had to stop here and now. "You guys each know the break you've been given," he said. "Stuff like this is gonna goof it and you're gonna be back behind the eight-ball. We're gonna leave you alone for five minutes. Find the blade!"

154

The moment the door closed out the screws, Franko jumped from the rank of prisoners and turned on them. "Which one a you bastards done it? Get it up!" he demanded. "You seen what they done to me. You know I don't have it."

Maggot spread a crooked smile on his face. There was a score to settle with this nigger-lover, but not all at once, not now. "Who in heyll put you in chahge, boy?" he scoffed. "Ah doan take no awduhs fum you!"

"You got the blade, Reb?"

"Sheet . . . ah doan have no blade," said Maggot, shuffling toward him.

Sawyer moved quickly from the rank and stepped between them. His broad frame and the unexpectedly defiant thrust of his big, square jaw effectively kept them apart. He felt a crazy thrill of duty again. "No point getting excited," he said softly. "Why don't we just look around. Maybe we can find it."

It was the opening Lever needed. He had his duffel bag and toilet kit emptied in seconds, and the blade effectively palmed. "Here's my stuff," he said to the room at large. "You're welcome to look."

The rest of them followed suit while Samson and Franko, the acknowledged innocents, inspected them. They had gone through only half the group, when a sudden sound— a barely audible sound of a small thing striking the hard floor—drew Samson's eyes. "There!" he called out triumphantly. The wrapped blade lay on the floor near the sinks. That it had not been there before, he was sure. Where it had come from, he did not know. But he was glad that he had found it.

Maggot darted for the blade. As he bent to retrieve it, Napoleon's foot came down on it hard, just missing his fingers, and he looked up in fury.

"Yo hungry, Massuh Archuh?" said Napoleon.

Maggot looked suddenly bewildered, as much by Napoleon addressing him by name as by the new way he spoke. But he nodded yes.

"Ah's hungry, too, Massuh Archuh," Napoleon mocked, "an ah wants mah breakfus wit no fudder trub'l. Ah says we all leave it right wheyah it is an let the gennilmuns fine it when they come back!"

Stuart Kinder was waiting alone in the Commandant's office when Reisman arrived at the prison. Kinder was wearing double rows of silver bars on his shoulders.

"What did I tell you!" said Reisman, smiling. "Congratulations, Captain."

"Thank you, Captain," said Kinder. "It's something I've been looking forward to for a while." He paused just long enough to allow Reisman any further small talk he might feel appropriate to the occasion. There wasn't any, so he went on. "I'm eager to hear what you've accomplished. I've been here since 0600."

"Don't you bother to sleep?" asked Reisman.

"Couldn't. I took a late train down last night . . . or maybe it was an early train this morning," said Kinder and laughed thinly. "Depends on one's point of orientation. Saw our jeep outside but didn't know where you were. The Commandant said he didn't think you'd stayed on the post last night."

Kinder's subtle chiding didn't escape Reisman, but he found it humorous rather than irritating. "I managed to find more hospitable quarters," he said, winking mischievously. But then he was sorry he had said that, for he felt suddenly that he had in some way slighted Tess. "What's up? What are you doing here?" he asked quickly.

"There's some testing I want to do right away. I hope it will be convenient for me to meet your selectees." He hesitated a moment, searching for the most tactful words. "By the way, John . . . that incident on the drill field yesterday . . . it didn't upset things any, did it?"

The question stumped Reisman momentarily, but then he realized what was meant. "No, it didn't," he replied tartly. He took a package of cigarets from his coat pocket and stuck one in his mouth. That was the second small reproof from Kinder, and Reisman wondered what in hell the man was attempting to establish. Kinder certainly had no authority over him, and Reisman preferred, in fact, to think of him as a glorified errand boy and aide-if-needed. "As a matter of fact, it helped," he said. "Who told you about it?" He lit the cigaret and snapped his lighter shut sharply in irritation.

"This fellow Morgan . . . the Sergeant," said Kinder. He picked up a sheet of paper from Colonel Tarbell's desk, at which he had made himself comfortable. "The Commandant let me have your transfer roster to save time. I

156

sent for Morgan. He's gone off to eat now, but I've already had a nice chat with him. He told me about another nasty incident this morning . . . something about a razor blade. Don't know how it came out, but I'm afraid you've got a very uncooperative bunch there."

"Good God, man!" Reisman exploded. "What in hell did you expect, a Boy Scout troop?"

Kinder backwatered a bit. "No reflection on you, of course," he asserted, smiling. "There is one other important point, though . . . if I may. Do you think it was wise picking Sergeant Morgan for your topkick? You do know he was the hangman, don't you?"

Three strikes and you're out, thought Reisman angrily. "Let us understand something, Stu," he said. "The personnel of this operation were to be left entirely to my discretion, were they not?"

"Why, yes," said Kinder, his voice falling off. "I didn't mean to . . ."

Reisman reversed field. "Now then . . . what can we do to help you?" he asked pleasantly.

"Well . . . I'd like to know how far along you are . . . what your plans are . . . that sort of thing." Then, in a tentative voice, "Maybe we can see where I can fit mine in."

In a few words Reisman brought him up to date, evaluating as best he could the potential of each of the prisoners. "Maybe this is as good a time as any for you to start your end of the project," he concluded. He hoped he didn't sound condescending, for he didn't intend it that way. "I'm leaving today to look for a training site."

"Fine! That's why I'm here—to help!" said Kinder eagerly. "I agree with you completely about getting the men away from here. Where did you have in mind?"

"I'll try Devon first," answered Reisman. "There's a jump school down there not far from the coast, and I'd like to be close by. The C.O. is a son-of-a-bitch named Breed I had a big hassle with in Italy a while back. He was a pompous ass then as a Major, I can only imagine what he's like now he's a Colonel. But I understand his training setup is excellent, and that's all that matters. Also there are some other bases nearby where I can get help and supplies in a hurry if I need them. As for a place to hide away our bully boys, we've always managed to find a nice quiet spot in our branch for this kind of work. A lot of the gentry have made estates and country houses available for the duration. I'll find one."

"What about the men while you're away?" Kinder asked.

"I'm going to have them run through as rugged a refresher course in Basic as can be set up right here—minus the weapons, of course. I want them marched and drilled and run through calisthenics from dawn till sunset," Reisman outlined. "You can have them today right after my pep talk, if you want them. I'll be meeting with them in a few minutes. While I'm away, make your arrangements with Morgan or Bowren. Bowren, incidentally, is the noncom to depend on. I'm just bringing Morgan along as a bogey man. He isn't worth a shit for command. Bowren's only a Corporal, but I intend to correct that as soon as I feel the time is right."

"Well . . . you seem to have things pretty well in hand," said Kinder. "Anything more I can do to help you?"

"Sure," said Reisman joking. "Tell me who thought up this mess."

He hadn't really expected a reply to that, and was amazed when Kinder eagerly offered one.

"I don't really know this to be fact, but I suspect the success of the British Army with their Special Training Units was one of the generating thoughts behind our plan, at least as far as personnel is concerned," related Kinder. "I've been ordered to confer from time to time with British Army psychologists active in that program."

Reisman asked, "Was that your specialty in civilian life, Captain?"

"Why, yes," acknowledged Kinder. "Clinical psychology, and I also dabbled a bit in sociology."

"What's with these Special Training Units? You don't mean the Commandos, do you?"

"Oh, no. I'm sorry . . . I thought you knew," responded Kinder. He was pleased to elaborate. "They're composed of men withdrawn from regular training or line companies where they either have been unable to adjust to discipline or have been criminal offenders. They're not prison camps, but are exactly what their name implies—outfits where an attempt is made to rehabilitate men with special and individual attention. They've had about seventy-five percent success in posting men back to regular companies." Kinder allowed Reisman to absorb that, then eyeing him with mischievous humor, as though he was telling tales out of school, he went on, "I have a feeling that somewhere recently a top U.S. officer and a top U.K. officer got together at lunch, and after hearing about the STUs, our man probably decided we were not to be outdone and ought to go it one better."

Reisman suspected this was the closest Captain Kinder would ever come to knocking the brass. The stuff about the British was interesting, and he thought he might look into it further himself.

"One avenue of approach I'd like to try has worked rather well with the British," Kinder continued. "You see, they make every effort to make their STU men feel like individuals again. They strive to touch them not only at the physical level, but the moral and mental levels as well." His voice rose excitedly to command level. "They must not be made to feel they are failures. For instance, one of the first things I would suggest is getting rid of these awful fatigues the prisoners are required to wear here with the letters painted on them. I'd get them done up in Class A's and replace missing clothing and equipment. You know . . . make them feel you're really interested in them. It's psychological . . . like a woman buying a new dress and hat or going to the hairdresser's . . ."

Reisman interrupted. "Captain Kinder," he said, smiling, "I think we really are going to work well together. I couldn't agree with you more. Shall we go?"

12

THEY STRODE briskly into the room where the prisoners had been brought, and Reisman called out, "Good morning, gentlemen!" startling them.

Some of them answered, "Good morning, Captain." One or two of them loud enough, the others feebly. Wladislaw called out "Hey-ey, Chicago!" thinking to ingratiate himself before all of them, but it died in his throat as Reisman gave him a cold stare.

He ordered the guards outside and they left, puzzled. Sergeant Morgan looked angry, as though he doubted the legality of his being excluded. Stuart Kinder, more perceptive than Reisman had given him credit for, also headed for the door.

"I'll wait outside until you want me," he said.

Reisman looked at them for a few moments composing his thoughts. They sat on wooden chairs in a day room on the ground floor of the prison—the twelve chosen ones, a cross section of cutthroat America. Not far above their heads, Enos Gardiner had dangled on a noose short days before. They were alone together now for the first time. It was just him and them.

"We'll be leaving here in a few days," Reisman began slowly. "Of the many things you must learn in the next few weeks, there are two that must never leave you. For if you break faith with me on these, you are finished."

His voice was soft, making them come to him. It rose slightly now in volume, for emphasis:

"First, is absolute secrecy. You must never reveal to anybody the things you are doing, the things that are told to you. That goes for the guards as well. Tell them nothing. Listen to them. Obey their orders. Answer them on questions of discipline and routine, but tell them nothing which I tell you is secret. It goes for any officers or noncommissioned officers with whom you come in contact, no matter how high their rank. It goes for the Commanding General: You must not reveal to each other things told to you in secrecy as individuals. Anyone who breaks this rule is finished. There are no second chances. You each know who you are, what you have done, and what your sentences are. I know these things too. The penalty for breaking secrecy will be immediate execution of sentence. There is no appeal.

"Second. You must not attempt to escape. You must not even think of attempts to escape. You will have enough to occupy your minds without it. For anybody caught attempting to escape, the penalty will be immediate execution of sentence. There is no appeal."

He could tell they were listening—not just hearing, but listening intently, riding up and down with him as he spoke, on a scale of hope and depression.

"As for who you are and what you've done, that is your privilege to keep or reveal to each other as you choose. I know it, you know it—that is sufficient. As to the nature of our work, the nature of our missions, you will learn more as you deserve to learn it. Let me say only this about it for now. It is important. It is very important. As much to you as to your country. Do it well and you will have atoned for anything your conscience tells you must be atoned."

Listening to himself—really listening—Reisman was startled to hear what he had said. He hadn't planned it. It had just flowed out of him. And hearing the words, he sensed the rightness of them.

"We will be together many weeks. It is my hope that you will get to like one another and work well together," he concluded, softly.

Whether he had reached them or not, he didn't know. He could imagine most of them muttering obscenities under their breath. But maybe one or two . . . maybe more . . .

They were silent as Reisman went to the door and summoned Captain Kinder and the guards. The MPs took their stations around the room. Kinder leaned a very large leather portfolio against a table up front, unchained his briefcase and placed it on top of the table.

Reisman introduced him. "Captain Kinder will be working with you men from time to time in the next weeks. He will ask you questions about yourselves which you must answer. I exclude, of course, those things which I tell you must be excluded. He will give you certain tests which will help us to help you."

He left Kinder standing there alone, walked to the back of the room, and took a seat. He intended to stay, at least for the beginning, to observe Kinder at his work silently but critically, and see also if maybe he could not learn something himself.

Stuart Kinder felt their eyes on him, figuring, evaluating; and the guards sizing him up as enlisted men always sized up men they were required to respect and follow at pain of punishment or their lives. He was pleased by Reisman's introduction, for he hadn't thought the man had so good a grasp of what he was to do. But he was also nervous and hoped it didn't show.

How different it was here at the sticking point, beyond the realm of theory, face to face with men who had done what these had done; who had entered a world of experience that must, praise God, be forever alien to him, though

161

he had striven to understand and to know them, and had experienced vicariously, in the reading, those thrills and horrors they had lived; men who had committed crimes of such magnitude that he did not know how he would speak to them or look at them without revealing the awe in which he held them. The extra bars hadn't really helped.

He admired the way Reisman handled these men, the way he could talk to them with command in his voice, and make them listen.

He looked for one face, one sympathetic face. There, the thin, pale boy with glasses. And he began to speak . . . it had to be a game . . . it had to be pleasant . . . nothing about psychology . . . nothing about tests . . . nothing to stir antagonism toward him or skepticism . . .

"I would like you all to help me in a little experiment," said Captain Kinder. "You might even find it to be fun . . ."

Reisman listened to him, and it was as though he sat among a group of children. Kinder's voice contained a smile, and gently he asked them to do things until each of them had a task and the room became a ludicrous beehive of cooperative schoolroom activity. Three tables were joined in a semicircle; twelve chairs were spaced evenly behind them; one man put test booklets and pencils at each place; others put still another table where Kinder indicated, and a chair on top of it as a backrest for the covered stack of large cards he took from his portfolio.

"Do not open your booklets until I tell you to," Kinder instructed.

They sat quietly at their places, attentive and obedient.

Napoleon had wondered what nonsense the man was up to. For one indignant moment, with all the moving around and rearranging, he had thought he might have been tricked into some simple test of motor skills, such as one might give to a class of retarded children, or clever apes. In Captain Kinder, he recognized a type—the social service agency man. He had seen enough of them around college, and elsewhere, for that matter—for in his experience their most self-supportive and justifying function had been to gather up the people and problems of his race for professional probing, picking, tearing and rendering.

But now, with the booklet before him and the stack of cards beside the Captain, Napoleon had a certain glimmer of what was being done, although he had never seen it done quite this way.

"Now all of you, I am sure," said Kinder, "at one time or another, have accidentally spotted ink on a piece of paper. Maybe you were writing a letter, or doing schoolwork, or maybe you even have done it intentionally as a game . . . I know I have. I've spread the ink around by folding the paper, and then, for fun, I've looked for pictures and forms and figures in the inkblots. Well, that is more or less what we've got here. I'm going to show you, one by one, a group of cards that are reproductions of inkblots. Most of them are in shades of black and white and gray. Others have colors in them. There are ten cards in all. Now, you will notice also . . . when I tell you to . . . that these cards are reproduced in the same way in the booklets you have before you, and that there is a blank page opposite the inkblot. Your task is merely to write on the blank page anything you see in these inkblots . . . pictures, forms, figures, anything the splotches remind you of, resemble, or might be. We will all take each card in turn, and there is no hurry. Take as much time as you need for each card. It makes no difference at all if somebody else has finished a particular card and you haven't. I would like you also to circle the parts of the inkblot you write about and to put a number there and the same number beside what you write about it on the blank page. Are there any questions?"

There were many, and it necessitated Kinder's going over the same instructions a number of times.

Napoleon marveled at the stupidity of these men with whom he had been grouped. When, finally, almost as an afterthought, the Captain asked if anybody had ever played this little game before, Napoleon started to raise his hand—to explain in positively clear and technical terms that yes he'd taken the Rorschach test before, at college, and knew it well in theory and practice, and therefore his results would not be very valid, and wasn't it passing strange that a rather sacrosanct procedure requiring quiet, individual isolation was being violated here by a group situation—but he thought the hell with it and he kept his hand down.

He remembered the story of the wise guy who screwed up a professor's research by getting everybody in a class to respond in the same way—a female pelvis—to every inkblot during private tests. But that was too easy. He looked at Card One . . . and it looked like a big black elephant with fanning, frazzled, batlike ears, sitting with its back to the viewer, as a curious cat would sit, waiting for two gray donkeys, reared back, to begin a fight—or a minuet. But he didn't write that. He began to write the most obscene and evil things he could think of—until he paused, realizing he was actually enjoying himself, he was with it again, he was functioning, and he didn't know if he was glad or mad or sad or what . . .

Victor Franko poised anxiously as the covering card was removed and the first inkblot exposed. The fink had said it was an experiment, but it looked more like a test to him, a test you had to figure to get good marks or bad, a test in which there had to be ups and downs, winners and losers, and he girded up all his mental faculties to do well, though he had no idea what well should be.

Myron Odell blanched at sight of the first inkblot. It was an evil, dirty mess and he didn't like it, but he had to write something. He liked Captain Kinder. He wanted to co-operate with him. He wanted to be good for him. He wanted to show him, in some way, any way, that he was innocent!

Roscoe Lever saw some of the others starting to write and he wondered what in hell they were writing about. He didn't see anything. It was some kind of trick. Well, screw them. He'd show them. That's what he'd write. It's nothing.

Archer Maggot wondered too what in hell they were writing about, but what got him mostly was that the nigger was busily scratching away at his booklet as though he knew what he was doing. Then it came to him suddenly what he was seeing there in the inkblot, and he snickered inwardly, remembering women black and white and wondering if that pipsqueak captain up there could ever know what he was really thinking, and then feeling the pain of his want again, unfed so many months, like a kick in the nuts. But he didn't think he ought to write down anything about a woman's black crotch or a black woman's crotch, so then he saw something else there, and it was the damnedest thing and it made him want to laugh, so he wrote that down—a big black nigger cat.

Victor Franko wrote—a ghost behind a window.

Myron Odell wrote—a dirty mess.

Luis Jimenez wrote—part of a woman.

Calvin Ezra Smith wrote—a butterfly.

Ken Sawyer, Vernon Pinkley and Glenn Gilpin wrote—a bat.

Joseph Wladislaw wrote—an X ray.

At the back of the room, Reisman looked at the inkblot card in the distance, shook his head, and looked away. He didn't really want to know his own reaction, and so he told himself he was seated too far away to make anything of it. He watched the prisoners and sensed their involvement with their task—and that alone was good, and sufficient. He looked for Samson Posey, found his broad back and massive head, and wished he could see his face.

Samson had asked no questions, had followed obediently. He understood what was expected of him. He saw many things in these inkblots—things to make him laugh, for he appreciated at once the humor in this strange game; things that were like visions seen in a peyote dream; things that brought him memories of times and people past. But how should he write down what he saw? He knew some words, but not others. He tried desperately to remember . . . to bring back the times that were good and . . .

He sat on a blanket beneath the big shade tree near the trading post at Towaoc. There were eight of them playing poker, and a crowd of men and women standing around watching, often switching places with a player who had gone down in defeat. Billy No-legs wasn't there; he was away at the white hospital again, getting his legs fixed up. Samson had been playing all day, with his usual good luck. All day, there had been the sounds of hammering and banging coming from where they were putting up the Bear Dance corral.

There was excitement in the air, anticipation. Crowds of men, women and children were coming in—by horse, by wagon, in pickup trucks. Utes from Allen Canyon in Utah; Utes from Ignacio, at the eastern end of the reservation; Navajo from Shiprock, New Mexico; Jicarilla Apache from their own reservation, southeast.

By the old ways, it was late for Bear Dance, his grandfather had warned. Almost two months had passed since Old Charlie had heard the first thunder of spring and said, "Bear is getting up. He is weak, he needs food, he doesn't see well. Somebody should organize Bear Dance right away. We have to help bear, to help ourselves."

But though The People held tenaciously to the old ways, they did it now when they could take time from their meager herds and flocks, or from their farms if they had become farmers like the white men. Around Towaoc, the end of May was a good time.

Samson had helped his family move the sheep down to the watering troughs at Navajo Springs and then had ridden up to Towaoc to be early for the gambling. His family would come later, when they found someone to look after the sheep.

Before he had left them, Old Charlie had looked up at his great height admiringly and said, "It is a good name we call you now, isn't it? A strong man. A warrior."

"It is a white man's name, but it is a good name, and I like it," he had answered respectfully.

"You must dance all the Bear Dance to show you are strong," his grandfather had said. "You should get married. Bear Dance is the time to get married. It is a good time."

It was a good time to get married, and Samson felt it strongly in his blood. Under the shade tree at Towaoc, he was intent only upon his poker, and nothing else really mattered, but at the back of his mind were yearning thoughts of the dance. For him, it would have to be the time.

He was eighteen, very much a man—yet still a boy. For two years he had fought a terrible battle within himself, hearing the sounds of courting flutes on a summer night, knowing the other young men were philandering around the camps—but knowing, too, about the lovesickness many of them got, and how it destroyed a man and woman. If he had risen to his great height and strength in these bad times, by some grace of Creator-of-Humans, then he would not give in to the temptations of Sunavawi, the wolf, and be tricked into a pleasure that destroyed. Yucca, his father, had cautioned him. Billy No-legs had warned him. He believed them. Wanting to remain strong and healthy, he had turned his eyes and his mind away from women and women things. But now the stirring within him was very strong. He was eighteen, and as Old Charlie had said, "Bear Dance is the time to get married."

166

Bear Dance leader came riding up on a great white stallion. He was handsomely dressed for his role—moccasins, beaded gauntlets, breastplate, riding chaps, eagle plumes in his black sombrero, and long black braids wrapped in otterskin bouncing on his chest. The gambling stopped and they listened to him declaim:

"We must make this dance a good dance like in the old times. Everybody must dance. You will enjoy yourselves, and you will keep away sickness and bad things from The People."

He told the story of Bear Dance: how, at the beginning, a Ute hunter had become friendly with a bear woman and she had come to his camp and shown The People how to dance, how to make music with the rasp, and how to sing the right songs.

How often Samson had heard that tale and the variations of it—as a child, a boy, and now a man. Yet each time it absorbed and thrilled him. It gave him a sense of the history and destiny of himself and his people. It was a reminder of his innate affinity to his land and the creatures that inhabited it—though the Utes were a conquered and destitute people.

"Bear Dance is for a good time," declared Bear Dance leader. "We are glad to have passed the long winter. Everybody go now to bear's cave. You must not drink! It is bad to be drunk there!"

Samson did not drink, but other Utes did. They couldn't buy whisky at the trading post because it was against the rules, but they went off the reservation and brought it back. It made them happy. It helped them forget. Lately there was peyote, too. But that was different. That was the Indian's religion.

Bear Dance leader rode off to repeat his oratory elsewhere, to gather stragglers and urge them to the corral he called the bear's cave. Samson pocketed his cards and his winnings—the coins and dollars that had once been blankets, buckskin, horses, cattle, sheep, pension and dole checks until traded into money and wagered in the chief recreation and endeavor of Towaoc. He mounted his horse and rode to the corral. Waving on a pole above it was an elaborately painted cloth in black and white, a bear standing in the center with his arms raised, and the words—UTE MOUNTAIN BEAR DANCE—1938.

The rhythmic rubbing of the cottonwood rasps began very softly. The musicians moved their cow bones, sticks and pop bottles up and down, urging the sound into the sheet-iron resonator set in a hole in the ground. Samson sat on a log on the north side of the corral with the men, listening to the beginning songs. They were good songs, some new, some old—and then it was time for the dance.

Half the women rose up in a body on the south side of the corral and moved toward the men. At first he was bold and looked them over carefully—the old ones, the middle-aged and the young, especially the young, especially Eva Pavisook. But then they came closer and he dropped his eyes shyly.

"You," he heard a girl call. "The big fellow over there."

It was one of the girls from the camps on Ute Mountain. But then Eva was there too, suddenly ducking under the other girl's outstretched arm. Eva took Samson's hand in hers and turned on the other girl with a look of challenge. The girl picked another man. Samson and Eva moved opposite each other into the separate lines of men and women in the center of the corral.

The muted, insistent background rhythm of the rasps burst into a roar. The singers' voices rose excitedly. The dancing began—two steps forward, two steps backward, the women aggressive, the men hesitant, the lines swaying back and forth, back and forth, again and again and again.

They danced that way for a while, neither Samson nor Eva speaking, concentrating on their movements, stealing an occasional glance at each other. He wore Levis, a loose denim jacket open to show his brightly decorated red cowboy shirt; on his feet were a good pair of cowboy boots; on his head a black cowboy hat, peaked low, not like the way the old men wore theirs. It was the costume he had been wearing all day under the gambling tree, but he had bought it new for Bear Dance week. Eva's dress was a yellow cotton print, cut straight and loose, as buckskin once had been cut, gathered at the waist with a broad leather belt. Her legs were covered sedately in dark cotton stockings, but on her feet were brightly trimmed white moccasins. Against the late afternoon wind, she wore a green wool shawl on her shoulders. For gaiety, a silver Navajo bracelet jingled on her wrist.

The lines became too long as more couples joined them. Samson and Eva separated from the lines. He moved his right arm to encircle her waist as it was allowed when couples danced alone. But he was too tall—it was awkward to reach so far down.

"You are much bigger this year, Suh-gatz," said Eva, smiling at him.

"So are you, Eva Pavisook," he answered in embarrassment. "But I am no longer Suh-gatz. I am called Samson now."

"Like in the Bible?"

"Yes."

"What do you know about the Bible?" she challenged.

He knew nothing. But Eva Pavisook knew—because her father was assistant tribal agent, and they lived in a frame house and went sometimes to the Presbyterian Mission, though they believed more strongly in the Indian ways, they said.

"I know about Samson," he answered proudly. But he really knew very little—only what he had heard from the black-suited Mormon missionary who had come to their camp that winter, and engaged Yucca and Old Charlie in oratory. The missionary had spoken the language of The People well. Looking at Suh-gatz, he had said, "He reminds me of the Hebrew warrior Samson. You should call him that." Old Charlie had asked who the Hebrews were, if they were another Indian tribe. The missionary had said they were an ancient and powerful desert people as were the Ute. They had lived in a faraway land, been defeated and dispersed all over the world. "This book," he said, tapping the black book of religion in his hand, "tells about the Hebrews, the lost tribes of Israel." Then he had astounded them by declaring, "You are descended of those people, of Samson and his tribe."

The dancing quickened—four steps forward, four steps backward—as the singers sang of bear and Ute, man and woman, the history of The People, the past and the present. Samson's arm pressed gently against Eva's breasts, his hand gripped her shoulder lightly. He was aware of where he touched her, but she didn't seem to mind. He stole quick glances at her face, and she returned them stare for stare. If he was to marry, then he would want to marry someone like Eva Pavisook. Whether she would have him or not, he did not know. Bear Dance was one thing, but marriage was another . . . yet she had sought him out, picked him for a partner, and during those times when cutting-in was allowed and other girls came to him, Samson saw her angry glances at the other girls.

Each day during the week of Bear Dance, Samson played poker and Spanish monte. Each afternoon until sundown he danced with Eva Pavisook. Each night he courted her.

In the frame house—one of the few near Towaoc—he discoursed at length with her father upon the problems of the times, their great need for water, from wells, from irrigation long promised by the government in Washington and overdue; because the winter run-off seemed always to be less and less and dried up quickly in the creeks and washes, leaving unpalatable alkali pools, and in the mountains streams were reduced to a meager trickle. He complimented her mother on the meals she prepared. He brought food and gifts purchased at the trading post, for Samson earned much more at gambling then the salary of her father, the assistant Indian agent. And he walked and talked with Eva outside in the star-roofed cool night of the high desert, but always within sight and hearing of her house.

They held hands.

"I like your new name," she said. "It fits you well."

"Now we both have white names."

"Yes. Do you like mine?"

"It is a good name."

They kissed shyly and held each other's bodies. She was slender as an aspen tree, yet round where it was necessary for a woman to be round. And though the top of her head came only to his mid-chest, that was a good height for a Ute girl, and maybe she would grow more, since she was only sixteen years of age.

"Have you known many girls?" she asked boldly.

It was the time to speak a lie, to crow of many conquests in the scattered camps of the reservation. But he didn't want to.

"No. This was the way I wanted it," he said, bending to her lips again.

"I am glad," she whispered, smiling. "I am glad my father and mother were strict. This is the way I wanted it too."

Afterward, he returned alone and aching in his loins to the tent he had pitched among the other camps near the Bear Dance corral.

When his family came to Towaoc later in the week, Samson asked Yucca, his father, to show him how to carve a courting flute from a willow rod. Yucca smiled knowingly. Old Charlie rose from the blanket-covered bedspring on the dirt floor of the tent, where he spent most of his time, and to which he had permanent and proprietary rights as the throne of his old age. Grinning wide and toothless he said, "Bear Dance is the time to get married." Samson did not appreciate the bawdy tone of the conversation that followed between the older men.

That night, when he left Eva at the door of her frame house, he did not return to his tent. He lingered within sight of her house, waiting for all the family to retire and the kerosene lamps to go out. Then, softly as a brave on the hunt, he crept to the window of her room. He raised the flageolet to his lips and the mellow tones were words secret and importuning, special to The People and known but to lovers.

In long notes and short, punctuated passages of trills and staccatos, the flageolet sang, "Eee-va . . . Eee-va . . . Eee-va Pa-vi-sook! . . . Com-m-m-m-e out! . . . Com-m-m-m-e out! . . . I-I-I lo-o-o-v-v-v-e yo-o-o-ou; . . . I-I-I lo-o-o-v-v-v-e yo-o-o-ou!"

She raised the window, but didn't step out. When he tried to climb in, she stopped him.

"My father and mother," she whispered.

"They heard," he said. "By their silence, they approve."

"But it is I you wish to marry, not my father and mother, is that not so?"

She was confusing him. "Very much," he answered shyly.

"Do you have three dollars?"

"Of course. I have more."

"Then we will go to Cortez and get married in the white way," said Eva.

"I am a Ute, not a white man," he protested angrily, "and this is the Ute way."

"Then you will not marry me," she said softly, and she closed the window between them.

Alone again in his tent that night, Samson felt the stirring in his blood beyond what he thought he could endure. Better to have followed the temptations of Sunavawi, the wolf, than this. Yet Eva came to him again the next afternoon, as though nothing had happened, and chose him for her partner; and though he was angry with her, he could not refuse. A man was not allowed to refuse—bear would come after him in the mountains; and there were Bear Dance assistants with cedar branches to gently whip those who refused, for the amusement of all.

When dancing ended for the day, Samson no longer was angry with Eva. How could he dislike someone so . . . so . . . He felt only longing and love for her. Late that night he came to her house again with his courting flute, and she raised her window for him.

"I will go to Cortez with you," he offered reluctantly, "if that is the way you want it. It cannot hurt me."

She leaned from her window and kissed him long and sweetly, and Samson felt terribly weak and helpless. "It is not just a game with you then, Samson," she said happily, "as it is not with me. Your love is true."

He started to lift his long legs over the window sill into her room, but she held him back gently. "Let us talk," she said.

"About what?"

"Gambling is a bad way to spend all your time. You must have cattle or sheep or a farm, and someday we must build a house better than my father's."

He pulled away from her, angry and astonished. "Gambling is my way," he said. "It is the old Ute way."

She reached her hand out to touch his cheek gently. "Don't be angry," she begged. "I want only you for my husband. You are strong and handsome and there is no one like you on all the reservation. In the beginning I will live in your tent and go wherever you say. But we must do better for ourselves . . . for our people . . . for our children."

"There is nothing wrong with gambling," Samson insisted. "I earn more than the farmers and the cattlemen. I bring food and clothing for my family, more than my father brings with the sheep."

"Then continue to do as you please," said Eva sadly, and she closed the window between them.

The next afternoon, Samson left the gambling early, went back to his tent, and changed into his most elaborate buckskin finery. He wished now that his hair was long, as the older men kept theirs, and that he could tie red cloth around braids on his chest, but his hair was cut in the fashion of the young whites he had seen in Cortez.

The Bear Dance corral was crowded when he got there —everybody excited and dressed in finery; if not buckskin, then the best clothing they owned. Men and women wore eagle feathers in their hair.

The dancing began, but Eva Pavisook did not choose him. She chose other young men—men Samson knew were bad for her. Other women came to Samson and he danced with them, but without that joy he had known with Eva. He waited until those dances when men too were allowed to cut in, and he tapped Eva's partner on the shoulder and urged him away with an angry look.

"Why did you not choose me?" he asked, scowling at Eva.

"It is your choice to make," she answered haughtily.

"I should leave you to dance with these coyotes," he mocked. "They will lead you into trouble and then you will be satisfied."

"No. It is still you that I want for my husband," she said softly. "I will dance only with you now, if you want it that way."

At sundown this day, they did not stop the dancing. The growl of the rasps filled the corral and swept outward toward the high mountains where bear could hear. The singers' voices chanted strongly. Fires were lit in the corral. The dancers moved vibrantly, faced with the challenge ahead, when those who were strong and those who were brave would dance through the night.

Four steps forward, four steps backward, again and again and again.

Samson saw the prideful looks of his father and grandfather who sat with the men. He saw the approving look of his mother who sat with the women. He looked into Eva's face and she looked strong and determined. Without words being said, he knew she would dance as long as he did, and he resolved neither one of them would fall.

As the hours passed toward sunrise, it seemed to Samson that her face became more lovely and radiant, her lithe, buckskin-clad body more desirable, swept onward in the ancient rhythms of their dance. Something very strong and very true passed between them this night.

Other dancers fell exhausted and Bear Dance leader came to them, walked round them, and rubbed them with his rasp to exorcise the evil from them, to prevent sickness from befalling them. Samson and Eva danced through the night, and when, at sunrise, the rasping and singing slowed and stopped, white clay was rubbed in their hair as a sign of their bravery and strength.

In the afternoon there was a feast, and though they ate well and were happy, Eva left early to go to her frame house and rest, and Samson retired early to his tent. Later, in the night, when the camps were silent, and only the night sounds were heard, Samson rose from his blankets and rode to the frame house of Eva Pavisook.

Again, the flageolet played, "Eee-va . . . Eee-va . . . Eee-va Pa-vi-sook! . . . Com-m-m-m-e out! . . . Com-m-m-m-e out! . . . I-I-I lo-o-o-v-v-v-e yo-o-o-ou; . . . I-I-I lo-o-o-v-v-v-e yo-o-o-ou!"

She came to him then, soft as a doe, wearing a blanket over her nightdress, through the front door of the frame house. She took his hand.

"You are a man, Samson," she said, "and you must do as a man must do. If you want to go to Cortez, we can go sometime. It does not matter. If you must gamble, then gamble well—and maybe also we will own sheep and cattle and a house."

They rode together to his tent near the Bear Dance corral, and there, with a gentleness that belied his great strength and need, he took the blanket from her shoulders and the nightdress from her body, and made her his wife. And in the morning, shy and happy, they came out into the bright sunlight together, where Eva prepared his breakfast over a campstove, and it was seen by all of The People who were there that Eva Pavisook and Samson Posey were married . . .

"Posey!" he heard someone call . . . and Samson was torn from his reverie, trying to hold desperately to the vision of Eva. "Posey!" It was the officer who was showing the strange pictures.

"Are you having trouble?" he asked.

"Yes," said Samson sadly. "I do not know how to write."

13

THERE WAS a great nothingness there on the Devonshire cliff, as of the edge of the world. It swept up and out to the rim that hung over the fog-welling sea, and dropped to the narrow beach below. Reisman threshed through the thick gorse that was rooted there waiting for spring, resisting, clutching out at him like a field of half-born-half-dead supplicants, yielding to the beat of his legs. It was an old habit of Reisman's. He was compelled to scout an area, to know all entrances and exits before going to a place or a city, or to the heart of a problem.

Beyond the Channel—so close that he might almost see them if the mists cleared—lay the Germans in their Fortress Europa; coming this close, knowing they were there, made him uneasy, uncomfortable.

The wind carried to him the sound of a barking dog. Looking down the beach, he saw a huge animal bounding in and out of the surf, racing up and down the sand. There was a woman, too—small, solitary and lonely in the distance, bundled in a coat and flying muffler, staring out to sea, walking, staring out to sea, ignoring the dog, though the animal raced past her, bounded to her and away in great leaps and starts, teasing her.

Reisman watched them until they disappeared into the face of the cliff, apparently taking a trail up from the beach. Then he too turned from the sea, and walked back through the gorse to the road where he had left his jeep.

It was just a short drive to Stokes Manor. They had given him good directions in the village, and he had stopped to scout the area as soon as he had seen the chimney tops of the great house sticking up above a dense grove of trees.

When he came to the tall iron gates, Reisman found them chained and padlocked. He tugged at the lock ineffectually; he shouted and honked the horn of the jeep to no avail. There seemed to be no one around. He reached into the jeep for his .45, aimed carefully from a few feet away, and blasted the lock and chain apart, shattering the gray early morning silence of the countryside.

At the house, there was still no answer to his ringing, banging and shouting. But he hesitated to use the gun again. Destroying a chain and padlock was one thing; smashing the lock mechanism and wood of the front door was another not so easily countenanced. The door was old and dark and beautiful, of oak studded with nailheads. It might have been there for two or three hundred years. He had been in enough houses such as this since coming to Britain, so that he was no longer as much in awe of them as he once had been—yet it was the sort of place he might have dreamed of as a child and called *palace* or *castle*, peopling it with fine ladies and gentlemen, dukes and duchesses, queens and kings, as in the movies.

It was an immense building, of native stone, with Gothic arches, and mullioned and leaded windows. He walked the graveled driveway around to the back. There were weed-clogged lawns, and overgrown hedges, trees and flower beds. It had been years since they had been cared for. The place had an air of tragedy about it, as though somebody had died and anybody else who cared had gone away to forget. About forty yards from the back of the house was the cliff, dropping away steeply to the sea. From where he stood in the driveway, he could hear surf pounding against rocks.

It was not the house itself, however, that interested Reisman, but the extensive acres of rolling fields and thick woods confined within the privacy of the estate. He had no intention of quartering his prisoners in the comfort of an old English manor house.

In a large clearing within a grove of oaks, alders and chestnuts, he found a likely spot where he could build a stockade. The trees would screen it from the main house, the rest of the estate, and even the chance of observation from the distant road. What went on there and who was housed there could be kept secret.

He decided to try once more at the main house before driving back into Stokesmouth. He would tell the town clerk that no matter what the man had said earlier in the day, there really seemed to be no one at all in residence at Stokes Manor.

This time when he rang, Reisman heard a dog barking

within the building, and finally the oak door opened. A young woman stood there, holding the door in such a way that she could still slam it shut quickly. At the level of her waist the growling face of a Doberman pinscher appeared, trying to force his way out between her and the door. Reisman gripped the butt of the .45 he had slipped into his coat pocket at the gate.

"What do you want?" challenged the woman.

Reisman realized she was the woman he had seen in the distance on the beach. She had not had time to remove the coat or the muffler. He had seen coats like that before—on young Nazis in Germany before the war, and on dead German officers.

"Miss Strathallan?" he said. "I didn't think anyone was home. Didn't you hear me before?"

"Yes, I'm Lady Margot," she replied. "No, I didn't hear you. I've just come in. Who are you and what do you want? How did you get in here?"

Her attitude seemed the human equivalent of the growling dog's. The animal lurched at him with bared teeth, restrained only by her hand on his collar and her leg squeezing him away from the open threshhold.

"In which order would you like me to answer your questions, Miss Strathallan?" he asked.

"Lady Margot, if you please," she insisted. "And there is no need to be rude . . ." She looked him over speedily, saw the bars. " . . . Captain."

"I'll start with the name," he said. "'I believe that's proper. My name is John Reisman. Your father has granted permission to my organization to train a group of men here . . ."

"My father does not live here," she interrupted. "I do."

"I was aware of that, Miss Strathallan . . ."

"I told you I am to be called Lady Margot!"

He looked at her more closely—a reedy girl with pale, powdered cheeks and auburn hair—certain that whatever strength she had did not go very deep. She was the sort who would resist somebody, something, anything with great strength, not bending at all but finally breaking.

"Lady Margot, then," he said, "permission has been granted by General Sir Howard Stokes Strathallan. It has been cleared through all the necessary channels, and we have been made very much aware of your being in residence here. We will not require any of the facilities of your house, merely a secluded section of the grounds."

"How did you get in?"

"Through the main gate."

"It was chained and padlocked."

"Came apart in my hands," said Reisman. "Wartime product . . . just don't make things like they used to." His eyes kept wandering back to her coat. "That's a lovely garment you're wearing," he said. "A bit large, but handsome. Great for tramping on the moors and all that. Did you liberate it yourself?"

"That is none of your business, Captain," she retorted. "Your crude attempt at humor is just that . . . crude. I am not amused, and I would appreciate it if you would leave."

"May we start again, Lady Margot?" said Reisman. "Seriously . . . your father has made Stokes Manor available to us to train a small group of men. Americans, that is . . . you were aware, weren't you, we've come into the war on your side?"

"That entitles you to be rude to me, then, does it?"

She must have relaxed her grip on the dog's collar, for he jerked forward, barking, and it was all she could do to hold him.

"I'd appreciate your getting rid of your friend," said Reisman. "We might be able to communicate better without the distraction. If I've been rude, I apologize. Chalk it up to my being tired and ignorant."

"Tell me exactly what it is you require of Stokes Manor . . . and me."

"Of you, nothing but your good will," replied Reisman, "and . . . and let me emphasize how important this is . . . your complete secrecy. It's necessary you maintain absolute secrecy about our presence here. Nobody must know."

He gave her some idea of the number of men he would be bringing in; the need to run vehicles over fields; they would be constructing some installations in the clearing in the wood, and bringing in their own power, mess and toilet facilities.

"Any damage done to your property will be repaired or compensated for," he assured her. "And there is one more thing . . . my men will be under firm instructions to stay away from your house. It will be necessary, too, that you don't come near the area where we're bivouacked. It's far

178

enough away from the manor so I don't believe it will inconvenience you if you like to stroll."

"Sounds ominous," she said.

"Not really," he answered casually. "Just necessary. I'd like to make this whole business as painless as possible for you. We wouldn't impose upon your privacy, and I'm sure we could arrange to bring in additional rations to share with you and your staff . . . things you may not have been able to obtain lately. That would be the least we could do for your courtesy in putting up with us."

"Don't play dumb with me, Captain," she said angrily. "You know perfectly well there is no staff. They've all gone off to the war or the factories or some damned-fool thing and good riddance! I am not a child to be won over by promises of sweets and cigarets and coffee. That is one of the vilest habits you people have."

Reisman turned back to the jeep, muttering to himself, "Jeezuss Christ, lady, you've just bought it!" Then louder, so she would be sure to hear him, "We'll be setting up camp here Sunday."

part
three

THE
DIRTY
DOZEN

14

THEY LEFT Marston-Tyne prison in a convoy early on the morning of Sunday, March 5, 1944.

Victor Franko drove a truck loaded with barbed wire, lumber and a huge crate. Corporal Bowren sat beside him, a .45 caliber grease gun in his lap and a .45 automatic pistol on his hip. There was another guard in the back of the truck armed in the same way.

Franko was point vehicle in the convoy, and Bowren kept yapping at him to slow down and take it easy. The feel of the pedal under his foot, the wheel in his hands, responding to his touch, answering his need to move, to fly, to break free and away, filled Franko with the sort of exhilaration he had thought only a woman or complete freedom could have brought him. When he saw women walking or cycling on the country roads, he tooted, hollered and whistled until Bowren told him one more time and he'd give up the wheel to one of the other prisoners.

Franko had a pretty good idea who and what was in each vehicle. All the prisoners and guards had helped load and he'd filed away the information in his head for whatever use it might be. Sawyer drove the truck behind him with just one MP in the cab, the back loaded with more barbed wire, posts and lumber, and mess gear, fuel drums and rations. That Polack from Chicago—Joe Slaw or Ski —drove the third truck, with Morgan in the cab and an MP in the back with building tools, training gear, weapons and ammo.

Pinkley—what a name!—that gawky hick from up in Vermont or New Hampshire or someplace like that, drove the truck with the rest of the men and guards and their duffels. Pulling up the rear where he probably spent all his time was the fink Captain in a jeep towing a water trailer with the nigger driving. Franko figured the CO had brought along the nigger to make him his private servant and do all the crap jobs wherever they went.

Corporal Bowren, too, felt good being out on the road away from the prison duty he had never wanted or liked. He made it look casual the way the submachine gun sat in his lap, but he'd have the safety up and the muzzle in Franko's belly in less than a second if he had to. It was a good idea of the CO's, replacing their rifles and carbines with the beefed-up firepower of the grease guns. The new CO was okay—strange and tough, but he knew his job and how to go about it, though Bowren couldn't swear to anybody, even if he was allowed to, exactly what that job was. The whole guard detail had met for briefing the day before —Bowren and the six MPs, the Captain and that slob Morgan—and the Captain had covered everything except the reason for the whole business.

"You've all got two jobs," he had told them. "First is to see that none of the prisoners get away from us and that they toe the line exactly as I order. Your second job is to help me train them. We'll work out a duty roster so some of you are always on guard and a few working with me. You'll run through some phases of the training as if you were recruits, but there'll be tougher stuff later on, such as jump school, which you can take if you want to but don't have to."

They had gathered around a table where Captain Reisman spread out maps of their training site and the surrounding countryside and towns. He also had shown them his drawings for the barbed wire stockade, watchtowers and a simple wooden barracks. As for commandeering supplies, the CO seemed to have the Number One priority in the Army for getting what he wanted. Except for a few items they would run in when needed, they were a self-contained, self-sustaining unit aboard the trucks, right down to a small field generator for electricity, a field kitchen and a water-heating unit to go into the barracks for a makeshift washroom, shower and laundry.

The Captain's last remarks had been: "You are to tell nobody what you're doing. You're to keep your mouths shut. You're not to question the prisoners about things I tell them that are none of your business. If you learn anything or see anything that gives you a clue as to what we're up to, you're to come and tell me about it—and nobody else. If any of the prisoners blab to you or anybody else, you're to come to me immediately and let me know."

Reisman and Napoleon, after the initial exchange of formal directions, had driven along in silence in the open jeep at the end of the convoy. Reisman had hoped that singling out Napoleon to ride with him, and giving him the responsibility and trust of handling the jeep, would improve his morale and attitude. But it didn't seem to be working. Napoleon drove sloppily, alternately heavy and light on the gas and brake, skidding the jeep and water-trailer around curves and corners like some crazy kid hot-rodder with a chip on his shoulder.

After one particularly irksome skid, Reisman snapped, "You intend getting us where we're going in one piece or you trying to break up the act before we start rehearsals? You want to kill yourself, buddy, count me out. I've got work to do."

"Scared?" Napoleon challenged above the wind.

"When I go, I'll pick my own way," said Reisman. "Start driving this damned thing like you know how."

"Yes, sir, Mr. Captain, sir!" Napoleon said.

"What in hell's bugging you anyway?" demanded Reisman. "Besides the usual thing, that is."

"How come you put me in here with you?" asked Napoleon, angrily. "Afraid I'll contaminate the white trash up ahead!"

"So that's it!" said Reisman in sudden understanding. What he had done had had the exact opposite effect he had intended. "Goddammit, White, short of getting down and kissing your ass, I thought I made myself pretty clear last week. I can't guarantee you're going to be loved and accepted, but with me everyone starts even. I'm not going to baby you. You'll just have to take your hard knocks like the rest of us. You agreed to do a job and I'm holding you to it."

Napoleon drove along, grim and silent, but his driving was smoother and he kept the jeep the regulation distance behind the truck they were following. They moved under gray skies, heavy with the threat of rain, through Devonshire farmlands that had been plowed and planted, though spring was still more than two weeks off.

"What do you say, Lieutenant? Do we declare a truce?" Reisman persisted. "Do you stop fighting the world . . . and me?"

"Not yet, Captain," answered Napoleon, turning his head briefly.

"You had your vengeance. Now you've got a reprieve. What in hell more do you want?"

"I see things differently now, Captain. Let me tell you a little story so you'll know what I mean."

"Go ahead, but watch your driving."

"I can do both." He had to shout what he was saying, so that Reisman would get the details above the noise of engine and wind, but he raced on in the bitter, angry voice Reisman had come to accept as normal. "There was a man who used to come to see me after my court-martial. Lieutenant Dewey Robinson, a Negro chaplain. He'd been aboard the *Île de France*, had heard what I'd done and was determined to lead my eternally damned soul back to the path of the Lord. He was an educated man—sharp and articulate, not one of these Low-Church hell-and-damnation preachers. His method was reason and logic liberally laced with all the schoolbook philosophy he found appropriate. He believed strongly in Jesus Christ, not in a mystical or magical way and all that jazz about bread and wine and body and blood—hell, we agreed that was no better than some of the witch doctor mumbo-jumbo our African cousins practice today! But he believed in Jesus the same way he believed in Gandhi, his modern hero. Turn the other cheek! Nonviolence! That was the way the American Negro was going to get anywhere, he insisted. He told me what I'd done was wrong, no matter what the provocation. By God, he almost had me believing it, too. He didn't want to see me hang, he said. He told me to be contrite, tippy-toe around from then on like some back-door plantation nigger, and he would do all he could to make the JAG Review Board aware of the motivating factors of my case so they would soften the sentence."

"That still might have happened," Reisman interrupted. "Hell, they don't want to hang anybody, anyhow. That's one of the reasons behind this mission. It doesn't look good on the record or in the newspapers. They'd rather use a man the best way they can."

"I smell a rat, Captain," said Napoleon, turning his eyes from the road to look at Reisman. "I think what they need is some cannon fodder and maybe it's better politics to let the Germans do the killing since it's got to be done."

"Every soldier faces that possibility, White," said Reisman. He leaned toward Napoleon and spoke loudly to make sure the meaning and conviction of what he said didn't disappear into the wind or engine roar. "And if you stay with me, you're going to soldier like you never did before. This hate thing of yours was pretty cozy for a man about to die, but what would you have done if they'd turned you loose at the court-martial?"

Napoleon was silent a moment, as though shocked by some new and baffling thought. "Let me finish my story," he said finally.

"Go ahead."

"You know about this off-limits business for Negro troops down in the Shires, don't you? Some towns are ours, some are theirs."

"No. I've been away fighting a war," said Reisman. "I don't know about that sort of thing."

"Well, maybe you wouldn't know anyway. I didn't know until Robinson told me. It was unofficial. It was done at the division level and down. Negro troops were getting too friendly with the natives. They were having them home to Sunday dinner and taking out the girls, and the white cocksmen were bitching. When an outfit moved and tried to visit back in a town that was changed to a white recreation town, there was trouble. Pitched battles with guns and knives. Then SHAEF must have heard about it because they said No more divvying up the towns, and you search every man for weapons before he goes on pass."

"Doesn't sound like Robinson was helping you any, telling you about stuff like that," said Reisman. "What was he trying to prove?"

"He needed help himself by then," answered Napoleon. "Funny how he came to me looking for it. Me with a rope around my neck. You see, our boys were being frisked clean since we're notorious knife-killers, but somebody was goofing on the white boys. They were ganging up on Negroes they found where they didn't want them. Robinson kept telling them to turn the other cheek, but I could tell on his last visit he was beginning not to believe his own philosophy. He kept digging into me for all the reasons that had committed me to the act of violence that landed me where I was. One day he told his men, Go ahead and defend yourselves. Forget the rules. Sneak out weapons if you have to, but promise you'll use them only for defense. Somebody reported him. He was court-martialed. Imagine the sons-of-bitches court-martialing a man like that. Inciting to mutiny, they said it was. Twenty years at hard labor, cut to fifteen by the Commanding General. So I don't tippy-toe, Captain. I tread hard."

Reisman reached across and turned off the ignition key. "Brake it!" he ordered.

The jeep slowed to a stop at the side of the road, Napoleon staring straight ahead sullenly, his hands gripping the steering wheel.

"Look at me, White," ordered Reisman.

Napoleon turned. Reisman found his dark, angry eyes and held them.

"Just don't tread on me, buddy! I warn you!" he said. "Try it and I turn you off just like that engine. Do we understand each other?"

"Yes."

"Yes, what?"

"Yes, sir."

"Now drive. We've got a hell of a lot of work to do before sack time."

It was raining lightly when the convoy reached the gates of Stokes Manor at mid-morning. Corporal Bowren double-timed back to Reisman's jeep. The other guards were already flanking both sides of the line of trucks.

"Well, I navigated us here okay, Captain," said Bowren, waving a map. "But it looks like we're not welcome."

"What do you mean?"

"Gate's chained and padlocked and there's nobody around."

"Lousy bitch!" muttered Reisman.

"What did you say, sir?"

"Nothing. Bring him up with the others," he said, indicating Napoleon.

As he passed Sergeant Morgan, Reisman told him, "Fall in the prisoners and guards in two semicircles around the gate, Morgan. Guards on the outside. Have everybody wearing their coats."

Reisman led the way up to the tall iron gates and saw that a new chain and padlock had been installed. He unsnapped his holster and took out the .45. "Your training starts now, gentlemen," he said. "You may have gone through this somewhere else in the Army, and you may know all about it, but we start fresh now. This is an automatic pistol, caliber .45, M1911A1. Its maximum range is about sixteen hundred yards, but if you ever have to use it at that distance, don't bother. Its effective range is about seventy-five yards. Up closer, it packs one hell of a wallop and you never want to be on the receiving end. In addition to his other weapons, each member of the guard detail will always carry a .45 fully loaded and cocked. It takes only a fraction of a second to press down the safety and put the pistol to work."

He moved the semicircles of men back and held them about twenty feet away. Then he wiped the rain from his face and eyes, aimed carefully and fired twice at the lock, smashing it apart. Some of the men swung open the double gates.

"I'll bring up the jeep and take the point from here, Bowren," said Reisman. "Tell the drivers to use their four-wheel drive and stay in low gear. We're going cross-country a way."

Reisman was still standing beside the last truck, waiting for all the men to get aboard, when he heard Bowren call out, "Say, Captain, lookee there, willya. Look what's comin at us."

Margot Strathallan's dog, his dark coat glistening wet, was racing down the driveway from the manor, coming like an express train and looking mean enough to take on the whole convoy.

"That's the end of him," muttered Reisman, taking the pistol from his holster again. "All of you stay back," he yelled.

The dog must have heard his voice or smelled him, because he veered suddenly and came right at Reisman. The Doberman started his open-fanged leap ten feet away and Reisman had the .45 raised and aimed when somebody smashed his arm down from behind, shouted, "No! Don't kill!" and hurtled past him on top of the dog.

Samson Posey rolled on the wet ground with the gnashing, growling dog, and then he stood up, cradling the struggling animal against his chest like a puppy, one fist clamped over its trembling jaws.

Reisman's arm ached where Samson had hit him. Those of the prisoners and guards who had seen what happened watched to see what would follow. The Indian waited stoically—to be lashed at physically or verbally—yet there was something of a look of pride, too, that said to Reisman without words: See what I have done for you . . . I have saved you from harm . . . and from an act that was shameful.

"Bowren, take Posey and the dog in the jeep up to the manor house," said Reisman. "Ring until you get an answer. That's where the dog lives. When you come back down the drive, you'll see our tracks cutting across the fields. You shouldn't have any trouble finding us. We'll be about half a mile over that way," he said, pointing, "in a patch of woods."

It was easier getting to the bivouac site than he had anticipated. The light rain continued and the fields were wet but not muddy. They had to do some fancy weaving through trees and knock down some saplings and brush, but Reisman got each of the trucks around the perimeter of the clearing in the wood, their tails facing in ready to unload. He waved Morgan over and they walked aside.

"The camp must go up in one day, Sergeant," said Reisman. "We'll break for chow around noon, then no more breaks till we're finished. Get all the prisoners back with their duffels in Number Four truck and have them change into fatigues and raincoats. Then let one MP change at a time till everybody, including you and me, is changed and ready for work. Got it?"

"I don't have any fatigues, Captain."

"Figured you'd never need them again?"

"That's right, Captain. No offense meant, but when I volunteered for that special job up at the prison, they said I had only that one job and that was it, so I got rid of all that extra stuff I was carrying around with me."

"You're going to get dirty, Morgan. This is a small outfit and everybody is going to work. You've got six stripes on your arms and you're going to work to keep them."

"Yes, sir," muttered Morgan.

"Look after the men now."

"Yes, sir," muttered Morgan again, turning away.

Corporal Bowren and Samson Posey came through the woods in the jeep while the men were changing. Reisman had been anxious about them—not because he thought the Indian would try anything funny—he was sure he wouldn't

—but because Reisman thought maybe he should have gone up to the manor himself, that it was his responsibility and his alone, and he had shirked it.

"How'd it go?" asked Reisman.

"Mission accomplished, sir," answered Bowren brightly. He looked around the clearing and commented, "Ain't much, but I guess this is home for a while, sir. Too bad you couldn't swing a couple of rooms for us at the big house."

"Nobody goes near that place, understand, Corporal!" Reisman snapped. His voice sounded a lot more irritated than he had intended it to be. "Neither you nor I nor anybody else in this outfit. It's off limits and out of bounds."

"Sure thing, Captain. Just dreaming out loud, I guess."

"You'll be cozy enough once we get the stockade and barracks put up." Reisman hesitated a moment before going on. "What did she say?" he asked.

"Nothing, sir. Just took the dog and locked the door on us. She's a strange one."

"Yes, I know. I've met her."

Reisman divided the prisoners into two work gangs of six men—one for the fence work, the other to put up the barracks and watch-towers. He singled out Glenn Gilpin, remembering a civilian history that told of odd jobs in the Southwest—construction, oil fields, ranch hand, a drifter who'd finally drifted into the Army Engineers when the war started. He was twenty-eight—a rangy, rawboned man with a scowling, black-stubbled face that would never look fresh-shaved.

"You ought to know about this stuff," said Reisman. His foot nudged a roll of barbed wire that had been unloaded from the trucks and stacked in the clearing.

"Yeah, I know about cattle-fencing, Captain," said Gilpin, "but I don't fancy putting this one around myself."

Reisman ignored the remark. "You work under Corporal Bowren," he instructed. "What he doesn't know, you show him, and you show the other men, and then see that they do it. We've got the posts, the wire and the tools. You do the job."

Besides Gilpin, Reisman assigned Posey, Maggot, Jimenez, Sawyer and Pinkley to the fence detail. Three MPs stood guard. Sergeant Morgan took charge of Franko,

Smith, White, Odell, Lever and Wladislaw to start clearing brush where the barracks would be going up. The other three MPs watched over them with grease guns slung at the ready.

Reisman was sitting in the cab of a truck studying his building sketches when he heard Morgan arguing with somebody. He stuck his head out the window into the drizzle and yelled, "What's the matter, Sergeant?"

Morgan led a prisoner up to the truck, holding him by the arm. It was Calvin Ezra Smith.

"He says he won't work because it's Sunday, Captain," explained Morgan.

"That's right, Captain," Smith affirmed. His long face tilted up so he could look at Reisman in the truck. The rain washed down his cheeks and off his pointed chin in a little river that connected him right to the ground. "It says in The Book, 'Remember the sabbath day, to keep it holy.' "

Reisman opened the door and hopped down from the truck. "It says a lot of other things too, Smith. You tried to kill an officer, didn't you . . . that's why you're here. I think this religious revival of yours is an excuse for gold-bricking."

"No, sir, Captain," protested Smith. "I had lost God then, but now I've found Him and I'm going to live by His Word."

"You're going to live by my word, fellow," snapped Reisman, "and the promises you made back at Marston-Tyne." If he allowed one single liberty, one goof-off without crushing it, then one of the others would be next, and then another. But he suddenly thought of a better way to handle this.

Reisman stopped all work and gathered the prisoners together in the clearing. Smith and Morgan stood by his side. "You men have all started to work and we've got a lot to do and it's got to be finished today," Reisman declared. "Mr. Smith here says he doesn't want to work because it's Sunday. Now I don't mean to impugn his belief in his God, and some of you other men might be religious too. I don't know. So I'll leave it up to you. Smith here can stand aside or walk about reading verses to us from his Bible, and if that will inspire you to make up for his loss of labor, okay. But if you vote that he works, he *works*!"

"Make him work!" yelled Lever. "Who the hell does he think he is!"

"Work!" some of the others called out.

"How bout waitin till the rain stops, Cap'm?" asked Archer Maggot. "Home we doan even work the fiel hans in the rain much less the white folk."

Reisman saw Napoleon White tense up and thought for a second he was going to jump Maggot. But what he did instead was walk up close to him and ask, loud enough for all to hear, "Have you ever heard of the Romans, cracker?"

"Yeah, ah heered a tha Romans, boy," said Maggot. "So what?"

"Have you ever heard of the Roman historian Tacitus, cracker?"

"Mebbe ah have, mebbe ah haven't. What's it to you, boy?" He was trying to brazen it through, but he had a perplexed and angry look on his face.

"The historian Tacitus," Napoleon went on, "wrote about the year one hundred A.D. that the climate in Britain is disgusting from the frequency of rain and fog, but the cold is never severe! You just keep that in mind, cracker, and you'll be all right."

Reisman burst out laughing and then because he did so did the others, even the ones who didn't know what the joke was or who it was on. Even Maggot laughed, if somewhat lamely. Napoleon smiled as he turned away from Maggot. It was the first time Reisman had seen him smile.

"You're outvoted all around, Smith," said Reisman, finally. "You work, or you don't eat when we break for chow."

Smith shuffled off with the others, looking somewhat put upon. Napoleon came past, walking alone, and Reisman stopped him with a hand on his arm.

"Handle that redneck the way you just did," said Reisman gently, "and you'll do yourself and maybe him more good than if you hit him with a sledge hammer."

"Maybe so, Captain. Maybe so," answered Napoleon wearily. "But you know, I don't think the stupid son-of-a-bitch even knows what I'm talking about."

"That's exactly what I mean," said Reisman.

By noon the rain had stopped. The oppressive gray

cloud vault which seemed sometimes by its persistence and familiarity to have never been anything else and therefore eternal, began to thin and break here and there with promise of blue sky. Some of the prisoners even seemed to be enjoying their work. Once Glenn Gilpin had showed him how to use it, Samson Posey proved to be exuberantly effective with a post-hole digger. His long arms rising and falling, his great chest and back heaving into the thrust, he had stubbornly refused to relinquish the tool to anyone else for even a moment's rest.

They ate lunch sitting around on the ground and the barracks platform: dry K-rations and coffee made with packets of powder and water heated on a gasoline stove. Then they went back to work.

It took all six men in Sergeant Morgan's detail, plus Morgan and Reisman, to ease down the huge crate Franko had hauled from Marston-Tyne in the back of his truck.

"What in hell's in there?" Franko griped as the box hit the ground.

Morgan handed him a hammer and chisel. "Open it!" he ordered.

"Do it carefully," directed Reisman. "We need the lumber."

Franko sprung an edge board, got the claw hammer under it and pressured it up. The others stood around watching, waiting to go ahead with whatever was in there. The nails screamed coming out of the wood, making some of them wince. Reisman saw the look of relish and greedy anticipation on Morgan's face, the way he'd looked in The Butcher's Arms slobbering over his food.

Franko got another board up and another.

"You!" said Morgan to Myron Odell. "Get another hammer and get these nails out of the boards and straighten them."

"Yes, sir, Sergeant!" replied Odell. He hopped right to it, gashing his hand on a nail as soon as he reached for the first board, wincing and licking the blood off delicately.

Finally all the top boards were off the crate, revealing a dark waxed waterproofing paper. On top of it lay a storage-stained, folded square of heavy white paper. Franko picked it up curiously, unfolding it once, twice, three times until he saw that it was a construction plan. And then he went white with terror and he screamed, "You bastards! You dirty, double-crossing bastards! Look a' that!" he yelled to everybody in the clearing. "Look a' that!" He shoved the plan at the nearest prisoner, Joe Wladislaw, almost knocking him down, and with his fingers he clawed at the dark waxed waterproofing paper in the crate, ripping it into a fury of shreds and ribbons.

There was wood under there: lengths and widths and thicknesses of white Vermont pine, and a rope of Manila hemp, boiled and stretched and laid neatly up and down and up and down the length of the crate, filling a place of importance among the posts and cross-beams and stair rails and risers.

"Look at it, you guys" yelled Franko, his eyes wild. "It's all there! A scaffold! A fucking hanging scaffold!" Morgan's face swam into focus before him, terrifyingly disembodied from his squat, broad frame.

There was sudden and deathly silence in the clearing. The fencing detail dropped their work and walked toward the crate. The guards didn't try to stop them. They kept their guns trained and followed along, carried by morbid fascination.

Archer Maggot snatched the damning paper from the strengthless hands of Joe Wladislaw, who felt its horror though he was not sentenced to be hanged. Maggot lost it without protest to Roscoe Lever, who looked and shrugged because his crimes had stopped just short of earning hanging. Smirking, he handed the scaffold plan to Kendall Sawyer, whose fate it still might be.

Franko moved slowly, as in a trance. Reisman came into focus. Franko bent to the ground and picked up the hammer he had dropped. He moved toward the Captain. "You lying, double-crossing fink!" he spat out.

Morgan was closest to Franko. Morgan could have stopped him, jumped him, done something—but he didn't. He watched him hungrily, eagerly.

"We're getting off, are we?" snarled Franko, waving the hammer. "We made a deal, did we?"

Reisman saw some of the MPs zeroing their gun muzzles. "Don't fire!" he shouted, moving in to meet Franko.

Napoleon White sprang low, left shoulder leading the rest of him—*Go for the shinbones, said the coach, and the laws of nature take over . . . ass over teakettle!*—and hit Franko just below the knees, sending him sprawling. Reisman's booted foot stamped hard on the wrist that held the hammer, and Bowren appeared swiftly out of the crowd, landing on Franko's back with both knees and twisting the other arm up behind him in a judo lock.

Napoleon rolled his body and snapped upward, breathing hard and angry, ready for anyone who came at him.

"Thank you, Lieutenant," said Reisman without looking at him. "I owe you a favor."

"Then give it now, Mr. Captain!" answered Napoleon. The words poured out in agitation. "I didn't do you any favors! I just want you around for the answers!" He bounded to the huge wooden crate and yanked out the heinous rope. "What in hell is this? What in hell you trying to pull?"

Nobody else spoke. They held their places—the prisoners stilled by fright; the guards curious, not wanting trouble, yet feeling the tension there in the clearing within the barbed wire stockade that bound them all together.

"What you have in your hands is a rope," said Reisman, speaking softly. "That's all it is . . . a rope. What's in that crate is lumber . . . nothing but lumber." He walked to Napoleon and took the rope from his hands. "This is England and there's been a long war on. Supplies are hard to get." Reisman's gray eyes went from face to face. "We need lumber to build our camp." The tense, wary, frightened looks on their faces began to change—still not certain, but they began to change. "Morgan!" he called . . . and wondered if the others knew, as Franko knew and feared, the hangman in their midst . . . as Reisman wanted them to know, though never telling them outright . . . for Morgan was a constraining evil more effectively left to feed on rumor from man to man and guard to prisoner . . . never acknowledged or confirmed, except by more rumor and the natural course of events.

Master Sergeant Morgan came forward slowly, the idiot-grin of sensual, secret excitement gone from his face. "Captain," he acknowledged.

The scaffold plan lay at Kendall Sawyer's feet, its lines and arrows and sizes and directions flouting at them its ugly perfection.

"Get that and burn it!" ordered Reisman. Those who knew the hangman would understand . . . those who didn't would learn eventually and remember this.

Morgan picked up the large white paper. "I don't carry matches, Captain," he said.

Reisman took his cigaret lighter from a pocket of his fatigue jacket. Morgan spun the wheel a few times reluctantly before the wick ignited, and then he jumped back as the scaffold plan erupted from his fingers and was devoured in a fiery pyre.

Reisman turned back to Franko, conscious that each prisoner waited now to see punishment meted out, and that unless it was done immediately, they would know for certain there was a permissible gap in their discipline. "Let him up, Corporal," he directed.

Bowren pulled Franko to his feet and held tightly to one arm. Franko's fatigue jacket hung open, his dark hair was wild with matted sweat and dirt, and he wouldn't look up.

"You dig latrines, Franko," said Reisman. "You ever try a stunt like that again and I'll bury you in one! Put him to work on the slit trenches, Corporal. If he looks slantwise at you, put a bullet in his head."

Reisman bent to the ground, picked up Franko's hammer and handed it to Sergeant Morgan. "The rest of you back to work," he ordered.

They shuffled off slowly, Morgan and the MPs taking over and urging them on to their jobs. Reisman carried the hangman's rope to a truck and threw it violently into the back, his hands feeling clammy from its touch.

—

15

—

THE CLEARING in the wood echoed with the noises and shouts of men at work—digging, sawing, hammering, cursing, ordering. New sunlight mixed body odors of labor and tension with smells of damp, warming earth, brush, trees and flowers evolving to bud; from the southeast, beyond the wood, beyond the manor house, came the drift of sea smell.

By late afternoon the stockade was finished. It was a double enclosure eight feet high—an irregular-sided box within an irregular-sided box—its shape determined by the perimeter of the clearing and the supply of barbed wire and fence posts. The outer fence followed the perimeter thirty feet in from the nearest trees. The inner fence was twenty feet in from that. The barracks was erected in the corridor on one side, filling the width but not the length. To enter or leave the inner compound it was mandatory for prisoners and guards to pass through a barrier line of five check-points under constant surveillance; barbed wire gate, wooden door, barracks, wooden door, barbed wire gate. On one side lay maximum confinement; on the other, dubious freedom.

An interior ladder in the barracks led to the roof where one MP would always be on duty when the prisoners were in the compound. It was in this ladder, and in the two watchtowers—narrow, railed platforms raised above the height of the stockade and reached also by ladders—that the wood from the portable scaffold was most in evidence. The watchtowers were placed at strategic points beyond the outer fence, providing a field of fire through the compound and the corridor between the fences. They, too, would be manned day and night when the prisoners were in the stockade.

There were two slit-trench latrines, each dug by Victor Franko, his weary body charged by rancor, his brain festering with putrescence, as soon would be the ditches. The prisoners' latrine was within the stockade at the farthest possible position opposite the barracks—made even somewhat farther and distinctive by a little bowed-out cul-de-sac artistically created there by arching the double fences around it. The two watchtowers commanded an excellent view of it. The second latrine was in the woods about fifty yards from the barracks, for the use of the guard detail.

When everything else had been secured to his satisfaction, Captain Reisman ordered a formation of the prisoners within the compound. They brought with them from the truck their duffels and full field equipment.

Trudging through the barracks, Victor Franko, stinking of dirt and sweat and lye and fury, swept his eyes quickly through the building, and in the twenty feet across the wooden platform from one door to the other, he got the picture: cots—though not nearly enough for everybody in the outfit; basins on a wooden shelf, water taps above them connected to the heater outside; field kitchen set up in one corner on another shelf; a tiny room partitioned off from the rest of the barracks, its partially open door revealing cot, chair and table—probably Reisman's.

Within the compound the prisoners stood at ease in a

single rank, their duffels and field equipment at their feet. Three MPs were on sentinel duty on the barracks roof and watchtowers. Sergeant Morgan, Corporal Bowren and the other guards waited before the barracks entrance. Every man looked as though he needed a bath, a meal and a good night's sleep. Morgan's Class A ODs were rumpled and caked with streaks of mud.

"You've done a good job," Reisman announced. "We'll pitch tents, clean up, and there'll be a good hot meal for you."

Archer Maggot muttered, "Whut the hell yo mean tents . . . ain't got no tents!" He hadn't meant it to be so loud, but Reisman heard him.

"What's discomposing you, brother Maggot?" Reisman said.

"Ah thot we wuz stayin in thet hen house yo made us put up," replied Maggot. "Ah doan see no tents aroun, Cap'm. Even theah was, ain't fair makin us do all thet work f'nuthin."

"You're sleeping on the ground under canvas right where you're standing," Reisman revealed to all of them for the first time. Most of them looked surprised, some disappointed, some angry. "The barracks is for the guards and special occasions. We're in the field and we'll operate under simulated combat conditions as much as possible. If you've forgotten, after being coddled in that cozy English jailhouse, there's a shelter half in your field pack. Put it together with another one and you've got a puptent. We'll pitch tents every night and strike them in the morning. Wherever we go, whatever we do, we'll move with full field pack including shelters. I'll allow leeway tonight, but in two days you're going to be pitching tents by the numbers in regulation time."

He assigned tentmates, making it seem casual the way he rattled off the names pairing men together, but he had given considerable thought to it all that day, knowing them better, watching them work. He put together Maggot and Jimenez, Franko and Posey, Odell and Smith, Sawyer and Lever, White and Wladislaw, Gilpin and Pinkley, and though they griped, they started pitching their tents and digging shallow rain trenches around them. As long as he could keep the troublemakers apart—maybe even put a worse one in with a better one and hope for the best—his job might go easier.

199

Reisman borrowed a shelter half from Corporal Bowren, buttoned it to his own and pitched a tent for himself closest to the barracks entrance. From then on, as much as possible, he would do what they did, sleep where they slept, eat as they ate, and they would know it. Morgan, Bowren and the MPs would be apart; he would not.

Reisman worked alone in the tiny room partitioned off from the rest of the barracks, writing out the training schedule for the next day. In the compound the prisoners were in their puptents for the night. Soon he would go to his tent, hopeful for an undisturbed night's rest. On the flat roof he heard Morgan's heavy footsteps taking the first four-hour watch. Bowren would relieve him at 0200. The next night Bowren would be off, Morgan would take the second watch and Reisman the first. For the MPs on the watchtowers it would work the same way—alternating their on-duty hours and getting one night off in three.

There was a knock on the partly open door. Reisman looked up. Corporal Bowren stood there looking a bit hesitant about what he wanted to say. He held a trumpet in his hand, its golden, brightly polished surface firing off glints of light.

"What's up, Corporal?" asked Reisman.

"Sorry to bother you, sir," said Bowren. "You remember I told you I played this thing."

"Sure, Corporal."

"I was wondering, Captain, if I might blow Tattoo and Taps? You know . . . make them feel they're really back in the Army . . . it might be good . . . something for morale. I know it sounds corny, but I always get a shiver up my back when I hear the calls. Not counting Reveille," he added with a smile.

"It's a fine idea, Corporal," answered Reisman. "I like it very much." He paused a moment, thoughtfully, before going on: "If you want to . . . and please don't think you've let yourself in for it . . . I'd like you to play the other calls, too, starting tomorrow. Reveille, Flag Raising . . . I brought a flag along just to remind them which side they were on when the time was right . . . We can rig up a pole on the roof . . . Chow . . . the whole works right through Retreat, Tattoo and Taps. It's a fine idea, Bowren. Thanks."

The last notes of Taps floated away on the night wind.

"Smith?" whispered Myron Odell. He had been almost asleep when the bugle started and woke him. He stirred now in his bedroll. "Smith, you awake?" he whispered again.

"That was real nice," said Calvin Ezra Smith softly. "There's religion in that tune. 'God is nigh.' Did you know them were the words that end it? And it sure is the truth."

"It reminds me of a long time ago," said Odell.

Damned if he didn't sound like he was gonna bust right out and cry, thought Smith. "When was that?" he asked.

"Boy Scout camp . . . that's when I first heard it. Were you ever a Boy Scout, Smith? We had a troop at the orphan home where I grew up," he rambled on without waiting for an answer. "One year they took us to a real Scout camp out in the woods and lakes. It was nice. I only went that one time. After that summer I couldn't be a Scout anymore. I was punished . . . but I remember it."

"What'd you do?" asked Smith. "To be punished."

"I can't say."

"Makes no difference to me," whispered Smith. "Nothing you done is worse than what I done. Anybody can make it right with the Lord. That's what it says in The Book. Where you from, Myron? That's your name, ain't it, Myron?"

"Yes. Cleveland, Ohio . . . that's where the orphan home was, so I guess that's where I'm from."

"I'm from Tennessee, Myron. You know where that is?"

"Sure I know where it is, Smith. I've never been there, but I know where it is. I went to school."

"You call me Cal now, you hear. You got anything troubling you, you just come right out with it and tell me and I'll see if I can find the answer in The Book. It's all there. Everything you wanta know is in there."

"I'm Innocent, Cal . . . I'm Innocent," Odell said. "I've been telling them and telling them, but nobody believes me."

Damned if he wasn't blubbering, Smith realized uncomfortably. "Why sure," he said. "And so was Jesus . . . innocent as the lamb. Now I know you're a religious man, Myron. The minute I see'd you I knowed that. You believe in God and Jesus, don't you?"

"I was brought up a Catholic. It was a Catholic home."

"Well, I'll be damned!" Smith said. "I wouldn't've knowed. But I'll say something for you, Myron, and I don't think it's gonna hurt you none. Now you listen . . . 'the Lord is my shepherd; I shall not want. He maketh me to lie down in green pastures: he leadeth me beside the still waters . . .'"

"Son-of-a-bitch, ain't they never gonna let us sleep!" whispered Archer Maggot. There was no response from Luis Jimenez, so he went on. "Goddamn if they ain't given us a little chickenshit music. Now ain't that cute!" There was still no response. "Howcum yo volunteer f'kaypee t'night, Looey?" challenged Maggot.

"Not KP," answered Jimenez drowsily. "Cook!"

"Sheet, thas the same thing. You ass-kissin that Cap'm aw somethin, Looey?"

"You take it easy what you say, my frien. I like to cook, thas all."

"You a cook in civilian life?"

"Sometime yes I cook," said Luis. "I was dishwasher-assistant cook in diner in Salinas. Bad times, I get fired, so I go back to fields. My father, my mother, all my brothers and sisters, everybody, that's what we do. I want to be Army cook but they don't let me."

"Hey, Looey . . . you a mesican?"

"No, not Mesican . . . Mexican . . . But I'm American born on California side of border. I'm citizen."

"Thas what I said, Looey . . . you're a mesican. That's bettern bein a nigger or a wop or a jew or an indian, thas f' damn sure. You okay, Looey. What'd y'do t'git caught-moshalled?"

"I kill a fucking Lieutenant!"

"Oh! . . . goddam!"

"What you do, gringo?"

"I din do nuthin. They say I did . . . I say I didn."

"Thas life, amigo . . . You shut up now an go to sleep . . . I'm tired."

"Sure! Sure thing, Looey! You okay!"

"How come that Captain called you Lieutenant?" asked Joe Wladislaw.

"None of your damned business," said Napoleon. The

202

bugle had reminded him of other times again . . . of Fort Huachuca and his regiment. Man, they'd been sharp!

Wladislaw weighed his words carefully. It hadn't been often in his life he had been called upon to think so hard about the rightness of what he was saying and how he should say it. "Look, feller," he insisted softly, "don't get me wrong. I'm not tryin to make fun of you or sumthin. I just asked, that's all . . . friendly. If it's none a my business, it's none a my business, that's all . . . you just tell me. I doan know who you are . . . you doan know who I am . . . but we're livin here in this tent, so I figure I talk to you, okay? Like at home when I go into a joint for a beer it's not because I want a beer . . . Christ, I can sit at home an drink all the damn beer I need . . . it's because we use to talk, kid aroun, chew the fat . . . you know, all the guys in the neighborhood . . . we had some fun."

Napoleon rose up on one elbow and stared through the darkness of the puptent. "You're from Chicago, aren't you, Joe?" he asked.

"Yeh, sure. How'd you know?" responded Wladislaw happily.

"Because I've got ears, Joe, and eyes, and a brain," answered Napoleon, "and I'm accustomed to using them. After you got all that good beer in you, Joe, how many times you and your friends go down the South Side to beat up a coupla niggers, huh?"

"Never!" retorted Joe Wladislaw indignantly. "What the hell'd I wanna do that for? I worked with a coupla colored guys on the trucks and they was okay. Sure I said things sometimes when I got mad . . . and I even had a coupla fights . . . but I never done anything like you said. What the hell'd I wanna do that for?"

"Fun, Joe . . . just fun."

"Oh the hell with it, feller," said Wladislaw, turning around in the darkness. "All I asked you was you a Lieutenant? Now is that bein disrespectful? Is that puttin you down?"

"You asked me why the Captain called me Lieutenant . . . not whether or not I had been a Lieutenant." Napoleon smiled in the darkness. He enunciated clearly, slowly, as though to a child, really feeling no rancor . . . and wondering why. "Now there's a difference there, isn't there, Joe?"

Wladislaw turned back again. "Yeh? I suppose there's a

difference. So was you a Lieutenant or wasn't you?"

"I was a Lieutenant."

"That musta been sumthin," said Wladislaw, with uncertain admiration. "That really musta been sumthin. You want me to call you Lieutenant? You want me to tell the other guys?"

"Call me Nappy," Napoleon answered with a pang of warm memory. "That's what they called me at school."

Samson Posey's heart beat to a different tune, a lullaby soft and gentle sung in the sweet voice of Eva Pavisook—*"Apuikwai, apuikwai,"* she crooned to the child, "Go to sleep, go to sleep. You'll go hunting when you get big . . . hunting for rabbits . . ."

He spoke softly, "You married fellow?"

Victor Franko squeezed to the farthest side of the canvas away from his companion, waiting for sleep dreamless and unhaunted.

"You married fellow?"

"Hell no!" Franko muttered tightly. "That's all I need, an old lady round my neck like my old man an mudder always fightin wit seven kids in a stinkhole. I got enough troubles a my own."

"I have wife Eva, baby Little Charlie, grandfather Old Charlie, mother Anna, father Yucca."

"Then why the hell ain't you home takin care a them. What're you doin in the Army? Hah! Go get yourself a dependency discharge or sumthin."

"I volunteer in Army. Go to Cortez and enlist to be a soldier. Good for my family. Good for my People. Government send money take care of them."

"Enlist! Hell, you must be crazy!"

Samson stirred angrily. "Crazy? . . . No, do not say that to me. You are crazy."

Franko was sorry as soon as he had said it, feeling rather than seeing the Indian rise up threateningly in his bedroll. "Okay, okay, don't get excited. I'm sorry. So I'm crazy, too!"

It was the burgeoning time of night when day things were gone into memory and there was only darkness and night things ahead and to be gotten through. In the tents of

Sawyer and Lever, Gilpin and Pinkley there was the silence of armistice, hearing each other's breaths, wondering at each other's thoughts, but each keeping his own counsel.

Captain Reisman walked out through the barracks, beyond the perimeter of the clearing, threading his way softly through the trees and brush. One last check, he excused himself. One last check before sleep . . . restless with thoughts of Tess Simmons . . . needing her then or someone like her . . . and he wandered out beyond the wood, beyond where he had intended to go, to where he saw the dark silhouette of the blacked-out manor against the clear night sky, and turned back through the wood, through the barracks, into the compound of prisoners.

The Corporal woke Reisman at 0600.

"Shall I give em a blast, sir?" asked Bowren, shoving his trumpet through the puptent flap.

"Sure, but you don't have to look so damned happy about it," replied Reisman, smiling. "Give me a couple of minutes to get out of here, then blast away." He was alert, dressing as he spoke, quick to the memory of his day's plans. "I'm going out scouting a bit, but I ought to be back by 0730. I'll give the day's schedule and duty roster to Sergeant Morgan before I leave."

"Yes, sir," said Bowren, pulling his head out of the puptent.

"Corporal!"

Bowren stuck his head back in. "Yes, sir?"

Reisman was lacing his boots and searching for the right words to say what he had to say. "I want you to know how much I think of your work . . . I appreciate it . . . taking on more than your two stripes call for."

"Thank you, sir. I don't mind."

"You may have to do even more, starting today. We go right to soldiering and Sergeant Morgan's going to have to pick up what he needs to know along the way. He's had limited experience at this sort of thing, so jump in where you have to, diplomatically. Do you read me?"

"Sure, Captain. I understand," said Bowren.

The Corporal pulled his head out of the puptent and Reisman crawled out after him into another soggy gray dawn. He washed quickly in a basin in the barracks,

205

skipped shaving and eating until later, and was moving quickly through the wood, out into the open hilly downs toward the sea before the first notes of Reveille sounded.

Franko curled up tighter into his bedroll, drawing his knees up into his belly, his head down upon his chest where his fisted hands pressed. The bugle stopped, but he still didn't get up. For a few moments longer, he fooled himself into thinking he didn't know where he was. Then a massive hand pressed at his back—gentler than he had imagined it might—and nudged him. During the night, the Indian had thrashed around and moaned and Franko had wakened to feel the sleep-heavy deadweight of his arm across him, and had been too terrified to shove it off, and so had slept badly.

"You get up now," said Posey. "Sergeant come around maybe there be trouble for you. You got enough trouble yesterday."

Franko got out of his bedroll and started dressing. The goddamn Indian took up so much room, his head bulging up into the canvas, Franko could hardly move without touching him. He had barely gotten his socks on when he heard Corporal Bowren yelling, "Roll call! On the double! Get the hell out right *now!*" About five minutes had passed since Reveille.

Franko stumbled outside, his damp, curled, unlaced boots making him move awkwardly. Bowren brought them to Attention, dressed the rank and called the roll.

"Present!" yelled Franko. What the hell was the need for this crap! Did they think anybody had snuck off in the night! He saw the two MPs up on the watchtowers, their submachine guns pointing down, and knew there was a third one behind him up on the barracks roof. Damn, but they had the place secured. For a while yesterday there'd been that heady burst of freedom when they were out on the road, and he'd thought of escape, escape, escape! But now it was maybe worse than it had been at Marston-Tyne. Sleeping on the ground with the Indian, run-ins with that goddamn Captain, digging slit trenches, and always feeling maybe there was the rope after all no matter how much crap he had to take. That Captain! That goddamn Captain! He wondered where the hell he was.

Franko watched Morgan standing out there like some

206

fat-assed General taking the morning report from Bowren. What's the matter, couldn't the son-of-a-bitch count to twelve himself! And how come he wasn't wearing fatigues like the rest of the guards?

The hangman came down the rank and inspected them, his head bobbing from fatigue caps to combat boots. Bowren followed along with the roster. "Boots unlaced," said Morgan, staring into Franko's eyes. "Put him down for the first crap detail that comes along today."

Franko shivered with morning cold and frustrated rage.

Morgan and an MP ran them down to the slit trench four at a time, while the others struck puptents and filled in the rain ditches.

Archer Maggot looked up from his squatting position at Franko buttoning his fly. "Whah if it ain't the Cunnel in chahge a this heah latrine!" he mocked. "What's the mattah, Cunnel, tighten up on yo?"

"Shut your mouth, Reb!" snapped Franko. "You ain't funny." He'd tried but he couldn't do a damned thing—not with Morgan standing there staring at them—though his bowel and bladder ached for relief.

"Cap'm say we gonna eat it we go anyplace else cause it ain't healthy lyin aroun," Maggot ridiculed. "No chance a me doin that. Whah you done a fine job here, boy. Real cozy. Weah all right proud a you, ain't we, boys?" The prisoners and MPs snickered. Sergeant Morgan stared with a sardonic grin. "Fars ahm concerned the job's yours permanent," Maggot taunted.

Franko started for him.

"You!" pronounced Morgan.

Franko pulled up in mid-stride.

Morgan's finger quivered at Archer Maggot and he was smiling. "You have a big and foul mouth," he said quietly. "You stay here. When everybody is finished, you sprinkle lye and you shovel in one inch of dirt. One inch exactly— not under, not over. You go down in that ditch and you measure it, every inch of the way."

Franko wanted to laugh, but he dared not!

Bowren took down the Captain's puptent—unintendedly vouching that he really wasn't in there still asleep, that he had slipped off quietly—and demonstrated how shelter halves were to be rolled and field packs made ready for quick forced march. Toilet kits and mess gear were left out, waiting for them to wash and shave, waiting for them to eat breakfast. Extra clothing and equipment not authorized for that day's march and training were packed in their duffel bags to be stored in the barracks.

One of the MPs came through the gate carrying a five-gallon can of water.

"Come and get it," Bowren ordered, beckoning the prisoners over, "and bring your helmets."

"What's that for?" asked Roscoe Lever suspiciously.

"Washing, shaving, brushing your teeth, . . . you can even take a bath if you want to," explained Bowren. "Or heat your rations and boil your water. One of the most useful pieces of equipment in the Army, the helmet."

"How come we can't use the hot water and basins in there like the Captain let us do last night?" demanded Lever, pointing to the barracks. "We ain't corpses yet."

"You want water, Lever?" asked Bowren, starting to tip the five-gallon can. "Or you want to shave dry?"

Lever had to bring up his helmet fast to catch the cold splashing water or it would have spilled all over him. The other prisoners held up their helmets, crowding in around Bowren, but they didn't look as though they liked it, and the Corporal could smell trouble brewing. He was just following orders: the CO to Morgan to the Corporal. This was the way the Captain wanted it this morning. He wasn't going to coddle them anymore and it was probably a good thing.

Archer Maggot came up from the latrine, Sergeant Morgan stalking contentedly behind him. "Ahm gohna need some hot wahtah an lotsofit t'git this stink'n stuff offin me, Cohp'ral," complained Maggot.

"You get just what the others get, feller," said Bowren. "Get your helmet."

"Well then yo jist know whut yoall kin do then, buddy, don't yo!" Maggot blurted out angrily. "Ah'll jist stay the way ah am an we'll see'f the stink bothus yo lack it do me!"

Sergeant Morgan circled around in front of Maggot quickly, pointed his finger at him and started to say something, but it never got out. Maggot lashed out at Morgan's hand, smashing it down. "Yoall keep that goddamn finger o yourn outen my face, Sergeant, yo hear!" he yelled.

Everything seemed to stop there in the stockade for a

moment, more in surprise than shock. Bowren waited to see how Morgan would handle it. If it had been anyone else, Bowren would have jumped in to help him and landed on Maggot hard, but Sergeant Morgan had no call to do some of the things he'd been doing. He seemed to get his kicks out of squeezing them unnecessarily, sometimes stupidly, enjoying the bogeyman terror he kicked up in some, besides the obvious enjoyment of throwing around the weight of those six goddamn stripes.

Sergeant Morgan pulled back with a startled look, rubbing his smarting hand. Then he tucked both hands under his arms, maybe to keep from pointing again, maybe because it made him seem relaxed and confident. "You're on latrines the rest of the day," he said to Maggot in an unexpectedly calm voice. "This one in here and that one out there. When we get back later that's what you take care of, if you wanta eat." The Sergeant moved away toward the barracks, his cheek muscles twitching.

"Get your helmet, Maggot," ordered Bowren, "and start washing and shaving."

"Ah'll jist stay the way ah am an we'll see," Maggot repeated.

"Then get over there by your gear," ordered Bowren, "at attention." He could feel the tenseness building in the air around him. The fuse of anger and fear and resentment had been lit for the day. Maybe he could make it sputter out, maybe he would only make it worse, but he had to do something, be ready for the explosion, keep the guards ready.

Victor Franko watched the Corporal move around counting out razor blades to the prisoners and he took one. He squatted beside his helmet, juggling on his knee one of the little shaving mirrors the guards passed around watching what they did with them like maybe they were hand grenades. He looked up quickly at the stupid Reb standing there by himself and he hated him—hated him although, and maybe because, the Reb had done something he hadn't done: he'd stood up to the hangman! But would he have done it if he'd known?

Franko recoiled from his own bloodshot eyes in the mirror! He tried to lather shaving cream with the icy cold water in his helmet and it felt clammy as toothpaste. His eyes darted to the nigger Napoleon, hating him. He'd tried to make friends with the guy, he'd tried to help him, but he

209

hated him now for interfering yesterday, hated him for not digging latrines. He winced from the scrape of the blade—dull! dull again, goddammit! hated *them* and the screws and the finks!—and his head ached trying to remember what it was to be a man again and he slammed down the razor in the dirt and cursed, "The hell with it!"

"What's the matter with you, Franko?" demanded Bowren.

"I ain't shaving . . . no more, that's all . . . I ain't shaving!"

"You shave, Franko!" ordered Bowren, shoving his face close to him, tasting the growing tension, angry that discipline was cracking, fueling the virulence himself though he wanted to smother it. "You shave whether you like it or not!" And he saw the others watching him, watching Franko, waiting to know what they could get away with.

"No!" yelled Franko exultantly. "None of us are gonna shave!" It had just struck him in that moment. He looked at the others—faces lathered, faces damp, faces half-scraped, razors poised—immobilized. Even the guards. And he moved quickly. Like a madman he darted from prisoner to prisoner. "Stop! Goddamn it, all of you!" he shouted, "They can't make us shave or wash . . . that's *us,* not *them* . . . not if we stick together. They're not gonna hang us for that!" He snatched razors, slammed them to the ground, half knowing half not knowing what he was doing, half believing they would follow him half fearing they would not, kicking over helmets, eluding Corporal Bowren and the suddenly galvanized guards . . . and the prisoners dazed at first by his outburst, not understanding, then getting it . . . Napoleon White comprehending and wanting the simple rebellion . . . Lever, Gilpin, Wladislaw, Jimenez, Smith, Pinkley, Odell liking it, believing they could get away with it, believing it suddenly their right, maybe the only right they had left and they'd find out soon enough if it was usable . . . Posey not caring one way or the other, not even certain what was going on, then sensing they wanted him to be part of them, to do what they did, and following . . . Sawyer who wanted to do what he was told, who didn't give a damn about cold water and helmets and dull razor blades because he knew battle none of the others could conjure in their wildest fears, yet going along because he didn't want to go against the group . . . throwing toilet kits, soap bars, lather-smeared towels

210

in the dirt with the razors . . . and Archer Maggot laughing, watching the guards herd them together because now they'd share whatever he got!

Reisman came through the outer gate and into the barracks a little before 0730, a route of march penciled on his terrain map, the places marked where they would stop for field demonstrations, lectures and calisthenics. No one was in the barracks and what he felt first was the unusual silence over the stockade, a lack of activity that he had expected. He strode across the floor, opened the door facing the inner compound. They were all there—the prisoners standing at rigid attention; Morgan and Bowren and the guard detail surrounding them, guns leveled as though something had happened to make them extra nervous.

"Corporal Bowren!" he yelled.

Bowren looked up, startled, and came on the double. Reisman went back into the barracks and was running warm water into a basin for shaving when the Corporal came in, locking the door carefully behind him. He looked worried.

"Glad to see you, Captain," said Bowren. "I'm afraid we've got trouble. They refuse to shave or wash."

"All of them?"

"Well, it started with Franko and Maggot, and the others picked it right up, even the ones you'd figure'd have better sense. All we could do was keep them settled down until you got back."

"How long have they been out there like that?"

"Almost an hour."

"That's a lot of time wasted."

"I'm sorry, sir."

"I didn't mean it that way," said Reisman. While he talked, he stripped down to his T-shirt and started lathering his face. "It's not your fault. Any of your men get to eat?"

"Nobody, Captain. There wasn't a chance."

Reisman scraped away the dark stubble on his cheeks in long quick strokes. He turned aside from the mirror to look at Bowren. "Don't worry about it, Clyde," he said. "You've got the situation in hand. Put up some coffee for us. I'll get cleaned up and take over."

Reisman went out in a few minutes into the silent inner

stockade. He nodded to Sergeant Morgan, who looked rather nervous—worried, no doubt, about the tenure of his six stripes—but no words were spoken. Reisman walked down the rank of prisoners seeking the eyes of each man. They avoided his gaze. He finished his inspection, strode off a few paces, turned and faced them.

"If you want to stink, *stink!*" his voice boomed out. "If you want to itch, *itch!*" He had to work at it to make his voice sound angry because he really wasn't. What they had done was a flagrant break in discipline, but it was the first sign they were a group that might be bent to work together, a first indication of *esprit de corps* among this motley gang of convicted cutthroats. Whether the *esprit* and the cutthroats were real or pseudo he still didn't know, though he knew he'd have to have the real thing soon enough. "If you were in combat you'd stink and you'd itch!" he said. "Ask Sawyer sometime if you want to find out. He knows. He's been there and back!" Ken Sawyer looked embarrassed, his eyes cast down. "But you'll get no more hot meals from now on—not after this morning's business! Nothing but K-rations . . ." He'd never intended feeding them anything but K-rations except when they'd earned better as a reward. "Any of you want out now, say so! You know what's waiting for you at Marston-Tyne!"

Victor Franko knew. Though he had led them to rebellion and was glad of it, a tremor of fear ran through him. His eyes rose to the empty watchtowers . . . riveted on the posts and cross-beams, stair rails and risers . . . and he ached with the truth of Master Sergeant Morgan and the memory of one night of his work.

16

CORPORAL BOWREN'S trumpet call filled the clearing. Reisman's eyes fastened on the flag as an MP raised it over the barracks roof. The colors caught in the sea-damp morning breeze, snapped taut and fluttering over the stockade, and a sudden and unexpected thrill of pride gripped Reisman.

Ludicrous as it was, this was his Command, his Post. His eyes dropped down to the men. They were slumped, unkempt, most going through the salute haphazardly, some openly contemptuous of him and the guards, if not the flag.

"Snap to attention, goddammit!" he lashed out at them.

A few stiffened their backs, some tilted their chins up, the rest just shuffled their weight. The trumpet notes fell away, the flag was tied to the pole.

"Parade rest!" ordered Reisman.

They slumped a bit lower into themselves, but that was the only real difference in their stance. They looked like what they were: prisoners. And he had expected more from them after their previous day's good work—an eagerness to begin, to learn, to strive, to improve. Every one of them had been through Basic or better, and Bowren had put them through an intensive refresher at Marston-Tyne.

"Stand to attention!" Reisman roared at them, and they snapped to, startled by the violence in his voice.

They reminded him of himself! He felt a taint of guilt by association, and it hit him with unsettling clarity that regarding this flag, this being an American, he might be as guilty as they, never concerning himself much beyond what he'd learned by rote as a schoolkid and used as his prerogative in his wanderings abroad; taking the birthright for granted but never replenishing it; and developing almost beyond the edge of acceptability and legality that uniquely American perspective which generated its own protective bravado in expatriate patriots and malcontents, even allowing room for mockery of itself. What a mockery then—or how fitting?—that he be their warder . . . divined by what unknown and finely attuned brain of authority or coordinance of fate!

Reisman glanced at his wristwatch. It was almost 0800. "We move out in thirty minutes," he announced coldly. "Before we do, you are going to learn the things you should have learned in the beginning. How to stand up straight is one of them! You fight me and I'll break you one by one and send you back where you came from! Learn fast and you eat. Otherwise you march out on an empty belly!"

He sent Morgan and half the guards into the barracks to cook their own chow. Then for ten solid minutes without pause, Reisman ran the prisoners through "Attention!

213

Right dress! Left dress! Eyes front! Salute! Attention! Parade rest! At ease!" while he and Corporal Bowren and three MPs moved up and down the rank tapping stomachs, chests, chins, legs, arms, asses, backs, making them "Pull it in!" or "Stick it out!" until he was satisfied with their performance.

One by one, Reisman dispatched the three MPs outside the compound to the watchtowers and barracks roof, waiting for one guard to get into position before releasing the next. The rank of prisoners held fast. Even their breathing was silent and motionless. They looked less like prisoners to him and more like soldiers. Reisman turned his back on them and strode away toward the gate. He beckoned Corporal Bowren to follow.

"Get their rations," he instructed, "and blow chow."

Reisman watched the prisoners from a short distance. Not one of them moved. Not one of them shifted the forward-set focus of his eyes. They held formation even as Bowren sounded mess call, as though uncertain what the sounds meant or whether the call was for them.

"Come and get it!" shouted Bowren.

They slumped back into themselves, broke the rank uncertainly, and looked like prisoners. K-rations packages for the day were distributed at the gate and they shuffled back to their packs and sprawled sulkily on the ground, warily unwrapping breakfast bars. Reisman sat near them, chewing his bar of dry chopped fruit, dry chopped pork and eggs, crackers that reminded him of dog biscuits, and tried to look as though he enjoyed every bite of it. The prisoners stole quick glances toward him: ugly, suspicious, peevish. Reisman scanned the perimeter of the stockade: the MPs alert on the watchtowers, the barracks roof, Bowren at the gate.

Sergeant Morgan came into the compound and relieved Corporal Bowren for chow. An MP carried in a kettle of hot water for the prisoners' coffee. He put it on the ground near them without comment and walked back through the gate into the barracks. Reisman watched him rising up through the hatch in the barracks roof to relieve the guard on duty there. He watched the two MPs walking around the exterior fence to relieve the watchtowers.

"Double-time it!" he called out.

They trotted to the towers, scaled the ladders quickly,

and the guards they relieved climbed down and jogged toward the barracks for breakfast.

Reisman waited for one of the prisoners to pick up the steaming kettle, to serve himself if not the others, but none of them moved. He knew they needed coffee, if only to wash the unpalatable stuff they were eating past their gullets. He got up and took the kettle.

"Who wants coffee?" he asked.

They looked toward him, startled, embarrassed and confused. A few fumbled with their packets of powdered coffee, powdered milk, and sugar. "I'd like some, Captain," Kendall Sawyer finally blurted out. "Me too, sir," said Myron Odell quickly. The others responded, some audibly, pleasantly, some with muttered grunts. They held up their mess cups. Reisman moved among them pouring out the water. When he had served them all, he squatted on his haunches in their midst sipping his coffee.

"Listen to me," he said softly. "Believe me when I tell you this . . ." They looked at him with suspicion again, some still smarting with the anger of his discipline, some bored because they had heard it all before. "If all this means to you now is an escape from what you were facing back there at Marston-Tyne, then quit now and go get yourself hung or put away in some detention barracks for twenty years or the rest of your life or whatever the hell your sentence is. You'll never make it here." They looked at him with quickened interest. "But I tell you this: you've got a chance in this outfit a lot of troops would give their left nut to get. You don't know what I mean now because you don't know what's ahead of you. But you will know as soon as you start shaping up like soldiers instead of prisoners. You can go from the ass end of this man's Army right up to the top with nobody out ahead of you, and I don't mean you're all going to be Generals or anything like that." If he had expected laughter, he didn't get any. "We've got enough Generals. What we need is soldiers."

"Then what'd you bring him along for?" challenged Victor Franko nervously. He jerked his head toward Morgan. "He ain't no soldier. You know what he is."

The others continued chewing, sipping their coffee, staring from Franko to Reisman, sensing there was something they ought to know about what Franko meant.

"Thas right, Cap'm," put in Archer Maggot, keeping his

voice low. "Ah doan usjully agree wid no one lak him." He glanced at Franko with a sneer, then back to Reisman. "But thet Mohgen's the goddamndest noncom ah evuh did suhve undah. Wah yoall know whut thet man did this mohnin t'git me so riled up ah . . ."

"That ain't what I mean, Reb," Franko poured out hoarsely. "You doan know nuthin yet. Go ahead, Captain, tell them who you brought along to keep them company!" He rubbed his stubbled cheek and neck apprehensively.

Reisman's eyes scanned the perimeter again. The guards were alert, watching the prisoners, though they probably couldn't make out all the talk.

"What's he mean, Captain, about the Sergeant?" asked Joe Wladislaw. He took another bite of his breakfast bar.

"Sergeant Morgan was the hangman at Marston-Tyne prison," said Reisman calmly.

Joe Wladislaw stopped chewing. No one spoke. No one moved. No one dared look toward Morgan. In split-second changes of mood they huddled to each other, to Reisman, apart. A derisive laugh, almost obscene in that moment, broke the silence.

"You mean that fat, funny little man?" scoffed Napoleon White. "You're kidding."

"He ain't!" blurted Franko savagely.

Archer Maggot laughed weakly. "No wunduh you so scairt a him, boy!" he said to Franko.

But it was uneasy laughter, stark and feeble, picked up by some of the others to still their own apprehension— even by some not sentenced to meet the hangman professionally, except Roscoe Lever who laughed and found succor in all their discomfort and the fact of his own legal exclusion from the hangman's circle.

Myron Odell tried to laugh, but he gagged and felt sick. Kendall Sawyer and Luis Jimenez didn't laugh at all.

Samson Posey didn't laugh. He understood what had been said, and found courage to raise his head and stare at Morgan. He would be wary of that one from now on, for betrayal, if it was that, was a thing he knew too well. Having the evil thing there, knowing it, he would work against it: work hard, think pure thoughts, pray to Creator-of-Humans, and summon the power of Billy Three-legs to help him.

"I knew there was something sinful about that man,"

whispered Calvin Ezra Smith. He glanced quickly at Sergeant Morgan and away.

Waiting tensely for another wild and angry scene, Reisman breathed easier, still not sure if he was relieved or disappointed by their reactions.

"Laugh, you fools!" Franko said, scowling, his fear an open wound for all to see. "What do you know? I was there! I saw him!"

"So was I!" Reisman said. The memory of execution came fresh to his mind and etched on his face as he looked from man to man and back to Franko. "You didn't see enough! It isn't pretty. It isn't easy. You should worry about what you do here."

He drained his cup of coffee and stood up. There was fear enough there now, even among those who had nervously laughed. And Franko, if he had been angling to be their spokesman and leader, had lost his chance by his own words and terror.

They finished chow and Reisman yelled, "Piss call!" and led a bunch of them down to the slit trench.

Franko could have kissed the Captain's ass. He was in a bad way by then, the K-rations working on him like Ex-lax, and he made it all right this time because Morgan stayed up near the barracks.

They formed a single line at the gate and Bowren and Reisman came down the line checking equipment. "Help one another," said Reisman. "Check each other's packs. Remember this in my outfit and you'll get along okay: look after yourself the best you can, then look after the guy next to you." He moved behind Franko and heaved up his knapsack a few inches, carrying the auxiliary pack with it. "Tighten the straps, Franko," he said, "or your ass'll be dragging in half a mile."

They moved out of the stockade through the barracks and the outer gate and formed a double line at the edge of the wood, tentmates together. Reisman held them there.

"One more thing before we move out," he warned. "Anybody thinks he's gonna make a break for it now because he's on the outside is gonna get a bullet for his trouble. There is no escape. You can't get away. And if you could, where the hell would you go?" He pointed back to the stockade. "Turn around and look at it. That's home. You built it yourselves and you did as good a job as the Engineers. Ask Glenn Gilpin. He can tell you because he was with them for a while." Gilpin scowled at Reisman for having been singled out. "We'll stay together on the march," Reisman continued. "It's not a combat patrol and nobody's out there shooting at you yet. Now you show me if you've got any more stamina than a Boy Scout troop . . . if you're as gutsy as you think you are!"

"Horseshit!" muttered Victor Franko under his breath.

They moved through the wood onto the fields and downs of Stokes Manor in a line of march away from the manor house, inland from the sea cliff and roughly paralleling it, the Channel hidden by an upland rise. Reisman was at the point, the MPs on the flanks, Bowren moving up and down the line. Master Sergeant Carl Morgan brought up the rear behind Franko and Posey.

Reisman was determined to test their endurance that day. To break them. He would use guile or shame or force or contempt, or any device that came to hand to gain his end: to change them from what they were into what they had to be. If he had to, he would break them and build them and break them and build them time and time again as he had done that morning, as he had done the day before. And if every petty problem in discipline led to rebellion, then he would take daily reassessment of them and of himself, and fight daily their hates, their fears, their ignorance, their outbursts of temper, and readiness to goof off. He had to show them the lousy shape they were in, the things he could do that they couldn't, and the things they would have to learn to do to lower the odds against them when they were dropped into the Nazi war machine—and they still didn't know about that.

The prisoners were overweighted with field equipment riding on their backs and butts and dragging down their web belts. Folding-stock shovels were tied into their knapsacks. Reisman carried the same plus fifteen pounds of weapons and ammunition—the M3 submachine gun slung over his shoulder and the .45 pistol at his hip. The guards traveled light: weapons, rations and water for the day, but no heavy packs to slow them down. Bowren and a couple of the MPs carried coils of rope and axes for the field problems.

There had been no time or personnel for Reisman to

218

create obstacles and problems of the sort trainees had to overcome daily in the OSS schools that assessed and prepared men for behind-the-lines operations, so he made use of every natural obstacle on the estate he could find. If there was a hill to climb, he led them up it at the steepest point; where there was a ravine to cross or a stream to ford, he made them make use of logs and branches and ropes and human chains, refusing them the easy way across, always pointing them to the difficult and the dangerous and the more fatiguing. He began to feel the muscle-pulling strain of his heavy packs, the straps gouging and chafing his skin through his fatigue uniform, but he knew the prisoners felt it more, except maybe for Samson Posey who didn't seem to tire, who looked as though he could carry himself and maybe one or two more the rest of the day.

The prisoners dropped exhausted at each break he allowed them, but he wouldn't let them just sit panting for breath or sprawled on the ground. He made them sit in formation, packs neatly beside them, and he lectured them: first the basic, simple stuff—military courtesy, discipline, personal health, sanitation—in ten-minute capsules, once every hour, followed by five minutes of calisthenics, stripped down to T-shirts in the cool, gray morning, and then they dressed quickly to keep the sweat from the cool wind, heaved up their packs and marched. They griped to each other, muttered at the guards and Reisman, but they tried.

During one lecture, watching them closely, trying to sense if they were really listening and understanding, Reisman realized he had overlooked something. He suddenly interjected, "From now on, each of you will carry with you a notebook and pencil and take notes at lectures and summarize what you have learned on field trips. There will be a review test each night after chow to see if you've learned your lessons properly. You're going to need minds besides bodies."

There was the language problem with Posey, and maybe some of the others weren't much better at it, but, if not, they could draw pictures or scribble or do something to indicate they thought. And he would try to get the smarter ones like White and Gilpin to help; and where he needed strength and endurance, he would get the stronger ones like Posey and Sawyer and maybe Maggot, and White, too, to help, and in that way build confidence and ability and interdependence, which was really all a working unit was anyway. They had to think *soldier*, think what they were doing and learning, about what was ahead of them—want to make it good, and in that way grow beyond the past and their own selfish, petty and miserable existences.

Reisman led them to the farthest reach of the estate, traversing back and forth across the inland side of the sea cliff to use up as much land and as many obstacles as he could, pressing the prisoners almost beyond the point of endurance, and then took them down a trail to the beach where they finally broke the march for chow.

They opened their mouths and nostrils to drink in the fresh sea breeze, and dropped into the soft sand, shucking packs from bruised and aching shoulders. Screaming seagulls floated and turned on the wind.

Samson Posey followed their flight enviously, and stared at the pounding surf of the English Channel in awe. He had seen other waters, small and large, since leaving Towaoc, and felt always this same awe that was almost disbelief; he had come far across the unimaginable ocean to the very place from which the white men had come; but he had never done what he wanted very much to do: go into it, immerse himself, feel it wash over him and cleanse him, feel its power against him and absorb it. There had never been the chance.

He went up to the Captain. "Can I go there?" he asked, pointing to the sea. "Wash . . . drink."

"Well, you can't drink it, Posey," answered Reisman, managing a smile. "It's salt . . . but you can wash if you want to. You know how to swim?"

"Swim? No."

Franko listened to the exchange and blurted out hoarsely, still trying to recover his breath, "Nobody washes, Chief! None of us! You remember this morning?" He swept an angry look around at the others, seeking support, ignoring Reisman and the guards and even Morgan, making his point again for simple, harmless, continued revolt that was *us* against *them*. "We agreed no wash, no shave, Chief! You savvy?"

Samson looked at him in puzzlement, and at some of the others nodding agreement, murmuring "Yeh!" "That's right, Chief!" opening their little packages of food, sipping from their canteens, watching him, more interested than he

220

would have imagined in what he was going to do. He understood, though he expected anger now from the Captain, or an order against them.

Reisman watched and listened acutely, and he shrugged his shoulders casually as though none of this little organized rebellion really meant anything to him. "Go ahead, Posey, if you want to," he said. He'd give them their head on this particular thing, he'd already decided.

Samson was torn between his desire not to offend his fellow prisoners, his need to be part of their bond, and the powerful lure of the sea.

"Just drink!" he said quickly, turning away and running down to the surf.

"Hey, don't you know there's salt in that water?" yelled Wladislaw.

Samson bounded to the frothy edge of the sea, scattering a flock of perched and cocky gulls. He watched one wave withdraw and another surge in to where it just touched the soles of his boots. He scooped up a double handful of water, tilted it against his lips and into his mouth, let it slosh guiltily on his face and wrists, gagged and spat.

He came running back to the group, rubbing his mouth in distaste and puzzled disappointment.

"Salt!" he said.

They ate their dry K-rations and drank the metallic-tasting canteen water and were glad mostly for the extended rest it gave them. Some ate quickly and sprawled out to catnap, turning their faces up to the weak sun struggling through the cloud layer for another day of tepid warmth. Some ate slowly, leaning against their packs, and watched the soothing rhythms of the sea. Samson threw bits of crackers to the gulls and drank in the joy of their sounds and movements.

They had half an hour and then Reisman ordered, "Fall in! Same formation as this morning."

He kept them on the beach now in a straight line of march without hills and obstacles, but it was just as punishing if not worse in the soft sand that grabbed at tired, aching legs and made them twice as heavy to raise, and the pace was quickened: five minutes double-time, five minutes walking.

Men started to stumble and fall out: Odell first, looking lost and bewildered; Franko—Posey grabbed him firmly by an arm to sweep him along, but he cursed, "Lemme alone, ya big ape!" and broke loose; Maggot and Lever with a screw-it-all look on their faces; Pinkley and Wladislaw a little more reluctantly because they would have liked to keep up; they all dropped into the sand for a stolen moment's rest, were prodded up by the tired MPs and staggered forward at a slower pace, which was all right with Sergeant Morgan bringing up the rear because he'd about had it himself. It had been a long time since he had done anything like this.

Reisman called a halt. He was damned tired, but he would have continued if all of them had stayed with him. White, Sawyer, Jiminez, Smith and Gilpin dropped into the sand against their packs, panting, not even bothering to slip out of the straps. They'd kept up with him and that was good. Samson stood there, face gleaming with sweat, tired at last but far from expended, waiting to be told what to do.

"You can sit down, Posey," said Reisman.

They had come only a mile and a half down the beach and there was that much more to go to the part of the sea cliff nearest the stockade. The morning's zigzag march had covered nine miles. Reisman waited for Bowren and the MPs to bring up the stragglers, and for Morgan, breathing heavily through open mouth.

"Tired?" taunted Reisman, looking from face to face. His eyes lingered on Napoleon White.

Napoleon caught the challenge. "I can do anything you can do!" he snapped back, his chest heaving with the effort. "Maybe more!"

"Suppose you take over and lead the march then, wise guy!" retorted Reisman. "You set the pace. You give the orders. We'll follow. You ought to know what to do. You've done it before."

Archer Maggot heaved himself to his feet, his face livid with rage despite his exhaustion. "Now, Cap'm, that damn Sahgent awreddy put me on shit detail foh the day an ah doan know whut in hell moh youall kin do ceptin starve me or hang me. Ah doan much give a damn bout all this marchin an trainin an crap cause lak the nigguh say ah kin do anythin youall kin do an do it bettuh, but ah'll be goddamned ef ahm gonna take any ohduhs fum him!"

Napoleon started to slip out of his packstraps and struggle up, but he took a good look at Maggot standing there panting with frustration and he dropped back into the sand. "Cracker, you're not worth the energy!" he jeered.

Reisman moved between them. "How long have you been in the Army, Maggot?" he demanded.

"Bout a year."

"You ever been on a night attack . . . a commando raid?"

"Hell, no."

"Then I'll tell you something, boy," said Reisman softly, as though he was revealing confidential information. The others were listening, too, from positions of sprawled exhaustion. "You see, in a night attack we all do ourselves up in blackface and it's a real advantage, and that's one of the times when White here's gonna have an edge on you, boy. There's others, too, but you're gonna have to learn those for yourself the hard way. You want to lead this march?"

Maggot was shaking his head back and forth in bewilderment, his jaw hung open. "Hell no, Cap'm, ah doan wahna lead no mahch."

"Then shut up and pay attention and maybe you'll learn something," Reisman said icily.

He gave them ten minutes of silent rest this time, and then he stood up. "All right, White," he said. "They're all yours. Show us what you can do."

Napoleon got up slowly, staring at him. "You mean it, don't you?"

"That's right, buddy. It's put up or shut up."

"Well, all right, Mr. High and Mighty!" Napoleon flashed back at him. "Everybody on your feet! Same marching order . . . Captain beside Wladislaw . . . Bowren three paces behind me to my right . . . Morgan, set up your straggler posts and keep them moving . . ."

His voice was firm, confident, professional. The guards and prisoners fell in where he wanted them—Maggot in a fury, the others amused, curious or indifferent. Reisman moved into the line next to Joe Wladislaw, and his presence in close among them had a stilling effect. Before they could do much thinking, Napoleon had done it for them . . . For*harrd haarrch!*" and turned the formation down to where the tide had gone out. He swiveled to face them, marching backward, keeping time without faltering, wanting to spit at them that he had an outfit once that could have marched the pants off any one of them, and he sang out, "Hut, hup, hip, haw! Hut, hup, hip, haw! Your left! . . . Your left!

223

. . . You had a good home when you left! . . . Your left! . . . Your left . . . You had a good home when you left! . . ." But they weren't his old outfit and they didn't pick him up on it . . . trudging dully . . .

. . . Archer Maggot raging silently that the others didn't explode and stand with him against that goddamn crazy Captain—what's the matter with him, didn't he know what a nigger was?—and that sassy black bastard . . . Maggot feeling the ache now more in his head and his guts than his legs and his back . . . and almost recognizing there was a difference here . . .

. . . and Victor Franko muttering "Horseshit!" under his breath like he would at any command . . . but thinking that was one smart nigger leading them down on the damp, hard-packed sand where the marching was easier . . . and getting away with it . . .

. . . and Captain John Reisman feeling pretty good about what he had done . . . moving along confidently at the brisk, steady pace Napoleon set.

They rounded a headland and Reisman saw the chimney tops of Stokes Manor in the distance. He stepped out of line and double-timed up front.

"Get back with the others, White," he ordered.

Napoleon hesitated, expecting some additional comment, but there was none and he fell back into line beside Wladislaw.

"Pick 'em up!" yelled Reisman. "Let's go!" He thrust his balled fist into the air twice and turned the formation onto the soft sand, jogging quickly.

The cliff rose more than one hundred feet above them where he called a halt. Cut into the red sandstone was a climbing footpath he had used that morning. Far down the beach around a point, he knew the place where sea smashed against rocks beneath the lonely manor house windows; and miles farther where river met Channel was the village.

The prisoners dropped into the sand at Reisman's order to fall out. "I need a volunteer!" he called.

Only the screaming gulls answered him, and the sound of the surf. No one came forward. They sprawled out full length or slumped exhausted against their packs, seemingly past caring. Reisman glanced at his watch. They had been working less than five hours, had come a lousy twelve miles and, except for Posey, looked as though they'd never make it home.

"Morgan!" he called.

The Sergeant came up to him suspiciously.

"Post your men in a semicircle thirty paces from us," Reisman ordered. To the prisoners, he said, "Sit up and move closer together."

The guards moved off, watchful. Reisman dropped his packs and squatted Indian fashion, the grease gun across his thighs. In the near distance, Morgan strained his ears to hear what was said.

"I asked for a volunteer," Reisman repeated quietly. "What I want him to do is very important. Our lives will depend upon it when we leave the beach. I'll work with him."

He looked from face to face and they stared back at him curiously or blankly or averted their eyes. No one raised a hand or spoke. Kendall Sawyer almost did, but he remembered the first axiom of the soldier: Never volunteer.

"Do you know what it is to soldier and mean it?" Reisman challenged. "Some of you did once, and that's why I picked you. I expect you to set the example, to help the others. All of you can do it. None of you are stupid. None of you are crippled or weak. If you were, you wouldn't be here." But they were stupid, they were weak, they were crippled—if not physically, then in pride and perspective—and it was for those very reasons, he knew almost for certain, that he had committed himself to them finally and irrevocably. He went on, "You got into trouble, so what! I've been in trouble too!" making confession before he knew he was making confession, wondering if this was the way—to make them know he shared their evil, they shared his good. But where did cunning end and truth begin? "Whatever you did before has nothing to do with what we do here. You have only one job . . . making yourselves into soldiers . . . and you have precious little time in which to do it. What we do together, what I teach you today, tomorrow, these next weeks, can save your lives and settle any debt you owe the Army, your country, yourselves. Who will volunteer?"

Kendall Sawyer, Glenn Gilpin and Samson Posey raised their hands. Napoleon White might have, but he didn't want to overdo it, seem too eager. Calvin Ezra Smith almost did, but he didn't trust this man, this Captain that mocked God and Sabbath and spoke lightly of evil.

"Posey, you're it!" said Reisman. Samson stood up, looking immensely pleased. "Sawyer, Gilpin, I'll use you another time." They had looked disappointed, even hurt. "The rest of you start looking for your second wind, and your guts. You're gonna need both pretty quick now. The day's only half over."

He called the guards in close. "Let me have all the line," he said, "and one axe."

Some of the MPs took from their light packs the ropes used that morning in field obstacle problems. Samson went from one to the other taking the rope, thrusting the coils down his long arms. Bowren handed Reisman an axe he hooked onto his web belt.

Reisman and Samson climbed the steep, twisting footpath. At the top, the path cut behind an overhanging edge of cliff and came out onto the plateau of gorse and heather. Part of the manor house could be seen more than half a mile away. Reisman looked around for a stout tree or large boulders, but there was nothing usable.

"We're going over the cliff on the rope and then climb up with the others. Do you understand, Posey?"

"Yes."

"Got any ideas how we can anchor the line up here?" Reisman gestured with his hands to indicate tying a rope and pulling on it.

Samson looked around. "No trees . . . no heavy rocks," he said. He tapped the folded shovel on Reisman's pack. "I dig hole . . . stand in it. You tie rope around me."

"I don't think so, but you have the beginning of a good idea," responded Reisman quickly. He unhooked the axe from his belt, pointed with it to some trees a hundred yards back from the cliff. "Cut me six thick branches and bring them here." He held the axe out to Samson. Samson reached for it . . . hesitated . . . their eyes met in understanding that there was trust between them. Samson took the axe, dropped his packs and the coils of rope and made for the trees at a run.

Reisman tied four ropes together and started digging a trench ten feet back from the overhang. Samson returned with the branches. They lashed together two simple anchors, tied the rope to them, wedged them securely in the trench and buried them. They strained on the rope with all their might and the anchors held.

"I'll go first," said Reisman, putting on his packs again.

"No, me!" Samson insisted.

"I'll go first. Wait until I signal you," Reisman told him. He slung the M3 diagonally across his back and tightened it. Peering over the edge, he shouted a warning to the men below and threw the rope.

It snaked out at the bottom with room to spare, but he realized suddenly that the taut, flat way it lay at the top made it more dangerous than he intended, particularly as the last few feet of the climb would be under the overhang, away from the dubious comfort and toe holds of the cliff face.

He sent Posey for more thick branches and they sank a tripod fulcrum for the rope near the rim of the cliff. It raised the rope high enough so that a man coming up could get a grip over the edge with his arms and legs.

Reisman looped the rope once around his seat, went over the edge backward and started down the face of the cliff, sliding the line slowly through tightly gripped hands and legs. Where the overhang fell away, he kicked himself out and swung in again lower down, putting his feet on a ledge for a moment's rest then swinging out again on the slack line. Twice he was able to swing in and stand on parts of the twisting footpath. When he got to the bottom, the prisoners were standing, watching him apprehensively. The guards had one eye on him, one eye on them. He moved out from the foot of the cliff to where he could see the top.

"Okay, Posey!" he shouted. "Come on down!"

Samson came down with less care and more bravado, stopping only at the knotted places that halted his slide. His hands, arms and legs were wrapped around the line, controlling his rate of descent. He hit bottom with a splash of sand.

"Get your packs on and fall in!" Reisman ordered.

"How about the trail?" muttered Roscoe Lever. "I ain't no goddamn mountain climber!"

"There is no trail!" snapped Reisman. "This is the only way up! Your life depends on it!"

They moved reluctantly . . . jittery about the climb.

"Hop to it!" Reisman prodded. "Bowren, run 'em

through a few deep-knee bends and push-ups just to loosen the kinks and make sure they're still alive."

He sent Sergeant Morgan and a guard up the footpath to the top, and three MPs to points on the trail where they could reach out to help a climber if necessary. Then he gathered the prisoners around him at the bottom of the rope.

"There is a right way and a wrong way to do this," he told them. "This is the right way." He demonstrated as he spoke, moving up the rope. "Haul with your arms and lock yourself there with your legs. Haul with your arms, lock with your legs." He slid down. "If you get nervous, don't look down! You're carrying fifteen pounds less than I am, so consider yourselves lucky you haven't been issued weapons yet."

"Just give us the guns! You ain't got the nerve!"

"Some other time, Franko!" Reisman said. "Not today. How'd you like to follow me up this thing, show the others how good you are."

"I'll wait my turn, Captain."

"Understand this!" Reisman said. "Anybody who fails to negotiate this obstacle is finished, kaput like the Krauts! I won't tolerate gold-bricking. If you can't do this, either alone or with the help we can give each other, you won't be able to do the other things that will be required of you and your value to this outfit will be zero." He paused to let that sink in sufficiently. "Who's going to follow me up?"

Samson pushed through the group and there was no denying him. Reisman handed him the slack end of the rope.

"All of you pay attention to what I show him now," he said carefully. "The man at this end is as important as the man climbing. He's got to hold the line rigid with his arms and legs." He moved Samson's arms and legs into position on the rope, making positive he understood exactly what was meant. "If that line holds stiff as a fireman's pole, the going is easier. If anybody on the rope gets into trouble and needs a toe hold, he calls down to the anchor man to move him in like this." He forced the line slack in Samson's hands and showed him how it should be swung into the cliff like a pendulum. "Anybody tries to get off the rope before hitting the top is gonna come right back down and negotiate it all over again, so take my advice and do it right the first time. Now, one more thing and this is the

228

most important. Look up, all of you! You'll notice how the cliff overhangs. The line is rigged so you can get over the top, but the man down here can help you by doing this." He drew Samson slowly back on the rope, making him pay it out tightly through his hands until he had used up the slack and the rope was held taut at an angle away from the cliff. "Walk the rope out just right and you ease your buddy over the top." He jerked the line out of Samson's hands. "Lose it and you can kill him! Bowren, you watch the anchor man and lend a hand. Grab the rope, Posey!"

He started up fast, calling down instructions as he climbed. "Haul with your arms, lock with your legs! Haul with your arms, lock with your legs! Don't look down and don't panic! There's lots of help around if you need it." At the mid-point he called, "Swing me in to the trail, Posey!" The MP posted there grabbed him as he moved close, held him there to show them, then released him to climb. At the overhang, Reisman inched up carefully, felt the rope angle away from the edge so that he was partly lying on it as he passed the hump. Morgan and the MP were staring down at him a few feet away, their hands extended. He waved them back and hauled himself over the rim.

Posey came up fine. Sawyer next, struggling past the overhang with a wild, desperate look on his face, then dropping in a heap onto the plateau, his nerves and muscles still vibrating. Gilpin was next, played out but throwing a damn-you-I-did-it look at Reisman. Then nobody. Reisman peered over the edge. They were arguing whose turn it was.

"Keep them moving, Bowren," he called down. "Franko, get on the line."

Franko came up slowly, taking advantage of every toe hold, spending more time resting than climbing. At the overhang, he slipped, spun around on the rope so that he was hanging down backward. "Captain, goddamn you!" he screamed. "I'm going down. I can't make it!" He started to slide back.

"Franko, stay where you are!" yelled Reisman. He couldn't see him because of the overhang. "You go back now and you're finished. You hear me? There's no tomorrow for you in this outfit. You'll be taken back to Marston-Tyne tonight!"

Franko's fingers came over the hump, scraped raw and bleeding, then his head, gasping for breath.

"Give him a hand, Sergeant," ordered Reisman.

Franko's face wore a look of horror as Morgan reached for him. Reisman grabbed the Sergeant's belt to make sure he didn't lose both of them over the cliff.

Smith, Wladislaw and Jiminez came up carefully, conserving their strength by signaling the anchor men to swing them into the cliff face to rest just before they reached the overhang, then scampering up the last few feet with do-or-die looks on their faces.

Myron Odell made it okay to the last toe-hold ledge and then he froze. He clutched the rope to him but wouldn't go any farther, neither up nor down. Reisman raced down the footpath to where he could see him.

He shouted angrily to the men on the beach. "Well, goddammit, don't just stand there! Somebody get up there and help him!"

It was Maggot's turn. "Damned if ah'll go up theyah and git muhself kilt helpin thet yelluh-bellied Yankee!" he muttered. "Wha the hell doan he jus jump an end it all!"

Napoleon moved before he was fully aware of what had possessed him. He grabbed Maggot's shoulder and jerked him back. "Stand aside!" he ordered, and started up the rope.

Maggot came back at him fast, grabbed his ankles and yanked him off the rope into the sand, smashing his fist again and again into Napoleon's body and head.

Through his haze of frozen terror, Myron Odell saw the fight, felt the rope jerked out of his hand, almost toppling him from his narrow perch. He saw the others separate the flailing bodies and hold them apart, heard the Captain shouting at him, first from the trail, then from down on the beach.

Reisman swung the rope into the cliff. "Grab it, Odell!" he called.

Odell crouched, petrified, alone, not caring if he stayed there forever, died there.

"Handle the rope, Corporal," ordered Reisman grimly. "There's only one way to make that son-of-a-bitch move." He unlimbered the grease gun from his back, flipped up the safety cover and aimed. "Odell!" he shouted. "In five seconds, lead is gonna start climbing the cliff. Grab that rope and move!"

Odell heard the words, saw the figures moving one hundred feet below him, heard the rattling explosions, and with fascinated disbelief watched the bullets chewing into the cliff, spitting out bits of sandstone as the stream moved upward toward his perch—and he jumped! his hands and arms and legs enmeshed with the rope, flying upward out of the welling of noise and dust and exploding rock with a new kind of fear that galvanized him scurrying past the overhang as though it wasn't there—nobody helping him because they'd all jumped back from the chattering gun!— and he dropped trembling and exultant beside the bug-eyed prisoners on the plateau. He had done it! He had done it, and more! Fired upon! *He!* Tasted what surely was *heat of battle!* Felt tiny shards of death speed past and leave him unscathed! Oh God, he'd showed them!

Reisman heaved a terrible sigh of relief.

"All right, dammit!" he snapped at the others. "Get moving!"

Maggot, White, Pinkley and Lever climbed the rope with surprising ease.

Bowren handed Reisman the slack end of the line. "I'm next, Captain," he said. "I don't want any of these jerks thinking they can do anything I can't."

He went up fast and over the top. Reisman trotted up the footpath to join them.

Odell stared at the Captain with feelings compounded of hatred and respect because of what he had forced him to do, and of admiration, even affection, he would have denied. But what if the Captain had killed him? Then this very minute he, Myron Odell, listening to the Captain's lecture on fieldcraft and living-off-the-land, would be lying dead, bleeding and broken at the base of the cliff—and he was Innocent! It was the concept of nothingness that he found difficult to understand and terrifying to accept. Going into nothingness, would he have clutched his wound, twisted and turned and grimaced "Ya got me!" as they did in the movies, or would he have screamed an eternal scream all the way down as they also did in the movies? He had done neither and so didn't know how he was to feel now—good or bad, shamed or proud. The Captain had not helped. He had come up the footpath, thrown him one curious glance, and then ignored him.

The lecture over, they stripped down again for calisthenics. Would the man never let them rest? Odell ached in every muscle and bone of his body, yet he marveled at the untapped wells of strength he had found within himself.

They went to relieve themselves before the march home, moving for some dubious degree of privacy a short distance from the place they had sat and the prospective line of march. *Home!* That was what the Captain had called it that morning. It was as much home, Odell knew, as any other might have been.

Franko stood beside him waving his penis freely among the gorse and heather, wondering if he would ever use it again for anything but peeing. He looked at Odell strangely, and Odell looked away—and gasped!

"My God, a woman!" he uttered, and wet himself in his haste to cover up.

It was a woman!—or part of one visible from the waist up, standing transfixed a few feet below where the footpath mounted the plateau. Victor Franko started toward her, oblivious to the presence of the others. Then he saw the dog.

Reisman heard the dog bark and looked up to see Margot Strathallan standing on the footpath about thirty yards away, holding the straining Doberman tightly by a short leash.

"Franko, get back here!" he shouted.

Franko turned, a look of ugly, angry pain on his face.

Reisman grabbed Bowren. "Go tell that woman to get back on the beach till we clear the area!" he ordered. "Morgan, get the men over here quick and line them up!"

The prisoners milled around, some curious, most darting hungry, envious glances at the woman. Samson looked anxiously from the Captain to the dog. Sergeant Morgan ordered them to attention, facing away.

Bowren jogged back and whispered to Reisman, "She says it's her property, sir, and nobody is going to tell her where she is to walk. She wants to see the officer in charge."

"Get them out of here, Bowren. Double-time back to the stockade. I'll catch up with you."

The Doberman lurched at him, growling his frustrated hatred, as Reisman came near.

"*Ruhig,* Sigismund," said Margot soothingly, stroking the beast's head and flanks.

The dog whined and sat down obediently, though still suspicious, his eyes following Reisman.

"Er gehorcht Ihnen gut!" Reisman said dryly.

"Sprechen Sie deutsch?" she asked in surprise.

"Yes, I speak it, but the sound of it always rubs me the wrong way—sometimes anger, sometimes laughter!"

She turned back to the dog. "The nice officer won't hurt us. He just wants to talk." The dog quieted. She smiled at Reisman. "I heard gunfire. Were you playing at one of your little games?"

"I asked you to stay away from any area in which we were working," said Reisman coldly.

"That's rather a common bunch," she mocked. "Americans, are they? And you expect to win the war with that? You'll have to do better. I know."

"I will tell you now just this last time," he said softly, struggling to control himself. "You are to stay away from my men. Out of sight and sound!"

"Out of sound?" Margot laughed. "That's rather difficult with the noise you've been making. Gunfire on my beach, and bugles at all hours. Am I to stay locked in my room just to please you?" she flashed angrily. "Let me remind you this is my home and you are here on my forbearance."

"If you prefer," said Reisman, calmer now, "I will do something I had hoped to avoid. I'll notify the War Office it would be in our best interests to have you removed."

Her face fell and she bit her lower lip nervously, but when she spoke it was haughtily. "That won't be necessary. I had no intention of surprising you at your work, as you call it. The sight of you galls me. It will be my pleasure to avoid you."

Margot pulled the dog past him onto the plateau, and he watched them move across the downs toward the manor house. He would not follow through on his threat, at least not for now. He raced after the men, hours of work still ahead of them.

17

ALL OVER the Great Kingdom that night people held fast together, clinging in love and fear and tenderness and passion as weapons against all that palled and frightened, in beds if they were blessed or lucky or well set up . . . snuggled into cold street-level window ledges in Belfast . . . standing up against dark brick walls in Liverpool . . . in the aisles and seats of railway carriages in transit . . . pound-Sterling taxi-jobs in London where the whores went through Piccadilly like the net of a purse seiner, few fish escaping their mesh.

Some made do with themselves.

Archer Maggot made do with his memories. He lay in his bedroll on the hard ground, muscles and bones aching, stinking of the latrines he'd mucked through, thinking of the woman on the cliff all bundled up in her great big coat so he couldn't tell if she had tits or an ass or legs or anything, and lusting for her in his own remembered way, wondering if she lived nearby, in the big house, if the Captain was getting some of that.

"Youall git much, Looey, when you wuz at home?"

"I get enough."

"You mesicans pretty hot stuff ah unnerstan."

"Sure we hot stuff. Whattayou tink?"

"Man, ah useta have suh much of it, made me sick just alookin at it."

"You talk big."

"That's cawz ahm a big man at home, Looey."

"Yeh?"

"Thas right, Looey. All the pussy ah evuh wahnned. All thuh fresh young poontang comin in off thuh fahm come alookin fust fuh Ahchuh Magit t'break em in, t'show em thuh ropes. All thuh likka ah evuh wahnned, too, an maw money in mah pockets than you prob'ly seen in yo whole life."

"What you do, man, run a whorehouse?"

"A whouhhouse? Hell, you doan know nuthin. Aint you nevuh heard a Phenix City?"

"Where's that?"

"Where's that! Goddamn, Looey, you doan know nuthin. Ah thot ev'ry man in thuh Ahmy been through Phenix."

"Arizona . . . my cousin work there once picking grapefruit."

"Boy, you a real country boy, ain't you. They ain't no Phenix City in Arizona ah huhd of. This heah's in Alabama. Thas wheah ahm fum down in Russell County. Right

234

across the Chattahoochee Rivuh fum Columbus, Geohgia. They's whouhhouses an strippin and drinkin an slots an cahds and craps an evuhbody playin thuh bug . . . even thuh nigguhs we let em play . . . an cockfightin an if'n a man hadda have a needle aw a pill wha we got it fo im. Anythin a man could want in thuh whole damn wuhld wuz right theyuh."

On Fourteenth Street and Dillingham Street and Seale Road ablazing with neons and filled with suckers pouring across the bridges from Columbus; pouring in from the County and downstate and Birmingham; from all over the South, up from Miami and Tallahassee and Mobile and New Orleans; and Yankee gamblers coming down from Chicago and New York and Detroit; and cowboys from Reno and points west . . . and mostly the Army . . . thousands and thousands and thousands of them from Fort Benning coming over those bridges with pockets full of pay, and hardons leading them right to where the girls were waiting in the honky-tonk cafés and night clubs and hotels and motels and spilling over into the County into old frame houses and corncribs and rabbit hutches and fish camps on rutted dirt roads. And Archer Maggot a big man in all of that. Not the biggest, not a kingpin, though he fancied he was sometime or he'd be sometime—but moving up, taking care of things for the Big Boys who owned the rackets, seeing that operations ran smooth, recruiting talent, keeping the girls in line, carrying the pay-off to the cops and sheriffs and politicians, taking care of the suckers that squawked about crooked games or watered booze or not enough time with the broads they'd paid for, working over the troublemakers with knucks or chains, palm-slappers or blackjacks, or sometimes just his big meaty fists and stomping boots, and he got a real pleasure out of that —though sometimes he and the boys went too far and somebody would find a bloated body floating in the Chattahoochee . . .

"Bullshit!" said Luis Jiminez. "You do all that stuff where I come from and the law get down on you fast. There ain't no place like that."

Maggot reared up out of his reverie. "Doan nevuh say bullshit to me lak that!" he whispered angrily. "Thuh law an politicians they wuz wuhkin fo us thuh way we had it goin, and they'd come sniffin aroun aftuh pussy an moonshine an a bit a fun jus lak anyone else."

235

"You such a big man what you doin here, huh?"

"Thas a long story, Looey . . . a long story."

"Shit, man . . . I have a rough day an that goddamn Captain he say he ain't gonna let up on us. I'm gawna sleep."

Archer Maggot couldn't sleep for thinking . . . for hurting flesh . . . for screaming nerves . . . for remembering how their juices ran and they began to squirm and sweat and moan and smell and grab and gasp and cry and then lie still, hair all wet and stringy, bodies soaked. He couldn't sleep for remembering the one in London who'd screamed "Rape!" against him though a thousand men had used her before, and made it stick at his court-martial, exhibiting the bruised face and body he'd inflicted upon her. A whore! Not even pretty or good in bed like the ones he'd trained and ruled in Phenix City. A cheap whore mocking him toward the gallows and putting him in jail with a nigger and an indian and a mesican!

He couldn't sleep for thinking of that morning in Phenix City he'd been handed his draft notice by a courthouse flunky . . . not mailed to him but handed to him so they'd know for sure he got it and he'd know for sure where it came from . . . and he'd gone downtown to the courthouse to find out who the hell had goofed, and they'd looked at him with blank faces like he wasn't somebody and said he had to do what the paper said and go in the Army . . . and he couldn't understand that because he'd always had protection from the top no matter what he'd done . . . and when he'd gone to see the Big Boys who could fix anything they'd told him there'd been too many beatings, too many bodies, too much branching out on his own . . . there'd been too many complaints and the heat was on from Fort Benning and maybe they were going to put some places off limits and that was bad for business . . . this was the way the important people had decided to settle it . . . to squeeze him out . . . they were doing him a favor . . . there were those who'd have liked to see him in Kilby Prison for the things he'd done . . . or in the Chattahoochee . . . or dug in a hole . . . but the Big Boys liked him too much for anything like that, they said, so he'd just have to go in the Army like all the other patriotic boys of their fair city and sovereign state . . . and he'd damned well better keep his mouth shut about how things were run in Phenix City . . . because if he blabbed they had lots of ways of getting to him . . . but if he was a good boy and did what he was told, there just might be a job waiting for him when he got home.

Since that first day he'd put on the uniform, Archer Maggot had nursed the grudge, vowed he'd come home a bigger man than he'd gone away, get even with the ones who'd put him in the Army. But the Army had never let him stay put in one place long enough to do more than start up some payday craps or poker—and having to play honest against guys who knew what they were doing had never paid off for him. Not until he'd come to England and settled in with a transportation outfit near London had he hit on his big idea: Organize the whores in London like they'd done with their women at home. Set them up somewhere and keep them under control, bring the men to them and take the cream off the top of their money, and slap them around when they needed it. His own empire, with him the kingpin!

And then that first whore he'd grabbed in Piccadilly . . . No! That wasn't right! It was her grabbed him, like he told the court-martial! . . . Laughed in his face when he'd put the proposition to her—not asking her but telling her. Her naked on the bed hurrying him and him still with his pants on telling her what he'd do for her and her girl friends . . . Though he didn't tell the court-martial that—only she'd picked him up, taken his money, given him nothing in return and if maybe he'd hit her a little bit it was because she'd taken advantage of him . . . She'd laughed in his face! Independent she was. Didn't go for pimping and didn't need one. Pimp! He weren't no pimp, dammit! That was cheap Yankee talk! And her coming back at him with the filthiest language ever come out of a woman, getting dressed without him getting what he'd already paid for—and that's when he'd let her have it good, ripping the clothes off her, taking what he'd paid for, working her over to show her she was taking orders from him and there was one thing he just couldn't abide and that was being laughed at. And she'd screamed so loud the neighbors called the limey cops and the MPs and they all said, every damned one of them, he'd raped her.

He'd get her! Yes, by damn, he'd get her! His blunt brain dwelt on the sight of her there naked and him putting it to her and beating up on her and putting it to her and beating up on her . . .

Samson Posey could not sleep. He rose from his blankets, took from his pocket the small, sharp shells he had found on the beach, and with great effort cut slivers of nails from his fingers and toes. He crawled forward, lifted the front flap of the puptent and held the slivers heavenward. *"Inusakats!"* he called softly to the old and familiar God of Benevolence. "Give me long life and help me, *Inusakats!"* he intoned. He threw the slivers to the night wind, went back to his blankets and slept.

Victor Franko huddled bug-eyed and sleepless against the far side of the tent. The crazy bastard gave him the willies.

Captain Reisman walked the flat roof of the barracks, scanning the compound, hearing whispers of conversation he couldn't make out, watching movements he couldn't really see . . . cursing whatever it was in him that made him take these hours of the watch, though as Commanding Officer he didn't really have to, it would never be expected of him . . . wondering when, if ever, he would be able to shake off this feeling of imminent trouble and impending doom that weighed upon him. What was it that drove him so? Remembered times of inadequacies? Fear of more? Would he never be able to trust the prisoners fully, ease up on himself and the guard detail? In a way it was toughest on them for they too had been placed under sentence by their assignment here, had to be almost always at work except for insufficient hours of sleep broken by night watches, and their one night off in three. Tonight Corporal Bowren and the three MPs off duty weren't even getting that.

After Taps he had sent them to Marston-Tyne—with appropriate warnings about loose talk concerning where they were stationed and what they were doing—to return three of the four trucks and drive back to Stokes Manor in the jeep. They had gone eagerly, if only to get away from the heavy oppression that clung to this place and the men in it —though they needed sleep most of all, or might have preferred a few hours' relaxation or dubious excitement in Stokesmouth Village or elsewhere if given a true choice. He wished he could have gone himself . . . a night with Tess . . . even a few hours or a few minutes to nurture himself on her loveliness, her softness, her passion.

238

Marston-Tyne was for him a place of such fantastically antipodal memories . . . fear, repugnance, death: love, beauty, life . . . Did Tess wait for him faithfully to come to her when he could? . . . as she had said simply, sweetly, in her young and vibrant way, though he had never asked it and wouldn't, and felt no right to expect it. She was a most wonderful phenomenon to have happened to him . . . but what could he possibly be for her? . . . on the evidence of his past . . . on the prognosis of his future. He felt a moment of great yearning, akin to anguish, in the thought that someone else might have become for her what he had become . . . and someone else might still become.

Why could he not learn to do without? . . . and like it!

He thought of Margot Strathallan . . . so close. In the grip and challenge of his work, he had almost forgotten she was there . . . until she had shown herself on the cliff . . . disturbing the men . . . My God! What an inopportune, inelegant time for her to appear! . . . Laughable! —unless it was maybe, pathetically, opportune after all, if still inelegant, depending upon the nature of whatever aberration it was that afflicted her . . . Yes, and unsettling him, too, dammit! . . . there in her strange, lonely world that seemed to mock everything . . . in what seemed to be a prison of her own making . . . and for what reason he still didn't know . . . might never know . . . Bitch!

For three days Reisman drove the prisoners ruthlessly through a schedule of toughening, learning, discipline. Training they might have gone through under other circumstances in weeks and months—as, indeed, most of them had—they had to relearn, reassimilate, reaccept in hours and days: forced marches up and down the vast estate and along the beach; clambering up and down ropes on the sea cliffs, or up, down, under, over and across any other obstacle he could find or dream up; close-order drill within the compound, calisthenics when they yearned for and expected the traditional "take ten," quick night hikes when they thought they were through for the day and were ready to drop; and constantly, incessantly, Reisman's voice commanding, coaxing, goading, threatening, lecturing, changing in tone and rhythm and timbre and pitch as the situation demanded, as his choice of word and phrase required—now the gruff patois, the Army talk, the buddy-

buddy talk; now the slow, careful articulate officer-gentle-man-part-time-intellectual speaking above some of them, yet pausing to lift them up, make sure they understood.

The lectures he varied and repeated, broadened and refined, adding new subjects as he felt they could absorb them: first aid, map reading, compass, fundamental infantry tactics, weapons familiarization. He didn't let them handle the weapons, much less use them—not yet. But he instructed them in the M1 rifle, the carbine, the .45 automatic pistol, the M3 submachine gun, grenades—reacquainting them with the basic, simple weaponry of the foot soldier that they would eventually have to relearn, requalify in before they could go on to anything more complicated and interesting . . . if they earned the right to use them again . . . if he found them worthy of it . . . if he could trust them.

Weather varied and was immaterial. They had to learn to operate effectively over all types of terrain, in all kinds of weather, by day and by night—until such time as he was told for certain what their missions were. From hour to hour the weather changed. It rained great slanting sheets of water that lashed at men and equipment, that tore at the fabric of the little tents in the night, overflowed the rain trenches, soaked everything, filled the compound with the stench of the latrine, leaked through the roof of the guards' quarters, and made miserable the MPs who had to stand sentinel outside. Other times the weather was mild and almost pleasant—harbinger of spring . . . and Invasion.

It was Corporal Bowren who gave the prisoners their name . . . their rallying cry . . . their identity, as it were.

He came to the door of Reisman's little office in the early morning four days after training had begun, and announced with mock and gracious gravity, "The Dirty Dozen await your pleasure, sir!"

Reisman glanced up from checking the training tests he had given the prisoners the night before. Some of their written responses were excellent, some adequate or poor, and some of the writing almost illegible—Samson Posey used words and little drawings—but Reisman was pleased with the way this phase of the training was progressing. He was getting through to them, they were working, trying, thinking. His concentration interrupted, he answered more abruptly than intended, "What's that, Corporal?"

"The Dirty Dozen, Captain . . . they're waiting." Bowen tried again, with a bow and sweep of his arm, smiling, yet suddenly wondering if he had overstepped the camaraderie the Captain had allowed to develop between them.

"Have they heard you call them that yet?"

"I don't think so, sir," answered Bowren, suddenly serious. "I was only kidding. I hope you don't think I'm riding them . . ." He meant the way Morgan rode them sometimes . . . without reason . . . unnecessarily crude or cruel . . . to satisfy himself more than do any good for the men or the Captain.

"You can ride the hell out of them!" Reisman declared unequivocally. "When you think it'll do any good. I want them lean and tough and mean. If they can't take it here, they can't take it where they're going. I wasn't thinking of it that way. I actually think they'd like a nickname like that. That's why I've let this washing and shaving bitch ride. Let them hear it . . . tell the guards to use it . . . Hell, it sure fits them, doesn't it!" he said, chuckling, getting up to go out to them into the compound. "They're really beginning to stink."

They did stink—though not so badly that they couldn't be approached, which was what they hoped for in secret and prideful discussions among themselves, and looked to happen if they kept it up long enough. But they did stink of the sweat and grime of unwashed bodies, slopped rations, fear and anger, and no plumbing. Beards and mustaches—really just short hairs at this stage that grew helterskelter on some, full and dark on others, matted with dirt —made them look fierce. Posey looked fierce anyway. Odell was trying hard with the little bit of fuzz he could muster.

Each day they had been offered the opportunity to bathe and shave, but they had refused. It was the only moment of undiscipline Reisman allowed. It had become a ritual each morning as the guard came out with the five-gallon can of water and offered it to them to wash and shave, for one of the men to take it, spill it on the ground to the general refusal and laughter of the others. Then Reisman would show himself and the laughter would subside and things

241

get back to normal. It was a little safety valve he allowed them.

Reisman stood before them in the compound. The prisoners sat on the ground, camp broken, rations eaten, packs lined up neatly behind each man, ready to move out if that was what he ordered. He thought of them now as the Dirty Dozen—as he was sure they would soon think of themselves, with an inverse, perverse sort of morale that would work for *them*.

"I'm going to teach you how to kill a man this morning," he said simply.

Some of them looked at him startled, a few actually embarrassed! He realized then how ludicrous that sounded. On the record, White, Franko, Posey, Jimenez and Sawyer had been convicted of murdering men, Odell of murdering a woman; Maggot, Lever, Smith, Pinkley, Wladislaw and Gilpin of mayhem sufficiently close to murder to warrant their being there.

"I'm going to teach you how to kill a man with this." He held up his pinky. "And these." He held up three fingers rigidly, crossing his thumb and pinky across his palm. "And how to defend yourself, though unarmed as you now are and will be for some time, against attack by gun, club, sword, knife, or a guy twice as big as you are . . . like Posey there. Never, incidentally try to kill a man or even hit a man with this." He balled his fist. "It is likely to do more damage to you than to him, maybe even break your knuckles and finger bones. Very painful."

He held up his little finger again. "When I say kill a man with this, I'm stretching a point, of course, merely to illustrate. It is the flat edge of the hand"—he demonstrated as he spoke—"running through the little finger, which makes a superb weapon when the other fingers are held close against it, the thumb stretched out at right angles to tense the muscle ridge that runs between your wrist and finger. Get out your notebooks and pencils. Sergeant Morgan, would you please find me a branch or a piece of wood . . . something about two inches thick and a foot or more in length."

The prisoners had rummaged through their packs for notebooks and pencils and were ready now, notebooks on their laps, pencils poised, looking like a class of schoolchildren whom time had ravaged and assaulted yet somehow left behind.

"What I'm going to teach you," Reisman continued, "is a science of unarmed offense and defense which the Japanese call jiujitsu and judo. You've heard of it, of course . . . maybe you know something about it . . . maybe you've been taught it sometime in your Army career and have used it. Maybe, too, some of you gentlemen have your own methods of killing which you prefer . . . or have used. You'll have an opportunity later on in your training to contribute what you can to the group. Meanwhile we'll go about it my way. There are variations and refinements that will amaze you!" He looked at Napoleon White to make the old point between them.

"The Japs, incidentally . . . just to make you a little smarter about what you're doing . . . didn't invent judo and jiujitsu," Reisman lectured. "It was developed by Chinese monks around the twelfth century. You see, their religion didn't allow them to use weapons . . . Mr. Smith, you ought to understand and appreciate that . . . but what were the poor guys going to do when they were constantly being attacked by nomads and bandits? They lost a lot of men, but over a period of years they worked out a system that made them really tough to tangle with in the in-fighting. That's when all war was pretty much face-to-face and hand-to-hand. You had to have real guts then to be a soldier, and real skill to come out alive. The Japs copied what the Chinese monks started . . . they're pretty good at that, you know . . . and they improved on it and refined it. But they've got no patent on it, or any secrets that make them any better or stronger than we are. And that goes for the Nazis too! I've fought against both of them and they've got no monopoly on terror or fighting or being supermen."

Sergeant Morgan came up to Reisman with a thick branch, as the prisoners scratched busily away at their notebooks. Morgan didn't look too happy about it, but Reisman showed him how he wanted him to hold the branch outstretched, gripped firmly with a hand on either end.

"Watch!" Reisman called to the prisoners.

In one smooth, powerful chop, he sliced his hand through the wood.

"Any of you should be able to do that in a few weeks," he said. "You too, Sergeant. All you've got to do is tough-en that ridge muscle by practicing. Every opportunity, every odd moment you have, hit the edge of your hand against any hard surface that's available. Let's do it now . . . come on . . . on the ground." They each tensed their hands and stretched out their thumbs as he had showed them, and began striking the ground with relish. "As for the practical uses, let me show you." Morgan backed away warily, still holding the two pieces of the branch. "Don't worry, Sergeant. Trust me. I'm just going to touch lightly. I won't follow through."

He showed them where to strike a man between the eyes just above the nose to break a paper-thin bone and drive a sliver into the brain to cause instant death; and where to strike just under the nose, chopping diagonally upward toward the ears to cause concussion or death; and how to strike the larynx with the full force of the body behind the blow—killing. Then, prodding Morgan's full belly below the base of his breastbone, he showed them where to ram three fingers stiff as daggers, palm upward, into the celiac plexus to burst the aorta and cause death from massive internal hemorrhage.

Some of the prisoners laughed at the sight of Morgan's discomfiture, playing the role of victim.

Reisman stopped and stared at them. "Don't laugh," he said coldly. "Don't ever laugh at death or injury or human suffering. It's not easy. It's not funny. To be meaningful, it must serve a purpose. Defending yourselves . . . fulfilling a mission. None of you are ever to follow through on any of these blows . . . do you understand? When you work with each other on offense, you are to identify and touch lightly the area of the blow . . . No more! There are ways, too, of putting a man out of action . . . incapacitating him . . . silencing him . . . without killing him or seriously injuring him, and I'll teach you those. You will use them for the purpose for which they were designed only when I tell you to. Any man who thinks he's a wise guy . . . who intentionally injures his opponent in practice . . . or to satisfy some personal grudge . . . will deal with me personally. And I warn you, I won't hold back. We'll forget about offense for now, and concentrate on defense. Posey, get up."

Samson stood up and came forward eagerly. Reisman drew a trench knife from a sheath at his belt and held out the hilt. Samson backed away from it bewildered.

"Take it!" ordered Reisman. "And attack me!"

"No," said Samson softly, shaking his head.

"Take it, I said, goddammit, and come after me!"

Samson took the knife and held it limply at his side, looking bewildered and embarrassed.

"For crying out loud, don't go soft on me now, Chief. What's the matter with you?"

"I hurt you . . . you good man . . . good officer . . . I don't want to hurt . . . I kill a man last time I fight."

"You killed a man because he didn't know what I know. Come on, damn you . . . fight!"

Samson stood there silently shaking his head.

"What the hell kind of an Indian are you, Posey? Sioux? Apache? . . . No, Navajo! . . . maybe squaw!"

Samson's face contorted in disbelief and anger as he tried to shut out the unexpected insults. "I'm Ute!" he said loudly, standing up to his full height. "Not Navajo . . . not white man . . . Ute!"

"Then the Utes are squaws, their women whores, their children beggars in the dust!"

Samson lunged forward with an animal cry, the knife hand raised in a reflex action. In one swift, practiced movement, Reisman's right forearm flashed up and blocked the downward-striking knife arm . . . his left forearm smashed into the crook of Samson's elbow, bending the arm backward . . . his left hand locked on his right wrist, trapping the knife arm in a vise . . . he drew his elbows close in to his body, bent swiftly from the waist and forced the knife arm backward, Samson with it. The brute strength of the man, tembling against him, almost broke the hold, but Reisman held it, pressuring Samson downward.

The knife dropped. Samson fell to the ground with a grunt. Before he could reach for the knife or get up, Reisman kicked it to Bowren and stood ready. Samson came at him like a raging bull, uncoordinated, unthinking, the perfect patsy for the next step.

"You want fight . . . I fight!" he shouted.

Reisman's left hand closed on Samson's right wrist . . . he turned and bent . . . reached for the upper arm with his right hand . . . and letting Samson's momentum and weight do the job, flipped him neatly over his head onto the ground.

245

Reisman bent over him to make sure he wasn't really hurt. "Thanks, Posey," he said, smiling.

Samson struggled up slowly, new understanding draining the anger that had taken possession of him. "Not funny," he said, knowing he really would have killed the Captain if he had not been able to defend himself—and that certainty frightened him, for then surely they would have hanged him. He went back to his place. None of the others had laughed. Maybe that was good. They had respect for what they had seen.

Reisman retrieved the trench knife. Tapping the hilt against his palm, he eyed them one by one. "Anybody think he can take me, come ahead!" he challenged. "Franko, how about you? You've got a big gripe to get rid of. No? White, how about you? You told me you'd jump at the chance if you could. Come ahead."

Neither one moved. Archer Maggot stood up, smiling. He jerked his thumb at Samson. "Sheet, Cap'm, that warn't nuthin but a big ole dummy not wantin t'fight. Tell yo boys dere t'stan back an hole dem itchy trigguh finguhs. Ah'll take y' by damn lak y' oughta be took, an theys t'say y'got stuck in a accident, y'hear?"

Reisman tossed the trench knife toward him hilt first in an easy arc. "You're on, Reb!" he said.

Archer Maggot caught the knife and came forward warily, crouched low, left foot leading, left arm extended to ward off any blows, his knife hand held close to his hip, ready to strike any opening. Reisman knew in that instant he had a man against him who knew what he was doing. Maggot wasn't bluffing. He was extremely dangerous, inching closer. Reisman stooped, reaching for a handful of dirt, and Maggot followed him down. Reisman pulled back, knowing he couldn't afford the fraction of a second he would need to uncover himself.

Within arm's length, Reisman sprang! . . . feet first . . . twisted to the left . . . hooked his left instep behind Maggot's left ankle . . . slammed his right foot against Maggot's right thigh . . . scissored him backward and down . . . broke his own fall with his hand, and in that instant raised his right foot and smashed the heel down viciously into Maggot's belly!

Maggot's hands clutched at his stomach, the knife dropped and forgotten. His mouth opened and closed with-

246

out sound, groping for breath. Reisman picked up the knife and leaned over him.

"You did okay," he said. "Later on when you're feeling better, you can show that trick to the other boys. Give him a hand, Morgan."

Morgan and an MP lifted Maggot. He was breathing again, able to groan. They helped him back to where he had been sitting. It had all been too quick. Maggot still didn't know what had happened to him, and that was what bothered him more than being whipped. There was more to that damn Captain than bullshit and brass, that was for sure—and he vowed he would learn it and beat him at it some day.

Reisman waited for his heartbeat to slow, his breathing to even out, the telltale signs of fear and tension that always showed in his voice after action to leave him. Then he spoke.

"There are more than a hundred different unarmed defenses like the sort of things I just demonstrated with Posey and Maggot . . . ways to protect yourself and gain the upper hand when you're attacked with weapons or without . . . ways to escape from a grip when you're taken by surprise or being held tightly by different parts of your body or clothing or in a wrestling hold. But there are only five simple and basic principles to the whole art of unarmed defense. It makes no difference how big or strong your opponent is, or how small or weak you are. Learn these principles and you will be able to handle yourselves with confidence and skill. You're not going to learn everything today or tomorrow or the next day or in a month, but we'll work on three new tricks every day from now on, and before you're finished here, you'll know something."

He beckoned Corporal Bowren over and told him to take as solid a stance as he could.

"The first principle is balance," said Reisman. "No matter what position a man is in, he's off balance in some direction. That's the direction in which he's working for you . . ."

Using Bowren as a partner, Reisman illustrated in slow motion the five basic principles: how to use an opponent's imbalance; how to use his strength and momentum against him by directing it instead of opposing it; how to use the internal oblique muscles in the lower abdomen as the source of power for every defense; how to concentrate maximum strength against maximum weakness; and how to prevent injury in practice by consciously separating defenses into major and minor operations—getting out of danger and getting the essential part of a hold, without applying the pressure that was the counterattack.

"It's not like pointing a gun at a man," he told them. "With a gun, you should never point unless you mean to shoot, and never shoot unless you mean to kill. With unarmed defense, you have a choice of being judicious. In practice with each other, I warn you again, you must exercise that choice. It doesn't mean you can't rough it up and attack or defend strongly. It means you have a split-second choice and the knowledge and training to exercise it like men instead of animals. For example, at this moment Mr. Maggot might be bewailing the loss of his testicles instead of a slight bellyache, or Mr. Posey's arm or hand might be broken . . ."

Myron Odell had listened and watched with mounting feelings of panic and dread. He hadn't minded the other training so far, though he regretted having to be dirty and smelly and the close association with others who were the same. He didn't mind the relentless physical activity that left him usually exhausted but sometimes feeling stronger, more competent, even prouder in a way he had never been before, like when the Captain had fired the grease gun burst toward him. He liked best the lectures—they were educational and the Captain made them so interesting. But the hand-to-hand physical contact, the brutal fights just witnessed had made him wince, feel nauseous; and the instructions that had preceded the raw violence and were now following it, the matter-of-fact talk about maiming and killing—which left little doubt as to what soon would be expected of him—made him ready to proffer by long habit his wall of old fears and inadequacies behind which he could take refuge and find some measure of security, though both cause and effect of his cowardice made him feel physically sick.

The Captain finished demonstrating the five basic principles and the three defensive tricks they were to practice now, and Odell felt helpless. He understood them, he could see how they worked, but how could he ever do them against men such as these who would never make allowances for him, who would never give him a break, if only to keep him from being sent back to the prison and the unimaginable horror that waited for him there.

"All right, on your feet and pair off!" ordered the Captain. "Tentmates together. Posey, you work with me. Franko, you work with the Corporal."

That was good. Odell didn't feel about Calvin Ezra Smith the way he did about most of the others. He wasn't afraid of him. He smiled at Calvin standing opposite him, and Calvin smiled back. Cal understood about him. Cal would take it easy.

The Captain demonstrated for them again the trick he said was the easiest, though it looked the most spectacular —the one he'd used to flip Samson Posey. This time he let Posey flip him, showing them how to land easily so they wouldn't be hurt. Posey's stoic face broke into a grin when he'd done it.

Cal ran forward with the attacking squad at a signal from the Captain. Odell grabbed his wrist hard, harder than he had expected to . . . grabbed his upper arm even harder . . . twisted . . . slammed his hip into Cal's stomach . . . and sent him flying over his shoulder. Cal slammed onto the ground on his back, the wind knocked out of him, and Odell went to help him, horrified and apologetic.

"There was no call for you to do it so hard, Myron," gasped Smith angrily.

He gave it right back to Odell in kind even stronger, when it was his turn, but Odell landed well—expecting it with some new sixth sense directing him, and he snapped right up. They practiced one wrist hold and break, and one body hold and break, not too rough on each other, and Odell felt better about the whole business than he had expected. Then the Captain made them switch partners.

"Anybody feel strong enough to take on Posey?" he asked. Nobody answered. "All right, we'll save him for graduation exercises. Let's run through the repertoire again."

Odell smiled at Archer Maggot who was now opposite him. Maggot glowered.

Reisman heard Odell's yelp of pain and rushed over.

Odell was hopping around, his hand pressed against his back.

"You chop him on the kidney, Reb?" asked Reisman angrily.

"Heck no, Cap'm. Musta bumped hissef accidental with mah elbow or sumthin," answered Maggot. "Ah was jus pertectin mahsef strong lak youall said t'do."

"What about it, Odell?"

"I don't know, sir," he answered hoarsely. Odell was still bending up and down, rubbing his back, his face contorted, but the pain was easing. Maggot had gotten rougher and rougher with each new hold, but he couldn't tell the Captain that . . . not in front of all the other guys . . . and leave himself open for more punishment from Maggot. "If that's what he says, I guess that's what it was."

"Take a break!" Reisman called out to the prisoners.

He led Odell away from the group and spoke softly so the others wouldn't hear. "You afraid of him, Odell?"

Odell hesitated, then admitted reluctantly, "Yeh . . . I guess so."

"But you weren't afraid of Smith . . . Why's that?"

"I don't know. Because I know him, I guess. He's all right."

"Because he's your tentmate . . . you talk to him . . . you're friendly, right?"

"Yeh, sure, I guess so."

"And because he was taking it easier on you, right?"

"A little . . . I guess."

"And you on him. I could see you guys pussyfooting around from where I was standing."

"Not every time."

"You know how much good that's going to do you both when you need it most, don't you? Nothing. Nothing at all!" said Reisman sharply. "Let me tell you something about fear, Odell. I've been scared more damn times than I care to remember. Anybody says he hasn't is a liar, is sick in the head, or he's dead. You don't have to be ashamed of fear, Odell. It can actually be a good thing for you. It makes you more alert. It opens the pupils of your eyes so you can see more. It makes your breathing and heart stronger. It gives your body that extra bit of strength and courage you need in a tight spot. What the hell do you think made you fly up the cliff the day I goosed you with the lead? Fear—that's all it was. But good fear, working

250

for you. All you've got to do is learn to control it."

They walked back to the group. After a few minutes' rest, the prisoners switched partners again and went back to work.

Napoleon White held Odell in a tight front body hold, while Odell struggled to get loose as Reisman had shown them.

"I don't know what the great brain told you, boy," said Napoleon, his lips up close to Odell's ear, "but if you wanta whip that loud-mouthed cracker so he eases off on you, you listen good now."

Odell broke the hold, started to apply the counterpressure as Reisman had demonstrated, then eased off before making it effective. It was Napoleon's turn. Odell was holding him strongly and he had to work harder than he'd expected.

"First thing you remember is you've gotta hate," grunted Napoleon. "You've gotta hate so big you don't know or feel anything else but that hate. Maybe you think of him beating up your mother or raping your little sister."

"I don't have any mother or sister," Odell squeezed through clenched teeth, fighting to maintain the hold.

"Well goddammit then, you little jerk, you think of something else that makes you mad," muttered Napoleon.

Odell squeezed tighter, feeling anger.

"And then you do something he doesn't expect," Napoleon said, breaking loose. "Like this." He crossed his hands quickly, grabbed Odell's open collar, fingers inside, thumbs outside, scissored his arms so Odell felt the strangling pressure and understood.

Every few minutes they switched partners again except for Posey and the Captain. Each time he broke a hold, took a hard knock, or gave one of his own, Odell felt stronger, more confident. He faced Maggot again and this time Maggot smiled and Odell didn't.

"Jus a li'l bit closuh, boy," Maggot sniggered, reaching for him.

Odell looked at him and hesitated, wondering what he could hate him for most. Maggot darted his hand out, down low.

"No balls atall, yo goddamn fairy. No balls atall."

Odell felt the probing hand jab his crotch and in that instant red fury burst in his brain, hearing the mocking *No balls atall*. . . hearing the girl again in the prophylactic station in Glasgow jabbering at him in her imbecile way *Are ye then a sissy-boy,* reaching for him there with him backing away . . . remembering again the terrible beating of his boyhood and feeling again the pain of fire and hate in his groin . . .

From a great distance separated by thicknesses and blacknesses, he heard a voice shouting "Odell!" felt strong hands chopping at him, dragging him.

He shook his head, dazed, aching . . . saw the Captain . . . Archer Maggot had been there a moment before, and he didn't understand . . .

"What in hell got into you, you stupid son-of-a-bitch? You could have killed him!" It was the Captain again.

"Killed her? . . . No . . . I told them I didn't kill her . . . I don't know what happened."

"Not her! Him! Maggot! What happened?"

Odell looked, became more aware, saw Maggot slumped on the ground, Corporal Bowren bending over him helping him, the others staring.

"What happened?"

"You were strangling him . . . he passed out . . . you almost killed him!"

He remembered it all then . . . Maggot, whom he feared and hated, cursing him, reaching for him . . . the red explosion in his head all mixed with terrible remembered pain going back . . . the poor dead girl in Glasgow . . . he'd hit her . . . yes, he remembered striking out at her . . . but kill her the way they said, No! . . . and the woman who came to him still in nightmare memories . . . the vile vicious vindictive vengeful virtuous eyes-blazing teacher of lessons to little orphans who peeked at naked women . . . beating him where it did the most good, the most harm . . . making his head explode red and black and forget . . .

"I'm Innocent," he whimpered, his face contorting desperately, "oh, my God, I'm Innocent . . ."

18

CAPTAIN STUART KINDER drove up to the gates of Stokes Manor late on the afternoon of Friday, March 10, in a state of some anxiety. He was not expected, but Captain Reisman had given him precise directions for getting there if and when the need arose. He carried with him in his briefcase the shocking and incontrovertible analyses of those few projective and psychometric tests he had been able to give the prisoners before they left Marston-Tyne. He hoped there was still time to make changes in the group.

The gates to the estate were closed forbiddingly. Kinder heaved and struggled at the heavy vertical latch bar, relieved to find it was not locked—though as an afterthought he wasn't sure he approved of it from a security point of view. He had declined for security reasons the use of the chauffeur to whom he was entitled, and had driven all the way down from London alone in a staff car from the SHAEF motor pool—a decision in which he felt certain Captain Reisman would concur.

Kinder swung the gates open and drove through, troubled by the thought that anybody else might have done the same thing. He wondered if he should pay his respects first to the English gentlewoman who lived there—her father was a General quite high up—but then he decided not to, since Captain Reisman had specified that one of her primary requirements for allowing use of the estate was that she never be disturbed. Kinder turned the car off the driveway, bumped a short distance across the field in the direction he believed the stockade lay, and parked. He walked back to the gates, closed them, and concealed himself behind some brush from where he could observe the road.

He waited impatiently for twenty minutes, glancing at his watch frequently, then smiled with satisfaction as a Signal Corps truck drove up and a telephone team went to work. It was gratifying to witness so concretely the results which the prestige of his task and connections, if not his rank, could bring.

He had tried to reach Captain Reisman by telephone, and had been appalled to learn that none had been installed at the training site, nor had any other speedy line of communication been established, other than to have one of the guard detail drive out as courier. There was a telephone at the manor house, but he had been specifically forbidden to call there, as had everybody else connected with Project Amnesty.

Captain Reisman apparently had a mania for isolation, though it didn't seem to disturb his immediate superior at OSS, with whom Kinder had discussed it anxiously. Major Armbruster had jokingly suggested carrier pigeons at either end. "We use them occasionally in our line of work, you know," he had said, smiling. "But don't worry about Johnny. He's used to going it alone once he's given orders. And he gets the job done. He'll be in touch with you if he needs you."

For Stuart Kinder that hadn't been at all satisfactory. He had taken matters in hand. The soldiers now working on the telephone lines out on the road had been sent there through an indirect, though high priority, chain of command, to arrive at a specific hour, cut a field telephone into the vast Signal Corps network, bury or camouflage the wires as much as possible, and depart quickly, leaving behind at the gate a live field telephone and enough wire on reels to extend two miles. They had no knowledge of the original source of their orders nor who would be using the phone.

When the Signal Corps truck left, Kinder walked back to his car and drove on across the field. He found a vehicle track and followed it through the wood, right up to the stockade. He got out of the car and, hearing the commands of close-order drill and the beat of marching feet, he walked past the barracks that blocked his view, around the perimeter, quickly observing the setup of barracks, fencing and watchtowers, and marveling at the job Captain Reisman had done. Then he saw the prisoners—and gasped!

"Nice to see you, Stu," lied Reisman. "What brings you down here? News of the missions, I hope."

Kinder settled himself grimly on the cot—the only other

254

place to sit besides Reisman's chair—waiting for the door to the little headquarters room in the barracks to be shut by the MP who had escorted him in. "No," he said, shaking his head, "nothing like that yet, thank God. It's worse than I feared. These tests I gave them . . . There's a marked predominance of the explosive and more primitive types of emotional response over the more adjusted and well-integrated ones . . ."

"No!"

"Yes! Some of them . . . maybe most of them . . . are the worst possible choices psychologically for what we intend them to do."

"But I thought that was the point of this whole operation?"

"It was . . . It is, I mean . . . but I hadn't been prepared for so much . . . Psychoneuroses, hysteria, anxiety states, obsessive-compulsive states, psychopathic personalities, mental deficiencies . . . Name it and one of them has got it. My God, some of them don't even belong in the military, much less undertaking missions of trust!"

"Stuart, Stuart, Stuart," said Reisman softly. Kinder looked so completely disconsolate that he felt genuinely sorry for him. "I could have told you that without all those tests. Matter of fact, I did . . . I told you and everybody else, but nobody'd listen to me."

"There's only one thing we can do, John," said Kinder. "We've got to get in some new men . . . replace the worst of them."

Reisman reared up like a mother tiger. "The hell you say!" he roared. "Not after what I've been through with them. I'll listen to you just so far, but it stops before it gets to that point. I am committed to them and they are committed to me! Wasn't that the way you wanted it? You and the General and the Colonels and the rest of that bunch at the meeting in Baker Street . . . and your mysterious friends at SHAEF or Washington or wherever the hell this thing started. The ground rules are set and the game is on. There'll be no changes made unless I make them for my own good reasons. The men know what those are, and they don't include any of your psychological-sociological mumbo-jumbo. In a manner of speaking, what Reisman has joined together, let no man put asunder! That's it!"

Kinder was startled by Reisman's explosive defense of the prisoners, and somewhat hurt by the angry, unthinking derogation of his profession, but he decided to ignore the slight for now. "But don't you *need* help?" he asked. "Look at them. Obviously even discipline has fallen apart."

"The hell it has. What do you mean?"

"I didn't expect spit and polish, but I did expect them to at least look as well as they did when they left Marston-Tyne . . . washed, shaved and clean. They look as if they've been in combat for a month under the most primitive conditions."

"That's morale," said Reisman. "Wait until you smell them. And it's going to get worse before it ever gets better." He explained finally about the Dirty Dozen.

Kinder listened anxiously as Reisman told him of the progress of the training and the reason for the men's appearance.

"They're doing well, you say?" He still found it hard to believe.

"Sure they are. They're beginning to function and think as soldiers again . . . even if they don't look and smell so good."

"That's wonderful," Kinder said with relief. "By golly it might work, John!" he exclaimed, brightening. "It's different . . . it's contrary . . . but it just might work." He stuffed one sheaf of papers back in his briefcase, took out another, and waved it. "A motto . . . a group identity . . . Yes! If you can then mold that negative rallying point to our purpose, the group can truly be made greater than the sum of its parts . . . with the competence and confidence of good, tough training, of course . . . Then we'll have something! A motto . . . a banner . . . Yes! How clever! That's correct . . . that's sound psychology. Don't you remember what Napoleon did at the siege of Toulon?"

"No. What did Napoleon do at the siege of Toulon?"

"He was just an artillery officer then, but what a marvelous natural psychologist! He built a battery in such an exposed position he was told he would never find men to hold it. But he put up a placard reading, THE BATTERY OF MEN WITHOUT FEAR, and those guns were always manned. That's wonderful, isn't it? You know, this is the sort of thing I'd really intended to come down here for until I got frantic about the test results . . . Motivation! I've got dozens of plans and ideas . . . films, reading, slide shows, lectures . . . material I want to bring down later . . . and more tests . . . I'm not through with the testing by any means." He remembered the phone suddenly and said accusingly, as though talking to a naughty boy, "I tried to call you a few times!"

"No phone," said Reisman.

"So I learned . . . to my chagrin. I took the liberty of having one brought out . . . very circumspect, of course. You'll find it all set up and waiting for you down at the gate, with enough wire to run far beyond here out into the field if you care to."

Reisman accepted the inevitable gracefully, though he didn't really want a phone. They were noisemaking, bothersome things that never let a man do his work. "That was very thoughtful of you, Stuart," he said. "I *had* wanted to telephone my girl and find out how she was."

"Well, I had hoped it would be used for something more serious than that."

"For instance?"

"Keeping in touch with headquarters in London."

"Stuart . . . this is headquarters. You're sitting in it."

"Yes . . . I suppose it is," acknowledged Kinder wearily. "Where do I bunk, incidentally? You have room for me, I hope."

Reisman hadn't planned on him staying around very long—but then again, he hadn't expected him either. Maybe it would be a good thing. He could certainly use another man to ease the work load on himself and the guard detail, if he could keep Kinder from upsetting things —and there were some questions troubling him that maybe Kinder could provide the answers to.

"You can sleep right in here, Stu," he said. "I think you'll be comfortable."

"No, that's very kind of you, but I certainly don't intend taking your bed away from you."

"I don't use it," explained Reisman.

"But where do you sleep?"

"Out in a puptent in the compound with the prisoners."

Kinder hesitated but a moment and then, as though throwing all caution boldly to the four winds, he said, "Then, if you don't mind, I'll do the same. If I'm to learn as much as I have to learn about the progress of our little group, then I ought to share as much of your experience as I can . . . within limits, of course."

Up close the prisoners now appeared more fearsome to Kinder than they had before, and yet outwardly they were behaving as Reisman had said they were. He watched them as they ended their day's training in the compound, pitched their tents and dug rain trenches with speed and efficiency, and stood Retreat. They were ramrod stiff, saluted well and had their eyes fixed on the flag respectfully. Luis Jimenez handled the colors, Reisman having explained to Kinder that each day he granted one of them this privilege.

Kinder ate K-rations with Reisman and the men, passing up the offer of a hot meal in the barracks with the guards. He confessed *sotto voce* that he had never had the opportunity to eat iron rations such as these before, and therefore welcomed the experience, particularly since he understood that K-rations were much maligned by enlisted personnel, felt it his duty to try it, and really should have long before.

"Not bad," he commented, chewing each mouthful long and carefully. "I can't see what they gripe about."

It began to rain.

"Hope you came prepared," said Reisman.

"Yes. I left my gear in the car. I'll only be a minute," said Kinder, moving toward the barracks.

"Hope you brought fatigues, too."

"Yes, I did."

"Better put them on now, Stu."

"To sleep in? Don't be silly. I've got pajamas."

"To hike in," said Reisman. "Working hours aren't over yet."

Reisman gathered the prisoners and guards in the barracks, everybody wearing rain gear and light field packs. The tents were left standing. In the close, damp quarters, Stuart Kinder wrinkled his nose distastefully. There was, indeed, a rather pungent and unpleasant onslaught of body odors.

"This will be a night reconnaissance patrol, and you'll be on your own," Reisman announced to the prisoners. "Captain Kinder, the guard detail and I will go along merely as observers and to see that you don't get into any mischief. You're to solve any problems that come up yourselves. The purpose of the exercise is to demonstrate your proficiency in map-reading and compass."

Kinder noticed how the guards ringed the prisoners—casual but alert, weapons ready for instant action. Three of them seemed to be missing—the Corporal and two of the MPs. He stared at Sergeant Morgan and felt a shiver. Odd fellow. There was one he'd love to subject to the minutest psychological scrutiny. He wondered how his presence was affecting the prisoners.

Reisman took out a terrain map of the estate he had drawn himself and spread it on a table. His finger followed the course of a red line he had drawn on a transparent grid overlay. "This is the route you will take. The object of your mission is to verify the accuracy of the terrain along your route of march as drawn on this map, or to refute it and come back with corrections marked on the overlay. It should be easy for you . . . you've been over the same terrain enough times already. Gilpin, you take command of the group and issue all necessary orders of march and deployment." He would have liked to have made it Napoleon White as a more dramatic illustration for Kinder, but he couldn't show favorites. He had to give the others a chance—and Gilpin, too, had good potentials. "Sawyer, you're Number Two man. Posey, you're Number Three. Bring up the rear and keep them moving fast." He checked his wristwatch. "You ought to be out and back here in less than two and a half hours."

"I don't have a watch, sir," said Gilpin.

"Captain Kinder, may I borrow yours?" asked Reisman.

"Of course," said Kinder, flustered. He handed it over and Reisman gave it to Gilpin.

"All right, Gilpin, take over. They're all yours," declared Reisman.

Gilpin hesitated a moment. "It's probably none of my business Captain," he said, "but where's the Corporal and the other two guards? They off tonight?"

"That's right, Gilpin," said Reisman. "It's none of your business. Let's move out the troops."

Following them out, Reisman halted Kinder and whispered, "Don't worry about the watch, Stu. They didn't get him for stealing." He unslung his submachine gun and held it out. "Can you handle one of these?"

"Never used one."

"Well, just put it on, anyway," said Reisman. "They'll never know the difference."

Stumbling along in the dark, noisy, rain-filled night, keeping the man up ahead of him just barely in sight, Victor Franko wasn't certain if the idea struck him just then because the time was beautifully opportune, or if it was just part of something bigger he'd been nursing for a long time. He hadn't really thought seriously about escape for days, though the idea was always present as a taunt lurking somewhere in the fringes of his mind. He believed the Captain when he said there was no escape: he said it often enough and made the penalties terribly clear.

But finding himself momentarily alone, it hit Franko how easy it might be to disappear—to just drop down into a ravine and stay there, or lay low behind some brush, or go off in a direction of his own choosing—not to stay, but just to go through the motions of it, goof off, test it and see how far he could get without getting caught, and join the others on the return route when they came back near the stockade. He'd never be missed. They were spread out in a thin pattern with him somewhere near the middle. The Captain and the guards were way out on the flanks and in the rear. Even if he was caught—after all, he wasn't really trying to escape—all he had to say was he got lost in the dark. How would he know for sure he couldn't escape if he didn't try?

He dropped into a ravine, but instead of coming up the other side and following the patrol, he moved off along the defile toward the manor house, stopping momentarily hidden among some brush, holding his breath and feeling exultant as the last of the prisoners and guards stumbled past through the wet night.

The manor house—and the woman. He figured he could make it there and back in plenty of time. If any of the men saw he was missing, they'd cover for him just like he'd cover for one of them. If the Captain or one of the guards missed him then it was just tough titty—he'd be back in his own good time.

He'd tell the woman up there at the house he was on some special mission—taking special training. Sure, he didn't look so good—but, what the hell, there was a war on, wasn't there, and everything for the boys in uniform. Here he was out busting his back on a night like this. All he wanted to do was talk to her, see how nice it was inside her house. Maybe she'd offer him a drink or give him something decent to eat. Maybe more . . . maybe more, and Jesus Christ the thought of it started him running so he wouldn't lose time and miss out, tripping frequently over unseen obstacles and smashing into the ground, oblivious to brush grabbing at his legs, higher growth whipping into his face as he tore by . . . feeling only a bigger ache, tasting victory already and the unimaginable joy of putting one over on *them* as he saw the dark shape of the big house through the wind-lashed rain and started across the driveway . . .

Corporal Bowren hit him so hard and fast, he never saw him coming. Franko was suddenly on the ground, his teeth grinding against the gravel of the driveway, his right arm twisted painfully high up on his back, and then he felt, above the cold of the soaking rain, the ice-touch of gunsteel pressed into his neck.

"Don't move, Franko!" ordered Bowren. "And don't even think of any of that judo we've been teaching you."

Suddenly Franko was whining. "Please, Corporal, don't! I got lost. I didn't know where I was going! I didn't know what I was doing! Honest to God, I didn't!"

"You've had it, buddy! You're finished here, you lousy bastard!" Bowren said. "Now you'll get what's coming to you. Get on your feet!" He let go of Franko's arm and backed away from him slowly, keeping the .45 on him. "That's it . . . nice and easy . . . and don't make one wrong move or you won't live to be hanged! Oh, buddy . . . you and your pal Morgan were just made for each other . . . now you'll be going somewhere together, all right!"

"No . . ." gasped Franko.

"Yes, you yellow-bellied, sneaking son-of-a-bitch!" Bowren spat at him. "After all the Captain's done for you . . . after all you've been told . . . you try to get away!"

"No! Honest! You got it wrong, Bowren!" pleaded Franko. "So help me God I wasn't tryin ta get away. Lemme go back! Jus lemme go back an catch up with em! You take me back if you wanna! Nobody'll know the difference!"

"Start moving toward the stockade, Franko," ordered Bowren. "We'll wait for Captain Reisman there."

Franko fell to his knees on the gravel driveway in the rain and he begged, "Please! Doan tell the Captain! Please doan tell the Captain! You know what he'll do! He'll send me back! Morgan! They'll put me in that room! He'll put a

261

rope around my neck. He'll hang me! Please! I'll do anythin ya say . . . anythin ya wahn me t'do!"

In that moment, Bowren wanted him to die . . . to disappear as though he'd never been. He was filled with revulsion for him and fought an overwhelming urge to sock him . . . to explode the .45 in his face and end it right there!

The moment passed . . . he could do neither. The instant of heat, the passion of action waned, leaving cold pity and contempt . . . diminishing, too, the certain conviction of duty. It hit Bowren sickeningly that the power of life and death had been passed suddenly to him. He wiped irritably at the rain streaming into his eyes and face, he strained to know what was right, he stared at Franko, seeing him at the end of the rope—dead and ghastly as he had seen the others.

"One chance," he said softly. "That's all you get from me, Franko. Never again! I didn't see you. I don't know anything. Get on your feet and take off fast. Find the others and stay with them."

Franko ran and Bowren watched him. He knew the awesome responsibility of the Captain, and he didn't want it!

Stuart Kinder stood at the stockade entrance with Reisman counting the prisoners through. They were all there, though at times on the march they had been so spread out Kinder had never been certain, and in fact had been rather concerned but hadn't wanted to interfere and say anything. He had worried, too, about using the submachine gun if circumstances had made it necessary. Would he have had the courage . . . sense of duty . . . anger . . . or whatever it was that enabled a man to pull the trigger with intent to hurt or kill? Against an armed enemy—yes, he was sure he could. But against any of these twelve?

Reisman glanced at his watch. "Not too bad," he commented, "provided they found all the errors I put on that map." He took a signal pistol from his pack and fired a flare high into the rain-filled, cloudy sky toward the sea.

"What's that for?" asked Kinder, startled.

"The lambs are safely home," said Reisman. "There's a cold, wet MP cursing me out down on the beach, another one at the far end of the property. Corporal Bowren's between here and the main gate. Which reminds me . . .

I don't have a TO for this outfit. I want you to fix it so I can give Bowren another stripe."

"Be glad to," said Kinder. "Write it up and I'll have it put through soon as I get back to London."

In the barracks Kinder followed with interest the debriefing of the prisoners. They stood around a table on which the terrain map lay. Glenn Gilpin, as patrol leader, reported for the group but took great pains to comment on how well they all behaved on the hike and stressed the contributions made to the corrected map by various of the men. He seemed embarrassed and reluctant in his role of leader, though he had apparently performed it well.

Reisman let them lounge around the barracks, smoke and talk afterward. Coffee was brewed and a box of cookies opened and passed around. To Stuart Kinder it all seemed very pleasant and reassuring, except that the guards still stood apart, watching, weapons ready, and there was none of the easy banter and laughter among the men that might have characterized a more normal outfit after a night training mission.

Reisman took Kinder aside. "Understand, Stu, we don't have these pleasant little *Kaffeeklatsches* every night. If you want to work with them, you can have them in about fifteen minutes. The pick-me-up ought to make them more amenable."

"Tonight!" said Kinder incredulously. "Don't you let them sleep? It's too . . ." He started to glance at his wrist.

"Gilpin . . . the watch," Reisman called out.

"Much obliged, sir," said Gilpin, hurrying over in embarrassment and handing it to Kinder. "Hope the rain didn't hurt it."

Kinder waited for him to go back with the others. "It's too late for anything I'd want them for," he told Reisman, strapping on the watch. "I'm tired . . . I'm sure they're tired. They'd have to be mentally sharp. I can work with them tomorrow, if it's all right with you."

"Fine, then you can help me with one of *my* tests now."

"Tests? Now? Not you, too?"

"I guess I caught it from you," said Reisman, smiling. He explained about the nightly written exams he gave the prisoners to make sure they were really paying attention to lectures and absorbing the material.

"Excellent, John, excellent," said Kinder. "You've kept

them, I hope . . . to note progress, improvement, that sort of thing."

"Sure."

"Good. That's wonderful. I must have copies for my own records."

They sat in the little office later, after the prisoners turned in and the night watch was set. Kinder was exhausted, filthy, wet and wanted more than anything a hot bath and sleep—but when, after checking the tests together, Reisman said, "Let's talk," Kinder rose to the occasion, determined to be as indefatigable in his energies as Reisman was in his.

The bath was out, of course, though he earnestly wished now that Reisman had extended his liaison with the manor house to the point where room and bath would have been available. After all, he understood that in that entire mansion there was only one solitary woman in residence. What a waste! He could look forward only to a hot shower—the guards had promised to keep the water heater going for him—and afterward, no doubt, a case of pneumonia caught dashing back into the barracks from the outside shower booth. Before dismissing them finally for the night, Reisman had casually suggested to the prisoners they might like to shower and shave after so strenuous a day—for his illustration, Kinder supposed—but they had stuck together and declined, though Kinder was certain a few of them did so extremely reluctantly. On a cold, wet night like this, Kinder could easily see the merit of their refusal. He somewhat regretted, too, his rash announcement that he would share a puptent and the hard ground with Captain Reisman. He would have preferred, after the last few strenuous hours, to have stayed right there in the damp, leaky barracks.

"Tell me, Stuart," said Reisman. "In all your psychological and sociological mumbo-jumbo, is there some way by which you can divine innocence?"

"You ask me that in all seriousness, I take it," replied Kinder irritably. He was tired of being baited.

"Yes."

"Then your phrasing is certainly not calculated to win friends and influence people," Kinder said. "Matter of fact, it's insulting. You're entitled to your opinion, John, but

264

psychology and sociology are not mumbo-jumbo. Also, your choice of words is rather poor. There are tools, yes, by which the probability of guilt or innocence might be evaluated, but they're only indicative at best, certainly not exact and foolproof. And in referring to these tools, whether they be a combination of searching interviews and projective and associative tests, or the use of a so-called lie detector, which is not my field, or narcoanalysis, which might be done by a qualified psychiatrist, I certainly wouldn't use the word *divine*. That belongs to the Chaplains Corps, not my department. It belongs to the world of myth, magic and religion . . . and there is great value in all of them . . . but not to the world of science."

"Thanks for the lecture. Now give me a simple answer in basic English. Is it possible to figure out if a guy is telling the truth when he keeps saying he's innocent of a crime, even if the evidence is loaded against him?"

"Yes . . . but not conclusively."

"Then I want you to set up whatever is necessary for Myron Odell."

"Why only Odell? Why not the others? I think they all pleaded innocent at their trials."

"Yes, but that was only a formality . . . part of the machinery of military justice . . . that's what the rulebook says they're supposed to do in major offenses against the Articles of War. Odell still insists he's innocent. He's bugging everybody with it. He's bugging me."

"Some of the others still claim they're innocent too, don't they? I know Franko and Maggot did."

"Okay, if you want to, set it up for them too. Maybe we'll get some surprises."

"You know about Franko, don't you?"

"As much as any of the others," answered Reisman casually. He knew Franko well. "According to the court-martial transcript, he shot and killed an English gentleman who caught him poaching on his property—though he's never admitted it, insists he didn't intend to do it, it was an accident. Strange thing is, from the setup, it well might have been. But with his record going against him, he didn't stand much of a chance. You remember General Worden telling us about the five thousand ex-cons who came over on the *Empress of Scotland*. He's one of them."

"And Maggot?"

"Says he was mousetrapped by a prostitute, so it wasn't

really rape. He's a mean son-of-a-bitch and probably deserves hanging for half a dozen things he's never been caught at, but any man could probably be held for legal rape at some point in his life. That's a tough one to define."

"No, it isn't," Kinder contended. "The law is as specific about it as psychology is."

"And what does psychology say?"

"Don't tell me you're really interested?" asked Kinder doubtfully.

"Sure. If I've got to live with these guys, play housemother to them, and make something out of them, I want to know what's bugging them."

"What's bugging them is something else again," explained Kinder. "All I can tell you about is how they act . . . their behavior patterns. There are three different kinds of rapists. There's the man whose pent-up sexual impulse suddenly explodes and he commits assault. He's the true sex offender. There's the sadist. His aggressive sex life becomes so exaggerated he loses control and it takes over. And there's the man who's more a working criminal than a true sex offender. He'll rob or kill or rape and it's all the same to him."

"All nicely categorized," said Reisman.

"Yes, all nicely categorized. I'd say Maggot probably fits into that last category. Probably Franko too . . . even though they didn't get him for rape this time."

"You haven't answered me yet, Stu," Reisman prompted. "Will you do what I ask?"

"I don't think we ought to, John."

"Why not?"

"It's just not within our authority, that's all. The question of their guilt or innocence was decided long before they got here. Otherwise, they wouldn't be here. And it was decided by more competent authority than we."

"Coming from you, Stu, I would imagine that should convince me . . . but it doesn't. There were still reviews pending. I guess I want to be convinced beyond any doubt . . . because of what we're doing here . . . because of the danger . . . not only in the missions, but now in the training. Particularly with Odell."

"There was a confession, you know."

"Yes, I read it. It was appended to the trial record. But

that was after days of questioning . . . and later he repudiated it."

"On the advice of counsel."

"Maybe. But he's a strange one . . . weak, cowardly, terrified of life . . . and probably more of death and physical pain, but he's changing, too." Reisman revealed to Kinder some of the disturbing incidents in which Odell had been involved.

"How did he act after what he did to Maggot?"

"Terrified. He's gone out of his way to be friendly ever since, but Maggot's carrying a big grudge. It only happened yesterday. We've got to watch them closely whenever they work together. Maggot's raring to get back at him. He'd probably kill him under ordinary circumstances. It was strange . . . Odell seemed to black out and become a completely different person . . . someone actually capable of killing . . . and then when he came to he had no memory of it."

"It's not unusual," said Kinder. "It could have been what happened with the girl in Glasgow."

"Maybe. But I want to be sure," insisted Reisman. "And if he really did murder her, I want him to know it beyond any doubt and face up to it. It'll make a better man of him . . . maybe even make my job easier."

"All right," said Kinder reluctantly. "If it will help you, I'll see what I can work out. But I'm against it."

"On the q.t.," said Reisman.

"On the q.t. What other problems have you got?" He was warming to the task now, glad Reisman was opening up a little bit at last, glad for the opportunity to talk.

"You still have no word on how these men are to be used . . . what their ultimate mission will be?"

"No."

"Nor even whether it will be individual missions as Colonel Denton indicated at the briefing, or one mission for the entire group?"

"No."

"Standard operating procedure," said Reisman acidly.

"You still have your doubts about them?"

"Doubts! I've had nothing but doubts since this business started."

"But you said they're working out, they're behaving," Kinder said nervously. He wondered if Reisman was holding something back from him.

"Sure they are," answered Reisman quickly. "You could see that yourself tonight. But how can I ever be sure? Any one of them could blow it any minute . . . who knows when? They aren't normal, and what we're doing with them here is neither punishment . . . they'd understand that . . . nor rehabilitation. We're using them and they know it. They could go through the whole damn period of training and blow it when we send them off to work for God and country. Maybe if I knew what they had to do in the end . . . what the point of the whole thing was . . . maybe I'd feel better about it."

"I wish I could help you there, but I can't . . . about the missions, I mean," said Kinder. "I could devise some sort of trustworthiness test, if you'd like."

"Trustworthiness test! What in hell would that be?" exploded Reisman, and it hit him in the same moment how damned tactless he was being, how offensive! "No . . . I'm sorry, Stu . . . I don't mean it like that. Go ahead and explain."

"It's been done before . . . a test to measure their tendency to abide by instructions without supervision or checkup."

"Sure, go ahead, Stu, if it's not putting you to too much trouble," said Reisman. He glanced at the time irritably. "Look, I've about had it. I've got a four-hour watch to pull at 0200. I'm going to hit the sack. Okay?"

"Sure. Do you want to use the shower first?"

"No, go ahead. Good night."

"Good night," said Kinder to Reisman's retreating back.

After his shower Kinder entered the prisoners' compound, shivering and cold. He smiled up at Corporal Bowren on the barracks roof and waved at the sentinels in the guardtowers, wondering what they thought of this whole business, what they thought of Captain Reisman, whether they regretted the harshness of their assignment. They stared back at him through the rain. Kinder felt rather ludicrous in flannel pajamas, trench coat and hat, his uniform bundled neatly under his arm, and Reisman's submachine gun hanging awkwardly from his shoulder.

In the puptent, Reisman was fast asleep, snoring, in a blanket bedroll. Kinder felt around quietly in the dark, found the sleeping bag he had brought down with him from London. It was a thick, down-filled officer's model he had bought at a famous sporting goods store in New York just before sailing, and had never used before. He had never slept in a puptent before, either. It was awkward, cold and damp. He finally settled down, zipping himself into the bag cozily, the submachine gun inside with him.

He couldn't sleep. He felt the criminal presence of the other men all around him in the other tents. He unzipped his sleeping bag and slid the weapon out. He still didn't really know how to use it. Maybe it would be better to put it on the ground between them so that Reisman could get to it in a hurry if he needed it. He did remember reading about various weapons at times, though. This particular one, he recalled, couldn't be fired unless the little hatch through which the cartridges were ejected was first raised. He ran his fingers along the gun. His eyes had adjusted to the dark so that he could just barely make out the various parts if he held it close to his face. He found the little hatch and pulled at it. It snapped, quite audibly! And almost in that same instant—so swiftly and incomprehensibly that he was filled with a fear such as he had never known before—there was Captain Reisman awake with a .45 automatic in his hand pointed at Kinder's head.

"Oh, no!" he blurted out hoarsely. "It's me! Kinder!"

"Yeah," acknowledged Reisman sleepily. He turned over and in moments was sleeping again as though nothing had happened.

Just before drifting off himself, after what seemed like hours of physical and mental discomfort, Kinder suddenly remembered the telephone. Captain Reisman had never had it strung to the barracks. It was still sitting out there in the rain.

—

19

—

REISMAN ARRANGED the prisoners' training schedule in the next few days so that Stuart Kinder could have each of them alone a number of times. As for giving an opinion on Odell, or any of the others, for that matter, that might convince him he should probe further into the question of guilt or innocence, Kinder insisted it would take many days of study after the tests, comparisons with norms and abnormals, and consultations with others in London. The psychological testing, he had intended to do anyway—all Reisman's request meant was that Kinder would now look for additional indices within the results.

Napoleon White was alternately bored and amused by his sessions with Kinder. It gave him a chance to goof off from the physical demands of training, but he wasn't really sure he wanted to do that anymore. He had found, to his chagrin, that there were aspects of the training that he enjoyed—maybe because they turned his mind outward again and set physical challenges for him to conquer as well or better than any of the others. He had always been an athlete, proud of his top conditioning, and the lack of muscle-toning activity for many weeks since his arrest and court-martial had made him feel soft and logy.

He wondered how long it would take for Kinder to see through the intentionally twisted performances he gave on the psychological tests, and call him down for it. When Kinder didn't, but continued to treat him with the properly professional, courteous and gentle aloofness he might also use toward a child, a mental deficient, or somebody completely ignorant of what was going on, it grated upon Napoleon even more.

The session Kinder started holding up the picture cards of the Thematic Apperception Test, asking him to recite little stories about what was going on in the pictures, Napoleon rebelled completely. "I don't see anything, Captain," he responded angrily. "It's all a lot of crap and nonsense. Whatever the hell you're trying to figure out, you're wasting your time on me."

"I don't think so, White," stated Kinder gently. "We really are trying to help you and the other men. Why don't you just try to the best of your ability." He went on holding up the cards, his pen poised to take down Napoleon's stories verbatim.

Only when he held up the one completely blank white card, did Napoleon respond positively. His answer was vigorous and bitter. "It's black," he said. "A solid black piece of cardboard. Black as the ace of spades. Black as a nigger in a coal bin at night."

"White, don't you appreciate at all what's being done for

you? The opportunity you've been given?" asked Kinder wearily. "You're a clever man . . . an educated man . . . don't think any of this nonsense you've been pulling has fooled me for one moment. However, in this particular area, I think I know more than you do. Even those phony answers you gave to the Rorschach up at the prison were indicative to me. Obviously you were familiar with it and thought you'd have some fun at my expense like a college sophomore. You've got enough hostility in you to take on the whole German Army, I'll bet. Why don't you ease it off? It can destroy you, you know. Why don't you co-operate like the man you really are? What is it that's bugging you, anyway?"

"Same thing that put me in here, Captain. None of it's changed." He tapped the picture cards with one hand. "You and the great brains that cook up these things start putting black men and women in these pictures and I'll give you some stories that'll curl your hair or make you puke!"

For Myron Odell the picture cards opened a great door to his most private and innermost self. So much that he had wanted to reveal about himself to others could now come out safely without fear of ridicule or reprisal, in the form of made-up stories.

Captain Kinder had said to him, "Take as much time as you like for each card, and tell me as much as you can possibly imagine about what is going on in the picture, who the people are . . . their backgrounds and futures if you have thoughts concerning them."

There was a close-cropped drawing of a woman's head against a man's shoulder, part of each face illuminated out of darkness by slanting bold light . . . "They are very much in love," said Odell. "It is a very tender moment. The woman has just told her husband that she is going to have a baby. They are very happy."

A woman sat sideways on a chair, her arms resting on its back, her chin cupped in one hand; part of her body was obscured by the chair back and a garment thrown over it; she was staring off into space. This was a card meant for girls and women, but Kinder was curious about Odell's reaction . . . "This is the same woman from the other card. She is resting after a hard day's work at home. She is waiting for her husband, whom she loves very much, to come home from work. She is thinking of the joy of having a baby. She loves the baby very much, even though he is not born yet."

In another drawing, a woman was standing on the threshold of a room, her hand on the knob of the door. She wore a somewhat shocked expression on her face, as though something she saw in that room had startled her. Odell was very slow in responding.

"Well, what do you see, Myron?" asked Kinder, gently.

"A woman standing on the threshold of a room, her hand on the knob of the door."

"Yes, but what does she see, what is she thinking, where has she come from, has she said anything, is she about to say anything? Is she a young woman or an old woman? Who or what is in the room?"

"I don't know."

"Can't you come up with anything at all? You've done very well, you know. I'm quite pleased with the answers you've given me so far, Myron."

Odell smiled. "Well, I want to help all I can," he said. "I don't know what this all means, but I want to be cooperative. I guess the only way people are going to believe I'm innocent is if I do everything I'm told, and don't get into any more trouble. All these tests you've been giving me . . . can they prove I'm telling the truth I didn't kill that girl?"

"Do you really believe you're innocent . . . that you've been wrongly convicted, Myron?" asked Kinder, staring directly into his eyes.

"I don't *believe* it, sir," answered Odell, "I *know* it. It's the truth."

"Let's get back to the picture card," insisted Kinder quickly. "Is the expression on the woman's face a happy one?"

"No . . . I don't think so."

"What is it then?"

"I don't know."

"Why don't you take a guess, Myron? I know you're tired, but you're doing so well, it would be a shame to stop."

"Shame, maybe . . . yes, maybe she feels shame. That could be it."

"Why?"

"I don't know," insisted Odell, shrugging his shoulders and looking away.

Kinder flipped to the next card. They were numbered, but he had not kept them in any particular order and, in fact, had tried to rearrange them differently for each interview. This particular card was almost totally black, except for an open window in which was silhouetted the figure of a youth . . . "He's been punished," said Odell. "He has to stay in that dark room all alone. He'd like to go out, but he can't. He has to stay there."

"Why?"

"Because he's been punished."

"What for?"

"I don't know."

"Who is he? What kind of a boy is he?"

"Well, I don't know who he is. He could be anybody. And he really isn't a boy anymore. He's growing up, you know what I mean . . . he's a teen-ager, I guess . . . maybe a little younger. Anyway, that's the way he looks to me."

"Would he jump out of that window?" asked Kinder. "Would he try to escape?"

"Oh, no!" exclaimed Odell. "It's too dangerous. He couldn't. He just has to stay there."

Kinder flipped cards and Odell blanched and turned his head away. "Oh, my God!" he cried.

"What's the matter?" asked Kinder with great concern.

"It's awful! Just awful! I won't look at it!" gasped Odell.

It was a drawing of a young man standing with downcast head pressed against his arm. Behind him on a bed a woman lay sprawled, her arm dropped to the floor, her face darkly shadowed, her high, full breasts thrust naked above the blanket.

"What's awful about it?" asked Kinder softly.

"She's dead! You're trying to trick me!"

"No, Myron. Not at all," said Kinder soothingly. "It's just a drawing like the others. Tell me about it."

"No. I can't."

"Why not?" Kinder was writing as he spoke. Odell's head was averted and he had his hand over his face.

"I don't want to look at it again. It makes me feel sick."

Tuesday afternoon Reisman brought the ten prisoners he had with him in from the field early to pick up Maggot and Jimenez. They had been left at the stockade for interviews with Kinder. Sergeant Morgan and an MP had stayed to guard them. As they rejoined the group passing through the barracks into the inner compound, Reisman saw Maggot and Jimenez make finger-twirling motions at their heads and grin sarcastically at the other prisoners. It made him wonder how seriously they all took their sessions with Kinder. They apparently liked him and respected him. A few even seemed to hold him in that same awe of respect reserved for doctors, lawyers and official representatives of God. There had certainly been no untoward incidents with Kinder. But who knew what really was going on in the minds of these characters? He figured Kinder might by now.

Reisman turned the prisoners over to Sergeant Morgan and Corporal Bowren, with instructions to keep them busy for a while in the compound with hand-to-hand workouts, calisthenics and close-order drill. He knew Morgan would like that. He was actually becoming fairly proficient in giving marching orders, breaking the men up into squads and directing them into unpredictable patterns and directions that seemed as though they'd never come out right at the end, but always did, probably because the prisoners themselves were developing a zealousness to excel.

Through a window in the office, Reisman kept his eye on the men and talked with Kinder. Reisman was sprawled on the cot, smoking a cigaret. Kinder sat relaxed in the one chair. The desk was covered with neat piles of his work.

"Tell me about it," said Reisman, waving a hand at the desk. "Or is it top secret?"

"No, of course not," said Kinder, smiling. "Although what you say isn't as far-fetched as you might think. I've heard of cases in my own branch, Psychological Warfare . . . particularly in Washington . . . where plans were classified so secret they were never revealed to the men at the operational level who were supposed to execute them."

Reisman cringed. "Stuart . . . don't use that word *execute* around here," he said, trying to sound offhand. "It has such a nasty connotation."

"Oh . . . I'm sorry. I didn't think anything bothered *you*."

"It's getting through," said Reisman softly. He changed the subject quickly. "Speaking of Psychological Warfare . . . this isn't the only project you're on now, is it? I mean I know you haven't been spending all your time on it since we met, so I figure you must have other duties."

"I do . . . I've got an office back in London where I have some plans and studies going. But nothing," he said with relish, "as important as this. Nothing as exciting!" He looked concerned suddenly. "You're not suggesting I've overstayed my welcome, are you?"

"Heck no!" answered Reisman quickly. He meant it, too, now. "I'm glad to have the help you've been giving me. What about this stuff?" he said impatiently, waving at the papers on the desk again. "Find anything?"

"You mean about Odell?"

"All of them. Any of them."

"It's hard to tell about Odell," said Kinder. "His responses bear out what you've said about him. Also, I hate to say it but he's either a latent homosexual or . . ."

"There!" said Reisman, jumping up excitedly. "How the hell could a homo rape a girl?"

"It's been done," said Kinder matter-of-factly. "You can't jump at things like that. He hasn't shown any signs of it around here, has he? If he has, I'd get rid of him. That spells trouble, but good, in any prison situation."

"Hell, I don't know what goes on in his tent at night . . . but I'd say there wasn't anything like that going on. He isn't much of a man, but I wouldn't say he was a working fairy."

"There, you see!" said Kinder. "You're grabbing at straws. In the space of ten seconds you've jumped in swinging on both sides of diametrically opposite conditions, proved nothing and resolved nothing. Let me fi—"

"An old habit of mine," said Reisman, smiling. "The logic of the uneducated and uninformed."

"Let me finish what I started to say," insisted Kinder. "He's either a latent homosexual or he spends so much conscious time worrying about his manhood he sounds like one, or maybe there's a bit of both traits there. Also, there are blank spots in his responses . . . particularly in reference to violence. I'd say he has a habit of running away from reality, escaping to fantasy. He's probably easily swayed and he's got no id . . . no real self to speak of."

"Could a man like that commit murder?"

"Consciously, I'd say not . . . Unconsciously, yes. You've already had one example of that."

Reisman got up and paced the floor nervously. "More important then . . . could he kill as a soldier? The hell with his guilt or innocence! Will he fight? Is he going to do his job under fire or run?"

"I'm not a prophet, John," answered Kinder with deep concern. "You're the one that's got to weigh the probabilities for us when the time comes . . . and for him too. For all of them. That's *your* job. Odell's neurotic, unstable, immature, under great internal and external tensions . . . maybe he's psychotic, I'm not sure. In a month . . . two months . . . depending upon what you do with him, what he does for himself, it can still go either way. That's only a quick, offhand opinion, though. I'll follow through as I said, if you want me to."

"Sure, go ahead," said Reisman. "*¿Quién sabe?*"

He squashed out his cigaret butt in a tin can and got up to leave. "Better get back to the troops," he said.

That night Reisman wanted to leave the stockade so badly he could taste it. He argued with himself that he couldn't, that he had no right to. Then he argued with himself on the other side that he hadn't really allowed himself any rest, and certainly no relaxation, for ten days, since they had come to Stokes Manor. Each of the guard detail had been out one or more times and he surmised and hoped that they had struck up suitable liaisons in the villages and countryside of South Devonshire. How the hell the prisoners stood it without some softness and beauty in their lives . . . without release . . . he didn't know. It was, of necessity, a de facto part of their punishment. He knew he'd have to ease up on them soon . . . introduce some sort of leisure activities . . . basket-weaving or some such nonsense, he supposed.

Finally he went to Stuart Kinder after Taps had sounded and asked, "How do you feel about taking full command of the camp overnight? I don't have any watch to pull tonight and I'd like to get away for a while."

"I thought you didn't trust me," replied Kinder. He smiled to take the sting out of it, for he believed he understood Reisman.

"I trust you in this way," said Reisman. It rankled him to be on the defensive.

"I would be honored, Captain," continued Kinder sarcastically.

"Oh, knock it off, Stu," snapped Reisman. He smiled too, now. "You know you're just dying to get rid of me and take over the whole operation."

"That I have sense enough to know I can't do. When will you be back?"

"I should be here by 1300 tomorrow. The duty roster and training schedule are all made up. Bowren and Morgan and the MPs know their jobs, and our charming charges know their place in life by now, I believe. I've got the schedule set up so they won't have to leave the stockade until I get back. Okay?"

"Okay," said Kinder, winking. "Have fun."

Reisman showered and shaved, dressed in a clean uniform, and put his toilet kit and a few items of clothing in a small bag. "I'll talk to Bowren and Morgan on the way out," he said to Kinder when he was ready to leave. "I think it will be best if the men don't know I'm away. Let them think I'm working in here or out on the downs or the beach somewhere cooking up some new hardships for them."

"I understand," said Kinder, "Goodbye."

He had to stop at the front gate to open it, and it was this act in itself, he told himself, that made him look up the driveway toward the manor house and think momentarily of Margot Strathallan. He drove the jeep out, closed the gate, gave an Italian salute in her direction and squeezed both her and the Dirty Dozen from his mind with thoughts of Tess Simmons.

He stopped in Stokesmouth and telephoned Tess from a public house. Whatever adolescent trembling and awkwardness he felt in the uncertainty of what her reaction would be, or whether she would even really be there, was swept away by her cry of pure joy.

"I've missed you so. Where are you?"

"I can be there in two or three hours," he said. "Depending on the roads, the traffic, and your bloody English weather."

"Come quickly," she said. "Fly like the wind . . . I love

277

you . . . I want you so much . . . No, John, drive carefully . . . please . . . I don't care how long it takes . . . just
come to me."

"Shameless hussy," he whispered into the phone, feeling
foolish at making love like this in a public place through
an inanimate object.

"Yes," she said. "I'll be waiting for you. Goodbye."

He drove fast, but not recklessly, feeling like the high-
wayman of Alfred Noyes's beautifully sad poem, riding,
riding, riding down a ribbon of moonlight to his one true
love. Though there was no moon. It was dark and wet
through Devonshire into Somerset, and that was just as
well. There'd be no stray Luftwaffe out taking potshots at
stray lovers moving on the English roads.

Tess greeted him as she had done that first night of the
execution—with a fire going for them in the dark, empty
taproom, with books she had been reading to keep her
awake, and with a steaming mug that was fire of rum,
blaze of cider, ignited by sticks of cinnamon. She wore the
robe he had bought her. Before they even got before the
fire, they grasped at each other hungrily and kissed again
and again. Reisman felt the tension drain from him and
knew that even this with nothing more, with nothing of sex,
would be enough. It was the feeling of hearth and home
that she generated, and the feeling of wanting only him.

"Oh, how I've missed you, how I've missed you," she
whispered. "Why didn't you write? Why didn't you
telephone?"

"I couldn't," he said, and knew it was a lame excuse.

"It was not knowing that was worst of all," she went on,
clinging to him. "Not knowing really when you would
come again . . . or if you would."

"I told you I would," he said, "and I've driven half the
night to prove it."

"I believe you now," she said, pulling away, leading him
to the fireplace, her eyes glowing happily.

They had their drink and he told her he was stationed
now in Devonshire, that he'd thought of her often and
wished she was there.

"Is there an address? I've never had a boy in the Forces
I could write to."

"I think not," he said. "I do have a London address for

278

mail, but this place where I am is rather isolated, and by the time a letter reached me from London, I'd probably turn up here again. I'll tell you what, though. I promise to telephone you at least once a week from now on. How's that? And drive up every chance I can."

"Then I'm really your girl?" she said softly.

"Yes."

When they made love, in that same room where he'd stayed before, she overwhelmed him with her need and passion and drove every other remaining thing and person from his mind.

20

REISMAN FOUND himself alone in his room at The Butcher's Arms when he woke up Wednesday morning. It was almost nine o'clock. He shaved and dressed hurriedly and went downstairs. Tess, looking radiant, was already at work between the kitchen and the public room where some people, military and civilian, were breakfasting. He didn't quite know how to greet her, but she solved it for him by coming to him, flushed, and taking his hand.

"I didn't have the heart to wake you," she whispered. "Should I have?"

"It's all right," he said. "I have a little time. Can you have breakfast with me?"

"I have to work," she answered. "What would you like?"

"Coffee, to start with, and a telephone."

She led him to the phone and, alone for a moment, he kissed her as he had wanted to do. Then he turned her around, pointed her toward the kitchen, and said, "Coffee . . . good and hot . . . lots of it."

It took awhile for the civilian and military hookups to be made, and while he waited impatiently Reisman had fleeting, guilty thoughts about one of the prisoners or all of them picking last night or this morning to create some new trouble or try to break out or in some way take advantage of poor Kinder. Then Kinder answered the phone, assured him everything was perfectly fine, and kidded him about behaving like a mother hen.

Tess served him his breakfast, and then nothing would do but he had to chat with her uncle, whom he had met formally that last week end he had stayed there; and with Mrs. Culver, the cook, who clucked over him and told him how much like a daughter Tess was to her. He wondered how much they knew about Tess and him.

Then it was time to go. Tess walked outside with him to the jeep. It was cool and windy, but there was good, yellow sunlight. The sky held promise and threat of almost any type of weather to come, with mountains of clouds piled high here and there on the horizons and the wind scudding cumulus squadrons at lower altitudes across spaces of blue. Tess wore the coat she had worn that first night of discovery. Her hand was under his arm and he covered it protectively with his own, rubbing it, intertwining their fingers in reluctant parting.

"Is this the spring your poets write about?" Reisman joked.

"Oh no," she said. "There's a saying, 'It ain't spring until you can plant your foot upon twelve daisies.' "

"Then we'll go out and look for them each time I come."

"I'd like that very much, John," she said. "And if I find them one day when you're not here, I'll mark the place and take you there . . . where I found spring."

He kissed her softly, with his hand on her cheek, said goodbye and drove away, turning just once to see her watching him and waving.

He had always had this facility for quickly wiping his mind clean, changing perspectives to meet new demands, almost instantaneously readjusting his thinking to meet what lay ahead—yet the glow of Tess stayed with him all the way back to Stokes Manor, while he began to turn over in his mind the afternoon's work, and his arrival there at the gates seemed even more of an ugly letdown by comparison.

Pleasantries between him and Kinder were quickly gotten through, as Reisman changed into his fatigues. Everything had been routine, and Kinder was now eager to get away himself and drive back to London.

"I've done about as much as I can this trip down," he said. "I'd like to observe the men training a while longer this afternoon, discuss a few things with you, and get off before dark. I've even learned to operate this thing," he said, handing over Reisman's submachine gun as though it was a token surrendering of his command. "Corporal Bowren gave me some private weapons instruction back in the woods for a few minutes this morning. Makes a lot of noise, doesn't it? I agree with you about Bowren. He does deserve more stripes. I'll add my own recommendation to yours when I get back to London."

"Fine. Why don't you hang onto this until you leave, Stu," Reisman suggested, handing the weapon back.

Kinder took it. "All right," he said, smiling. "It does lend one a certain jaunty air."

Within a few minutes of his arrival, Reisman ordered a formation in the compound, loaded up two of the MPs with rifles that had been stored in the barracks, took a couple himself, and went out to the prisoners. He was amazed at the shock effect—after only so brief an absence, and though he had no reason to be even surprised—to see and accept the prisoners' filthy, disheveled, smelly condition as anything resembling a military outfit. Yet they snapped to smartly when Sergeant Morgan—glowering, as was his usual condition now in lieu of terror—dressed them in two ranks and left them standing at parade rest. Stuart Kinder stood just inside the inner gate, observing.

Reisman faced the prisoners with one rifle slung on his shoulder, the other held in his hands. Woman-softness and sweet memory were gone as though they had never been. Tess Simmons was gone. There was only the very real immediacy of the men and him and the weapons. "You're about to be promoted from kindergarten to the first grade," he announced. His eyes darted among the men and settled on Vernon Pinkley. He was a thin man with a long neck and prominent Adam's apple and a matted shock of brown hair that fell over his eyes and ears. Reisman had hardly ever singled Pinkley out for anything before. He was generally taciturn by nature, volunteered nothing, and had done just what was expected of him and nothing more. "Mr. Pinkley!" Reisman called out.

Pinkley looked at him startled. "Yes, sir," he answered warily.

"What am I holding in my hands, Mr. Pinkley?"

"A gun."

"The hell it is!" snapped Reisman. His eyes darted elsewhere among the men. "Mr. Sawyer, what am I holding in my hands?"

"A rifle, sir! U.S. rifle, caliber .30, M1," said Sawyer. Not until he had gotten it all out did Sawyer realize he had snapped to attention, and he hoped the others didn't think he was trying to show up any of them, or was brown-nosing.

"That's right. Thank you," said Reisman. He turned back to Pinkley. "You've been in the Army better than two years, took basic training, learned how to use this piece, took advanced training, went on maneuvers, and theoretically paid attention to what I had to say about weapons all last week. Then how in hell can you still call this a gun?"

"Sorry, Captain," answered Pinkley in embarrassment. "I just didn't know what you meant."

Reisman held the rifle high in one hand. "None of you are recruits. Every one of you has handled this weapon before, and you've all heard the speech about you take care of it and it'll take care of you. It's the truth. Believe it. When I hand you this weapon, you're soldiers again, do you understand? The weapon is yours to use in an honorable way in defense of your country under orders from your superior officers. It is not a toy. It is not an object of personal vengeance. It is not a tool to be used in the commission of a crime."

He glanced down the rank. "Mr. Jimenez, what else can you tell me about this rifle?"

"You pull the trigger, somebody get in front of it, you kill him," said Jimenez laconically.

Some of them snickered, and Reisman realized he'd opened himself wide for that and there was only one way to end it. "¡Ven acá, Luis . . . pronto!" he ordered.

Jimenez stepped forward slowly, confused by Reisman's speaking to him in his family tongue.

"Take it!" Reisman ordered, holding out the rifle.

Jimenez took the piece reluctantly and stared at it glumly.

"Now turn around and tell your laughing friends what you did the last time you held an M1 in your hands!"

"No," said Jimenez, shaking his head.

Reisman grabbed Jimenez' right elbow with his left hand and spun him. He kept his right hand ready, pinky ridge stiffened, thumb out taut. "¡Digales lo que hizo, Jimenez!" he snapped.

Jimenez held the rifle loosely, glowered at the ground.

"Pick your head up and tell them like a man!" Reisman spat out. "Tell them how proud you are!"

"Maté un hombre," whispered Jimenez. His eyes were still downcast and his voice barely audible.

"You killed an unarmed officer, didn't you? You shot your superior officer for giving you orders in the legitimate performance of his duties! Isn't that right, General Jimenez? You shot and killed him because you thought you knew better than he did and wanted to prove it!"

"He was not unarmed," murmured Jimenez. "He had a gun."

"Was he threatening you with it?"

"No."

"Where did he have his gun?"

There was no answer.

Reisman slapped the .45 holster at his hip. "He had it here, didn't he?"

Reisman stood behind him, barking into his ear, watched him take it, watched him tremble and say nothing.

"If you ever point that rifle at anything or anyone you are not ordered to point it at, *amigo*," said Reisman softly, "I shall personally ram it up your ass and pull the trigger before they hang you! *¿Comprendame?*"

"Sí," replied Jimenez quietly.

"Now get the hell back in rank and keep your mouth shut unless you've got something worthwhile to contribute!" ordered Reisman. "Hold on a minute. Bowren, get the serial number of his rifle and have him sign for it."

When the other rifles had been issued, numbers recorded and vouchers signed, Reisman asked, "Who thinks he remembers the manual of arms well enough to demonstrate?"

Both Napoleon White and Ken Sawyer raised their hands. Reisman told them to step out and face the rest of the men, and had Bowren run them through it slowly a couple of times. They did very well. Reisman separated the prisoners into two squads, put Napoleon in charge of one, Sawyer in charge of the other, making sure Maggot was in Napoleon's squad.

"You've got half an hour to work on the manual," Reisman explained. "Then we'll have a little competition. Whichever squad does best gets a full night's sleep tonight.

The losers will have the honor of inaugurating a new phase of your training. The MPs tell me they're pretty lonely up in their towers at night. Beginning tonight, you men will start keeping them company and guarding yourselves by walking a post within the compound. A four-hour watch just like we pull, three men to a shift."

He left Bowren to police one squad, Morgan the other, and headed for the barracks. The prisoners had gotten through a night and morning without him and without trouble, and the more they worked willingly and hard now without the threat of his eyes upon them and his punishment hanging over them, the better they would all be for it.

"Quite a performance," said Kinder, opening the gate for him.

"Good or bad?"

"I liked it," acknowledged Kinder, following him into the headquarters room. "There's nothing like public confession to humble a man and make him regret his sins. And nothing like a little responsibility to give a good man his head."

"That was the easy part," said Reisman, dropping into the chair. "The day I've got to issue them ammunition is the one I worry about." He lit a cigaret, inhaled deeply and blew out a cloud of smoke.

Kinder stood at the window looking out and spoke without turning. "You know, one of the things I've been looking for is a clue to some additional mechanisms that will motivate each one of them in the same way to the same purpose."

"Ridiculous and impossible!" stated Reisman flatly. "They're not machines."

Kinder turned from the window, glowing, "Ah, but that's just the point! You'd be amazed at just how much like machines people are—with habits and actions and reactions and motivations that can be planned, scheduled, programed and twisted."

"Like Herr Schicklgruber?"

"The arch example and the most horrible. But even you have done it with this permissive attitude of yours toward their shaving and bathing. I agree with you . . . if it gives them a sense of belonging, some crazy sense of pride to be bearded and dirty, let them be for now. But there's got to be something more than that. Mother, God and Country certainly won't work for this bunch. Yet, if there's any single thing that stands out in all their personalities, it's that every one of them feels he's a failure—and you can't do much with that as a motivational mechanism. All we can do is work against it."

Reisman wondered what had become of the fiendishly clever and eager Lieutenant Kinder he had met in London less than three weeks before. "What about the individual?" asked Reisman. "Isn't that a better approach with this bunch? Reach the man inside, find out what makes him tick, get his blood and pride moving again, allow some of them initiative. Let the ones that can, lead sometimes, exert themselves, feel a little manhood and self flowing back into them in areas where they're qualified and competent."

"Yes, but that's where the danger lies, too . . . in *self!* . . . as it does with all of us. Too much *self* is what got them into trouble in the first place. None of them had that certain something, completely unselfish maybe, beyond themselves to drive them, carry them through, sustain them. Each was too selfish and wrapped within himself and it is *self* that destroys!"

"Then I am as guilty as they are . . . and I am not destroyed."

"Yes, I suppose you are," said Kinder, with an optimum mixture of diffidence and tact that was completely lost on Reisman.

"Then what would you suggest? Religion? Country? The pride that comes from seeing the flag on foreign soil, that makes strong men weep?"

"You're not likely to change any of their temperaments, you know," said Kinder, a sudden thought disturbing him and making him somewhat devious. "You can't."

"Why not?"

"In the first place, it would be impossible in so limited a time. In the second, it might not be a good idea. It wasn't really what we wanted in the beginning."

"I know. It was the bad ones you wanted. Let me quote. 'Their proven capability for viciousness is to be cultivated under rigid controls.' There's an anomaly and paradox in there somewhere, I'm sure."

"But you can change a trait or two in each of them," Kinder rambled on. "The dynamic traits that will respond to incentives. And you've got to change abilities. There's no question about that. And maybe attitudes . . . enough of each man's attitude so he'll behave himself now, learn his lessons well, and we'll have a fair idea which side of the war he's on. That's what you're doing, isn't it?"

"I'm sick of driving them, I'll tell you that much," Reisman snorted. "I'm not used to this sort of thing. I can do a dirty piece of work myself, I can lead if I have to, but I don't like driving."

"A few more rewards might help," Kinder threw in. "What would they like to do if they had any free time? I know they don't have any . . . well, maybe they ought to. There's a totality and complexity to human experience that they're thoroughly cut off from. As soldiers they were cut off from some of it anyway. And as prisoners they're cut off from most of the rest of it. Letting some of it back into their lives would make them less resentful, more willing to work hard, less likely to explode."

"They'll earn their time off . . . and their rewards," asserted Reisman. "As for attitudes, there's one damned important thing you've reminded me of."

"What's that?"

"What in hell do they think of the Germans? That's what they're training for, isn't it? To fight and kill Krauts. Well, maybe they love 'em. That's something we can work on, isn't it? After all, we're not down here just to have them play guinea pig for you or me or some high brass experiment, are we?"

"Of course not!" answered Kinder almost indignantly. "I would have gotten to that eventually. In a way I consider it the second phase of my work . . . certainly not primary at this time, and something to which they can be properly molded later on. But if you'd like, I'll prepare some questions for my next visit."

Reisman remembered then the imminence of Kinder's departure, surprised to realize that he might actually miss his being around.

In the compound, Napoleon White snapped out commands to his squad, directing their rifles through the studied positions and patterns of the manual. He'd started slow, picked up the pace after a while, and now there was a good rhythm to it that they were getting at last—never as good as his old outfit, but what did these sorry bastards know about rhythm . . . the castanet smack of palms against barrels and stocks, the almost sound of the vibrating steel, the tambourine jangle of the swivels, the taut-leather slap of the sling. His boys had been good at it. They'd been the best. Because like the good white folks said, wrong as they were but wanting to be nice, "Man, if a nigger ain't got nothing else, he's sure got rhythm!"

Then Archer Maggot started fighting him with what he probably supposed was subtlety—delaying his timing, bringing his rifle up to left shoulder arms when Napoleon had distinctly said right shoulder arms, and once even dropping his piece in the dirt, which in any other outfit would have meant he'd have had to eat, sleep and shit with it in his hands for a week.

There was Joe Wladislaw, Samson Posey, Victor Franko, Luis Jimenez and Archer Maggot in his squad, and only Maggot—though somewhat chastened and reconstructed in recent days—was not taking kindly to Napoleon's orders. And it made Napoleon wonder if maybe he wasn't doing the wrong thing, because no matter how hard he tried there'd always be some son-of-a-bitch like Maggot around, and maybe he should have refused to put himself in any position where he was anything more than an automaton getting by with no inner drives, and as little response to externals as he could manage in order to stay out of trouble and keep up the fiction of the repentant criminal and regenerated soldier. But that damned Captain—both damned Captains—were doing a snow job on him, leading him up to something. He wasn't sure what, but he did like coming alive again, coming out of the forced vegetable state he had buried himself in. He liked demonstrating his proficiency and giving orders, and maybe feeling a little something besides the hatred and misery that had been the only emotions to pierce his defenses for so long.

"Huh-orr-daah haahms!" he sang out. "Pa-ra-aade rest!"

Archer Maggot went into a slumped at-ease position instead of parade rest.

Napoleon was going to let it go, like he'd let the rest of Maggot's fouling up go by without lacing into him—because it would only lead to more trouble, he knew, maybe a fight, and then shit details for both of them, and what was the use. But then he saw the two officers coming out of the barracks, and he wanted his squad to win the competition, so he called out to Maggot, "Massuh Ahchuh, how kin youall be so danged stupid? Ah said parade rest, not at ease."

Maggot didn't see Reisman and Kinder coming through the gate. "Yo stop givin me thet cheap niggah talk, niggah!" he spat out.

Napoleon walked up to him slowly, holding his own rifle at port arms, ready to block or thrust with it. He saw the two officers stop a short distance behind the squad, watching and listening.

"Whah thas not niggah talk, Massuh Ahchuh," said Napoleon. "Thas po white trash talk. Youall nevuh huhd me talk lack that ceptin t'yo so'd y'unnerstan me, did youall?"

The terrible frustration on Maggot's face burst suddenly. He snapped his rifle up, reared back, and lunged the weapon toward Napoleon's head, stock first. Napoleon sidestepped, twisted the stock of his own rifle up hard, smashed it against Maggot's weapon near the trigger guard and sent it flying. He aimed his rifle stock again, coldly, without the blindness of anger, about to bash it into Maggot's face—and stopped, inches short of what he'd intended to do. For Maggot stood there unflinching, sneering in that cocksure, ugly way of his. And Napoleon knew it would do no good. If he hit him again and again and again. If he ground his head to bloody pulp in the dirt, it would do no good. Maggot believed the things he said, the things he felt, the things he did with every fiber of his being. He believed them with the naïve purity of God-blessed religion, and there would never, never, never be any changing it.

Captain Reisman was suddenly there between them. "Having trouble, Mr. White?" he snapped.

"No, sir," replied Napoleon. "I was just showing Maggot here one of the advantages of being proficient in handling an unloaded rifle."

"Pick it up, Maggot," ordered Reisman, pointing to the rifle on the ground. "After our little game, you take it apart, clean every speck of dirt from it, oil it properly, and bring it to me for inspection. Got me?"

"Sure, Captain. Sure," muttered Maggot, retrieving the rifle.

Each squad was given three minutes to show what it could do, with Reisman, Kinder and all the guard detail looking on critically. Napoleon's squad went first. In the middle of the drill, Archer Maggot suddenly brought his rifle up to right shoulder arms instead of left shoulder arms, smashing his elbow against Joe Wladislaw's and making them both drop their weapons.

"You dumb, stupid, Rebel son-of-a-bitch!" Wladislaw spat at him as they bent quickly to the ground. "Now you've done it!"

Maggot glowered at him, but said nothing. He hadn't meant to do it, but who would believe him? It really had been a mistake—because instead of paying attention to Napoleon's commands, all he could think about was the nigger out there barking orders at him.

Ken Sawyer's squad wasn't nearly as snappy in their movements. But nobody goofed on their positions and nobody dropped a rifle. They won the contest.

Captain Reisman came over to Napoleon's squad. "You're to continue as squad leader for the rest of the day, White," he told him. "Prepare a guard roster for the night watch, and then get your men ready for a hike with full field packs and rifles."

Watching the Captain's retreating back, Napoleon wanted to call out to him, Enough! Let's stop this nonsense! I don't want to play soldier anymore. But he turned to his squad instead and said, "Sorry, fellows. Who wants the first watch?" He hadn't meant to say *sorry* to anyone ever again. It just came out.

"You did okay, Nappy," muttered Wladislaw. "It wasn't your goddamn fault."

"My frien here not so good soldier," said Jimenez, pointing to Maggot. "You pretty good, Nappy."

"Sure he is," declared Wladislaw, who felt he had a proprietary interest in his tentmate. "He useta be a Lieutenant, didn't he?"

They all wanted the first watch, so that they wouldn't be awakened in the middle of the night and be ready for the sack again when Reveille sounded at 0600.

"I'll take second watch," said Napoleon. "Who else? Let's have two volunteers."

"Okay, me," said Samson.

"You're number three, Maggot," stated Napoleon, finally, when nobody else volunteered.

Maggot took a threatening step toward him. "The hell you say, niggah!"

Samson put his hand on Maggot's shoulder and jerked him back. Wladislaw and Jimenez boxed him in.

"Let's take a vote," said Franko. He was out of it and didn't give a damn, but he knew where the others' feelings lay. If he couldn't be Numzer One, then he wanted to be on Number One's side. And he hated Maggot more than he hated any of the others. "I say Maggot pulls second watch. It was his fault we lost, anyway."

The vote was five to one, and Archer Maggot began to know what it was like being a pariah, though he had never heard of the word.

—

21

—

IN THE DARK, wet night, Victor Franko stood at his unaccustomed sentinel post in one of the watchtowers, cursed his lousy luck, the weather, the United Kingdom of Great Britain, the Army of the United States of America, and that son-of-a-bitch of a Commanding Officer for sticking the prisoners with this new duty.

He winced and jumped at every crash of thunder and lightning, frighteningly aware he was a damn good target stuck up in a high place.

In between his fears, he thought it was a pretty damned funny thing he was standing up there in that watchtower on guard duty. Him! Even if it was only with an unloaded rifle on his shoulder. Who the hell was he supposed to be guarding? Himself? The other guys? He sure as hell wasn't going to rat on any of them or try to stop them if they wanted to try a break. The MPs? That was even funnier. He had to stand out there in the goddamn rain doing nothing so one more of the lousy MPs could lay in the sack undisturbed all night, if he wasn't in town or somewhere screwing some farmer's daughter. The CO? That was funniest of all. Guard him, hell! He'd like to kill the son-of-a-bitch!

Oh, but he was a clever one, that Captain. When he first put them on night watch, the prisoners had to walk a post down in the compound, and the MPs were still on duty in both towers, and Reisman or Bowren or the goddamn hangman was up on the barracks roof. But a couple of nights later, Reisman had pulled one of the MPs off night duty and stuck a prisoner up in his tower to stand around looking important. "It'll teach you a little something about responsibility," he'd bullshitted them. "You haven't earned the right to carry ammo yet, but every one of you has got a pair of eyes and a pair of ears and a good loud mouth to use if trouble comes up."

But Franko knew the real reason he'd eased up on the MPs. Franko had heard them muttering and bitching about the hours they had to work, how the CO was as tough on them as on the prisoners, and Franko had laughed at them. They deserved it! In every pen he'd done time the screws and finks were always bitching about how rough they had it. It served them right for being finks!

Another clap of thunder and flash of lightning, closer, made his flesh crawl. He huddled deeper into his raincoat, the rain poured off his helmet liner onto his face and neck and deep into his clothing and he shivered with the cold wetness of it. He moved around on the little platform, trying to keep warm, darting glances down into the stockade and off into the woods, seeing nothing. Only when the firebolts came could he see distinctly the puptents in the compound, make out for an instant the MP on the other tower, and barely discern the figure of the Captain walking the barracks roof far across the stockade.

Stupid son-of-a-bitch! What in hell was Reisman trying to prove? He didn't have to stay out there on a night like this. He was the boss, wasn't he? Yet he'd gotten out of the sack in the middle of the night, posted the guard for the second watch, and was standing up there playing warden for all of them.

In the light of another thunderbolt, Franko saw him again, or thought he saw him, and it gave him an idea. A little game to help him pass the time. He took the rifle off his shoulder and ran his hands along it. He liked the feel of it. He liked the promise of power it fostered. His fingers stopped at the muzzle end and played with the rubber condom that kept the rain out of the barrel. When Morgan, red-faced and snapping, had passed the condoms out the first time it rained after they got their rifles, the guys had told him they had better uses for things like that and he'd been so mad he'd made them drill an extra hour in the dark after they were supposed to have turned in—and that son-of-a-bitchin CO had let him do it.

Franko pulled his fingers away. The touch of the rubber made him think, and the thinking made his nerves tremble and his balls ache. He pulled the bolt, cocking the piece, and squeezed the trigger. He did it again and again and again. Then he kneeled on the platform, rested the rifle barrel on the railing and pointed it toward the barracks roof. Lightning illuminated the clearing and he tried to find Reisman through the gunsight in that instant, but he missed him. He felt the tower shake, ever so slightly, jumped up startled and peered down the ladder. It was empty.

He got into his kneeling position again, liking the game, eager to see the Captain down the barrel of the M1, eager to squeeze the trigger, imagine the explosion, picture him falling, no longer the big man, no longer so cocksure of himself.

Again the crash of thunder came that made him wince, and the stab of light over the stockade, and in that instant he zeroed on something there on the barracks roof, not really certain, but thinking it was him, squeezed the trigger with a sigh of exultation, heard a noise behind him on the platform, felt a terrible pain at the base of his neck and went reeling sickeningly into blackness . . .

Reveille revealed the scene.

And the wonder of it and the horror to all the prisoners, including those two who had been on guard posts down in the compound, was that none of them had any awareness of it until Corporal Bowren's trumpet blasted through the first bare light of wet dawn.

Myron Odell saw it first as he crawled out of his puptent, or at least he made the first and most noise about it.

"Oh my God, look!" he shouted.

Calvin Ezra Smith came after him, looked, and ducked back into the tent for his Bible. Luis Jimenez and Joe Wladislaw crossed themselves. The others stared.

Victor Franko was hanging from the watchtower, his mouth gagged, his arms and legs trussed, suspended by a rope that circled his chest under his armpits. He looked dead.

Reisman came up behind the men, threading his way through the puptents. On his shoulder was slung his submachine gun. In his hands he held Franko's M1. His voice, hard, unfeeling, ice-cold, broke through their stupefaction: "Cut him down!"

Ken Sawyer and Samson Posey started forward, realized suddenly they wouldn't be able to get through the barbed wire to reach Franko, and turned back to Reisman bewildered.

He handed his trench knife to Sawyer. "Go on out through the barracks," he told them. He shouted to Bowren up on the barracks roof, "Take a guard with you, Corporal, and shag after them!"

The other MPs and Sergeant Morgan poured out of the barracks into the compound with their weapons ready, some half dressed, uncertain what was happening. They stopped cold when they saw Franko. A little smile played around Morgan's lips, then disappeared as he saw Franko kick his bound legs.

Samson reached the top of the platform first and hauled on the rope that held Franko suspended. Sawyer got there with the trench knife, cut away the bindings on his arms and legs, and untied the gag from his mouth. Franko stood up shakily, leaning on them, then he fell against the railing, almost toppling off the platform, but they caught him.

"What happened to you, Vic?" asked Sawyer. "Who done it?"

Franko steadied himself on the railing. "I doan know what happened . . ." he whispered hoarsely.

At the foot of the tower, Bowren and an MP waited, looking up at him curiously, without sympathy, almost laughing now that they saw he was alive.

"Bring him down easy," ordered Bowren, moving part way up the ladder.

Franko stared down into the compound. The crowd of faces were fuzzy and reeling. He found Reisman's face, smug and unconcerned, the eyes mocking him, and he knew it had to have been him, it could only have been him.

Waves of nausea floated over Franko, trying to claim him, but he refused to give in. He forced himself erect with one hand on the railing, and with the other hand stabbed an accusing finger at Reisman. His voice burst over them in a sudden hysterical shout: "Ask *him* what happened! Ask the son-of-a-bitchin Captain what happened! *He* done it."

Prisoners and guards turned to Reisman, looking for rebuttal. There was none. They turned back to the watchtower in time to see Franko snatch the trench knife from Sawyer's hand. The men around Reisman had an instant in which to flee before Franko heaved the knife with a desperate curse. It smacked onto the ground ineffectually and bounced with a metallic ring.

Reisman walked over to it slowly, picked it up, wiped it carefully on his fatigue pants and jammed it back into the sheath on his belt.

"That's what you should have done last night!" he roared up at Franko. "You were on guard duty, you stupid son-of-a-bitch! If it had been a German, he'd have spilled your yellow guts all over the place!" Yet even as he laced into him, Reisman sensed that he was losing the other men, that they were looking at him as much with contempt as with anger. An officer didn't strike an enlisted man, didn't brutalize him as he had brutalized Franko—not without just cause.

Franko was starting down the ladder, the others helping him.

"Keep him up there!" Reisman ordered. He hefted Franko's M1 in one hand like a spear. "Bowren, catch this," he called, and arched it neatly over both fences. "Hand it to Franko. It's his."

Franko took the rifle reluctantly.

"Okay, killer, show them what you were doing last night on guard duty!" Reisman called out.

Franko stood there, looking around at all of them, feigning confusion.

"Show them, killer, or you'll be back in Marston-Tyne before the day is out!" Reisman warned.

Franko kneeled to the platform slowly and rested his rifle barrel on the railing.

"Now aim, killer!" commanded Reisman. "Aim just where you were aiming last night!"

Franko pointed the rifle, guilt and fear and anger all mixed up in him at the same time. The others watched, saw the barrel lined up on the barracks roof where the Captain had walked his post in the hours before dawn.

"Now one more question, killer!" Reisman demanded. It was a question for all of them—for the prisoners whose respect he might have lost; for the guards who might think he had overstepped his authority; for Franko; for Reisman. "Think about it real hard, Franko! And then keep the answer to yourself! I don't want to know it! What would you have done if the rifle was loaded?"

He didn't know the answer to that one either. And somehow he doubted that Franko did. In the silence that followed, he let them all find their own answers—for it was a problem they would all soon have to face.

"All right, Bowren, get them back in here!" he commanded. "Playtime is over! Let's have some chow and get to work!"

Three times that morning, Reisman made the prisoners fieldstrip and assemble their M1's. Then he made each man do it again blindfolded, working against a watch. They did well. The next step should have been dry runs for technique on a firing range, then issue live ammunition, stand back and shoot the works! Instead, Reisman sent two MPs down the ranks collecting their rifles, giving no explanation why he was taking them back.

When he and the MPs came out of the barracks a few minutes later carrying a dozen carbines and a dozen .45 automatic pistols, some of the prisoners were still griping —looking and sounding like a bunch of dirty, overage kids who'd just had their bat and ball confiscated by the cops for breaking somebody's window. They stopped when they saw the new, light rifles and holstered .45s. A few faces lit up with anticipation.

"—You're being promoted to the second grade," Reisman told them, as the MPs passed out the weapons, recorded serial numbers and had the men sign for them. "Carry these awhile. Get the feel of them. Learn to handle them until you can take them apart and put them together again blindfolded. What I told you about the care and respect of the M1 goes for these too. Work hard the way you have been and you'll soon earn the right to fire them again."

His big worry now, Reisman figured, was boredom, the sameness of their routine and their physical surroundings. These men weren't raw recruits faced with the challenge of new skills and duties which in themselves were fresh and exciting enough to keep them eager and hopping. They were proving more knowledgeable than anybody might have imagined from the sight of them. Whatever they had learned before in their military careers, coupled with the refinements Reisman was teaching them, the tight reins of their discipline, and the constant drive of their schedule were making them sharper than Reisman had dared hope with his awareness of who and what they were.

But on the moral and mental levels, he was still unsure of them. Whether Stuart Kinder was doing them any good or not, he didn't know. All Reisman was really certain of was that on the practical, physical level—his level—the men were toughening, were soldiering better. Even the frightened ones—like Myron Odell who whined and Victor Franko who blustered.

In unarmed offense and defense, they had come along to the point where they really knew what they were doing now, and none of them—not even Odell—chickened out when it came to taking their hard knocks from Samson Posey or from Reisman himself. He had to laugh sometimes at the way they went around whacking the flat edges of their hands against the ground, trees, branches, fence posts and each other, toughening their muscle ridges for judo—even a guy like Archer Maggot who had thought he was tough enough and knew it all already, until Reisman and Odell had shown him otherwise.

There were still fights among them if one of them thought he'd been chopped too hard, or didn't want to play, or was rubbed the wrong way, or just blew up because that's the way he was—but it was no longer a senseless, brawling thing. They knew how to defend as well as attack, and hand-to-hand combat between them, even in anger, had become a combination of tough, studied, scientific, almost graceful movements. And none of them ever went too far, never went for the kill—knowing he'd get it back in kind.

Still, Reisman couldn't move as fast as he would have liked to, as fast as he had been accustomed to in readying other men for OSS assignments. Not knowing the what and how and where of the prisoners' ultimate missions, he could only take them along step by step in his own way. He wasn't ready yet to set up a firing range and issue them live ammunition, or put a live grenade or demolitions charge in their hands. And not until he had brought them through that stage—qualifying them in every light and heavy weapon of the infantryman's arsenal—would he set up their jump training.

Somewhere along the way, enough of the physical, mental and moral would have to blend in these men so that

Reisman could really trust them, so that he could truly believe they were capable of undertaking the still vague and nebulous missions he was training them for. He wanted to believe in them. It was much too late for him to go back now.

In the library at Stokes Manor early Sunday afternoon, Margot Strathallan sat beside the telephone, wanting to ring up Captain Reisman, yet afraid to.

She thought surely, it being Sunday and all, he would understand her calling and asking if he and his men would like to come to tea. They'd have to clean up, of course . . . but how nice it would be to have them there to tea, and then they would be friendly and it would end the fear under which she'd lived these many days, that he would have her forcibly removed from her own home.

Margot reached for the telephone, pulled her hand back, rubbed her thin fingers over her lips and chin, gnawed at her knuckles. She got up and paced the room nervously, strode determinedly back to the telephone—and went past it, out into the hall. Sigismund, who had been watching her with questioning eyes from the rug before the hearth, padded after her sadly, whining to go out. She opened the great oaken door a thin crack and peered out apprehensively. The Doberman barked and danced excitedly, wagging his tail. She pushed him away from the opening, slammed the door shut and locked it. She glided upstairs restively—into her bedroom and out, along the silent corridors, opening and closing doors suspiciously. The dog padded after her, whining, his great head swinging from side to side, as restive as his mistress.

For two weeks Margot had felt a prisoner in her own home. It was silly, stupid, maddening—but since the humiliating meeting with Captain Reisman and his disgusting soldiers above the beach trail, she had been afraid to go much beyond the immediate vicinity of the building on her walks within the grounds of the estate. A number of times she had gone quickly down the driveway and through the gate, to walk on the public road with Sigismund. But it was demeaning and she didn't like it. People going by had seen her. Farmers, people of the village, strangers, soldiers. They wondered about her, talked about her, as they did when she drove the old Riley into the village with Sigismund to shop once a week. Nobody delivered things anymore. Not even to her. It was the petrol rationing, they said. Rationed like everything else. Well, they had bicycles, didn't they, damn them!

Margot walked downstairs again, into the library, and sat down beside the telephone, staring at it with a haunted look on her face. It was one thing to be a hermit of one's own design, for reasons that were precious and ennobling, and another to be a prisoner. She had to end it. She had to ring up the Captain now and invite him and his soldiers to tea. The anxiety of what he had threatened weighed upon her terribly. She knew the Captain could indeed have the War Office remove her—and, no doubt, her father would pin a medal on the man for doing it.

Quickly, before she could change her mind again, Margot picked up the telephone. She knew there was a telephone because she had seen the lines. She had first to contact the operator in the village, ask for a connection to the nearest American military exchange, and have the call routed back from there.

She waited irritably, listening to operators making connections, afraid to stay on the line, afraid to hang up, listening to clicks and buzzes, and then the dull, continuous ringing of the Captain's telephone. She imagined she could almost hear it somewhere back there in the wood, and see him reaching for it.

Nobody answered.

She tried again ten minutes later. And again half an hour afterward, and every half hour throughout the long, agonizing afternoon.

Late Sunday afternoon Reisman and the men came in from the field. He stood at the exterior gate to the stockade and watched them file through. They were tired, sweating, filthy, stinking—but he was pleased. The same march, over obstacles and up the rope on the cliff, that had taken them five hours the first time, had taken less than three today. Even Sergeant Morgan and the MPs seemed to be in better physical shape, though, of course, they weren't carrying full field packs and didn't have to take the obstacles if they didn't want to.

Reisman heard the phone start to ring and shouted into the barracks for Corporal Bowren to answer it. When he got there, Bowren had his hand over the mouthpiece, waiting for him. "It's a woman," he said. "Asked for you."

His first thought was Tess! Reisman took the phone and covered the mouthpiece.

"You and Morgan take over," he told Bowren. "Have them set up their tents, then ask for volunteers for KP. We'll all have a real dinner and the evening off for a change."

He waited until Bowren had closed the door behind him, then uncovered the phone and said hello. It somehow didn't surprise him at all that it was Margot Strathallan at the other end.

"*Tea*, Lady Margot!" he exclaimed, unable to keep the incredulity out of his voice.

Her conversation came on all at once, and it was as though there had never been anything at all regrettable between them.

"How kind of you," he said. "No, I'm sorry, but we couldn't. We've all just come in and none of us are presentable at all." He was determined to be civil and as diplomatic as possible. "Yes, of course. I understand. I'm sorry for my rudeness of the past, too. What? The War Office? No, of course not. You have been most kind in your cooperation. I appreciate it very much. No, not at all. Yes, maybe another time. Thank you. Goodbye."

He sat there for a long while afterward, smoking a cigaret, wondering what in hell had come over her. She'd been all sweetness and light, if somewhat frantic and tremulous of voice. A rather ludicrous and admittedly fiendish thought crossed his mind and he laughed. To have turned the Dirty Dozen loose in the aristocratic rooms of Stokes Manor, at a tea party hostessed by an English gentlewoman probably suffering from a case of hot pants, would have been a most decisive test of their trustworthiness, indeed. It gave rise to another idea, for if the Lady Margot really wanted to be nice and play USO, there was a way she might help.

He went out into the compound and yelled for Napoleon White. Napoleon came up to the gate on the double.

"You got that book list?" Reisman asked.

"No, sir."

"You still want some books, don't you?"

"I suppose so, Captain," said Napoleon, shrugging. "If there's ever any time to read."

"You'll have time tonight . . . and there'll be other times if everybody behaves. Look, do me a favor, will you? Check each of the men and find out what he'd like in the way of reading material or games or some relatively simple recreational equipment. Check the MPs, too. Then join me in the barracks in ten minutes, ready for a little trip. Tell the Sergeant I asked you to help me."

Napoleon came in with the list and presented it to him with a straight face. There were no names, just items: magazines, *Stars and Stripes* and some Stateside newspapers; checkers, cards, equipment for baseball, football and volleyball; cold beer, good booze, steaks, candy, cigarets and cigars; and quite a few requests for women, with rather intimate and explicit descriptions of sizes and shapes.

Reisman called Margot back.

"You've changed your mind, Captain?" she said eagerly. "How nice."

"Not exactly, Lady Margot, but I was wondering if I could come up now and borrow a few books from your library. Maybe a deck of cards or a checkers set, if you've got them, and any newspapers or magazines you're throwing away."

She was trying to sound munificent, but he could sense the uncertainty and alarm in her voice. "Of course," she answered. "Please come."

Reisman hung up and said to Napoleon, "You are about to meet Aristocracy up at the manor house, Mr. White. Sure you don't want to clean up and shave?"

"I'd rather stay here, sir, if you don't mind," answered Napoleon diffidently.

"I'd rather you came along!" Reisman snapped. "And you can look like a slob if you want to!"

Reisman shaved for the second time that day, showered and changed into a dress uniform. Only briefly during the few minutes it took him to make himself presentable, did it occur to him that it really wasn't necessary, that he didn't have to impress Margot Strathallan, or pretty himself up as he had done for Tess Simmons, like a lover going courting.

Margot greeted Reisman with a nervous smile at the doorway. The dog was not with her. "How nice to see you again, Captain," she said.

She was trying too hard at something she didn't mean. There was no warmth in her voice. She was thinner than he remembered her and had that same haunted look behind the forced smile. Something really bugged her, and Reisman pitied her. He really wished he could help her.

Then Margot saw Napoleon standing just back of Reisman in the twilight. "Oh! . . . I thought you were coming alone. How do you do?" she said.

"Good evening, ma'am," said Napoleon. In the half-light of the shadowed doorway he tried to read her face and eyes quickly, but saw nothing . . . except maybe fear, and he didn't want to dwell on that.

"This is one of my associates . . . Mr. Jones," said Reisman.

"Come in, please," she said. "Can I offer you a drink, Captain . . . or the tea you turned down earlier?"

"No, thank you. How about you, Jones?" asked Reisman solicitously as they came into the great entrance hall.

"No thank you, ma'am," said Napoleon.

"The men are waiting for us, Lady Margot," Reisman hurried to explain. "Holding dinner as a matter of fact. Told them we'd be right back. Maybe some other time."

"Surely," she replied, and to Reisman she sounded somewhat relieved. "Why don't we go right into the library and you can select whatever books you'd like. I'm sorry I don't have any newspapers or magazines. I don't read them. The wireless is bad enough."

Napoleon crossed the threshold of the room and the sight of the place, the shelves of books, the dark paneling, the heavy chairs and tables, the very smell of the place filled him with so great a wave of nostalgia that the sigh of remembrance reached his lips almost as a sob, and made the woman turn to him and ask, "Something wrong, Jones?"

"Nothing really, ma'am. It's nice, that's all. There were reading rooms and lounges like this at the University."

"University?" She looked at him doubtfully. "You don't look much like that now, do you?" she said, wrinkling her nose distastefully. "Where was that, Jones?"

Napoleon caught Reisman's sharp look. "Just a dream, ma'am. Just a dream," he whispered. He moved around picking books off the shelves at random if they were fat enough to catch his eye or if quickly-seen titles stirred any excitement in him. He wanted to get out of there fast.

When he had five books in his hands, he turned to the woman and asked, "Will these be all right, ma'am?"

"Anything at all," Margot answered. "Provided they're returned in the same condition they're lent."

She had waiting for them on a table two decks of cards, one checkers set, one chess set and a cribbage board.

"Do you play chess, Mr. Jones?" asked Reisman.

"Yes, sir."

"Good . . . then we'll borrow these with gratitude, Lady Margot," Reisman said to her. "I think the cribbage can stay, though. I doubt that we have any players."

"Well, send them up for lessons some evening, Captain," Margot said lightly.

Reisman insisted upon making up an official list of the borrowed items in duplicate, signed both lists and asked Margot to do the same. He handed her one copy and folded the other into his coat pocket. "Thank you again, and good night, Lady Margot," he said, walking hurriedly out of the library with Napoleon.

She followed in their wake and put a hand on Reisman's arm, holding him at the open front door. "Can I speak to you a moment alone?" she whispered.

He shouted down to Napoleon, "Be right with you!" and turned back to Margot. She was biting her lips nervously and had that frightened, pitiable look in her eyes again. "What is it?" he asked softly.

"Is it all right if I walk on the beach again?" she blurted out. She tried to smile. "Poor Sigismund is so cooped up . . . and I . . . and it was really the only pleasure we had . . . the long walks . . . and now . . ." She ended with a helpless shrug.

"Better not," he answered, sorry now that he had come. "I think it would be best for all of us if you stayed fairly close to the building for a while. I can't explain why. I wish I could. If there was some way I could make it up to you, I would."

"There is!" she snapped, eyes suddenly flashing angrily. "Take that . . . that . . . *person* with you . . . and leave me alone!"

She turned and slammed the door after him.

"Who's she mad at?" asked Napoleon as the Captain climbed behind the wheel.

"The world. Forget it!"

"Sure, Captain. My mind's a blank . . . and my name is

Jones. I would have hoped that *you* would have been just a little more imaginative . . . sir."

Reisman turned and smiled at him, digging in where it would hurt the most. "I think maybe she's got the same problem as you . . . persecution complex."

Napoleon stewed in silence while they bounced across the field toward the wood. But Reisman felt expansive and wanted him to talk. "That's quite a variety of books you borrowed," he said. "Why'd you pick them?"

"Does it make any difference . . . sir?" Napoleon retorted. He wasn't even sure now what he had there. He juggled the books on his knees, wondering why the hell Reisman bothered drawing him into a conversation like this. It threw confusion on the simple relationship of officer to soldier, and keeper to kept.

"Curious, that's all," said Reisman. He reeled off the titles from memory. "*A Study of History* by Arnold Toynbee, Volume One . . . *The Nigger of the Narcissus* by Joseph Conrad . . . *The Collected Poems of Rudyard Kipling* . . . *The Seven Pillars of Wisdom* by T. E. Lawrence . . . and last but not least *Winnie the Pooh* by A. A. Milne. I'd like to read Lawrence again, and Kipling, when you're finished with them. As for *Winnie the Pooh,* I've got a hell of a confession to make. I never read it. Underprivileged childhood, I guess."

"I never read it either, Captain," said Napoleon. He picked up the small, thin book and laughed. "I didn't even know I had it here. I was just grabbing things to fill up my hands."

"The hell you were. There was a reason behind every one of your choices. It may have flashed across your nimble brain in an instant and vanished, but it was there all right. Come on, dredge it up. Let's see what makes you tick."

"I thought mind reading was Captain Kinder's department," Napoleon shouted above the engine noise.

"Sure it is, but I'm bucking for his job. Come on, White. You afraid to talk?"

"No, I'm not afraid!" Napoleon flashed back. He held up a thicker book. "Toynbee . . . Volume One. That's probably all I'll have time for. You ever read him?"

"No."

"Now there's a man with a broad point of view. Great reading for when you're feeling glad for yourself or sad for

303

yourself, big country or little country, big man or little man, black man or white man. It's all passé . . . yesterday, today and tomorrow . . . and it makes no damn bit of difference. The world is up for grabs and may the best man win!"

"How about Lawrence?" Reisman urged.

"I read him a long time ago. I admired him. Reading him again ought to prove something to me," Napoleon answered.

"What's that?"

"That I was a sophomoric jackass then! Now I've lived, too. I've killed a man, and I've lain in a ditch half dead myself. Now Lawrence should reinforce everything reprehensible to me about the white man's burden."

"White man's burden, my ass!" Reisman rapped out. "Maybe in Kipling, if you look for it, with all that empire-building and soldiering among their lessers, but not in *The Seven Pillars*. Lawrence was too sensitive, too compassionate. He identified too closely with the slobs he led . . . and even the men he killed. He was a scholar, a romantic, a bit of a nut and fanatic, but never a racist or bigot."

"I didn't mean he was outwardly a bigot," Napoleon ran on. "But the supercilious gall of the man! A white-skinned Englishman lording it over people in a country where he had no right to be in the first place!"

"Boy, you've got it bad, White," said Reisman. "Like I told you once before, you want somebody to hate, you better start thinking of those Krauts across the Channel. I'll personally give you five bucks for every Nazi throat you slit. With your hatred, White, you ought to finish the war a rich man."

"All right, Captain, what did *you* think of him?" Napoleon demanded. He was loosening up, eager to talk again, hungry to pit his mind against another.

Reisman shrugged his shoulders. He was hunched over the steering wheel, snaking the jeep along the rutted roadway through the trees. "I never could figure out if I was for him or against him," he admitted. "He had a mind that made me feel like an ant . . . and he was braver than any one man had a right to be and still survive."

"Brave? So what!" Napoleon mocked.

Reisman turned his head quickly to see if Napoleon's expression mirrored his words, and was disappointed to see that it did. "To me, a great deal, Mr. White," he affirmed.

"In a soldier, I would say it was an admirable and advantageous, if not absolutely necessary, commodity." He turned his head back just in time to avoid bashing the jeep into a tree. "I read the book in a hospital in Spain . . . wounded in a war *you* might say I had no business being in. There were a lot of us there . . . some who knew what they were doing and why . . . some of us who didn't." He had a sudden, vivid memory of the Englishman a couple of beds away from him in that abattoir who had loaned him the copy of *Seven Pillars* . . . and he remembered, too, the things Lawrence had written about war and killing that had made him feel uncomfortable . . . made him think too hard about the way he lived and was likely to die . . . the men he'd killed . . . what was the good of it? . . . right or wrong? . . . that sort of thing. Though it hadn't really made any difference because a year after Spain he was in Palestine training Jewish settlers and fighting beside them against hit-and-run raids by the same Arabs Lawrence had led to their short-lived glory less than a generation before, so maybe that was the real reason he could never figure out if he was for the man or against him.

"What were you looking for in Spain, Captain? Glory?" Napoleon taunted, though he couldn't help feeling now a new and grudging respect for Reisman.

"Maybe the same thing you were looking for when you slit the throat of that man aboard the *Île de France*. Vindication." He was surprised to hear himself say it, surprised at how easily he was opening himself up. "Maybe a little glory, too," Reisman admitted with a smile. "It's in all of us when we're young enough and strong enough or angry enough. You've got it, White. The glory quest. So have the others. Don't knock it. Use it. Captain Kinder tells me you're a pretty good amateur psychologist."

"If I were any better, I wouldn't be here, Captain," declared Napoleon cockily.

Reisman braked the jeep to a stop beside the stockade and leaned toward Napoleon. "Let's finish with these," he said, tapping the stack of books. "What about the Conrad novel?"

"*The Nigger of the Narcissus?* The title . . . its ugliness infuriates me," Napoleon commented with unexpected candor. "I've always refused to read it before. Every time I saw it on a library shelf or in a card catalog, I'd want to destroy it. Because whatever it was, I didn't want other people . . . white people . . . to see it and spoil the life I was leading."

"You don't think you're going to destroy one of Lady Margot's books now, do you?"

"I intend to read it, Captain. With your permission . . . sir," Napoleon added with mock dignity.

"And *Winnie the Pooh?*"

Napoleon laughed. "Just a gag, Captain," he said sarcastically. "I figure I'll read a bedtime story to the boys some night. Okay?"

"Sure. They'll love it," muttered Reisman. He got out of the jeep, lifted the engine hood and removed the rotor from the distributor.

Napoleon preceded him through the gate. He waved his hand around at the double barbed wire fence pointed at the rotor and said bitterly, "All this, and you still don't trust us, do you, Captain?"

"Would you?" demanded Reisman, pausing at the barracks door. He hadn't missed the fact that Napoleon had said *us* and not *me,* including himself with the others and them with him, maybe for the first time.

Napoleon met the Captain's calm gray eyes, but refused the challenge in the question. He shrugged his shoulders noncommittally.

Reisman unlocked the barracks door and motioned Napoleon inside ahead of him. "Wait for me in there, White," he ordered him, indicating the smaller room. "I want an answer to that question."

Napoleon carried his armload of books and games through the office door, sorry now that he had allowed himself to be drawn out at all.

At the far end of the barracks, Reisman saw Luis Jimenez happily at work in the corner that was the MPs' kitchen. Myron Odell bustled about helping him. Master Sergeant Carl Morgan guarded them, salivating.

"That all for KP, Sergeant?" Reisman called out.

"They all volunteered, Captain. Every last one of them," answered Morgan. "Some peeled spuds. The rest are going to clean up the mess after these guys get through. The Corporal's got them outside now. They're just sitting around waiting for chow."

Luis Jimenez turned from the table where he was cutting up chickens. "I doan cook no mess, Sergeant," he flashed angrily.

He waved the knife in his hand. Morgan backed away a step.

"Luis, *mi amigo*, don't be so damned temperamental!" Reisman snapped, moving toward him. "Get back to work and prove it!"

Jimenez turned back to his creative labors, murmuring Mexican obscenities, only a few of which Reisman caught and was able to enjoy as he walked toward his room. He could believe that Jimenez had indeed volunteered, and maybe Odell and a few of the others, but as for all of them having volunteered for KP, as the Sergeant said, he doubted it. It was probably Morgan who had volunteered them in the old Army way, though it made no difference to Reisman. The MP detail was entitled to a change, too. They'd been griping about doing their own cooking and KP in addition to their long hours on guard duty. None of them were good cooks, and on top of that, having expected the prisoners would be doing all their crap jobs for them, they were disgruntled it wasn't so. Reisman had tried to make up for it by keeping the quantity and quality of food for them high. To supplement the canned goods, Corporal Bowren and one of the guards picked up fresh bakery and dairy products, meat, fish and fowl twice a week at a supply and mail drop that had been set up for the outfit under a cover story at a Quartermaster Depot twenty miles away. They even had the luxury of a refrigerator, powered by the same field generator that fed juice to the barracks lights and to the floodlights in the compound which were rigged for an emergency but never used because of the coastal blackout.

Reisman entered the office and closed the door behind him. Napoleon had put on the overhead light, a large, bare bulb hanging in a socket at the end of a wire that had been tacked along the wall and ceiling. He was sitting on the cot, thumbing through the books distractedly. Reisman glanced quickly at the unshaded window and strode toward it.

"That's not very bright, Mr. White," he snapped. "There's a war on, remember? And there are still Jerries flying around up there." He untied the heavy blackout curtains and let them drop into place.

Napoleon looked at him and at the covered window as though he really didn't give a damn, and the idea of a German air raid might be amusing. Reisman stood in front of him and took a pack of cigarets from his jacket. "Smoke?" he asked.

"Sure. Thanks, Captain," said Napoleon, taking one.

Reisman lit it for him, lit one for himself and sat down in the chair at his desk. "Now I want an answer to my question, Lieutenant," he said softly. "Can you be trusted yet . . . all of you . . . completely?"

Napoleon drew deeply on his cigaret, feeling almost as though he could truly relax, but knowing deep down that he couldn't, maybe never could again. He recognized the question as much for a forthright appeal for help as it was a challenge. And if he were to answer it honestly, it would have to be a rueful No, not yet.

"Maybe," he said. "If we knew what you were up to. What we were really doing here. What this big deal is we're supposed to be involved in." He rubbed his coarse-bearded face and gestured to himself. "Maybe you can't tell on me, Captain, but I'm dirty, real dirty, and I stink. You don't think I liked having that woman up there look at me like I was filth, do you? I don't like being this way one little bit, and neither do the rest of us."

"Sure you do," countered Reisman archly. "You love it. Otherwise you'd clean up and shave. You know what the guards are calling you, don't you?"

"The Dirty Dozen . . . so what?" Napoleon parried. "You know that kid stuff about sticks and stones, don't you? Matter of fact, we kind of like it."

"Sure you do. That's what I said. You're the new elite of the Army," Reisman mocked.

"Then when are we going to stop all this Boy Scout crap you're running us through and get on with the real business of it?" demanded Napoleon.

Reisman got up from his chair and paced the floor. "Maybe soon . . . maybe never," he muttered. "You ought to know. You were the Plans and Training officer for your old outfit, weren't you? Given a squad of convicted murderers, rapists, thieves and thugs, how would you turn them into disciplined soldiers, Lieutenant? At what point would you trust them?"

Napoleon looked up. The Captain was in front of him, no longer pacing, yet even standing still he seemed to be in motion, compelling an answer by force of will. Napoleon was drawn to his eyes, startled by the way they changed color and mood from moment to moment. "I'd say the point at which you have to, Captain," he answered, still trying to hedge, still trying to remain aloof from the other man's problems.

"Would you trust them *now?*" demanded Reisman.

Napoleon held his gaze, meeting the challenge honestly at last. "No," he said softly. "Not yet."

"Let me know when you do, Mr. White," said Reisman, "and we'll take it from there."

In the manor house, Margot Strathallan still smarted with humiliation. She felt debased, degraded, used, and the longer she dwelt on it, pacing the empty corridors and rooms of the building with the dog padding and whining after her, the angrier she became, until she knew she had to do something physical, something to assert herself against that which oppressed her and those who oppressed her—or she would go out of her mind.

She put on her coat and scarf, snapped a leash to the collar of the prancing dog, and opened the great oaken front door. The night was quiet. The gravel driveway and nearby fields empty. A cold, penetrating fog hung over the downs, and quickly she and the dog went out into it, enveloping herself in it, liking it, making straight for the gate and through it to the road and the telephone pole where, on one of her frenzied walks, she had seen the wire running down and off through the roadside brush, barely hidden, into the estate.

In the brush on her hands and knees, Margot felt around for the wire, found it and took it up into her hands. Sigismund, black upon black in the night, circled her, pawing the ground, sniffing, growling, and from the nights and days of their years together she sensed the taut curiosity, wonderment, eagerness to please, and held the wire up to him.

"Take it, Sigismund!" she commanded. "Bite it! Tear it!"

And the Doberman's white teeth flashed at the telephone line, enjoying the unexpected game, snarling his pleasure as he tore and jerked at it while Margot held it tightly, and they played at tug of war there until Sigismund had gnawed the wire through.

22

THE PRISONERS tore into Luis Jimenez' chicken dinner like starved animals; the guards ate with an excess of relish and dearth of decorum. Jimenez accepted, with nods and shy smiles, the compliments shouted at him, and when he had served everybody, sat down to his own food and showed by the slow, gentlemanly way he dined, his disdain for the grotesque table manners of the others.

The men sat at plank tables and benches, on cots and floor, prisoners and MPs intermingled and talking to each other—only two of the guards standing on armed alert at any one time, while the others ate.

Outside in the night, wet fog enveloped the land around and the close sea and finally became rain. Inside, Captain John Reisman sensed a mood of camaraderie diffuse among the prisoners, extending even to the guard detail, and had to remind himself, after savoring the mood too briefly, that it was an illusion of wishful thinking imposed upon a full belly. He belched discreetly, which returned him immediately to reality, rose from his seat at the table, went to Luis Jimenez, and clasped him disarmingly about the shoulders.

"*Muy bien,* Luis," he complimented. "Someday you will make some woman a fine husband."

For Luis the *abrazo* was food itself. "Thank you, Captain," he said softly. "I do this every day if you like."

"Not a chance," said Reisman, laughing. "K-rations and C-rations. Otherwise we get soft."

While he scrubbed at pots and pans and mess gear, Samson Posey's eyes and ears filled with the sights and sounds of a poker game in progress among the relaxing MPs at one of the plank tables. The Captain had said everybody would have the night off after KP until Taps, and Samson hurried at his work, hoping that he, too, might be allowed to play. How long it had been since he had held a deck of

310

cards in his hands! Yet he knew the skill could not have left him, and he yearned to show these others, so superior to him in all things but brute strength, that the Utes were their masters at gambling. And he vowed, too, that among these men he would use only skill—and put out of his mind all those tricks Billy Three-legs had taught him.

He finished his work and went to stand beside the card players. It was a noisier game than that to which he was accustomed. They laughed and joked and cursed, and played poorly, filling the air with the smoke of cigarets and cigars—but that was the way it had been wherever he had played in the Army. The money they used was also strange to him. It was the money of this country, but he had not used it enough to learn its values. It would place him at a disadvantage if they did allow him to play. Then it struck him suddenly that he had no money at all, and nothing else of value, so how could he play? He turned away from the table, looking for something he could do, lost in an over-whelming wave of nostalgia. Some of the men were writing letters with paper and pencils the Captain had given them, and Samson wished he could write well enough to send a letter home to Eva . . . something for his son, who surely would learn to read and write. But could he write them of his shame? It was better left unsaid. He gazed around at the other men. Napoleon, the Negro . . . Black Buffaloes his ancestors had called them for the fierceness and power of their charges when they had served in the cavalry of the white man against the Indian . . . Napoleon sat apart against a wall, reading books. Once he had been an officer, Samson knew, until he had slain a white man in anger. He was a person of great learning and ability, different from him—yet he knew, too, the anguish of apartness and the uncontrollable fury that was murder, and for this and other reasons Samson admired him and felt close to him. The frightened one, Myron, a cross between a rabbit and a coyote, went up to Napoleon, spoke, was offered two books which he took and sat down to read. Samson promised himself that one day he would ask Napoleon to teach him to read. In exchange, maybe he could teach him how to gamble. He turned back to the poker game.

Reisman came out of his room and called to Master Sergeant Morgan. "Do you play chess, Sergeant?" he asked.

"No, sir," answered Morgan.

"Too bad," said Reisman in mock disappointment. "How about checkers?"

"It's been awhile, but I think I remember."

"Good," said Reisman, handing him the box of checkers and the board. "Find one of the prisoners to play with you."

Morgan took the game and stared around the room, feeling uncomfortable. He would have preferred to remain aloof from things such as this. His eyes fixed on Victor Franko, who had taken over a cot for himself, lying upon it, smoking indolently, as though he hadn't a care in the world. Morgan walked up to him. "You!" he said softly.

Franko jerked up startled.

"You play checkers?" asked Morgan.

"Not too good."

"That's good enough," said Morgan, sneering. "Move over."

They sat on the cot together and set up the board between them. Morgan looked around and saw nobody paying attention to them, the others involved in their own amusement.

"If you win," he taunted, with an ugly laugh, "you can hang *me*."

Franko could not meet his eyes. The proximity of the hangman made him tremble and he had all he could do to keep his hands steady to make his moves. He played badly —and knew that he would lose.

Reisman squeezed in among the men standing around the poker table. He had the second deck of cards with him, and the chess set and board. He had hoped to play chess with Napoleon White, but seeing him absorbed in his reading, had left him alone.

"Anybody want to play chess?" Reisman asked.

There were no takers.

He drew the pack of cards from his pocket. "How about getting up another little game?" he suggested.

The men turned to him eagerly, Samson Posey in the forefront, his hand raised, his face excited.

"Do you play, Posey?" Reisman asked in surprise.

"Yes, Captain, but I do not have money."

"You don't need any," said Reisman. He dropped the deck onto another plank table. "There's room for six players, including me. Be right with you."

He came out of his office in a few minutes toting a metal box of .30 caliber ammunition. Posey, Maggot, Gilpin, Sawyer and Pinkley were seated at the table, waiting for him eagerly.

"This is better than money," Reisman told them, tilting the box's contents onto the table. "It'll keep our minds on our work. Six hundred rounds . . . worth a buck apiece for betting. Count out a hundred to a man, Sawyer. When the game's over, there'd damned well better be six hundred rounds back in the box."

Reisman took the middle place on one bench. On either side sat Glenn Gilpin and Ken Sawyer, directly opposite was Vernon Pinkley, on Pinkley's right Samson Posey, on his left Archer Maggot. Reisman picked up the deck, shuffled it once and put it down in front of the Indian. "Dealer's choice," he said.

His eyes widened in amazement as Posey snapped up the deck, shuffled it flat-wristed and light-fingered against the table like a professional, placed it in front of Gilpin and ordered, "Cut!"

Posey swept the cut deck into his huge hands, flicked his eyes coldly from man to man. "One dollar to play," he said, moving a bullet forward. "Five-card draw . . . jacks or better . . . joker wild . . . three-dollar limit . . . three raises . . . okay?" As he spoke, the cards sped from his fingers in soft, faultless motions, flat against the table, and skidded to a stop before each man.

The game varied from draw to five-card and seven-card stud and a few hands of blackjack. Occasionally someone would suggest a more complicated game and would be shouted down by the others, who would ultimately turn to Reisman for the final word of, "Let's keep it simple, huh!" Reisman was a better than average player. Thousands of shipboard and waterfront games lay behind him in his seagoing days, and he had made his modest deposits at most of the popular gambling spas of the world. But he could not get over the superior skill demonstrated by Samson Posey. It obviously wasn't fool's luck, for he handled the cards too well for that, bet judiciously, and was in full charge of every game he dealt. After an hour, Posey was high winner, Maggot second, Reisman third.

313

Archer Maggot didn't like being second in an occupation he figured he knew better than any one of these amateur suckers. He'd started the play figuring that before long there'd be six hundred bullets piled in front of him, and they'd know damned well who was top dog at this and give him the respect that was his due, including the CO, who shouldn't have been playing with them in the first place if he was such a stickler for regulations. Most of all, Maggot didn't like being second to that dumb cluck of an Indian. Posey's uncanny run of luck infuriated him, but he knew ways to take care of that.

A monotonous succession of hands in which he had absolutely nothing worth betting on, and lost his ante each time plus some bluff bullets, convinced Maggot he should make his move. In a game of five-card stud, he found himself staring at the ace of spades as his hole card, and when nothing good showed in two upcards, he folded, palmed the ace in his left hand, covering the movement by leaning forward and extending his right hand far out to place his discards in the dirt. When the deal came to him two hands later, the card was tucked safely behind his left knee. The game he called was seven-card stud. He played it through, knowing he was beaten by what was showing, throwing away bullets to keep pace with the betting, just to get the three downcards to play around with. It came out nothing, but there was an ace of hearts in there and a ten of spades.

Maggot folded the hand quietly just as the last round of betting and bumping got started, and had a quick decision to make: to go for aces—which might be missed if they didn't turn up occasionally in somebody's hand; or go for the big flush—which might take longer, might never even happen, but would look more legit if he played it right. He palmed the ten and got it behind his knee, and threw the ace of hearts away with the discards. He had a royal flush going for him now, covered at both ends. Each time he got the deal, his game was seven-card stud. He got more cards that way, more opportunity to steal. He won a little, lost a little, and kept about even.

It took quite a few rounds until finally all Maggot lacked behind his knee was the king of spades. It never came to him. Three times he saw it in other people's hands when they threw down sloppily at the end of a game, and watched it get lost in the shuffle, until finally it landed close

314

to him, and on the pretext of pushing cards back to the center of the table, he stole it.

Maggot got the deal. "The game is five-cahd droah," he announced softly, riffling the cards expertly. He looked at them all challengingly, particularly the Captain. "What say we play pot limit fo a change, Cap'm? Thet way they's big winnuhs and big loozuhs an we sep'rates thuh men fum thuh boys."

"I'm game," said Reisman. "It's getting late, anyway. We've got to break it up soon. How about the rest of you?"

They all nodded approval or muttered their yeahs. Reisman smiled at them. They all looked so damned grim— poker grim—though there was, thankfully, none of that depressing, all-pervading aura of the death cell clinging to the stockade this night.

"Okay. You can bet or raise any amount up to the limit of what's in the pot. Understand, Posey?" asked Reisman.

Samson said, "Hm!" just as they figured an Indian should. Maggot dealt the cards. Sawyer wanted to open, but asked first, "I don't *have* to match the pot, do I?" There was only the six-bullet ante in there. "No, suh," said Maggot. "Youall kin still open f' one, two, three, aw thuh whole danged pot. Suit y'sef. Yo gottem, bettem!" Sawyer moved one bullet forward. Maggot figured Sawyer had only jacks for openers. Now he wished he'd been able to rig the deck so one or two of them would think they had sure things and would come out betting strong.

The CO stayed in for one bullet. Maggot figured he had nothing or a low pair. Gilpin put in one and raised it three. Maggot figured him for a high pair or a prayer. He felt his blood start to pound now. And then he like to bust a gut when the Indian met the raise and reraised the pot limit with a straight face that told them absolutely nothing. Thirty-two bullets in the pot now. Maggot figured Posey had two high pair or three of a kind queens, kings or aces. It was Pinkley's turn. "Too rich for my blood," he said, and folded.

Maggot came out strong, counting bullets and moving them forward. "Lessee now . . . it's gawna cost me twenny t' stay in thuh game . . . an ahm gawna raise thet lil ole pot by whutevahs in theyuh now."

"They's fifty-two in theyuh now, Mistuh Kingfish," mimicked Reisman. "So all told its gawna cost youall sevenny-two pieces a lead."

Maggot laughed. A high, raucous, but genuine laugh that cracked his set, scowling face into something almost pleasant and likeable. "Ah gottem, Mistuh Cap'm, suh! Ah gottem!" he crowed. He counted bullets excitedly, pushing them forward. "An now we sep'rates thuh men fum thuh boys!"

There were one hundred and four bullets in the pot. Ken Sawyer stared flabbergasted at how the pot had soared away from his lousy one-bullet bet. It would cost him seventy-one more to stay. He didn't have that many, but he had an ace, a king and the joker, and he felt lucky. "Can I play light?" he asked.

"How will you back it up if you lose?" Reisman asked him.

Sawyer tossed in his cards with a shrug. "I'll save my money," he said.

Reisman counted out seventy-one bullets from his pile. "I'm in," he said laconically.

"Wassamatta, Cap'm? Ain't yo gawna bump me?" challenged Maggot.

Reisman looked across at him and smiled. "After the draw, Kingfish," he promised.

Glenn Gilpin went down with a muttered, "Damn!" Samson Posey added fifty-two bullets to the pot to equal Maggot's raise.

"Ain't yo gawna bump me neithuh, Chief?" taunted Maggot.

Samson sat silently, his cards squared neatly in a pile before him, one hand covering them, the other resting lightly on the table. Though inwardly he was excited, his face revealed nothing, and to chatter nonsense at this moment was unthinkable to him.

Maggot picked up the deck. "How many cahds, Cap'm?"

"One."

Maggot couldn't contain his look of surprise. He wondered if by the wildest chance the CO was going for a legitimate royal flush. He dealt the card, and saw absolutely nothing in Reisman's face to indicate whether he had made what he was going for or not. Maybe the betting would tell him more, but if their hands were tied at the call, they'd have to split the pot. He turned to the Indian. "How many cahds youall want, Chief?"

Samson kept his hands on his neatly-squared cards. He didn't even bother to look at Maggot. "No cards," he replied.

Maggot's heart skipped a beat. There were sharp intakes of breath around the table and low murmurs of amazement. What the hell did the Indian think he was doing, Maggot worried? Pat hand, huh? Pat hand, my ass! Nobody could hold a pat hand good enough to beat what he had stashed behind his left knee! He went into his covering act, fidgeting and shifting on the bench, puffing up a nervous smoke screen with the cigaret that dangled from his lips. "Ah'll take just one," he muttered. Carefully, in plain sight of them all, he placed one card in the dirt and removed one from the top of the deck. He fanned out the cards in his hand to make it look good, squared them, and locked them tightly in his left hand. He was actually surprised to find he had a full house, sevens over threes, but he sure as hell wasn't going to play with them. "Your bet, Cap'm," he said softly.

"There're two hundred and twenty-seven bullets in the pot," Reisman stated. "You and Posey have a few more than me, but none of us can match it. I'm betting what I've got left here . . . seventy-eight."

Slowly, painstakingly, Samson counted out bullets to match the bet. And while all eyes were on the Indian, Maggot fidgeted and shifted, puffed his ciagaret nervously, and used the precious seconds to exchange the cards in his hand with the cards behind his left knee.

When Samson had met the Captain's bet, he counted out all the remaining bullets he had and put them in a pile apart from the main pot. "Raise fifty," he said.

"Ah cain't meet it, Chief!" declared Maggot. "Youall know bout tapping out?"

Samson pointed to his separate pile of fifty bullets. "How much you got, fellow?" he challenged.

"Ah got sevenny eight t' meet thuh Cap'm's bet." He pushed them into the pot. "An twenny five t' meet half yo raise." He pushed them toward Samson's separate pile. "An I'm tapped out."

Samson swept back in front of him the extra twenty-five. It was the Captain's turn and Samson felt embarrassment for the Captain because he could not meet any part of the raise. He wished he could lend him the bullets with which to bet, but he knew that was not proper.

"I'm tapped out," said Reisman calmly. "I play only for the main pot."

"Awright, Chief," chortled Maggot. "You high bettah. Ah call!"

Samson fanned his cards out in front of him, his face expressionless. There were a few muttered curses from those who had dropped out.

"Wha yo doan have nuthin but one ace an garbage!" said Maggot in amazement. "You wuz jus bluffin!"

"What you got, fellow?" said Samson.

"Ah got these! Thas what ah got!" snapped Maggot. He fanned his cards on the table, angry that he had worked so long and hard to win a pot crookedly which he might have won honestly.

"Holy mackerel! A royal flush!" exclaimed Pinkley. "Hot damn!"

Sawyer and Gilpin stared bug-eyed, glad now they had dropped out. Samson looked once, assuring himself what was there, then looked to the Captain, waiting for him to show his cards.

"Yo hand, suh?" asked Maggot in mock gentility that belied the gloating expression of his face.

"Three sixes," said Reisman, "and that ain't enough. Take it, Maggot."

Maggot let out a Rebel yell of triumph, startling guards and prisoners all over the barracks. "Man, oh man, oh man!" he crowed, sweeping in the massive pile of ammunition. "All ah needs a rahfle an ah kin take on thuh whole damnyankee ahmy!"

Samson Posey stretched and yawned. He stretched so long and hard that his left arm extended behind Pinkley to where it could just reach Archer Maggot. And working his leg muscles against the floor, Samson suddenly thrust, toppling the bench backward as though it was an accident, spilling Pinkley and Maggot and .30 caliber ammo—and the hold-out cards Maggot had cached behind his left knee. Which was the way Samson had figured it.

He came up from the floor with Maggot clutched in one hand and the hold-out cards in the other. "You cheat!" he bellowed.

MPs and prisoners were moving in on them and Reisman shouted, "Leave them alone! He's got it coming!"

Maggot hung limp but a moment, surprised at being discovered but no longer afraid of the Indian because of his size. What he knew about dirty fighting before, he knew even better now—thanks to Reisman, who'd showed them there was use for their talents. He brought his right knee up hard into Posey's crotch, felt the Indian's hold on him break with his cry of excruciating pain. "Cheat, you say!" he roared back, smashing a judo chop into Posey's jaw. "Wal yo goddamn injun it takes one to know one!"

Samson reeled and fell against the table, overturning it. He heard the accusation, and the shame of its half-truth fed his rage. He tried to gain his footing and slid on the hundreds of bullets rolling around the floor. He steadied himself, picked Maggot out of the diffused maze of darting, shouting figures, rushed toward the cheater, forgetting that once before he had murdered in this same way, forgetting everything Reisman had taught him about fighting as he lunged forward arms extended.

Maggot grasped the Indian's wrist, twisted, smashed his hip into his stomach and flipped him over his back. The building shook as he crashed onto the floor. He got up quickly, just as Maggot, overlooking his own lessons for the moment in his haste to follow up his advantage, came at him full gallop. They collided, struck at each other blindly, overturned tables, benches and cots as they banged against them, and fell apart on the floor.

Samson rose and shook himself, a roaring of voices in his ears. "Give it to him, Chief! Give it to him!" He focused on the others cheering him, their faces eager, their eyes lit up with excitement, and he felt good that all these white men were with him against one of their own. He saw the cheater circling him warily, left arm extended, right arm crooked to block or strike—and he remembered now his lessons. He took his stance, moved forward slowly, feinted a blow with his left, and as Maggot's arm shot out to block it, Samson chopped hard into his belly with his right hand, and a fraction of a second later sent Maggot sprawling across the barracks with a powerful left-handed cut to his shoulder. The men roared their delight!

Reisman leaped between them. "Break!" he commanded. They stood apart, panting heavily, circling, each aware now that the other knew what he was doing. "Bowren, get at the door and send a man out to open the compound gate!" Reisman called out. "Morgan, take one MP and start picking up bullets. There's six hundred rounds of .30 caliber ammo rolling around on the floor and I want every round accounted for." He turned to Maggot. "You want to continue the fun, Kingfish?" he challenged.

"Yo damn raht ah do, Cap'm!" Maggot spat out. "Git thuh hell outen thuh way!"

"Posey?"

"I fix him he don't cheat no more! You bet I fight!"

"Open the door, Corporal!" Reisman called. "We'll do it outside so you don't wreck the barracks. Everybody out one at a time. Search them for ammo as they go through, Bowren."

Outside, in the black rain and mud, with prisoners and guards egging them on, Reisman set Posey and Maggot at each other again. He gave them two rounds, three minutes each, and they fought it to a bloody, bone-rattling, mud-splattered stalemate that was more fun for the watchers than it was for them. Then he made them shake hands.

"I teach you poker without cheating," Samson offered magnanimously. He was surprised the anger in him was spent . . . burned out in the violence of the fight. "I cheat better, too," he added proudly. "You stink!"

Maggot pulled his hand out of the Indian's. "Balls!" he muttered.

Everybody broke into laughter, softening the tension, violence and bloodlust that had been there a moment before, that was always there just below the surface in all of them, ready to subvert, pervert, destroy. Reisman figured it was a good moment to end it. "That's all for tonight, gentlemen," he announced. "Sack time."

The night watch of MPs and prisoners was set, and Reisman stood on the barracks roof and looked out over the wet stockade as Taps sounded. He wondered if guys like Maggot could ever change for the better, at least to the point where they believed faithfully in honor among thieves. It had been one hell of a night of recreation. He imagined Stuart Kinder would have classified it under Therapy.

Tuesday morning, after three days of drilling with carbines and pistols, studying parts and nomenclature, dismantling and assembling, Reisman made the prisoners take the blindfold test. Not that he expected they'd ever have to do it that way some black, bloody night in combat; but it was another challenge to make them sweat and strain, as in every task and exercise he led them to or drove them to, to force them to use the utmost of their bodies and minds—and in this test even their sense of touch and digital dexterity. And it was another way—an aggravating way—to force them to commit themselves to regimen, routine and doing things by the numbers the way the Army wanted them to do it. Reisman aggravated the test further by playing a trick on them.

The prisoners were seated in a rank on the ground in the stockade, their shelter halves spread out in front of them as groundcloths. To the left were their carbines, to the right their .45 pistols. The parts were to be lined up in order on the groundcloths. When they were blindfolded with their scarves, Reisman gave them the signal to dismantle both weapons as speedily as possible and then stop. As they worked, he walked quickly from man to man, his movements lost amid the clatter, and shifted small parts from the carbine file to the pistol file and vice versa. When every man had finished breaking down his weapons, he gave them the order to assemble. Within seconds, there were curses, cries of anguish and confusion, and blind groping of fingers for the right parts on the groundcloths.

"Come on! Come on!" Reisman yelled at them. "Time's running out. What the hell's the matter with you guys?"

Some of them panicked and were immediately all thumbs. Ken Sawyer—more weapon-wise, proven in battle—was the first to get it, put the right parts in the right place, and raised his hand. "Finished, Captain," he called.

Reisman checked his weapons. "Good work, Sawyer," he commended. "You can take off your blindfold now and get a laugh out of watching these other lamebrains. But keep your mouth shut."

Napoleon got it next, and it made him sore to think Reisman would stoop to such trickery. He started to speak out, as much to warn the others as to let Reisman know he was on to him. "So that's what the hell you did! You swit—"

"Keep your mouth shut, White!" snapped Reisman before Napoleon could get it all out. "This isn't a gabfest! Just let me know when you've done the job, that's all!"

Napoleon went back to work, finished assembling both weapons, and was about to call out when Archer Maggot beat him to it with a loud, "Heeyah, Cap'm!"

Reisman checked Maggot's weapons. "Well, Reb," he said with satisfaction, "youall gittin smartuh evruh day."

"Thas right, Cap'm," Maggot answered cockily. "Ah been learning mah lessons real good. It'll take a lot more'n yo got t' fool me. Ah been shooting since ah wuz knee high t' a tadpole anyway. When yoall gonna give us some ammo an let us shoot away?"

"When you stop cheatin at poker, Kingfish."

Reisman moved on to check Napoleon's weapons, then Lever's and Gilpin's. The rest of them never got what he'd done until he called time, had them remove their blindfolds, and they saw how he'd disarranged the parts. They were griping to each other about how unfair it all was when he called them to order.

"Just remember this!" he told them. "The Heinies across the Channel aren't going to lay things out for you nice and neat and tidy. Think, damn you, think! One of these days when your life depends upon it you're going to find a mountain, a river, a village, or a whole damn German division out of place . . . or find a rat where you thought you had a friend. Use your brains! Never accept things completely the way you imagined or were told they were going to be. Put two and two together and if it reads five instead of four, figure out why and then make it work for you. Think!"

Reisman made them put on the blindfolds and run through the drill again—this time without disarranging the parts, even though they expected it now and were wary of him. When they proved to him they really did know the carbines and pistols backward and forward, he took the weapons away from them and issued them new M3 submachine guns that had been crated and waiting for them in the barracks armory.

It startled Morgan, Bowren and the MPs—and even made Reisman more nervous—and all of them more watchful, seeing the Dirty Dozen all bright-eyed and bushy-tailed, handling the same grease guns they used—murderous, ugly, short-barreled weapons without grace, capable of spitting out enough lead in a few seconds to cut a man in two.

Early Tuesday afternoon Corporal Bowren returned from the QM Depot with provisions, some mail for guards and prisoners, and a tightly sealed Manila envelope for Reisman from Stuart Kinder that had been delivered at the cover address by motorcycle dispatch rider early that morning.

Reisman finished reading one of the messages from Kinder, picked up the telephone and held it to his ear a few moments. "Damn if he isn't right!" he muttered.

Bowren was sitting on the cot entering a record of all the other mail—whom it was for, whom and where it had come from—in a notebook Reisman had ordered him to keep for this purpose. He picked his head up. "What's the matter, sir?" he asked.

"Line's dead."

Kinder's frantic message related he had tried to telephone Sunday night and all day Monday without getting through, and had been reluctant to send out any Signal Corps linemen to track down the trouble until Reisman had indicated his approval.

"Better follow the wire out to the road, Clyde, and see what you can find," said Reisman. "Take one of the men with you. Gilpin ought to be a help. He probably knows more about this sort of thing than any of the others. Play it for real and let him do the scouting and the work if he finds anything and can handle it. You just keep an eye on him."

"Sure, Captain," Bowren acknowledged. He finished recording the day's mail and got up to go out into the compound where Sergeant Morgan and the guards had been left apprehensively overseeing the prisoners practicing sighting and aiming, position and trigger squeeze exercises with their grease guns.

Reisman opened another envelope that had been in the Manila folder. It contained a personal note from Kinder, an official order and two pair of buck Sergeant's stripes. Reisman's eyes glowed warmly. "Hey . . . hold on a minute!" he called after Bowren. "Here's something for you . . . Sergeant!"

Bowren stuck his head in the doorway. "Did you want the Sergeant, sir?"

"You're it!" said Reisman enthusiastically. He stood up and held out the mimeographed order. "Uncle Sam decided to give you a raise in pay and status."

"Well I'll be damned," said Bowren softly, coming back into the room. He took the order, read it and tried to get used to the idea, shaking his head back and forth slowly. Then he looked at Reisman and said simply, "Thanks a lot, Captain."

Reisman handed him the two pair of buck Sergeant's stripes. "Captain Kinder wants you to have these as his gift, and he sends his congratulations."

Bowren took the stripes and slipped them into his pocket.

"Got a needle and thread?" Reisman bantered.

"Later, sir," said Bowren. "Gotta get used to the idea first. I'd better see to that phone line now."

In less than half an hour, he and Gilpin were back in the compound from their scouting patrol, and he summoned Reisman aside to whisper to him, "You'd better come with us and have a look at this, Captain."

"What did you find?"

"There's a break all right . . . beyond the wall, just off the road. Gilpin says he can splice it together good as new if we bring out some tools and tape."

"What the problem then?"

"It doesn't look like any accident to me, and it sure as hell didn't wear out!"

Reisman went with them. In the brush beside the public road, he picked up the parted strands of telephone wire and examined them.

Gilpin stood close to him and pointed with a finger. "I'd say a critter was at it," he suggested. "See here on the insulation. Looks like teeth marks . . . like something bit down on it and gnawed away. If they got coon or coyote hereabout, I wouldn't be surprised. Even a big fat jackrabbit or a frisky deer could do that sometime."

The implanted thought took root and jarred another one in Reisman's mind. He looked in the direction of the manor house, hidden from him here by trees and brush and the stone wall, and he knew that what he was thinking was truly possible—outlandish and unlikely as it seemed.

"No . . . no coyotes, Gilpin," he muttered. "Maybe just a frightened bitch."

Reisman reached Stuart Kinder in London by telephone.

"It was a break in the line, Stu," he explained. "Ersatz war material, I suppose, or one of the linemen may have goofed. We fixed it ourselves. What was it you were trying to call me about?"

"Corporal Bowren's promotion . . . and I just wanted to keep up with how things were going," came the reply.

"Oh," said Reisman, his voice reflecting both disappointment and sarcasm. "I was hoping maybe the great brains had decided how we were actually going to use the bully boys."

"No, not yet," Kinder told him. "They're not really ready for anything like that anyway, are they?"

"No, but they're getting warmer every day. They're keeping their noses fairly clean and working hard. I'm going to start setting up a firing range, and I figure by Saturday I ought to be able to turn them loose on it and see which way they send the lead flying."

"I want to be there for that, John," said Kinder. " 'Fact I ought to come down a day or two in advance . . . make sure they're in the right frame of mind . . . Information and Education . . . motivation."

"Glad to have you. Just bring a helmet and a bullet-proof vest," Reisman said.

"John . . . don't kid me. You don't really think it's going to be that bad, do you?"

"Actually, I don't . . . but *¿quién sabe?* Anything else for me?"

"Yes. There was a strange fellow around asking for you yesterday. He showed up just after I'd sealed the dispatch and was sending it off. That's why I didn't write you about him," explained Kinder. "Seems he turned up at Baker Street and Major Armbruster sent him over to me . . . told him I'd be able to put you in touch."

"Who was it?"

"CID man named Osterman."

Reisman's heart skipped a beat. He hadn't really been prepared for it, despite his father's letter. And hearing the old name again, conjuring up and catalyzing in the instant the whole rueful business he'd fled fourteen years before . . . and knowing Osterman had actually come into this new, far distant, different life and place to see him . . . set the adrenalin pumping stronger.

"Leon Osterman," Kinder went on. "Identified himself

as an agent with the Seventh CID. Got his badge number here . . . 840.”

"Did you tell him where I was?"

"No. Of course not. I told him I'd be in touch with you and would give you his address, that's all. Do you know the man, John?"

"Yes, I know him," Reisman answered. "It's all right." Yet, in answering, he realized that he really didn't *know* Leon Osterman . . . and it really wasn't *all right*, for he wasn't sure he wanted to see him now . . . to revive old memories interred and maybe best left that way. Remembering, he wasn't even sure if he liked or disliked the man. There was always a tendency to hate someone who has done you a favor you can never repay. Nevertheless he jotted down the London address and phone number as Kinder read them off, telling himself he should at least send a note to Osterman acknowledging that his message had been delivered.

Then he got off the subject quickly. "Listen . . . since you're coming down anyway," he asked Kinder, "can you round up some things for the men and bring them down with you?"

"Delighted to," Kinder answered. "Pencil's ready . . . shoot!"

Reisman asked him to requisition some games, athletic equipment, and all the recent copies of *Stars and Stripes* and *Yank* and any other newspapers and magazines he could get hold of through the various service organizations that provided that sort of thing. "One other thing," he added. "And you probably know more about this than I do. I want to help Samson Posey learn to read and write. Are there any simple primers or instruction books you can get for me?"

"Yes, indeed, John!" Kinder told him enthusiastically. "The War Department has put out some very good, basic manuals on reading, writing and arithmetic. They're just what you want. Pictures, drawings, simple words, problems and answers, relating in particular to the military life. I'll requisition them immediately. It's a wonderful idea! I should have thought of it myself."

"Well, I'm sure you would have, Stu," Reisman said with an unaccustomed glimmer of tact. "I'm closer to the man now, that's all. He's not dumb, by any means. In fact, he's pretty sharp. But he's groping in a world he doesn't

326

quite understand, and I think this is one way we can help him, and help ourselves at the same time." Reisman wanted to hang up now and get back outside with the men, but there was still another matter he'd hoped Kinder would bring up without being pressed. "How are you making out with Myron Odell?" he asked. "You remember what we talked about, don't you?"

"Of course I do," Kinder acknowledged. "I was going to save it until I saw you in person."

Kinder seemed to be backing away from it, and that only made Reisman more anxious. "Why don't you just brief me on it now?" he said.

"Well . . . I've personally gone over every aspect of his record . . . and the records of the other men, just as you asked," said Kinder. "A complete analysis of his psychological tests showed nothing more than what I'd already indicated to you. I've also discussed him with other men here in my field. Very discreetly, of course, without revealing his name or current circumstances. To throw off any suspicions, I posed him as a sample case . . . an imaginary conglomerate put together for purposes of one of my studies."

"What did they think of the chances of this Frankenstein actually being innocent?"

"Not much. We all felt that in the specific situation I posed, this Mr. X was very capable of committing criminal violence," Kinder said. "I used as an example the actual circumstances of Odell's case . . . the background and psychological state of the man, what he remembered of his meetings with the victim prior to the night of the crime, and what he related of the events of that night up to the point where he went blank. But I didn't tell them it had actually happened. I offered it as a fictitious situation. We all felt Mr. X was indeed very capable of rape-murder. And that, of course, bears out what the court-martial decided on the basis of the circumstantial and physical evidence they had in hand . . . rather than this fantasy of innocence which Odell goes around inflicting upon everybody, including himself."

"But shouldn't there have been grounds then for a strong insanity plea?" argued Reisman.

"Not by the legal definition," Kinder told him. "All the prosecutor would have had to do to prove he was legally sane was show he'd been carrying out his duties in a satisfactory way . . . which he was . . . and that he knew the difference between right and wrong . . . which he does. It certainly wasn't made an issue by his defending officer at the court-martial."

"Defending officer, hell!" snapped Reisman. "He was probably an insurance salesman or a college kid in civilian life!"

"Not in a case of this seriousness," Kinder contended. "It's true that just about any officer can act as a defense lawyer in a court-martial, but the Army's got many good lawyers in uniform now and they're the ones who get the serious cases, defending and prosecuting. I'll grant you they're probably harried and overworked and don't have the same time and facilities to prepare their cases as they would in civilian life, but I'm certain Odell and the rest of your men got the best legal aid available for them."

Reisman found himself incomprehensibly defending Odell heatedly, as though it was Stuart Kinder who had prosecuted him and somehow done him wrong. "But what if the circumstantial and physical evidence was wrong!" he insisted.

"I'm afraid that reopening his case . . . or any of their cases . . . from an investigative or legal point of view won't be possible," Kinder replied.

"Why not?" demanded Reisman. "I thought you'd promised to try it on the q.t. You seem to be in a good position to get things done well and fast."

"I did try," reported Kinder. "But it's not the sort of thing one can do completely on the q.t., John, unless I were to undertake the legwork and labor of it myself, which would put me way beyond my authority and responsibility, not to speak of the time away from my own duties. I approached certain people in the Judge Advocate General's department, the Military Police and the Criminal Investigation Division . . . and let me say that it was an extremely difficult thing to do without revealing my motives."

"What happened?"

"We're completely blocked, John," said Kinder, his voice sounding almost reluctant to reply. "Despite any personal feelings or opinions we may have, there is nothing we can do for them except train and qualify them for their assignments to the best of our abilities. I didn't make that decision for them. You didn't make it. And the Army didn't make it. They made it themselves."

"What do you mean?"

"We seem to have forgotten," said Kinder gently, "that when they volunteered for Project Amnesty, they gave up for the duration of their assignment all claim to review, appeal, new investigation or retrial."

The words sank in, and Reisman realized he had forgotten—or wanted to forget. And though he still didn't understand fully why he should be trying to find an out for Odell, or any of the others, or why he should even care, he only knew that he did. "Well, thanks for trying, Stu," he said softly. "I appreciate your efforts. I guess you might say we're in a state of limbo down here, and that's the way it's got to be for a while."

Only when he'd hung up did he realize he'd used the wrong word. In Limbo there were only innocent souls. This was more like Purgatory.

—

23

—

LATE WEDNESDAY afternoon Reisman brought the men in from the field where they'd started laying out the firing range and excavating target pits, and found a staff car parked outside the stockade. He waited until all the prisoners and guards had passed through the barracks into the compound, then walked into his office, expecting to find Stuart Kinder.

"Hello, Big Shot!" said the man sprawled comfortably in his chair. "The door was open so I came in and made myself at home."

Reisman stared dumfounded. It was no longer necessary to give occasional, annoying thought to how and when he should contact Leon Osterman. There he was, dressed in tweedy English country clothes, hands crossed contentedly across his stomach, an unlit cigar stub in his mouth, and a big grin of satisfaction on his florid, beefy face.

"The door was locked . . . and so was the fence," said Reisman.

"All right . . . so the door was locked," agreed Osterman with a shrug. "I learned breaking and entering from the best pros in the business."

"How did you find me? Nobody is supposed to know."

Osterman bounced up from the chair, his right hand extended. "How the hell you think I got to be the best detective on the Chicago cops! Chrisakes, kid, you look grimmer than the police commissioner on a bad day. Where's your manners? First say hello, then ask questions."

Reisman stared at him stupefied, unable to respond for a moment, while he tried to organize his feelings. It had been a long time since he had found himself so inadequately prepared to handle a situation. Finally a broad, spontaneous grin spread across his tired face. Though he still wasn't sure what he felt about this brass, profane, flesh-and-blood wraith who had suddenly materialized out of his remembered past, it was no longer alarm. "Hello, Sarge," he said, taking his hand. "Long time no see."

"Too long, Johnny! And you recognized me, huh, after all these years!" Osterman responded warmly. He pointed to his head and his paunch. "Less hair, more gut, this worn-out, ugly puss, and you still knew the old Sarge, huh!" He clapped an arm heartily around Reisman's shoulders. "Your old man sends you a kiss, but you ain't getting it from me. You got a girl, I'll give it to her, she gives it to you."

"How is he?" Reisman asked, managing to extricate himself from the bear hug by pointing Osterman back to the chair he'd just vacated, saying "Sit down!" and seating himself on the edge of the cot—thankful there had been no reason to bring any of the guards or prisoners into the office with him.

"He's fine, kid, just fine," said Osterman, settling himself, comfortably in the chair. "I seen him about two months ago and he's okay. Still driving a hack . . . making a living. Only complaint is you don't write often enough."

Reisman laughed softly at that, and though questions demanding more immediate answers still raced through his mind, he delayed them a bit longer with pleasantries. "I got a letter from him a month ago . . . maybe the first one I ever got from him in my life," he related. "Even I do better than that." But visualizing Aaron again—his world and image brought into the room by this visitor—he added guiltily, "I've got to answer it soon."

"Heck, kid, you know how the folks are," said Osterman. "They can never get enough no matter how much you write. It ain't the letters. It's the boys they want back. God knows there's enough with the same complaint these days . . . not only your old man." He looked around the room, tossed his dead cigar stub into a butt can on the desk and took a fresh one from his breast pocket.

Reisman refused one for himself, lit a cigaret quickly, and held his lighter out for Osterman. "Pop mentioned you were in the Army and came to see him before shipping out," he said.

"Yeh, I told him I was gonna look you up," said Osterman between deep puffs on the cigar. He got it glowing well, took it from his mouth and stared pensively at the new gray ash. "He misses you, Johnny. He's real proud of you. Talks about you all over the neighborhood. I'm supposed to tell you to send a picture so he remembers what the hell you look like. It's been a long war for you, ain't it, kid? He told me you joined up right away . . . even before Pearl Harbor."

Reisman nodded, but he didn't know what to say. *Before Pearl Harbor* sounded strange and meaningless to him, and the years of his wars went back too far and were too complex to be covered by the simplicity and implied patriotism of the slogan. He didn't know what he was expected to explain now or if he was expected to say anything. No doubt, for his father, the phrase covered so many blank spots he didn't know anything about, for though he'd always had some inkling of what his son had been doing all these years, he didn't really *know;* and the extent of those years and blank spots, therefore, Leon Osterman had no way of knowing. Reisman was here now in this war for those same reasons he had been anywhere and everywhere else in all his other wars, and Osterman's look of genuine sympathy and concern, fashioned on a wrong perspective, was embarrassing.

"You look great, kid, just great!" Osterman ran on, brightening again to Reisman's relief. "Sure, you're a man now . . . no more a kid, but I would've knowed you anywhere. And you're doing okay, huh? A Captain, goddammit! That's something! I knew I wasn't making no mistake steering you straight when you was a punk kid. Tell me all about yourself, Johnny. What in hell you doing way out here in the sticks?"

"Whoa! You're going too fast!" Reisman said. "First you

tell me, Sarge, then maybe I tell you. Pop gave you my mail address, and I heard from London yesterday you were looking for me up there, but I know damned well nobody gave you the guided tour to this joint. It's strictly *verboten!* How the hell did you find me out here, and what are you doing in mufti?"

"I'm a tourist on vacation, kid. It's a hell of a racket. I got the only job in the Army they let you wear civvies, ain't that something?" Osterman said. "Even the Generals gotta wear their zoot suits, but me and the other guys in the outfit wear whatever we think'll do the job."

"And sniffing around the Devonshire countryside looking for Johnny Reisman you figured you'd better look English tweedy?" asked Reisman.

"Yeah, that's it . . . sort of."

"Driving a U.S. Army staff car?"

"You know, kid, that's the one thing I ain't figured out how to change yet!"

The both laughed at that, and Reisman asked, "What are you doing in the Army anyway? You sure as hell weren't drafted at your age. I'd have thought you'd still be keeping the boys in line in Chicago."

"They needed a coupla tough old bastards like me to keep you guys in line over here," Osterman explained. "They were going around to cops all over the country looking for volunteers, so when I heard about it, I told them I wanted in. I got no close family, you know. Still an old bach . . . they used to say I was married to the force . . . so it don't make no diff. The fact I was in the Army the first time we took a crack at these bastards probably helped, too. That's why I did so good on the force. You know, being a GI . . . only we called them Doughboys back then . . . and being active in the American Legion and the Jewish War Veterans and half a dozen Lodges . . . even the same synagogue where your old man's a member. It's all good politics for a cop. But I never saw any action in the First War, and this time I really wanted in. It's too big to stay out of, and it's more personal this time, too. I get the angry shakes every time I think of that son-of-a-bitch Hitler. I'd like to be the guy that nabs him, and get in a few licks myself before they string him up. It ain't likely in my line of work, but what the hell, at least I'll be a part of it. Somebody's gonna get him."

"They give you guys some kind of rank, don't they?"

asked Reisman. "I figure you for at least a Major or a Colonel. Maybe I ought to be saluting you and calling you sir instead of Sarge."

"Nah! It's still Sarge. But, you know, they offered me a commission. I should be a Major. What do you think of that, kid, huh! I would've outranked you. Wouldn't that have been something! Major Sergeant Leon Osterman, or maybe Sergeant Major Leon Osterman! I told them Nah! All my life I been a Sergeant . . . maybe twenty years . . . and I told them I wouldn't know who the hell they was talking to if somebody yelled, 'Hey, Major!' So I wanted to be just a Sergeant in a cop's job and that's what I got, CID. I go out on a case just like I was home in Chicago, and I'm pretty much my own boss, seeing as how I know more than the brass about this business, anyway!"

"You're not on some kind of a case down here, are you?"

"No. Like I said, I'm a tourist on vacation. I had a coupla days coming to me, so I decided to look you up."

"You're not kidding me, are you?"

"No. Christ, kid, you're awfully suspicious in your old age. You do something I ought to know about?"

"No. The point is, Sarge, I'm doing something you shouldn't know about. How did you find where I was?"

"You got time now, huh, Johnny? I mean, can you talk or you got something important to do?" Osterman asked. The sounds of orders being shouted and the men setting up camp drifted in to them, and he, too, had been glancing through the window. To Reisman he seemed to be backing away from a direct answer. "I mean I wanted to surprise you and all that," Osterman went on, apologetically, "but I know you got a job to do, kid, and if I'm interrupting something, don't feel you gotta be nice or anything. I'm in the way, you just tell me and I clear out. I could meet you in town later, buy you a coupla drinks and a good dinner, and we could really have a time!"

"Sure I've got something important to do. But I'm making time," Reisman told him, trying to hide the rising irritation he felt. He got up, paced to the window and back, and stood there waiting. "What I ask you is not just idle curiosity. It's very important to me."

"Sure, Johnny. I got nothing to hide," Osterman declared, with a mischievous grin. "It was kind of funny, anyhow."

The way he explained it, it had been ridiculously easy for him—and the only consolation for Reisman was that it wouldn't have been for somebody else. Using his position as CID agent, Osterman had traced him through the Army Post Office to the Baker Street office of Major Max Armbruster. Max had checked his credentials, and apparently not feeling there was any breach of security involved, had directed him to the office of Stuart Kinder as the quickest, though purposefully still indirect, way of being put in touch with his "old friend from Chicago." Kinder, whom he called "that snotty kid," had given him the run-around, but Osterman had already caught a glimpse of Reisman's name and the QM Depot address on the dispatch envelope as it was being sent off, so he had more or less accomplished his mission there anyway.

"What did you learn up in London about me?" Reisman interrupted. "About my work and the outfit I'm with."

"Nothing. What the hell you think I was asking you all those questions for your old man for? They were pretty tight about it up there . . . that Major with the handlebars and that snotty kid. So I figured I'd leave that part of it alone, except for finding out where you were so I could see you."

"How about this place and the men here? What do you know about it?"

"Nothing. Jeezus Christ, kid, let me finish my story, will you. I'm getting to the good part."

"Yeh, I'm sorry. Go ahead."

Osterman related how he had taken some leave time that was coming to him and had driven down to the QM Depot, only to learn there was no Captain Reisman there, it was just a mail and supply drop. But at that point he was one very tenacious cop who had no intention of being led on a wild goose chase. Using his CID card, some phony story about a black market ring, and the tactfully threatening manner of the experienced detective, he had inveigled the noncom whose job it was to hold Reisman's mail and supplies, into helping him. When Bowren had showed up at the cover address the day before, Osterman had been parked in a convenient lookout spot, had been given the high sign by the noncom and had tailed the truck back to Stokes Manor, going past the gate and back into the Village to make inquiries about the place and spend the night.

"They told me in town the place belonged to some English General and his crazy daughter was staying here alone," said Osterman. "Nobody said nothing about soldiers being out here, so whatever the hell you're hiding, kid, you're doing a pretty good job of it. But I say to myself, Jeezus Christ, it sure looks fishy, and even besides wanting to look you up because I promised your old man, maybe I ought to come out here and see what's going on anyway."

"It's a good way to get shot sometimes," said Reisman. "Well, now that you've seen, what do you think?"

"I don't know, Johnny. Maybe you ought to tell me. Is it honest?"

Reisman had to smile at that. "Always the good cop, aren't you?" he chided. "I'm not sure if it's honest or not . . . but not in the way you mean. You didn't stop at the manor house, did you?" he asked suddenly.

"No. Soon as I come through the gate I seen where the trucks been cutting off the road so I followed it . . . and here I am, surprise! I was just getting tired of waiting for you when you come in with that Boy Scout troop. That's quite a bunch, Johnny. What in hell you up to out here?"

"It's some experimental training work," Reisman said. "Sort of an endurance test . . . that's why some of them probably looked pretty bad to you. They're the test group. The others are the standard group against which we evaluate them. It's sort of classified, so I can't tell you anything more about it." His tone was almost apologetic, trying to make it all sound inconsequential.

"Don't give me that crap, Johnny," said Osterman, getting up and going to the window. "I can smell a con a mile away . . . by the look of them, the walk, the stink of them inside and out. You don't want to talk . . . you're not supposed to talk . . . okay. Maybe I shouldn'ta stuck my nose in down here. But don't try to give the old Sarge no fairy tales. Half of those guys out there look like they been doing time on Devil's Island or Joliet."

"How about me, Sarge?" Reisman said defensively. "Do I look like a con to you, too?"

Osterman turned back. "You look great, I told you. I'll give a good report to your old man."

"But I could have been a con, huh, Sarge? Or maybe I should have been?" He regretted saying that as soon as it was out. But saying it, he realized he hadn't just dredged it up out of nowhere, or pulled it out of thin air to make small talk. It was one of the things that had been there all these years gnawing at him. It was what had really bothered him in the beginning about getting this assignment.

"You're not the type, Johnny," said Osterman, looking at him quizzically. "That's why I stuck out my neck to help you. What you did when you was a kid back then in Chicago wasn't a crime. If it was, I wouldn'ta helped you. You did what you did because you had to, because you had guts, moxie . . . call it whatever you want . . . and what you did was right. And what I did, I did because it was the best way to handle it. It's the years since that count. Like you see, it done no harm to nobody. Nobody was ever the wiser."

"Except you and me . . . and my father," said Reisman, and it struck him now, with Osterman there to bring it home to him and to clarify it for him, that one of the reasons he had committed himself so completely to the Dirty Dozen, to the point of trying to prove guilt to be innocence, to make the unredeemable redeemable, to turn debasement and dishonor into pride and glory, was that he was trying in a way to repay the unrepayable favor Osterman had done for him so long ago, and thereby expiate his own guilt.

"It still bothers you, don't it, kid?" Osterman's voice broke in.

Yes! Reisman wanted to cry out . . . But not only, as Osterman probably thought, the residual guilt of a justified killing in self-defense performed by a hysterical sixteen-year-old. What bothered him more was the guilt of the cowardice that had preceded it and for which he had never forgiven himself . . . the guilt of not facing up to the consequences afterward . . . the guilt of running away as Osterman had arranged for him to do after erasing his connection with what was publicized then as another mobster killing . . . and the guilt of all the *justified* killings since then, driven to seek his own form of vindication in his own way. "Doesn't it bother you?" he challenged. "Isn't that why you're here? Isn't that why you've always asked my father about me? Isn't that why you went to see him to get

336

my address? To make sure again you'd done the right thing?"

"Yeah, I guess you're right, kid. But I didn't think you was gonna make no Federal case out of it after all these years. Would you have wanted me to turn you in, have a record and a trial? You would've got off anyway because no judge or jury in the world would've convicted you for defending yourself. And if you'd have stayed around Chicago or if your name had come into it, self-defense or not, your life wouldn't have been worth a plugged nickel. I couldn't have helped you. The whole damn force couldn't have helped you. The mob that guy ran with would've come after you, and maybe even your old man. What the hell! That's ancient history anyway. Look, you want to meet me in town later?"

"No. I'd like to tell you about this place and the men in it," said Reisman, surprising himself as much as he did Osterman. "I'd like you to stay . . . and help me." He could trust him. He was sure of it. Osterman had just the right touch of larceny in him to make him honorable.

"Hey, Pope!" one of the MPs called. "The CO wants to see you."

Odell crawled out of his puptent, where he'd been hoping to catch a few minutes' rest before chow. He hated it when they called him that . . . *Pope Innocent!* . . . and they were all doing it, guards and prisoners, mocking him because he wasn't guilty like the others. He went with the guard into the barracks, into Captain Reisman's office.

"I'd like you to talk to this gentleman, Odell," said the Captain, not bothering with formal introductions. "He's going to ask you some questions about yourself . . . about what happened up there in Glasgow, and about your court-martial. We're going to try to help you. We'll do everything we can to check out your claim that you're innocent."

The suddenness of it made Odell's heart pound massively against his ribs, throbbing and echoing to his ears.

"It will take a lot of time," the Captain went on, "and I don't want you getting your hopes too high . . . but, believe me, Odell, if you're telling the truth, this man will be

337

able to help you, and we'll do everything we can to clear you. If you're not telling the truth, you can only help yourself."

Odell felt strange, the air constricted in his nose and throat, his eyes moistened. "I'm telling the truth, sir," he squeezed out hoarsely.

"You are not to tell anybody about this meeting, or what was discussed. Do you understand?" said Reisman.

"Yes, sir. I understand, sir."

Leon Osterman took over, and for Reisman it was a revelation to watch him work.

"Tell me about yourself, Mike," said Osterman. "That's your name, ain't it . . . Mike?"

"No, sir. It's Myron."

"Well, you look like a Mike," said Osterman, smiling. "Pretty rugged guy, I'd say."

"Well, I've learned a lot, sir, these last few weeks training with the Captain. Before that I wasn't too rugged. He taught me a lot."

He smiled at Reisman shyly as he said that, and Reisman didn't know if he was putting it on or not.

"Give you a bath and a shave and I bet you'd look like one of them tough Hollywood movie stars, huh?" Osterman kidded him.

Odell shrugged and fidgeted and actually blushed. Any guile he had hoped to use was drained out of him and he was left limp and open and naturally responsive.

"You know, Myron, I've worked with a lot of young fellers like you over the years," said Osterman, "and I've been able to help a lot of them. There's only one thing I ask, and that's that you play it straight with me right down the line. Tell the truth, the whole truth and nothing but the truth, like they say in court. Being in trouble ain't half as bad as trying to lie your way out. It never works. You make a mistake . . . okay. Best thing you do is face up to it like a man . . . you do your time, and you never make that mistake again. Now tell me about yourself, and what you did up there in Glasgow."

Glasgow? Odell seemed hardly to remember that he had ever been there. It was another world, and the man there maybe another man. Yet he talked frankly now about the history of that other man to this stranger in the tweed suit who imparted to him the firmness and gentleness and interest of a father . . .

He was in the medics . . . because he'd told every classification officer and noncom he'd run into in those early days of induction back in the States that was where he belonged and could serve his country and the Army best. He'd believed that, too, because he knew he couldn't have taken any of the other branches with the weapons and explosions and having to learn to fight and kill. He'd known medics went into the front lines, too, and sometimes were in even worse spots than the soldiers they had to help, and were wounded and killed, but he'd face that if and when it came—which he didn't think it would in his case, and because he'd do everything he could to get out of it—as long as he didn't have to go out there with a gun in his hands to kill and maim and give the enemy the right to do the same to him. Contrary to the old Army game, the classification people had believed him, too, and he'd actually been assigned to the branch he wanted and where he really did fit best.

After his medic training, they made him a hospital orderly. He was pretty good at it, made T/5 in a short while, and really had no ambition to do or be anything else in the Army. He didn't mind ministering to the sick and injured —though at one hospital where he'd been stationed, he took care of his first cases of combat wounded and they made him nervous by their pain and their wrecked bodies and their memories, told to each other in comradeship he couldn't share, or screamed out in nightmares that filled him with fear that there were things like that out there waiting for him.

In his off hours, he kept pretty much to himself—usually staying on the Post, going to movies, walking, looking, hanging aimlessly around day rooms, service clubs, PXs, or walking around towns by himself staring at people and things and places—not open-faced, but in a curious sort of slantwise way or darting quick nervous glances that tried to appear not to be too interested, so as not to invite an answering look; feeling a small hunger for something but not knowing what it was, minding his own business and staying out of trouble. He didn't buddy around with any of the guys, or go after women the same way they did, though he listened hungrily to hospital and barracks tales of sexual conquest. He knew he wasn't particularly liked, that some of the guys he worked with thought he was strange or there was something wrong with him, and a few even questioned his manhood with snide remarks that made him angry and almost got him into a few fights, but never quite, because he never let it go that far, backing down before he was ever brought to the point of testing himself—with men or women. He supposed later that stuff like that was maybe noticed and kept in a secret record by the noncoms and officers.

He hadn't wanted to go overseas—it meant he would be closer to the reality of the war, the coming Invasion, and the test he knew he would fail—but there had been nothing he could do to prevent it. Trained medics were needed to fill Tables of Organization overseas, and there was no officer or noncom who liked him enough to try to keep him in his last Stateside post. He hadn't minded then, and had been glad at first, when, after debarking at Greenock in the Firth of Clyde, he had been assigned, in one of those crazy quirks of the Army and the fortunes of war, to Glasgow to a small branch prophylactic station for the prevention of venereal disease, instead of to a line outfit readying for the Invasion, as he had feared.

Guys came into the station for treatment after they'd had intercourse with a woman. They came in directly, matter-of-factly, by plan, order or both; they came wandering in shyly, just happening to find it, and thinking maybe they'd better make use of the facilities after all; they came staggering in drunk, obscene and obnoxious, and lucky to find it; and they came terrifiedly racing in, remembering the grim horrors of their *Mickey Mouse* movies. It was Odell's duty to give pros to these sexually sated, happy, bragging, sometimes griping, sometimes panicky, sometimes sad members of the American and Allied forces, or help them give themselves one: internal prophylaxis of the penis with a syringe squirting sulfa ointment, and general external prophylaxis of the testicles, scrotum and pubic area, rubbing in the excess sticky ointment. It was a crazy place for him to be. It made him feel strange all the time. He never ceased to be amazed, awed or cowed by these cocksmen, though it was with the sad or panicky ones he felt most closely allied.

The place was kept open round the clock, though there was only one medical technician alone there on duty at a time. Odell worked various shifts, and there was generally a fairly brisk trade, tapering off to a bare trickle around

0300, picking up again as men roused themselves from strange beds, nesting places and gutters to rush back to Reveille calls and military duties in the hours around dawn, and then falling off again to almost nothing in the morning hours of the day when the women no doubt took their deserved and needed rest.

Penises! That was what he remembered most about Glasgow. Thousands and thousand of sets of virile, hairy-framed penises and testicles—short ones, long ones, circumcised, uncircumcised, fat, thin, dark, light—mocking him because he, in that place, was an impostor who had never made proper use of his own.

His duties had finally begun to get through to him, making him more nervous, depressed and irritable than ever, and he had been trying to work up enough courage to ask for a transfer—knowing fearfully that it might be to a line outfit—when the poor half-witted girl had showed up at the pro station the first time. It had been during one of the quiet times when he was completely and gratefully alone with nobody to treat, sitting in the anteroom of the clinic reading a magazine, maybe dozing, when she came in. His first reaction was one of shock and embarrassment seeing a female in that place and having her see him there. Then the odd sight and sound of her focused for him, startling him in a different way—though afterward, when he realized she suffered from some defect, some mental impairment probably, he felt sorry for her, something of the delicately balanced empathy-sympathy of love-hate that one cripple might feel for another.

She was unkempt, with long dark hair falling over her face and shoulders, dirt on her face, hands and worn clothing, and was jabbering away strangely so that at first he couldn't really understand her and thought maybe she had been in an accident or had been attacked and had come in there asking for help. She was big, her body mature, but it was hard for him to tell then how old she was. Her face was not vacuous, but struggling in halting speech and uncertain emotion; and looking into that face, into her eyes, he imagined she could be any age from fifteen to twenty-five—but what did he know of the ages and problems of girls and women? Only later, at his court-martial, did he hear her described as a mentally defective nineteen-year-old virgin—though there was nobody who

341

had thought it necessary to also describe him as a psychologically disturbed virgin who wasn't sure if he was twenty-three or twenty-four.

Finally coming out of his bewilderment at the sight of this female apparition, and understanding what it was she was saying to him, he was even more startled and embarrassed than before. She was asking if that wasn't the place where a girl came to find a boy friend to love her and make love to her.

Somebody had to have put her up to it, or brought her there, Odell realized later. A cruel and heartless joke, maybe by some soldier to whom she had made her witless proposition. But if there was such a somebody, or group of them, he was never to learn who. His first impulse was to get her out of the pro station as speedily as possible. He ordered her to go home in an authoritative, if somewhat frantic, voice that startled her and actually sent her scurrying back out through the doorway. But when he went to see if she had really gone, there she was lurking timorously in the street, trying to work up enough courage to come at him again. It gave Odell a strange feeling, for rarely had anybody allowed him to feel that there was any such power of command in his rather weak voice and uncertain manner.

His relief came on then, and sizing up the strange tableau of Odell in the doorway and the extremely unappetizing girl on the street, the man leered at them in a knowing way that really knew nothing at all, and said something inane like, "So that's your girl, eh, Myron. I was telling the boys you wasn't queer like they said!"

Odell turned back into the clinic in embarrassed anger. "She's not my girl!" he insisted to the other medic. "She came in here looking for somebody. Maybe you!"

The man dropped into the chair Odell had vacated, put his feet up on the desk they used for their clerical work, and picked up the magazine Odell had been reading. "Go on, beat it!" he said, laughing. "You're relieved. Every man to his own taste. You can use one of the back rooms if you want. I won't watch. It'll be quiet for a while. If it gets busy, maybe I'll sell tickets and we can split the take."

Odell cursed him, but the man just sat there comfortably and jeered, "Go on, quick, Myron, before somebody else gets her!"

"Can't you see the poor thing is sick?" said Odell, going

342

out the door and feeling slightly ill himself, his heart hammering. The girl was still there. "Go home!" he shouted at her. "Go home and clean yourself, for God's sake . . . and comb your hair and change your clothing!"

She stood there on the quiet street in the gray morning, frightened, but trying to understand—and then she smiled at him.

"Go home!" he shouted. "Or I'll call the MPs! I'll call the police!"

She scurried away with determination on her face then and direction in her movements, with him feeling terribly sorry for her, and he went in the opposite direction, taking a roundabout way back to his quarters. He wondered where she lived, who she was, what was wrong with her, if she would go back to the pro station, and if somebody else with less consideration than he would take advantage of her. In his barracks bed, he fell into a fitful sleep, filled with sexual fantasies in which the girl became all mixed up with the woman at the orphan home in Cleveland who was the only woman he had ever seen naked. He woke up with a start, feeling a strange quiver going through him. His pajamas were wet. He had had an emission for the first time in many years, and he felt very ashamed and frightened.

The girl came back to the pro station the very next shift Odell was on duty. She knew his name. "Mahh-run! . . . Mahh-run!" she said in excited recognition. Somebody had to have put her up to it this time, if not the first, too—possibly one or more of the other medics, or soldiers who used the facilities often. She probably had come back there looking for him in her pitifully eager, expectant way during the hours he'd been off, and had been coached when to return and what to say and do. Still, he didn't chase her away, as he knew he should. She had actually done what he had shrieked at her to do the day before. She was far from being pretty, but she was scrubbed clean, and her chestnut hair was no longer matted and stringy, but seemed to have been washed and brushed, and looked nice falling down her shoulders and back; and her dress, which she proudly showed immediately she took off her worn coat, was a bright sort of party thing.

His heart pounding excitedly, Odell told her to sit down, and went out into the street to see if there was somebody lurking there to observe the fun of her being thrown out again, or to crash in on them together with filthy, mocking insinuations. There was nobody. It was the quiet time in the street, as it was for him alone in the pro station. He came back inside again, really not knowing what he was to do or say next. He looked at the girl and she smiled at him, brushing her hands nervously along the fabric of her dress, tugging at the hem to pull it down over her knees and appear demure.

"What's your name?" he asked nervously, sitting on the edge of the desk, looking not quite at her but at a spot beyond her on the wall. He couldn't meet her eyes, and if he looked down he would be looking at her bare white legs and knees and a bit of fleshy thigh, for she had leaned over to place her coat on another chair and this made her short skirt slide up again.

The girl leaned forward and stared at him, smiling eagerly with her jaw open. "Cat-the-rine . . . Cat-the-rine . . . Cat . . . Cat," she said.

"Your name is Catherine . . . and you're a cat," said Odell, chuckling to cover the agitation he felt, and quite pleased with himself for the cleverness of his little repartee.

She shook her head vigorously, first yes and then no, while she moved her hand rapidly in front of her, pointing to herself. "Cat! . . . Cat!" she said.

"Your name is Catherine and you're called Cat for short," he said.

She bobbed her head in assent, saying "Yes! Yes!" happily.

They talked for a little while, and with each minute she seemed to be calmer—as Odell was surprised to find he was himself—and her speech was less jabbering and more clear. He asked where she lived and she waved her hand outward and named a nearby section of the city. He asked if she had parents or brothers and sisters and she said she did. She never volunteered anything—except for the distressingly guileless invitation of her face and eyes and flesh —but when he asked her something she would respond eagerly, as though grateful for this chance to talk. No, her family didn't know where she was, though they probably knew by now that she was out and might even be looking for her to catch her and bring her home and punish her, for none of them really loved her or were kind to her.

"I understand," Odell said softly. Out of terrible depths

344

of loneliness and loveless memories, he was drawn to her. But what she had said also made him nervous and wary, for he surely didn't want any trouble to arise over what for him was a perfectly innocent situation. When he asked her why she had come in there and what it was she wanted, she repeated what she had said the day before, that she had come there to find a boy friend to love her and make love to her. But he did get from her this time that the idea of coming there was not her own—though the idea of love was—and that it was "some nice soldiers" who had told her where to go. He asked her if she didn't already have a boy friend at home or maybe in the Service, and she shook her head and looked very sad.

"Do you know anything about men?" asked Odell, his voice quavering. "About lovemaking?"

She wrapped her arms around herself tightly, hugged and swiveled her body, and puckered her lips in the shape of a kiss, her eyes closed. Odell, trembling, reached his hand out and might have touched her gently then, except that he suddenly became aware of boisterous voices outside and the harsh stomp of combat boots on pavement. He rushed to the doorway fearfully. Two soldiers were coming toward the pro station, arms about each other's shoulders, swaying drunkenly, singing, "A ring-dang-dooooo . . . Now what is thaaat? . . . So round and faaaaat . . . Like a pussy caaat . . ."

Odell came back into the anteroom of the clinic in great agitation. "Go home! Somebody's coming! You've got to go!" he shouted.

She shook her head, smiling at him eagerly all the while. He could hear the men practically at the entrance, and, panicstricken, grabbed up the girl and her coat in a flurry of movement, uncertain whether to hide her in one of the treatment rooms, rush her down the corridor to the rear exit which opened onto an alley and was kept bolted and never used; or propel her out past them forcefully with a great display of indignation. "Come here quickly!" he ordered, taking her damp hand.

But it was too late. The soldiers came in and saw her. "Hey now, ain't you got a racket here, buddy," one of them called out, leering at Odell and the girl. "She ain't much, but it sure is convenient! Man, how do you get a job like this?"

"You treat *him!*" said the second soldier, pointing to Odell then his companion, and giggling. "I want *her* to treat me!"

The girl smiled at all of them. Odell moved between her and the soldiers. He pointed to the open door of one of the treatment rooms where packets of sterile equipment were laid out in trays on a table, and opening off the room was a latrine with sink, shower and toilet. "In there, both of you, and get ready," he ordered with as much strength and determination as he could muster. "Close the door behind you!"

To his surprise, one of them muttered, "Sure, Corporal, no need to get your dander up. We were only kidding." They both moved into the other room complacently and closed the door, and he could hear them laughing and bantering as they got undressed.

Odell took the girl's hand again and led her into another room. She gripped his hand hard and followed without protest. It was a plain white hospital-like room illuminated by a bright white globe, furnished with a steel cot, a couple of chairs, a table on which were trays of prophylaxis equipment, and a first aid cabinet with medicines, bandages and some surgical scissors and knives. "Wait in here and keep quiet!" he whispered harshly . . . and realized suddenly, My God, what am I doing! With the way open and business at hand, why didn't he throw her out! "If you say one word or come out before I tell you, I'll call the MPs. I'll call the police. Do you understand?" He put a finger to his lips to emphasize the secretiveness of the game they were playing, and she did the same thing. She was so willing! So wanting! Yes, she was sick. As he was sick. But would she let him only look at her naked? To go back again to the time it had all gone wrong for him. "Do you want one of those soldiers?" he blurted out. If he could see what it was really like, maybe some of the fear would go out of him. Maybe that was the beginning he needed.

She shook her head vigorously, tossing her long hair around her face and shoulders. "You! . . . Mahh-run! . . . Mahh-run!" she said excitedly. She hugged his arm tightly and tried to caress him. She was as tall as he was and strong. He had to struggle to break away from her, but not before she had squeezed her wet lips against his cheek, and the woman touch of her and the warm, damp breath sent a tremor through him.

"All right . . . but you must be quiet!" he sputtered, keeping his voice low, covering her mouth with his hand. She bit at his palm, a wild animal look in her eyes, and he pulled his hand away. "Keep still, for God's sake, or we'll get in trouble! Stay here, but don't make a sound! I'll come back when I get rid of those two!" He staggered out of the room, pulling the door tight behind him. Every pulse in his body beat like a drum, he felt faint, and could hardly see straight. He took a few deep breaths and steadied himself.

The door to the room where the two soldiers were, opened. "Hey, Corp, I don't wanta rush you or nothing, but we gotta get back," one of them called out.

"Yes, sorry," said Odell. "I had to chase that girl out. That's the second time she's come around here looking for trouble."

"Jeez, Corp, she wanna bang why don't you give her a bang! I'll give her a bang you want me to. I ain't particular."

Both of them stood there naked in the doorway of the treatment room, staggering against each other and the doorframe. Somehow, despite his inability to focus properly, despite his trembling, Odell managed to help them treat themselves—but this time he was revolted by the whole process and felt as though he was about to throw up.

Then they were gone and he was alone, and behind the closed door the strange girl was waiting for him. He started toward the room, excited, yet calmer than he had been, trying to think and reason. He went back to the entrance of the clinic and bolted it. The hell with them! Let them go elsewhere or let their damn penises wither with disease and fall off! He opened the door to the room and gasped. The small throbbing ache that had been there in his groin leaped suddenly and hurt more painfully. She had taken all her clothing off and was sitting on the cot completely nude, leaning back against the wall, holding her heavy breasts up in her hands, her fleshy thighs spread, opening to his fear-filled, awestruck eyes a blurred vortex of dark hair—he hadn't known women had so much hair there—and slit through it the strange beckoning wet lips that were the entrance to God knew what! He took all of her in at once in one quick all-absorbing glance and hissed, "Get dressed! You must get dressed and go!" He felt ill and revolted. She was disgusting. Covering her plump white flesh were welts

347

and bruises and discolorations—marks, no doubt, of ill treatment and beatings.

She moved, but not to dress and leave. It was a body-arching move of seduction and supplication. Odell groped for a chair, rattled it back to him against the closed door and dropped into it heavily.

"You like me, Mahh-run?" she murmured, caressing herself. "Come here . . . love Cat . . ."

Her smile was awful to him now. "I'm sorry . . . I think you'd better go now. Go home!" he gasped, locking his thighs together to squeeze the anguish from his loins.

She raised herself from the cot toward him, taking one hand from her breast and beckoning him. "Mahh-run's afraid," she said, laughing. "Cat's not afraid . . . Make love to Cat . . . Please love Cat . . . Nobody never, Mahh-run," she entreated, babbling words of love and love-making he was sure she couldn't understand.

"Please go!" he cried out in agony. "I can't help you!"

She came toward him, gasping heavily, the wild animal look in her eyes and contorted face. Odell sprang up to protect himself, knocking his chair over, pressing against the door, and as she reached out and grabbed his genitals hard and mocked, *Are ye then a sissy-boy!* the terror and fury of that terrible boyhood beating burst within his brain and he felt again the fiery lash of the strap cutting pain and hate in his groin, saw the wild, exultant look of the woman who beat him, and struck out at her screaming, "Leave me alone!" smashing her hand away, then the soft flesh of her body that absorbed and rebounded from his fist . . . and from that moment on, whatever it was that happened in that pro station in Glasgow exploded in his head all red and black and unremembered, for they found him later in his quarters cowering beneath the blankets of his bed, and he couldn't tell them how or when he'd got there.

"What about these . . . uhh . . . fadeouts . . . these blackouts, Myron? They happen often, huh?" Leon Osterman asked, leaning forward. He knew such things happened, that they could be legitimate, but most of the time in his years of police work, he hadn't believed in them. They were too easy an excuse; a fuzzy medico-legal device to cop a plea.

Odell, still faraway, struggling with his memories and the awful things he'd been induced to tell about himself, focused on the man in civvies, hearing the first questions only as the next were being asked.

"Is there any record of them having happened before? Any medical record . . . or police record?" Osterman pressed.

Odell looked at him rather indignantly. "I don't have any police record!" he snapped out.

"Okay, Myron, take it easy! I didn't mean nothing nasty by that, kid. I've gotta ask you these questions if I'm gonna help you. Okay?"

Odell relaxed and smiled at him. "I'm sorry, sir," he said softly.

"Did it ever happen before that time in Glasgow or since then?"

"It happened here a couple of weeks ago during training. Captain Reisman knows about it." Odell looked at Reisman for help. "He told me I was berserk and went blank for a while. I was fighting with Archer Maggot, one of the guys . . . we were practicing judo like the Captain taught us, and he got kind of rough where he wasn't supposed to and I guess I gave it right back to him . . . only I didn't really know what I was doing till the Captain brought me around."

Osterman looked to Reisman for affirmation, and Reisman nodded. He hadn't said very much since the interrogation began. It hadn't been necessary and he had stayed out of it, not wanting his voice or presence to jar the mood while Osterman worked his magic and Myron Odell poured out his story.

"How about when you was a kid . . . at home with your parents, or in school?" Osterman asked.

"I never had any parents. I grew up in an orphan home. I never even found out who my mother and father were. Nobody did. They told me they found me on the steps of the home in a cardboard box one night. I was a baby, but they didn't know how old I was exactly."

"Where'd you get the name?"

"I don't know. They just gave it to me there. I think it belonged to an old priest who taught there and died before I was there. They just gave it to me, I guess. I think they were hoping I'd become a priest too. Maybe I should have been."

349

"Did you like it there?"

"It was okay, I guess." He'd hated it, so why did he lie? He decided suddenly, The hell with it . . . to tell this man everything! Why not? It couldn't hurt any worse anymore. "No, that isn't true," he blurted out, shaking his head. "I hated it. Nobody liked me. I was always being picked on. I was just a skinny little kid most of the time and I was always getting beat up for something by the supervisors and the other kids. The nuns and priests weren't much better either. They were pretty tough sometimes. I don't think I ever had a friend in that whole damn place . . . not even in church . . . not even God . . ." He was caught up in his memories now and he ran on and they didn't try to stop him. "You know what they used to tell me, those kids? You know, not all of them were real orphans like me . . ." He said this boastfully, with a ludicrous tone of pride. "Some of them had parents who were just too poor or didn't give a damn to take care of them, or they came from what you call broken homes, or some of them had only one parent who couldn't keep them, and even those who didn't have any parents usually had a relative or something or at least they knew who they really were, where they came from and what their names were. Me, I had nothing and nobody. The only kid in the whole damn place who didn't even know where the hell he came from. Maybe I really wasn't even a Catholic, I don't know. You know what they used to say to me . . . just to show you what kind of lousy kids they were . . . they used to run after me and tease me and yell at me I was queer and the way I got there was a drunken bum going past the Queen of Angels . . . that's what it was called . . . masturbated in front of the place and a few minutes later they said I came crawling up the stairs. Well, you know how long I believed that damn story!" Odell exclaimed, his voice rising in pitch and volume as he got caught up in the overrighteous, self-immolating anguish of the memory. "I believed that damn story for years and I didn't even know what the hell the word masturbate meant! Would you believe that, mister?" he asked Osterman.

"Sure, kid. I know it's rough sometimes on a kid. But what the hell, you can't go the rest of your life feeling bad about something like that or letting it ruin your life. These blackouts, they ever happen to you when you was a kid?"

"No."

"How about when you was older? A teen-ager, or when you got out of school and before you got in the Army?"

Odell remembered now. "Yes . . . maybe two or three times when I got real mad about something or somebody in the home. I'd come to after a while like I'd been away somewhere or I'd been unconscious . . . but I never hurt anybody . . . I don't know, maybe they hurt me and that's why I couldn't remember things."

"How old were you then?"

"Maybe fifteen, sixteen, seventeen . . . I don't know. I'm not even sure how old I am now, or when my birthday is. You know, because of the way I was found there on the steps, they were never really sure."

"You ever get into any serious trouble before this?"

"No."

"You sure? How about kid stuff, Myron? You know, I don't think there's ever been a kid ain't been in trouble a couple of times. How about girls? There's trouble enough . . . ain't that right, Captain?" Osterman asked, winking at Reisman.

"I never went out with girls," answered Odell, somewhat self-righteously. "I don't know any."

"You must have been a pretty good kid then," said Osterman. "Hey, what's the worst punishment you ever got, huh? I mean before you was in the Army . . . back when you was a kid."

Odell wanted to tell him, but he was ashamed, so he skipped what had led up to it. "I couldn't be a Boy Scout anymore," he said, his eyes averted.

"That serious, huh?" Osterman kidded him.

Odell shrugged, looked up and smiled, thinking he'd gotten away with it.

"Why? Why couldn't you be a Boy Scout anymore, Myron?" Osterman insisted.

Odell looked panicky for a moment and fidgeted around in his discomfort. What did all this have to do with Glasgow and the trouble he was in now? Maybe it had everything to do with it. He didn't really know. "I got caught peeking at one of the women supervisors when she was undressing!" he blurted out, and added immediately, as an ameliorating factor, "All the kids used to do it . . . particularly with this one. She was the youngest and the best-looking, and I got dared to do it one night. The other kids said she knew about them sneaking around outside her window or her keyhole and she liked it." As he talked he began to feel the pain in his groin again and his legs trembled as he forced his thighs together. "Yeh, boy, she sure liked it all right!" His voice rose frantically. "She caught me at the door, and you know what that crazy woman did? You know what that lousy crazy woman did? She dragged me in her room and she made me take down my pants and underwear . . . and her still standing there naked like she was . . . and she took the strap off my pants and she beat me with it! She beat me and beat me and beat me until I was screaming for mercy and I passed out from the pain! That's why I couldn't be in the Boy Scouts anymore! They punished me. They said I was a dirty kid and they punished me. And I was in the hospital there almost two weeks . . . and I've still got the scars, you know, down here." He pointed, in embarrassment, to his crotch and his rear. "Even when I talk about it, it hurts."

"Gee, that's rough, kid," said Osterman in calculated sympathy. "What you done was wrong, you know that now, but she shouldn't've beat you like that. That wasn't right. You gotta figure there was something wrong with her too!"

"I'll say!" agreed Odell bitterly. "She was gone by the time I got back to the dormitory from the hospital. She was fired. But they still punished me on top of what she did to me. And everybody knew about it. The supervisors, the priests, the nuns, the lousy kids . . . and none of them ever let me forget it. Don't worry, boy, I never went near another woman again. Till that crazy girl came into the pro station in Glasgow."

"Did you kill her, Myron?" Osterman asked suddenly.

Odell looked at him aghast and disbelieving. His eyes flicked from Osterman to Reisman and back again. "You're tricking me, that's what you're doing. You're trying to trick me!" he accused, suddenly on the verge of hysteria.

"Nobody's trying to trick you, Odell," snapped Reisman in irritation, "so knock it off. Goddammit, you're a man now, not a little kid. Answer the question!"

"I'm innocent," Odell whispered, his eyes cast down.

Reisman ran on, while Osterman tried to signal him frantically to shut up. "The girl was found naked, raped and with a surgical knife up her whatsis after it had been slashed across her throat, her tits and her belly! Your fingerprints and the girl's were the only clear sets on it, Odell, so how the hell do you explain that?"

Odell sat there on the cot trembling. "The same way I explained it to the lousy, stupid court-martial!" he cried out. "I handled those instruments. It was part of my job. We gave first aid sometimes if there was an accident or an emergency. Sure my fingerprints were on there. They were supposed to be . . . but the girl's weren't!"

"If she fought you for the knife they would," said Reisman, unable to keep a new feeling of contempt from his voice. Listening to Odell . . . dealing with Odell . . . worrying about Odell . . . made Reisman feel dirtier than the foulest excrement . . . and in moments like this, he hated him for it. "If she died trying to pull the knife out, they would!"

There was a great silence in the room.

"Is that the way it happened, Myron?" asked Osterman gently.

Odell looked up at each of them in turn. "So help me God, I don't know . . . I don't remember . . . but I couldn't have . . . I couldn't have . . . It's too awful . . ." His eyes were wide, guileless, pleading. "Can I go now, Captain? I don't feel too good."

"All right, you're dismissed, Odell," said Reisman resignedly. "Report to Sergeant Morgan and tell him the men can go ahead and eat without me. I'm not to be disturbed here unless there's an emergency. And remember what I told you about keeping your mouth shut. We'll do what we can to help you, just as I promised."

Odell, too, was resigned, as he had been, to his fate. "Sure Captain, I understand," he said softly. He turned to Osterman. "Thank you, sir . . . for talking to me."

When they were alone again, Reisman hunched forward on the edge of the cot and asked, "What do you think?"

"I think he convicted himself . . . right up to where he says, 'I didn't do it,'" Osterman replied. He picked up a thick folder from the desk. "Just like the stuff you showed me in here . . . the court-martial record . . . the confession he took back later."

"Then you don't think it's worth looking into?"

"I've worked on screwier cases. Frame-ups . . . suicides that came out looking like murder . . . phony rapes where the girl or her relatives should've gone to jail instead of the guy. Some things come out in the wash eventually and we try to set 'em straight. Some never do, I suppose. You got a feeling about the kid? Okay. Sometimes a good hunch . . ."

Reisman interrupted, "It's not that I think he's necessarily innocent. It's that he *might* be innocent. If he is, I want him cleared and out of here fast, before it's too late. And if he isn't . . . if he's guilty . . . I want him to remember it. I want him to see it in front of his eyes and face up to it like a man."

"Maybe what you want is a head doctor, Johnny, not a cop," suggested Osterman. "One of them psychologists or psychiatrists or something."

"Maybe," agreed Reisman, "but right now I'll settle for a good cop." He was as reluctant to reveal to him that the *snotty kid* in London was a psychologist who had been looking into the same problem, as he would be reluctant to reveal to Stuart Kinder he had confided in Leon Osterman.

Osterman got up from the chair and walked to the window. He stood there staring out, chewing his cigar which had gone out. "You remember what it was like, don't you, Johnny, being in trouble, being scared? Back in Chicago when you was a kid. That's why you feel for these guys, ain't it?"

"I've never been out of trouble, Sarge," Reisman answered flippantly. "It's been my way of life since the last time you saw me. And I've been scared more times than I care to remember."

Osterman turned from the window to look at his face. "You're saying that like it was a joke, Johnny, but you mean it, don't you?"

Reisman stared back coolly. Why was it so difficult to say Yes . . . and then to explain? He shrugged his shoulders. "Yes, I remember," he said . . . and the mere saying of it seemed to lighten the heavy oppression weighting him, and open a floodgate of memories. "Do you remember it all?" he asked.

"Sure, like yesterday," answered Osterman, nodding his head solemnly. "The summer of 1930. How old were you? Seventeen? Eighteen?"

"I was sixteen." Reisman lit another cigaret, stood up and started to pace again . . .

That fall he would have gone into his last year of high school, and afterward maybe even college if he could have made up his mind what and where he wanted to study and how to go about financing it. His father had gotten him a part-time summer job at the cab garage washing cars and helping out the mechanics. "It's always good to know a trade, even if you're gonna be a college boy," Aaron had said, looking at him proudly . . .

"I spotted you the minute you come into the station house," said Osterman. He was still standing by the window, his arms folded, talking through the stogie. "I knew your father a little and I'd seen you around with him sometimes, but I didn't really know you. I could tell right away you had trouble bad. You were scared stiff and you looked like you'd been up all night, maybe even crying a little."

"Yes, I was scared, but it was anger that was strongest by then . . . that brought me in, I think," said Reisman softly. And there had been tears, too, tears of shame and anger for himself, tears of sorrow for poor, dead old man Tanner . . .

Everybody in the neighborhood knew Tanner. He was a nice, friendly guy who ran a candy store on Kedzie Avenue, and it wasn't really what you'd call a bookie joint but you could play the numbers there—nickels, dimes—quarters were a real big deal. Johnny Reisman never really understood how they worked, how you became a winner, how you could really trust a guy with your hard-earned pennies; if it worked on the horses or the stock market or like a lottery or if Tanner or some other guy just pulled a number out of the air and said that was it, that was the winner. His father played sometimes, always talking about how one day his ship was gonna come in. "Jacob, my son, do me a favor, huh," Aaron had said to him that day at the garage as Johnny was leaving work. "Go to Tanner's and put a nickel on a number for me. I got a lucky hunch. You wanta be a sport, make it a dime. Risk a nickel yourself, maybe. Who knows? Between you and your old man maybe we can make enough to send you to college" . . .

"Don't think I'm knocking you, kid, because I'm not," said Osterman, pulling the cigar from his mouth. "You had good reason to be scared. It took guts to come in there and tell me what you did."

"Guts, hell!" muttered Reisman in self-derision. "If I'd had any when I should have, old man Tanner would have still been alive!"

"You still blaming yourself for that after all these years? That's nonsense!" exclaimed Osterman in sudden understanding. "I still say it took guts to come in to the cops and finger three hoods on a murder rap" . . .

The three hoods had come into Tanner's while Johnny was sitting at the counter sipping a soda, talking to Tanner after placing the bet. Nobody else was in the store. Tanner's face filled with fear. One of the men locked the door and pulled the blinds. The other two swaggered to the counter. Johnny didn't know any of them, but he recognized the type—gangsters, dressed sharp, out for trouble. He thought maybe it was going to be a holdup, until one of them reached across the counter and grabbed Tanner by the collar, spitting out, "We told you nobody handles numbers but us!" smacking him back and forth across the face. The boy reacted instinctively, out of the physical toughening of his hundreds of kid fights and street fights and school fights in the crowded, sharply neighborhooded, expanding city . . . *Yid! Wop! Kike! Guinea! Jewboy! Ginzo! Polack! Heinie! Spic! Nigger!* . . . out of his emotional toughening in the ambivalent private world in which he'd grown up and kept himself whole. "Hey, leave him alone!" he yelled. "What the hell you think you're doing!" He grabbed the hood's arm to yank him away from the old man. A blow struck him from behind, sending him reeling off the counter stool, ears ringing, face tingling. Another hood was on him, dragging him up by his hair. "Out, kid!" he snarled. "Outside if you know what's good for you! You weren't here, understand? You don't know us, we don't know you. Got it?" Behind the counter, Tanner was being worked over methodically, pleading for help, yelling, "Run, Johnny! Get the cops! Get the cops!" The boy struck blindly at the hand gripping his hair. The hood let go and backhanded him with a full swing of his body. Johnny fell backward and heard the mocking voice say, "Tough kid, huh? You wanna fight, huh! Let's see you fight this!" Johnny started back at the hood and stopped cold! There was a gun in the guy's hand pointed at his heart and the fear of it froze him in sudden new terror! "No," his adolescent voice quavered. "Don't shoot me," he pleaded. The hood laughed, jabbed the gun muzzle into the boy's belly and shoved him backward with it toward the door. Tanner was still yelling. He was being pummeled into the back room. "Run, Johnny! Run! Get the cops! Get the cops!" he screamed. The hood moved the gun from Johnny's belly to his head and the touch of it against his skin overwhelmed him with fear and nausea. "You mind your business, you understand, boy?" the hood mouthed. "One word to the cops and you're dead! You get out of here now and you keep your mouth shut! You say nothing to nobody! Now or never! No mother, no father, no friends, nobody, no cops! Open your big mouth and you get this!" The gun waved threateningly in front of the boy's misted, fright-bulged eyes. The door was opened, his arm wrenched savagely behind his back, and he was thrust out with the sharp pain of a kick that caught him just below the spine, hearing Tanner still yelling behind him, running, running, running . . .

"I ran away, Sarge, and they killed him," whispered Reisman stopping his agonized pacing in front of Osterman, staring at him almost beseechingly, his face twisting with the fresh torment of his memories. "I didn't get any help and they beat the old man so bad he died. My father was at his funeral right then when I was talking to you. It's where I should have been . . . only I was too ashamed."

"Ashamed of what!" exclaimed Osterman. "If you'd done any different, your old man would have been at your funeral instead of Tanner's."

"I've been at my funeral many times since then, Sergeant," said Reisman bitterly. "Only I'm never dead. That's the penalty one pays for cowardice."

"What do you mean cowardice, Johnny? I suppose you was a coward when you come into the station house and told me what happened? That's nonsense!" snapped Osterman, tapping a finger on Reisman's chest for emphasis.

"But it was too late then. Old man Tanner was dead," said Reisman softly, starting his nervous pacing again.

"There was nothing you could have done about that, Johnny," insisted Osterman. "Believe me, it was already too late when those strong-arm guys worked you over and threw you out of his store. Whatever they did to Tanner those first few minutes was what killed him, and there was nothing you could have done to save him even if you'd brought the whole damn police force back there. He was already a goner when we got the call later after his wife found him. He just took a little longer to die, that's all" . . .

And Johnny Reisman had not known he was dying. He had run in terror . . . saying nothing to his father when he got home, even lying to him that Tanner's had been closed

357

. . . saying everything was all right when Aaron looked at him with concern and asked him what was wrong, if he was feeling sick . . . thinking of running to his Uncle Pete for help . . . Pete was tough, Pete had a gun, he had connections, he'd know what to do . . . then remembering the threats about telling anybody, and fearing for himself and only secondarily for his uncle, and wondering if maybe Pete ever did things like those hoods, and discarding the thought as reprehensible, impossible, for Pete wasn't that kind of a gangster. In the morning Aaron showed him the item in the newspaper, with appropriate curses in English and Yiddish for those responsible, and Johnny added a few of his own in Italian to cover the turmoil he felt. Tanner had been found beaten up and unconscious in his store . . . he was in the hospital in critical condition, unable to talk. "No wonder the store was closed," said Aaron, in his absolute innocence never connecting his son with the event he was reading about . . . and it took a terrible effort for Johnny to control his emotions, and only later, when his father left the apartment, did he weep and get sick. It took Tanner all that day to die, and every moment of it was agony for Johnny Reisman, willing the old man to live, to recover, to tell his own story to the cops if he wanted to, and that way take the responsibility away from him . . . but in a tiny, newly discovered, cruel and awful part of himself, aware that if Tanner died nobody need ever learn of his part in it. The next day the newspaper reported Tanner's death. Aaron left the apartment saying he would take time off from work later to go to the funeral. Johnny Reisman wrestled with his fear, his sorrow and his anger, and went to the police station . . .

"If he'd lived, maybe I never would have come in," said Reisman.

"Maybe. Maybe Tanner wouldn't have talked either, out of fear. But you did, Johnny, and that's what counts," said Osterman. He strode past him to the chair and lit his cigar again. "I've always been glad it was me and not some meathead you talked to. I went right out with you when you told me what it was all about, remember? And we went right over to Tanner's so I could see if you was really telling the truth. Not that I thought you was lying or anything, but you know sometimes a lot of hysterical people or cranks think they got important information, or sometimes even a guy tries to cover up for what he done himself, and you were pretty scared and nervous, so I wanted to check it out quietly first. I said nothing to nobody, not even the cop outside guarding the store, and it was a damn good thing, the way things turned out. I don't know, maybe I was also trying to protect you because of what you was doing, or bucking for a commendation, trying to be a big hero and solve one myself. I never even wrote out a report later, thank God, so there was nothing to connect you with the Tanner case or what happened later." Osterman paused and took a long, deep drag on the cigar, waiting until Reisman turned and was pacing back toward him again. "I suppose you're gonna tell me you was a coward the next day, too, how you handled that torpedo, huh, Johnny?" he asked softly.

Reisman leaned over the desk and jabbed the short remnant of his cigaret down into the butt can. "It was all part of the same thing. It scared the shit out of me," he muttered, searing his fingers as he twisted and crushed the hot embers . . .

Fear had been his constant companion. He felt it as a palpable thing all around him once he committed himself . . . once he went to the police station; to the murder scene to reconstruct the happening for Osterman and describe the hoodlums; walking back to the station house with nervous, furtive glances at faces they passed, at loiterers in doorways and alleyways; looking at mug shots in secret with Osterman, fingering those who looked enough like the killers to be picked up for questioning . . . and afterward alone with himself . . . "Be careful, kid! Lemme know if you see those guys around! I'll be in touch!" said the detective . . . and Johnny was out on the street again, alone with himself and his fears. And that was the worst of it. He didn't go to work. He went to a movie theater to lose himself, to forget, to become involved with the lives and emotions of those other people up there on the big screen. When he came out, it was night, and he hadn't forgotten at all. His fear met him at the exit and walked home with him, keeping him wary, jumpy, unusually attuned to sights and sounds and movements. The gunman came at him suddenly out of an alleyway leading to the elevated train embankment between buildings. It was the same hood who had worked him over in Tanner's store. If he had fired right then, Johnny would have been finished, but his gun was still holstered, the guy wanted to get in a few good licks first, wanted to play with him, wanted the boy to know for sure who he was, what he was giving him and why he was getting it. Complete and absolute terror was first—there was no denying it—draining every drop of strength from Johnny's mind and body as the hood clamped a hand over his mouth and dragged him into the alleyway, cursing him for having gone to the cops. But for Johnny there was nowhere to go with terror, nothing he could do with it, and as the guy worked him over viciously, the goading pain of the blows, the accusing ghost of Tanner, the aching memory of cowardice, all joined with his most primitive drive to save himself, and he turned upon the hoodlum in a fury such as he had never known before. The guy fell back in surprise, reaching under his jacket for his gun, leaving face and body unprotected from the desperate, telling onslaught of hysterical rage. The thug cracked against a building wall, tripped, fell, the gun was knocked from his hand and Johnny snapped it up, trembling, and pointed it. He heard one terrible scream of "Nooooo!" as a rush of noise and stabbing lights roared into the alleyway from a passing train on the elevated embankment at the other end. The feel of the gun in his hand was one of heart-pounding, supreme and unbelievable power, heightened by the sight of the hoodlum's new and utter terror. Johnny felt no fear, no sorrow, no sympathy or empathy for a man—only his consuming need for self-vindication, vengeance for Tanner, and an almost calm and positive awareness that he must destroy his attacker. He fired, hardly aware of the explosion as it melded with the roar of the train. He fired again and again and again, knowing what he was doing and exulting in it, stopping only when he realized the gun was finally empty and there was an awesome silence in that confined space. He moved slowly to the bullet-torn, bleeding corpse on the ground, stared at it through the darkness so that its image burned itself into his mind, dropped the gun with an agonized, horrible sob of awareness and fled . . .

"So you was scared. So what! Big deal!" Osterman said. "Why shouldn't you be scared? It ain't every day you kill a man. I never had to do it, thank God, but even a cop gets nervous about it."

"That's not what I mean," murmured Reisman from far away . . . He'd learned since then . . . it didn't make him

360

nervous anymore . . . he'd fought and killed him in all his forms and guises in every part of the world, and every time it had been easier. "You don't understand, Sergeant. I didn't have to kill him. I wanted to."

"No, Johnny. You had to. You can't blame yourself for that, either," insisted Osterman. "It was him or you . . . maybe even an accident like your father said when he called me at home and I came running out to your place."

"That's one thing I never really understood then or since," said Reisman sitting down on the cot again. "Why you covered for me. Why you went to all that trouble. Making my father stay in the apartment and swear he'd never say a word to anybody. Dragging me back to that goddamn alleyway where I threw up my guts all over the place while you were futzing around with the gun and the body. Then down to the docks, and the next morning I was stoking coal for a living on an oreship way out on Lake Michigan. Not that I'm complaining, Sarge," said Reisman sarcastically, holding up his hand. "After all, these are the little maturing experiences that one has to go through to make a man of him, and—"

"I owed it to you," said Osterman, shrugging, staring at his cigar ash, but not looking up. "What was it, after all? A nothing. A no-good bastard was dead where he belonged . . . you even saved the taxpayers the cost of doing it. We got the other two eventually. You were a good kid. You'd done a pretty brave thing and could've gotten into trouble two ways . . . minor trouble with the cops and the law and investigations and all that . . . major trouble with that hood's mob. Like I said before . . . no harm was done doing it my way."

"But you were taking a chance. You could have gotten into trouble, serious trouble."

"I suppose so," said Osterman, rising heavily and walking to the window again.

"Why did you owe it to me?" Reisman pressed.

"Guilt," murmured Osterman, staring into the compound. "Just like these guys. Just like you." He turned to face Reisman squarely. "But mine was the guilt of stupidity. It was my fault what happened to you . . . that hood almost shooting you. It was only your guts . . . maybe a little luck, too . . . maybe a little God, who knows? . . . that you got him and lived to tell about it. I should never have let you leave by yourself once you came in and told me about Tanner's killers. I should have put you in a hotel in protective custody, or put a tail on you day and night to see nothing happened to you. I should have known once I started moving after those guys the word would be out and they'd be after you. Maybe they even saw us together on the street. Who knows? So . . . you stuck out your neck, I stuck out mine. What your old man tells me . . . what I see here . . . you haven't changed. You're still sticking it out, huh, Johnny?"

"Aren't you?"

"Sure. Why not? That's half the fun of living, ain't it?" said Osterman, smiling at him. "What have you got to eat in this joint? I'm hungry."

"I eat K-rations with the prisoners."

"Balls! How about coming into town with me?"

"Can't. I've got a watch to pull later."

"So we say goodbye for a while, okay, kid?" said Osterman, holding out his hand. "I'll do what I can about Odell and I'll be in touch. I'm glad to help . . . but it's gotta be strictly on my own, in my own way. Nothing official."

Reisman grasped his hand warmly. He did like Leon Osterman, and at last he felt he *knew* him, and it was more than *all right* . . . it was good. "That's the way I figured it, Sarge," he said. "It can't be official. Otherwise I would've thrown you out long ago."

—

24

CAPTAIN STUART KINDER came back to the stockade at Stokes Manor on Thursday, March 23. For two days he indoctrinated the prisoners with pep talks, propaganda and morale pamphlets, and films entitled "Why We Fight!" interspersed with their regular training and intended to put them in the proper frame of mind for Saturday morning when Reisman was to issue them live ammunition on the firing range. Except for occasional snickers when Kinder slipped unconsciously into Mother, God and Country, the men paid strict attention and showed great interest in the material, though Reisman suspected it was more because they were being entertained and it cut into the tedium and sweat part of their training, than it was due to any salutary effect Kinder's efforts were having.

If the threat to all their lives wasn't there already, as Reisman believed, in the festering fear, hate and frustration of at least some of the prisoners, then the time had come now to induce it—if only to bring it to a head immediately, wipe it out or, at minimum, lay it to rest more securely for the duration of their training.

Friday evening after chow Reisman split the prisoners into two patrols and assigned each group specific scouting missions and objectives in different parts of the estate. It was not that they needed this sort of night drill on the grounds of Stokes Manor anymore. By now they had been over every inch of the land many times by day and night, could recall exactly upon demand particular contours, features and obstacles, and could probably have done their marching and reconnaissance blindfolded.

Victor Franko—to his own and everybody else's surprise —was assigned to command one group; Ken Sawyer the other. The patrols moved out fifteen minutes apart, each under orders to move silently and avoid the other as if they were on opposite sides of the war—yet Reisman had arranged lines of march on their separate terrain maps so they would cross at a number of places. For the first time, they went out alone. Just the prisoners. No guards.

Standing at the exterior stockade gate with Reisman watching the unguarded prisoners vanish into the dark wood, Stuart Kinder felt a great anxiety about the advisability of the night's training missions and the effectiveness of his own work. "Do you really think this is wise?" he whispered.

Reisman glanced at his watch, then at Kinder, dressed in fatigues and carrying a submachine gun on his shoulder again. He looked more comfortable with it this time. "They'll have about two hours out there to themselves," Reisman said. "Enough time to plot any mischief they might have in mind for tomorrow."

"Why let them?" asked Kinder incredulously. "You don't want them to, do you?"

"No . . . not really. But we don't know. Let's say it's my own version of the trustworthiness test you once mentioned, Stu."

"I'm working on it," Kinder explained hurriedly. "It's

quite difficult, and would be only an experiment, but . . ."

"We've got to give them enough rope to hang themselves now," stated Reisman flatly. "Our entire assessment of them could be wrong. Everything I've taught them, everything we've done together could be a mockery, and three weeks of training could go down the drain . . . or worse. But how else do we find out if what we're doing is working? Would you rather they showed their dirty hands tomorrow . . . against us, if that's what any of them have in mind; or when we drop them on the Krauts depending on them to do a job?"

"Tomorrow," Kinder answered weakly.

They turned back into the barracks together and Reisman tapped the barrel of Kinder's weapon and warned, "Just make sure you remember how to use this thing if you have to."

Kinder felt suddenly a more acute and terrible reality in this business than he had ever felt before.

Victor Franko led his patrol directly to the firing range they had completed that day. It lay in a natural depression on the landward side of the sea cliff near the far edge of the estate. Moonlight illuminated the target pits, the frame supports and posts for the targets, and the heaped earth embankments and sandbags behind which the markers would take cover. Napoleon White, Archer Maggot, Roscoe Lever, Myron Odell and Luis Jimenez were in his patrol.

"Take ten," Franko told them. "You can light up if you want, but let's play like real soldierboys and keep the matches and butts covered so nobody sees 'em."

"Big deal," muttered Lever. "Who the hell you think you are, telling us what we can do, punk?"

"You wanna march all over this fucking place tonight, stupid?" Franko threw at him. "Or you wanna sit on your tail and take it easy till it's time to go in? Reisman won't never know the diff if we keep our mouths shut."

"What the hell are we doing here anyway, Franko?" Napoleon challenged, dropping to the ground and relaxing against an embankment. He'd seen the map and the line Reisman had drawn on the transparent acetate grid overlay, and knew the patrol was supposed to skirt wide of the area.

"Look, White," snapped Franko, "I doan give a shit if you was an officer once or not. You ain't no more. You're just like the rest of us. When that fink Captain puts you in charge, I follow you, do what I'm told and I keep my mouth shut, doan I?"

"More or less," answered Napoleon. When Franko was making up to him, putting on his buddy-buddy act, he also called him *Nappy*—now it was *White*.

"Okay. You do the same," Franko ordered petulantly.

"Thas right, boy, y'heah," muttered Archer Maggot. He had wanted to say, He ain't not lack thuh rest of us, yo stupid wop! Ain't yo got eyes t' see? . . . But he'd learned that his festering bigotry got him nowhere with the others and did no good for himself, so he held back.

"You shut up, too, Reb! I doan need your help," Franko rapped out.

Napoleon ignored Maggot completely, for he'd found it the best way of handling him. Franko he mocked with a snappy salute from his reclining position, and a "Yes, sir, General!" He felt slighted that Reisman had appointed Franko patrol leader tonight. Though they had all been given a crack at it, Napoleon had been put in charge more frequently lately and he had come to look forward to it, if not actually expect it as his due. Sticking a cigaret in his lips, he shielded it with his helmet liner, cupped a matchbook in there with his palms and lit up. If Franko wanted them to sit there the rest of the night, that was okay with him. He was just taking orders. Franko would catch it if Reisman found out and that would be the last time he'd be put in charge of anything besides latrines.

But Victor Franko didn't just want to sit there. He wanted to talk about tomorrow. He let them sit around awhile relaxing, bull-shitting and smoking, while he tried to work through in his mind the details of a plan, and how to sell it to these jerks.

Out on the downs nearby, Samson Posey scouted ahead of Ken Sawyer's patrol, heard the voices, followed them stealthily to their source, then moved back quickly to report Franko's patrol sitting around the firing range. It roused Sawyer's curiosity and he signaled the men in his group to him. Besides the Indian, there was Calvin Smith, Glenn Gilpin, Vernon Pinkley and Joe Wladislaw.

"Let's see how close we can get without them knowing we're here," Sawyer whispered. He felt good about being a patrol leader, grateful to Reisman for the frequent chances he gave him to demonstrate his proficiency or experience in some part of their training. And the guys, even the foul-ups and the hard-nosed bastards who were always talking and acting tough, seemed to respect him and follow him without bitching because he was the only one among them who had ever been in combat.

His men deployed quickly and silently through the brush, following Sawyer's hand signals to separate positions on the hilly perimeter of the firing range, each crawling in to where he could see and hear the other patrol without being observed.

"I got a plan," said Victor Franko, "for tomorrow."

"What do you mean?" asked Luis Jimenez suspiciously.

"We come out here tomorrow and they give us real ammo," said Franko slowly. His head moved from man to man and he held his submachine gun out toward them in both hands as if it were a votive offering. "There's twelve of us against nine of them."

"There's ten. That other Captain's around, too," Roscoe Lever reminded him, moving in closer.

"Nine, ten, what the hell makes the difference! Three of us could take them screws on and wipe the floor up with 'em!" Franko said. There was a nervous excitement in the air now as he realized the others were listening intently, no longer sprawled around lackadaisically.

Myron Odell opened his mouth to say something in protest, but no words came out. The small stirrings of kinship he had begun to feel with these men in their long days and nights together, evaporated in new fear. He fell back and was silent.

"Sheet, youall nevuh had any eyedeeuh wuth talkin about in yo whole lahf, Franko," scoffed Maggot.

"Then what are you listening so close for, Reb?" Franko challenged.

"You talk big trouble, man! I think maybe you better shut up," spoke up Jimenez.

"No, let him talk, Luis," insisted Napoleon. "Let's hear what he has to say. I'm sure it will be brilliant."

366

"First off, they're not gonna be expecting nothing," began Franko.

"First off, you're wrong," said Napoleon. "You think Reisman is as stupid as you are?"

"For Christ sake, listen to me, Nappy, will you?" said Franko, his voice now more pleading than demanding.

"That's right, boy," put in Maggot. "You jus let him talk hisself to death."

"We surprise em . . . knock em all off . . . and nobody knows what happened cause nobody ever comes here," Franko ran on.

"You mean kill them?" Odell uttered in shocked disbelief.

"What the hell you think I mean, Pope?"

"But they've got machine guns. They'll shoot us. We'll be killed!" protested Odell.

"Not if we get the drop on em, they won't," Franko rapped out. He patted his weapon affectionately and a smirk grew on his scowling face. "Four hundred and fifty rounds a minute. That's what the Big Man taught us, ain't it?"

"But only thirty rounds to a magazine," Napoleon reminded him.

"Three times more than I need by myself . . . three bullets for each of them . . . maximum range, one thousand seven hundred yards . . . effective range, two hundred yards . . . I learn my lessons good, don't I? I'm gonna be a lot closer to the son-of-a-bitch than that."

"I told you it would be brilliant!" mocked Napoleon.

"Stop needling him, goddammit!" growled Lever sharply, turning to Napoleon. "Listen to him!"

"All right," said Napoleon reasonably. "We surprise ten guys watching every move we make every second. We kill them all. Then what do we do?"

"We bury them . . . in there!" Franko spat out, pointing to the target pits. "And if it wasn't too much trouble, I'd say take em up and dump em in the shit trench! That's where Morgan goes!"

"What next, Franko? . . . and make it good," said Lever. His fingers played nervously with the safety catch of his grease gun, snapping it up and down.

"Like I said, nobody ever comes to the stockade. I got a plan, sure . . . but we're gonna have time to move around a bit and figure things out even better. Any of you get hurt, we can take care of you."

"Yeah, Franko, ah kin jus see youall playin nuhsmaid t' me with a bullet up my ass . . . thas a joke!"

"What do we do after the funeral?" Napoleon asked. "What's your big plan? Swim over to the Germans?"

"We hole up in the big house till after dark. Take care of the woman and . . ."

"Kill her too, I suppose!" flashed Napoleon.

"What's thuh mattuh, boy? Ain't yo got guts t' do it?" demanded Maggot.

"Guts!" exploded Napoleon with contempt. He spit on the ground at Maggot's feet. "That's for your lily-white raper's guts!"

Maggot lurched toward him, but Franko grabbed his arm, jerked him back, and Roscoe Lever, eager to hear more, helped hold him.

"That's right. Kill her too, and take anything we need to help us get away," Franko talked on frantically. "At night we leave . . . with all the guns and ammo and food we can carry. We don't go out on the road . . . we go on the beach. We look for a boat and take it. And we get across the Channel, or go to some island somewhere . . . or maybe even to Ireland. They're not in the war."

Napoleon was surprised Franko knew even that much. "That's what I call a really well-thought-out plan," he said, smiling.

"It ain't bad. You got a better one?" challenged Lever.

"Yes. Keep playing soldier," answered Napoleon without humor. He thrust out his submachine gun. "I bet we don't even have these tomorrow. I bet Reisman takes them away and we start out with the M1's again. Single shots . . . eight bullets to a clip . . . What do you think you can do with those, Franko?"

"Makes no difference!" ranted Franko. "You with me or not?"

The others looked toward Napoleon expectantly, even Archer Maggot, as though keying their answer to his. "You make your move first, killer," said Napoleon, "and make it big enough for everybody to see you . . . and maybe I'm with you."

Ken Sawyer wanted to rise up from cover and shout

368

something at them, but he didn't know what he could say. Quickly he slid back from his position and scurried from man to man in the circle of eavesdroppers, signaling them to follow him away from there. Out of earshot of Franko's patrol, back on their assigned line of march, he called a halt and asked, "What do we do about it?"

"They want to kill Captain," said Samson, shaking his head.

"It ain't all of them. It seems to me like it's just that Franko. He's no good," declared Calvin Smith in a hushed voice. " 'Jesus said, Thou shalt do no murder.' That's what Saint Matthew wrote."

"Save it for church, goddammit," snapped Sawyer. "What do we do about it? Tell the Captain?"

"You can't do that," said Gilpin. "I don't like it either, but nobody rats on nobody else."

"They'd hang him," said Joe Wladislaw nervously. "Maybe all of them, just for listening."

"Then what the hell do we do?" demanded Sawyer. He knew what he would do if it came to that. He'd stop it himself, but he was afraid to tell them. "You want to go back there and tell them we're in on it with them? That's crazy!" he exclaimed.

"I say we keep our mouths shut and sleep on it," said Gilpin, "and see what happens tomorrow. We don't know that any of them are in on anything. All we heard was Franko spoutin' off."

Each looked at the other suspiciously, for it was suddenly no longer a matter of *We*, but of *I*. Victor Franko had introduced a new element into whatever unity they had attained, and no one of them was willing to commit himself to another.

Captain Stuart Kinder was so nervous he couldn't shave in the morning for fear of cutting himself. He felt ratty and imagined he looked as bad as the prisoners. Before they left the stockade, Reisman issued him and the guard detail six more full magazines apiece for their submachine guns and briefed them on the positions they were to take and the procedures to be followed on the firing range—both in the event everything went well, and in an emergency. On the march out, the prisoners toted the heavy ammunition boxes in addition to their full field packs. The early morning was clear and windy and the day gave promise of being sunny. Yet Kinder sensed a mood of greater tension, anxiety rather than expectation—as great as his own—in the dogged plodding of their movements and the grim silence that hung over them as a pall, smothering the banter that usually passed between them, and between them and the MPs. His eyes shifted constantly between the two men he was assigned to watch personally. Though it was against all safety rules, he carried his weapon loaded, cocked and locked—as all the guards were required to do, as though they were moving through a combat zone in imminent danger of being attacked.

At the range Reisman left the group near the entrance to the long, shallow valley and made a quick survey of the area. He nosed around both sides of hillocks on the perimeter, in and out of gullies, around the pits and embankments and target posts, looking for signs of anything out of order, some indication of mischief that might have been laid the night before. He found none, except for squashed and shredded cigaret butts near the pits that told him they had been there, though neither of the patrols was supposed to have been.

They stood silently in a single rank waiting for him now, apprehensively eyeing each other, the guards and Reisman as he strode toward them. Knapsacks were lined up neatly on the ground behind them. Ammunition boxes were stacked under guard some distance away. Master Sergeant Carl Morgan waited somewhat less than eagerly for his orders.

"Bring them to inspection arms," Reisman told him.

The prisoners still carried the grease guns they'd been drilling with these last days. Though he had originally planned to start the live firing with rifles, which would have been more in keeping with standard training procedure, Reisman had changed his mind and let them keep the submachine guns, strengthening their hands and putting greater temptation in their midst in the tangible form of firepower.

He passed down the rank, snapping their weapons smartly from their hands, inspecting open chamber and barrel, and the face of each man as he returned his piece. None would meet his eyes directly, but looked past him or through him. Victor Franko was gripping his gun so tightly, Reisman had to tug at it three times to get him to relin-

370

quish it properly. When Odell's gun was handed back to him it skidded from his hands and would have landed in the dirt if Reisman hadn't caught it. All the men seemed unusually tense and anxious—whether with eagerness to begin firing or with fear about something else, he couldn't tell. Reisman intended, however, to demonstrate something very real for them to worry about now.

"The guard detail will shoot first," he announced. "They'll show you the speed and accuracy with which this weapon can be brought to bear on a target. They'll fire at drab silhouette targets from fifty yards. That's a distance considerably further than we're standing from you now. White, Gilpin, Jimenez, Wladislaw, Pinkley and Odell will come with me. We'll set up targets and then take cover. Captain Kinder will act as range safety officer and will ascertain from his position behind the firing line whether any of us in the pits are in danger. Sergeant Bowren will be in command of the firing line. His order to fire will be followed by one short blast on his whistle which will be the signal to execute the command. The order to cease fire will be preceded by a series of long, loud blasts on the whistle, from either Sergeant Bowren or Captain Kinder. You are not to leave cover to mark or change targets until ordered to do so by me after the cease-fire command has been executed. If you men in the pits value your asses, you'll be eating dirt while the lead's flying. The rest of you . . . Franko, Lever, Maggot, Sawyer, Posey and Smith . . . will stand behind the firing line with Sergeant Morgan and observe what happens closely."

With the target men and one MP, Reisman moved out onto the range. It had none of the niceties of a regulation setup designed specifically for the submachine gun, with rope-controlled silhouettes twisting and popping out of concealment, but it would do nicely for all their weapons, with sufficient width for four men to fire at once. The targets would be stationary, diversified between drab silhouettes in prone, kneeling and standing positions and Standard A rifle range cards. Firing distances would be varied up to two hundred yards.

From behind the safety of one of the heaped earth embankments where he huddled with Captain Reisman and two of the other men, Myron Odell strained to hear Ser-

geant Bowren run through his sequence of commands . . .
"Ready on the right! Ready on the left!" . . . He heard the
command to fire, the scream of the whistle, and then the
immense horror of the exploding submachine guns, and he
trembled and felt an uncontrollable urge to get up and run.
He pressed his face into the dirt, pulled it up, and his eyes
darted hysterically from side to side.

Reisman pressed close to him. "What's the matter?
They're not gonna hit us. We're safe here!" he yelled.

"I've never been under fire before, sir!"

"Sure you have. The day I goosed you up the sea cliff."

"That was different, sir."

"Didn't you ever run an infiltration course back in the
States?"

"No, sir. I've never even fired a weapon before, sir!"
Odell shouted back, his voice quavering. "We didn't take
that kind of training. We—"

The staccato pandemonium of the guns stopped . . . as
startling in their sudden silence as they had been in their
noise. Sergeant Bowren's whistle sounded the all-clear. The
heavy concentration of fire had lasted less than a minute.

"That wasn't so bad, was it, Myron?" asked Reisman.

"No, sir," replied Odell, now sheepish at his panic.

"Think you can get used to it?"

"Yes, sir. I think so, sir."

"Do it often enough and you'll come to love it, on both
sides of the line."

"Sure, Captain," said Odell nervously. "I know I've got
to get used to it."

Reisman picked his head up, peered over the embankment and hopped out. The four guards who had fired had
their submachine guns loaded with new magazines, cocked,
locked and pointed at the sky. Around their feet were lit-
tered the six magazines each of them had emptied. The
stink of gunpowder was in the air.

"All right, out of the pits. Let's look at the targets,"
Reisman ordered. "Morgan, bring that crew down here
with you and let them see what's left of these things."

There was very little left. Victor Franko stared at the silhouettes that had been sliced and gutted and chewed to
shreds as the concentrated bursts of .45 slugs passed
through them and slammed into the hill behind. He
reached out his hand, picked at bits of cardboard tatters,
ran his fingers over the splintered gouges and deep holes of

the thick target posts, and felt a shiver of fear, as though he had fondled his own corpse.

Reisman didn't think there was any need to repeat the demonstration with the rest of the guard detail. The message was clear enough. "Franko, White, Sawyer, Odell . . . On the firing line!" he ordered. He regrouped the others. Six to the pits. Two behind the line to observe. MPs in place. Bowren, Kinder and Morgan in place. New targets were posted. The markers took cover. Reisman moved down the firing line—Odell, Sawyer, Franko, White, in that order, left to right—issuing each of them two full magazines. "One in your pocket. One in your hand," he ordered. "Don't load until I tell you to." Then he turned his back on them and strode out into the middle of the range, stopping and turning to face them next to the first grouping of targets. He took his grease gun from his shoulder and held it at his hip, pointed at the ground. Accidents happened, and he didn't want to start one. He was pushing them to the limit of temptation, and he felt again in these moments that special kind of brazen, heart-pounding fear that sharpened senses to their most acute, that tensed every muscle for action.

Captain Stuart Kinder stood ten yards behind the gunners to their left, looking between them at Reisman, his gaze glued there in horrible fascination instead of on the men in the pits to assure their safety—seeing what was happening as though it was being done in slow motion.

Master Sergeant Carl Morgan stood ten yards behind the gunners to their right, cursing Reisman silently, zeroing the muzzle of his submachine gun on the backs of the prisoners. He didn't want trouble. He was close enough to their guns to be hurt or killed if they turned on him. But if trouble came—and that cocky, son-of-a-bitch of a CO was just asking for it—he hoped one of them would kill Reisman, and he hoped it would be Franko so he could hang him.

Sergeant Clyde Bowren inched his way down-range from his position at the far edge of the firing line, putting himself almost at the periphery of the field of fire, his eyes darting among the gunners, examining their faces, their eyes, the movements of their hands and bodies—afraid that in the next seconds he'd have to kill someone.

"Load, cock and lock your guns . . . then keep them pointed at the sky!" Reisman commanded.

Metal tapped against metal. Magazine catches clicked as

373

they were shoved home. Bolts snapped as they were drawn taut and locked.

Victor Franko's hands grew clammy. Sweat stood out on his forehead despite the breeze. His eyes misted with anger and frustration, and down-range Reisman's taunting figure swam in an unfocused haze, calling out to them, "You will fire these first two magazines merely to get the feel of the weapon. You can shoot as fast or as slow as you want. Later on, you'll learn the touch of the trigger well enough to get off one shot at a time and make every bullet a hit. If your gun jams, remove the magazine immediately, raise your hand and keep the barrel pointed down-range. Captain Kinder or Sergeant Bowren will immediately blow the cease-fire whistle and come to your assistance. Follow their instructions explicitly."

Franko rubbed his free hand over his forehead and eyes, wiping the moisture from them. He saw Reisman turn his back again, start to walk slowly toward the safety of one of the sandbagged embankments. Franko swiveled his head hesitantly, almost imperceptibly. He saw Bowren to one side facing him . . . Morgan and Kinder on either side in back of him . . . the MPs fanned out in the rear, at the sides, on the hillocks above him . . . all with their guns aimed at him.

Then Reisman was gone. Disappeared into a pit. And Bowren had taken over, moved back up even with them, and was running through his sequence of commands.

"Ready on the right! . . . Ready on the left! . . . Ready on the firing line! . . . The range is clear! . . . *Fire!*"

The spit-wet, piercing burble of Bowren's whistle filled the air, but only silence followed it. Nothing happened. Nobody fired. The gunners stood immobilized.

Victor Franko felt himself trembling, unable to sight a target, unable to touch the safety, unable to finger the trigger. He looked to Sawyer . . . to Odell . . . to Napoleon . . . felt their eyes seeing him though they weren't looking at him . . . saw their stances shifting ever so slightly to bear on him!

"Fire, goddamn you, you stupid sons-a-bitches! Fire!" Bowren roared.

The trembling stopped. Franko's thumb lifted the safety, his finger hit the trigger, and his fear and frustration spewed out of him as the weapon bucked and chattered in his hands and the stream of bullets smashed down-range into a cardboard silhouette. In seconds the magazine was empty. He heard the silence—his own and that of the other guns—before he was even aware he'd spent the bullets. He was breathing heavily, as though from deep physical exhaustion—and yet a gentle flood of relief, rising to pleasure, to exultation, began to swell in him. He swiveled his head to the others . . . to Sawyer, Odell, Napoleon, all looking at him . . . to Bowren, Kinder, Morgan, the MPs . . . and he wished Reisman was visible too . . . and he smiled for them all. There would be another time for reckoning, another time for freedom. This now, in and of itself, was power sufficient. This now, in and of itself, was a small measure of escape.

Slowly, calculatingly, knowing every movement he made was agonizingly scrutinized, Franko unsnapped and dropped the empty magazine, withdrew the full one from his pocket, inserted it, raised the gun to his shoulder, and in short, carefully aimed bursts began to play with his targets.

25

IN THE DAYS and nights they spent together shooting up the firing range, Reisman came to admit the Dirty Dozen to a new level of trust. It was nervous work . . . but, for them, he soon realized the intensive target practice was as much genuine pleasure and therapy as it was military necessity.

For most, it was an element of manhood, pride and self restored. For Myron Odell, it meant the confidence of new skills. Gun shy at first and way off target, he learned to handle submachine gun, rifle, carbine and .45 automatic pistol with almost the cold efficiency of the others. And though Reisman had been dreading grenade practice—not so much fearing an attack by the prisoners anymore, as knowing the tendency of men like Odell to freeze up, kill themselves and others—by the time they began tossing grenades, Odell handled them with no more fear and no less respect than did his cohorts.

In some ways Reisman eased up on the men now. There was an occasional hot breakfast or dinner with the guards in the barracks, and a few more evenings for leisure.

Victor Franko, knowing he held the power of life and death over them each time he was issued ammunition, felt more the equal of Reisman and no longer trembled at the checkerboard with Master Sergeant Morgan. He tasted the excitement and pleasure of actually beating him once, and dredged up the courage to refuse to play again, though Morgan hounded him.

For the card players, there were new decks, and instead of bullets there was play money from a Monopoly game included by Captain Kinder among the recreational equipment and reading matter he had brought down with him. Samson Posey, sorely tempted by the cards, denied himself this pleasure and struggled with reading, writing and arithmetic manuals. Kinder wanted to tutor him, but Reisman asked him to hold off and was rewarded with the desired result: Napoleon, then Odell, realizing Samson's difficulties, began to take turns working with him.

"They're ready for the next step," Reisman told Stuart Kinder, midway through the week. They were in his office, after the night watch had been posted and Taps blown. Reisman fingered a calendar as he spoke. "I'd like you to have orders sent from the highest possible echelon to Colonel Everett Dasher Breed, telling him we'll be at his camp Monday morning, April 3, to start parachute training. I could do it through my usual OSS channels, but I'd rather keep them out of it and you went up to London and handled it personally through your people there. Besides," he added, smiling, "I'm sure you know more Generals than I do."

He was surprised when Kinder put a damper on it. "I wish I could feel as optimistic about their progress," he said. "I don't mean their physical progress. Lord knows, you've done wonders with them, John."

"Then what's wrong? Wasn't it your infectious optimism and enthusiasm that helped get this thing rolling?"

"Yes . . . but I had hoped and expected there would be some deeper changes in them by now, but there aren't," Kinder explained. During these past days, he had been probing the prisoners' attitudes toward the Nazis, as Reisman had asked him to, using a combination of word-association tests and personal interviews, and he reported now what he had learned.

"*Enemy* to most of them, I'm afraid, is still as much the United States Army, the MPs, Morgan, Bowren, you and me, or any other form of demanding or confining authority . . . or even the World for some of them, or some mysterious, unspecified *They* . . . as much as it is Hitler, Mussolini, Nazi, Fascist, Wehrmacht, SS or Gestapo. Despite the chance the Army has given them, despite what you've done for them, despite my talks, my films, my propaganda and morale pamphlets," he said, shaking his head. "The war against the Germans really has no meaning to most of them. Inside they're still fighting their own private wars. Posey, Jimenez, Maggot and Franko, for instance . . . they've lived in personal worlds so narrow and limited their thinking can't possibly encompass, emotionally or intellectually, anything quite so big and grand as the events building up around us. They say they have nothing against the Germans . . . though Posey, to our benefit, nurtures a dream about becoming a great warrior. Maggot and Lever even give some indication of admiring the Nazis. White has his own cause and is still too blind to see another. Smith prattles about being glad to atone for his sins, but he's not sure he's really engaged now, with this outfit, in the Lord's work. As for the others, they feel various degrees of being put upon, and nothing so nebulous as a righteous crusade. Only Sawyer has a positive feeling about the Germans as enemy, and I suppose it's really just a latent one left over from combat in Italy."

Yet none of this really distressed Reisman as much as it did Kinder. "It doesn't really make any difference now," he said. "They may change . . . they may never." He knew them, he felt, for he was one of them—as Kinder would never know them—and with these men, *enemy* would be anybody that came against them or anybody they were sufficiently goaded to go against. "They're still ready for the next step," he repeated. "I want Colonel Breed's orders to be very specific. Take some notes, will you, Stu? He is to roll out the red carpet as to treatment afforded us. Don't phrase it that way, of course, but that's the idea I want gotten across to him. He is to delay any other programs he has going, and all jump school facilities, aircraft and instructors are to be placed at my immediate disposal for a crash program. Other than that, he and the members of his command are to mind their own business, ask no questions of my men or about my men, other than those pertinent to the actual training. He is to defer to me, to my noncommissioned officers and enlisted cadre in all matters of discipline and procedure relevant to my personnel."

"Isn't that a bit too much to ask for?" said Kinder, glancing up from his notebook. "I mean with a full Colonel . . . and you a Captain. Shouldn't it be phrased a little more diplomatically?"

"Not with this bird," answered Reisman. "With him, there's going to be trouble."

"What was the hassle about in Italy? You mentioned it at Marston-Tyne when you told me you'd be bringing the men down here."

Reisman grinned with the memory of what had happened between him and Breed in Italy. The rancor had long since disappeared so far as he was concerned, but he doubted that it had with the Colonel. "He was a Major then," he said. "He and his glamor boys had just jumped in and saved the bridgehead in the mountains north of Salerno. They'd been through some tough fighting. One good thing I'll say for him is he's probably a damned good soldier, even if he's not my type. He earned a Silver Star and a Purple Heart for that round. He was still working, with his arm in a sling, when I met him. In fact, that's one of the big troubles with him, he probably doesn't know how to relax, and he won't let anybody else if he can help it."

He told Kinder the rest of the story—how he had come through the German lines dressed in Italian civilian clothes, to link up with American advance units and make his report about what the enemy was up to out ahead of them. Parts of a village from which the Nazis had been chased had come to life again and Reisman had paused for some food and wine in a *trattoria* that had opened for business amid the rubble. The place was crowded with paratroopers taking momentary advantage of the respite from combat, enjoying being alive, buying what little food was available and much wine, accepting the gratitude and enjoying the conviviality of the local citizenry and especially the women who had come there to see the American liberators. Reisman had sat among them, for his own amusement still not revealing his identity but speaking a thickly accented, labored Americanese to them. Then Major Everett Dasher Breed had come in, cleared the place out in a high-handed manner and ordered his troops into a bivouac position outside the village.

Reisman, almost alone in the *trattoria* within minutes, had dropped his act and said, "Why the hell don't you let the boys have a good time, Major? They could be dead tomorrow, you know."

"Who the hell are you?" Breed had demanded.

Reisman had identified himself then and asked for a jeep. "I've got a report to make and I want to get down to the coast in a hurry."

Breed had placed him under arrest. He had doubted Reisman's identification and story of how he'd gotten there, out of both suspicion and pique. He had accused him, during the hours he'd held him close by in custody, of being everything from a Nazi spy to an American deserter to an Italian Fascist. Finally, Reisman's identification had been confirmed by higher echelon, Breed had been chewed out by someone up the line for holding him up and keeping him from making his vital report, and he'd been ordered to give Reisman his own jeep, driver and armed escort to get him quickly and safely to his destination. That was the part that had rankled—especially when in parting Reisman had told Breed off in choice language, and the Major had known there wasn't a damned thing he could do about it.

"I'd avoid trouble with him this time," Kinder said. "Lean over backwards to be nice and friendly, even play upon his vanity if you have to."

"Why, because he's a Colonel now?"

"No, because we've got to remain as inconspicuous as we can about Project Amnesty, and Colonel Breed sounds like trouble, as you say."

Kinder left for London in the morning, and Reisman was relieved he would be away for a while again. He didn't delude himself about what the prisoners' acquiescence to discipline and their improved abilities meant in relation to the ultimate purpose of Project Amnesty, or more immediately, the next phase of training. It had been one thing for them back there at Marston-Tyne prison, under the immediate shadow of the gibbet or facing lengthy terms in a penitentiary, to say Yes, I'll do anything! But when confronted with the actuality of it, how many would balk at the jump training? It was not an easy thing for a man not constituted and eager to do it—and Reisman had been pondering matters both of the spirit and the flesh, as reward for their progress so far, and as inducement and inspiration for what was to come.

With these men, he believed matters of the flesh were of greater concern and would be more effective, though possibly also disruptive. He was toying with a very practical, though unorthodox, idea of his own, but he intended to give it considerably more thought before putting it into action. He did know that he had to get away from the stockade again himself for a night, before the pressures, dangers and uncertainties of the parachute training began. It was more than two weeks since he had been with Tess, though he had telephoned her once a week as promised.

Reisman half rose in the bed and stretched beyond Tess to the table where his cigarets and lighter lay. His belly touched against the soft full giving warmth of her and he nestled himself down across her stomach, thinking nonsensically that there really should be something one could do with navels—then becoming suddenly aware how long it had been since he had last thought and felt the simplicity of untrammeled nonsense.

"Am I hurting you?" he asked.

"No, never," she answered. She spread her fingers upon his back and pressed him down harder. "I love the weight of you on me," she said.

In *their* room again, bathed in the warmth of a good fire, he felt good, relaxed, whole, no longer nibbled at by the conflicts, tensions and events of these last weeks and those to come—at least momentarily. Though he had not come to her tonight lightly, but with determined and serious mien, so that she had teased him and begged him for a smile, as she might have of a child—he was feeling guilty, not so much for her as for those he had left behind who were not free to do as he was doing, though he knew their need.

"Do you smoke?" Reisman asked now. "I've never seen you."

"No, but I'd like to try," said Tess. She raised up and took the cigaret from his mouth and put it in her own. She puffed on it, blowing out great clouds of smoke, until finally it stung her eyes, she inhaled and choked, and handed the cigaret back to him, coughing. "I think I'd rather watch," she gasped.

She asked him to blow smoke rings and she laughed when, both sitting up now, he spiraled them onto her nose, her puckered lips, her breasts. They lay down together again when he finished the cigaret, and he held her softly to him in the cradle of his shoulder. And now the others rose up to haunt him—or mock him, he wasn't sure—as though they were already dead.

He hadn't expected to ask Tess, or anybody, for advice, but suddenly he found himself saying, "Would you think it was wrong if I tried to bring to men living a lonely, frightened, brutal existence, a touch of something like you?" He went on quickly, not even giving her a moment to answer, for he felt he must explain further. "They're these men I'm working with. Lying here with you, I realize how much they're missing . . . to make them strong . . . to help them feel like men again. They don't really feel completely that way . . . and they must, to do what they have to do."

"No, I don't suppose a man ever does unless he has a woman," Tess whispered. "I've heard it . . . oh, so many times . . . and now I know it, from you." She moved her head and pressed her lips against his neck.

"It wouldn't be lovely," Reisman went on, "because that's not the sort of thing I have in mind, and there wouldn't be time for it, as we've made our own times together. And they can't go out to find such a person themselves. But it's something I think they really need . . . a woman . . . to play at liking them, and trying to satisfy them."

"All other male things are rather secondary, aren't they, when held alongside his relationship with a woman?" She said that proudly, boastfully, in the full knowledge of what it was she did for him. "Of course, if it's a shoddy relationship, it's too bad . . . but there is that purely physical thing that lets a man know he's a man, I suppose."

"It would be breaking all sorts of rules and regulations."

Tess picked up her head. "If you mean as we are breaking them, then it really doesn't matter."

"No . . . military rules . . . by the code . . . that sort of thing,"

"If it doesn't hurt them . . . if it does good . . . if it doesn't hurt the women, as this doesn't hurt me . . . if it does them good, as you do me, then what is the harm?"

She wrapped an arm across his chest and hugged him to her tightly. "I love you, John. I believe you're fond of me. We may each die tomorrow . . . today. What loss to the world? None. But how much greater the loss to ourselves without this."

Once in Macao before the war—or was it in some God-forsaken whorehouse in the Caribbean?—Reisman had thought how nice it might be to give up the sea as a living —after all, one did have to work hard at it, and there were always dangers—and open a pleasant little whorehouse of his own, testing and retesting all the wares personally, and merely sit back comfortably and let his living come to him instead of going out to seek it. He supposed it was the gloriously impractical dream of all young cocksmen at some point in their lives. Thinking of it again now in the barracks at Stokes Manor Sunday night, he remembered it had been some such wild scheme as this that had brought Archer Maggot to his present low estate. And yet here he was himself now the planner of something equally crazy.

No sooner had he returned to the stockade Saturday morning than Reisman had given Sergeant Clyde Bowren some money and sent him off on a unique mission, for the performance of which he was to stay away overnight and not return until after dark on Sunday. "It must be someone who lives more than fifty miles from here and has no knowledge of the area," he had instructed. Then, trying to joke, though they both realized the seriousness of what they were doing, "Bring someone with impeccable references . . . someone you've tried yourself and approved."

And since in the morning he would have to begin to contend with Colonel Everett Dasher Breed, there also came to Reisman's mind now that memorable discussion about women and soldiers they'd had in Italy when Reisman had been Major Breed's temporary prisoner. Reisman had really set him off when he'd suggested—after Breed had cleared the troops out of the *trattoría*, arrested him and taken him to his CP—that what the Major really needed to improve his disposition, if not his soul and body, was a good night in the sack with a woman.

"Whoever the hell you are, fellow," Major Breed had exploded, "you're an impertinent son-of-a-bitch with an evil mind! I had a wife once for that sort of thing, but there's no room for that in a soldier's life. It must be a total effort! It has been a total effort! This is what I've trained for all my life, and the day we went to war, the very day I knew for certain, I refined my life, my very thinking, to purity which nurtures strength and is itself beautiful and self-sufficient. That sort of thing has no part in my life any more. And if you're an American Captain as you say you are, fellow, it shouldn't have in yours either."

"What did your wife think of your sudden conversion to monasticism?" Reisman had said.

"Not monasticism. Celibacy. Isn't that what you mean?" Breed had demanded.

"Yes."

"I should say it is none of your business . . . but I won't," Breed had said disdainfully. "Let it be part of your education. We were divorced, my wife and I, shortly afterward. What she has done since is none of my concern. I trust she has found her own brand of happiness elsewhere."

"And you've found yours in war?"

"Yes, completely."

"Your philosophy on this subject is probably unique, Major," Reisman had told him.

"I believe my thinking is partly known to some of my colleagues, junior and senior," Breed had said. There had been an undeniable sound of pride in his voice as he spoke, an abstract, almost fanatical look in his eyes, in the dedicated set of his features. "Though I don't have evidence of effort to support me. I don't pry into the private lives and thoughts of others as long as they do their jobs as well as I do mine, and my men do!" He had said this last with vehemence and pride. "But don't think I'm alone and unique in my philosophy. I remember a distinguished military psychologist, Dr. G. Stanley Hall, who wrote that, 'War of all the occupations of man, because it is the most exciting and the most strenuous, makes not only possible but imperative for its supreme success the highest degree of chastity.' "

"Hah! Try selling that to the Army!" Reisman had scoffed at him in that stinking, rubble-strewn CP in Italy. "Obviously we've read different books, Major. Do you know of the great Russian General, Aleksei Nikolaevich Kuropatkin? He was more of a realist. He had the perspicacity to observe that on the eve of a great battle which might be fatal to his soldiers, many complained of painful erections which it was necessary to reduce by the use of drugs. My own particular psychologist—I forget who he was just now—analyzing this military problem, said it seemed to him that, confronted with death, the urge to life and procreation became stronger."

Remembering, Reisman laughed silently, derisively. For the Dirty Dozen there was even more to it than that.

Bowren had driven in with the woman after dark and had taken her, slightly drunk and gaily blindfolded for the game they were playing, directly to the smaller room in the barracks. Reisman had cleaned out the place, locked away all papers in the desk, and removed anything that might give her a clue to where she was, or be a temptation to the men. The window was heavily curtained, the lights throughout the barracks kept barely visible. Reisman didn't want to see her or have her see him; nor did he want to see the faces of the men or have them see his. Master Sergeant Morgan had been sent far off in the truck on a phony errand, for Reisman particularly didn't want him around for this night's amusement. The other guards had all been posted on duty within the compound, so that they would have no personal knowledge of what was going on in the CO's office.

Now Bowren came out of the office and said the woman, a prostitute he had picked up in Plymouth, was ready and eager for the party to begin. "This one would've done it for nothing," he said, "when I told her there were twelve very hungry fellows, all heroes, all just back from some terrible work against the Heinies . . . and not even time to bathe and shave, for this was the way we felt they'd get their minds off their horrible memories the quickest."

Yet the prisoners themselves still didn't know. They'd had a good dinner, and Reisman had then sprung on them suddenly the announcement that they'd be driving out from the stockade in the morning to start their jump training. Then he'd ordered them to bed early, with the excuse that they needed plenty of rest for the work ahead. There'd been little grumbling—mostly an air of nervous tension. He doubted that any of them were really asleep out in their puptents.

Odell was brought in first. Reisman sat at a plank table in semi-darkness near the kitchen side of the barracks, as far away from the office door as he could get. Bowren went outside again to stand between the barracks door and the inner compound gate, available when needed.

Reisman knew he was taking an awful chance with Odell—but, Christ, he was taking a chance with all of them. He had no way of knowing how Odell would act—whether he'd be gentle with her or scare the shit out of her and ruin everything, or whether he'd do anything at all.

"How do you feel about the jumping, Myron?" Reisman asked.

Odell's face looked pitiful under his scraggly layers of hair and dirt, and even in the dim light Reisman could see the fear in his eyes.

"We're not really going to do it tomorrow, are we? Don't they teach us about it first?" he blurted out.

"No, you won't be jumping tomorrow," said Reisman quickly. "You'll have a week of preparatory stuff first. When you do go up, Myron," he said reassuringly, "I promise you, you'll be ready, if not eager."

"Sure, Captain. What was it you wanted now?"

"There's somebody in my room to see you. You're not to say a word about who it is or what goes on to anybody, not even your tentmate. Do you understand?"

Odell's face brightened and his glasses picked up and reflected little glints of the dim light as he turned his head toward the office and back again. "He's come back," he said. "That man who was going to help me. He's found out something good."

"No, it's not that. It's someone else who might be able to help you in a different way. There's a clock on the desk in there. You're to stay no longer than fifteen minutes. Go ahead. Close the door after you."

Odell was hardly in the smaller room, with the door closed behind him, than he came bursting out again, trembling. "I'm sorry, Captain. I can't," he said. He reached for the barracks door to flee back into the compound.

"Odell, come here!" snapped Reisman.

Odell walked toward him slowly, his face looking as though he'd seen a ghost. "It's not fair of you to do something like this to me!" he muttered.

Reisman sensed an angry tone growing in his voice, and that was good. "You're a man, aren't you?" he asked.

"Yes, I'm a man!" Odell flung at him. "I'll shoot your guns . . . learn to jump . . . do what I have to . . . but not this!"

Reisman held a cardboard box toward him. "Pro kits. Would you rather help the others when they come out? You're an expert on this sort of thing, aren't you?"

The anger rose in Odell now so that the words sounded strangled as they burst from his throat. "Fuck them all, Captain!" he gasped out. "I'm nobody's pratboy, and I never will be again!" He turned and walked slowly from the barracks, and Reisman let him go without another word.

Victor Franko was brought in.

"Would you like to take a quick shower and shave?" asked Reisman.

"What for?" said Franko suspiciously.

"There's a woman in there," said Reisman, pointing to the office. "Sort of a reward for being a good boy. She might find you easier to take if you were clean and sweet-smelling."

Franko's jaw fell open. "You're kidding, Captain," he said hoarsely.

"No. See for yourself . . . but once you open that door, you're in and you've got fifteen minutes. Who knows? She may not even want you, looking and smelling like you do."

Franko hesitated, walked to the office, opened the door and closed it behind him. His head reeled at the sight. *That son-of-a-bitchin Captain!* The naked white skin of the girl picked up the dim light and seemed spotlighted. He searched her face, sought her eyes for reassurance—more a woman than a girl, about thirty, not bad-looking, a little on the plump side . . . but that was good . . . oh, looka those tits, looka those tits! He stared at her—lying spread-legged and beckoning on the cot—and he was unable to move.

"Cor, but ain't you a mean-looking one," she said, smiling.

He grinned at her weakly, his fingers plucking at the coarse hairs of his beard.

"You afraid of me too, honey?" she asked, pouting.

She was a little drunk, he could tell, and there was a bottle of whisky and a glass on the desk near the clock that had already ticked off a minute and a half of his allotted time, and he looked at it longingly.

"Go ahead," she said, nodding to the bottle. "Help yourself, if I'm so hard to take straight."

"No, ma'am, no, not at all," he managed to get out. He

poured himself a drink with trembling hands and belted it down quickly. "Something for you, ma'am?"

"Cor, no. I've had enough," she said. "Come on. Get your pants off. Party's paid for."

Franko overstayed his time and Reisman had to summon Sergeant Bowren to go in there and get him out. He looked embarrassed and docile as a baby as he shuffled through the barracks buttoning himself up again.

The others were brought in one by one and most stayed their full allotted time, then came out for an embarrassed exchange of words with Reisman as he handed them their pro kits, told them to make damned sure they used them, and to keep their mouths shut about the night's recreation.

Luis Jimenez wasn't embarrassed at all. "Man oh man, Captain, you okay!" he said happily. "I doan need no parachute to fly!" And then, lapsing into Spanish, he boasted, "Twice I came in ten minutes. What you think of that, hey!"

Calvin Ezra Smith came shuffling out of the office toward Reisman and looked at him accusingly. He knew every chapter and verse exhorting against what he had just done—yet he had done it, lusted like an animal in the doing, and filled now with remorse, he needed someone to blame.

"What's the matter, Smith?" asked Reisman. "Don't you feel better now?"

"No," he whispered, shaking his head. *The time cometh,* he thought, staring strangely at Reisman, *that whosoever killeth you will think that he doeth God service . . . That's Saint John, you whoremonger . . . John 16:2 . . .* and he shivered with so righteous a thought.

Two others never touched the woman. Samson Posey came out of the office as quickly as he had gone in. "I have wife," he said sadly, and left the barracks. Napoleon White came out in a fury. "What makes you think I would touch that filth!" he spit out. "Bring me a black woman!"

Archer Maggot was last. Jimenez had come back to the tent singing, and saying over and over again, "Man oh man!" and Maggot had tried, without success, to pry out of him what was going on. He had peered from the tent often and seen men coming and going and finally Bowren had come for him.

In the Captain's office he couldn't believe his eyes. There was a little booze left in the bottle and he took that first to quiet him down a little and so he wouldn't come so fast, because he could feel himself going just looking at her. Then it suddenly struck him—*the nigger!*

"That black bastid ain't been in heeyuh, has he?" he demanded.

She laughed. "In and out so fast I hardly saw him. Cor, honey, but I sure would have liked *him* to stay. I've had plenty of bucks like that. They've got real big ones, you know . . . and they sure can use them. Come on, soldier," she cajoled, "let's see yours. Give me a good time, honey. I'm hardly warmed up."

Maggot threw himself at her, grabbing, slapping, punching, yelling, "Nigguh lovuh! Lousy stinking goddamn nigguh lovuh!"

She screamed loud and clear and often, and the next thing Maggot was aware of was Sergeant Bowren pounding on him and dragging him, with his arm twisted up behind his back painfully, back into the compound.

"You never learn, do you," Bowren muttered. "You stupid son-of-a-bitch."

When the woman had left with Bowren in the jeep, Reisman walked slowly into his room and surveyed it—the empty whisky bottle and filthy glass; the damp, stained, rumpled bedclothes that reeked of the woman and the men. He felt a sudden revulsion, yet no regret at what he had done. Each of them had made of it what he wanted. For some it had been good. He tore off the blankets and sheets and, with the bottle and glass, carried them outside the barracks to the trash can to be burned and buried.

part
four
KRIEGSSPIEL

26

VICTOR FRANKO felt good driving. His hands and arms hugged the steering wheel of the truck tightly. He felt the throb of its big engine as a sensual thing coming up through his body. He exulted in the sense of control over power, speed and direction. He felt cocky, almost happy: a free woman and booze the night before, and now they were out on the open road again in the early morning in fine, bright weather, giving him that elusive taste of freedom once more after four weeks cooped up in that stinkhole of a stockade. If the good things kept up, he wouldn't mind this outfit at all. Except every now and then, looking through the windshield at the Captain and the nigger driving the jeep up ahead, he felt like jamming down the gas pedal, smashing right over the jeep and the Captain, and the hell with the nigger, he was too damn smart for his own good anyway.

Franko wondered if Bowren, riding shotgun beside him, would kill him if he tried to ram the jeep, or let him do it, afraid they'd all be killed—Bowren and him and all the rest of the guys and the MPs in the back—if he was shot at the wheel. He snickered silently at the paradox, then slowed the truck and turned off the highway following the jeep down a dirt road toward an MP checkpoint and gate and beyond it what he now saw to be a big Army base of tents and Quonsets and wooden barracks and buildings, stretching out over a vast plain toward a distant airfield.

He braked the truck a few feet behind the jeep, watched Reisman take a salute and get directions from the gate guards; then he was waved on. The unpaved road wound past buildings and tents, camouflaged dumps of equipment, ammo, massed pools of vehicles and guns, and men—paratroopers in singles and clusters, squads and platoons and companies. The moving vehicles raised clouds of dust around them.

Out of the corner of his eye, Franko saw something huge and imposing on the landscape. He jerked his head toward it and felt a sudden clutch of fear that iced his growing composure and cockiness. It was a steel-girdered tower a couple of hundred feet high, with four long arms sticking out at the top. Troopers were working around the bottom of it, others were positioned in the surrounding field, and suddenly Franko saw a man being hauled up one of the arms, dangling helplessly from a harness beneath an open parachute. And it hit him that he was going to have to pay for all the joy he'd had the night before, and pay even more for having gotten out of jail.

The jeep slowed and Reisman raised his hand to signal a stop. Franko watched him hop down to the road and trot back to them, shouting, "All of you out of the truck for a minute."

Prisoners and guards dismounted and gathered around Reisman.

"Take a good look at that," he said, pointing to the tower. "That's the fun part. You're in harness when you go up and your descent is uncontrolled. By the time you get to this stage, you'll know exactly how to handle yourself. Going out of a plane afterward will be a hell of a lot easier."

Franko's eyes glued in horrible fascination upon the man being hauled slowly up the tower. Roscoe Lever squeezed close to him and said, "Boy, you get hanged here, Franko, they sure hang you high!" Lever said it lightly, but he did so only to share his own fear, for the reality of the jump training had hit him hard right in the gut.

Franko watched the man on the tower, heard a loudspeaker somewhere boom out, "Are you ready?" saw the iron ring holding the parachute go up a few more feet and then the dangling man suddenly drop, falling free at first before the chute filled out—and Franko turned away from the sight, from the guards and prisoners around him, leaned against the side of the truck and fought to keep from chucking up his breakfast.

Two platoons of smartly dressed paratroopers were drawn up in parade formation on either side of the roadway leading to the entrance of the big, barnlike structure that was the main building of the training center. As Napoleon White drove the jeep past the troops, Reisman stared at them curiously, wondering if he was blundering into some sort of ceremony. There was a band, too, partly hidden behind a platoon on one side of the road. They began to play just as Reisman saw Colonel Everett Dasher Breed come out of the building toward the jeep. There was a commanding height and lean toughness about the man, and his eyes projected a bright, startling blueness even at a distance. Out of an aura of strength and competence, an awareness of experience and status, and an undeniable magnetism that exuded from him and marked him as leader, the eyes seemed to say first of all, Where do you fit into the scheme of things, little man, and how do you balance with my world?

Reisman hopped out of the jeep, threw a salute; it was returned. Above the loud, martial music, the Colonel said, "Welcome to the Manor, Captain. I had hoped I would run into you again someday, under my Command." There was a contemptuous smile on his face, as though he had just eaten a division of Krauts for breakfast, and Reisman wondered, among other things, about his use of the word Manor. "Where's the General?" Breed asked. "From the tone and priority of the orders I got, I figured there would be at least one or two with you. I'd like him to review my troops, at his pleasure, of course."

Reisman didn't know what the son-of-a-bitch was up to, but if Colonel Breed wanted to play games, and if he wanted a General, he would give him one. "The General's in the truck, Colonel," Reisman snapped. "He's traveling incognito on this deal and I'd have thought you'd have gotten that point from your orders."

Breed looked dubious, but also a little bit as if he might be forced to eat crow any second. "General who?" he asked.

"That's right, sir," replied Reisman politely. "General Who, that's what you can call him. He's got no other identification, except a number, just like the rest of my group. That's the way it's got to be . . . secret . . . just like your orders stated, Colonel. Kind of you to arrange this big welcome, but stupid pointing the big finger at us when we wanted to come in quietlike. If you'll wait here a minute, I'll go back and talk to him."

Breed bristled and flushed red with anger, but said nothing as Reisman strode away from him. At the back of the truck, Reisman tossed the canvas flaps aside, dropped the tailgate and peered in at the mixed bag of MPs and prisoners. All insignia of branch and rank had been removed from the guards. Dog tags had been taken from everybody and left back at the stockade. Everybody was dressed the same in fatigues, helmet liners and stiff new jump boots that creaked. They all carried carbines, but none of them were loaded, and the MPs kept their ammo clips hidden. The only obvious difference between the guards and prisoners was that the Dirty Dozen were bearded and stank.

"Sawyer, how'd you like to be a General?" Reisman asked softly.

The men laughed. Archer Maggot asked, "What's all thuh band music bout, Cap'm? We gonna have a peerade?"

Sawyer answered, "Sure, Captain. What do I have to do?"

"Look stiff and straight and like a son-of-a-bitch, and no matter what you do . . . even if you want to fart . . . do it with style and authority, like that's the way it's done by damn and screw everybody else. I'll line the rest of these bearded bastards up behind you. You MPs get into the line between every other man. There's a chickenshit Colonel out there, Sawyer. When he throws you a salute, you give him one back. If he holds out his hand to shake, ignore him and don't even bother talking to him. Look at him and his troops with contempt. You're better than him and you're better than these tin soldiers out here . . . do you understand . . . every one of you? All you have to do, Sawyer, is walk past one of his platoons, look them over, and disappear into the building. We'll follow you, and I'll take over from there."

The band music stopped. The paratroop platoons, dressed in Class A's, looking sharp and tough and competent, were brought to attention by an officer. Reisman looked at them and wished that twelve of them—any twelve picked at random—could be his. For they'd go in and do the job that had to be done and do it well, and though they'd know fear as all soldiers did, they'd do their work with zest and pride and confidence, and with no danger of copping out, killing each other or their leader.

Ken Sawyer rose to his crazy bluff with unexpected magnificence. Colonel Breed threw him a salute, he returned it with hauteur, and he strode quickly past the rigid paratroops, with Reisman, the Dirty Dozen and the MPs trailing in a ludicrous shuffle behind him. Gaining the shelter of the vast, barnlike building, some of them broke into helpless laughter. Luis Jimenez slapped Sawyer on the back. "Man, you sure make damn fine General!" he shouted.

Reisman silenced them. Neither Breed nor any of his men had followed them into the training building yet. "Look around you," said Reisman. The high-ceilinged room, big as an airplane hangar, was surrounded by balconies and filled with parachute harness and cables and ropes and training gear. "That was your last laugh," Reisman said ominously. "By the end of this day, none of you will have the strength to weep. What went before was Boy Scout stuff. This is for the money now!"

A paratroop Lieutenant came through the door and told Reisman, "Colonel Breed would like to see you in his office now, sir. It's at the other end of the building."

It was really in a separate Quonset, built smack up against the training building. Reisman was escorted through the orderly room quickly and shown to a door with a sign on it that read, Colonel Everett Dasher Breed, Commanding Officer. The escort knocked, Breed called, "Come in!" and Reisman went in alone. He decided to play it straight, cool and formal, as though the phony reception incident had never taken place. He strode front and center before Breed's desk, saluted and stood at attention.

"Captain John Reisman reporting, sir," he said, "with a complement of twenty men to begin parachute training."

"At ease, Captain," said Breed, leaning back in his chair and swinging his legs casually onto a corner of the desk.

Reisman's eyes swept over him appraisingly, separating the details, refreshing his memory of the man. The jump boots were not mere swagger or public relations, but well-used tools of his trade, of fine leather made supple and creased by hard wear, and polished softly to perfection. On the Colonel's breast, above a row of campaign ribbons and awards, was the silver badge of the paratrooper. He was about forty years old, Reisman estimated. His close-cropped hair was black and gray—probably war-induced gray. Reisman had seen men's hair turn color and their faces line with age in a matter of days. Breed's face was lined and had the look of always being thrust up into the wind and the sun or any other elements his time and place threw at him. He seemed poised now between anger and humor and had a curious way of looking at Reisman as though he were some sort of inexplicable specimen. "Is that filthy slob really a General or are you trying to give me a snow job, Reisman?" he demanded.

"You thought I was giving you a snow job in Italy, too, didn't you?"

"Still haven't learned any manners either, I see, or military courtesy."

"Colonel, you asked me to present a General and I did. That's as much as I can say about it. I am not allowed to divulge the identities or organizations of any of these men. Those are my orders, and as far as I have been informed, they are also yours. And if you'll read your orders carefully, sir, you'll also see that I'm not under your Command as you phrased it during that little show you put on outside."

"From the orders I got, I thought you'd be bringing a whole regiment over," snapped Breed. "What the hell do they mean by tying up all my instructors, training equipment and aircraft?"

"To show you what a good sport I am, Colonel," said Reisman, relaxing and smiling at him, "you can have most of it back. I can tell you exactly what it is I'll need now."

"That's damn big of you, Captain!" Breed exploded. "If you didn't have friends in high places, whoever the hell they are, I'd have you and your crummy crew off this post in half a minute. This isn't a regulation training center, you know. It's mine. I built it for my regiment by scrounging every piece of wood and steel and equipment out of somebody who thought he needed it more than I did."

"That's commendable, Colonel. It's a real nice place you have here," said Reisman pleasantly. "But now I need it more than you do."

Breed rambled on as though he hadn't really heard him. "This outfit got pretty badly mauled in Africa, Sicily and Italy, Captain. The men that survived are tough and good and they'd follow me into hell itself if I asked them to. We weren't getting the right kind of replacements from the parachute school at Fort Benning and we weren't getting them fast enough, so my officers and I went all over Britain and scavenged the best material we could find, got them transferred and we train them ourselves . . . our way. Sometimes another regiment or division asks to use the facilities, but they observe the courtesies, Captain. I've never been ordered to let an outside group in here before, and I sure as hell don't like it!"

"We're in the same Army, Colonel," Reisman stated.

"So far I've seen no evidence to support that, Captain," said Colonel Breed. "Who the hell are these men and what are you up to?"

"You know I can't tell you that."

"And another thing, Reisman," Breed rapped out angrily. "Most of them are filthy, stinking and unshaved. What the hell kind of an outfit do you run? I run a clean, taut, efficient post. My men shave, bathe, get haircuts and keep their persons, uniforms and equipment spotless. How the hell do you think I'm going to explain to them why I should allow your group to come over here and be any different. They're a disgrace to the Army, as far as I'm concerned . . . if they're even in the Army."

"Colonel . . . you're the Commanding Officer. You don't have to explain a damn thing to them. And I'm the Commanding Officer of my group and I don't have to explain a damn thing to you. My orders are to bring them here, train them, qualify them as parachutists, and move on. I'd like to begin immediately . . . with the Colonel's permission, of course."

Breed smiled at him from behind the desk, but it wasn't a friendly smile. "Reisman, I sure wish I had you in my outfit," he said. "I'd have you busted down to a buck-assed Private in ten seconds flat."

"At this point, Colonel, I'd probably thank you for it. May I proceed with an outline of my plans and requirements now?"

"Sure, go ahead, Captain," muttered Breed in disgust. "I guess the sooner you get started, the sooner we get rid of you."

Reisman outlined how he wanted to conduct the training over a two-week period, combining elements of the American method as taught at Fort Benning, Georgia, which he'd briefed himself on, but had never taken, and elements of the British method, particularly its swiftness, as taught at Ringway, where he'd taken his own training.

"I'll lead my group through and do the teaching and demonstrating myself," Reisman explained. "I'll need only two of your instructors . . . any grade you can spare, it doesn't make any difference. I'll want them to keep a sharp eye on my boys to see that they follow instructions explicitly, and I'll want them to do a little personalized coaching where it's needed. During the time we're here, they're to be attached to my Command and under my orders exclusively."

"What makes you think you're qualified to instruct, Reisman?" Breed challenged. "I don't even see any jumper's wings on you."

"You needn't worry on that score, Colonel," Reisman answered, smiling pleasantly. "You're welcome to join the class and observe any day you've got the time. At Benning you had five weeks to learn your trade. I'm taking only two weeks to teach these boys the basics and qualify them with five jumps . . . and I'll want wings for them when they're finished. If you don't think they've made it, you can tell me and we can take it from there. Some of them are here only to observe, but twelve of them have got to learn to jump, whether it scares the shit out of them or not."

"Hop to it then, Captain," ordered Breed coldly. He rose from his chair stiffly and pointed to the door. "And God help you if you don't know what you're doing. I'll send one of my Lieutenants and one of my Sergeants next door to the torture chamber to show you around and help you out. I trust I have your permission to use any of my facilities you're not using at any given moment . . . for instance, my C-47s. You don't mind if I take some of my troops up for a refresher jump every now and then while you're our guest, do you?"

"My pleasure, Colonel. I'll send a report up to SHAEF that your cooperation has been magnificent. That ought to make up for the last time."

Reisman started through the door when Breed brought him up sharply with, "By the way, Captain Reisman, I *have* been informed of your recent activities in this area from time to time. Lady Margot Strathallan is a friend. She has already complained to me a number of times about the use you're making of Stokes Manor. Regrettably, there was little I could find out, except that it had been authorized, and nothing I could do about it. You see, when I brought my regiment down here I had somewhat of the same idea you had, find an old country place to set up headquarters and live like a squire. I knew there were a few of these places around and available. But when I broached it to Lady Margot and she said No, I accepted her answer, and we've been good friends ever since."

"Why that's just fine," Reisman said. "It makes for better Anglo-American relations and all that. But when you came looking for your baronial headquarters, Colonel, did you have authorization from SHAEF?"

"I was acting on my own," said Breed crustily. "If I had found an agreeable situation, I was going to suggest it up through channels. You know we don't billet our troops in private homes without permission, Captain. What the devil do you think we are, Nazis?"

"Nor am I living the life of a country squire there, Colonel," said Reisman. "I do have authorization from SHAEF, and from Miss Strathallan's father, who owns the property. I have a job to do and I intend to do it without interference."

"And what is that job, may I ask?" pressed Breed.

"I am not at liberty to say."

"Perhaps you are at liberty to give me an explanation as to why Lady Margot rang me up last night very disturbed. She was out walking near a patch of woods where your camp is supposed to be, and she said she heard a woman screaming. I told her it was highly doubtful—just to reassure her, of course—although I had no way of knowing for certain myself. Did you have a woman in your highly secret, impregnable little fortress last night, Captain?"

Reisman met the Colonel's probing blue eyes and held them without flinching. "Probably one of my men, sir," he said, "undergoing torture."

In the vast, high-ceilinged training building the paratroopers called the torture chamber, Reisman briefed the Lieutenant and Sergeant assigned to him by Breed, and was in turn apprised by them of all the equipment and facilities available for jump training there in the building and elsewhere on the post. Far across the room, Sergeants Morgan and Bowren called cadence as prisoners and guards limbered up with simple calisthenics.

"The ones you watch and worry about are the bearded ones," explained Reisman. "This is an experimental group and the stress is mostly on them. The others should be able to take care of themselves. Some will go through parts of the program, some may not go through any of it, and one or two may go all the way. Nobody has a name, rank, serial number or organization. They're to be identified only by the numbers by which they'll report to you. Anytime you see one of the Dirty Dozen goofing off, report it to me, I'll give you the go-ahead, and you land on him hard. The rest of them I'll discipline myself, if it's necessary. Do you read me clearly?"

Two "Yes, sirs!" assured him they did.

"All right, let's begin!" said Reisman.

He stood on a raised platform with a paratroop instructor on either side of him. Prisoners and guards intermingled below him. Besides their individual identification numbers, he had secretly split the twenty men into three groups. X group was the Dirty Dozen, Y group was Sergeant Morgan and three MPs, Z group was Sergeant Bowren and three MPs. Y and Z would alternate in different parts of the program, particularly in the beginning, to make it look good, but any of the guards could beg off, with permission from Reisman, if he didn't feel up to competing with his charges—in which case he was to fall back into observer status and take notes on the training and behavior of the prisoners, besides keeping his eyes peeled for possible mayhem or attempted escapes.

"Your work here will proceed in four stages," Reisman's voice boomed out. "The first will be physical conditioning and familiarizing yourselves with getting in and out of harness and handling the risers on your chutes. The second will be a series of exits and controlled jumps off the balcony in here, and learning to drive and steer your parachute under simulated airborne conditions." He pointed to parachute harnesses suspended from cables that slanted downward from the high balconies to poles implanted near sawdust pits. "During stage two, you will also begin to practice parachute packing, and you'll continue to practice it right through stage four. The chutes you jump will be the chutes you pack yourselves, so you'd damn well better learn to do it right. Stage three will take you up the tower we saw on the way in here, and you'll begin to learn the refinements, and how to save yourself if you get into trouble. In stage four, you'll fly and jump for a target. There'll be four daylight jumps and one night drop. Any questions?"

He was sure there were hundreds of them, but nobody asked any.

Reisman went on: "I'll repeat. There are four stages. Thousands and thousands of men have gone through this program and come through without injury as qualified parachutists. Ordinarily a man can repeat a stage if he washes out and wants to go at it again. But we don't have that kind of time. If you goof off on the first stage, you might kill yourself on the second . . . but nobody gets left back! You know the alternatives open to you if you decide to cop out!"

After the rugged weeks of field training at Stokes Manor, Napoleon White had thought he was in pretty good shape physically, but Reisman and the two T-shirted robots working with him drove the group through a so-called conditioning program that first day that seemed designed to break them down rather than build them up. Outdoor runs along the base roads and across fields were made at lung-searing speed, without letup and without apparent reason other than to make men drop in their tracks, be dragged up and driven on mercilessly. Napoleon noted with pleasure that the MPs were now the first to lag behind and fall out, and he tossed mocking obscenities at those of the guards who alternately chose to use the jeep to catch up with wherever the Dirty Dozen were working.

Between runs, there were calisthenics—performed for fifty minutes without letup in a huge sandpit, where the gravitational pull on limbs and bones and muscles seemed quadrupled, and Napoleon watched guys collapse with their noses and mouths buried in the sand, turning over to breathe again only with the contemptuous lift of an instructor's foot. Few of the MPs took part in this phase of the game; certainly not fat-assed, full-bellied Master Sergeant Morgan; though Sergeant Clyde Bowren did, keeping up with and sometimes surpassing everything the prisoners had to do. Napoleon knew Bowren didn't have to take all this crap if he didn't want to—but because he did, because he shared it as Reisman did, Napoleon felt a grudging respect for the man.

Everywhere, there seemed to be ropes that had to be climbed, though none as high or as terrifying as that first rope on the cliffside Reisman had made them climb the first day of training. Napoleon often glanced toward Samson Posey when he felt he could not go another step or take another breath, and the sight of the seemingly inde-structible, tireless giant would give him new energy to go on. If there was any humor at all that day for Napoleon or for any of them, it was when Indian clubs were issued for a drill period that threatened to tear arms from shoulder sockets, that left hands wet and trembling, and fingers nerveless; and everybody knew what the damned things were called, except Samson Posey.

Reisman was right—what went before had all been Boy Scout stuff, Napoleon realized as they drove back to the stockade at the end of the day. He was so completely exhausted he'd told Reisman he didn't think it would be safe for him to attempt to drive the jeep back, and so Reis-man had taken the wheel himself. Napoleon had been rele-gated to the flesh pile in the truck, and a proud and wake-ful Samson Posey had been given the privilege of riding up front with the Commanding Officer. Victor Franko, too, had gladly turned the truck wheel over to one of the guards, and rode in the back.

The men were grim, silent, ungriping, many asleep in twisted, tortured postures against each other in the truckbed. Napoleon was drained of the energy it might have taken to weep.

The second day the conditioning was the same, but now it was interspersed with the practical stuff of the fledgling jumper. In the big training hall and spotted in key loca-tions all over the post, usually at the end of a hard run, were jumping platforms up to fifteen feet high. Reisman led them up the scaling ladders, knelt on the platforms, drilled into them the exit command sequence they'd use aboard the plane, and sent them off. If they balked, as a few of them did, he pushed them. Below, depending on the height of the platform, they landed on canvas mats, dirt, sawdust or rocks, and an instructor was waiting for them, screaming into their ears, "Legs together! Bend your knees! Tumble, goddamn you, tumble!"

In the torture chamber, they climbed in and out of parachute harness again and again until they could do it with their eyes closed as easily as putting on their pants. Then they swung on risers suspended from a moving system of pulleys and cables, to get the feel of being airborne. It was hard on their arms and shoulders, and hardest on their testicles if they hadn't buckled on right and their straps slipped.

Once in the morning and once in the afternoon, Reisman let them go to the latrine, always a few of the guards and a few of the prisoners together. The latrines here were elegant compared to the slit trenches back at the stockade. Joe Wladislaw found himself lingering admiringly over a real toilet bowl, time enough to put him a couple of beats behind the group as they exited the building. The door slammed in his face as he started toward it, and he felt two pairs of arms clutch at him from behind.

Wladislaw turned. Two burly paratroopers—a Corporal and a Pfc, in Class A's, bemedaled and beribboned—were holding him. "What the hell you doing!" he squawked, trying to jerk loose.

They dragged him off balance on the edge of his heels back against the far side of the latrine. "Take it easy, fellow," said the Corporal, smiling at him. "We just want to ask you a few questions." They pushed him against the wall and kept holding him.

A warning signal to keep his mouth shut and try to fight his way out of there went off in Wladislaw's head. The deal stank of something Reisman would try to do, some kind of entrapment. "Sure," said Wladislaw, relaxing his tensed arms and smiling back at them reassuringly. "Get the claws off. What'd ya wanna talk about?"

"Let him go," said the Corporal.

The instant their hands came loose, Wladislaw went at them. He ducked, brought interlocked fists up against the jaw of the Corporal, side-stepped to chop downward against the other one's neck, but suddenly the guy wasn't there and he felt the sledgehammer edge of the Pfc's hand in his kidney and he went down gasping for breath. He knew damn well then he wasn't up against any amateurs. While he groped for air, the Pfc was on him and had his right arm twisted and locked behind his back, forcing him back up on his feet again. But Reisman had taught him how to get out of that one, and the instant he had his breath back he brought his right heel down hard on the

Pfc's arch and slammed his left elbow back into the guy's solar plexus, heard the trooper's cry of pain as he released his arm. In the next seconds of give and take, as the Corporal came back up off the floor to join the fight, Joe Wladislaw suddenly realized he was enjoying himself. Then they nailed him to the ground, but good, arms and legs unmovable.

"All right, you filthy bastard, talk! Who the hell are you? What's your name?" barked the Corporal.

"Number Six," Wladislaw gasped. He kept up the struggle, trying to move, twisting his fingers, his feet, bouncing his rump up and down on the hard floor to try to dislodge them, letting them know he hadn't given up, because if this was Reisman's deal that's what he'd want.

"That ain't your name! Give us your name!" demanded the Corporal.

"Number Six!" Wladislaw threw back at him.

"All right, wise guy, we'll do it our way!" the Corporal muttered. He yanked Wladislaw's arm down to his side. "Hold him there!" he ordered the Pfc. With one hand freed from the fight, the Corporal undid Wladislaw's fatigue jacket buttons, searched around his neck and chest, and not finding what he wanted, he grabbed the neckline of Wladislaw's T-shirt and ripped it down. "Where in the hell are your dog tags, soldier?" he demanded furiously. "Ain't you in the goddamn Army?"

Wladislaw raised his head a couple of inches off the floor and spit in the Corporal's face. Then he reviled both him and the Army with the full lexicon of the gutter.

Anger got the better of the Corporal in that instant and he started to backhand Wladislaw's face. "You filthy son-of-a-bitch!" he cursed. "I want your name, rank, serial number and your outfit!" He beat a tattoo with every word.

His left hand unexpectedly freed when the trooper started to work him over, Wladislaw put it to good use. His fingers probed and he found the right spot quickly. His thumb dug into a point at the base of the man's neck, just above the clavicle bone, and he squeezed with all his might —so calmly aware of what he was doing that he could visualize Reisman demonstrating it, identifying it, spelling it: subclavian nerve pinch.

The paratroop Corporal screamed in agony and fell backward off Wladislaw on top of the other trooper. In that moment of respite, Wladislaw spun to his feet and made it out the door of the latrine.

Reisman had just noticed Wladislaw's absence, was chewing out Master Sergeant Morgan, about to send him in search, when Wladislaw came racing up wildly to join the group.

"What the hell happened to you?" Reisman barked, inspecting his torn clothing and bruised face. "You been in a fight?"

Wladislaw hesitated a moment, then retorted angrily, "You ought to know, Captain!"

"Now what the hell's that supposed to mean?" demanded Reisman.

"You sent those two guys after me, didn't you?" asked Wladislaw, doubt beginning to creep into his mind.

"What two guys?" Reisman countered.

Suddenly he got it. He took Wladislaw's arm, led him aside and got the full story. "You didn't tell them anything, did you?" he asked quickly.

"Crap, no!" answered Wladislaw indignantly. "I figured you was pullin a fast one on us! I was just beginnin to have some fun when I cut out a there."

"All right, get back with the others," Reisman ordered. Then, as an afterthought, knowing he should say something more, he called out, "Wait, Joe." He put a hand on Wladislaw's shoulder and said, "You did all right. Tell the others what happened. Spread it around. Warn them to watch out, and yell for help if they need it. It wasn't my doing . . . I promise you that. I think I've got it figured."

He decided, however, that he would say nothing to Colonel Everett Dasher Breed, nor do anything about it for the present.

Wednesday, April 5, the third day of parachute training, they moved into Stage Two. It was fast, but not the fastest it had ever been done. Reisman had known men to learn the whole jump course in four or five days when their missions were pressing.

Myron Odell moved slowly near the end of the line on the balcony, forty feet above the floor of the torture chamber. He was trembling, butterflies danced in his stomach, and he wanted to go to the toilet. He watched as the first man went out the mock-up door of the plane, dropped sickeningly about twenty-five feet, bounced halfway back up at the end of his harness and risers, and slid down the inclined cable on a pulley wheel to slam into a pile of sawdust at the other side of the building.

It was like a scaffold. Odell was glad he hadn't been first, to freeze in the doorway and exhibit his cowardice again for them all to see. But it grew even worse waiting and watching the others go out, seeing some of them lock their fingers on the frame of the exit, refuse to go, while Reisman slapped at their legs, coaxed, cajoled and threatened or pushed until finally they went. By the time it was his turn, Odell was in an absolute sweat of bug-eyed terror. His fingers fumbled with the harness, unable to buckle it on right.

"What the hell's the matter with you, Mike?" Reisman whispered harshly in his ear, trying to make it as private as possible. "Nine guys have gone off here, some of them just as scared as you are, and every one of them is still alive without a scratch on him down below. For Jesus Christ's sake, lemme help you, will you?" he said, fiddling with the straps and buckles to make sure Odell really had them on and they wouldn't strangle or emasculate him when he dropped.

Odell moved in a fog, his muscles and nerves limp, letting Reisman push and prod him, position him in the mock-up frame of the aircraft doorway. He felt the slap on his leg, heard the "Go!" knew that a few more seconds passed as he stood there limply rather than frozen, felt the extra push from Reisman at the small of his back and he fell like a deadweight sack of potatoes—neither mind nor muscles nor nerves functioning to brace himself and remind him what to do right, until he felt the shock of the harness grabbing at his crotch and armpits, yelled "Ouch!" and came alive again just as he slammed into the sandpit all wrong with fingers and feet out ahead of him to intercede for the rest of him. A thumb on one hand and a pinky on the other ached painfully. They were sprained badly, but that was the worst of it. He knew he could go back up now and make the exit again and again, as he would have to, and do it right.

That night, after a hot dinner, Reisman gathered guards

and prisoners together informally in the barracks.

"I am reminded that tomorrow is Good Friday," he said deferentially. "Any of you MPs who want to go to Mass while we're at the jump school can do so. I've got a schedule of both the Catholic and Protestant services. You can do it in staggered shifts so nobody gets left out." His eyes moved among the others as he went on. "As for you other men . . . there is no reason in the world why you can't go too, if you want to. I personally would like very much for you to go. It's a good time in your lives to think of something bigger than yourselves for a change. I don't mind giving you a short break, if it's legit, but anybody who thinks he's going to answer church call just to goof off has got another think coming! Who wants to go?"

He was surprised to see that they all raised their hands except Samson Posey.

"Very well," said Reisman. "You will, of course, shower and shave in the morning before we leave here. I don't want any of you standing out in a crowd. You know, already, what happened to Joe Wladislaw earlier in the week."

Slowly the hands began to come down. First one, then another, then another, as they looked at each other.

"The hell with it!" muttered Victor Franko, speaking for all of them.

"Suits me," said Reisman. "Tomorrow, we go up the big tower just as planned. I advise you to say a few prayers on your own tonight."

27

VICTOR FRANKO'S fingers felt thick and unresponsive as he and the other men attached Reisman's parachute to the ring that would haul him up the 250-foot tower. He gave the silk canopy an extra tuck and pat, surprised that he cared, and stepped back as the two instructors moved quickly around the circle, double-checking their handiwork.

A jeep drove up. Reisman saw Colonel Breed get out of

it and stride toward him. He had stayed pretty much out of the way and out of sight all week, but now he'd apparently decided it was the moment to make his weight felt again—or to heckle.

"Anybody been up yet, Captain?" he asked.

"No. I'm going to test the wind," replied Reisman.

Breed wet a finger in his mouth and held it in the air as he gazed up at the four arms of the tower. "I think you picked the right one," he said.

"That's what I'm about to find out, Colonel." He looked away abruptly. "Send me up," he ordered one of the instructors.

An engine started, a windlass began winding steel cable, and Reisman rose skyward. Franko stood under the tower, his head tilted back, his eyes fixed on Reisman's swinging body as it went higher and higher. Suddenly he realized he was standing there alone. The others had moved out to better vantage points away from the tower to watch. Franko trotted after them and found himself standing with a group near the chickenshit Colonel.

High on the tower, Reisman looked at the widening vista of the Army base, the airfield, distant farms and roads. He didn't like this part at all—being captive on this damn contraption with no control over it until he was electrically released at the top, and he wasn't even sure about it then. He hadn't told anyone, but he'd never been on one of these before. All he knew about it, he'd read in technical manuals and picked up by subtly questioning the two instructors. There had been no intermediate step such as this where he had taken his parachute training. They had just jumped.

The ring stopped and he hung there helplessly in the wind. "Are you ready, Captain?" the loudspeaker blared. It was Colonel Breed's voice.

"Go ahead!" Reisman shouted. If he'd picked the right arm, the wind would push him away from the tower. If he hadn't, he'd have to start climbing his risers fast or risk making a damn fool of himself—or worse.

Nothing happened. Reisman still swung there. He looked down. It was a long way to go without a chute. He heard Breed's voice again just as he began to wonder if something had gone wrong with the controls.

"Speak up, Captain," the loudspeaker boomed. "You'll have to say it louder. I can't hear you."

Victor Franko, standing near the Colonel, wondered what in hell was wrong with the hard-nosed bastard. He'd heard Reisman's shout loud and clear.

"Pull the goddamn plug!" Reisman bellowed angrily.

Still, Breed didn't release him. "I certainly hope you know how to handle that thing, Reisman," he cooed into the microphone. "Whatever happens, don't panic, fellow. And when you land, take a little roll. Don't try for a stand-up grandstand play. You'll smash your legs. If you're ready now, we can proceed. Just give the signal, Captain, any time you think you're ready to try it. There's no hurry now, if you think you want to get used to it awhile up there first. It happens that way sometimes."

Reisman gritted his teeth in fury. His arms and legs were beginning to ache from hanging there. As loudly as he could, he shouted down, "I'm ready! Go ahead!" and restrained himself from adding an obscenity.

He felt the ring go up ten more feet and then he dropped. The parachute whooshed out full at two hundred feet, and he saw, with relief, that the wind was pushing him away from the steel spider's web. He came in softly, legs together, knees bent, did a little roll and stood up gathering in the lines and silk, about fifty yards from the tower and a little farther from the group around Colonel Breed. He moved toward them. "Wind's just right," he called to no one in particular. Even at this distance he could see that same cynical smile on Breed's face that he'd worn that first day at the phony band reception. "There should be no trouble at all. Who's next?"

Sergeant Bowren trotted forward to relieve him of the parachute and harness. "I am, Captain," he said.

"Could you hear me all right when I was up there, Clyde?" asked Reisman, jerking his thumb upward.

"Right from the first, sir."

"That's what I thought. Fall in the men around you at the tower. I'll be right there."

Bowren gave the order, added, "On the double!" and Colonel Breed and one of his instructors were suddenly alone at the microphone observation post.

Reisman came up to them. "Get over to the tower with the others, fellow," he ordered the instructor.

The man hesitated, looked at Breed.

"Do as the Captain says," muttered the Colonel.

The microphone was picking up their exchange, adver-

409

tising it all over the area. Reisman reached past Breed and switched off the loudspeakers. "I don't wish to embarrass you in front of the men as you tried to do to me, Colonel," he said evenly.

Reisman faced him squarely, feet spread, poised ever so slightly up on his toes, as though for a fight. Breed's eyes met his and held them, wary and ready.

"Colonel Everett Dasher Breed," said Reisman, as though he was beginning a heroic citation, "besides being a first-class soldier, officer and gentleman, you are a first-class prick. I warn you, Colonel," he continued without raising his voice, "if you ever try anything like that again, those eagles on your shoulder are going to shit all over you."

Breed smiled at him. "You realize, Captain, that I can now have you arrested and court-martialed for insubordination?"

"Try it, Colonel, and your job here is finished," said Reisman softly. "You'll be doing your barking and jumping from a desk somewhere in the ass end of the Pentagon." Whether he could do it or not, Reisman didn't know, but he thought he could. Everything he'd wanted so far in Project Amnesty had been granted him. "Your rank means absolutely nothing to me or the work we're doing here. Anything you do to impede that work will be known in the highest command before the day is over and would be sufficient justification for your removal." He reached for the loudspeaker switch again. "If you'd like me to, Colonel, I'll turn this on now and repeat everything I've just said. That way, you'll have witnesses for your little court-martial."

"No need to be crude, Reisman," snapped Breed. He was no longer smiling. His face was blank, revealing no emotion whatsoever. "For a while you amused me, but no longer. I'll merely add this incident to the bill of particulars and present it to you for a final accounting at some future date." He turned away with a majestic air of dismissal and strode back to his jeep.

Reisman felt a wave of relief flood over him.

It was Victor Franko's turn on the tower. Sergeant Bowren had gone up and floated down in one piece, beaming when it was over. Franko had watched Napoleon

White and then Samson Posey, each nervous as he was being hooked up, despite their seeming eagerness to volunteer—each swaggering a little bit, grinning like a kid as he unhooked the harness after landing, and earning a bit of Franko's grudging respect for having gone up on the damn thing and come down alive. Now it was Franko's turn and he was scared silly. Master Sergeant Carl Morgan was there in the crowd hooking the silk up to the hauling ring, and Franko fought away thoughts that Morgan was in reality fashioning a noose about his neck and that this whole business was some fantastic and unbelievable cover-up for a hanging.

He had to go to the toilet, and he felt nauseous—afraid he was going to spew his guts all over the men working around him.

"Ready to go, Vic?" called Reisman, smiling at him reassuringly, and Franko wondered why the hell he was so friendly all of a sudden . . . he never called him Vic . . . maybe once or twice . . .

"Yeh . . . sure, Captain . . . sure," he answered, his voice cracking.

"Just think about the landing, that's all," Reisman ran on. "Do it by the numbers . . . feet together . . . bend the knees . . . easy hit . . . take a roll and come up spilling air. The breeze is good. There's nothing to think about this first time but the landing. Sing out loud and clear at the top."

"Yeh . . . sure . . . sure," said Franko again, and suddenly he was going up, panic rushing in on him from all sides, and he knew he had to stop it, had to control himself or he'd screw up the drop, forget how to land, hurt himself. Hurt himself . . . Why not? . . . Suddenly he had an idea to fix upon, to still the fears that gripped him and capitalize on what was happening to him. If he banged himself up, he'd be a hero, hurt in training, wouldn't have to go on the mission, wouldn't even have to finish jump school, risk getting killed falling from the plane. And they couldn't hang him. He'd be hurt . . . and you had to be whole to be hanged. He still remembered that.

"Sound off when you're ready, Franko!" Reisman's voice boomed through the loudspeakers. The cable had stopped. He was up there and he hadn't even known it. He took a good look around. What a view! Goddamn, what a view! This wasn't so bad. Not if going down was as easy as coming up. Lectures, films, demonstrations spun through his head. He knew how to drive this rig . . . how to steer . . .

"Go ahead!" he shouted.

The sudden drop put his heart where his mouth was and he almost screamed, thinking this was what being hanged was like. Then he heard the *whoosh* and *snap* of the parachute filling out, his descent slowed, and he took one quick look at that beautiful canopy over his head. He was all right . . . moving away from the tower. He tugged at the risers, testing them, pointing himself back toward the bottom of the steelwork . . . he knew how to do it . . . how to make it look good . . . maybe just a bad sprain . . . or a little break . . . or a big fat bruise that looked worse than it was . . . and he saw the ground coming up fast . . . too fast! . . . and the scattering mob of uniforms trying to get out from under him . . . and there was Morgan with a disbelieving look of horror on his face . . . and Franko tried to climb back up into the sky as he hit him a resounding wallop with legs and back and skull and caved into the ground unconscious . . .

Myron Odell bent over Franko and moaned, "Oh God, is he dead?" He'd been steeling himself, getting ready, knowing he'd have to do it, feeling better as each guy floated down out of the sky and told how great it was—and now this!

Reisman turned from the dazed Master Sergeant Morgan, sitting up now, and snapped at Odell, "Goddammit, man, don't you know? You're a medic, aren't you?" He was glad Breed wasn't there.

Franko groaned and opened his eyes. Myron Odell and Roscoe Lever were peering into his face. Others were hovering near, looking worried. Somebody was poking at his legs, saying, "Is it broke? Is it broke?" He pulled them up. No, they weren't broke. He ached all over, his head was spinning and there was a lump on it, but nothing seemed to be broken.

Reisman came at him angrily, helping Sergeant Morgan along to his feet. "What in hell do you think you were trying to do?" demanded Reisman. "Of all the numskull tricks I've ever seen, that takes the cake! I ought to let the Sergeant beat the crap out of you, Franko!"

Morgan, leaning on Sergeant Bowren and an MP now, didn't look as though he was in condition to beat the crap out of anybody, but he made a sudden lunge toward Franko. "You trying to kill me?" he bellowed. "You did that on purpose, didn't you, you slimy son-of-a-bitch!"

Reisman stepped between them, facing Franko. Sergeant Bowren and the MP eased Morgan away. "Apologize . . . tell him you're sorry," Reisman muttered softly to Franko.

"Sorry?" echoed Franko. He felt stronger—bolder since coming down off the jump tower where the hangman had never been—edged his way around Reisman and spit. "Sorry, hell!" he rapped out. "I wish I had killed him! What was the fat-assed bastard doing in my way?"

Roscoe Lever was next on the tower. Then Ken Sawyer. Then Myron Odell, and once again it was the fear of chickening out, of making a public coward of himself, that bothered Odell more than any terror of being maimed or killed. If only he'd volunteered first like Nappy and the Chief, he'd have been up and down and all right now. But there were still two men ahead of him, the way Bowren had set up the line, and the longer he waited, watched— seeing Franko almost get killed—the farther back he wanted to go, the more he was beset by doubts of his ability and fears of disaster—or cowardice!

Reisman came over with a new parachute and harness. "Who's next?" he called.

Roscoe Lever held back. Screw it. He didn't want to go. A guy could really get hurt . . . maybe killed . . . even without going on a plane. The sight of Franko crashing into the ground had shaken him badly. He wanted no part of this. He didn't have to do it. He wasn't under the hangman's noose like Franko and Sawyer and Odell and the others. Let them put him back in jail. He didn't give a damn. "You go," he muttered to Sawyer.

"Lever! Let's get with it!" snapped Reisman.

"I ain't going!"

"The hell you're not!"

"I said I ain't going, Captain, and I mean it," Lever blurted out nervously. He backed away, trying to push himself in among the startled group.

Ken Sawyer ambled in front of him. "I don't mind going first, Captain, if he's too chicken."

"Get back in your place. Lever, come here!" ordered Reisman.

Myron Odell listened to the exchange with growing excitement, pushing himself forward, almost without will. It was as though Lever's public fear was absolving him of his own and replacing it with a crazy surge of blind courage.

"What's the matter, Roscoe? Scared?" said Reisman coldly.

Lever turned back to him angrily. "No, I ain't scared!"

"Then you're a coward and you don't belong here with us. Tonight, you'll be taken . . ."

"Let me go, Captain!" It was almost a scream from Odell. He had pushed himself through ahead of the others and grabbed the harness. "Now! Let me go now! Please!"

Reisman looked at him, startled, recognized the struggle going on within Odell. "Okay," he said. "Now." He pointed at Roscoe Lever. "You're next, yellow. Odell will show you how it's done."

They hooked up his parachute to the ring, and Reisman barked, "All right, all of you, clear away from here." He saw the glazed look in Odell's eyes, the forced calmness, and it worried him. The guy was scared stiff and he shouldn't let him go up like that. He coached him gently, out of hearing of the others. "Now, Mike, listen to me. The day couldn't be better for this. Don't look down. Close your eyes and take a nap if you want. Think of it as an elevator. I'll wake you when you get topside. Take one look around and then sing out loud and clear. You'll like it. I promise you. I'll coach you every inch of the way down, but you're not gonna need it. The wind is good . . . your chute is gonna blossom without a jolt . . . and you're going to float easy. I'll tell you when to set your legs for the landing. That's all you'll have to think about . . . the landing. The chute'll take care of itself. Just the landing . . . legs together . . . bend your knees . . . roll . . . and come up spilling the air out."

Odell nodded, his eyes closed tightly, not even wanting to look at the Captain or the others or the world around him. "Now. Quick. Send me up now," he murmured.

He felt himself rising, hanging free, thinking only of the Captain's last words . . . his eyes still closed, pretending he was asleep. And then the cable stopped with a jolt that swung him back and forth in the harness, and with his eyes still closed, he screamed out, "Pull the goddamn plug!" and he dropped, and only then opened his eyes, thinking it might be his last sight, looking down not out, because it was down that worried him, seeing the open field and uniformed figures rushing up to meet him, slowing as the chute filled, and he thought to look up and remark how beautiful the white silk canopy was above him, as he heard the Captain's voice on the loudspeakers, "Good . . . you're doing good . . . one fifty . . . one hundred . . . drift's perfect . . . look down . . . judge your distance . . . fifty feet . . . legs together . . . don't try to climb . . . not so stiff . . . don't fight it . . . stay with it . . . twenty feet . . . legs together . . . legs together . . . bend your knees . . . bend your knees . . . roll!"

Odell came out of the tumble, his hands on the lines, gathering them in, spilling the wind out of the silk—feeling ten feet tall! And as he came trotting back to the base of the tower, he couldn't help looking triumphantly at Roscoe Lever, who met his gaze and moved reluctantly forward to go up.

Sergeant Clyde Bowren was up before the sun Easter Sunday. He was showered, shaved and dressed in his Class A's, ready for church by the time he blew Reveille. He wanted very much to pray this morning. He didn't relish going with these goons, but Reisman had told him he could take one shift over to the parachute camp and Morgan another. At roll call before chow, he listened as the Captain made the announcement to the prisoners.

"You all know what day this is . . ."

Bowren wondered if any of them really did, or felt it as he did now . . . that whole wonderful business about resurrection and hope, although he'd never quite thought of it like this before . . . Some of them must, he supposed, for surely they needed it more than he did . . . If there was damnation, then they were damned and this was their purgatory . . . Sharing it with them, guiding them through it to God knew where, was making him think too damn much these days . . .

"You have all been invited by the Chaplains at the parachute camp to attend the church of your choice," Reisman went on. "Those of you who want to take Communion can go with the first shift and pass up breakfast until later. Each of you have done well these last weeks, and I trust you to behave well and follow the orders of the men in charge of your group. As your Commanding Officer, I urge you to go. For those who don't want to, this will be a free day here at home. There will be no training schedule today. Those of you who want to go, raise your hands."

They all did. Samson Posey raised his hand slowly at the last after seeing that he would be alone.

Sergeant Bowren couldn't figure that one out, or, for that matter, figure what had come over the rest of them—particularly since they'd been offered a goof-off day right there and were turning it down. He wondered if it was because tomorrow was their first real jump and if there was any peace to be made with a God, any praying that might have an effect, this was the propitious time for it in their scheme of hedging their bets.

"You'll have to bathe and shave, of course," said Reisman.

The hands came down.

"Suit yourselves," he said.

For Reisman it created a problem, though. All the MPs wanted to go as much to get away from the prisoners and have extra time off, as to pray, he suspected. He could have split the guards into shifts as he had intended if the Dirty Dozen were going with them, but it suddenly occurred to him that here was his first opportunity to be really alone with them for an extended time. Twelve to one odds to sweeten temptation. Ultimately, on their missions, they'd be alone; or he would lead them—which was what he wanted to do, despite what Major Armbruster had said about him not going in anywhere for a while.

He called the Sergeants aside and told them they could take all the MPs over to church with them now, if they wanted to go. "There's no need to hurry back," he said. "Let your men have a day off. You've all earned it. Go into town if you'd like, or take a long drive. Be back before 2400 to get some sleep."

"How about you, Captain?" asked Sergeant Bowren.

"I'll stay here."

That didn't sit well with Bowren. As the guard detail was climbing into the truck, he looked back at Reisman standing alone in the barracks door. "You take them," he muttered to Morgan, and strode purposefully back inside the gate.

"What's the matter?" Reisman asked.

"I'm not going," said Bowren. "You can't stay here alone with these slobs."

"Of course I can. We've got them gentled down just fine now," said Reisman. "Go ahead. There's nothing to worry about." He knew Bowren by now, knew his desire to go to church this day was strong and genuine and that it would do him good.

Yet Bowren insisted, almost angrily, "I don't have to go if I don't want to, Captain."

"Okay, Clyde. Come on in and we'll have some breakfast," said Reisman warmly, "I can't order you to go to church. That's in the rulebooks somewhere, I think."

Once they were sure it was really all right, most of the prisoners went back to sleep. Later, after a sumptuous, leisurely breakfast catered by Luis Jimenez, they lounged and loitered around the barracks or the compound—talking, griping, reading, playing checkers and cards, or staring wordlessly beyond the fence into the wood that screened the world where spring and freedom lay. None had any desire to exert themselves with the athletic equipment Stuart Kinder had brought down, and Reisman couldn't really blame them. He and Bowren alternated between the barracks and the compound, strolling about to make their presence felt, stopping here and there to chat. Bowren carried his weapons loaded and cocked. Reisman, for the first time, went unarmed.

Napoleon White noticed it. He had set up his bedroll outside his tent and was lying there reading, luxuriating in the warm sun, when Reisman came by. "You look naked, Captain," he remarked. "Aren't you carrying your need to trust us a bit too far."

"I don't think so," said Reisman, squatting down beside him and offering a cigaret.

Napoleon sat up, took one, and Reisman lit it for him.

"Do you really think I need a weapon to protect myself from you?" asked Reisman.

"No, I guess not," said Napoleon, matter-of-factly, blowing out a stream of smoke.

"We discussed the subject of trust a few weeks ago," Reisman went on. "I told you we'd talk about it again. What do you think now? Would you trust them?" he asked, nodding his head at the rest of the stockade.

Napoleon didn't avoid the question this time. Whatever Reisman was training them for, he was doing an impossible job well, and Napoleon felt a greater empathy with him. "More so now . . . I think," he answered. "They're tougher . . . but with more substance and less bullshit. In ways, I think we can be quite competent."

"But what about trust itself . . . dependability . . . the faith it will take to let you go in and do an important, dangerous job without a gun at your heads?"

"Depends on the job, Captain. What is it?"

"Not yet, Nappy."

"When?"

"Depends on you . . . on them . . . what you all do in these next days. How do you feel about tomorrow? Nervous?"

"Sure. Who wouldn't be?" said Napoleon with a grin. "It isn't man's natural estate to come floating down out of the sky. That's for birds and angels, and I'm neither." And, also, he'd seen no other Negroes around the parachute camp and he'd sworn he'd make it there and make it good. He was scared, sure, but it was a challenge to something deeper in him.

Reisman started to get up, but Napoleon didn't want him to go yet. He blurted out, "You were right about this, you know." He held up the copy of Lawrence's *Seven Pillars of Wisdom* that he'd borrowed from the Englishwoman's library weeks before. "I'm afraid I admire him as much now as I did when I was a kid. More so, maybe. I understand him better as a man, and there's a power and beauty to his writing. I can see now what you meant about it being a disturbing experience when you first read it in Spain. It's not designed to make a man want to go out and make war. Rather the opposite effect in parts, I think . . ." He flipped back pages quickly. "Here, listen to this," he ran on. " 'With man-instinctive, anything believed by two or three had a miraculous sanction to which individual ease and life might honestly be sacrificed. To man-rational, wars of nationality were as much a cheat as religious wars, and nothing was worth fighting for: nor could fighting, the act of fighting, hold any meed of intrinsic virtue. Life was so deliberately private that no circumstances could justify one man in laying violent hands upon another's: though a man's own death was his last free will, a saving grace and measure of intolerable pain.' "

Napoleon examined Reisman's face to see if he'd really absorbed the full import of the lines. "Certainly not something one should read before going into battle, is it, Captain?" he remarked. "Definitely not the kind of get-in-there-and-fight stuff our psychologist friend would want me to be lapping up."

"No, I guess not," said Reisman, smiling at him. "But I think you're big enough to discount it."

Napoleon wouldn't let go of it, wouldn't let it end there. "Man-instinctive . . . man-irrational . . . that's me," he expounded. "That's what I did in anger to put me here with you and them. Man-rational . . . it strikes me that you might be the quintessence of that, Captain. How do you square it with your past and future of blood and guts, and your zest for the glory quest?"

Reisman wondered if he was being mocked. "Man-rational, my friend, isn't born that way," he said. "If he is unlucky enough to reach that estate . . . and I haven't yet . . . then he does so only after years of pandering to his instincts. Have you torn up *The Nigger of the Narcissus* yet?"

"No, I read it!" Napoleon flashed back.

"Good. Then you're improving . . . moving toward man-rational," said Reisman sarcastically as he stood up. "Don't go too far, though. Remember . . . we still want you to kill some Nazis before you're off the hook. How'd you like the story?"

"I hated it and I liked it," Napoleon said passionately. "There were moments I envied the Nigger's dark power over his shipmates. I hoped he'd lead them all to their doom and somehow rise out of it himself, whole and reborn."

"But he didn't and you didn't like it," offered Reisman.

"Hell, no! That wasn't it! I hated it because as an acceptable hero . . . as men go, for that matter . . . he was a leech of a man . . . contemptible in his whining. But! . . . when he died . . . when he died at last, so that even I heaved a sigh of relief . . . that world around him trembled! They knew he'd been there, by God, and they'd never forget him!"

"And you liked that?"

"Yes!" said Napoleon defiantly.

"Then you've passed the book on?"

"No. It's in my tent. Odell has Toynbee's *History* and *Winnie the Pooh*. Sawyer has the Kipling poems. But the *Nigger's* in my tent," he said, and suddenly he couldn't help himself, he began to laugh and Reisman joined him.

"Better let me have it, since it's still in one piece," Reisman told him.

Napoleon crawled into his puptent and brought out the book.

Reisman took it and started away. "Let me have the one you're reading, too . . . as soon as you're finished," he said, turning back. "I wouldn't want Myron Odell reading it . . . particularly the part you read me. His head is muddled enough with doubts already."

Leon Osterman turned up later that day. He telephoned first from Stokesmouth Village this time. "It's the Easter bunny, kid. Can I pay you a visit?" he asked.

Reisman was delighted to hear the familiar Chicago patois. "Sure. We're not working today. Anything new on Odell?" he asked hurriedly.

"It'll keep a few minutes," answered Osterman. "I'll be right over."

Reisman cleared the men out of the barracks and told Sergeant Bowren to keep them amused in the compound for a while. He was almost tempted to let Myron Odell stay with him in the office, but changed his mind. It would be premature, if not cruel—for Osterman, after all, had given no hint of anything on the phone.

Osterman was in uniform this time. "Just to prove to you I really am in the Army," he said, laughing. "Here, I brought you a little something to celebrate." From a paper sack, he produced a bottle of fine Scotch whisky. "Glasses I didn't bring."

Reisman went out into the barracks and brought one back.

"Who's not drinking?" asked Osterman.

"I'm on duty, Sarge," said Reisman apologetically. "My boys wouldn't like the smell. There's just two of us holding down the fort for a while. But go ahead . . . enjoy."

Osterman put the bottle back in the bag. "Here, put it away . . . a present from the Easter bunny. Save it for a happy occasion. I don't like to drink alone."

"You've brought some news, I hope . . . about Odell."

"Nothing good . . . nothing bad," said Osterman, putting the bag on the desk and taking the chair. "Just a report on what I've been doing, so you wouldn't think I forgot. As far as the girl is concerned, what Odell said was true. She was a nutty kid, treated bad at home and everywhere else. So bad, in fact, she tried to kill herself a few times . . . and that never came out at the court-martial."

Reisman leaped at the possibility. "Then she could have killed herself there at the pro station when he not only rejected her but beat her up, couldn't she?"

"Maybe. At least we now have reason to believe that could have happened. But prove it!"

"How?"

"There is no how. The girl is dead and buried. The evidence when it was fresh said murder. I've been up there in Glasgow. I talked to the MPs and CID men and the limey cops who were on the case. I even talked to her family. They were very uncooperative. As far as they're concerned, Odell killed her. I had a hell of a time getting them to admit she'd tried suicide."

"Why should they be uncooperative? What the hell have they got to lose?"

"Well, they might have a good case against the Army to collect damages . . . I don't know. There's been a few cheap frames . . . damages . . . allotments. If this was straight rape, we'd have a better chance. Sometimes a girl's married and playing around, so she yells rape when she gets caught or knocked up. But murder's something else."

"What do we do now?"

"Figure for the time being it wasn't suicide. We save that for last, since we can't prove it, and work on it like it was a murder case. If Odell didn't do it . . . and on the books it's still an open-and-shut case against him . . . then we look for another guy who could have. I'll say this much . . . before the court-martial, particularly since they had that confession he later retracted, they didn't do so good on this end of the investigation. If Odell didn't kill her, he at least left her there all beaten up, maybe unconscious. He's admitted hitting her. Okay . . . he blacks out, opens the door, gets out of there and back to his barracks somehow. The door is open, the girl still there, somebody comes in."

"Who?"

421

Osterman shrugged. "One of the medics who worked there . . . somebody who'd been treated there or wanted to be . . . somebody who'd gotten laid in that part of the city that night. Go find them all. It's one hell of a job. I know, because I been trying. Those two soldiers who saw the girl there with Odell, they're okay. They testified at the court-martial and I talked to them. Their stories check out. I also talked to one of the medics who works there and remembers Odell. His story checks. A few of the medics, including the one who found the body, have been transferred. Getting to them is gonna take time . . . particularly since this is all unofficial. If you wanted to do it through channels, we could bring all these guys together and go at them again. We could check every cocksman on the record who was treated there . . . and maybe even find a few who weren't."

"I can't do it through channels," said Reisman bitterly.

"Then I'll keep at it just the way I have. Okay, Johnny? Only you should understand it's gonna take a lot more time . . . and maybe there ain't gonna be enough before you . . . you know, before he has to do whatever the hell he has to."

"You're doing a fine thing, Sarge," said Reisman warmly. "Whether it works or not . . . I appreciate it . . . and yet all I can do in return is say thanks."

"Aghh, the hell with that!" scoffed Osterman. He waved a hand, brushing it away in embarrassment. "There's one more thing maybe you want to try. Take him back up there where it happened. Let him look around the place . . . try to remember. Maybe we could tell if he really did black out . . . I don't know. Sometimes just seeing a room or a person or an object again, or getting a feeling about a place can open a guy up . . . bring things back . . . start him talking."

"You sound more like a psychologist than a cop now," said Reisman, "but it's a good idea if he's got the guts to go through with it." He glanced out the window, searched the compound for Odell, but couldn't see him. "Not yet, though . . . not this week anyway," he went on wistfully. "It's strange . . . In the beginning I was afraid the guy would either kill himself or chicken out before he got this far. Now I don't want to stop him. He's changed. He's stronger. He's still afraid, but he's learned to live with it, control it, use it . . . and he's developed a determination, almost a dedication, that he didn't have before. If he makes his first jump all right . . . if he doesn't chicken out . . . he'll be even stronger. Nobody's really the same afterward . . . it's a bit like combat that way. By the end of the week, he'll have something . . . a bit of stature . . . maybe a bit of swagger . . . a bit of contempt . . . something to face the truth with if he is guilty."

28

IT WAS A GOOD DAY for flying and jumping. They'd packed their own chutes Saturday, lingering over them a long time, and now, dressed in new jump suits and helmets, there was nothing more they could do except go up and jump—or turn yellow. At the airstrip, filing aboard the C-47, nobody balked—except Master Sergeant Carl Morgan.

"I don't know nothing about flying, Captain," he said weakly at the door of the airplane as they started to load.

"I'm not asking you to pilot it, Sergeant," snapped Reisman cruelly. He could see Morgan was suddenly scared stiff and he meant to rub it in in front of everybody. "I just want you and two of your detail to sit there and keep an eye on the men after I go out. One of the instructors will act as jumpmaster, Sergeant Bowren will drop at the tail end, and I want you there watching that the boys behave."

"I don't get no flying pay," retorted Morgan. "I don't have to fly."

Reisman ordered him into the plane and he refused; and Reisman thought how amusing it might be to have a few of the Dirty Dozen testify at a court-martial reducing the hangman to buck-assed Private—for they and the guards were keen and amused witnesses to the dialogue. He asked for three volunteers from among the MPs and watched them board the plane. To Morgan he said, "I'm noting this on your fitness report and it might have a bearing on how long you'll be allowed to keep those stripes. Take the rest of your men back to the truck and drive over to the drop zone."

Morgan tried to stifle his hate and fury against Reisman.

Through these last weeks he knew he had become to all of them less a figure of terror and respect than of contempt and derision. He saluted, tried to make his acknowledgment a retort, but his voice came out obsequiously, "Yes, sir . . . but I . . ."

"No buts . . . just git!"

Samson Posey watched the Captain stand up and come toward him. Though he had volunteered to be first, he had been placed next to last in the jump stick, just before Sergeant Bowren. The Captain looked into his eyes now, saw the eagerness there, and smiled.

"You're one guy I don't have to worry about, do I, Chief?" he said.

"Okay, Captain," Samson answered. He would follow anywhere this man who had taught him the skills of the soldier . . . and more . . . this man who had restored his pride.

The Captain moved from man to man, speaking words of encouragement, until he was back at his place.

"Stand up!" the jumpmaster ordered. "Hook up!"

Samson fastened his static line to the overhead cable.

"Check your equipment!"

Samson's eyes and fingers probed and poked at the equipment on the back of the man ahead of him, examined carefully his own harness and the reserve chute on his chest, and felt Sergeant Bowren poking around with the stuff on his back.

"Sound off for equipment check!" the jumpmaster called.

Bowren first, then Samson, then the others, reported by number that their equipment was in order. Samson watched the two small lights over the open doorway. The red one came on as they neared the drop zone.

"Stand in the door!" ordered the jumpmaster.

Samson watched the Captain position himself, turn once and give them all a smile and a thumbs-up sign. The jumpmaster yelled, "Ready!" The green light came on. He slapped the Captain's leg, yelled "Go!" and the Captain leaped out into the wind.

Samson wished he could see him, watch the parachute blossom and carry him safely down, but he couldn't. They were going out this first time in slow singles, not together in a stick. The airplane turned and circled back over the drop panel.

Samson marveled at how Myron, the frightened one who was a cross between a rabbit and a coyote, now stood bravely in the doorway. "Go!" and Myron, unprotesting, was gone. And as the plane circled back and forth across the drop zone, Samson shuffled closer and closer to the doorway behind the others, a prayer to *Inusakats* formed upon his lips, until it was his leg that felt the slap, his body that answered "Go!" and suddenly it was true—he was plummeting from the sky like an eagle upon its prey, heard a crack like that of Yucca's old rifle in a high canyon on Ute Mountain, felt himself seized and snapped like a heifer lassoed and bulldogged in full flight . . . and with a smile of exquisite pleasure looked up to see the full-blossomed parachute floating him safely and serenely to the ground, and knew that the old prophecy of Billy Three-legs, the old signs of eagle and airplane and Army had this day indeed come true.

On the ground, Master Sergeant Carl Morgan watched the first dark figure plummet from the airplane, and knowing it was Reisman, he wished it would keep on plummeting until it smashed into the ground. But the white parachute billowed out, and then, as the C-47 flew back and forth overhead, another chute billowed and another and another and . . .

"That's a wonderful sight, isn't it?" said a deep voice behind him.

"Maybe," muttered Morgan.

He looked behind him then, startled to see the paratroop Colonel, and flustered that he had answered him the way he had. "Sorry, sir," he apologized. "Yes, that sure is a great thing to see."

"You part of this bunch, soldier?" the Colonel asked in a friendly manner.

For a moment Morgan wondered why he wasn't being addressed as Sergeant, and then remembered none of them were wearing stripes or insignia. "Yes, sir," he replied.

Breed extended his hand. "I'm Colonel Breed," he said with a disarming smile.

Morgan shook hands eagerly, amazed and pleased at how friendly a guy like this could be. "Morgan, sir," he said automatically. "Master Sergeant Carl Morgan, sir."

"You're not a trooper, are you, Morgan?" pressed Breed, examining him closely, still gripping his hand.

"No, sir. I'm . . ." With a sudden clutch of fear, Morgan heard himself speaking, realized he had divulged his name against Reisman's strict orders and warnings. He pulled his hand back, almost rudely, and tried to get out of it. "No, sir . . . I'm not anything, sir . . . I'm just observing, Colonel, for my own outfit."

"What outfit is that, Sergeant Morgan?"

Morgan hung there limply, staring at the Colonel, not knowing what to say. "I'm . . . I'm sorry," he stammered. "I'm not . . ."

"That's all right, Sergeant," Breed interrupted, his manner more overbearing now, his voice more curt. "I understand perfectly. Thank you."

Morgan found himself ridiculously saluting the man's back as the Colonel brushed by him toward where the jumpers were landing.

Close to the drop panel, Reisman bundled his parachute under an arm and watched Odell touch down by the numbers. His eyes flicked skyward for the others, and he felt a surge of pride as the air filled with his men, while the voice of an instructor on the loudspeakers commented, warned, corrected and coached each man down.

Reisman trotted over to Odell, pointed up excitedly, and asked, "Again?"

"Not today, Captain," gasped Odell, still shaking with tension. "My God, that was something!"

Reisman clapped him on the back. "But you did it, goddammit, Myron, and you did it good!" he burst out jubilantly, and moving on to the others, he complimented, joked, offered a handshake here, a warm grasp of a shoulder there.

Few of them had landed perfectly. Some were rubbing at bruises, kneading sprained ankles and wrenched shoulders. Victor Franko sat on the ground, massaging an aching kneecap and moaning obscenities. Reisman feinted a kick in jest at the injured member and Franko rolled swiftly out of the way and was standing on his two feet before he even realized he really didn't want to gold-brick now and probably couldn't get away with it if he tried.

Some of them, like Roscoe Lever, looked shaken; some, like Napoleon White and Archer Maggot, looked cocky and triumphant; and a few looked just plain awed, as though they were in shock. But there was also something of a glow of pride about all of them that hadn't been there before.

Sergeant Bowren came along helping Samson Posey to walk, Posey limping like a Monday morning quarterback —the result of trying to make a forbidden stand-up landing.

"How'd it go upstairs, Clyde?" asked Reisman.

"Never would have believed it," muttered Bowren, smiling broadly, exuding the excitement of what he had just done. "Jumpmaster didn't have to push a one of them. They all went out on their own."

"You gonna be in shape to jump tomorrow, Posey?" asked Reisman.

"Damn right, Captain," said Samson, taking his arm from the Sergeant's shoulder and hopping away on one leg.

"All right, fall it in and let's get back to school," Reisman's voice boomed out. "You're not experts yet. You've still got a lot to learn."

Exchanging wisecracks and comments on their performance, they straggled in a disorganized, happy group toward the waiting vehicles and MPs. Reisman was surprised to see Colonel Breed there, too.

As they came abreast of him, Reisman ordered, "Eyes right! Salute!" The men were unprepared for it and it came out a sloppy mockery just as he'd intended.

Breed returned the salute reluctantly and stiffly, then stood there silently scrutinizing the men closely as they climbed aboard the vehicles. Finally, as Reisman strode past him, ignoring him, and took the wheel of the jeep, Breed commented, so that they could all hear, "That's the crummiest-looking bunch of men I've ever seen in my life, Captain!"

Reisman started the engine and rose to the bait. "That's the point of it, Colonel," he retorted defiantly. But as he drove away, he saw a satisfied little smile playing about Colonel Breed's lips that worried him.

They jumped once each day for the next three days. They learned how to tie down weapons, grenades and heavy field packs so they wouldn't lose them or kill themselves. They attended lectures and watched films on the fine points of parachuting—how not to drown if you landed in water, or be dragged to death along the ground by a stiff wind, or be hung up helplessly in a tree. They continued the tedious and hated calisthenics, running, close-order drill, the unexpected forced marches in the dead of night, and the sentinel duty in the stockade, robbing them of longed-for sleep.

There had been much humorous repartee in the training program when Reisman had learned to jump years before —humor to leaven the seriousness of the deadly business most of the candidates would be engaged in behind enemy lines, humor that was part of the courage and fear of supremely dedicated men. But there was no humor here. The entire complement of the stockade moved back and forth between Stokes Manor and the parachute school in a perpetual state of exhausted silence. From early morning to late afternoon, and into the night, it was grim, hard work —leavened only by the new feeling of competence and pride the prisoners had earned.

On Thursday, Captain Stuart Kinder, summoned from London by Reisman, witnessed the fourth jump.

"Magnificent!" he exclaimed to a sullen Sergeant Morgan and six bored MPs. Only Sergeant Bowren had gone up with Reisman and the prisoners this time, and though Kinder had horrible visions of them maybe overpowering their superiors and the plane crew and flying off somewhere, he thought it magnificent, too, that trust had now been extended to them to this degree.

He watched, awe-struck, as fourteen men spilled out of the low-flying airplane in a tight stick, one after the other, in one pass; and wished he had had nerve enough to take the training and jump with them. It seemed so effortless, so beautiful.

It seemed less so Friday night, and Kinder felt a tight, gnawing fear for them instead. He waited at the drop zone in a hellish storm, with Morgan, the six MPs, a ground coach on the loudspeakers, a crash truck and first aid team. Wind-whipped flares, nose-thumbing any Germans zealous enough to be out flying in this weather, marked the target panel. Kinder's eyes and ears tried to pierce the black, slashing rain for sight and sound of the C-47.

This one was the qualifying jump. Earlier, when the weather had turned fierce, he'd asked Reisman if he was really going to jump them.

"Sure, why not?" had been the answer.

"Isn't it dangerous?" Kinder had pursued.

"So are bullets and flak and the rest of the shit they're going to throw at them if you ever come up with a mission. Watch closely tonight, Stu," Reisman had challenged. "That's why I sent for you . . . and then you go up there to London and you tell your friends we're ready now!"

Kinder saw the bucking, slow-moving C-47 in a flash of lightning before he ever heard it, and he was damned glad now he hadn't been fool enough to take the training and jump with them. Another firebolt illuminated the cluster of descending white chutes, and he saw with relief that some of them were already safely on the ground.

He rushed forward to where the jumpers were rallying on Reisman, and he heard him shout above the storm, "That was the worst of it! After tonight you can do anything!"

"The hell you say!" boomed a deep, challenging voice.

A tall, ramrod-stiff figure Kinder hadn't seen before, loomed suddenly out of the darkness beyond the flare-lit target panel. The silver eagles on his raincoat reflected glints of the light.

"A rain jump is a cushion job, the air is so heavy," said Colonel Breed. "And if you knew anything, you'd know that, Reisman!"

Reisman felt too good to argue. "Five jumps, Colonel. They're troopers now! You want a band and parade for graduation tomorrow, or do we get our wings tonight?"

"You can buy them in any PX, Captain, if you've got the nerve. As far as I'm concerned, you and your filthy crew could have dropped a hundred times. Until I find out who and what you are, you'll wear no wings on this post!" With that he turned back into the darkness as suddenly as he had appeared.

Reisman looked at the rain-soaked faces of the prisoners, elated a moment ago, and now, like children, hurt and resentful.

"What's eating him?" asked Napoleon.

"He doesn't like us," answered Reisman with a broad smile.

429

"Well, screw him," muttered Franko, giving an Italian salute to the darkness. "I doan like him neider."

They walked toward the waiting vehicles in silence, their brief elation deflated. Stuart Kinder, still shocked by the exchange, finally found his voice.

"Breed?" he asked.

Reisman nodded.

"Who in hell does he think he is!" exploded Kinder angrily. "There was no reason at all for that!"

The outburst, so completely unexpected from Stuart Kinder, brought a smile to Reisman's face—and a satisfying awareness that Kinder, too, had become emotionally involved with the Dirty Dozen.

Saturday morning, after Kinder drove off to London, Reisman gave Sergeant Bowren some money and sent him out to buy paratrooper wings for the prisoners and himself, and to bring back another whore after dark. Then he telephoned Major Armbruster at the OSS branch in Baker Street.

There had been very little contact between them since the beginning of Project Amnesty and Reisman felt good now being able to say with confidence, "We're ready to go operational, Max. Kinder's on his way up to report to the Powers That Be."

"That's fine, John," Armbruster responded with enthusiasm. "You have no more reservations about them then?"

"No," Reisman lied. There would always be reservations, but he was willing to contend with them. "How about letting me in on the deep, dark plot now?" he asked.

"I still haven't the foggiest notion what the job is," Armbruster told him. "Kinder's our only liaison with whoever dreamed this up or approved it at SHAEF. He's very pleased with you, I know, and he's let the people he's working for in Grosvenor Square know it right along. It's a good thing, too. There have been some inquiries about you. I gather you've been leaning too hard on a certain Colonel. I'd ease up if I were you, John. We don't want him poking around where he shouldn't be, and he's too good a man to ease out of there unless it's absolutely necessary."

"Since you brought it up, Max, I ought to tell you . . . I'm afraid Colonel Breed is working himself up to something he shouldn't be," Reisman said. "He just won't let go of it gracefully. You know we've always disliked each other. But the hell with him. Except for a couple of refresher jumps if we have the time, my business is finished over there. Do what you can for us, Max, will you?" he urged. "Just a vague idea of where they're going and what they're going to do, to get me started. I've done my part, now it's up to you. My boys are sharp and ready, but I don't know how long I can keep them this way without telling them what this is all about. I'm getting itchy too."

"Do you want to leave them and go on to something else?" asked the Major.

Reisman knew it was asked out of simple considerateness and without malice, but it startled him. "No," he answered quickly. Such a thought was inconceivable to him now.

He rang off, but the prospect of just waiting around now for word from Kinder—with nothing real and active and important as an immediate goal, and with the danger of that mood being transmitted into letdown and lethargy among the prisoners—bothered Reisman. It was the fifteenth of April, and if, as rumor sometimes had it, the Invasion could come off early in May, it worried him that there was precious little time left to learn what their mission was and to set up a new training program for the specifics of the job. And there was also the gnawing concern about the part that he was to play in it.

Feeling restless and at loose ends, he marched the men out to the firing range for a few hours' work just to get the sound and smell of gunfire back into their systems.

In the manor house, the sound of gunfire on the estate again, after a silence of two weeks, startled Lady Margot Strathallan and set the dog to barking furiously until she shouted at him and silenced him with a smack on the rump that sent him scurrying under the bed in shame.

She telephoned Colonel Breed. "They're shooting again," she whispered. "I thought you'd want to know."

The Colonel thanked her, and after a few moments' conversation rang off—rather abruptly she thought. Certainly more abrupt than he'd been the evening before when he'd telephoned with an idea he said would be of help to both of them. He'd been somewhat embarrassed to speak of it, but the point of it was that he'd been giving additional thought to her suspicion that there had been a woman in Captain Reisman's camp one night. If her suspicion was true, and he felt more strongly now that it was, then he felt the incident was likely to be repeated—possibly this very weekend. And if she could, indeed, verify such an incident as fact and be prepared to give testimony to that effect to himself and the proper authorities, he felt confident Captain Reisman and his men would be severely disciplined, and most certainly removed from the scene, which he unnecessarily reminded her had been her most urgent wish and therefore his.

Margot had seen the camp at last, more than a week before, when Colonel Breed had asked her to look it over for him, assuring her the Captain and all his men were away. She had left Sigismund at home, and in the daylight had snuck up on the camp through the wood like a red Indian —which she often did at night, though never so close. She had walked all the way around the stockade, made skittish by the slightest sound and breeze; had stood rooted in nauseated fascination beside the foul ditch of their excrement, and had almost stumbled into another one in the wood; but she had been unable to get into the barracks and compound past the locked gate and barbed wire fence, and had been glad for that as an excuse because she was genuinely afraid. She had reported afterward to the Colonel that the place, with its double fences and gates and watchtowers and ugly look of doom, struck her more as a prison than a training camp.

Margot seated herself now at her lookout post in the window of an upstairs room that gave her a view of the main gate and the rutted field the vehicles crossed coming and going to Captain Reisman's camp. Later, after nightfall, maybe she would be brave enough to go into the wood, and maybe closer, but it would have to be without Sigismund again, for he could run away and bark and sound the alarm.

Master Sergeant Carl Morgan walked his sentinel post in the darkness on the flat roof of the barracks, burning with anger and frustration.

He was losing them the closer they came to the finish of this damn business. The prisoners were slipping away from him the longer they trained, the longer Reisman brought his influence to bear upon them, and that damn Captain Kinder, too. And now they were strutting, chest-thumping, wing-wearing, goddamn paratroopers, and Morgan worried if there was anybody left in all of England to hang.

But something could happen yet to bring them back to him again. He knew the dirty business going on below his feet this very moment, the girl they had down there, and he'd heard it had happened that night the son-of-a-bitchin Captain had sent him off on some phony business a couple of weeks before. This time the lousy CO had made an announcement about it, like it was time for chow or something, telling them they ought to wash the stink and dirt off themselves and shave their beards to please the goddamn whore and celebrate they were big deals now.

But none of them had wanted to clean up. They'd as much as thumbed their noses in Reisman's face, and Morgan had wanted to laugh. That uppity nigger had even said he wanted no part of no white woman—right out loud where they could all hear him; and the big Indian had said he was married and didn't want to get in trouble—the stupid jerk, where did he think he was; and that four-eyed queer they called Pope Innocent, he said he wanted no part of it either. But that left nine of them down there having a shot at her one at a time, and maybe a couple of the guards, and maybe that brown-nosing bastard Bowren, hanging around on his night off, bucking for still another stripe. And maybe even the goddamn Captain was gonna dip his thing in there too. He wasn't no better than the rest of them.

Suddenly Morgan dropped down into a crouch and peered intently into the fringe of the wood. He thought he'd seen something move out there. Nervously he raised his submachine gun and sighted narrowly along the barrel —and there it was again, flitting quickly from tree to tree: a woman, coming closer to the clearing between the wood and the gate, then stepping across the clearing and standing beside the gate itself. It was the woman from the manor house, the one they'd all seen out walking with the dog many weeks before. Morgan dropped prone, laying his weapon aside. He watched the woman pause indecisively, listen intently for sounds from the stockade, and stare at the barracks as though trying to see through it. Then, at the sound of the coarse, brazen laughter of the whore. inside and the answering laugh of a man, the woman at the gate turned in terror and fled.

Morgan stood up again, breathing heavily, as though it were he who was running or he who was in the barracks with the whore—and he decided he would report nothing to Reisman about what he had seen.

Sunday morning, because Reisman feared the danger of a letdown now, because he sensed the prisoners would want to goof off, might even expect to be left alone—since there had been no startling announcements from him, no clues as to their fate, no rah-rah-let's-get-in-there-and-fight stuff—he rousted them from their puptents even earlier than usual, and before the sun was up had them out stumbling across the estate on a forced march, with full field packs, weapons and ammunition, that lasted for five hours before they staggered back into the compound and were permitted to eat.

The most gratifying thing to Reisman was that none of them seemed to think it unusual that Morgan and the MPs were left behind sleeping, and only he and Sergeant Bowren represented the presence of authority among them.

The call from Stuart Kinder came that afternoon while Reisman was in the compound instructing the prisoners in detonating and explosive devices. He put down the gammon grenade he'd just assembled from plastic explosive, cloth, detonating cap and fuse, and odd bits of nails, spikes and metal refuse. It was fully armed and he placed it on the ground gently. "Don't anybody move," he told them. "Stay exactly where you are. I'll be right back."

Kinder was calling from Max Armbruster's office in Baker Street. "We've got the go-ahead, John," he said. "We're to be briefed here tomorrow morning at 0900."

When he hung up, Reisman wanted to laugh as he pictured the terribly grim expression that must have been on Kinder's face to match the tone of his voice. Then he remembered the grenade, went to the window and looked out. The men were still frozen in their places, hardly breathing. He'd told them one had to be extremely careful with a gammon, for the slightest jar or contact could set it off. But he'd neglected to tell them a release string had to be loosened first.

REISMAN FELT a familiar surge of excitement as he leaned forward in his chair and stared at the big map that had just been uncovered by Colonel Denton. They were in the large, handsome drawing room of the OSS branch in Baker Street where they had met more than seven weeks before to launch Project Amnesty. Besides Colonel Denton from Base OSS in Grosvenor Square, who was conducting the briefing, there were only Major Armbruster, Captain Kinder and Reisman in attendance this time.

The Colonel swept his arm across the map. "As you can see, Allied Intelligence has been extremely busy," he said. "This is the German order of battle as we now know it."

Reisman felt the same tremble of anticipation he had each time the specifics of a mission were revealed to him at last, brought down to the basics of place on the map, date on the calendar, time on the clock. It was combined now with a feeling of awe at being made privy at last to something the entire world was waiting for. The map showed the south of England, the Channel, and the western part of the Continent from the Netherlands to the Spanish frontier. On it were marked the locations of dozens of Nazi divisions: static and reserve divisions for manning the coastal defenses; attack infantry, panzer and parachute divisions.

He was disappointed then when Denton said, "I cannot reveal to you just yet where the exact area of the Invasion will be, for security reasons. Nor can I tell you the date, which I don't know. At this point I suppose it is still variable and the Commanding General himself isn't certain of it. All I can tell you now is the part in the operation to be played by Captain Reisman's group . . . the Dirty Dozen, as I understand they're called. And that, incidentally, Reisman, is something that can't be allowed to go on much longer. They can't go in anywhere looking as they do now. I understand the smell alone would give them away."

"They won't," commented Reisman curtly, throwing a

wry look at Kinder. "May I ask you a question now, sir?"

"About what . . . I haven't even begun."

"The answer belongs here, Colonel. Does the success of the Invasion hinge upon our mission?"

Denton stared at Reisman as though he couldn't make up his mind whether he was being sarcastic or serious. "Surely you don't mean that?" he asked. "Would your assessment of their capabilities be less if that were the case, Captain?"

"More," answered Reisman quietly. "The opportunity to be important, to be heroes, would make them so. I'm sure of that."

"Psychology is Captain Kinder's department, not yours," contended Denton pointedly. "You don't think SHAEF is completely insane, do you? Their assignments can be of utmost importance to our overall success, depending entirely on what they do with them . . . just as the assignments of our other units and individuals in Special Operations and the assignments of the French Underground. But they are sort of frosting on the cake. If they get licked off it doesn't really hurt the whole of it."

Reisman remained silent now, wanting him to get on with it, contenting himself with the amusing thought that sugar coating was a considerable step upward in simile for men who had been the dregs of the American Army.

Colonel Denton returned to the map. "There are almost sixty enemy divisions identified and pinpointed here," he stated, "about half of them either dug in already on this extended northwest coast or within a few hours' striking distance. However, we have learned that a high percentage of these troops occupying France are foreign prisoners forced by the Nazis to fight with them. Russians, Poles, Czechs and even their erstwhile allies the Italians, have been impressed into everything from labor and service battalions to first-line shock troops. Many, however, are merely second-rate occupation troops used to pad out or supplement existing crack Nazi divisions. Here, in these foreign troops, many of them there against their will, we have a ready-made weak spot to probe.

"The plan then is this. Two days before the Invasion, your men will be dropped at certain points far behind the coast, wearing the uniforms and carrying the identification, weapons, and equipment of troops such as those the Germans have impressed. They will carry forged papers and orders of transfer that will make it plausible for them to keep pretty much on the move and not have to tie up with any one outfit. Their job is to infiltrate the enemy and strike at every target of opportunity: kill enemy personnel and collaborators, pillage supplies, destroy vehicles, sabotage roads, rails and bridges. They are to do anything and everything to create confusion, undermine enemy morale and effectiveness, and sow terror."

Reisman could hardly believe what he was hearing. It was heroic, yes, there was no doubt of that. But to what purpose? It seemed to him it would be a suicidal gesture with no specific tactical importance. To his way of thinking this sort of assignment had as little chance of being carried out successfully by a group of supremely dedicated, superbly trained, battle-wise, educated strategists and linguists, as it did by the twelve convicts he had trained.

"Colonel!" he interrupted loudly, half rising from his chair. "My men aren't prepared for anything like that!"

"Hear me out completely before you comment, Captain!" snapped Denton. "I realize you'll have opinions of your own. You're the guerrilla expert, aren't you? The best we've got, I'm told. That's one reason why you were chosen for this. You take the time you've got left and you teach them the whole lovely business . . . everything you know. I understand you've done quite an adequate job so far."

Reisman dropped restlessly back into his chair, but Denton made the bitter gall rise in him again when he continued, "We had considered dropping them singly, but now recommend they go in pairs to support one another. I surmise you still have your bad eggs among the lot . . . those less trustworthy than the others. I'd team a bad one with a good one, a weak man and a strong man, a dummy with a smart one."

Reisman couldn't contain himself. It was worse than he'd thought. In a group, with him leading, they could fulfill a tactical mission successfully, and have a chance of coming back, at least some of them—but not alone or in pairs. For men like them it was an open invitation to surrender and save their hides—and if they tried to do what had just been described, they didn't stand a chance.

He blurted out absurdly, "What do you recommend, Colonel Denton, where the bad ones are also the smart ones?"

"Well, you know your group. Work it out the best you can," answered Denton, completely missing the sarcasm. And he ran on, "As for the language problem—and of course we realize there is one—do you have any men who speak any of these foreign languages? Not fluently, necessarily, although that would be a godsend, but enough to fake it if they have to."

"Yes," Reisman answered quickly. There was at least Italian and Spanish, and Napoleon had studied French and German in school, and maybe Wladislaw knew enough Polish; and besides the languages he knew fluently himself, there were those he had been in close touch with often enough to learn a bit of.

"That's a break," said Denton. "We have available a variety of simple phrase books in all these languages to help you further. I would suggest they learn some German, too. The fact that they will speak it badly will only serve to support their identifications as nationals of other countries allied with or overrun by the Nazis."

Only then did Reisman realize the impossibility of that with Napoleon White and Samson Posey. "Are you aware that one of my men is a Negro and another is a Ute Indian? How am I supposed to pass them off as Germans or Europeans?"

"Then get rid of them," said the Colonel sharply. "Replace them in the time you've got left. There are at least two or three weeks . . . maybe more."

"Replace them!" exclaimed Reisman in disbelief.

"Yes, replace them," repeated Denton in irritation. "If they're not right for this mission, why not? No man is unreplaceable in the Army, Reisman. You ought to keep that in mind for yourself, too."

The anguish of the thought that this could indeed be done tempered Reisman's voice as he said, "I can't do that, Colonel. I won't do it. You know what the alternative is for them. I made a deal with these men . . . all of us were party to that deal and we can't go back on it now. I'll work it out somehow. Why can't they go in American uniforms as American soldiers? Why can't they all go in that way? Then if they're captured they won't be executed as spies."

There was a tense silence in the room, until Denton said, "It would make no difference in that respect. Hitler has ordered all parachutists summarily executed, whether in uniform or not. Why this humanitarian concern for them?

What difference does it make to you what these men do? What are they to you? Besides, if I may continue the briefing you interrupted, Captain, for them to go in American uniforms would defeat our purpose. Wherever possible, they are to fall back with the retreating Germans and continue their work."

"Until death do them part!" muttered Reisman.

"What's that, Captain?" demanded Denton.

"In other words, you don't want to see them again. That's not a plan. It's an execution, Colonel."

"Captain Reisman!" thundered Denton. "You carry your tactlessness too far with me!"

Major Armbruster turned to Reisman and said calmly, "Ease up, John. Colonel Denton's on our side, you know. We'll all work it out together."

"And where do I fit into it?" Reisman pressed. "Where and how do I go in and keep control of them?"

"You don't, Captain," replied Colonel Denton with finality. "Nobody ever said you would. You are to train them, assign drop points and see them off—that's all!"

It was this that Reisman had seen coming and had dreaded most of all . . . and he resolved now that he would never let it happen that way, and that he would go with them. For how could he send his men where he would not go himself? He sat through the rest of the briefing in silent turmoil, listening but making no comment.

It was over quickly then, and with a curt "Good day, gentlemen!" and a curious, almost sympathetic glance at Reisman, Colonel Denton was gone, leaving the myriad of details for them to work out.

Reisman rose wearily from his chair, went to the map, stared at it, touched it with tense, trembling fingers as though he might crush it, and turned upon Stuart Kinder, seething. "How much of this insanity is your work, Captain?" he demanded. "Why don't you try something like that yourself? Are you afraid?"

Kinder stared at him appalled. Armbruster reacted angrily.

"Enough of that, John!" he snapped. "There's no need to make that sort of personal attack. You owe Captain Kinder an apology." Armbruster remembered now what Kinder had told him in the beginning, before he'd transferred Reisman to Project Amnesty, that the key man for the assignment had to be composed of equal parts of bru-

439

tality and compassion. But he had never imagined Reisman would become as emotionally involved as he had.

"That's all right, Major," said Kinder. He faced Reisman down without flinching. "No more of it is mine than yours, John," he replied. "And as for being afraid . . . yes, of course I am. How do you think the war would go if our roles were reversed . . . if you had to do my job and I had to do yours? In modern war, there must be roles to suit the personality and the ability, not only the situation. Some yearn for action, others don't . . . but that doesn't make them cowards."

"I'm sorry, Stu. I had no right to say that," Reisman apologized.

"The choice of missions was never my responsibility. I am as distressed by it as you apparently are," said Kinder sympathetically. "In the beginning, to me, this was more just an experiment to see if we actually could train and inspire such a group of malcontents, than it was anything else. But when you insisted so vehemently there be a mission now . . . when I saw for myself and realized what you had done for them . . . then I, too, insisted. I pressed the issue for you, and for them, just as you wanted me to. But, believe me, I didn't know what the mission would be."

"Then there never was any mission to start with," Reisman accused.

"I knew as much about this part of it as you did. It seems to me it has never been any more nor less than it is now."

"The original paper on this, John," reminded Major Armbruster, "merely said they were to be delivered secretly onto the European mainland prior to the Invasion to wreak havoc upon segments and personnel of the Nazi war machine. That's what we have here, isn't it?"

"Then you've got to get them something else, Max," said Reisman fervently. "And I must go with them. As a group, they can succeed. Apart they're lost."

"I must agree with him on that, Major," Kinder put in. "Here is a classic situation where the group is greater than the sum of its parts."

"There is nothing else," said the Major. "I take orders too, John. I'm not running the war, thank God. My job is to supply you with what you need and help you get ready for the missions Denton just outlined."

"Then make something! Anything that gives them a chance! They'll listen to you at Base," Reisman poured out. Groping, clutching at straws, he suddenly remembered. "How about Rosedale? Do you remember Rosedale? You had me looking for personnel for it before this came up. Did you fill it? As a matter of fact, what was Rosedale?"

"A rumor," said Armbruster. "We decided it was too chancy to pursue. Couldn't put together the right team on the basis of such a rumor anyway."

"What was it?"

The Major strode to the map and pointed. "Do you know Rennes?" he asked.

"In Brittany," said Reisman. "On a river . . . the Vilaine. I've been through it a few times, but I don't know it. What's there?"

"That's what we don't know," said Armbruster. "We're aware it's a big railroad switching center and road hub, and it's being bombed regularly by the Air Corps on that account. But the rumor has it that a group of Generals and high-ranking aides of the German Seventh Army meet at a château there from time to time for mapboard *Kriegsspiels* —war games—combined with a certain amount of relaxation and private fun and games."

A surge of new excitement grabbed at Reisman. "That's it!" he exclaimed. "That has to be it!"

"It's nothing of the sort, John," argued the Major. "We can't send a group in there on the strength of a vague rumor."

"But what if it's true?" pressed Reisman. "What an opportunity to catch them there!"

"If we ever did know for certain that they were there," mused Armbruster, staring at the map, "I'm sure SHAEF would send in a first-rate group . . . not yours, John. Or the bombers would take care of them. How could we even be certain they're going to be there when your men are due to go in? The Wehrmacht is certainly not going to schedule a *Kriegsspiel* for our convenience."

"Max, I've never asked you for anything," said Reisman quietly. "I've done your dirty work and done it rather well. Now I want something, and I want it bad enough to steal it if I have to. Find out, Max. Get word to the Underground. Bring somebody out who knows the place and knows what goes on there. You've done it before. Trace the rumor back to its source. Do that much for me, Max," he implored. "Because the way it stands now, all the great brains have done is change the method of execution—and I am their executioner!"

There was an awful silence in the room. Armbruster hesitated. "What do you think, Captain?" he asked, turning to Stuart Kinder.

Kinder didn't want to answer. He gestured helplessly. He didn't want to answer because, mostly, he wanted no feeling of even partial responsibility for the consequences. The way it stood now, the prisoners would go in . . . and God be with them, their fate would be whatever it would be . . . better maybe than it might have been. But with this other thing, if there was anything to it, Reisman the damn fool would throw himself away. Kinder feared that and he didn't want it to happen. "I don't know, sir," he answered finally. "It's really not my field. I don't think I'm qualified, nor is it my place to say."

Armbruster nodded in resignation. "All right, John. I'll look into it," he said softly. "Meanwhile, you are to follow orders and prepare your men for the jobs Denton outlined. I'll get everything down to you right away . . . German uniforms, weapons, identification papers, orders, language primers . . . the works. And get the sons-of-bitches to bathe and shave, will you?" he concluded angrily.

Reisman smiled at him. "Thanks, Max," he said. "They will . . . when they have to."

It was still before noon when Reisman left the Baker Street building and drove away into the noise and bustle of London. Kinder had asked him to lunch at an Allied officers club he frequented, but he'd declined, saying he was eager to drive back to the men immediately. From a public telephone, he called the CID office out of which Leon Osterman worked. Now, more than ever, he realized they had to settle the matter of Myron Odell's innocence or guilt. But Osterman wasn't there, and the feelings of futility and apprehension with which Reisman had come away from the briefing were compounded when he was told the detective had been sent to Scotland suddenly on a case and would be away for two weeks.

All during the long drive from London across the south of England, these feelings clawed at him. Though he was wracked, too, by the great urgency now to get back to the stockade and mount the new, intensive, almost hopelessly overwhelming program of training he'd been building all these hours in his mind, by the time he came to a crossroads in Somerset where he would have turned south to Devonshire and Stokes Manor there was a need, too for private succor, and he drove north instead to Marston-Tyne and Tess Simmons, excusing it on the grounds that he wasn't expected back at the stockade until morning.

In the late afternoon, in a gentle world of soft wind, setting sun and young flowers, Reisman walked hand in hand with Tess as she led him happily along country lanes and across fields. She took him up a little hill and beyond into a meadow and said excitedly, "Here . . . here is where I found it."

"What? A treasure? The crown jewels?" he asked, trying to join her lighter mood, yet still too much filled with his own depression.

"Much better," she said, pointing at what she meant. "Spring. I told you I would save it for you."

Reisman remembered and raised his foot to see if he really could plant it upon twelve daisies.

"No!" she cried, dropping to the ground and gently circling with her arms the stand of flowers. "Please don't hurt them."

"No, of course not," he said gently. "How stupid of me."

He reached down his hand and raised her up. The ground was green and lush, but cooling now as the sun sank away. They were alone there and he kissed her. If it were warmer he would have dropped beside her into the grass and flowers and lost himself.

Tess looked into his eyes as he held her. "You want to make love to me now, don't you?" she asked.

He nodded, feeling almost embarrassed. "Yes," he said.

They walked hurriedly along a road leading back to The Butcher's Arms. "Stop!" Tess suddenly cried, holding him still.

"What is it?"

She pointed to a rather noisy bird sitting alone on the branch of a tree. "A magpie. Raise your hat and make the sign of the cross on your breast," she urged. "It's bad luck if you don't."

"That's silly."

"Yes, but I like it," she said, "and if you won't do it then

I must do something else for you." She turned and spat three times over her left shoulder.

"Is it all right now?" he asked.

"Yes."

"Who taught you that?"

"Mrs. Culver. She's very good about things like that. She says the magpie was the only bird that refused to enter the ark with Noah. It perched on the roof of the ark by itself and jabbered over the drowning world."

"By itself? Didn't there have to be at least two of them, to carry on the species?"

"Hmmmm," she mused. "I suppose you're right. I never thought of that. Well, maybe it was she who went in and he who stayed out then. But Mrs. Culver says that so defiant and rebellious a bird must be considered unlucky."

"Why that's me," said Reisman, smiling. "All but the part about being unlucky. I'm very lucky, you know." He turned and raised his hat to the magpie and made the sign of the cross on his breast. "Suddenly I like the little fellow after all," he said.

Colonel Everett Dasher Breed sped toward the estate of Stokes Manor Tuesday morning in a rage. He rode beside the driver of the truck and in the back was a squad of his armed paratroopers, sworn to secrecy.

Sergeant Morgan had been the key. Knowing the man's name and rank, he'd been able to have him traced. A hangman! A goddamn bloody hangman! And having uncovered that on the fifth of March, Morgan the hangman was detached from Marston-Tyne prison with a detail of guards and prisoners, Colonel Breed was almost certain of the rest.

They were the convicts! And Reisman their keeper! With all his airs and pretenses, their keeper!

And adding to Breed's anger was the pitiful call from Lady Margot that a whore had indeed been imported into Reisman's camp. Not only against all the rules of propriety but against all military regulations—and flaunted in the face of the tactful warning Breed had given him!

Once through the main gate of the estate, he didn't bother to pause at the manor house, but ordered his driver across the field toward the wood. Lady Margot would be aware of their arrival and would stay in the building as he

444

had instructed her. They bounced along between the trees and suddenly there in the clearing was the barbed wire stockade and barracks and watchtowers just as she had described them. A prison! He had no doubt of it now—and God knew the manner of men who had been brought here to endanger Lady Margot and be let loose to contaminate the unsuspecting.

The truck stopped in front of the barracks, Breed hopped out and took in the setup at a glance. There was no need to deploy his squad. He wouldn't give Reisman the satisfaction of making it seem a military operation. He strode up to the gate in the barbed wire, his men massed around him.

"Stay right where you are!" came a loud command.

Breed looked up to see a soldier standing on the barracks roof aiming a submachine gun down at them.

"Want me to wing him, Colonel?" muttered one of the troopers, unslinging his carbine.

"Don't be a jackass!" snapped Breed, looking at the trooper distastefully. "There's to be no firing . . . and no rough stuff till I tell you."

Sergeant Bowren held his weapon on Breed, whom he recognized. "This is a restricted area, sir," he declared, "and you have no right being here."

"Where's your Commanding Officer?" demanded Breed.

"He's not here, Colonel," answered Bowren.

"Damn!" muttered Breed. "Who's in charge, soldier?"

Bowren started to say Sergeant Morgan, but caught himself in time. "One of us is, Colonel."

"Well, dammit, don't just stand there looking stupid, soldier. Send him out."

Bowren descended into the barracks and opened the inner door to the compound. Sergeant Morgan and some of the MPs and prisoners, who had been lounging around awaiting Reisman's return, were moving toward him, aware of something going on outside.

"It's that chickenshit Colonel from the paratroops, Sergeant," Bowren told Morgan. "He wants to talk to whoever's in charge. I guess that's you."

"Stay here with them," said Morgan, jerking his thumb back at the prisoners.

"No, I'm going with you," Bowren told him.

They went through the barracks to the gate where Breed waited impatiently. His presence there worried Morgan and he recoiled guiltily when the Colonel looked at him with that phony smile of his and said, "Sergeant Morgan. Nice to see someone here who knows what he's about. Open the gate."

The hangman hesitated.

"We can't let anybody in here," insisted Sergeant Bowren.

"You see these eagles on my shoulder!" Colonel Breed rapped out. "Open the goddamn gate, Morgan, or you'll be a buck-assed Private before the day's out."

For Morgan the threat was sufficient inducement. Before Bowren could stop him he'd unlocked the gate. Bowren jumped back to the door of the barracks and leveled his weapon at Breed and his troopers. "You don't scare me, Colonel," he shouted. "First man tries it, gets this!"

Breed walked toward him smiling, and Sergeant Bowren's finger trembled on the trigger. But he couldn't bring himself to shoot. Breed came right up against the gun, brushed it aside and looked right through him as though he didn't exist. "I didn't think you would, soldier," he said.

Two of the troopers grabbed Bowren and disarmed him, and the mass of them pushed on through the barracks into the compound where Colonel Breed ordered prisoners and guards to line up in two separate formations.

Napoleon White couldn't figure out what the hell was going on, until the Colonel braced them at attention and announced, "One of my men will pass along the rank in front of you. You are to report to him your name, rank, serial number and military organization."

"Keep your mouths shut," Napoleon muttered to the men next to him. "Don't tell him anything. This is one of Reisman's goddamn tricks!"

"I don't think so, Nappy," Wladislaw whispered back. "Two of these guys are the ones that jumped me at the parachute camp!"

"Screw them, too!" Napoleon snapped at him. "This stinks of Reisman's trickery. Pass it along quick, you jerk. Anybody opens his yap now is finished. I just know it, buddy!"

"Silence!" shouted Colonel Breed, stepping closer to them. "Don't you sons-of-bitches know enough to keep your mouths shut in ranks!"

But the word had passed quickly enough so that when Breed's trooper passed in front of them with paper and pencil demanding their identification, they each replied only with a number. The MPs got the idea quickly and also reported by number. Colonel Breed took each man aside and questioned him individually. He used every trick of cajolery and intimidation at his command, but he got nowhere. Napoleon thought he put on quite an amusing performance.

Finally Breed singled out Master Sergeant Carl Morgan. "You! Come with me!" he commanded, and took him to the far end of the compound away from the others. "I want you to tell me exactly who each and every one of these men is, Morgan," he demanded. "And I want you to tell me the exact nature and purpose of their training."

Morgan was frightened and he did his best to bluff his way out of it. "I don't know anything about them, Colonel," he mumbled.

"What are you afraid of, Sergeant?" Breed cajoled. "Is it Reisman? He's only a Captain. This is a Colonel talking to you now."

"I know that, sir. I ain't afraid of him."

"Then you're afraid of losing those six stripes you don't get a chance to wear around here anyway. Is that it, Morgan?"

"I ain't afraid of nothing."

"In that case, Sergeant, it will be my pleasure to reveal to your Captain Reisman that it was you who admitted us to this camp, and that it was your stupidity in divulging your name and rank some days ago that enabled me to find out that these men are convicts and guards from Marston-Tyne prison and you are the resident hangman."

"No . . . please, Colonel . . . don't do that," stammered Morgan.

"Then talk."

"It's just like you say, sir. We're from Marston-Tyne. That's about all of it."

"Why are they here?"

"They're training . . . that's all, sir."

"I know that, damn you. Training for what?"

"I don't know. That's the truth, Colonel."

"Is it for the Invasion . . . or something else? Talk, damn you, Morgan, or I'll have your stripes."

447

"I don't know, sir. If I did, I'd tell you. Honest . . . you've got to believe me."

"How about the whore, Morgan? I suppose you don't know anything about that, either. Wasn't there a whore brought in here for the pleasure of this swine?"

"That wasn't none of my doing, Colonel," Morgan protested. "I didn't like the idea and I didn't have nothing to do with her."

"But they did! Many times!"

"Yes. Twice, I think."

"And Reisman?"

"I don't know nothing about him."

"What are they training for, Morgan?" Breed demanded again.

"I don't know. Nobody knows. Not even the CO maybe. Some kind of a mission I think."

"In the Invasion?" pressed Breed, incredulous.

"I think so."

A wave of self-righteous indignation enveloped the Colonel. "Lunacy!" he murmured, his voice trembling. "Unimaginable lunacy! Convicts! Filth!" He got control of himself. "They're the convicts . . . the dirty ones, aren't they, Morgan? The Dirty Dozen? Why is it permitted? Why are they allowed to go around like that? Does it have anything to do with their mission?"

"I don't think so, sir," Morgan told him. "One day they just made up their minds they wasn't gonna shave or clean up no more, that's all."

"And your Commanding Officer let them?"

"That's right, sir. It didn't seem to bother him none."

"Then they will bathe and shave before we leave here, Sergeant, if I have to do each and every one of them myself."

Breed summoned the trooper who'd been trying to get identifications from the men. "Their names, Morgan. Give this soldier the names and serial numbers of every one of them . . . prisoners and guards," he poured out. "I want their names, ranks, serial numbers and military organizations. Do you understand me, Sergeant?"

"I don't know all that stuff, Colonel."

"Then give this man what you do know," ordered Breed in a voice of controlled rage. "And when you're finished with that, I want a statement from you about the whore . . . and you are to sign it!"

30

REISMAN MOVED silently and undetected through the fringe of the wood around the stockade, paying out the wires of the demolitions charges. Now he was in his element again, almost happy.

He worked quickly, goaded by the sound of Colonel Breed's voice still berating the men in the near distance. He led the wires back to the barracks and up the ladder to where he could just see from the hatch in the roof without being observed himself.

In the compound, Napoleon White was less amused now by the lengths to which Colonel Breed was going. He still felt certain it was a stunt instigated by Reisman to demoralize and test them. Breed sent a trooper down the rank tearing off the jumper's wings they had all worn so proudly. He held one up. "This badge is an insignia of honor!" he said. "You have no right to it! You debase it by your very touch! You insult those courageous men who by their deeds ennoble it!"

"Horseshit!" muttered Victor Franko.

"You!" thundered Breed, pointing a quivering finger at him. "Get the hell out of that rank!"

Franko moved forward hesitantly, frightened now to be singled out.

"You will now demonstrate for the rest of this scum the proper procedure for bathing and shaving in the field," Breed ordered. He motioned forward one of his men carrying a can of water, soap, towel and shaving gear.

Franko went rigid.

"Will you shave and bathe?" demanded Breed.

"No, sir I won't," answered Franko.

"Then we'll do it the hard way. Dry shave him!" snapped Breed.

Two of the troopers moved forward at the Colonel's orders and pinioned Franko's arms and legs. A third man knocked off Franko's helmet, grasped his matted hair and laid the sharp edge of a bayonet against his cheek.

An uncontrollable rage swept through Napoleon. He had no love for Franko but this was too much. If the Colonel got away with it, he and the others would be next. Even Reisman, who had more reason to, hadn't dared to violate them this way. He rushed at the soldiers holding Franko. "Take your goddam hands off him!" he shouted.

In that instant, two tremendous explosions rocked the stockade. Napoleon hit the dirt beside Franko. He picked up his head to see everybody else down including the Colonel, and a third explosion made him eat dirt again.

Reisman's voice, from the direction of the barracks, ordered, "Everybody stay exactly where you are!"

Colonel Breed started to get up. "That you, Reisman?" he called out.

"That's right, Colonel. You get up nice and slow now and move toward me."

Napoleon saw some of the paratroopers starting to move also, swinging their carbines around to bear on the barracks, uncertain yet exactly where Reisman was. A long burst of submachine gun fire revealed his position in the roof hatch, but the bullets thudding into the ground just beyond where everybody lay served notice they were all effectively covered. Only Breed continued moving, contemptuously. Napoleon trembled with excitement and a little fear.

"Stay where you are Colonel," Reisman commanded. "Tell your boys to toss aside their guns."

Breed looked up at him in amazement tinged with honest fear. "You're mad!" he shouted.

"That's right buster . . . I'm mad! And you're trespassing in a maximum security area and can be shot . . . with no regrets on my part. Order them to drop their weapons."

Breed hesitated. He recognized that Reisman would actually kill him if necessary, and he had no desire to go out so stupidly. But he never had to give the order. All over the compound his troopers tossed aside their guns on their own.

"Clyde . . . Nappy . . . gather up the hardware," Reisman ordered.

Napoleon moved fast, filling his arms with carbines. Sergeant Bowren personally liberated the Colonel's .45 and it gave him great pleasure to do so.

"Come into the barracks, Colonel . . . alone," Reisman called down.

He was at the door opening it by the time Breed got there. The anger he had felt earlier had been expended in action. "Your boys sure do worry about you, Colonel," he said caustically.

"That's one of the joys of a good command, Captain. I doubt very much whether you will ever inspire such loyalty in your swine."

Reisman led him into the office and closed the door. "Now tell me what brought about this adolescent little adventure of yours. What exactly do you want here?" he demanded calmly. He seated himself on the cot where he could keep his eye on the compound and indicated the chair at the desk for Breed.

"There's no need for you to try covering up anymore, Reisman," snapped Breed, continuing to stand. "I know what they are."

"What are they, Colonel?"

"Convicts from Marston-Tyne prison. And with Morgan the hangman as your associate, I imagine they're the worst. Murderers, rapists, thieves! How dare you bring this refuse into contact with my regiment!"

"They're soldiers of the United States Army, Colonel. Volunteers engaged in secret experimental training."

"You expect me to swallow that, Captain?"

"You'd better swallow it, Colonel, and keep to yourself anything else you imagine, if you value your own position."

"Are you threatening me?"

"Yes. I could prefer charges against you for this little caper, you know. And also for ordering two of your glamour boys to attack one of my men on your post in an attempt to pry secret information from him. That can be a hanging offense, you know."

"How dare you!" Breed exploded. "You're not fit for command! How dare you expose Lady Margot to this filth! Did you have a woman here, Reisman?"

"The rantings of a madwoman."

"I not only have verification of it from Lady Margot, Captain, but from one of your men . . . and I intend to use it to arrange your court-martial."

"Who?" Reisman demanded.

"An unimpeachable source, Captain. Your hangman . . . Master Sergeant Carl Morgan."

"He tell you the rest of it, too?"

"He merely confirmed what I already knew."

"How did you find out?"

"That is my business. I want to know exactly what it is you and these convicts are involved in."

"Colonel, what we are doing here is none of your goddamn business."

"But it is, Reisman, it is," said Breed icily. "Aside from your insulting behavior toward Lady Margot, and your endangering her safety . . . aside from the whores you brought in here, which alone would earn you a court-martial . . . this is very much my business. It's obvious to me you're preparing for a parachute mission in the Invasion. I want to know what it is. I demand to know it! Do you think for one moment I would allow you and that criminal refuse out there to do anything that might affect the safety and success of my regiment . . . if not the entire operation? What lunacy! What unforgivable stupidity!"

"You're insulting the intelligence of your superior officers, Colonel, and showing grave disrespect," mocked Reisman. "That's also a court-martial offense."

"I would be derelict in my duty to my men, to the Army and to myself if I didn't get to the bottom of this," declared Breed. "You wouldn't dare prefer any of these ridiculous charges against me, Reisman, and you know it. You're wide open for counterattack. Your position is too untenable."

Reisman stood up and paced toward Breed. "We seem to have reached a stalemate, haven't we," he said. "You a betting man, Colonel?"

"Bet on what?"

"Yourself and your troopers."

"Anytime, Captain."

"Good. You want to play games like today? Let's play one fair. Set up an exercise. My boys against yours. If we succeed, you'll keep you mouth shut and that will be the end of the affair. If we don't succeed, my experimental training program will end here at Stokes Manor."

It was a groping stab in the dark, but to Reisman's relief Breed rose to the bait with relish. "I think I would enjoy that even more than your court-martial, Reisman. Do you have a map of Devonshire?"

452

Reisman got one from the desk. The Colonel spread it on top and sat in the chair. "There's no need to set up an exercise. There's a war game scheduled for May 3 near Slapton Sands." He pointed with a pencil and marked the map. "One battalion of my regiment will be holding a fixed, defensive perimeter from here to here. Make arrangements through your own channels to join the maneuver. Somewhere in that perimeter will be my Command Post. Take it or destroy it and you're off the hook."

Breed and his squad drove away but behind them they left the angry tension of mistrust. Reisman waited in the barracks until Sergeant Bowren returned from making certain they'd cleared the grounds.

"How'd he get in, Clyde?" he demanded.

"Putting his belly up against this," said Bowren, fingering the muzzle of his grease gun. "Maybe this just isn't my line of work, Captain. I've never killed a man . . . and whether he was right or I was, that isn't the way I want to do it when the time comes."

"Morgan told Breed about the women," said Reisman. "Did you know that?"

"No, sir," Bowren replied. He went on hesitantly, for the old injunction against ratting on a fellow soldier to the brass ran strong in the grain. "But the Colonel knew him when he came up to the gate, sir . . . greeted him like an old asshole buddy."

They went out into the compound. Even the MPs seemed shaken and angry, and Sergeant Morgan had that same skittish air about him that Myron Odell had once worn. Napoleon White called out, "Like the Seventh Cavalry in the movies, Captain! Just in the nick of time or we'd have been scalped!" It was part admiration, part sarcasm.

Reisman nodded acknowledgment. He saw the hangman trying to lose himself back in the crowd. "Fall in the men, Morgan. MPs in a separate rank," he ordered. He couldn't allow himself to call him Sergeant anymore.

Reisman stepped from man to man, saying something personal to each, commending them for their conduct under pressure, apologizing for not having been there sooner. He did the same with the MPs—except for Morgan. He ordered him front and center to face the others.

"Let me have your weapons," he told him.

As the hangman hesitantly shrugged the submachine gun from his shoulder, Reisman grabbed the barrel and transferred the gun to his own shoulder. He reached one hand to Morgan's waist. "This, too!" he snapped. To undo the holster belt holding the heavy .45, he jerked the leather tightly so it dug into his belly and made him grunt.

"What's this all about, Captain?" Morgan asked apprehensively.

"An ancient and honored military tradition. Imagine you're on formal parade and you hear the roll of drums." Reisman turned to the men. "The hangman is leaving us today. Before he does, he has a few words to say."

Morgan looked at him in confusion. "I ain't going nowhere. Whatta you mean, Captain?" he challenged.

"You traded your soul for six lousy stripes, Morgan," Reisman said. "You betrayed your men and you'd hang your mother to keep them. Tell them who it was let the Colonel and his boys in here to put them on the rack."

"I couldn't help that. He pulled his rank on me," Morgan protested.

"His rank didn't scare anything out of them!" Reisman said. "You told the Colonel who these men are . . . against orders, against every warning I gave you!"

"He tricked me . . . all I told him was my name . . . so help me, I didn't tell him nothing else," Morgan stammered.

"Then besides everything else, you're stupid. And your stupidity, your betrayal, your cowardice will be sufficient for your court-martial. You'll leave here now and be returned to Marston-Tyne in custody. It's my intention to have you charged, tried and convicted under the appropriate Articles of War . . . and to see that you never again rise above the rank of prisoner. Pack up your gear and get the hell out of my sight!"

Morgan looked around frantically . . . to Bowren, the MPs, the prisoners. Their expressions ranged from contempt to triumph and pleasure. He shuffled away toward the barracks. At the gate he turned and muttered in weak defiance, "You'll get yours, Captain . . . you'll get yours."

Victor Franko's eyes followed the hangman in awe. He felt the weight of a once intolerable, maddening burden rise from the constant anguish of his mind. "And now you'll get yours," he murmured.

An hour later Reisman watched Sergeant Bowren and the six MPs drive off with Master Sergeant Carl Morgan in sullen custody in the back of the truck. Bowren carried a letter to Lieutenant Colonel Tarbell, Commandant of the prison at Marston-Tyne, specifying the charges against Morgan and asking that he be kept in a cell until a court-martial could be convened. All of the guard detail except Bowren had with them their duffels, for it had struck Reisman while he was writing up Morgan's transfer that the Dirty Dozen didn't need guards anymore, and the fewer men who had access to what they would be doing from now on the better it would be. To Clyde Bowren, he had offered a choice: he could return to the stockade if he wanted to, or be reattached to the prison complement at Marston-Tyne. "I'll be back, Captain," he had said without hesitation.

Reisman walked back through the empty barracks into the compound, and for the first time in the many weeks they had been together he was completely alone with the Dirty Dozen. The men were standing together in a group near the inner gate, waiting for him eagerly, still somewhat in awe of all that had happened that morning.

"Move into the barracks, gentlemen. It's all yours," Reisman told them.

They moved in like excited kids, picking and arguing over the best beds among cots that were all the same, decided who was going to sleep next to whom, reveling in the luxuries that were now theirs, relishing possession of the barracks they had built themselves and coveted. Reisman gave them a few minutes, then called them together at the mess end of the room. They seated themselves quietly on the benches.

He looked at them a few moments, composing his thoughts. "You've earned your chance. You're soldiers now as far as I'm concerned . . . not prisoners," he said. "But that chickenshit Colonel we just tangled with intends to put you back in Marston-Tyne prison and stop you from getting the chance you've worked for."

He explained Breed's threat, told them about the war game and the deal he'd made. It set off a rumble of gripes and enthusiasms that infected and supported each other.

"I'd sure like to get back at that son-of-a-bitch!" muttered Victor Franko.

"Damn right, Cap'm!" said Archer Maggot. He was like a hound already sniffing with pleasure his promised new quarry. "Thet Cuhnel had no business messin roun with us!"

"Way I figure it, we've sort of got a score to settle," Glenn Gilpin spoke up.

Myron Odell summed it up practically, with grim determination. "We need the practice for the real thing anyway."

Reisman realized with satisfaction that in a curious way he was indebted to Colonel Everett Dasher Breed. By his high-handed acts, the Colonel had unwittingly done him a good service, provoking in them more of that *esprit* or even hatred that was *we* against *them*, besides having provided him the situation earlier in which to win more of that loyalty Breed had disparaged.

Napoleon White brought him back to the greater reality he had been putting off. "What about the Invasion, Captain?" he demanded. "Isn't it time you told us what they turned us loose for in the first place?"

The men leaned forward, half expectant, half fearful, to meet Reisman's next words. It was something they'd talked and wondered about among themselves since the beginning.

But Reisman had no intention of telling them about the missions yet. "If you don't prove yourselves in the war game, there won't be anything else," he answered.

He spread open on one of the plank tables the map Colonel Breed had marked for him, and gathered the men around him. "Somewhere within this perimeter is your target," he said, pointing to the area. "You have a single goal: to locate and then capture or destroy the Colonel's Command Post. You'll be on your own. I'll help you now. I'll get you anything you need to do the job. But I won't take part in it with you. In this operation, you've got to prove to yourselves, to Breed, to the Army . . . and to me that you can do it on your own."

"Do we jump?" asked Joe Wladislaw.

"If it's part of the plan you work out. It's up to you. Start thinking."

"Kid stuff!" muttered Napoleon. He was still smarting at Reisman's curt dismissal. "It's like little boys playing games." He remembered the great maneuvers in Louisiana where he'd come to his own personal grief, and the memory rankled.

"Kid stuff, hell, man!" protested Luis Jimenez. "I rememba maneuvas ina States, there was two guys in my outfit got hit by artillery."

"Killed?" asked Odell nervously.

"Nah . . . jus a lil bit cut up, thas all. They got outa the hospital okay later."

"Don't let it worry you, Myron," said Calvin Ezra Smith. "They let everybody know when they have a live barrage. We just stay away from there."

"I'm not worrying," Odell insisted. "I just don't know anything about it. How does it work? I mean, how do you tell if you're dead or captured? How do you know if you've won . . . like this CP we're supposed to take?"

"Umpires, dammit!" Napoleon said. He looked at Reisman uncertainly and Reisman nodded for him to continue. "They tag the casualties and determine ground gained or lost based on strength, position and fire power of opposing units in each action . . . sometimes right down to patrol level." He spoke with authority, as though he was in charge and not Reisman, and he felt good seeing how intently they all listened to him, even Archer Maggot with his usual half-mocking expression. The goddamn Captain had hooked him again and Napoleon knew it—and liked it.

Reisman urged him on. "Why don't you try working out a plan of attack?"

"Theoretically, it's easy," Napoleon said. "All we have to do is sneak up on the objective without being discovered . . . avoid contact, don't engage in wasteful firefights that might uncover our presence in the area and endanger the mission . . . and don't attempt to kill or capture enemy troops until we're in position to go for broke. Theoretically, it's also impossible."

"Then it isn't kid stuff," observed Reisman dryly.

Napoleon shrugged noncommittally.

"How many of you have been in a war game before?" Reisman asked.

Some had, but for those who hadn't he described how they were run. Each side would wear different color helmet bands and shoulder loops . . . umpires, neutral observers and their vehicles would be distinguished in a similar way

457

. . . also special couriers and ambulances for real casualties. "The rules are no actual physical contact between opposing units and no hand-to-hand stuff," Reisman explained.

Sarcastically Archer Maggot muttered, "Who say we gotta play by thuh rules?"

"You don't," replied Reisman, surprising him. "But that doesn't mean you're gonna kill anyone or blow anything up. Fire will be simulated or with blank ammunition . . . except there'll probably be live artillery and dynamite going off here and there to give it all a little real sound and fury. I'll get you all the information pertaining to this particular game, but in general terms. Those are the rules and procedures."

"What do you mean we don't have to play by the rules?" Napoleon asked.

"Seems to me you've got to use some kind of deception," Reisman suggested. "Like you said, it's an impossible assignment . . . particularly in a war game where you won't be able to see any visible signs of the damage you could do in combat just on the strength of sheer guts. In an ordinary unit-against-unit encounter you'd be heavily outnumbered and outgunned. You've got to be smarter than they are . . . do something they'd never figure on."

"Like what?" demanded Napoleon.

"It's your party, gentlemen. Start thinking," Reisman told them.

Roscoe Lever struggled with an idea. It had worked for him in dozens of armed robberies . . . except that once. He hesitated, unwilling to volunteer anything to Reisman or any of them, unwilling to share, afraid maybe it was too stupid . . . but the challenge caught him up, the chance to try it again. "We can disguise ourselves," he muttered.

"How the hell could you guys disguise yourselves?" Reisman ridiculed, laughing at them. "Breed and his troopers know you . . . what you look like . . . what you smell like, for that matter!"

They looked at each other's bearded faces, filth, matted hair, dirty clothes. Victor Franko didn't want to say it. He hated to be the one to go back on what they'd vowed together at his instigation. But he knew what the Captain meant. They were stuck with it. They all seemed to turn to Franko now for a sign.

Samson Posey thought he knew what was meant. He

458

spoke slowly with great resolve, rubbing the sparse hairs of his beard. "I will clean myself . . . shave face . . . but I must leave hair long in Indian way," he said.

"Good enough, Posey," Reisman agreed quickly. "It'll be hidden under a helmet anyway. There's even Biblical precedent in your case. How about the rest of you? You guys can hate Breed, hate the Army, or me if you must," he exhorted them in a gentle voice. "You can hate whatever it is that pleases you or damn the fates that brought you here . . . but whatever it is that bugs you, here's a chance to show Breed and his men and the whole damn Army you're better soldiers than any of them. Do a job on them just for fun and practice, and then we can go in and do a job on the Nazis for real, because they're the sons-of-bitches that brought you over here in the first place."

"I think we have to do it," Ken Sawyer said to all of them—and he, for one, would be glad for the chance to look like a soldier again. "Otherwise we don't stand a chance . . . in this, or the real thing."

"You don't have to do it just yet," Reisman said, "because we'll be going up to the parachute school for a refresher jump and we don't want to give it away. But if you shave, shower and change those rags you've got on the night before the war game, I think we can work out a plan together to win your objective."

Napoleon shrugged his acceptance. What the hell difference did it make now? "I'm willing," he acknowledged.

Victor Franko listened to more of them add their approval, and wanting it to be his decision, not theirs or Reisman's, said finally, "Okay, we'll do it."

During the next days, they developed plans and worked out tactics for the war game, and there was great excitement and enthusiasm now in what they did. Kinder sent down aerial maps of the maneuver area, pinpointing topographical features, permanent buildings, bunkers and emplacements. He wanted to come down himself to help in the training, but Reisman specifically asked him not to, for he wanted him to be a neutral observer during the game.

Napoleon White and Ken Sawyer came to be recognized among them as leaders, based simply on ability and experience, with a minimum of squawking from the others. Within the perimeter Breed had indicated, they singled out two buildings and a bunker he might use as his Command Post. Using blankets, earth, bits of brush and materials scavenged around the stockade, Napoleon showed them how to construct hasty terrain models of the key points where their planned action would take place. A little figure was made for each man and his movements plotted in various theoretical situations. They kept experimenting and settled finally on a plan. It didn't require a parachute jump, and it was based upon deception brazen enough to gladden Reisman's heart.

When the crates of German uniforms, weapons and papers from Major Armbruster at OSS arrived, Reisman still couldn't bring himself to tell the men about the missions. He left the hated gray uniforms in the crates. Only Sergeant Bowren would know about them for now. But he taught the men to use the weapons with the same skill they'd developed in American arms, explaining it as part of their special training. And he began to teach them, too, all the brutal, clever stuff he'd learned and used as a guerrilla —silent killing, fieldcraft, living off the land, how to plant mines and booby traps, blow bridges, trains and buildings, and clever little bits of noiseless sabotage that could be more effective than a demolitions charge.

They found it harder to understand why he wanted them to learn German, but they followed orders and tried. Each man was issued a German-language guide and phrase book. Napoleon took six men and Reisman six and they drilled a couple of hours each day. With Samson Posey, the strange phrases he was taught came to him no harder than the English reading and writing in the Army manuals. During certain tactical exercises, Reisman spoke to them only in German and insisted they do the same. Except for Napoleon, their most frequent words were *"Ich verstehe nicht."*

Two letters for Reisman arrived during these last days of April. One was from Leon Osterman in Scotland. He apologized for not contacting him sooner and for not being able to pursue the Odell matter for a while. He'd been given a new assignment that was going to take him longer than expected, but he promised he would get back and be able to devote time to Odell during the middle of May.

It had been many weeks since Odell had bugged anybody about his innocence, and Reisman said nothing to him about the letter. He hoped only that Osterman returned in time for them to make one final effort to help Odell before the Dirty Dozen parachuted into France.

There was a more maddening and frustrating letter from the prison Commandant at Marston-Tyne. It was a personal letter that tried to take some of the sting out of what he had to say.

Dear Captain Reisman,

I have considered this matter for many days now, and write you my decision only after seriously weighing all aspects of the case. I regret that I cannot convene a court-martial to try Sergeant Morgan on the grounds you specified, nor is he being held in custody as you requested. I believe my decision is for the good of the Service and that you will agree with me.

I have interviewed Morgan extensively and feel that in view of certain events he states occurred during his detached service at your camp, and in view of the coercion he claims was used against him at the time of the alleged breach of security, by a respected officer who outranks both of us, the offense you charged against him must be considered in a more ameliorating light.

Also, please do understand this—Morgan is a permanent and necessary member of my command. His rank was given to him in accordance with the duties he is assigned to perform. Since it is possible he will be asked to perform those duties again in the near future, I feel that it is in the best interests of the Army and the war effort to do everything to prevent this matter from going further, and to continue Sergeant Morgan indefinitely in his present rank.

Sincerely Yours,
Simon R. Tarbell, 0-2473629
Lieutenant Colonel, CMP

Reisman folded the letter away in a desk drawer. He understood too well. There was nothing further he could do about it. The hangman would still be waiting at Marston-

Tyne for the Dirty Dozen and others like them.

The call from Major Armbruster came Sunday evening, three days before the war game. Reisman drove through the night and they were waiting for him anxiously when he got to Baker Street. Armbruster, Denton, Kinder, and a strange, nervous-looking civilian were there.

Denton said with grudging respect, "You're not one for simply following orders and letting others follow theirs, are you, Captain?"

"No, sir. I doubt that any of us really are in this branch . . . would you say?"

"No, I suppose not." He glanced at Armbruster with a wry yet not unsympathetic look. "At your bidding, Max took it upon himself to pursue a matter I'm not sure we were quite ready for. However, you have set certain forces in motion and we must now deal with them."

He introduced the civilian. "This is Monsieur LeMaire. Until yesterday morning he was a caretaker at the Château de la Vilaine in Rennes."

He was a thin, wiry man dressed in coarse country clothes. He looked as though he hadn't had enough to eat for a long time, and he was very tired.

"Monsieur LeMaire has confirmed for us what was previously only a tantalizing rumor," said Denton. "The Château de la Vilaine is a meeting place of Generals of the German Seventh Army, their staffs, their civilian friends, and their feminine companions. It seems the château is part war college for mapboard *Kriegsspiels* and conferences, part hotel and recreation center and part whorehouse. According to Monsieur LeMaire, there has been under that roof a most formidable array of enemy authority, talent, and sympathizers."

"Lovely place for a vacation," murmured Reisman with a grin.

"Yes . . . ideal," agreed the Colonel with surprising good humor. "Provided we pick the right moment to vacation there . . . and send the right people. The moment, of course, is when the Generals are there. According to Monsieur LeMaire, that is usually for one or at most two nights in the first week of each month when the *Kriegsspiels* are held. It is an elusive moment we cannot control, nor can we time the Invasion to it. But perhaps this time we are in

462

luck, Captain . . . and I warn you, you are under the most severe restrictions not to breathe the slightest hint of this to a soul. D-Day is now scheduled for the first week in June . . . and what makes this situation even more interesting is that the place of the Invasion will be Normandy, the very sector where the German Seventh Army is waiting."

A surge of excitement and awe gripped Reisman. He started to speak, but the Colonel waved him to silence. "I think you'd better listen to Monsieur LeMaire before you say anything, Captain."

In a mixture of English and French, LeMaire spoke. Stuart Kinder took notes and drew rough diagrams, and a detailed picture of the château, its interior and its surroundings emerged. It was not one of the larger, better known châteaux to which attention was drawn naturally by history and tradition, and the Germans had done everything possible to keep it inconspicuous and the use to which they put it secret. Usually the place was lightly guarded by impressed foreign troops of the occupation army, but when the Generals were there crack elements of the nearest regular unit, the Fifth Parachute Division, were moved in. That was the giveaway that the Generals were there, for their comings and goings were kept relatively secret. Some came by car, others by boat on the river. There were always a number of high-speed limousines kept handy in the motor park, just in case, and a number of speedboats kept in a boathouse which connected to the main building by an underground passageway.

"What a setup! What a fantastic opportunity!" exclaimed Reisman.

"It's no piece of cake, John. It's not much better than the last thing as far as chances are concerned," commented Armbruster.

"But there's more substance to this, Max, more meaning. Just think of it . . . the dregs of the American Army going after the cream of the Nazi slime!"

"Nobody has said that yet, Captain," declared Colonel Denton impassively. "Two weeks ago you accused me of wanting to send your men out to be executed . . . which is what most of them deserve anyway. At Rennes they would be alone a hundred miles out ahead of the troops coming over the beach and for all practical purposes almost as far from the nearest airborne outfit. What's the difference?"

Reisman knew Denton was right. This, too, might be suicide, but . . . "At Rennes, Colonel, they could go in together and I could lead them effectively," he said quietly. "They would have a crack at a tactical objective of importance and then try to fight their way back. Who knows . . . if the Generals are there it might even turn out to be the single most important objective of the day. It could wreak havoc with their communications and chain of command."

"What if they're not there?"

"We can work out an alternate target before we go in. Maybe the railroad yards. Max said it was a big switching center and road hub. That means they'll be moving troops through there to the Invasion front. We can hit them there."

Denton considered that a moment. "My concern is neither in giving them an opportunity to be heroes, Captain, nor in saving their hides," he said. "It's considerably more important than that. This whole business is strictly a long shot, and the biggest maybe is your men."

"What in hell did you haul me up here for if you didn't intend this for us?" demanded Reisman.

"What assurance can you give me your men have the ability and can be trusted?" countered Denton. "If we're going to take this on, maybe we ought to try putting together a first-rate group of volunteers in the time we have left."

Reisman had the answer ready for that. "Come see for yourself, Colonel," he challenged confidently. "The Dirty Dozen are participating in a little *Kriegsspiel* of their own Wednesday. Captain Kinder will be there as a neutral observer. I would be very pleased if you and Major Armbruster arranged to be there too."

"Very well. We won't make any decision till then," said Denton.

—

31

—

REISMAN STOOD near a window looking-out across the stark gray downs, listening to the heavy rolling artillery barrage. It fought with the static and chatter of the open radios and low murmur of conversation and orders behind him in the war game director's headquarters.

Sergeant Bowren, also wearing the green helmet band and shoulder loop of a neutral observer, walked toward Reisman from the gigantic terrain model in the center of the room where he had been watching the markers move unit symbols into positions they now occupied, and eavesdropping on conversations.

"Breed's CP is in the bunker they picked. Red force is going to put a live barrage near there at 0855," he said anxiously. "Two batteries, three minutes, on grid coordinate C7P5."

Reisman glanced at a large map on the wall. The fire coordinate was a hill three hundred yards south of the bunker. To make their prearranged rendezvous, some of the men would have to sneak over the hill and down into brush on the bank of a stream.

"Plenty of time to get through there," Reisman said, checking his watch. "They'll be told about it by the umpires before the attack."

Through the window he saw Stuart Kinder drive up in the staff car that had brought him, Denton and Armbruster down from London. A green neutral's flag snapped on a standard over the hood.

Reisman met Kinder at the door. "They split up okay?" he asked.

"Yes. They blended right in. I don't know how you did it, John," Kinder said enthusiastically. "They looked beautiful. I actually had trouble recognizing some of them."

His job had been to shepherd the shaved, showered and freshly laundered men to companies to which they'd been temporarily paired. Armbruster was with Napoleon White and would follow him through the maneuver. Denton was at Colonel Breed's Command Post as an official observer.

"Let's hope Colonel Breed has the same problem," commented Reisman.

At the rendezvous point, Napoleon stared anxiously up the ravaged, desolate hill that had been pummeled again and again by practicing cannoneers over many months. Crouched in the brush beside him were Jimenez, Franko, Pinkley and Major Armbruster. By the rules, and marked

465

on the map Napoleon held, the target hill was out of bounds, nobody was allowed to cross. Yet Odell, Smith, Wladislaw and Lever had to come that way to escape from control of their temporary units. Major Armbruster had looked astounded and worried when Napoleon explained why they were pausing there, but had made no overt criticism.

Victor Franko muttered nervously for the third time, "Look at the time, goddammit, look at the time!"

They each had a watch, map and compass so their plan wouldn't go awry, but they'd agreed Napoleon was in charge. "0854," Napoleon said.

"Jeezus, let's get outa here," Franko pleaded.

"We get blow up, man," threw in Jimenez with a curious smile.

"Maybe they'll come through after the barrage," said Napoleon. "We can't leave without them. Let's just figure the artillery's got good aim."

They heard the whistle and scream of the first shells going over just as four distant figures topped the ridge running. They moved in darting, panicky spurts, hugging the ground, throwing themselves into old craters and behind blackened clumps of brush and trees as the ground shook from the explosions, then got up and ran again, the impact area creeping partway down the slope after them until they got out of range.

Myron Odell threw himself into the brush beside Napoleon, trembling with excitement. "Son-of-a-bitch! They were shooting at me!" he said. Then, seeing Armbruster, "Oh, excuse me, sir!" he stammered.

"That's all right, son," said the Major. "That was a close one."

Armbruster had expected to be ill at ease with these men, suspicious, but strangely he wasn't. He was very much caught up in what they were doing. It promised to be unusual, though he still couldn't put the pieces together. Reisman had outfitted them like a guerrilla's dream of a walking munitions dump. On the surface, in their unmarked fatigue uniforms, they were ordinary enough to pass for regular troops. They carried carbines, blank ammo and dummy grenades, and Jimenez lugged a BAR for heavier support. But their field packs each held a broken-down submachine gun and were crammed with dummy demolitions charges. They each also carried a concealed .22

466

pistol with silencer and a variety of time pencils and other detonating and explosive devices, all of which Armbruster had personally arranged to send down from OSS.

Napoleon shouted to penetrate the noise of exploding shells. "What about the houses?"

"Mine was empty," Wladislaw reported.

Lever crouched close to him. "There were some guys at mine with red bands on their helmets," he said, "but they didn't look like paratroopers."

Napoleon parted some brush and pointed across the stream toward a squat reinforced building in the distance. "That bunker's probably the one," he said. "Let's go."

He could make out tiny figures moving in and out; a motorcycle courier sped away on a paved east-west road; some trucks, jeeps and armored vehicles were parked off a parallel dirt road on the near side of the building; a few anti-tank guns and mortars were emplaced in good defensive positions, their troops standing by, and Napoleon was certain there were machine guns hidden, sited to sweep both roads and the broad fields on all sides. There should have been pickets out directly across the bank from him, but they weren't expecting anybody to come over the target hill to scout them.

"What makes you so sure?" challenged Franko. "What if it isn't?"

"Then we'll do our act in every damn building within Breed's perimeter until we find it," snapped Napoleon. "Put on your red force identification now."

From their packs they took the red helmet bands and shoulder loops and exchanged them for the blue ones they'd been wearing. Major Armbruster looked on curiously. What they were doing was thoroughly illegal in the standard operating procedures of the war game. He was tempted to speak, but again he didn't.

The shelling behind them stopped. "Come on, let's catch up to the other guys," said Napoleon. In the sudden silence his voice sounded unusually harsh.

They moved west along the bank, hugging cover until they were out of sight of the bunker, then forded the stream and hiked quickly toward the road intersection where the others were to meet them.

Ken Sawyer's group was waiting there with the stolen jeep and a heavy machine gun covered by a tarpaulin in the back. They displayed the green identification of neutral observers. Sawyer, tinkering with the engine as though it were out of order, was wearing a Major's insignia.

Franko plucked off one of the gold leaves. "This badge is an insignia of honor!" he recited in a poor imitation of Colonel Breed. "You have no right to it! You . . ."

"Knock it off, man," cautioned Jimenez, hitting him with his shoulder. He nodded back toward Major Armbruster.

Sawyer took off the other leaf and slipped both into a pocket. "Easy come, easy go," he said, grinning. He reattached the coil wire he'd disconnected and banged down the hood.

"How'd it go?" asked Napoleon. His eyes continued to scan the roads and fields. Nobody else was in sight, but he knew that wouldn't last long. The bunker he'd scouted was a mile and a half away and they were standing on the main road to it.

"Couldn't have been easier," responded Sawyer. "Like the CO said, most people believe what they see . . . even the enemy. It's amazing what you can do just on bullshit . . . and believing in yourself." He and Posey had showed phony orders to take the jeep from a blue force motor pool, then had picked up Maggot and Gilpin with the machine gun at a prearranged point. To get through the lines over a guarded bridge, theoretically bombed out, they'd changed their helmet bands and shoulder loops to neutral green and he'd posed as an officer to give it more weight.

"We're going to split up again, sir," Napoleon told Major Armbruster. "Do you want to go with the jeep or wait here with me?"

"Where will the key action be?"

"Ought to be great fun at both ends . . . if it works," said Napoleon. "We'll catch up to them for the climax."

"I'll stay with you," said Armbruster.

Sawyer, Posey, Odell and Gilpin put on red force identification and changed the flag on the jeep. Napoleon and Sawyer synchronized their watches.

"I'll allow a full hour for the ambulance," said Napoleon. "If it's not here by then, I'll figure Breed got onto you and we'll improvise something else. Lend me those Major's leaves, will you? You won't be needing them."

Sawyer took them from his pocket and handed them over. "What if it ain't the right place?" he asked.

"Then the Army's gonna lose a lot of vehicles today,"

said Napoleon, grinning. He slapped the side of the jeep. "Good luck."

Sawyer drove carefully, watching the mileage meter. No other vehicles passed and he hoped it stayed that way. After a mile and three tenths he pulled to the side of the road and sent Gilpin to scout ahead on foot. He disappeared on the double around a bend and was back in a few minutes.

"Two more curves," he said. "There's a good steep ditch just this side of the second one. They won't be able to see what happens, but they ought to hear the blast and see the smoke."

Gilpin stopped him when they got to the spot. Sawyer pointed the jeep down into the ditch. Gilpin slashed the right rear tire with a bayonet until the air came hissing out. "That's a real bad blowout," he said proudly. He put a few slices in his fatigues, then in the others'. Each of them rolled on the soft shoulder of the road and rubbed dirt on their hands and faces.

"Damn. I was just getting used to being clean," muttered Sawyer. "Give me your helmet and jacket, Chief. We'll broil them a bit to make it look better." He took the can of gas from the jeep, set it down next to Samson's jacket and helmet. "All right, over the top!"

The jeep went into the ditch and crashed on its side. Odell began wrapping wide swathes of gauze around Samson's head, chest and arms. Gilpin climbed down after the jeep, knifed the gas tank again and again with his bayonet until he split it and a stream of fuel gushed out. Sawyer poured a gasoline fuse from there back up to the road and splattered some of it on Samson's helmet and jacket.

"Hit the deck!" he shouted. He struck a match, held it to the end of the gasoline trail, ran after them and threw himself to the ground.

The fire raced along the fuse, hit the jeep's gas tank and it blew with a roar. They gave it about ten seconds. Sawyer leaped up and stomped out the fire on Samson's scorched jacket and helmet. He handed them to Odell. "Get him down in the ditch, quick," he ordered. "Start moaning, Chief. You've been hurt real bad."

Sawyer and Gilpin leaned close to the pyre of the jeep until the smoke stuck to them, then they loped up the road yelling, "Help! Help!"

They spotted Colonel Breed right away. The explosion

and column of smoke had made machine gunners rise out of concealment, and set up a stir of activity just outside the bunker. A jeep was already crawling out of the parking area toward the road. Gilpin blocked it to give Odell more time on the bandages. Sawyer raced toward Breed in the bunker doorway, yelling, "Call an ambulance! Call an ambulance!"

The Colonel grabbed him. "What's the matter, soldier?" he snapped.

"Accident, sir . . . bad accident . . . tire blew and we went in a ditch. One of my men's pretty bad off. Call an ambulance, sir, please!"

Breed barked instructions to a radioman in the bunker, then demanded to know who Sawyer was, what outfit he was with and what the hell he was doing cutting through his perimeter. Sawyer blurted out his story that they'd been spotting for the battery that laid on the barrage south of them, and had gotten lost trying to get back.

"Thank God your spotting's better than your driving, soldier," muttered Breed. "Stay out of the way. We'll bring your man in. Clear out when the ambulance gets here."

"Yes, sir . . . thank you, sir," said Sawyer.

Some of the paratroopers brought Samson in on a stretcher and laid him on the floor in an out-of-the-way part of the bunker. He moaned occasionally and Odell hovered over him, turning away all offers of help with the same answer. "Don't touch him, dammit! I was in the medics once and I know what it is. Just let him be till we get him to a hospital."

He took off Samson's boots solicitously, and stealthily dropped time pencils into each before placing them under the radio table. Sawyer and Gilpin wandered around the bunker with ingenuous expressions on their faces. They removed their heavy packs, loaded with demolitions charges, and placed them strategically. Once, Sawyer thought he saw an officer looking at him with too much interest, but the man, a Colonel wearing the green of a neutral observer, immediately turned away and became involved in a discussion with the war game umpire on duty there.

At the crossroads west of the bunker, Napoleon saw the ambulance speeding toward them. They moved from cover with the machine gun and blocked the intersection. Napoleon wore the Major's leaves.

"Bad accident up ahead, sir!" shouted the driver, looking

dumfounded at Napoleon's rank. "Got to get through."

"Sorry, soldier, this is as far as you go," snapped Napoleon.

A Medical Corps Lieutenant leaned out the other side. "There's a man badly injured up there, sir. They radioed for help. I'm a doctor," he said rapidly. "We've got permission to cross all lines and roadblocks."

"I'm sorry, Lieutenant. You're our prisoners," said Napoleon. "We were warned to watch for a blue patrol trying to get through with a yarn like yours."

"Yarn! Good God, Major, don't you know the rules?" exploded the doctor. "There's a real casualty up there . . . maybe dying for all I know." He looked around helplessly, spotted Major Armbruster wearing the green neutral's color. "Explain it to him, will you, sir?" he said anxiously.

"I'm just an observer, Lieutenant," explained Armbruster, "not an umpire. I can't interfere or make any rulings." He had a good idea now what was going on. It violated all the rules in the book, but he was curious to see how far they'd be able to take it.

"Out of the ambulance," ordered Napoleon. "We'll drive it through and check for you. If you're right, we'll bring your man out in a few minutes."

"It's your responsibility," muttered the doctor angrily. He and the driver climbed out.

"Take the gun," ordered Napoleon. "I don't trust these guys."

They picked up the machine gun and piled into the back of the vehicle, urging Major Armbruster in ahead of them. Victor Franko drove. Beside him, Joe Wladislaw took his grease gun from his pack and reassembled it. As they sped down the road, Armbruster watched the others do the same, and change their helmet bands and shoulder loops again, this time to neutral green.

"This isn't really cricket, is it?" he said.

"We were taught different," answered Napoleon cockily. Things were going beautifully and he was eager for the finish.

Calvin Ezra Smith wanted the officer to know he didn't really approve either. "It ain't right . . . that's what he means, it ain't right," he chattered. "This here's leadin us right back where we was. Jeremiah asked the sinners, 'Will ye steal, murder, and commit adultery, and swear falsely?' And you all know which a those we done awready and

471

which we gonna do . . . an there ain't no redemption from it, there ain't . . . not doin what that Captain wants us to do . . . cheatin like this . . . he's leadin us right down the road to . . ."

"Oh, shut the hell up, you holy-rolling son-of-a-bitch!" Franko said.

Ken Sawyer heard the ambulance outside and saw it backing right up to the doorway. He pulled some of the gauze away from Samson's eyes and put a carbine in his hands. Franko and Wladislaw, blocking the threshold, yanked open the ambulance doors. Napoleon leaped out and right behind him were two men at the heavy machine gun covering the interior of the bunker.

"Colonel Breed!" yelled Napoleon.

Breed turned sharply, spilling coffee from the cup that had just been handed him by an orderly. There was irritation on his face at the rude shout. The look changed to momentary bewilderment at sight of the colored Major striding toward him, then shock at sight of the strange soldiers and machine gun in the blocked doorway, and finally awareness and anger as Napoleon said, "Captain Reisman sends his compliments. Would you prefer to be captured or destroyed?"

In the war game director's headquarters, Reisman heard the radio signal from the umpire at Breed's Command Post.

"They've done it!" he yelled, and almost did a dance with Stuart Kinder.

But a minute later, the radio that had been ruled destroyed came on again: "Disregard last message . . . repeat . . . disregard!"

They waited an anxious hour, but when there was no further sign of action by the Dirty Dozen or any report of them as casualties or prisoners, Reisman, Kinder and Bowren took the staff car through the lines. The main attack against Breed's perimeter by blue force was under way, and they were held up at a roadblock by an extremely suspicious officer who told them, "This gag has already been tried once today!" He finally received orders from the Command Post to let them through.

They were taken directly to Colonel Breed. He was poring over a map table with a group of subordinates in the bunker. Neither the Dirty Dozen, Denton nor Armbruster were there.

"I shall expect you to honor our agreement immediately, Captain," said Breed, hardly looking up. "Your little experiment . . . whatever it was . . . will end."

"Where are my men?" demanded Reisman. "I know they took this position. I heard it on the radio."

"The hell you say!" exploded Breed. "What they did was a flagrant violation of the rules!"

"Colonel, these men and what they must do are outside the rules," retorted Reisman. "They're in this to fight dirty and rough and win. Did they or did they not destroy your Command Post?"

"I suggest you listen to the umpire's ruling on that, Captain," said Breed stiffly.

"Where are my men?" Reisman demanded again.

"In a truck out back . . . under guard as they should be."

Kinder and Bowren went out to check. Breed led Reisman to the Lieutenant Colonel in charge of the umpires within his perimeter. He stood at the radio, monitoring traffic.

"This is Captain Reisman," said Breed. "He'd the Commanding Officer of that silly bunch that barged in here before."

The umpire looked at Reisman disdainfully. "What in hell did you expect to gain with a crazy trick like that, Captain?"

"This headquarters."

"That's absurd," the umpire scoffed. "I'll admit they had me fooled for a minute . . . I even signaled the director . . . but as soon as Colonel Breed pointed out . . ."

"Did they take this position or not, sir?"

"They most certainly did not! This isn't a children's game, Captain. It's serious business. Changing sides at will . . . playing neutral . . . diverting a medical team . . . not to mention the wanton destruction of government property, for which you no doubt will be held to account!"

"Were there any observers present?"

"They're out back interrogating your crew," said Breed. "They've never seen anything like it either."

Reisman headed for the door. Breed strode after him quickly. "You're to vacate Lady Margot's estate immediately," he said. "Otherwise I'll make my report today . . .

and I'll take it all the way up to SHAEF if I have to. I'll break you . . . and them."

Reisman shrugged. "I'll need a little time, Colonel . . . two weeks to arrange a transfer and restore the grounds as I promised Miss Strathallan."

"Very well . . . two weeks," said Breed brusquely.

Reisman left the bunker to find the men. The ultimatum didn't bother him. He didn't intend to meet it. He never had, win or lose—and as far as he was concerned he had won or at worst reached another stalemate. He was more concerned now about the reactions of Denton and Armbruster to the umpire's decision.

He saw them waiting for him with Stuart Kinder. A short distance away the men were under guard in an open truck surrounded by a detail of paratroopers staring at them curiously. Sergeant Bowren had climbed up with them and they were all talking to him animatedly. Reisman joined the huddle of officers.

"That was quite a stunt, Captain," said Colonel Denton.

"Sneaky but effective," Armbruster remarked with a grin.

"Isn't that what the Rennes mission calls for, Max?" To Denton he said, "It wasn't a stunt, Colonel. It was a well-grounded and appropriate plan, competently executed. However, it didn't do any good. The umpire ruled them out."

"Oh, the hell with that!" snapped Denton, surprising him. "It doesn't make any difference. Take the chip off your shoulder, John. The Rennes mission is theirs."

The anger and tension in Reisman softened and he felt a sense of relief. Then he realized Denton had said *theirs,* not *yours.* "How about me?" he pressed.

Denton hesitated, looked at the others. "Work out a plan of attack," he said.

"I already have, Colonel," Reisman replied. "Why don't we all meet at Stokes Manor and discuss it. I'll arrange transportation out of here for the men."

"All right," Denton agreed.

Reisman walked toward the truck where the men were being held and heard Napoleon sing out, "Here comes the Seventh Cavalry again!"

In his office at the stockade, he outlined for the three

officers the plan that had been growing in his mind since his meeting with Monsieur LeMaire in London.

"Deception is the only way," he said. "Something combining elements of the guerrilla work you originally proposed and elements of the maneuver you witnessed today. A direct assault would never work with the limited firepower we could take with us . . . and it would tip off the Generals if they're there and give them a chance to escape. We've got to get into the building quietly and get close to them before showing our hand. As a starter we've got the German uniforms and weapons you sent down to us and the men have been learning German. I'll build on that."

"How about your colored boy? The Indian might pass, but not him," said Major Armbruster.

"Nobody gets left behind for the hangman," said Reisman. "We'll work that out somehow. You've still got that Frenchman under wraps, haven't you?"

"Yes. It's too risky to take him back now . . . both for him and us. He's available any time you want him."

"Stu . . . I'd like you to work with him. We know enough now to begin and you've got those rough sketches you made of the château. Now I'd like you to have them converted into an exact replica model of the château and the surrounding area. Have aerial reconnaissance get pictures . . . and I want maps, too. Question LeMaire again and again. Have him work right with the model makers. Pump him dry about every road, hill, ditch, tree and bush he remembers . . . and exactly where the Krauts set up their checkpoints and defenses . . . what weapons and strength. Then do the same for the interior of the building . . . power lines, telephone and other communications . . . and I want every room, hallway and closet he remembers duplicated in the model. When you've got that, start on the people. Who comes there, why, and in which rooms are they likely to be found . . . German and French . . . men and women . . . get up a dossier on each of them."

"A caretaker isn't likely to know much of that," commented Denton.

"I've found people often know more than they think they do, Colonel. The Germans do things, they talk . . . our friends watch and listen. Servants, workers, even collaborators and whores. LeMaire no doubt has seen and heard much that might appear inconsequential to him but would be of inestimable value to us."

"What about our friends . . . people like LeMaire who work there, or others who could be innocently caught in an attack?" asked Armbruster.

"Work out something with BBC. A radio message to evacuate as inconspicuously as possible. Signals are going out to the Underground all the time. I'm sure you've got one planned for D-Day. We can try . . . but nothing more overt than that."

"It's not going to be a pretty piece of work, John," said Armbruster. "Not at all like other things you've done for us. There'll still be civilians there, no doubt . . . some women, I suppose, according to LeMaire. Maybe wives . . . surely the usual mistresses and camp followers."

"That ought to be an incentive for this bunch," said Denton.

"What do you mean?" asked Reisman.

"I remember months ago, when we first met on this, saying there'd be certain dirty work to be done. I had no idea then, believe me . . . but this sort of thing shouldn't bother them as much as it would a regular group. I rather think they'd relish it."

"They're no more bloodthirsty than the rest of us, Colonel," Reisman said sharply. "They have the same fears, longings and hates. A little more lost, maybe, but they'll do what they have to do, and kill anybody who comes at them or gets in their way."

Sergeant Bowren had kept the men occupied at the mess end of the barracks out of earshot of Reisman's room, but they had sensed something big was up. When the three officers left, Reisman broke out the bottle of Scotch that Leon Osterman had brought him and poured a drink all around. With unexpected politeness they waited for him to pour his own.

Reisman raised his cup to them in a toast and flicked his eyes from man to man. "You did well today," he said. "My congratulations."

Napoleon raised his own cup high in countersalute. "*Ave Caesar, morituri te salutamus!*" he intoned.

"Now whut in heyll do that mean, boy?" demanded Archer Maggot.

Reisman touched his cup to Napoleon's. "Hail Caesar, we who are about to die salute you! It's what the old Roman gladiators used to say when they entered the arena. You wouldn't know about that, would you, Mr. Maggot?"

"Heyll no!" he responded, contemptuously proud. "Youall both real smaht, ain't you, Cap'm!"

Napoleon talked to Maggot but held Reisman's eyes. "To translate for you, cracker, what I mean is this: I think maybe we've earned the right to die in a more preferred manner than previously decreed."

"Drink up," said Reisman, and he made it sound like an order. He sipped at his drink, rolling the liquor on his tongue, letting it slip smoothly down his throat. Most of them gulped theirs in one long swallow.

"How would you gentlemen like to get yourselves a bagful of Generals?" Reisman asked.

Victor Franko felt the good hot booze hit his belly. He started to wipe the drops from his lips with the back of a hand but licked them off with his tongue instead so as not to waste them. "Theirs or ours?" he chuckled.

"Does it make any difference?" asked Reisman. He didn't really think it did.

Franko shrugged his shoulders . . . and feeling cocky and strong he answered truthfully, "No."

A few of them laughed nervously and Reisman wondered how many others really felt that way too, as Stuart Kinder had warned him weeks before. He sought the right words now . . . words that would be judicious, inspiring, optimistic . . . and then thought, Fuck em! and let them have it straight.

"We're jumping into France the night before the Invasion," he said impassively. "We'll be in first and far out ahead of anybody else. Our mission is to get into a château where a group of Nazi Generals may or may not be waiting for us with a bunch of their lesser friends and associates. Our job is to kill them . . . not wound them or take prisoners . . . but get in close enough to know damn well they're dead. We'll go in wearing Kraut uniforms, carrying Kraut weapons and identification. How does that suit you, Mr. White?" he challenged.

Napoleon was frozen in amazement, and Reisman saw by the way the others looked at him and each other that their reactions ran from dumb acceptance through awe to uneasiness. Samson Posey and Calvin Ezra Smith, who had only made a pretense of drinking, now drained their cups.

Reisman softened somewhat. "This mission you've been given is of vital importance to the success of the Invasion," he said. "As I told you when we started here, there are troops who'd give their left nuts for this job. Nothing you did before in your lives will count as much. Nothing you ever do again will equal it. Exactly where we will drop and when we will go must remain secret a while longer. But I give you the right now during these next weeks of preparation to criticize and make alternate suggestions within the framework of our assignment. You must contribute according to your experience and abilities. You must begin to think for yourselves, for each other . . . and for me. The key word is deception. Everything we do now in thinking, planning, practice, everything we do in the attack must be directed to convince the enemy we are what we are not . . . until we get close enough to kill him."

Archer Maggot raised his hand and Reisman nodded for him to speak. "Cap'm, hows he s'posetuh pass for a Heinie?" he asked, jerking his thumb at Napoleon.

"At night, all cats look black, Reb. We're going in at night. We'll work it out one way or another. Are you concerned about him?"

"Heyll no!" Maggot said, shrugging off any such possibility. "Ahm worried bout me not him. Ah doan wan mah ass cote caus a him."

"You may be lucky going with him, Maggot. He may have an advantage over all of you. He *sprechens* better *Deutsch* and *parlez-vous* better *français* that you'll ever learn. You've still got trouble with English."

Laughter from the others eased the tension in the room. Napoleon had listened to the exchange without really taking offense because the same thought had occurred to him. And it had also occurred to him there was something very fishy about this plan. It was too sophisticated in conception, too doubtful in the execution . . . he cringed at the word . . . for a group like theirs. But he'd go along with it . . . bide his time and see what it was really all about.

Victor Franko liked the plan the way it was. It was made to order in the Kraut uniforms. He could convince the others . . . or lose them . . . or kill them if he had to . . . and all he had to do was turn himself in to the Germans. He could sit out the rest of the war and no matter who won he could be safe and alive and a hero.

"If any of you would rather call it quits now, you can," Reisman told them quietly. "The alternative is still there . . . I can't do anything about that. But you're still volunteers, remember. You don't have to go if you don't want to."

"Isn't it too late for that now, Captain?" Napoleon challenged.

"No. The choice is still yours to make . . . regardless of the consequences," Reisman told them. "But I warn you now . . . I'll kill any one of you who tries to cop out once we go in."

The grim silence of that reality was broken by Victor Franko. "Hell, Captain, none of us wanta go back. Let's go on with it."

Nobody else had anything to say. It seemed to be the attitude of all of them.

"All right . . . sleep on it," said Reisman. "Dream about it. We'll start work in the morning."

32

STUART KINDER brought down the model of the château and the maps early the following week. The model was a thing of beauty built in sections they put together on a table in the barracks. Everything aerial reconnaissance had caught and everything Monsieur LeMaire had remembered were built into it in fine detail. There were even barges on the painted river, two speedboats tucked into the little boathouse, and tiny Mercedes limousines and some trucks in the motor park within the walled courtyard. Known defense positions and guardposts were marked and tiny replicas of heavier weapons emplaced.

The main building had twenty-three rooms, one of them a large ballroom where the *Kriegsspiels* were now played; and in the basement was a communications center, including radio transmitter. There were also a number of detached service buildings and an auxiliary power plant. The roof and second story of each building were removable so that all rooms and corridors could be examined from above. And a full complement of little figures, male and female, civilian and military, in painted Nazi and American uniforms, waited in boxes like neat rows of lead soldiers before the battle.

Kinder had been prepared to find the men rebelliously bearded and dirty again, but they weren't. They had shaved and showered every day without question since the war game. The Dirty Dozen were gone. But Kinder could not help wondering if maybe their new image was worse. During those hours they trained in their German uniforms, some of them went around goose-stepping like kids, *heil*ing Hitler and each other, and seeing them like that sent a shiver up his spine.

"Do you know what you have in this bunch?" he said to Reisman. "The perfect Nazi mentality . . . chronic delinquent adolescents."

"Sounds serious," Reisman muttered distractedly. He was more interested in watching Sergeant Bowren run the men through the German manual of arms and close-order drill. Though Bowren was technically an outsider, Reisman trusted him implicitly and he was a party to all phases of their training and briefings on the mission. The men had begun to address him mockingly as *Unteroffizier* Bowren, as they addressed Reisman as *Herr Hauptmann*.

Kinder persisted in his discourse. "Take Franko, for instance . . . there was really no reason for him to go bad . . . unless you blame a crowded tenement, foul smells, dirty streets, his neighborhood friends."

"I'm familiar with the environment," said Reisman caustically, turning his full attention to Kinder, "but I don't see it as cause and effect. It's too easy an answer. The old rhubarb about a rose growing out of a dunghill disproves it."

"There is no easy answer," said Kinder. "I've learned a lot about Franko, but I still don't know what really bugs him. There were all the influences around him of good. A father, a mother, sisters and brothers who went to school, to church, to work . . ."

"Maybe he went to see the wrong movies," suggested Reisman frivolously.

"That's not such a far-fetched idea, John," Kinder told him. "A gangster hero portrayed by some slick Hollywood idol . . . an identification with the sufferings of some swarthy youth on the way to the electric chair with the whole world against him."

"What about Napoleon White? He certainly doesn't fit your Nazi formula."

"In a curious way he does. He suffers from a bad inferiority complex that leaves him wide open for almost anything . . . much as the Germans did after World War One . . . do now, in fact. His inferiority complex is a failure to come to terms with reality. And the murder he committed was the gesture of an adolescent."

"Adolescent gesture, hell!" said Reisman harshly. "It was the necessary and reasoned act of a man. It has to be. Otherwise how can you justify what we're doing here . . . what we're going to do . . . the entire meaning of the Invasion and the war for that matter? It was an act of vengeance and purification."

He turned away. He didn't want to go on with the conversation. He felt uneasy in it and called to Sergeant Bowren to bring the men into the barracks. When Kinder left for London, he was glad to see him go.

"What the hell does a Kraut General look like?" asked Victor Franko as he studied the model of the Château de la Vilaine.

They were placing the little figures in various positions, working out their own approach to the target and movements through the building.

Reisman described the red tabs and gold-braided oak leaves on the collars, the gold epaulets on jacket shoulders, the red stripes down the seams of greenish-gray trousers. "You might even find one bare ass in bed with a broad," he added facetiously, "wearing an iron cross . . . and a swastika tattooed on his butt. Don't ask for an ID card, Franko. Kill anybody who gets in your way as quietly and quickly as you can. With a knife or garrote if possible . . . and we'll take the twenty-twos and silencers. Once the shit hits the fan and they know we're there we can use our heavier stuff."

"How many Gen'rals they gonna be?" asked Maggot.

"Eight . . . ten . . . maybe one apiece . . . maybe none. We won't know till we get there."

"What about the women, sir?" asked Odell.

"No one must be allowed to give an alarm," said Reisman obliquely. "Each of you will have a few rooms to cover once we get into the château. The goal is the Generals.

481

We must move in silence and remain undiscovered as long as possible. There's no way to take prisoners."

Odell felt all the strength he had built up these many weeks drain out of him. His heart pounded rapidly, sweat coated his palms, and nausea rose from his stomach and gagged in his throat. Here it was at last. They were asking him to do something they had sentenced him to hang for doing—and he was Innocent. They wanted him to kill . . . maybe to kill a woman. No, he wouldn't do it . . . he couldn't do it. *I'm Innocent!* he bleated silently.

In the dark in their cots they listened to Bowren up on the roof blow Taps into the gentle May night. The last notes signaled, as it did each night, the time of reverie past and future, the time of memory, of hope, of fear, alone with themselves, with each other, away from the eyes and ears of the CO and the Sergeant.

Victor Franko turned on his side and whispered, "Hey, Chief . . . you understand all that stuff he's been tellin us? You gonna scalp yourself one a them Generals?"

There was silence from the neighboring cot. Samson Posey was troubled by thoughts of this new thing he must do. It was one thing to go as a warrior . . . to fight bravely, kill or be killed by this enemy he didn't know . . . to seek out their leaders with the knife and the gun or his bare hands if necessary, for he understood about their evil . . . but it was another thing to sneak in the night as a thief and maybe kill a woman just to silence her. He was troubled, for this was a thing he had not expected. And yet the answer was there, was it not? Wasn't it said about the old days that the bravest of the warriors were not those who took the scalps of men in battle, but those who kidnaped or killed the women and children, for it meant they had entered the camp of their enemies where their strength was greatest. How much like the white man had he become . . . that he should forget this, that he should not know it and feel it in his heart and mind . . . that he worried it was not a warrior's task, that it would make him less of a man.

Victor Franko spoke again into the silence, "Well, maybe I'm gonna get me one . . . and maybe not."

Samson stirred in irritation. "What you mean?" he demanded.

"I'm just gonna think about it, that's all, Chief. I got ideas maybe." . . . to hold a knife to a General's throat, a gun to his belly and scream at him . . . Save my life, they're gonna hang me!

"Hey, Looey . . . I got me a hardon jus thinkin bout them Heinie girls," muttered Archer Maggot. "You know whut ahm gonna do if ah git me one . . . ahm gonna fuck er t' death be'fore ah kill er . . . an if'n it's a Frenchie ah'll jus do thuh same."

"You watch out, man . . . she gonna cut your cock off," answered Luis Jimenez gleefully.

"I mean I been in combat and I know what it is, Nappy," whispered Ken Sawyer. "You don't just attack a place and figure it's all going your way. You gotta protect yourself. You gotta have a way to pull out. All the CO talks about is going in."

From the other side of Napoleon's cot, Joe Wladislaw spoke softly. "Some a the other guys and me was sayin the same thing, Nappy. He ain't talked any yet about how we're getting back."

"What's the difference?" said Napoleon bluntly. "Maybe we're not supposed to. Maybe they figure it's better to let the Germans take care of us."

"But how about him . . . the CO?" protested Sawyer.

"Maybe he thinks he's immortal . . . maybe he wants to commit suicide . . . I don't know. We've got time. Let him work it out. Every day we get a little more of it."

Reisman was dissatisfied with the training. To stand around a model of Château de la Vilaine in the barracks and move little figures according to a plan was not enough. One night he took the books and games he had borrowed from Margot Strathallan many weeks before and distributed them among the men. He had ordered them into their German uniforms and full combat gear.

"Your assignment is to get into the manor house without disturbing the woman who lives there, and place these items in the library," he told them. "Nappy knows which room it is."

"What about that hound?" asked Glenn Gilpin.

"He's a German dog . . . I suppose he'd bite your head off if he caught you," said Reimsan. "But that's better than being caught by the Nazis, isn't it?" He was suddenly vexed by the memory of the time he had made a fool of himself by almost shooting the animal. "Don't get caught . . . and don't hurt him in any way . . . that's an order! Posey can gentle him down if he comes at you."

"How do we get in?" asked Calvin Ezra Smith.

"That's your problem. Any way you can . . . as long as the lady of the manor doesn't catch you."

"Don't worry . . . I'll get us in there all right," Roscoe Lever spoke up with relish. "It'll be a cinch."

"Keep your hands off the woman, Lever," warned Reisman. "All of you. We're too close to the pay-off to louse it up with a stiff prick."

"Hell, Captain I wouldn't try anything like that," retorted Lever. A quick image of the girl in the Birmingham jewelry shop flashed through his mind and he cursed silently.

"You did once before. That's why you're here," Reisman remarked.

Lever wore an ugly look as he went out the door, but Reisman knew the warning had been sufficient. They'd all keep a close eye on him—and each other.

Reisman called after them. "Nappy . . . better bring me Volume Two of Toynbee's *History* . . . just to prove you actually made it in there and didn't toss that stuff in the Channel."

Reisman and Bowren stayed behind in the stockade. The men were back in an hour. Napoleon handed Reisman the book sullenly. "I thought we'd learned to trust one another, Captain," he said, scowling.

"I do," replied Reisman. "But I don't intend getting careless either. How'd you get in?"

"Simple. Roscoe the second-story man picked the lock on the front door," said Napoleon. "I went in, did the foul deed and came out. The rest of them waited outside."

"How about the dog?"

"I could hear him kicking up a fuss upstairs . . . barking and scratching at a door, but he never came down."

"Tomorrow night, you take them back again," said Reis-

484

man. "I want a sketch of the layout inside the house. And I want every man to go into that building and bring back an item from a different room to prove he was there."

Lady Margot Strathallan stirred fitfully in her bed. The dog had begun to growl again, tearing her from the thin edge of sleep that allowed her mind to run wild but brought her no rest. She heard noises as she thought she had the night before when she had cowered in bed behind the locked door, unwilling even to open it to let Sigismund at the thing that excited his anger . . . telling herself it was only a figment of her imagination, born of her fears and isolation, and unwilling to find out it was not . . . or an incubus come to ravage her so she would no longer be worthy of her distant lover.

The dog barked loudly, pawed at the door. She called to him in a hoarse whisper to be silent, tried to soothe him so that she could separate the other night sounds. In desperation she rose from bed, put on a lamp, crouched fearfully beside him at the locked door, wrapped her bare arms tightly around his neck and squeezed his muzzle into trembling silence.

She heard footsteps, quick movements. But who? The Americans . . . the soldiers, filthy, bearded, ugly . . . their Captain. But no, he wouldn't dare! The Colonel had said they were leaving, their training was finished, they would be gone in just a few more days. They wouldn't dare break into her home like this! They wouldn't dare assault her! She heard running, whispered voices, doors opening and closing.

Terror gave way to fury. She released the dog. He threw himself at the door, flailed at it with his nails. She opened it, unable to cower there longer in uncertainty. The Doberman burst through with an angry snarl. Footsteps ran to her left in the dimly lit corridor, down the stairs. The dog bounded after them. Margot caught a flash of movement to her right. She turned . . . a fleeting glimpse of something . . . uniformed, helmeted . . . not the Americans, but a spectral shape of something remembered . . . an incubus conjured to her longing. She clutched her throat, knew terror and joy in the same moment, felt giddy . . . "Sigismund?" she called weakly to the shadows. She moved after it . . . opened doors into dark, silent rooms, pleading,

"Sigismund? Sigismund, is it you?" . . . heard the barking dog downstairs, the slam of the big front door suddenly cutting the sound, leaving it dim and protesting in the distance.

He was outside. Someone had opened the door and the dog was outside in the night. She was alone . . . attacked, invaded, defenseless . . . terror returned. She fled . . . down the stairs . . . tore at the great oaken door, flung it open and ran out into the night screaming, "Sigismund! . . . Sigismund!"

Samson Posey moved quickly. For an instant he had thought the woman was about to discover him. The others, clumsy in their movements, made too much noise. But now he came out of the room in which he had hidden and made his way swiftly into her bedroom. He was drawn to the nighttable on which the lamp was lit. There were books there, and he thought he might take one of those—then he saw the picture. He picked it up, peered at it curiously under the lamp, tucked it under his jacket and sped from the room.

Outside the big house, he met with the others. Each had some object to prove he had been there. As they made their way back to the stockade, they could still hear the sound of the barking dog and the woman calling after him.

Glenn Gilpin could hardly keep a straight face as he told Reisman how he and Myron Odell had decoyed the hound out of the manor house. "With them big damn sharp teeth a his getting ready to chomp on poor ole Pope's ass . . . man, it was a funny sight!" . . . and then how they skinned back inside and locked the dog out while two others on the outside took up the decoy according to plan, confusing the dog, leading him away from the building from man to man until each of them had managed to get back inside, steal something and add a few details to the rough sketch of the manor house Reisman now held in his hands.

They deposited on a table the items they had taken—an odd assortment of *objets d'art,* silverware, china, vases, paintings, books and clothing.

"German General," said Samson Posey proudly, displaying for them the framed photo.

Reisman took it and stared at it in wonder. It was a picture of a handsome young man in the uniform of a Lieutenant in the Nazi SS. He read the inscription, written in German, and the signature—Sigismund—and all at once so many puzzling and infuriating things about Lady Margot Strathallan fell into place.

"No, not a General, Posey," he murmured. "But almost as bad."

This then was her flaw . . . as he was flawed, as they all were flawed.

They were eating breakfast when Reisman heard a vehicle drive up. Sergeant Bowren opened the door and yelled back, "Trouble, Captain. It's Colonel Breed . . . and the woman from the manor house."

Reisman glanced around quickly. The men were in their regular fatigues. The German uniforms and weapons were out of sight and the model of the château covered. "Keep eating," he ordered. "Clyde, open the gate for them and show them into my office."

Margot hung back in the doorway. She was disheveled, her face haggard, her hair unkempt.

"Come in Lady Margot . . . please," Reisman said gently.

"Sigismund," she whispered hoarsely.

"Your dog?"

She shook her head.

"It's not the dog she's come for," Breed snapped. "We'll get to that in a moment. I want to know why you haven't broken camp yet, Reisman. Your two weeks are up today, you know."

Reisman closed the door and turned back to them. "We're not leaving, Colonel . . . not just yet anyway."

"Then you never intended to abide by our agreement," Breed accused.

"No, sir."

"I might have known. A man like you has no honor, Reisman. If it's the last thing I do in this Army, I'm going to see that you're court-martialed and your criminals go back to jail where they belong!" the Colonel exploded.

"Some things of Lady Margot's were stolen last night. Where are they?"

Reisman opened a footlocker. One by one he placed the items on the cot. Breed stared in angry disbelief.

"I intended returning them today in the same way they were borrowed. It was an exercise, Colonel," said Reisman finally as he rose from the footlocker with the framed photograph in his hand. "We got more than we figured on." He handed the picture to Breed. "I think you'd better tell the Colonel who this is," he said to Margot.

She leaped at it and grabbed it from Breed's hands, but not before his startled eyes had seen it and read the inscription.

"Sigismund," she whimpered, clutching the picture tightly to her.

"That's a German officer," said Breed. "Margot, who is he?"

She smiled and whispered, "My lover!"

"Your lover!" Breed echoed hoarsely, "My God!"

"Sigismund gave you his namesake, didn't he?" said Reisman.

"Oh yes . . . and that coat you admired . . . years ago in Germany. I went to school there . . . I fell in love with him . . . and all the wonderful things he was doing. Have you ever been to Germany, Captain? A lovely country. He was only a puppy then, and I had a terrible time bringing him home, but my father arranged it . . . only . . . only . . ." Whimpering, clutching the picture against her, she dissolved in tears on the cot. "Five years . . . five terribly long years," she sobbed. "And I've been good . . . so good . . . I've waited . . . and now . . . Oh my God, you're all going after him . . . don't hurt him . . . please don't kill him."

Colonel Breed rose heavily from the chair and walked up to her. He stared at her a moment, turned away and walked quickly from the room. Reisman went after him. The men at the tables gaped at them with more than idle curiosity, for they could not have helped but hear the commotion and wonder at it.

"I told you guys to eat, goddammit!" Reisman snapped. "Sergeant, get in there and stay with the lady till I get back."

Outside, the Colonel leaned against his staff car and

breathed deeply of the fresh air as though he had been strangling. "This place . . . this prison," he murmured, glaring at it with revulsion. "Damn you . . . and her . . . and your men . . . to have involved me like this . . . to have made a fool of myself."

"You involved yourself, Colonel!" Reisman said. "Why don't you accept the fact you're human like the rest of us?"

Breed stared at him.

"You were very wrong about Lady Margot," Reisman said. "Why can't you be just as wrong about my men? They've got a chance to redeem themselves, Colonel . . . with honor . . . the kind you prize . . . maybe with glory if they're lucky. Nobody has the right to take that chance away from them."

Breed said abruptly, "All right." It was neither defeat nor resignation. "I'll not say anything . . . to anyone . . . about anything." He hesitated a moment, asked, "What will you do about Lady Margot?"

"Nothing," said Reisman . . . and wondered that Breed was out of it already, absolved by himself of all responsibility, deferring it to him. "I'll see that she gets home all right. I don't think she represents any real danger to any of us . . . I mean from a security point of view. Her father would have said something. He wouldn't have allowed us to come . . . wouldn't have allowed her to stay on here all these years."

Breed smiled. "That's one on you, isn't it, Captain?" he said. "You're not infallible after all . . . you who make such a fetish of security . . . to have brought your men to train at Stokes Manor and risk exposure of your secrets to a woman in love with a Nazi officer." He started to get into the car, turned back and asked with concern, "Do you think she'll be all right?"

"Probably. She's done all right so far. She'll probably outlive both of us in good health, Colonel."

Breed looked past him at the blue sky over the English Channel. "Good Invasion weather," he said. "It won't be long now. In a way that makes life simpler, doesn't it, Reisman?"

He got into the car and drove off.

33

OSTERMAN FINALLY telephoned from London on May 20.

"Where the hell you been, Sarge?" Reisman asked edgily. "We could have been in Berlin by now."

"I didn't figure you was goin anywhere yet."

"How do you know?"

"Oh, I get around, I hear things," said Osterman. "Look, kid, I'm sorry it took so long. I'm available any time you want me now. While I was up in Scotland I went by that pro station in Glasgow again and followed up a few guys for Odell. Nothing . . . drew a blank all around. There's only one more thing I can figure. Like I said before, let's take the boy up there. Maybe it'll settle something for him, maybe it won't."

Reisman looked at the calendar. He would be cutting the time pretty thin. "How about Friday, the twenty-sixth?" he asked.

It was a long trip north to Glasgow—slowed and stopped and shunted for troop and equipment trains moving ever south—and Odell had many hours to think of what had gone before, what was now, and what he had to do. He watched the trains with fascination through the compartment window, sometimes feeling as if he were swimming the wrong way against a powerful, unending tide.

The Captain and his friend Sergeant Osterman, whom Odell now knew was a CID agent, sat across from him. They read newspapers and magazines, as he tried to do; they dozed, they talked with each other softly so he couldn't hear, but had little to say to him. He knew where he was going, knew what was expected of him, knew that both men were putting themselves way out on a limb to help him, even if it only meant he would find some peace of mind at last. He didn't think anybody in the whole damn Army could have a CO as good as Reisman.

When the CID agent had taken him from the stockade that morning, the Captain hadn't been there. Odell had been handcuffed to the car and felt dirty, small, criminal, despite the neat OD uniform he was wearing, the polished jump boots on his feet and the paratrooper wings proud on his chest. Leaving the car at the railroad station in Marston-Tyne—and coming that close to the prison again had made him agitated, made him want to run—Osterman had locked their wrists together, and despite the raincoat he had draped casually over the handcuffs, Odell had felt awful and worried what people would think. Then the Captain had met them in Marston-Tyne, where he'd apparently stayed overnight. He had peeked under the coat and said there was no need for that, and Odell had been very grateful.

He wondered what it would be like to be really free again, what he would do with himself if he was, if he had the freedom of choice. He envied the strangers who sat in the compartment with them—men and women, military and civilian, who came and went all through the long trip —and he was glad the Captain had decided it would be quicker for them to go by train. He liked being with other people again, engaging in small talk, or wondering in silence about their lives and feeling an ambivalent mixture of pride and anguish that they didn't really know about him, that they didn't know and he couldn't ever tell them the things he had done, the things he had accomplished these last months, the agony he was going through now, the mixture of hope, frustration and fear, the things he might have to do soon—if the results of this trip changed nothing for him, brought no new facts out of the darkest recesses of his mind, presented to the Captain, the CID man and the Army no reason to believe he was truly Innocent.

His mood fluctuated wildly.

Between Gloucester and Liverpool, a young mother and her two little boys shared their compartment, and Odell was made very nervous at first by her sitting next to him, by the smell of her, the occasional involuntary touch caused by the rocking car, the terrible awareness of her very presence so close to him. He sweated, felt terribly constricted in the close compartment, and little waves of nausea toyed with him.

The woman was plain, her clothing dark and sturdy, as well-worn as it was worn well, brushed and pressed for the trip as she herself was. Her little boys—and there was unbidden envy, admiration, wonder and pain here, too, for Odell—wore new navy-blue short-pants suits, white shirts and small red ties, and she clutched their little blue caps in her lap with her bag and other paraphernalia of travel, keeping her legs tightly together in a stiff and uncomfortable position so as not to impose upon Odell.

It was the little boys who made things easier for him, made him feel better after a short while. They were talkative, eager, excited by their trip. The older one, no more than seven, tired of sitting quiet and reading, stood up and started to thread his way past his mother among the legs in the narrow aisle, toward the window. He stopped in front of Odell, looked up at him and smiled. "Hello. Are you a Yank?" he asked.

"Yes," Odell said, smiling back at him.

The boy came closer, peered at the paratrooper's wings and asked, "What's that?"

His mother leaned over, making Odell flatten back away from her. "Hush now, David," she said. "You leave the gentleman alone." She smiled at Odell apologetically.

"That's all right, ma'am," he said desperately. He looked to Reisman for help and saw him nod approval.

The little boy was fingering the wings.

"That's a paratrooper's emblem," said Odell.

"My daddy is a sailor. He's gone away to fight the Boche," said the boy gravely. "Our house was bombed. Tell me about America."

He squeezed back onto the seat between his mother and Odell, and through the boy, Odell soon found himself talking in a relaxed way to the mother. She was shy, but very pleasant, and the way she looked at him and talked to him —sort of admiringly for being a young American soldier, and gratefully for the attention he paid her son—made Odell feel a man, took away from him the remaining vestige of nervousness at her proximity, and made his heart go out to her.

When the young mother and her boys were leaving, she offered Odell her hand and said, "God bless you!" and the warmth and spontaneity of it brought a tightening to his throat, fed an old, old longing, made him want to go with her, and left him with a terrible loneliness and nameless nostalgia when she was gone.

And alone, he thought again of what had gone before, what was now and what he had to do. And he worried about what had been written in the envelope Sergeant Osterman gave the Captain at the Marston-Tyne station . . . "Bowren said it was left at the mail drop yesterday by a dispatch rider, so it's probably important" . . . Reisman had read it quickly while Odell searched his face for some clue to what it said, sensing it affected him very personally in some way he would want to know about, disappointed when Reisman merely said impassively, "We're just getting this in under the gun."

It was night when they reached Glasgow, and Odell felt the terrible anxiety building in him again. Why were they taking him here? Why were they playing with him like this, like that Captain Kinder and his psychological tricks? What was he supposed to remember? Maybe he didn't want to. Hadn't he told them everything already . . . to the MPs, the police, the court-martial, Captain Reisman . . . he was Innocent.

They took a cab from the station after having a quick supper. Odell gave the directions and they got out a block away from the VD clinic. "It's the busy time," he said bitterly as they stood across the street watching the men enter and leave.

"You understand what we want you to do . . . why we're letting you go in alone?" Reisman asked.

"Yes, sir . . . I think so, sir," Odell said anxiously. "You want me to go in, look around . . . see if I can reconstruct in my own mind what happened that night. How long should I stay?"

Osterman answered that. "Fifteen . . . twenty minutes . . . till you get the feel of the place. Let it all come back to you. Then you come out and we all go in and talk it over."

Odell hesitated, glanced at Reisman once more.

"Go ahead, Mike," the Captain urged. "It takes guts to face something like this again . . . maybe more than it took to parachute . . . maybe more than it'll take for combat. You want to try it, don't you?"

Odell took a deep breath, tried to stand taller. He liked it when the Captain called him Mike. He had never really liked the name Myron. "Yes, sir. Very much, sir," he said, and walked quickly across the street.

His heart pounded so heavily his chest hurt, and he could hardly focus his eyes as he entered the familiar front room of the pro station and closed the door behind him. There were a few soldiers there waiting, joking with each other. The medical attendant stuck his head out of one of the treatment rooms, gave Odell a quick glance and told him to sit down and wait his turn. Odell was thankful he didn't know the man.

His eyes moved slowly around until they fixed on the closed door of the room where he had hidden the girl that terrible night. He started as the door opened. A soldier came out, walked past and left the clinic. Odell rose as in a trance and moved to the threshold of the open room, took in the plain white walls, the steel cot where she had sprawled naked, the table of prophylaxis equipment, the first aid cabinet with medicines, bandages, surgical scissors and knives.

Trembling, sweat-damp, cold, he turned and bolted down the corridor to the rear door. His fingers clawed in terror at the heavy latch bar, he raised it and fled away through the darkness of the alley. And as he escaped through the fog-gloomed back alleys and streets of Glasgow, he knew this was what he had to do, this was what he had intended to do—and having done it, he was glad, he was exhilarated by his daring, he was strong.

He thumbed a ride east with an Air Corps gasoline truck on the Edinburgh road. Why east, he didn't know . . . where he would go, he didn't know . . . but he had to get away from Glasgow . . . he had to be free for a least a little while . . . to do the things he had to do . . . to think the thoughts he had to think, unfettered. He thought of London, but it was too far. He thought of the young mother on the train who'd been so nice to him, who'd looked so lonely, and if he knew her address he knew he'd go to her. Where did one go? How did someone like him begin? He was ashamed to ask the truck driver.

At Coatbridge he hopped from the truck and went south. Why south, he didn't know . . . except he didn't want to go too long in one direction, in case they were following him. He had to cover his trail, fool them, find a haven where he could stop, do what he had to do. All Friday night and most of Saturday he was out on the roads. Lanark, Moffat, Carlisle, steadily south, undirected yet directed. He didn't eat, though he was hungry. He didn't rest, though he was tired. The military traffic was heavy, there was always a ride for a GI, particularly if he was going south. Penrith, Lancaster, MPs on the road at Stafford unsnarling and directing convoys, and he leaped from the back of the weapons carrier and fled across a field, knowing he was vulnerable, could be easily picked up in a spot check for IDs and passes, for he had neither. He made it into Birmingham on foot Saturday night, his eyes skittish for MP patrols and city police, and suddenly he knew this would have to be where he made his stand. He asked a civilian for directions to the nearest American service club.

It was a big place, crowded, hundreds of guys passing through the lobby, looking for a bed in the cot-crammed dormitories, looking for a shower and shave, a place to read and write, a bit of recreation, a rendezvous, a guided tour. Odell loitered in the lobby, looking for an identity, amazed at the brashness of his idea.

He figured he should get a paratrooper, so his own boots and wings wouldn't look out of place with a new ID and pass, but he knew he couldn't wait too long. He had to do it before he lost his nerve, before they found him. He settled on a guy in a group of artillerymen carrying little overnight bags, registering for a cot, telling the lady behind the desk they wanted to shower and shave and leave their things before going out on the town. The man was the right height and weight and looked a little like him, and wore no visible sign of rank.

Odell followed them into the big latrine and started to get undressed to make it look good, watching where the soldier hung his things in an open locker. He waited until the guy and his buddies disappeared into the steamy shower room, then moved quickly.

He didn't check the wallet until he got outside again and was moving quickly away from the service club. He felt guilty, but curiously satisfied, too, that necessity had bred action. The soldier was a Private. Besides an ID and pass, there was money in the wallet, and Odell stopped in a restaurant and had his first meal since the railroad station in Glasgow the night before. It was nice sitting there, ordering food and drink and being waited on. He almost bolted out the door when an MP patrol came in and started checking the servicemen, but he sweated it out, even when one of the MPs told him he had no right to be wearing paratrooper boots and wings if he was an artilleryman.

"I've got the right," Odell replied brazenly. "I took my training. I'm qualified. I'm entitled to wear them. I got transferred out when I was hurt. Hell, I was even in the medics once," he said, showing them the trim on his old cap.

When they asked him why he wasn't wearing any insignia or fruit salad for a guy who'd been around so much, he said, with a cocky grin, "Because I'm modest." His stolen papers were in order, though, so they left him alone and he finished his dinner, knowing he'd never have been able to bullshit his way through something like this if it hadn't been for Captain Reisman. Thinking of him, thinking of the other guys, he felt guilty, wondered what they were doing—then he forced himself not to think of them anymore.

Outside again, he hailed a taxi. He knew that much. The barracks cocksmen always said if you wanted to find a woman in a strange town always ask a cab driver. In fact, he'd met guys who'd said they'd done it right in a cab in places like London—but Odell knew he could never do anything like that.

"Where to, Yank?"

Odell made his voice sound strong, confident, knowing. "Where's all the excitement in this town, Mac? Where does a guy go for some fun?"

"We've got some clubs and theaters and cinemas and that sort of thing. Is that what you're after?"

"As a starter, sure. Take me to one of those night clubs where there's entertainment . . . and girls."

On the way, he struggled with how to say what was on his mind. Hey, Mac, where do I go to get laid . . . where do I find some . . . poontang . . . quail . . . like all the other guys? My God, where do I find a woman who will help me! But when he could finally bring himself to blurt it out, it was a nervous, "Sir . . . where do you think I might find a woman? You know . . ."

The driver half-turned and grinned. "Why didn't you say so, Yank? Cost you a pound now."

Odell leaned forward and handed him the money. The driver turned down a side street away from the bright, busy entertainment district. "There's a few old mopsies I

496

can put you onto," said the driver cheerily, falling into the spirit of the thing. "And a few young ones, too," he added, laughing. "How do you like em, Yank? Short . . . tall . . . skinny . . . plump . . . red . . . dark . . . I'm afraid I don't know any blondes."

Odell was glad it was dark in the cab and the driver couldn't see his face. "Someone a little older, I think," he said hesitantly . . . and then threw off the pose of bravado. It might work with other things, but he didn't feel it with this. "No . . . not a young girl," he mused, whispering it so the driver could barely hear him. "Someone not beautiful, but pleasant to look at . . . someone gentle . . . not eager, not demanding, but willing . . . someone who will be nice . . ." Someone who would help him do what he had to do, so he could know at last this thing that gnawed at his guts . . . so he could live . . . so he could die . . . for how could he face his death now without experiencing this, without knowing . . .

The driver pulled to the curb and peered into the darkness at him. "I know someone," he said. "A fine old girl . . . though not so old as that. How much money do you have?"

Odell handed him everything in the wallet but a pound note. He could steal more later if he needed it, he knew. The driver took some of it, gave the rest back. "This'll be more than enough for her," he said. "Wait here."

He disappeared into a building of cheap flats, and in those minutes waiting for him, Odell fought the urge to flee. The driver reappeared and opened the door for him. "It'll be all right now, Yank," he said. "She's expecting you. Second floor, back. A good girl . . . nice as your own mother, if you'll pardon me."

She opened the door to his knock, peering curiously from the lighted room into the darker hallway. "Come in, Yank," she said, smiling.

Thank God she had clothes on, Odell thought as he walked hesitantly into the flat. Thank God they were alone . . . it wasn't public . . . it wasn't one of those whorehouses with sloppy women lying all around . . . with piano players and raucous, leering, drunken men . . . and everybody knowing why you were there and what you were going to do.

She turned from the closed door and looked at him uncertainly. Odell's heart pounded like a triphammer, he felt the pain stronger in his groin. His eyes darted over the cheap furnishings, the floor, the lamps, the ceiling, the landscape prints on the papered walls of the sitting room, and he forced himself to think of those things.

"Let me take your hat," she said, coming toward him.

Odell started to back away, felt his head spinning, thought of running out the door, and it took a giant surge of will to keep him rooted there and stop his trembling. She took the damp, twisted cap from his sweating hand. There was a strong smell of sweet perfume emanating from her. Her face was plain, a little puffy with plumpness, though her skin was smooth. Her powder, rouge and lipstick seemed freshly put on. She was a woman in her late thirties, he figured.

"I'm Mrs. Barnes . . . but you call me Nora now," she said gaily. "What's your name, Yank?"

"Myr—Mike Odell," he said hoarsely, too late to pull it back and give the name on his stolen ID. He wondered if there was a Mister Barnes and where he was.

His eyes followed her as she moved away from him to put his cap on top of a cabinet. She had heavy breasts and he was glad for that, and broad hips and buttocks. He sucked in his breath thinking of them full under the cheap cotton print.

She turned back to him chattering away that she'd just been on her way out when her friend stopped by to say he had a nice young Yank looking for company . . . "That's a nice name . . . Mike Odell. Sounds Irish. Are you Irish, Mike?"

"I don't know."

She laughed. "You don't know?"

"No, ma'am. You see I never knew my mother and father. That's just my name. I don't really know who I am. In fact, my name isn't Mike, at all . . . it's Myron."

"Myron," she repeated musically, extending the vowels and hitting the consonants hard. "That's a lovely name. I like it better."

He brightened at that, felt more comfortable with her, and he came almost to the point of relaxing when she shook her head sadly and said, "No mother and father . . . you poor boy. And here you are fighting for your country . . . and ours, too. What a brave lad you must be." She came close to him and pressed her lips to his cheek. "There now . . . Nora will make you happy, if

498

that's what you want." She took his hand and started to lead him toward another room. "Come see the rest of my flat," she said proudly. "I keep it nice. You'll like it here, I'm sure. And we've got the whole night ahead for the two of us now that you're here. There'll be no going out and rushing about for me . . . and I can tell you I wasn't much looking forward to that sort of night, Myron."

Odell held back, making her turn and look at him again uncertainly. He said, "Can I go out and get you something, Mrs. Barnes? A bottle of whisky maybe . . . or something to eat?"

She smiled at him, and he sensed she understood his nervousness, and he blessed her for it silently.

"You call me Nora now, Myron," she said. "Not Mrs. Barnes. That's only a name . . . like yours. It doesn't mean anything. I've had my supper, thank you. But if it's a drink you want, I've got a bit of brandy here. No need to go out. Will that do?"

"Oh yes, thank you . . . I'd like that."

Odell dropped into a chair, his nerves fluttering, making himself sit up stiffly and look calm when she came to him with the glass and the bottle. He gulped the first drink quickly. She smiled and poured again. "Have another," she said, but as he lifted the glass she put her fingers over his mouth and said, "Slowly . . . It'll be all right . . . Don't you get drunk now, Myron." She winked, put the bottle on a table near him and sat in another chair. He took just one sip of the brandy this time, then held the glass tightly, stared into it so as not to look at her, felt the heat of the first drink spread out from his belly, diffuse through his limbs, calm his nerves. He stole a glance at her, and she smiled. She was so nice, he thought.

"Go on and tell me about yourself if you'd like, Myron," she said. "A lot of the boys like to talk a bit first . . . that's all right. Some of them want to talk more than anything . . . and that's all right too." She laughed heartily at herself. "Some of them even tell me I remind them of their mother. What do you think of that, Myron? What an awful thing to say to a girl, isn't it?"

"Oh, yes . . . No, I mean . . . I'd never tell you that," agreed Odell quickly.

She leaned back, hummed a tune, drummed her fingers on the arm of her chair. Odell took another small sip from his glass, met her eyes, looked back into the brandy, and with great effort he began to speak, very softly so that she had to lean toward him to catch his words. "You must understand, Mrs. Barnes . . . Nora," he said. "There is something I have to do . . . I'm not what you think I am . . . I can't tell you . . . I'm a virgin," he blurted out. "I don't know . . . I can't . . ."

"There now . . . that's all right, Myron," she said, coming to him. She kneeled, put her hands on his knees and looked into his face. "I was once, too, you know."

He trembled at her touch, felt the pain spread out of his groin, and to fight the anguish, the terror that gripped him, the shame, the unknown of past and future, his mind reached out and grabbed desperately at those things of strength and daring he'd accomplished these last months . . . this last day. He felt her fingers at his chest, playing with his paratrooper's badge.

"Are you really one of those jumpers?" she asked with something of awe in her voice.

"Yes I am," Odell said proudly.

"Then there's nothing in the world I'd think you'd be afraid of," she said, looking at him with genuine admiration that made his heart swell. "You'll be just fine. I know you will, Myron." She took his hand and tugged him lightly to his feet. "Come on now. Take your drink, if you'd like. Let me show you the best part of the flat. I keep it quite nice in there . . . real cozy."

He went with her, she leading him like a little boy by the hand, and he liked that, clung to her. There was a lamp on beside the bed. He hardly saw the room, but he said, his voice breaking, "Yes, it's very nice," and staggered, heart thumping uncontrollably, back into the sitting room to the chair, where he drained his glass again.

She stood in the doorway and looked at him with disappointment on her face. "Don't you like me?" she asked . . .

And in a terrible instant hardly recorded he saw the idiot girl in the pro station . . . heard her voice . . . Cat-the-rine . . . Cat-the-rine . . . Cat . . . Cat . . . You like me, Mahh-run? . . . Come here . . . love Cat . . . Mahh-run's afraid . . . And he shuddered, squeezed shut his eyes, opened them again to see the woman in the doorway . . .

"Oh yes . . . yes, very much," he said, his voice too loud, freeing himself from the apparition.

The woman smiled, started toward him.

"No . . . please . . . don't . . . stay there . . . I want to just look at . . . I'd like to just look at you . . . without any clothes on," he said agitatedly.

"That's all?"

"I don't know."

"Well now, sonny . . . I'm not much to look at if that's what you want," she said coolly.

"Yes, you are," he said with sudden strength, panicky that she wouldn't. "You're very nice . . . you're very beautiful."

She warmed to him again. "All right," she murmured almost shyly.

She disappeared into the bedroom and Odell wanted to run after her, scream at her No, not there where I can't see you! . . . I must see you and know what a woman is like! But she was back in a moment, her dress off, standing in the doorway in a slip, bending to her stockings, not looking at him, as though he wasn't there, and that was good, that was the way he wanted it, as long as she didn't touch him and make worse the burning pain in his hardened genitals, that mocked and taunted him, that conjured and made real the old shock, the old nightmares and fears.

He peeked quickly, deliciously, guiltily, at legs, knees, pale fleshy thighs, bare arms, shoulders, neck, breasts cleft deeply and hardly contained, and then she was gone, back into the bedroom, leaving him trembling, giving him a moment's respite. He heard her struggling with a garment, heard it snap against her skin, heard the bed creak as she sat on it and got up, and she was in the doorway, her slip bunched down around her hips, reaching with both hands back to the catch on her brassière.

Odell looked away, squeezed his legs tightly, looked back and gasped at the revelation of white, swinging, heavy breasts. She glanced at him and he dropped his eyes, ashamed.

"It's all right. Look at me. I want you to," she said. "Do you like me now?"

He looked up, not at her face, but at the darker swelling of her nipples, trying to see if they were hard and pointed like the barracks cocksmen said. He couldn't tell. He got up, trembling. "Stay there . . . please," he pleaded, moving toward her. Oh God, how he wanted to put his mouth on them. He bent, touched his lips to her skin, rolled his cheeks against her gently with a moan, squeezed his face into the cool mound of flesh, worked his way down, and then she, sensing what he wanted, lifted one breast from beneath with her hand and fed the nipple into his mouth.

He clung to her for what seemed eons of unbelievable happiness but could only have been seconds, felt her hand in his hair, pressing him tightly to her, heard her murmuring gentle, loving things in his ear, felt her lead him into the room, ease them both down onto the bed. Then she slipped his glasses off—"They hurt," she explained—and he knew he had to take command and she had to do things his way or it would all get out of hand, way beyond what he was ready for.

He drew away from her reluctantly. "Give me my glasses," he said.

"You don't really need them for this, sonny."

"I do. I want to look at you. I can't see you without them."

He put them on and asked, "Do you think I'm funny-looking?"

"No, Myron . . . of course not. I think you're quite handsome."

He blessed her again for understanding him and being nice and doing as he wanted, and excused her for calling him sonny, twice now, though he didn't like it, but if she did it, all right, for he didn't want to offend her, didn't want to risk spoiling this, didn't trust himself with anything resembling resentment or anger. He got up and tilted the lamp shade so the light shone full on her, and brought another lamp close to the bed.

"What are you doing?" she asked anxiously.

"I want to see you. Take that off," he said urgently.

She raised her hips and struggled off the twisted slip that had bunched between her navel and thighs. And hidden behind the lamps like an audience in the semidarkness of a theater—with Mrs. Nora Barnes the star-mother-sister-girl-friend-teacher-supervisor-whore-wife of his nightmares and dreams—Myron Odell sucked in his breath and searched with hungry, joyous, blood-pounding, guilty wonder her total, awesome nakedness.

And when he had examined at a distance very inch of her, every mound and hollow and orifice and secret, the knowledge and strength grew in him that he was born of a woman like this and it was all right now because he was going back there and he knew where he came from, he

502

could see that now and he never had before, and this made him so glad he didn't even mind anymore that he was maybe going to die.

He went to her still fully clothed, leaned over her on the bed, touched her flesh now warm and damp here and there, followed with gentle, wondrous, probing, kneading motions those mounds and flats and hollows of her body, and ran his fingers carefully, uncertainly into her orifices and secrets, while she squirmed and twisted, moved to him and away, and moaned with pleasure, "Oh, my God, you're marvelous, sonny . . . Myron . . . You've got it all backward . . . It's I that's to be giving you pleasure . . . Don't stop!"

Odell felt an enormous power, a control over her that he hadn't expected, that it was she who wanted and not the other way around, the way it had always been—and he was exhilarated!

"Take your clothes off, Myron!" she gasped. "Now . . . please . . . get undressed!"

The woman sensed his fear, and controlling herself with great effort, she took his hands from her, kissed his fingers and asked, "What is it you fear, Myron? I'm clean . . . I'm all right."

Odell sat on the bed, squeezing his thighs together tightly, shaking his head in anguish, letting her hold his hands, run them over her breasts again.

"Is it women you fear? Don't be afraid, Myron. You're strong . . . brave . . . good." She stood up and eased him gently down onto the pillows, speaking softly, reassuringly, caressing his face and neck with her fingers. She bent and kissed him full on the lips, ran her tongue into his mouth, around his tongue, along his cheeks and teeth, and now he moaned as she had moaned, reached for the great white breasts hanging over him, found safety, happiness with one in his mouth, while her fingers busied themselves about his clothes.

She was undressing him. Oh my God, she was undressing him. Exposing him. And yet she was gentle, unhurried, woman soft, mother careful.

"Relax," she whispered, breathing heavily, easing the trousers from his legs. "Let me do everything." Her clever fingers were a caress. "Oh my God, you're wonderful," she said, bending and kissing him there.

"It hurts . . . it hurts something awful," Odell gasped.

She saw the agonized look on his face, the tightly closed eyes, the clenched fists. "What does?"

"There!" he said, pointing. "It hurts so bad . . . I can't . . . I was hurt there once."

"In the war?" she said with sudden understanding and compassion.

"No . . . long before . . . when I was a boy. A doctor told me it was all in my mind, but it isn't. It's there . . . it hurts . . . I can't . . . I'm sorry, Nora . . . I can't."

From behind his closed lids, his pain-and-fear-muted consciousness, he heard her saying, soothing cooing, "Oh no boy, no boy no . . . You just lie there and don't move . . . don't say anything . . . don't think about it . . . I'll do everything . . . You'll love it, Myron . . . I know you'll love it . . . I'm good . . . I'm very good . . . You'll love it . . ." And he felt the bed move and creak and spring as she got back up onto it with him, and felt the un-believable ecstasy of warmth and wetness as she slid her-self up and down on him, up and down on him . . . and the old pain left him and an excruciating new one flooded over him, mounting and mounting, making him gasp and moan and thrash and thrust his hips and claw full fingers of her buttocks as she exhorted him, pleaded, "Keep it up, keep it up, hoo boy, keep it up!" and it was the fear that sustained him, held him back, kept him from letting go, kept him in control, kept him from going off as she lum-bered her weight up and down, thundered her flesh against him, driving him on . . . "You're good, you're good . . . hoo boy . . . Oh, Myron, you're good . . . the others come off so quick I never know they're there . . . but you're good . . . so good . . . aieeeyaaaaaa!" As he let himself go, felt the waves of orgasm sweep him to con-quest over shame and fear and pain and battle and death, Myron Odell came in a burst of exquisite glory.

By mid-morning Sunday he had swaggered his way fifty miles farther south to Gloucester. The church he entered— for this, too, had been part of his plan to prepare himself for whatever came after—seemed almost an anticlimax to the cathedral he had invested the night before. It was a beautiful old church, and sitting alone in a back pew, between the times of the Masses, he absorbed the stones and wood and saints and Jesus himself up there on the cross, and the grand organ music and the sweet holy smell and peace of the place into his flesh and bones and nerves, for he was unboundedly happy this morning and loved the world. And in a mood compounded of obeisance, gratitude and self-satisfaction, he relived in pleasurable, exhilarating detail the thing that had happened to him—no, the thing that he, himself, had made happen, and over and over again he murmured to himself, as though reciting a Rosary, I've been laid, I've been laid, I've been laid.

He asked for a priest to hear his Confession . . . "Bless me, Father, for I have sinned," he murmured by rote, and with barely reined joy, he ran through a proud accounting of what he had done the night before . . .

"And not only the first time, sir . . . Father, I mean . . . although that in itself was so much more than I thought God would ever grant me. And he didn't punish me. No, he rewarded me. I desired sensuality. Yes . . . yielded gladly . . . relished the pleasures of the flesh . . . and it was like the laying on of the hands I've heard about Jesus . . . this terrible pain . . . this terrible physical pain here in . . . in my privates . . . and not only the physical pain, but the mental anguish of years . . . gone suddenly . . . all gone, sir . . . Father. And I mean suddenly I was free of it and I was a man. And I slept like a baby . . . like a baby's supposed to sleep, they say, but I never knew, because when I was a baby I didn't have any mother and father and I don't think I ever slept like that. And then when I woke up and I realized what I'd done and where I was and she was there and the pain was all gone and . . . and I wanted her again . . . right then and there I did . . . and this time, knowing where everything went, how it was done, I went at it manfully . . . and she wanted that, Father, and I wanted it . . . and afterward I felt calm and wonderful. And then again later. Three times during the night, Father. And then I gave her all the rest of my money . . . you see, sir, it really wasn't my money anyway . . . and there I sinned . . . I know I sinned there . . . but I had to, and you don't know about that because that's another story and I can't tell you about that . . . not even you . . . and I gave her all that money because she was so good to me, and she didn't even want it, and I made her take it because where I'm going I won't need any money and like I said, it wasn't really my money anyway, and I kept only a pound of it . . . and I want to give that to the church, Father . . . I want to put that in the collection plate because I won't be needing it and I want to make it my offering . . . and I didn't eat this morning . . . I've been traveling since dawn and I didn't eat because I just had to confess and receive Communion because it may be the last time I can do it. And something else, too, Father . . . you see I'm Innocent . . . I know I'm Innocent now . . . and that may sound stupid to you for a guy to confess he's Innocent, and I can't even tell you what I'm innocent of . . . but, you see, all this time they've been saying I was guilty and I'd done something real bad, and I never knew for sure because I had these blackouts where I wouldn't know what happened . . . and I had one that time when they said I was guilty, but I didn't think I could do anything that terrible and I kept telling them I was Innocent but nobody would believe me . . . but now I'm sure because I got through what I did last night and it was good and wonderful, even if you say it's a sin, Father . . . and I didn't black out and I didn't hurt Nora . . . and I just don't see how I could have done it another time like they say . . . And there's more, Father . . . so much more . . . It would take me days to confess . . . maybe years . . . I don't know . . . It goes all the way back to when I was a boy . . . I haven't been to Mass . . . I haven't been to Confession . . . And that's all now, Father, because I've got to go now or I'll be in even worse trouble . . . I know what I have to do to make it right . . ."

Odell heard a deep sigh of understanding from behind the screen . . . a gentle question asking if he was feeling well . . . a sympathetic concern about his physical, mental and spiritual health . . . and a firm, but tactful urging that he seek the immediate aid of a doctor or his Commanding Officer . . .

"Oh, I'm fine, Father . . . just fine," he insisted. "Yes, sir, I'll talk to my Commanding Officer just like you say . . . I'll see him just as soon as I get back. But what's my penance? . . . so I can go to Communion. It's been a long time, Father. I want to very much. I need to. I may not have the chance again."

He was surprised at the lightness of his penance—to say five Our Fathers and five Hail Marys. And as the voice behind the screen began to cleanse him . . . "May our Lord Jesus Christ absolve thee . . ." Odell began to recite in counterpoint, with great feeling, his Act of Contrition . . .

"O my God, I am heartily sorry for having offended Thee, and I detest all my sins because I dread the loss of heaven and the pains of hell . . ."

He said his penance, stayed for Mass, received Holy Communion, put his last pound into the collection plate, and took to the roads again heading south.

Through the day and into the night, driven by something now that was larger than himself, he walked, trotted, ran and hitchhiked. And with him and around him moved the endless convoys of olivedrab trucks crammed with troops and guns and munitions and fuel moving to the southern coast of England; and the fields bloomed, not with greenery, but with the huge camouflaged dumps of military stores; and on the roadsides, mile after mile of camouflaged tanks and heavy artillery and weapons carriers and ammunition caissons roared to life; treads clanked ponderously, moved faster, merged into the massive streams. And Odell wanted to be part of it, in the vanguard with Captain Reisman and the Dirty Dozen. Innocent or not, he didn't care. He didn't want to be left out of this biggest thing that was happening or likely to happen in the world in his lifetime.

—

34

—

REISMAN WASN'T at all glad to see Stuart Kinder arrive at the stockade Monday morning. He'd had the wild idea that if only Kinder stayed away until after they had taken off, everything would somehow turn out all right in the days remaining, or it wouldn't make any difference anyway. Yet he had known Kinder was coming down from London to shepherd them from Stokes Manor, and there had been no way to head him off. The dispatch Leon Osterman had given him in the railroad station at Marston-Tyne had been from Kinder. It had placed him and the Dirty Dozen on alert. They were to prepare to leave Stokes Manor on Wednesday, May 31, fully equipped for their mission, to camp at the airfield at Colonel Breed's post.

Kinder was in the barracks more than half an hour,

watching Reisman and the men run through their attack plan for him with the model of Château de la Vilaine, before he sensed the worse-than-usual edginess in Reisman's voice and manner and it finally hit him that there were only eleven prisoners there.

"Where's Myron Odell?" he asked anxiously.

The men looked at him in stony silence. They knew Odell was gone, but they didn't know why or how or where. Reisman had told them nothing. Some suspected the worst—that Odell had been taken back to prison for execution, although they couldn't understand why; a few thought he had escaped, which they could hardly believe, and which made them mad—that he'd had the nerve to do it and they hadn't, and that he'd left them in the lurch at this late date.

Reisman took Kinder into the office, closed the door and told him what had happened—about Leon Osterman, about the unauthorized trip to Glasgow, and how they had waited half an hour outside the pro station before going in and discovering that Odell had escaped through the back door.

Osterman had run down the alley and back, angrily shouting, "Son-of-a-bitch! He's cut out. Ungrateful bastard! I'll get out an alert immediately. MPs, CID, city police, Scotland Yard . . . the works. He won't be loose more'n a coupla hours." He had reached for the phone on the medic's desk but Reisman had stopped him.

Kinder exclaimed, "My God! Why? This can compromise and destroy the entire plan . . . our months of work! What are you doing about it, John?"

"Nothing. Osterman's still out looking for him on his own. I've been in touch with him every day since. Not a trace . . . and I suppose we ought to give the little bastard credit for that," he said with a touch of curious pride. "Anything official would have caused a big stink. After all, we were a party to his escape. If it got out, maybe it would kill the whole operation. The search has to be made quietly . . . keeping the inquiries discreet. If anybody can do it, Osterman can."

"What if he isn't found?" demanded Kinder. "I've got to report it, John. We can't just leave him wandering around loose. He knows too much."

"You don't have to report it to anybody, Stu," Reisman

insisted. "I don't know why Odell ran off . . . but he isn't going to blab about Project Amnesty. It would be his finish. ¿Quién sabe? Maybe he was scared stiff of what's ahead . . . maybe he was really innocent and this was his way out for a while, to try and prove it on his own . . . maybe he realized up there he really was guilty, or maybe he knew it all along and was just waiting for a chance to make a break."

"No, he really believed in his innocence," said Kinder. "He couldn't have fooled me. Not with all the time I spent talking to him . . . testing him." He shook his head in disbelief. "Of all the guys in that bunch, he was the last one I would have thought would try to escape."

"Maybe," said Reisman pensively. But what he didn't say was that during these few days he had felt a curious sense of relief—that guilty or innocent, Myron Odell had taken his fate into his own hands and would work out his own destiny.

They were dismantling the barbed wire fences late in the morning, with Reisman and Kinder supervising the work parties, when Reisman heard a shout from Sergeant Bowren on top of the barracks roof. Bowren had put on his guns again and gone back on guard duty after Reisman had returned early Saturday morning without Odell and told him what happened.

The Sergeant had his submachine gun trained on something coming out of the wood facing the front of the barracks, and Reisman and Kinder raced around to see what it was. Reisman's heart leaped. "Son-of-a-bitch . . . look!" he exclaimed.

When Kinder could get his jaw working again, he muttered, "The return of the prodigal."

Myron Odell, exhausted, disheveled, dirty, stood there with his hands over his head in acknowledgment of Bowren's command, but with a triumphant look on his face. Reisman frisked him quickly, found only the stolen wallet.

"I'd like to send that back to the guy that owns it, sir," said Odell sheepishly.

Reisman handed it to Kinder. "Why'd you come back, Myron?" he asked.

Odell lowered his arms, rubbed a bruise on his face. "I

509

don't know, Captain . . . I just wanted to. I had to, I guess."

"Why?"

Odell held Reisman's gaze. "I found something here I never had before," he said softly. "You gave it to me . . . respect . . . pride . . . maybe courage. You trusted me . . . I didn't want to lose that."

Now it was Reisman who averted his eyes in embarrassment. "You find out anything out there . . . about yourself . . . about what happened?"

Odell shook his head. "No. I still think I'm innocent, Captain . . . but it doesn't make any difference any more."

Kinder stared at him incredulously. "How in the world did you get through to here from Glasgow?" he asked. "Besides the MPs, there are two thousand Counter Intelligence Corps agents cordoning off southern England."

Odell grinned, rubbed the bruise on his face. They noticed one of his hands gashed, crusted over with dried blood, the knuckles swollen. "I know, sir. I met a couple of them around dawn outside one of those barbed wire troop sausages near Taunton. I don't think I hurt them badly. Just enough to knock them out, tie them up and borrow their jeep. I left it near Stokesmouth Village and hiked cross-country." He held his injured hand out to Reisman. "You were right, Captain. It hurts when you use your fist. I've got to remember next time," he said, chopping the edge of the good hand against his forearm.

Walking into the barracks, Reisman let Kinder go ahead, and pulled Odell back a moment. "Did you get laid, kid?"

Odell looked at him cockily. "Damn right, Captain."

The stockade was dismantled, most of the material salvaged, even the nails saved where possible. "There's a war on, you know," Reisman lambasted them cheerfully, as they went about erasing traces of themselves, evidences of their occupancy of the estate.

Kinder had tried to make it easier for them. "There's really no need to do this," he told Reisman. "When things quiet down, I'll get a crew in here to take care of it."

"We'll do most of it. You can take care of anything that's left. I promised Lady Margot," Reisman explained.

But he also wanted something to keep the men occupied these last few days.

"Ever have much to do with her?" Kinder asked brightly, nodding toward the manor house.

"No . . . not very sociable," Reisman replied, dismissing the topic. Yet he was certain Margot must be aware of this last burst of activity on the estate, and he wondered if it made her glad at their going at last, or frantic at the portent of the hell that would soon burst across the Channel.

Kinder took personal charge of the dismantled model of Château de la Vilaine. He would take it to the airfield in his staff car, have it available for further drills and briefings, and afterwards take it back to London.

They all slept under puptents again, and a few of the hardier ones rolled up in blankets under the stars. The barbed wire fences, watchtowers and barracks became just so many piles of wire, wood and posts carted outside the confines of Stokes Manor in many round trips of their truck and jeep, and cached beside the road to be picked up ultimately by men whose job it was to worry about such things.

But not the wood from the portable scaffold which had served its double purpose by being an integral part of the stockade and being a constant fearful reminder to the men. These posts and cross-beams and stair rails and risers, and the boiled, stretched rope that had come with it, were piled and left in the center of the clearing.

When the other jobs were done, the firing range pits filled, the bullet and explosive scars healed where possible, the latrines neatly filled and covered with transplanted brush and saplings, Reisman assembled the men around the portable scaffold in the clearing.

"Franko!" he called, and sure enough the son-of-a-bitch jumped as though he'd done something wrong or was thinking something wrong. Reisman ignited his cigaret lighter, handed it to Franko, pointed to the scaffold and said, "Burn it!"

Wednesday, May 31, Sergeant Bowren placed the last of their extra provisions on Lady Margot's doorstep. He rang the bell, they heard the dog barking. Reisman saw movement upstairs at a window and knew she was watching them roll down the driveway. He got out of the jeep, trotted back and closed the gates. Glenn Gilpin waited for him beside the telephone pole where he'd reeled the wire.

"Still alive?" he asked.

Gilpin nodded, gave him the field phone and joined the others in the truck. Reisman rang the operator and it took a few minutes to get through to Tess at The Butcher's Arms in Marston-Tyne. He told her he'd be away awhile and wouldn't be in touch. "I've talked to a friend . . . Leon Osterman," he said. "He'll look after you."

"I don't need looking after," she protested. "There's my uncle and Mrs. Culver . . . but I'd love to see him anyhow . . . to talk about you. I love you. Think of me . . . wherever you're going . . . whatever you're doing . . . think of me when you're lonely, tired, when things go badly. Know you're loved."

"Same here," he said thickly. "I do love you . . . you're very dear to me." He hung up, took the trench knife from the sheath on his boot and cut the telephone wire.

They set up camp at the airfield at the paratroop base, right beside the tarmac where their C-47 waited with a squadron of others that would carry Breed's paratroopers to Normandy. Reisman and the Dirty Dozen wore regular fatigues, carried U.S. weapons—but in separate packs were the German uniforms and weapons they would put on when airborne. In other packs and containers were mines, extra explosives and ammunition, heavier weapons to be dropped with them on cargo chutes.

The weather was ideal. In the morning Major Armbruster and Colonel Denton flew in from London in a liaison plane for a final briefing. "It's on for Monday, June 5," said Denton as he returned Reisman's and Kinder's salute. And even he had a hard-to-rein note of excitement in his voice.

They spoke in soft voices, standing near the light plane. The pilot had gone to the ready room Quonset for a few hours' rest. Just off the tarmac, Reisman watched the Dirty Dozen lounging around their pitched tents, playing at cleaning guns, sharpening knives, but trying to tune in on the officers' briefing.

"You'll take off Sunday evening, long enough before the

airborne pathfinders to make your extra distance to Rennes," the Colonel continued. "In fact, you should be at your target about when they're leaving England. If there's a change, you'll receive the coded message *Bowsprit,* which will mean a delay of twenty-four hours. If there's a delay beyond that, I'm afraid it will be for a couple of weeks or even longer because of the tides on the beaches. They'll have to mount the whole damn thing over again. It would be hard to keep everybody bottled up for that length of time. Let's hope this weather holds. The long-range forecast, so far, is good."

Major Armbruster filled Reisman in on additional details. Air Corps was going to lay a bomb strike on the railyards in Rennes, coming in from the east, to cover the Dirty Dozen's approach from the west. "That eliminates the alternate target you proposed if the *Kriegsspiel* isn't on," said the Major. "You're to stay away from there."

Reisman tapped the map they were studying, indicating the headquarters of the German 5th Parachute Division. "Maybe we'll just go over here and take on these guys," he said. "If they're not waiting for us already at the château guarding the Generals."

"That's one thing you're not to do . . . before or after, John," said Colonel Denton brusquely. "I realize you have a predilection for that sort of thing . . . such as you did in the Mattarone last winter. Just do the job you've planned, if the Generals are there . . . and then bring your men out. And, more importantly, yourself."

"There is no alternate target, John," said Major Armbruster. "If you discover the Generals are not there, you're to start back immediately."

"Toting all this stuff we're taking in with us?"

"Bury it . . . destroy it . . . I don't care what you do with it. Just keep what you need for defensive purposes. And I know it will be hard for you, but avoid all unnecessary contact with the enemy." He looked at Reisman anxiously. "We can't give you any help getting out this time, you know. What have you planned? You've been tantalizingly, if somewhat alarmingly, silent on that subject."

"There are a number of ways," Reisman told him. "Probably best to split up. Some on the river through Brittany to the sea, using one of their boats. Another group using one of their lovely limousines and just drive like hell toward our nearest units. Or maybe even try a free ride aboard one of their troop trains heading to the Invasion front."

"You realize, of course, everybody will be after you," said Armbruster. "The Nazis . . . the French Underground will start shooting at anything that looks German . . . and our own people when you get close enough . . . and from the air. Maybe you ought to get rid of your German uniforms before you start back . . . try to join a unit of the *Maquis* and wait until Allied forces liberate their area."

"I'll play it by ear, Max," said Reisman, "depending on what happens at the château. We'll have to fight our way out no matter what."

"What about your colored boy and the Indian?" Denton asked. "I realize you're going in at night, but what if they've got to bluff their way in a face-to-face meeting and make the Nazis think they're some of their troops?"

"That part of it is mostly my job, Colonel . . . the deception. White and Posey are willing to take their chances . . . and I'll risk it. White's still my best man, and he can shoot French and German from the hip if he has to. As for Posey, let me show you something."

Reisman yelled for him, and Samson trotted over to join the officers beside the liaison plane. He saluted with great dignity and waited at rigid attention.

"What do you tell the Germans if you have to speak to any of them?" Reisman asked.

Denton and Armbruster listened in amazement as Samson spouted in German, "I am a Tatar from Siberia . . . The Russians made me fight with them . . . I was captured . . . I am a German soldier now . . . I hate Joseph Stalin . . ." And then he launched forth in a stream of chatter that neither officer could understand.

"Ute," explained Reisman. "As far as the Krauts are concerned it might as well be Siberian. They'd never know the difference."

Stuart Kinder set up the model of Château de la Vilaine in the back of a truck so the Dirty Dozen could run through their attack plan once more for Armbruster and Denton. It was crowded, dark and hot in there with the canvas down all around. Each man used his flashlight to illuminate and explain his assignment as his turn came.

Reisman began. "Here, half a mile from the château, is where we'll penetrate their perimeter. The countryside is lightly ringed by roadblocks and checkpoints like this, but this is the weakest one . . . two bored guards at a lonely outpost . . ."

Step by step Colonel Denton and Major Armbruster absorbed the plan. When it was finished and the officers were alone again out in the sunlight, Denton remarked, "I'm not so sure I hope the *Kriegsspiel* is on."

"What do you mean?" asked Reisman. "Don't you approve the plan?"

"Brilliant . . . but now I see why you had to go with them. You're the decoy all the way. Tell me *Herr Oberst*, have you ever played the part of a German officer before?"

Reisman clicked his heels smartly and raised his hand in the Nazi salute. "Occasionally . . . but never one of your exalted rank, *Herr Oberst*."

"And while you're inside the château with your neck stuck way out, what's to keep your Dirty Dozen from taking off . . . or the one who'll be with you . . . what's his name . . . the ersatz *Major?*"

"Sawyer."

"Yes . . . what's to keep him from turning you in?"

"Sawyer's a good soldier, sir. He saw many months of combat in Italy before he got into trouble. I trust him. I almost trust all of them . . . not quite . . . but almost. Enough to weight the odds in our favor."

Just before he and Denton boarded the liaison plane to fly back to London, Major Armbruster gripped Reisman's hand, wished him luck. "I'll keep the tub ready for you," he muttered weakly, feeling that no matter what he said now it would be inane, futile, inept. There had been hundreds of goodbyes like this, with many men, but he could never get used to them. With his other hand, he fumbled in his pocket for a small box he handed Reisman, and stammered out, "I know you won't . . . but just in case they're grabbed early enough to spill the whole deal."

Reisman slid open the box, saw the cyanide pills. "Not for this bunch, Max," he said, handing them back. "They may kill each other or me before it's over . . . but not themselves."

In the afternoon, while Sergeant Bowren and Captain Kinder sat with them on the ground within the semicircle of their pitched tents, Reisman divulged to the men the time and the place. He told them the name of the château and the nearby city, and they could see on the map he'd set up just how far out ahead of the rest of the Army they would be.

Victor Franko thought again about the advantages of a German prisoner-of-war camp. His eyes devoured the map of Europe, the symbols of enemy strength and deployment it advertised.

Joe Wladislaw waited until the Captain was finished and asked them, "Any questions?" Then he raised his hand nervously and said, "Yeh . . . how we gonna get back? It ain't only me wantsa know, Captain. We all been talkin about it . . . an we figure it's time we know."

"At approximately 0045 on the morning of June 5," said Reisman impassively, "after you've completed your assignments and have fallen back on me in the motor park of the Château de la Vilaine, you'll be briefed on your route of escape."

"Yeah, Captain," Roscoe Lever began to protest, "but what if you ain't . . ."

"What if I'm not there . . . what if I don't make it," Reisman finished for him. "Then you'll have to do it on your own . . . with nobody telling you how or when or why. You can work your way back living off the land and off the Germans. You can hit them as hard and often as you want . . . for pleasure or profit . . . or just to get the meanness out of your guts. But don't worry, Lever . . . I plan to be there, and in one piece."

"The glory quest!" mocked Napoleon, loud enough for them all to hear.

Reisman ignored the remark. "I suggest you all write letters now if you want to," he said. "Captain Kinder will give you the stationery and will mail them after we take off. Be careful what you say. We'll have to censor them before they're sent."

Reisman wrote to his father.

He went on for a few paragraphs, writing warmly of their long-ago days together and of his love for him now as then—rereading the February letter as a guide to what he felt Aaron would want to read, would need to know and feel for his own happiness. And he wrote lightly and vaguely about the war and his involvement in it. But he couldn't help inserting a gentle reprimand and small history lesson before he closed the letter.

Don't knock the *shvartzes*, Pop—to use your lousy expression. They were there before you. The first settler in what later became Chicago—when it was still savage Indian country—was a Negro named Point Sable. Too damned many scalps have been taken and there's been too much fighting over it and the rest of the world, since. Believe me, Pop, it isn't worth it.

When he finished the letter to his father, Reisman also wrote one to Tess, and then to Leon. In the evening, when the men turned in their letters, he saw that Samson Posey had proudly and painstakingly written one to his wife, the first he had ever composed. Napoleon White had written a letter to his family and to a friend in New York. Luis Jimenez, Kendall B. Sawyer, Calvin Ezra Smith, Vernon Pinkley, Joe Wladislaw and Glenn Gilpin had written. The words were different, but the tone of each was the same: loneliness, longing, nostalgia, and . . . just in case I don't get back.

Victor Franko, Archer Maggot, Roscoe Lever and Myron Odell didn't write letters.

Samson Posey dreamed that night about Sun Dance, and he knew what that meant. It was a sign directly from the sun. If he was home, he would have to volunteer to dance and try with all his might to seek power.

In the morning the sun rose strong again and he knew that soon, maybe in a month, they would be having Sun Dance at Towaoc and Ignacio. And it struck him in a moment of illumination that there were twelve of them there in his outfit, just as there were twelve poles required for the Sun Dance corral, and twelve disciples of Christ—although why there were twelve poles he didn't know, or which had come first. That sort of stuff had gotten all mixed up in the Ute religion and it was sometimes hard to tell which was the Utes', the Spaniards', the other tribes', the Americans' and all their different kinds of missionaries and holy men.

517

Even with that forked tree they put in the center of the corral, which represented Creator-of-Humans—some said it was God or Jesus or both. Things were always changing anyway, even in his lifetime, in the way they did Sun Dance and other ceremonies. There were always the changes in the old ways, always something new coming in, and objections by somebody who said it wasn't the way to be done, it wasn't the way they did it in the old days.

Samson went to the Captain, told him what he wanted to do, and asked him to bring him certain materials.

"A fan of eagle-tail feathers!" exclaimed Stuart Kinder. "An eagle-bone whistle! Red paint, black paint, yellow paint, fresh-cut willow trees. Is he kidding, John?"

"No, he's very serious," replied Reisman. "And you, of all people, I'd have thought would understand. It's very important to him, and I think we ought to give him the chance to get whatever strength or peace it will bring him."

"I can probably get the paints easily enough . . . and the drum," said Kinder, looking at the written list Reisman had handed him. "But this other stuff!"

"Improvise. He said it didn't make that much difference, and he'd understand. As long as he made the effort, his God would understand too."

Reisman saw the Chaplains drive up in a truck and rose to intercept them. He and Kinder had been sitting to one side, apart from the circle, watching the ceremony with great interest.

"We heard you and your men were out here," one of the Chaplains said after the introductions. They were from the airborne base, each ministering to a different faith. "Thought maybe we could be of help . . . talk to them . . . prayer meetings. There may not be much chance later. We'll have our own boys to look after."

"Not now," said Reisman. "I don't want to interrupt this."

The Chaplains were astounded by what they saw and heard. Squeezed into a clearing among the parked aircraft, the men to whom they'd come to minister were seated in a wide circle around a center pole that somewhat resembled a large crucifix, except that the crosspiece was nailed on crookedly and more nearly resembled a Y, and it was painted at eye-level in three broad bands of red-black-red. In the middle of the ring, a giant Indian, naked to the waist, his face painted, moved back and forth in a trance-like state, his eyes riveted to the fork of the Y. In his mouth was a whistle on which he blew staccato notes to the rhythm of a drum in the lap of a Negro soldier. In one hand was a bunch of feathers which he fanned over himself and the men in the circle from time to time in exorcising movements. Some of them seemed uncomfortable, bored, almost angry with what was going on, although the drummer was working at his role with relish.

"War Dance?" asked a Chaplain.

"Sun Dance. Part of Posey's religion," Reisman answered. "We had to improvise a bit to help him. Sergeant Bowren and the other men represent the twelve main posts of the Sun Dance corral. The feathers are chicken instead of eagle, and the whistle is MP instead of eagle bone."

"Twelve? Why twelve? What is the significance of that number?" one of the Chaplains asked pointedly.

"That's what Posey's people use at home, Padre," explained Kinder. He had questioned Samson hurriedly before he began, trying to sort out details and meaning: "I know what you're thinking . . . and the Apostles are part of it, too . . . although it's a little mixed up."

"He wanted me to be Creator-of-Humans," Reisman said. "Didn't think I qualified. We got that pole out there instead. It's closer to the forked tree they use at home."

"How long will this go on?"

The Chaplain's tone was amiable—benevolent without being condescending or patronizing. Each of them edged closer to the circle of men, absorbing the scene with more than professional interest.

"I don't know," Reisman said. "Posey said it takes days sometimes to know if it's working . . . and he's just begun."

The Chaplains watched awhile and then left, saying they'd be back.

Samson danced all the rest of the day, through the night of June 2 and into the morning of the third. He was Indian again and felt strong. His hair was long now, plaited into two braids like the horns of a bull, and tied with red cloth. He touched neither food nor drink, although at home it would have been permitted to rest occasionally and drink a little water. He prayed, he opened himself to power—that same power Billy Three-legs had got that made him walk again that time at Sun Dance after he'd come back from another trip to the white man's hospital. The white doctors hadn't been able to help him, but Sun Dance did. Billy No-legs was struck by the power just sitting there and listening and watching and praying and being fanned by that curing wand of eagle-tail feathers. And then he jumped right up and grabbed that old shaman's cane right out of his hand and he walked. And after that Billy Three-legs had more power than anybody.

As he danced, Samson was aware that during the night the other men left their places in the circle to sleep, but it pleased him that they thrust bayoneted rifles into the ground to mark the twelve main posts of the corral, and returned there in the morning.

It was a gray morning, however—and it got worse. It began to rain and the wind increased and then the downpour until it was like the gale-force storms of winter. Samson danced and prayed and tried to make it stop, but it did no good. The colors he had painted onto his face ran in mocking streams down his naked chest and stomach and stained his pants and bare feet. The ground turned to mud, his whistling and the sound of the drum became lost in the noise of the storm. The others sought shelter in their pup-tents and the Captain let them, but still Samson danced. He wanted power not for himself, but to help these men with whom he was going into battle, and to help the Captain.

Some of them mocked him. Not all, not the Captain and the Sergeant and the other officer and some of the men— but a few of them. He heard their taunts and catcalls, felt the rain slash at him like knives, shivered with cold, tasted the bitterness of defeat again, and in shame he finally stopped.

He sat beside the forked pole alone in the storm and wondered what had gone wrong. He had seen it happen once when rainclouds appeared during Sun Dance that those with power made them break up and go away. But not here. Maybe because he had everything wrong here, nothing of the eagle, nothing really of the land and spirit of The People—no paint ground from red ochre in Mancos Canyon, no shell gorget and beadwork on his chest, no Ute clothes, no fresh-cut willows, no singers, no storytellers, no dancers but himself. He had all the wrong things.

Or maybe there was really nothing to it. Maybe Billy had really been cured at the white hospital and had fooled them all. Samson had thought of that sometimes. But then, sitting out there alone in the storm, the thunder really got through to him and he remembered how, when the first thunder in the spring came, his grandfather used to tell him to get up and stretch so he would grow taller. Well, that had surely worked for him, and that meant there was power and there were things you could control.

Exhausted, soaked through to the bone, hungry, he crawled into his puptent. He put on warm, dry clothing, gnawed at his packaged rations, and fell into a deep, fitful sleep.

June 4. The weather was the same, maybe worse. Reisman was given the *Bowsprit* message postponing the mission twenty-four hours. A full gale was raging in the English Channel, along the Invasion coast of France and making itself felt in unfavorable weather far inland. He had gathered the men together in the back of the truck and had just told them about the delay when there was a loud banging on the tailgate and one of the Chaplains heaved himself up and stuck his head between the canvas flaps.

"We're available now if your men want to answer church call," he announced without preamble.

"All right," Reisman assented. He was almost glad for the interruption this time, for he could see the increased tension in their faces—even on Kinder and Bowren—and maybe this would ease it. "I suggest you all pray for clear weather so we can get the hell out of here!"

They started to scramble out of the truck when a shout of "Captain!" halted them.

It was Samson Posey, his face muscles working tensely as he said, "You want storm to end?"

"That's the general idea, Posey," said Reisman.

Samson stood up to his full height, towering over them all massively even though he had to stoop to keep his head from pushing through the canvas top. "I can stop rain!" he declared and he ran on, seeing the scornful faces of some, and fearful the Captain wouldn't give him a chance. "I

521

come from a place of much dryness . . . and when we are blessed by rain sometimes it is too much too quick and it must be stopped. I have seen it happen and I know how it is done."

Archer Maggot cursed, oblivious of the close presence of the Chaplain. "Sheet, Chief . . . ah think yoall got goofed up an brought the rain with yo damn Sun Dance!"

"Don't mock him, fellow!" barked the Chaplain angrily. "Whatever your beliefs . . . if you have any . . . do not mock him!"

Reisman uttered a silent thanks for that. "Sure, Posey, go ahead," he said. "What do you need?"

"Stick . . . this long," explained Samson excitedly, extending his hands. "Red paint . . . that's all. If I got power from Sun Dance . . . even a little . . . rain will go."

When he'd sharpened the stick, Samson crawled into his puptent, where he had cached the rest of the paints Captain Kinder had brought him. He painted the stick red, stripped himself to the waist again, and took the stick outside. Twenty yards from his tent, he thrust it deep into the muddy ground. He squatted nearby, letting the full force of the gale tear at him, and he prayed.

He was still there in the morning, seemingly impervious to the elements. They offered him food and hot coffee cooked over an open fire under a shelter half, but he refused and waved them away. It was still raining later in the day when a dispatch rider came sloshing through the quagmire and handed Reisman the message he feared would postpone the mission again or cancel it altogether. He read it, walked to where the Indian was sitting, leaned over him and said, not quite believing it himself, "You can stop now, Posey. It worked."

Samson tilted his face up into the rain and looked at Reisman in confusion. "Still raining, dammit!" he muttered angrily.

"Maybe now, Chief . . . but not later when it counts. Believe me . . . whatever you did, it worked. Weatherman says it will clear tonight over our target . . . clear for the Army on the beaches tomorrow. We're going."

It had stopped raining there at the airfield by the time they were ready to board their aircraft, and all the men had followed Reisman's example in congratulating a very proud Samson Posey. Though it was late evening, it was still daylight under British Double Summer Time.

Sergeant Clyde Bowren gripped Reisman's hand. He was to take the truck and report back to Marston-Tyne, and he hated the thought of it. "It's been a hell of an experience sir," he said. "Thanks for saving me from a life of boredom." He hesitated a moment, as though about to say something else. "I'll check the men again, Captain . . . make sure they've got everything."

Reisman watched him trot toward where the men were strapping on parachutes and equipment, and turned to Stuart Kinder. "I'll make a bet with you, Stu," he said. "You'll be a Major before I get back."

Kinder wanted to be flip also, but he couldn't. He didn't have the heart for it. He wished Reisman luck, his face grim. "I'll be in London . . . waiting anxiously," he said inanely.

Neither of them saw Bowren skirt the area where the Dirty Dozen were, nor did any of the men see the Sergeant heave aboard the aircraft the extra packs and weapons and parachutes he'd had ready, in the hope that he would have such a moment and the daring to take it.

All across the airfield, Reisman could see many trucks and jeeps moving now, and the airborne units beginning to gather at their planes. The day before, one of the Chaplains had said to him, a little guiltily, that Colonel Breed, knowing the Dirty Dozen were scheduled to take off earlier, wanted to know what Reisman's bunch would be up to. "He's particularly concerned," the Chaplain had pressed with very nimble tact, "as to whether you were among the pathfinders. As a matter of fact, he said he'd be damned if he'd drop on a marker your people had put in."

Reisman had grinned at the intractability of the man, and said, "No . . . assure the Colonel we're not among the pathfinders. We have business elsewhere." He had felt he owed him that much.

When they were airborne awhile, Reisman went forward to confer with the pilot about their route and the Estimated

523

Time of Arrival, and found Sergeant Bowren crouching in the compartment, watching in fascination the flyboys at their work.

"You can't come," Reisman shouted above the engine roar. "You've got to get the hell out of here now."

"I think the Channel's below, Captain. Would you like me to swim back?"

"This isn't Easter Sunday, Clyde. There are killers with guns waiting for us at the other end of this ride."

"There are murderers with guns right here with you, Captain, and I got a feeling you're gonna need help," said Bowren. "Besides, I've worked just as hard as these sons-of-bitches and I'll be damned if I'm gonna let them think they can do anything I can't."

As the aircraft droned south toward the Brittany coast, crossing the English Channel far west of the Cotentin peninsula to avoid that night's heavy traffic, Reisman, Bowren and the Dirty Dozen slipped out of their packs and parachutes and did a quick change. American uniforms were replaced by German, weapons were exchanged, and packs and cargo containers repacked.

Reisman was scared. He felt it in his stomach and throat. But that didn't really surprise him or bother him. He was always scared in these moments before action. Bowren was scared. Reisman saw it in his eyes, the itchy way he sat on the bucket seat along the wall of the plane. But there was a curious calm about every one of the Dirty Dozen that amazed Reisman. He had put them through so much, so many emotional and physical hurdles during training, that it struck him now that this, the reality, might be a snap—a release.

The jumpmaster came down the aisle and leaned over Reisman. "Better saddle up, Captain. It won't be long now." But the transformation in their uniforms was too much for him. He couldn't contain himself any longer. "What in hell did you guys do to deserve such a dirty job?" he said.

Reisman shouted back, "It's not so much what we did . . . it's that the jobs to be done deserve us."

The red light came on over the door and Reisman signaled for the others to hook up. He didn't like it, but he was going out last this time to make sure they all jumped. Bowren moved forward and took the leadoff spot in the stick. Reisman squeezed down the aisle from Bowren, double-checking equipment, touching hands, arms, shoulders, murmuring of all damned things, "God bless you!" to each of them. What in hell else did he say, except you'd damn well better be there where you're supposed to be in one piece when I get there.

He hooked up, checked the equipment of the guy in front of him and his own. The pilot throttled back the engines, making their approach over the drop zone quieter. Then they heard flak in the distance. The raid on the railyard was on, drawing the Germans' attention. The green light came on, Reisman shuffled forward and dived after his men. Behind him, the jumpmaster kicked out the cargo chutes.

—

35

—

MYRON ODELL stood trembling in the bedroom closet off the suite he was assigned to cover. The rooms had been dark and empty when he slipped in earlier. The closet contained a German officer's uniforms and a few items of women's apparel. Odell marveled that he was actually here in this place, prepared to do what he dreaded doing.

Elsewhere through the large building and on the grounds of the château, he knew the others must have reached their positions without mishap, for he had heard no sounds to tell him otherwise. The Captain and Sawyer, impersonating a Nazi Colonel and Major, had bluffed their way through the front door of the main building with their forged credentials and Reisman's fluent German. They had been shown to quarters and then had wandered through the building with impunity, opening prearranged doors and windows to admit Odell, Sergeant Bowren and others. Odell knew where each was waiting at this moment, and what each of those positioned outside had to have accomplished to be on schedule. The signal to attack would be the explosions of timed charges the Captain and Sawyer had left in briefcases in the *Kriegsspiel* room and the communications center, and a charge that Glenn Gilpin had by now affixed to the tall signal antenna mast on the roof, which he would detonate at 0015, when the first paratroopers would be on the ground in Normandy. Or the moment might come prematurely, dictated by the sound of gunfire, indicating one of them had been discovered. Odell was to burst into the rooms, kill anybody there or in the corridors as he swept through the building, then retreat to the motor park outside, from where Reisman would direct them. If he had to kill before that, he was to do it quietly.

He held a knife ready in his hand, and thought with pity and horror of the first blood they had drawn. He hadn't been expected himself to do it, nor could he have done it then in that way. But Maggot and Posey, Lever and Jimenez had volunteered, two to a man while the Captain had decoyed the Germans by walking boldly down the middle of the road. And Odell could still see now, as he waited alone in the darkness, the grisly sight of the stabbed and garroted bodies they had dragged from that roadblock half a mile before reaching the château, and had concealed in the orchard. The faces of the men had held a spectrum of revulsion, contempt, savage excitement over the kill. "They're Fifth Division parachutists. A *Kriegsspiel* is scheduled," the Captain had said exultantly, lifting his eyes from the corpses that had provided the necessary clue. "The Generals are on the way or there already."

Pinkley and Smith had made for the river, one to flank the château on the east, the other on the west, heading for the boathouse. The rest had moved out in two parties—Napoleon's squad, Odell among them, planting mines, booby traps and trip wires along the approaches Nazi relief troops would take when the battle at the château erupted. Sergeant Bowren had worked with them, fitting himself smoothly into the machinery of the plan he had known so well though he hadn't been part of it. The second group—*Herr Oberst* Reisman, *Herr Major* Sawyer, *Einfacher Soldaten* Posey, Franko and Wladislaw—had moved quickly toward the wooden gates that blocked the driveway into the courtyard motor park of the château. Odell hadn't witnessed it, but by the time he and the others had finished their work outside the wall and reached the motor park gates, the two German sentries who had been there to challenge *"Wer da! Zeigen Sie mir Ihren Ausweise!"* at the

Captain's imperious demand for entrance, were both dead. They had died quickly and quietly with bullets in their brains, fired through the .22 silencers at skin-touch range by Franko and Wladislaw, and they had been replaced as guards by the men who had killed them.

On the outside stairway of a detached service building that was the guards' quarters, Napoleon White peered through a window and watched a card game in progress among off-duty soldiers. The changing of the guard, he knew, would not be until 0200, and he felt curiously safe from danger, relaxed, remote from what he was doing. By now Pinkley and Smith must have killed the two sentries patrolling near the boathouse—Smith no doubt arguing with himself right up to the sticking point whether he was doing God's work or the devil's. There had been no alarm, and Napoleon could assume one speedboat had been silently and permanently put out of action and the other fixed so only they could start it by reconnecting the right wires. Smith would be in position near the auxiliary powerhouse to put it out of action when the outside power source was cut by Reisman in the basement of the château. And Pinkley had probably entered the underground passageway between the boathouse and the main building. With submachine gun, carbine and grenades, Pinkley could stand off an army there and stop anyone who tried to escape by the river.

Suddenly, unexpectedly, Napoleon heard footsteps on the iron stairway and there was nowhere to go. He turned away from the window and the nearby doorway and leaned against a railing, looking down into the courtyard toward the motor park. His hand gripped the .22 silencer, his finger tendons and muscles trembling, skin crawling, hoping he wouldn't have to use it now, prematurely. A voice in German greeted him from behind, he answered, and there was a brief exchange before the man entered the guards' off-duty room and Napoleon unglued his wet hand from the pistol and breathed a sigh of relief. In the darkness, the soldier had never seen his face and hands. He had been accepted.

Napoleon heard a commotion at the gates to the motor park. He watched as Franko and Wladislaw opened the gates and a limousine whisked through with a German

General's standard flapping over the hood. He watched the General and his aides strut across the courtyard and enter the main building. Then he went back to the window and observed the cardplayers. They were white men, they were Nazis, but he knew it would be difficult to kill them. He didn't feel the burning hatred he had when Reisman took him from the execution block at Marston-Tyne prison. He thought of the prayer of the freed Negro slave which his father had made him memorize when he was a boy: Lord, we ain't what we wanna be; we ain't what we oughta be; and we ain't what we gonna be; but thank you, Lord, we ain't what we wuz.

Roscoe Lever waited behind the blackout drapes of a bedroom on the second floor. He had a rope tied and ready to go out the window if things got too hot. A maid came into the room. He saw her, but she was not aware of him. The maid moved about nervously, kept checking her watch, seemed eager to leave. Lever sweated and trembled. He remembered the completely helpless woman in the jewelry shop in Birmingham. He had the same feeling of power over this one. He stared from his watch to the woman and back. It was 2350. The time was very near . . . but if he was going to get hurt or killed . . .

He moved toward the maid as she opened the door, coat on now, a cloth handbag clutched tightly. She glanced nervously down the hallway, as though preparing to run or do something she wasn't supposed to do. Lever grabbed her, stifled a scream with his hand mashed over her mouth, and in his pidgin French and German implored, threatened, cajoled. She fought him—a German soldier bent on rape—pleaded in French and broken German that she had to leave, that she would tell the officers if he didn't behave, that she would meet him the next night if he would only let her go now—none of which Lever understood. He wrestled her to the bed, fell upon her, and never saw her hand desperately grope in the cloth bag for the pair of shears she plunged into his chest.

Roscoe Lever died gurgling that he was on her side, that he was not a Kraut, that he was an Amer—

At his emplacement a short distance outside the château

grounds, Samson Posey proudly checked again the watch the Captain had given him. It was midnight—2400, as he had learned to say—and he knew the time was soon. He was alone now and glad of it, for he was not certain the Captain or any of the men would have approved his appearance. He had stripped the heavy, ugly German uniform from his body and wore now his own boots and the trousers of his American battle fatigues. His chest was bare, his long-braided hair uncovered, and his face painted for war in yellow and black. He had with him the heavy machine gun and ammunition they had taken from the German roadblock, and an arsenal of smaller weapons and grenades to hold off any Nazi troops and vehicles that moved toward the château once the fighting began. He was ready and eager for battle.

Myron Odell heard people enter the living room of the suite. He heard a man and woman speaking and laughing. He heard footsteps come into the bedroom, move toward the closet; he felt his bowel involuntarily begin to empty and with a tremendous effort of will and muscle stopped it. The closet door opened and he plunged his waiting, trembling knife into the belly of a young and attractive woman.

He stared, horrified, frozen, his hand still on the weapon, her blood oozing out all over him, and then he remembered the other time . . . *the naked girl, his pain, his blind rage, the surgical cabinet, the knife, the horrible squish as it sank into her body, the blood* . . . and he screamed, "I'm guilty! . . . My God, I'm guilty!" and he ran, pursued by demons, shouting hysterically, filled with blood lust. In the outer room he saw the blue of a Nazi officer, a weapon in his hand. He heard the gun explode, felt the lead smash into his shoulder as he rolled on the floor and came up firing his Schmeisser machine pistol. He ran down the corridor, waving the bloody knife in one hand, firing the Schmeisser with the other, raving, "I'm guilty! I'm guilty! I'm guilty!"

36

HEADQUARTERS
PSYCHOLOGICAL WARFARE DIVISION
OFFICE OF STRATEGIC SERVICES
UNITED KINGDOM BASE
EUROPEAN THEATER OF OPERATIONS
UNITED STATES ARMY
A.P.O. 400

15 June 1944

SUBJECT: Compilation and interpretation of Intelligence Reports to date pertaining to personnel and objectives of Project Amnesty.

TO: Commanding General, SHEAF, ETOUSA, A.P.O. 400.
Numbered Copy Two to Colonel Francis Denton, O.S.S., ETOUSA, A.P.O. 400.
Numbered Copy Three to Major Max Armbruster, O.S.S, ETOUSA, A.P.O. 400.
Numbered Copy Four retained by Major Stuart Kinder, P.W.D., O.S.S., ETOUSA, A.P.O. 400.

CLASSIFICATION: Top Secret

The project having been completed and sufficient time having elapsed to partially evaluate the success of the mission it encompassed, the following report is submitted:

1) Sources of Military Intelligence:

(a) Primary source is Bowren, Clyde, ASN 20467050, Sergeant, CMP. His story was recorded by G2 1st Division at Casualty Control Center, Carentan, Normandy, France, at approximately 1600 hours 14 June 1944. He had been picked up, gravely wounded and semiconscious, the previous morning at approximately 0800 hours by advance patrols 1st Division probing enemy lines north of St. Lô, and inadvertently identified as a German prisoner of war. At the time of making his report to an officer of G2 1st Division, Sergeant Bowren was not completely conscious and lucid due to his wounds and various medication prescribed therefor. (*Note re Sergeant Bowren*: He is currently carried as Absent Without Leave by his unit, the 51st Disciplinary Training Center, Marston-Tyne, Somerset, England. However, the undersigned wishes to state that he is personally acquainted with the record and character of Sergeant Bowren, and that this is not an ordinary AWOL that would or should be dealt with by standard operating procedures through disciplinary action and court-martial. The undersigned recommends instead that Sergeant Bowren be immediately transferred in the rank of Staff Sergeant to the jurisdiction of Psychological Warfare Division, Office of Strategic Services; that a suitable commendation be awarded him for the heroic action in which he volunteered; and that he be returned to permanent duty with P.W.D., O.S.S., London at the earliest possible moment commensurate with recovery from his wounds.)

(b) A secondary, but highly gratifying and relevant source of information—at least partially and temporarily confirming one very important aspect of this report: the survival of Project Amnesty's Commanding Officer, Captain John Reisman—is to be found in two somewhat cryptic and personal written messages (Copies appended) and a confirmed casualty list (Copy appended) found in a pocket of Sergeant Bowren's uniform when he was returned to Allied lines. One message, addressed to Captain (sic) Stuart Kinder, states, "What in hell was it again Napoleon said at the battle of Toulon?" The other message, addressed to Major Max Armbruster, states, "Keep the tub clean and the water hot, Mox'll!"

(c) Additional sources of information are Agents of the French Underground, and monitored German communiqués.

2) Casualties:

Sources of information include Captain Reisman's confirmed list, the verbal report by Sergeant Bowren, information from the French Underground, and tentative assumptions made on the basis of elapsed time between date of mission, 5 June 1944, and date of this report, and failure of individual personnel to return to Allied control.

(a) Dead: Odell, Myron; Lever, Roscoe K.; Smith, Calvin Ezra; Gilpin, Glenn; Franko, Victor.

(b) Wounded: Bowren, Clyde; White, Napoleon; Jimenez, Luis.

(c) Missing in Action: Posey, Samson; Sawyer, Kendall T.; Wladislaw, Joseph; Pinkley, Vernon; Maggot, Archer; Jimenez, Luis (also confirmed wounded); White, Napoleon (also confirmed wounded); Reisman, John, Captain (possibly wounded).

3) Evaluation of the mission:

(a) Objective: To take by surprise and kill an unspecified number of Generals and high-ranking officers of the German Seventh Army who might have been gathered at the Château de la Vilaine, Rennes, France, on the night of 5-6 June 1944 for a *Kriegsspiel*. Attack was timed for maximum effect for the hours just prior to the landing of the first Allied paratroopers in Normandy, without any certain knowledge by Allied Intelligence whether or not the enemy personnel would be there.

(b) Plans and Training: Superbly outlined and conducted under the leadership of Captain Reisman, as continually observed by the undersigned between 26 February 1944 and 5 June 1944.

(c) Personnel: Despite overwhelming obstacles presented by the character, background and ability of the personnel of Project Amnesty—the so-called Dirty Dozen—who were twelve General Prisoners convicted by courts-martial and doomed to be executed or serve lengthy prison terms for murder, rape, robbery, and other crimes of violence, it is the considered opinion of the undersigned that a more normal group or even a superior group of soldiers might not have been suitable and might not have performed their tasks as diligently or acquitted themselves as well under similar circumstances.

(d) Combat report on the mission: A separate and detailed report will be made as soon as Sergeant Bowren has recovered sufficiently, or as soon as personnel now listed as Missing in Action are returned to Allied control. Incidents and details reported herein are based almost solely on the verbal report to G2 1st Division by Sergeant Bowren on 14 June 1944, and partial corroboration of some points deduced from a survey of French Underground Intelligence and intercepted or monitored enemy Intelligence and communiqués.

1. Entry into the grounds and buildings of the château and reaching of assigned positions prior to the specified moment of attack—0015 6 June 1944—was gained successfully, in secrecy, according to plan. Known enemy casualties in this phase of the operation: six dead. The moment of attack, however, occurred prematurely by approximately ten minutes—though apparently without untoward consequences to the objective of the mission. Sergeant Bowren explains this by reporting what he heard in a conversation between Captain Reisman and Luis Jimenez when the survivors of the battle in the château rendezvoused with the Captain in the motor park prior to their escape from the vicinity. Captain Reisman asked the whereabouts of Myron Odell, a former medic, who was needed to dress the wounds of Sergeant Bowren and Napoleon White. Jimenez replied, "He's dead, Captain. He go crazy. He start this whole fucking (sic) business. I hear him running down the hall yelling, 'I'm guilty! . . . I'm guilty!' "

2. It may be surmised, therefore, that Odell was discovered in his hiding place by enemy personnel prior to H-hour, M-minute, and was forced to defend himself by means other than silent, which he had been ordered and trained to do in such an event—for it was this outburst that apparently began the battle within the main building of the château. (*Note re Myron Odell*: During the months when the undersigned knew and worked with him, Odell continued to claim he was innocent of the murder for which he had been court-martialed. It can only be assumed now, if Jimenez was correct, that something of profound psychological importance occurred to Odell in combat or just prior to it to reveal to him at last that he was indeed guilty of the crime for which he had been convicted.)

3. Regarding the objective of the mission—the elimination of certain important enemy personnel—it may be pointed out here that though Captain Reisman and his men were, through our foresight and planning, in the right place at the right time, and that although a *Kriegsspiel* was indeed scheduled, Sergeant Bowren reports that in the hour prior to the battle, Captain Reisman, moving about the château freely in his cover as a Nazi infantry Colonel, learned that the game in the war room of the château was

not actually scheduled to begin until 1000 hours the following morning 6 June 1944. For the Allied Invasion, it was a fateful coincidence that would never take place, but for Captain Reisman's group it was too long a wait. Though the full complement of enemy Generals were not to be there until morning, and only a few were to be staying there at the château that night, it was too late for Captain Reisman to alter his plan of attack.

4. Also regarding the objective of the mission—the elimination of certain important enemy personnel—it is known that Generals Stumpffeldt and Volkmann left their commands on 5 June 1944 for the *Kriegsspiel* at Rennes and that they never returned. Others, such as Generals Hellmuth and Von Stollwitz are known to have been there, and others never reached there or turned around en route when they became aware of Allied activity. It may be assumed that at least Stumpffeldt and Volkmann were killed at the château and that in this respect the mission was a success.

5. An incident privately related to Sergeant Bowren by Vernon Pinkley at the time of their rendezvous in the motor park appears to confirm that at least one General was indeed killed trying to escape via the river. Pinkley's assigned position was in the underground passageway between the boathouse and the main building, to prevent any enemy personnel from reaching the speedboats which had already been put out of action, or from attempting to escape via other means on the river. Pinkley told Sergeant Bowren that shortly after the firefight broke out he heard many footsteps running toward him in the dark tunnel. Hand-lights and lanterns were being used and Pinkley was able to fire at them slowly, deliberately and with great accuracy. They piled up on each other, apparently dead, and within seconds Pinkley said he heard someone else running toward him and shouting alternately in German and English, "General! . . . General! . . . stop!" and he almost shot him before he recognized the voice of Victor Franko and confirmed this by shining a flashlight on him. Pinkley rushed up to him as Franko, who was not even supposed to be in the tunnel, bent over the body of one dead officer illuminating it with his flashlight. Pinkley shined his light on four other dead Germans—two officers and two enlisted men. He told Sergeant Bowren that at that moment Franko shouted at him angrily, "You killed him, you son-of-a-

bitch!" and that he—Pinkley—then examined the uniform and remarked, "Well, I'll be goddamned . . . I got me a General. What the hell did you want me to do? Take him home as a souvenir?" Pinkley described them as both gasping, filled with the excitement of the battle, although they were momentarily alone, the sounds of firing in the distance, and that he then looked at Franko suspiciously and demanded, "What in hell were you yelling at him for? What did you want?" Franko is said to have replied, "You goddamn dumb hick! He was our out . . . maybe the only one." At which Pinkley claimed to have stuck his weapon in Franko's belly and said, "Don't try it, Vic. I warn you . . . you won't get away with it."

6. The above incident, which does appear to confirm the death of one German General, is also, regrettably, an evidential aspect of a negative part of this report which will be explored more fully below concerning the actions and death of Victor Franko. It might, however, be best first to give here what details were reported by Sergeant Bowren regarding certain other casualties:

Calvin Ezra Smith—Pinkley told Sergeant Bowren that while he and Franko were moving back from the river to the motor park they came upon the body of Calvin Ezra Smith shot to death near the auxiliary powerhouse he had successfully destroyed. There were six dead German soldiers in the vicinity, apparently killed by Smith with grenades and submachine gun fire; and three wounded whom Pinkley and Franko finished off, since there was no way for them to take prisoners.

Glenn Gilpin—Sergeant Bowren says that Gilpin successfully detonated the signal antenna mast on the roof within seconds after the firing erupted. He reports that he and Captain Reisman both saw the body of Gilpin while the Captain was helping the Sergeant through the courtyard toward one of the German limousines in the motor park. Bowren had been wounded in both legs by small arms fire and couldn't walk. Gilpin had apparently been firing at enemy troops from the roof and, while descending on a rope, had been machine-gunned and smashed to the ground.

Roscoe Lever—Sergeant Bowren states that earlier in the battle, before he was wounded, as he swept through the château in search of the German Generals he came upon the body of Lever lying on a bed, a pair of ordinary sewing shears plunged into his chest. Since it appears unlikely a German soldier or officer would have used such a weapon, it can only be conjectured as to what exactly did happen to Lever and who killed him.

Napoleon White—Sergeant Bowren says that when he and Captain Reisman reached the motor park, White and other men were already there waiting for them. White was bleeding from a serious wound in his side, but he was able to walk. Enemy survivors within the château had not yet come after them and relief troops from outside had not yet arrived. Though there was little time to spare, Captain Reisman insisted upon attending to the wounded men before splitting up the group for their escape. Kendall T. Sawyer, Joseph Wladislaw, Archer Maggot and Luis Jimenez were ordered to set up a defense perimeter while the Captain doctored the wounded and got them into one of the limousines. Vernon Pinkley and Victor Franko fell back on the group about this time. Samson Posey was a short distance from the château grounds waiting to be recalled from a defensive strongpoint to join the escape or to stand off Nazi relief troops should they appear. Regarding the assignment Napoleon White had carried out, during which he had been wounded, Sergeant Bowren recalls a conversation between White and Captain Reisman while he was putting sulfa powder and a compress on his wound. The Captain nodded toward the guards' quarters White had covered, and complimented, "You must have done a good job up there, Lieutenant (sic). I haven't seen anybody crawl out of there. It's real quiet." White is said to have answered derisively, "Yeah, I did all right . . . I did real good. But you know something, Captain . . . once again I killed for my own reasons, not yours. Those fucking (sic) Nazis took one look at me coming through that door and started yelling, '*Schwarzer! Schwarzer! Schwarzer!*' That's when I let them have it, but good!"

Luis Jimenez—Sergeant Bowren remembers that Jimenez, Sawyer, Pinkley and Wladislaw had just been ordered to the boathouse by the Captain to make their escape by the river when sounds of heavy firing came to them from the direction of Posey's position beyond the walls. While the other three headed for the speedboat, Jimenez raced out, without orders, to recall Posey and help him in falling back. Sergeant Bowren places himself, White and Franko in the back seat of the German car, Captain Reisman at

536

the wheel and Maggot beside him as they left the motor park driving toward Posey's position, which was being intermittently illuminated by enemy flares. During one such flare burst, Jimenez was seen to stagger and fall as he neared Posey, then rise and move forward again slowly in a crouch, clutching his thigh as though wounded there.

Samson Posey—Even making allowances for Sergeant Bowren's condition at the time of his oral report to G2 1st Division on 14 June 1944, his recollection of Posey at this time is vivid and startling, and reflects only the highest credit upon the Service. The men in the car were only able to catch short glimpses of him, but it appeared to them that Posey, a member of the Ute Indian tribe, had somehow contrived to dress and paint himself as an Indian warrior. (*Note* The undersigned had provided him with paints and feathers for personal religious use at the request of his Commanding Officer on 2 June 1944, and he probably had some of these in his pack when he parachuted.) Posey was seen to be firing furiously with a captured heavy German machine gun, and intermittently throwing hand grenades with great accuracy. Many Nazi troops and vehicles were seen approaching. Due to the heavy concentration of enemy numbers and firepower, Captain Reisman could not drive the car closer to Posey and risk its loss. He waited, instead, for Posey and Jimenez to fall back on them, and he and the men in the car, including the wounded, lent supporting fire with submachine guns and carbines. The Germans were apparently still unaware of their presence, for no answering fire and no flares were sent in their direction. The enemy seemed instead, according to Sergeant Bowren, to increase his efforts against Posey's strongpoint. Jimenez was seen to reach Posey, converse with him and point back along the line of retreat toward the waiting vehicle. At that moment, Posey was seen to thrust Jimenez aside, leap from his entrenched position and engage in hand-to-hand combat with two Germans who had slipped around onto his left flank. Jimenez was seen to recover and take over the operation of the machine gun. Napoleon White, despite his wound, started to get out of the limousine to go to the aid of Posey. Captain Reisman stopped him. Sergeant Bowren remembers the Captain shouting, "No, let him be! If he lived a hundred years he'd never have another moment like this!"

Victor Franko—The actions and death of Victor Franko regrettably introduces the only confirmed negative note in the entire appraisal of the loyalty and performance of the so-called Dirty Dozen on this mission. Sergeant Bowren states that the limousine careened down the road in the opposite direction from Nazi troops swarming around Posey's position. Within moments, however, the headlights picked up a strong enemy roadblock. Franko panicked—or possibly had intended this all along—and shouted at Captain Reisman to halt the vehicle and surrender to the Germans. The Captain, according to Sergeant Bowren, pressed the limousine to maximum speed in order to smash through a wooden barricade. Whereupon Sergeant Bowren heard Franko unleash a stream of obscenities and saw him place the barrel of his Schmeisser machine pistol against the Captain's neck. Sergeant Bowren, who had been holding his .45 automatic pistol ready for use against the enemy, shot Franko twice just as the German soldiers at the roadblock realized they weren't going to stop and began firing at the speeding car. Franko's body fell from the vehicle as they struck the barricade and broke through to the open road.

(e) Report on activities of the survivors and contacts with the enemy and friendly French civilians during period 6 June 1944 to 13 June 1944 and following:

1. This is an area in which we must wait for Sergeant Bowren to file a separate and detailed report, which can then be collated with details of French Underground Intelligence and German communiqués and Intelligence, and with the reports of those personnel of Project Amnesty who, now listed as Missing in Action, can be expected to ultimately come under Allied control again.

2. Regarding the activities of his three companions during this period, and their current whereabouts, Sergeant Bowren has reported few details, due to his deteriorating physical condition and semicomatose state during those days. He is fairly certain, however, that for a few days they continued to use the captured Nazi limousine as transportation toward the expanding Normandy lodgment, although there were many hours during which they were unable to travel due to Allied air activity, congested enemy ground activity, or the danger of discovery. He believes there were a number of brief firefights and believes he saw Captain Reisman's neck and upper left arm bandaged. He is also fairly certain that the Captain made a number of fruitful

contacts with friendly French civilians to whom he revealed their identities, and that during one of these contacts when they were offered food and shelter, Archer Maggot was ordered to remain behind and look after Napoleon White until the area was liberated by the Allies. Sergeant Bowren told G2 1st Division he believes Captain Reisman had become obsessed at this point with the obligation of personally returning him safely, and that he possibly believed he would be more certain of accomplishing this if they separated from White and Maggot who did not get along well with each other.

3. Sergeant Bowren reports that the last time he saw Captain Reisman was in the farmhouse some miles north of St. Lô where the Sergeant was found by American troops. Captain Reisman obviously knew that German troops had already retreated from the immediate area and that the first American soldiers would be arriving in minutes. In fact, it is entirely possible he saw them coming. Sergeant Bowren remembers the Captain urging him awake from his semiconscious condition and saying, "Clyde, this is the end of the tour. I'm going back to see how the others made out." When Bowren was found, the Captain was gone.

4) Recommendations:

(a) It is the recommendation of the undersigned that no project similar to Project Amnesty ever be undertaken again. An elaboration upon this view will be made if requested.

(b) It is the recommendation of the undersigned that all personnel records pertaining to the twelve American soldiers known as the Dirty Dozen be amended forthwith to record that they were returned to active duty in their former ranks 5 June 1944.

Stuart Kinder, 0-42280485
Major, P.W.D., O.S.S.

ACKNOWLEDGEMENTS

TO Russ Meyer for a memory of WW II; to Charles B. Bloch for vision and guidance, and for his personal enthusiasm and commitment; to Robert Specht, Jack Guss, Joseph Morhaim for advice and encouragement; to Ed and Shirley Duffy for being with me all the way; to Ira A. Greenberg for critical readings and for having so many of the right reference books in his own library. And to Lee Wright, my editor at Random House, for an infinity of patience and her dedication to the book.

The author is also indebted to many people who helped him with research, and others who contributed bits and pieces of their time and effort and knowledge. Among these are Dr. Ernest A. Weizer (Colonel, MC, USAR); Dr. Milton B. Asbell; Henry L. Peck (Colonel, MPC, USAR); Walter Dillon; Bud Kane; William G. McNamara (Lt. Col., USA Ret.), and various military and civilian personnel of the Department of Defense; Colonel Alan Beresford Todd (now Brigadier General, USA Ret.), and various military and civilian personnel of the Office of the Judge Advocate General, Department of the Army, and Mrs. Elizabeth Lee of their Law Library; Wilbur J. Nigh and associates in the World War II Records Division, National Archives and Records Services; George Rubenstein, Attorney at Law; Stuart N. Arkin, Attorney at Law.

I am especially indebted to Robert White of the United States Department of the Interior, Bureau of Indian Affairs, formerly with the Consolidated Ute Agency, Ignacio, Colorado, for his detailed and informative letters and for directing me to helpful research material.

I also wish to thank Nathan L. Schoichet, Attorney at Law, and Congressman James C. Corman for helping me to borrow a particular source book; and Merril B. Friend, M.D., for lending me psychiatric and psychological material and making himself available for interviews.

Many others answered correspondence, consented to interviews or did active legwork for the author, among these Miss Vivien Hughes in England; and many military people, retired and active, and ex-servicemen supplemented my research. To these many people who gave of their time and knowledge I wish to acknowledge my thanks.

In other matters, not connected with research but important to the work, I am deeply indebted to Paul P. Selvin and Saul Cohen, Attorneys at Law.

And to my most penetrating, faithful and best critic—my wife, Marianne Duest Nathanson—to whom I have dedicated this novel, I owe the largest debt of gratitude:

for her love, her inspiration, her devotion to my work, and for her many invaluable critical readings of the growing manuscript through the long, difficult years of its birth.

E.M.N.

AN ORIGINAL PAPERBACK SERIES • Edited by Don Congdon

COMBAT: WORLD WAR I

The story of the "war to end all wars" as it has never been told before—eye-witness reports of the great battles fought on land, at sea, and for the first time in the air. Foreword and afterword by William Manchester. Introduction by Herbert Mitgang. **75c**

COMBAT: WORLD WAR II

EUROPEAN THEATER These authoritative first-hand accounts recreate in full dimension the historic battle for Europe, from an overview of grand strategy to the fox-hole view of the individual rifleman. Introduction by Merle Miller.
60c

PACIFIC THEATER From the bombing of Pearl Harbor to the destruction of the Japanese fleet in Leyte Gulf, here is the war as recorded by the men who fought it. Introduction by Merle Miller.
60c

THE WAR WITH JAPAN On-the-spot reports of the war with Japan—the ships, the planes, and the men who turned defeat into victory. Introduction by Richard Tregaskis. **60c**

THE WAR WITH GERMANY From Dunkirk to the fall of the Third Reich—the war with Germany recreated in all its fury by the men who fought it. Introduction by Herbert Mitgang.
60c

Each volume complete with maps and running commentary.

DELL BOOKS

If you cannot obtain copies of these titles at your local newsstand, just send the price (plus 10c per copy for handling and postage) to Dell Books, Box 2291, Grand Central Post Office, New York, N.Y. 10017. No postage or handling charge is required on any order of five or more books.

Don't Miss These Bestsellers From Dell

THE FIXER Bernard Malamud 95c

TAI-PAN James Clavell 95c

THE LIE Alberto Moravia 95c

THE PLEASURE OF HIS COMPANY Paul B. Fay, Jr. 75c

LA CHAMADE Francois Sagan 75c

A DANDY IN ASPIC Derek Marlowe 75c

THE LAST PICTURE SHOW Larry McMurtry 75c

IN THE COMPANY OF EAGLES Ernest Gann 75c

THE PAPER DRAGON Evan Hunter 95c

THE EMBEZZLER Louis Auchincloss 75c

ODOR OF SANCTITY Frank Yerby 95c

CANNIBALS AND CHRISTIANS Norman Mailer 95c

If you cannot obtain copies of these titles at your local bookseller's just send the price (plus 10c per copy for handling and postage) to Dell Books, Box 2291, Grand Central Post Office, New York, N.Y. 10017. No postage or handling charge is required on any order of five or more books.

THE SECRET OF SANTA VITTORIA

by Robert Crichton

THE NATION'S #1 BESTSELLER

From time immemorial the Italian hill town of Santa Vittoria had existed as a world unto itself, hostile to strangers, wholly involved in growing and making the fat black wine that was its glory and its lifeblood. As the Allied armies approached, the Germans sent an occupying force to claim the town's great treasure—one million bottles of wine. At this moment a leader emerged—the clownish wine merchant Bombolini. Behind him the town united, forgetting ancient feuds, lovers' rivalries, the division between aristocrat and peasant, pooling its energies and resources to outwit the invader.

"This brilliant novel should be celebrated with a fanfare of trumpets, with festivals in the streets." —*The New York Times*

"Crichton tells his story with grace, pace, warmth, and a wonderful free-reeling wit that skips among the vineyards like an inebriated billygoat." —*Time Magazine*

95¢

If you cannot obtain copies of this title at your local bookseller's, just send the price (plus 10c per copy for handling and postage) to Dell Books, Box 2291, Grand Central Post Office, New York, N.Y. 10017. No postage or handling charge is required on any order of five or more books.